Acclaim for Philip Caputo's

ACTS
OF
FAITH

"A gritty, spellbinding epic that captures the human drama of civil war in southern Sudan in the 1990s.... Powerful, captivating."
—*The Seattle Times*

"Vivid and credible.... Caputo brings a reporter's instinct and a fiction writer's soft heart to a part of the world unexplored by most of his colleagues in both fields, and it pays off in a sustained, fierce depiction of a country riven by [war]." —*Entertainment Weekly*

"Nothing is omitted in this ambitious novel depicting the turbulent lives of several aid workers at the height of the Sudanese civil war.... Caputo may have set out to write an epic parable about the dangers of uncritical belief, but he ended up with, quite simply, a great story."
—*The New Yorker*

"Caputo . . . writes with astonishing authority, launching several complex plot lines and an enormous, vibrant cast of characters—aid workers, soldiers, militants, mercenaries, missionaries and corrupt officials. The plot threads join in a propulsive, satisfying finish, inevitably inching demon and deity ever closer together." —*The Baltimore Sun*

"Philip Caputo, from Vietnam onwards, has understood the hardest truths of the modern world better than almost anybody. *Acts of Faith* is a stunningly unflinching novel. On the surface it is set in Africa, but in fact its true landscape is the ravaged soul of the twenty-first century. Philip Caputo is one of the few absolutely essential writers at work today." —Robert Olen Butler

"*Acts of Faith* reads like firsthand observation.... A compelling, vibrant tale of war in Africa." —*Chicago Tribune*

Philip Caputo

ACTS
OF
FAITH

Philip Caputo worked for nine years for the *Chicago Tribune* and shared a Pulitzer Prize in 1972 for his reporting on election fraud in Chicago. He is the author of six other works of fiction and two memoirs, including *A Rumor of War*, about his service in Vietnam. He divides his time between Connecticut and Arizona.

ALSO BY PHILIP CAPUTO

A Rumor of War

Horn of Africa

DelCorso's Gallery

Indian Country

Means of Escape

Equation for Evil

Exiles

The Voyage

In the Shadows of Morning

Ghosts of Tsavo

ACTS
OF
FAITH

ACTS
OF
FAITH

Philip Caputo

Vintage Contemporaries
Vintage Books
A Division of Random House, Inc.
New York

FIRST VINTAGE CONTEMPORARIES EDITION, MAY 2006

Copyright © 2005 by Philip Caputo

All rights reserved. Published in the United States by Vintage Books, a division of
Random House, Inc., New York, and in Canada by Random House of Canada Limited,
Toronto. Originally published in hardcover in the United States by Alfred A. Knopf,
a division of Random House, Inc., New York, in 2005.

Vintage and colophon are registered trademarks and
Vintage Contemporaries is a trademark of Random House, Inc.

Permissions acknowledgments can be found at the end of the book.

The Library of Congress has cataloged the Knopf edition as follows:
Caputo, Philip.
Acts of faith / by Philip Caputo.
p. cm.
1. Human rights workers—Fiction. 2. Americans—Sudan—Fiction.
3. Conspiracies—Fiction. 4. Violence—Fiction. 5. Sudan—Fiction.
I. Title.
PS3553.A625A626 2005
813'.54—dc22   2004048982

Vintage ISBN-10: 0-375-72597-0
Vintage ISBN-13: 978-0-375-72597-5

Book design by Virginia Tan
Map by MappingSpecialists, Madison, Wisconsin

www.vintagebooks.com

Printed in the United States of America
10 9 8 7 6 5 4 3 2 1

*With thanks to my wife, Leslie, for her advice and patience
through a project that took more than four years;
to Asya Muchnik for her superb translation work,
and to Patrick Butler, Dale Roark, and Heather Stewart,
for their stories and insights.*

All things have I seen in the days of my vanity: there is a just man that perisheth in his righteousness, and there is a wicked man that prolongeth his life in his wickedness. Be not righteous over much . . . Why shouldest thou destroy thyself? . . . For God shall bring every work into judgment, with every secret thing, whether it be good, or whether it be evil.

—*Ecclesiastes*

It seemed to him that every conviction, as soon as it became effective, turned into that form of dementia the gods send upon those they wish to destroy.

—Joseph Conrad, *Nostromo*

Whoever tries to turn angel turns beast.

—Pascal

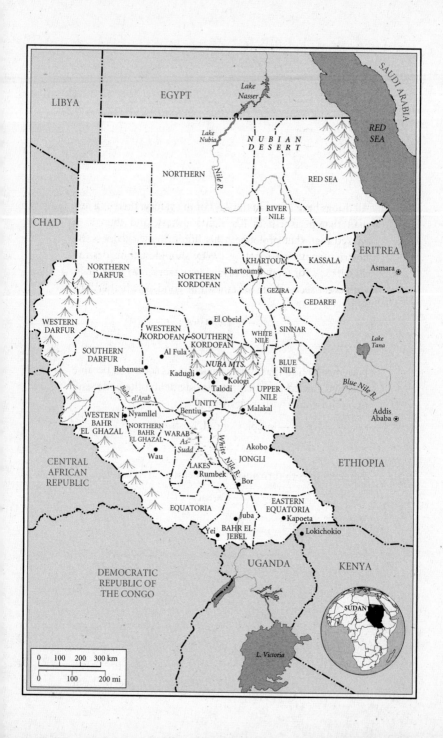

Cast of Characters

MAJOR CHARACTERS (*listed alphabetically*):

DOUGLAS BRAITHWAITE—American aviator in his early thirties, formerly a UN pilot, now managing director of Knight Air Services, an independent airline flying aid into Sudan

WESLEY DARE—Texas-born mercenary and bush pilot, Douglas's partner in Knight Air

QUINETTE HARDIN—mid-twenties evangelical Christian from Iowa, employed by the WorldWide Christian Union, a human rights group that redeems black slaves captured by Arab raiders in Sudan

IBRAHIM IDRIS—*omda* (chief) of the Salamat, a seminomadic Arab tribe; also a warlord commanding a detachment of *murahaleen*, irregular Arab cavalry used as raiders by the Khartoum government

FITZHUGH MARTIN—mixed-race Kenyan, a former UN relief worker

MINOR CHARACTERS:

JOHN BARRETT—defrocked Catholic priest, field coordinator for International People's Aid, a privately funded Canadian relief organization

LADY DIANA BRIGGS—wealthy middle-aged Anglo-Kenyan philanthropist and human rights advocate; one of IPA's principal donors

FATHER MALACHY DELANEY—Irish missionary priest, Barrett's old seminary classmate

KEN EISMONT—American human rights activist, executive director of the WorldWide Christian Union, Quinette Hardin's boss

MARY ENGLISH—young Canadian aviator, Dare's copilot in Knight Air

MICHAEL ARCHANGELO GORAENDE—lieutenant colonel in the Sudanese

People's Liberation Army (SPLA), commander of rebel forces in Sudan's Nuba mountains

HASSAN ADID—multimillionaire Kenyan businessman of Somali extraction, an investor in Knight Air

DR. GERHARD MANFRED—German physician who operates a hospital in the Nuba mountains for German Emergency Doctors, a nongovernmental organization

PHYLLIS RAPPAPORT—American TV correspondent, chief of CNN's Nairobi bureau

TARA WHITCOMB—Anglo-Kenyan bush pilot in the mold of Beryl Markham; managing director of Pathways Ltd., an independent relief airline and Knight Air's chief competitor

Also a host of walk-ons: ULRIKA, a nurse; BASHIR, an Arab slave-trader; NIMROD, Dare's Kenyan loadmaster; SULEIMAN, a Nuban guerrilla; TIM FANCHER and ROB HANDY, American missionaries; PEARL GORAENDE, Colonel Goraende's daughter; TONY BOLLICHEK, an Australian bush pilot; and others.

Note: This book is a work of fiction. It should not be taken as an accurate representation of the events that inspired it. None of its characters, whether modeled on real people or created wholly out of the writer's imagination, are intended to resemble any persons, living or dead.

ACTS
OF
FAITH

Introductory Rites

ON A HOT night in Lokichokio, as a generator thumps in the distance and katydids cling like thin winged leaves to the lightbulb overhead, he tells his visitor that there is no difference between God and the Devil in Africa. Whoever understands that in his blood and bones and guts, where true understanding resides, will swim in its treacherous currents; whoever doesn't will drown.

This observation has come from out of nowhere, during a lull in the conversation, and the visitor's first impulse is to brush it off as some random thought that has popped into Fitzhugh's beer-fogged brain and then out of his mouth; but because she is new to Africa, it occurs to her that he might be giving some advice, or a warning, and that she ought to pay attention.

She is a dark-haired American journalist in her late twenties, and a magazine assignment has brought her to Lokichokio, a town as squalid as it is remote, hidden away in the barren, bandit-haunted plains of northwestern Kenya, some thirty miles from southern Sudan. Years ago that accident of geography lifted Lokichokio out of obscurity and transformed it from a market town for local Turkana tribesmen into a headquarters for the armies of international beneficence. Just beyond its shabby shops and warrens of stick and straw huts, acres of warehouses, depots, and fenced compounds stretch away from an airfield where cargo planes land and take off every day, shattering the desert stillness. The planes fly for the United Nations and private relief agencies enlisted under its pale blue banner, delivering humanitarian aid into Sudan, where a civil war between the Muslim Arabs of the north and the Christian and pagan blacks of the south conspires with periodic droughts to create misery on a scale colossal even by African standards.

UN publicists have told the journalist that this mighty exercise is the largest relief operation since the Berlin airlift in 1948, but there is a peculiar wrinkle in it, and that wrinkle is what has drawn her to this backwater. The Islamic fundamentalists who rule Sudan from Khartoum have imposed an aid blockade on those parts of the south controlled by the Infidel's military forces—the Sudanese People's Liberation Army. UN planes are prohibited from entering these so-called no-go zones, Khartoum arguing that their cargoes would fall into rebel hands, though the actual reason is to starve the southerners into submission. The inhabitants of the no-go zones might well have perished long ago, if certain aid agencies had not decided to break the rules. Declining to serve under the UN, they operate independently and employ the services of small freight airlines to deliver food, medicine, and drinking water in superannuated planes flown by free-booting pilots willing to risk MIGs, ground fire, and dicey landings on bush airstrips.

The journalist is writing about these people—mercenaries with a conscience. The man she is interviewing, Fitzhugh Martin, is managing director of one such airline, SkyTrain Relief Services. He doesn't fit the image of an aviation executive, or for that matter an emissary of humanitarianism. An hour ago, when she entered SkyTrain's office, a small cinder-block building near the airfield, the journalist was greeted by a balding man wearing a rumpled T-shirt over cotton shorts, sandals, a wispy mustache, and a pair of gold earrings dangling from one ear. He looked like a beach bum or a pirate—a very big one, every inch of six-three and every pound of two-fifty, his torso resting on his brown legs like a fifty-gallon drum on sawed-off telephone poles.

Before the journalist could begin, he insisted that, contrary to what she might have heard, his business is only modestly lucrative. True, its steadiness compensates for its slender profit margins. The war, which has been going on for so long that *peace* has become a mere word, as meaningless to the inhabitants of Sudan's febrile marshes and sun-stricken savannahs as *snow* or *ice*, promises to go on forever, producing a perpetual stream of victims in need of the things his airline delivers.

"But I'm not in this to get rich," he declared.

"Then why are you in it?" asked the young woman.

His small black eyes squinted at her with the mistrustful look of someone who has learned not to take anything or anyone at face value. "Because there's a vacuum of mercy in southern Sudan, that's why!" he replied passionately. "And we help to fill it. We call it 'flying on the dark side.' I was with one of the first airlines to do it, Knight Air Services . . . Well, never mind, that was a long time ago. What I wish you to know is that it's damned dangerous. A year ago a Sudanese gunship blew one of our planes out of the sky. I have to pay my pilots a premium to take such chances. And think of my insurance costs. Of course, I'm in it to make money, but that's not the same as getting rich, is it?"

The journalist was silent, taken aback.

"I'm sorry," Fitzhugh said. "I'm a little touchy about—"

"Look," she interrupted, "if you're worried that I'm going to say you guys are war profiteers, don't be."

Thus assured, he pulled a can of Tusker beer from the cooler at his feet. "Okay, ask me whatever you want."

An hour later, after he'd tossed his fourth empty into the wastebasket and smoked half a dozen Embassy cigarettes, she paused to flip through her notebook and make sure she'd covered all her questions. That was when, apropos of nothing, he made his remark about the synonymousness of God and the Devil in Africa.

Now she glances at him, perplexed. To her, it isn't clear which God and which Devil he is talking about. There are a multiplicity of divinities and demons and demon-divinities in the vast forests, swamps, and plains lying south of the Sahara (north of which Allah has an almost exclusive franchise). Each tribe, and there are thousands—Xhosa, Zulu, Masai, Kikuyu, Tutsi, Hutu, Loli, Bembe, Yoruba, Fulani, Dinka, Nuer, Chagga—possesses its own pantheon of spirits that dwell in numinous trees and on sacred rocks: ancestral spirits, benevolent spirits, evil spirits, and capricious spirits whose goodwill can be bribed with certain sacrifices or charms, though such gratuities are paid without guarantees, for those supernatural beings reserve the right to turn malevolent on a whim, rather like African politicians.

Is Fitzhugh referring to them? she wonders. Or does he mean that the God of Abraham and the Prince of Darkness have joined forces to reign united over the continent?

He doesn't answer directly but tells her, in the metaphorical language he favors, that the word of Africa's Supreme Being is to be found not in the writings of prophets but in its great rivers. The slow, brown, resistless currents of the Congo, the white wrath of Nile cataracts—those are His scriptures. The Congo and the Nile create and destroy and create anew out of what they destroy, declaring the rule of God in Devil and Devil in God, a majestic duality who offers neither judgment nor mercy, neither reward for virtue nor penalty for sin. He nourishes the robber's fields while flooding the honest man's, bears the bloody-minded safely to their destinations while sinking the vessels of the guiltless, for He doesn't demand good behavior from humankind, only recognition of His dyadic sovereignty, and submission to it—

She interrupts: "Fitz, *what* are you talking about?"

"I'll admit the idea isn't completely my own," he replies, as if its originality were the issue. "It was inspired by something I read. In Isak Dinesen. In *Out of Africa*."

The journalist has never seen a photo of the real woman: a picture of Meryl Streep comes to mind; it doesn't help her understand Fitzhugh's meaning. She asks him to explain.

"Simple," he says, clutching a fifth Tusker. "If we were in front of one of those Nile cataracts right now, and I said, 'Well, that's bad, let's get rid of it and put it someplace else but keep the nice smooth stretches below,' you'd think I was crazy. That's how the African thinks of good and evil. It's foolish to try and separate the two. Foolish *and* dangerous. You have to give in to it, the oneness, I mean, but not entirely. No! You submit without surrendering. That's the difficult trick. That's how the African survives, physically and otherwise."

Fitzhugh is an African, albeit of mixed race, so she accepts his sweeping generalizations without argument, but she's grown impatient with his figurative lingo. He senses this and raises his hand to hold her in her chair, facing the Bob Marley poster taped to the wall behind him.

"Let me tell you about a friend of mine, an American missionary priest, Father Rigney. Jim Rigney. Maybe then you'll see what I'm getting at."

A political missionary as much as one who ministered to the soul, says Fitzhugh. An apostle of human rights who became known in Kenya for his intemperate public denunciations of official greed and nepotism and brutality. Bandits in Savile Row suits, Father Jim called cabinet members and members of parliament, fattening themselves while people in the villages he served went without clean water or electricity or proper medical care. He raised money back in Chicago, where he was from, built churches, schools, and clinics, had wells dug. He lived ascetically, in a small mud-brick house out in the Masai-Mara, and his veranda was neutral territory where disputes between Masai and Luo were settled, Father Jim presiding. He had exposed a land-grab scheme by a couple of cabinet ministers and sheltered the farmers who'd been driven off their *shambas* in a tribal clash orchestrated by the politicians. He was beloved by his congregations and seen as a champion of the oppressed, even as a kind of charmed figure because he got away with things that would have landed a Kenyan in jail or in the morgue.

"I loved the guy," Fitzhugh declares. "He did things that needed doing and said things that needed saying, but"—he pauses, contemplating the elephant on the label of his beer can—"he did them the way white guys do things over here, head-on, and he said them so loudly, so directly, even after he got a couple of death threats, even after the head of his own order sent him a letter, asking him to back off just a little. They were worried that he was going too far."

One afternoon about two years ago some of Father Jim's parishioners told him that two girls, fifteen and sixteen, had dropped out of school after they'd had sex with a powerful member of parliament, Daniel Mwebi. The sixteen-year-old was Mwebi's niece. The priest counseled the girls and hired lawyers for them. A lawsuit was filed against the MP, alleging statutory rape. The case made all the newspapers. Also TV and radio.

A couple of weeks later both girls were visited by certain gentlemen and strongly advised to withdraw the charges. They refused, their defiance encouraged by their lawyers, who belonged to an organization that defended women's rights in Kenya and had somehow deluded itself, as well as its clients, into thinking it could. The girls were summarily thrown in jail. Kenyan jails are extremely unpleasant places, and a week in one was enough to persuade the fifteen-year-old to do as she'd been told. Mwebi's niece, however, wouldn't quit. Her lawyer managed to get her out, and they went ahead with the case. The member was arraigned. More headlines, more stories on TV and radio.

In the meantime Father Jim had heard that several other underage girls in the parish had slept with Mwebi, and he mustered more lawyers to gather depositions from them.

At this point Mwebi, accompanied by two bodyguards, paid the priest a call.

"Now I know you'll wonder how I found out what happened at this get-together," Fitzhugh says. "But trust me, I'm sure it's true. The lesson is, African politicians, even the worst of them, can be subtle when they need to be."

Daniel Mwebi, himself a Roman Catholic, asked Father Jim to hear his confession.

"Clever, wasn't it? Anything said in confessional is absolutely secret. Can I swear that the MP confessed to having sex with all those young girls? No. But I'm pretty sure he did. Can I swear that Father Jim checked this move by telling Mwebi that he could not grant absolution without assurance that his repentance was sincere? And that the best way to assure him was for Mwebi to admit his guilt in court? No, but I'm pretty sure he did. But Mwebi had another move on the board.

"Yes, he would be willing to face the music to save his immortal soul, but he informed Father Jim of certain events that had recently taken place in Nairobi. First, the judge had decided to postpone setting a trial date for two months. Perhaps Father Jim had read that in the newspapers? Second, Mwebi's niece had privately agreed not to go ahead with the case. She'd had, oh, call it second thoughts, and did not want to disgrace her uncle's name any further—after all, he was going to stand for reelection in a few months. Soon she and her lawyer would inform the judge of the decision. In exchange for the favor, Mwebi would pay for the rest of the girl's schooling. So you see, said the member of parliament to the priest, he could not answer the charges in court because there would be no trial. Ah, but Mwebi truly wished to be cleansed of sin. So for his penance, he would pay for the schooling of all the girls involved—if Father Jim and the lawyers agreed to stop gathering evidence against him. Can you imagine? Old-fashioned African marketplace bargaining, right there in the confessional box.

"Now I can't fault Father Jim for being outraged, but here was his chance. Do you see what Mwebi was saying? 'We are in the confessional, Father. Nothing we say to each other can leave this little box. No one will ever know we made an agreement. My reputation will be saved, and your honor will be preserved, and the girls will all benefit.' Father Jim could have made sure that Mwebi did indeed pay for the school fees. He could have convinced Mwebi that if he so much as touched one of those girls again, the scandal would be revived. He could have submitted to the evil without surrendering to it. But he didn't. He kicked the man out. Mwebi walked straight outside to his car, but he made some sign to his companions, who remained in the office and suggested to Father Jim that he take his annual three-month home leave now. They were still giving him an out! He turned them down.

"The niece did drop the charges, no trial took place, and the other girls, for all their devotion to Father Jim, realized that they'd better keep their mouths shut. A few more months passed, and then one morning Father Jim was found beside his Land Rover on a road out in the bush. Head blown apart by a shotgun. Weapon at his fingertips. The spent round was never discovered, but a live one was found in his pocket. The assassins wanted to make it look like a suicide, yes? And the crudeness of the attempt didn't show they had no skill in planting false evidence. No! It showed their arrogance. They expected people to believe that a Catholic priest would commit the gravest sin, and would do it with the most astonishing flexibility and recuperative powers, shooting himself in the *back* of the head with a shotgun, then come up from the dead and get rid of the fatal cartridge. And I'm afraid they were right. Not that people really believed it. They simply knew the consequences of stating that they did not."

Fitzhugh falls silent, to again study the elephant on the black and gold can.

"And?" the journalist asks.

"And nothing. No one dared to investigate if the MP ordered Father Jim's murder. I'm sure someone could prove he did, and I'm sure no one ever will. But you know, I am sometimes inclined to acquit Mwebi in my own mind. Maybe Father Jim *did* commit suicide. He must have known he was in mortal danger from the moment Mwebi was arraigned, but he didn't take even the most elementary precautions. Didn't bother to change his routine. Said mass in the same places at the same time and went to them by the same routes, every week, and he was ambushed on one of those routes. His body wasn't discovered until Monday, with the vultures already going to work on him. His mass kit was found in the back of his Land Rover. Chalice. Paten. Hosts. Flasks of holy water and communion wine. He must have believed he was traveling under the protection of those sacred vessels, but their magic doesn't work over here, as it would in America or Europe. He had set off alone that Sunday morning. *Alone.* Did he do that because he was brave, proud, stubborn, and dedicated, or because he never understood the testament written in our waters?"

The journalist looks on, bewildered.

"I'm reminded of a couple of Americans I knew six, seven years ago. They definitely did not understand. I don't judge them for that. Anyway, I try not to. Douglas and Quinette. A pretty name isn't it? Quinette? I guess I should pass judgment on Africa." He gives a small, rueful smile, a philosophical shrug. "She isn't kind to people with good intentions, never has been."

"You're talking about Father Jim again, or what?"

"There are other ways to die over here than the way he did"—jabbing with an unlit cigarette—"and other ways to drown. You can suffer what Father Jim would have called spiritual death, you can drown morally but not know what's happening to you. It's not Africa's fault. All it does is provide enough water for you to drown in. Those two—well, they remind me of the scuba divers I'd heard about when I was a kid in the Seychelles. The ones who went too far down and caught nitrogen narcosis. The rapture of the deep. Good word. *Rapture.* Poor souls thought they were in their native element and the fish out of theirs, so they took out their mouth-pieces, offering help to the creatures who didn't need it. And when the divers' lungs cried out for breath, they sucked in water, thinking it was air."

"And this Douglas, this Quinette—"

"Took a few people down with them."

"Is it too much to ask what you mean?"

He fixes her with a steady gaze that makes her a little uncomfortable.

"It's a long story, right? Maybe some other time?" she says, explaining that she is to have dinner in half an hour with the UN director of operations.

"He'll lie through his teeth about all the great work the UN is doing."

"I'll keep that in mind," the journalist says, and adds, "Really, I want to hear the story."

"It's all about swimming and drowning, but it's history and you're not in the history business."

Wouldn't mind getting to know her a little better, Fitzhugh thinks after she leaves, and is reproached by the photograph of his wife and two children, smiling out of the frame on his desk. Static, only static—there are no planes in the air at this dark hour—hisses through the high-frequency radio atop a small table beneath a poster of Malcolm X, who with upraised hand glares through horn-rimmed glasses at Bob Marley, as if lecturing the dope-smoking singer. A schedule board hanging beside Malcolm X reminds Fitzhugh that he is to fly out at six tomorrow morning to the Natinga airstrip, just over the border. A mechanic and parts are being flown there to repair one of his leased planes, wrecked a month ago when it hit a pothole on landing. He should get to bed early, but he can tell that he'll only toss and turn, despite the beer. Some paperwork involving the wrecked aircraft holds his attention for a couple of minutes, no more than that. He can't focus and wishes he hadn't mentioned Douglas and Quinette to that reporter, for the mere utterance of their names has set the drama reeling through his memory, with all its emotions of regret and anger and disappointment, mostly in himself. It's as though a runaway videotape were playing in his restless brain, and as it spins forward, his thoughts turn backward in time. In a kind of surrender, he leans back in his chair and cracks another beer, his eyes on the slender green katydids, clinging to the light.

BOOK ONE

Outlaws and Missionaries

PART ONE

Man of All Races

IN HIS EARLY twenties, after two undistinguished and troubled years at university, Fitzhugh Martin had achieved a modest celebrity as center forward for the Harambe Stars, which are to Kenyan soccer as the New York Yankees are to baseball. A sportswriter had nicknamed him "The Ambler," because he never seemed to run very fast, his leisurely movements caused not by slow feet but by a quick tactical eye that allowed him to read the field in a glance and be where he needed to be with economy of motion.

He traveled with the club throughout Africa, to Europe, and once to the United States. He saw something of the world, and what he saw—namely the shocking contrast between the West and his continent—convinced him to do something more with himself than chase a checkered ball up and down a field. He'd heard a kind of missionary call, quit soccer, and became a United Nations relief worker, first in Somalia and then in Sudan.

That was the story he told, but it wasn't entirely true: a serious knee injury that required two operations was as responsible for his leaving the sport as a Pauline epiphany. Or maybe the injury was the mother of the epiphany; sitting on the bench with his taped knee, he knew his career was as good as over and wondered what to do with the rest of his life. Of course, if he hadn't had a social conscience to begin with, he would not have made the choice he did, and that conscience was formed by his ancestry. He had come to Kenya from the Seychelles Islands when he was eight years old, the eldest of three children born to a French, Irish, and Indian father and a mother who was black, Arab, and Chinese. The emigration took Fitzhugh from a place where tribalism was unknown and race counted for little to a land where tribe and race counted for everything. His family wasn't poor—his father managed a coastal resort near Mombasa—but he came to identify with the poor, the oppressed, the marginalized, because he grew up on the margins of Kenyan society, a boy without a tribal allegiance or a claim to any one race, for all the races of the earth were in him. He was the eternal outsider who was never allowed to forget that he was an alien, even at the height of his athletic fame. His skin was brown, yet the white Kenyans, children and grandchildren of colonial settlers, were more accepted than he, a tribe unto themselves.

After he worked for a year in Somalia, the UN promoted him to field monitor and assigned him to its operations in Sudan. Now a corporal in the army of international beneficence, he wandered in southern Sudan for weeks at a time, stalking the beast of hunger and devising strategies to hold the numbers of its victims to some acceptable minimum. That vast unhappy region captured him body and soul; it became the stage where Fitzhugh Martin played the role he believed destiny had assigned him. "The goddamned, bleeding, fucked-up Sudan," he would say. "I don't know what it is about that place. It sucks you in. You see some eighteen-year-old who's been fighting since he was fourteen and can tell you war stories that will give you nightmares, but drop a piece of ice in his hands and he's amazed. Never seen or felt ice before, never seen water turned to stone, and you get sucked in." He meant to do all in his power to save the southern Sudanese from the curses of the apocalypse and a few the author of Revelation hadn't thought of, like the tribalism that caused the southerners to inflict miseries on themselves. That was where his cosmopolitan blood became an advantage. He moved with ease among Dinka, Nuer, Didinga, Tuposa, Boya; the tribes trusted the tribeless man who had no ethnic axes to grind.

He loved being in the bush and hated returning to the UN base at Loki. It had the look of a military installation, ringed by coils of barbed wire. The field managers and flight coordinators and logistics officers—to his eyes a mob of ambitious bureaucrats or risk-lovers seeking respectable adventure—drove around like conquerors in white Land Rovers sprouting tall radio antennae; they lived and worked in tidy blue and white bungalows, drank their gins and cold beers at bars that looked like beach resort tiki bars, and ate imported meats washed down with imported wines. When Loki's heat, dust, and isolation got to be too much, they went to Europe on R&R, or to rented villas in the cool highland suburbs of Nairobi, where they were waited on, driven, and guarded by servants whose grandparents probably had waited on, driven, and guarded the British sahibs and memsahibs of bygone days. They were the new colonials, and Fitzhugh grew to loathe them as much as he loathed the old-time imperialists who had pillaged Africa in the name of the white man's burden and the *mission civilisatrice*.

When he wasn't in Sudan, he who had grown up on the edge of things dwelled on the edge of the compound, in a mud-walled hut with a *makuti* roof and two windows lacking glass and screens; it wasn't much better than the squalid twig-and-branch *tukuls* of the Turkana settlement that sprawled outside the wire, along the old Nairobi-Juba road. Inside were a hard bed under a mosquito net, a chair, and a desk knocked together out of scrap lumber. Fitzhugh's only concession to modern comfort was electricity, supplied by a generator; his only bow to interior decoration, the posters of his heroes, Bob Marley, Malcolm X, and Nelson Mandela. Asceticism did not come naturally to him. Self-denial is easy for people with attenuated desires and appetites; Fitzhugh's were in proportion to his size. He could down a sixteen-ounce Tusker in two or three swallows and inhaled meals the way he did cigarettes. He loved women, and when he came out of the bush, he would sweep through the compound, scooping up Irish girls and American girls and Canadian girls. (He stayed away from the local females, fearing AIDS or the swifter retribution of a Turkana father's rifle or spear.) Inevitably, he would feel guilty about indulging himself and go on a binge of monkish abstinence.

He met Douglas Braithwaite exactly two months and eighteen days after the UN fired him, an encounter whose date he would come to recall with as much bitterness as precision. Years later he tried to persuade himself that he and the American had come together for reasons he couldn't fathom but hoped to discover, hidden somewhere in the machinery of destiny or in the designs of an inscrutable providence. Who among us, when an apparently chance meeting or some other random occurrence changes us profoundly, can swallow the idea that it was purely accidental?

Over and over Fitzhugh would trace the succession of seeming coincidences that caused the path of his life to converge with Douglas's. He never would have laid eyes on the man if he hadn't lost his job; he would not have lost it if . . . well, you get the idea. If he could map how it happened, he would find out why.

Eventually Fitzhugh's mental wanderings led him back to the day he was born, but he was no closer to uncovering the secret design. So he was forced to abandon his quest for the why and settle for the how, a narrative whose beginning he fixed on the day a bonfire burned in the desert.

The High Commissioners of World Largesse, as he called his employers, occasionally overestimated the amount of food they would need to avert mass starvation in Sudan. Blind screw-ups were sometimes to blame; sometimes field monitors deliberately exaggerated the severity of conditions, figuring it was better to err on that side than on the other; and sometimes nature did not cooperate, failing to produce an expected catastrophe. Surpluses would then pile up in the great brown tents pitched alongside the Loki airstrip, tins of cooking oil and concentrated milk, sacks of flour, sorghum, and high-protein cereal stacked on pallets. Once in a while the stuff sat around beyond the expiration dates stamped on the containers. It then was burned. That was standard procedure, and it was followed rigorously, even if the oil had not gone rancid or the flour mealy or the grain rotten.

Mindful that cremating tons of food would make for bad press, the High Commissioners had the dirty work done under cover of darkness at a remote dump site, far out in the sere, scrub-covered plateaus beyond Loki. Truck convoys would leave the UN base before dawn with armed escorts, their loads covered by plastic tarps; for the Turkana, men as lean as the leaf-bladed spears they carried, knew scarcity in the best of times and were consequently skilled and enthusiastic bandits.

And it was the Turkana who blew the whistle. One morning a band of them looking for stray livestock in the Songot mountains, near the Ugandan border, spotted a convoy moving across the plain below and smoke and flames rising from a pit in the distance. The herdsmen went to have a look. That year had been a particularly hard one for the Turkana—sparse rains, the bones of goats and cows chalking the stricken land, shamans crying out to Akuj Apei to let the heavens open. The bush telegraph flashed the news of what the herdsmen had seen from settlement to settlement: The *wazungu* were burning food! More than all the Turkana put together had ever seen, much less eaten.

The word soon reached Malachy Delaney, a friend of Fitzhugh's who had been a missionary among the Turkana for so long that they considered him a brother whose skin happened to be white. Apoloreng, they called him, Father of the Red Ox, because his hair had been red when he first came to them. He spoke their dialects as well as they and was always welcome at their rituals and ceremonies. In fact, he was sometimes asked to preside, and anyone who saw him, clapping his hands to tribal songs, leading chants of call and response, had to wonder who had converted whom. Malachy had been reprimanded by the archbishop in Nairobi and once by the Vatican itself for his unorthodox methods.

A frequent topic, when Malachy and Fitzhugh got together over whiskey in one of the expat bars, was Fitzhugh's employer. Although Malachy was a man of the Left, he once told Fitzhugh that he admired the American senator Jesse Helms, probably the only man on earth who despised the United Nations as much as he. It had encamped in the heart of Turkana land to lavish aid on the Sudanese while doing nothing for his parishioners. Hadn't helped them dig so much as a single well.

When he learned that the UN was destroying food that could have filled Turkana bellies, he lived up to his nickname. His hair was gray now, but his broad, blocky face, scholarly and pugnacious at the same time, was scarlet when he appeared at Fitzhugh's tukul to vent his outrage. Destroying it! And it looks like they've been making a practice of it, did you know that? Fitzhugh answered that he'd heard as much, but of course he'd never seen it and couldn't prove it. Proof, if it's proof you're needing, here it is, Malachy fumed, producing a charred can of powdered milk from his daypack. The herdsmen had scavenged it from the ashes, he added, and sat down under the eave, on one of the crates that served as Fitzhugh's veranda furniture.

"More in there if you care to see it. It won't surprise me if some of the lads ambush a convoy one of these days and take the bloody stuff for themselves, and if they kill somebody in the process, I'll by God give them absolution in advance." Malachy looked out across the asphalt meadow of the landing field, toward the huts beyond the barbed-wire fence, their domed roofs leakproofed with green, white, and blue sheets of plastic. "Ah, Fitz, I just might nick a rifle and lead them to it myself." Malachy had a martial streak; Fitzhugh thought that a part of him regretted joining the priesthood instead of the IRA.

After he'd cooled off, he came up with a sounder plan. He had friends on the staff of the *Nation*, Nairobi's most influential paper, and at the Kenya Television Network. If he got advance word about where and when the next burn was going to be, he would see to it that reporters and cameramen were there to record it. A few of his Turkana lads could show them where to hide—it would be a kind of bloodless ambush. The whole sorry scene would be captured on film, and then the UN scoundrels would be shamed into stopping their unconscionable practice. Accurate intelligence would, of course, be critical to success.

Fitzhugh gave him his full attention. He'd returned the week before from the Sudanese province of Bahr el Ghazal, where he'd been sent to conduct a "needs assessment" after Khartoum mounted an offensive against the SPLA. The rebel army didn't suffer much, but the people did. Villages leveled by Antonov bombers, fields set afire, livestock slaughtered. They were mostly Dinka tribesmen out there, a very tall people with little flesh and fat to spare. Thousands filled the dusty roads: dead men, dead women, and dead children who did not realize they were dead and so struggled on through the heat, past the prostrate forms of those who had acknowledged their doom; struggled on seeking the brief clemency of an acacia's shade, the small mercy of a cup of water, a handful of sorghum. Each one of those dark, lofty figures looked as insubstantial as a pillar of smoke. *My goodness,* he thought, listening to Malachy, *a tenth of the surplus that had been put to the match could have saved them all.*

To abbreviate, his espionage was successful. So was Malachy's media ambush. The story made the front page and led the nightly news on KTN. Images of sacks, tins, boxes—forty tons of food!—consigned to the flames. The Father of the Red Ox went on the air to condemn the UN in the most florid terms, and to plead for the surpluses to be distributed among his beloved Turkana if they could not be used in Sudan. The foreign press was quick to pick up on the story. Detachments of journalists assaulted Loki. UN officials, feverishly trying to control the damage, issued denials and half-truths. Things were quite exciting for a while, but predictably the scandal died down, the journalists left, and nothing was done. The only actions the High Commissioners took were to bar Malachy from the UN compound and to launch a quiet internal investigation to find out who had tipped him off.

Fitzhugh's friendship with Malachy was common knowledge. He soon found himself undergoing a cordial but persistent interrogation in the security office. He told a few lies, thought better of it, and confessed, showing no contrition whatever. His supervisor, a Canadian woman, told him he was through. Naturally he did not merely nod and leave. He made a speech, detailing the UN's sins. She heard him out and, when he was done, told him that he possessed an "insufferably Hebraic soul," a reference not to his religious affiliation but to his judgmentalism. He expected too much of people and human institutions, she said. Not everyone could be a saint; nor was relief work a religion.

FITZHUGH HAD BEEN in the bush for so long that he'd forgotten the pleasant emotions the sea aroused in him. He had gotten used to living away from it but never stopped missing it. When he saw it again, from the balcony of his family's flat on the coast, he felt as if he'd been reunited with a cherished friend. During his first week of unemployment he spent two or three hours a day staring at it, not a thought in his head. The cobalt vastness of the Indian Ocean, the advance and recession of the tides, the surf's suck and draw, constant yet never monotonous, awakened vestigial memories of his island childhood. The salty winds cleared the oppressiveness that had been weighing on his soul. His work in Sudan had narrowed his vision and restricted his horizons; cut off from the rest of the world, caught up in the intense emotions fostered by bearing witness to war, starvation, and epidemics, he had almost lost the power to imagine places where people had futures that extended beyond the next day and had dreams of something more than finding a crust of bread. The sea's breath, scented with the promise of new possibilities hidden beyond the seam of water and sky, assured him that such places still existed and encouraged him to believe that peace and plenty might one day come even to Sudan. At such moments the colors and dimensions of the sea, its sounds and smells, seemed to be those of hope itself.

He loved being back on the old Swahili coast, full of mongrels like himself, children of the sea's human wrack. It was good to hear music and to wander Mombasa's sultry and intricate streets; good not to listen for the drone of approaching Antonovs. Maybe it was too good. Fitzhugh's tendency to swing between extremes kicked in. Having denied himself for so long, he now abandoned himself to the delights of Kenya's answer to the Costa del Sol or Miami Beach. A few club owners remembered him from his star-athlete days and bought him rounds on the house. An old friend from high school, the son of a local political boss, knew a Nigerian who supplied him with prime-grade cocaine, and the two schoolmates would snort themselves into blabbering insomnia a couple of nights a week. Fitzhugh danced in the discos and slept with English and German and Scandinavian girls as if he'd spent the last six months on one of the trading dhows that sail the monsoons from Mombasa to India.

His conduct appalled his parents. Bad enough that he was thirty-three years old, out of work, and living under their roof. His father told him that he would roll up the welcome mat if he did not find something useful to do with himself, and quickly. Kenya is not an ideal country in which to find employment, so he thought Fitzhugh should go to work at his hotel, starting at the bottom, as a doorman. He was the proper size for that job. The doormen at the Safari Beach Lodge were costumed to look like something out of *The Arabian Nights*. Fitzhugh could not imagine himself got up like that, grinning at fat tourists, hailing taxis, hefting luggage for tips.

He was saved by something that approached divine intervention and inclined him to believe that his partnership with Douglas Braithwaite had been foreordained. Kenya's phone service isn't famous for its reliability, yet Malachy, calling from Nairobi one afternoon, got through on the first try. His ring came as Fitzhugh was leaving his parents' flat to speak to his father at the hotel. Five seconds later, and he would have been gone.

Malachy had been summoned to the capital for what he called his semiannual dressing-down by the archbishop. During his visit (and here

was another coincidence that didn't seem coincidental to Fitzhugh in ret-
rospect), he happened to bump into an old classmate from the seminary,
John Barrett, who had told him about a job opportunity—

"I can't get away from Irish priests!" Fitzhugh interrupted.

"This would be a former priest," Malachy informed him. "A former
Catholic priest. John was a missionary in Sudan for, oh, I would say fifteen
years. It seems a Nuban woman persuaded him that celibacy was an
unnatural state. He got some official or other to marry them. Pretty common arrangement in Africa, but the wrong people found out and John
had to turn in his collar. So he switched. He's now an ordained minister in
the Episcopal Church of Sudan."

"And what is the job opportunity? Altar boy? Do Episcopalians have
altar boys?"

"John is at present unemployed as a minister," Malachy replied. "He's
just been hired to direct relief operations in Sudan for a nongovernmental
organization, International People's Aid. He's looking to hire someone
with field experience, and I recommended you. Feel a bit responsible for
your situation, don't you know."

Fitzhugh hesitated—he'd never heard of International People's Aid.

"They're fairly new on the scene, based in Canada, well funded I'm
told, all nongovernmental sources. They are planning to take some bold
steps. How soon can you get up here?"

Fitzhugh had read somewhere that the greatest happiness lies in living
for others. The self and its appetites, the satisfaction of which only yields
deeper hungers, are to the soul as mooring cables to an airship. To cut
them willingly and without regret is to know true emancipation, the kind
that cannot be granted by constitutions, proclamations, manifestos. Yes,
he needed a job, but in speaking to Malachy, he realized that seeing hungry mouths fed and knowing that he'd done his bit to feed them had been
more gratifying than anything else he'd done. Relief work *was* a religion,
at least to his way of thinking. In a way it was an act of faith that infused
his actions with spiritual value. He missed it and the freedom he found in
it from the inner tyrant who kept demanding, *I want, I want, I want.*

He booked a seat on the next morning's flight to Nairobi. One way.

THE REVEREND FATHER Malachy Delaney would have accused himself of speaking high treason if he ever uttered a civil, much less an admiring, word about English aristocracy. Inbred twits who could no longer
manage even to be interestingly decadent, their antics fodder for Fleet

Street tabloids, their sole achievement was the perpetuation of their titles and privileges decades after their class had outlived its relevance.

He made an exception of Lady Diana Briggs, partly because she was a Kenyan citizen, British by ancestry only, and partly because her title was conferred rather than hereditary, bestowed for her good works throughout Africa. An admirable woman, hardworking and selfless, was how Malachy described her as he and Fitzhugh drove from the airport to her house in Karen, the Nairobi suburb that remained a kind of game reserve for Caucasians. Lady Briggs had spent several years in refugee camps, laboring to repatriate displaced Africans, and when repatriation was out of the question, she helped them emigrate to whatever countries would take them in. She had sponsored scholarships for poor Kenyan children, served with the Red Cross in Rwanda, and had a genius for getting grant money. Now she was lending her expertise, her time, and some of her money to International People's Aid.

Fitzhugh wasn't sure how much time or expertise she had, but when he and Malachy got to her place, it was apparent that she didn't lack for money. Two *askaris* opened a steel gate, admitting them to a world as remote from grimy, crumbling Nairobi as the land of her ladyship's forebears. Acres of grass and garden, shaded by tamarind and eucalyptus; a rambling main house with white stucco walls, a clay-tile roof, and a veranda upon which wicker chairs practically begged you to sit down with a drink; a guest cottage; a carriage house with a Mercedes sedan and a Toyota Land Cruiser parked beside it; a small stable, an exercise ring. It was February, the beginning of the dry season, and the air at the foot of the Ngong hills was crisp and clear, scented by frangipani, hibiscus, mimosa. Fitzhugh recalled that perfume, and how it went immediately to his head, like good gin.

While a servant went to summon Diana, the two men waited in the foyer of the main house. Fitzhugh looked at Malachy and raised his eyebrows.

"Ah, now then, Fitz, I know your feelings about upper-crust do-gooders. Believe me, she's different."

"Different how?"

Malachy answered that her mind wasn't the usual hatchery of idiotic schemes to uplift the dark-skinned downtrodden. Diana was practical, hard-headed. She knew what would work in Africa and what would not because she was as African as any Kikuyu, her family having been in Kenya for three generations.

Fitzhugh pointed at the sepia photographs on the foyer walls: brutal sahibs standing over lions they had shot, memsahibs wearing white muslin dresses and severe expressions—you could almost hear them ordering houseboys beaten for trying to clean tarnished silver plate by rubbing it with gravel.

"Atoning for her ancestors' sins with all her charity work?"

"It isn't charity," replied Malachy. "And as for *why* she does what she does, well now, what difference does that make, so long as she does the right thing?"

"Apoloreng! You are late!"

Her tone was cheerfully scolding: a hostess greeting a habitually tardy but always welcome guest.

Malachy made a pretense of looking at his watch and pleaded heavy traffic. The bloody traffic in Nairobi got worse by the day.

"Everything in this country gets worse by the day," she said, embraced him, and gave him each of her cheeks to kiss.

Malachy made the introductions. Diana Briggs took a half-step backward and extended her hand as she looked Fitzhugh up and down with the bluest eyes he had ever seen.

"I'd heard you were a footballer, and I must say, you look the part."

Her smile fell on him like a gift, and her accent, thankfully, lacked the marbles-in-the-mouth mutter of the British upper classes. She spoke with the precision of a BBC news reader.

Fitzhugh was something of a sexist. To his mind, beauty forgave almost everything in a woman. Not that Diana Briggs was exceptionally beautiful; she only seemed so in comparison with the picture he had formed of a stout matron, Malachy having told him that she was in her early fifties. The body that suggested itself under a black cotton blouse and a pair of linen trousers, while it wasn't slender, was a long way from matronly. If there was any gray in her blond hair, it had been artfully disguised. Only the cat's whiskers at the corners of her eyes and the crescent furrows at the corners of her mouth betrayed her age, and you had to be within an arm's length of her to see them; otherwise, you would have sworn she wasn't beyond thirty-five. All this and the smashing smile made it impossible for Fitzhugh to dislike her, as he'd been prepared to do.

He couldn't resist complimenting her looks. She responded with a toss of her head and a short, self-deprecatory laugh before telling the servant, in flawless Swahili, to bring in a fresh pot of tea.

They followed her through a hall decorated with ancestral memorabilia—crossed elephant tusks, the hide of a leopard that appeared to have been slain back in the days when Denys Finch-Hatton and Isak Dinesen were loving it up. Diana's loose trousers flowed about her hips and legs as she walked, and the swirl of linen over flesh would have been erotic if it weren't for her brisk, straight-backed stride, like a sergeant major's on parade. They entered a study—a lot of old books, more old photographs and moth-eaten skins, a Masai buffalo-hide shield hanging over a fireplace, in front of which two men sat, backs to the door.

"John, Doug, the circle for our seance is now complete," Diana said.

The pair stood. One was in his forties, going bald, and stood five-six at the tallest. He wore wire-rimmed glasses, and his complexion was the color of uncooked oats. This was John Barrett. When, with a kind of reflexive respect, Fitzhugh called him "Father Barrett," he grinned tightly and reminded him, in a brogue less pronounced than Malachy's, that he had lost claim to that title.

"It's just plain John," he said.

The other man was about Fitzhugh's height, with thick hair hued like khaki, a slim frame, and a long, thin nose, slightly hooked, giving him the aspect of a handsome raptor. He might have been thirty, though he easily could have passed for an undergraduate. Straight away Fitzhugh knew he was an American. It wasn't the cowboy boots and Levi's that declared his nationality, nor the scrubbed, healthy complexion, as if he'd just stepped out of the shower after a game of pick-up basketball. It was the way he stood, chin cocked up, shoulders slouched just a little, projecting the relaxed belligerence of a citizen of the nation that ran the world. Fitzhugh imagined that a young Englishman would have struck a similar stance out in India a century ago, or a young Roman in the court of some vassal Gaul.

"Doug Braithwaite," he drawled, shaking Malachy's hand, then Fitzhugh's, gripping his forearm with his other hand, as though they were old comrades, reunited.

"Fitzhugh Martin." He flexed his arm after a moment to signal Braithwaite to let it go.

"Great to meet you. Been hearing a lot about you."

If it's possible for eyes to embrace another person, his embraced Fitzhugh. They had that effect on everyone, creating an instant intimacy. Clear and gray, giving off the appealing gleam of artificial pearls, they flattered you the moment they fell on you, the directness of their gaze making you feel that he was interested only in you.

"It's all been good," he went on. "We've got something in common. We're both on the UN's shit list."

"Doug used to fly for the UN out of Loki," Diana interjected.

"I prefer to say that I flew for an airline contracted to the UN. PanAfrik Airways. Copilot on Hercs mostly," he added, turning again to Fitzhugh. "I'm surprised we never ran into each other. It's a big operation out there, but not that big."

"Evidently it's big enough for us not to have run into each other. I was in the field most of the time."

"Got the heave-ho a couple of weeks ago." There was an undertone of pride rather than shame in the statement. "Ran afoul of regulations. You know what I mean, Fitz."

Actually, he didn't quite but was somehow embarrassed to say so. He asked whom Braithwaite was flying for now.

"Myself, if I can ever get my hands on an airplane," he answered, with a smile that looked a little forced.

"So what regulations did you run afoul of?"

"It would be quicker to tell you which ones I didn't, Fitz," came the evasive answer. "Sorry. Is Fitz okay, or do you prefer Fitzhugh?"

The American had very nice manners. Fitz was fine. Braithwaite insisted that he call him Doug.

"Brilliant," Diana said, displaying her brilliant teeth for emphasis. "Now that we're all on a first-name basis, shall we get on with things?"

"Things" turned out to be a kind of job interview, with Diana and Barrett asking what exactly Fitzhugh had done for the UN for how long and why he'd left. Malachy had told them all about that, but now apparently they needed to hear it from Fitzhugh himself. Barrett looked elfin, but there was nothing elfin about his manner. Pitched forward in a green leather armchair—the kind you see in men's clubs—he fired his questions like a prosecutor. There seemed to be an anger in him; he was a regular little kettle on perpetual boil, though the source of the flame wasn't immediately clear. Whatever, the man's intensity compensated for his size; it forced everyone to pay attention to him, and (Fitzhugh doing some psychologizing) maybe that was the reason for it.

The servant came in, quietly served tea, and stole out again. The nature of the questions changed. What did Fitzhugh think the southern Sudanese were fighting for? Independence? Autonomy? A unified Sudan under a secular government? No idea, he replied. He wasn't sure if they knew any longer. Sometimes he had the impression that the rebels were fighting out of sheer habit. After all, they had been at it, off and on, for thirty years.

"Out of *habit*, you say?" Barrett leaned farther forward, so that his body was bent like a stubby hairpin. "Oh, I cannot agree with that, not at all. They're fighting because those butchers in Khartoum don't give them any choice. Fight or die—it's that simple, and make no mistake about it."

"I suppose that's true." Fitzhugh, feeling a bit like a pupil who has given the wrong answer, glanced sidelong at Malachy for help, but he gave none; nor did Douglas Braithwaite, sitting directly across, long legs outstretched while he chewed on the tips of his aviator's sunglasses and looked as if he were weighing Fitzhugh's every word.

"There's no supposin' either," said Barrett. His pallid face glowed. "It's jihad for the Arabs, and there's no quarter given in a jihad. Allah gives his stamp of approval to mass murder." Barrett sat back and took a sip of tea, the color fading from his cheeks. "This war isn't like these other African dust-ups. It's a continuation of the Crusades. The crescent versus the cross. Comes down to that, wouldn't you say?"

The war was nowhere near as clear-cut as that, but a voice in the back of Fitzhugh's head cautioned him not to voice such an observation. Gray did not appear to be Barrett's favorite color.

"Pardon me," he said, wondering if it had been a mistake to buy a one-way ticket. "I've come all the way from the coast, thinking you were going to talk to me about a job."

"And that is what we are doing. Isn't that what we are doing?"

Barrett glanced at Diana, sitting alongside him, her legs crossed, hands clasped over a knee, hair aglow in the dazzle slicing through the casement windows.

"You've wandered a bit far afield," she said in a voice tinged with exasperation. Soothing the scrapes caused by Barrett's abrasiveness was probably something she did fairly often. "Your questions seem to be making Fitz uncomfortable."

Fitzhugh remarked that he did not feel uncomfortable so much as baffled. It was as if Barrett were examining him not for his qualifications and experience but for his political correctness. He said that as a relief worker he had devoted himself to filling empty bellies, not to politics. "An empty belly is an empty belly, and what I think about the politics of the situation doesn't have anything to do with anything."

"On the contrary. Politics has everything to do with it."

"That isn't what I said!" Fitzhugh's voice broke, like a fourteen-year-old boy's, as it usually did when he got angry. "I said that what *I think* about the politics has nothing to do with it."

"A Jesuit is what you should have been, John Barrett," Malachy said. "Why are you being so argumentative?"

"And look who's talkin'. Malachy, there's no man as contentious as you.

I'm not arguin'. It's dedicated people we're lookin' for, committed people. For when the goin' gets rocky, as rocky it is bound to get." Barrett removed his glasses, blew on the lenses, and wiped them deliberately with a handkerchief. "Relief work is full of dilettantes. Nice people lookin' to do some good in the world so they can feel good about themselves. They hand out a few chocolate bars and go home."

Fitzhugh offered a none-too-amiable smile. "What is it you're suggesting?"

Barrett, returning his glasses to his face, was about to reply when Douglas made a sound—not a sigh, an exhalation rather, long and slow. It was almost inaudible, yet it had the same effect as a judge's gavel in a noisy courtroom. The conversation stopped, everyone turned to him. Fitzhugh would always remember that moment distinctly, because it was the first time he'd observed the American's peculiar power to draw all eyes and ears to himself with nothing more than a vague gesture, a change of expression, or a breath. It was a kind of magnetism, too effortless to have been learned.

"Fitz doesn't seem like any dilettante to me," he said in his pleasing drawl. "Seems all right to me, and I'm the one who'll be working with him. So how about we end the inquisition and tell him what the job is?"

"Splendid suggestion." Diana, rising, moved in a whisper of cotton and linen to a desk, one of those old campaign things with brass handles and corner brackets, and withdrew a large map, folded up with its printed side out. "Stuffy in here," she murmured, and cranked a window open. Immediately the intoxicating scent from her gardens filled the room.

Diana spread the map over a table: a pilot's chart, Fitzhugh saw by the black vector lines fanned across the green of equatorial swamps, the reddish browns and yellows of highlands and arid plains.

He shook a cigarette from his pack and asked Diana if she minded.

"Not at all, now that the window's open. You are familiar with this neck of the woods?"

A lacquered fingernail fell on one of the brown patches toward the upper edge of the map, marked *Jebel al-Nubah* in transliterated Arabic, the Nuba mountains. The years that did not show in Diana's face, Fitzhugh observed, were revealed in the fissured skin of her hands. They disappointed him somehow.

"Never been there," he said. "I don't think anyone has, oh, not for some time. No one from the outside."

"Fitz, I'm gettin' to be fond of your voice. There's a smile in it."

He looked at Barrett, leaning into the table, both sets of knuckles resting on the map, like a general planning a campaign.

"A smile?"

"Your voice smiles, even when you don't. I believe it's the cheeriest voice I've ever heard."

"I'm told it's boyish."

"I delight in the sound of it."

"Does that mean I'm hired?"

Barrett made an impatient gesture. "We know you could not have been *in* the Nuba mountains. We're wonderin' if you're familiar with the situation up there."

"Not much news comes out of there. Very isolated, very backward. I'm told the Nubans go about naked as Adam and Eve, some of them."

"And not entirely by choice," Barrett said.

"I did hear the government's been bombing up there."

"And two reasons for it." His fingers spread into a V. "One ideological, the second more down to earth, under the earth in fact." He folded one finger and with the other traced a road leading southward from the mountains to a town near the confluence of the Bahr el Ghazal river and the White Nile.

"Bentiu," Fitzhugh said. "There's oil there."

"And lots of it," said Barrett.

Then there was something about an international consortium, in partnership with the Sudanese state petroleum company, something more about building a thousand-mile pipeline all the way to Port Sudan, on the Red Sea.

"Construction's well under way," Barrett went on. "That gets done, and Sudan joins the club of big-time oil-exporting countries."

"And it doesn't take a rocket scientist to figure out what the government plans to buy with the revenues," Douglas added.

Barrett said, "For years, Khartoum has been trying to clear people out of Bahr el Ghazal and other places in the south, as you well know. But now they've redoubled their efforts. You know, dryin' up the sea of people the guerrilla fish swim in. And why? Amulet Energy—that's what the consortium calls itself—wants to make sure the pipeline route is secure, and of course, so does the Sudanese government."

Fitzhugh was momentarily distracted by his cigarette ash, about to fall on the map. He tapped it into his cupped hand, then went to the window and brushed it into a hibiscus shrub outside.

"I feel like I've walked into a military briefing. What does all this high-flown strategy have to do with me?"

"Part of the pipeline will pass near the Nuba," Barrett said, his finger now tracking along the western border of the mountains. "Khartoum wants to make sure the area is firmly under its control. And so, yes, they've bombed. And also stirred up Arab tribes to raid Nuban villages. Those who weren't killed outright were driven out of their homes, and those who didn't die of starvation or disease were herded into internment camps and forced to convert to Islam. Would that jibe with what you've heard?"

Fitzhugh nodded, then thought to qualify his answer: What he'd heard about the Nuba wasn't any different or worse than what he'd *seen* elsewhere in Sudan.

"But it could well get worse. This is where the first reason, the political and religious one, comes in." Barrett, his face gone florid again, flattened one hand to cover the reddish-brown swath on the map. "What you've got up here are brown Arab tribes and black Nuban tribes livin' more or less cheek by jowl. Some of the Arabs support the government, some don't, some don't care one way or the other. And the blacks, some of 'em sympathize with the SPLA and some don't. Anyway, up until recently this mixed lot—Christians, Muslims, ancestor-worshippers, whatever else—more or less got along. Yeah, the odd tribal dust-up now and then, but mostly live and let live, and that mob of fundamentalists in Khartoum can't tolerate that sort of toleration. Want *everybody* to be reading the Koran, *everybody* to follow Islamic law. Makin' that bloody oil pipeline secure gives 'em a perfect excuse to do what they've been wantin' to do for a long time."

"But worse. You said it could get worse," Fitzhugh said. "Like I said, what you're telling me doesn't sound any worse than—"

"Because the Nuba is so isolated," Barrett said, cutting him off. "No pryin' eyes to report on what's goin' on up there. Khartoum has declared that the whole bleedin' place is a no-go zone, thirty thousand square miles, a million people. A few Nuban *meks*—that's what they call their big chiefs up there—somehow got word to the UN and appealed for 'em to send in some assistance. A couple of NGOs were ready to, but those outfits are under the UN umbrella, and the UN muckety-mucks said no."

"Another excuse to do nothing," Douglas interjected. "Sometimes you have to take sides."

He gave Fitzhugh a glance whose meaning was ambiguous.

"I have no problem taking a side, if I think it's right. I believe I've shown that."

Douglas eked out a thin smile that hovered between arrogant and self-assured. "Fitz, if you hadn't, we wouldn't even be having this conversation."

They were through testing him, if that's what they'd been up to, and at last clued him in. Barrett said he had presented the board of International People's Aid a plan for delivering assistance to the Nuba. Obviously the group would be operating independently, off the UN reservation. Barrett's strategy was to provide disaster relief at first and then development aid to rebuild bombed-out roads and devastated farms and above all St. Andrew's mission, where, after his conversion to Protestantism, he had preached as a guest minister.

There had been nothing like it in all the Nuba, he said, with its fine church of brick and granite quarried from the surrounding hills, with its clinic and primary and secondary schools, its guest house for visiting clergy, its training center where agriculture, carpentry, and tailoring had been taught. A lodestar of progress and education, a refuge for the sick. A prosperous town, called New Tourom, had grown up around it, and so the fanatics had had to erase it from the map. Bombed it first with cluster bombs, armed and incited a tribe of Baggara Arabs from the plains to raid it. The minister, the canon, and three teachers were killed, along with sixteen schoolchildren and an unknown number of townspeople. More were captured, to be taken to the camps or sold into slavery. Others fled deep into the bush.

Barrett had returned there a month ago to inspect what was left and was sickened and outraged by what he'd seen. He must have delivered electrifying sermons, for he painted a vivid scene of biblical desolation. The town that had once harbored twenty-five hundred souls now counted under a thousand. Houses had been devoured by red ants. Terraced farm fields had gone back to scrub. The ruined church was a nest for rats and snakes.

"The only bright spot," he went on, "is that the SPLA has opened up a Nuban front—War Zone Two, they call it. They've moved troops into the mountains and the rebel headquarters are near New Tourom. A full regiment, nearly a thousand men. Man in charge is a Nuban himself, Lieutenant Colonel Goraende. Splendid soldier. He'll provide you with security."

Fitzhugh wasn't sure he'd heard right. "Me?"

"Who else would I be talkin' about? Rebuildin' the mission, that's our long-range goal, but for the meantime there's more immediate needs to be addressed. IPA's board has to have an estimate of what those needs are and their costs. I can't give 'em the costs without knowin' the extent of the needs, and that's where you come in."

Fitzhugh was beyond incredulous. "You want *me* to assess what they are? I'm to go into the Nuba mountains? Alone?"

Everyone was silent for a moment or two; then Diana turned sharply to Malachy, who raised both hands in a mock plea for forgiveness.

"Told him you were planning to take some bold steps, that was all. Didn't seem prudent to say anything more on the phone, and once he got here, well now, I thought it best he heard it from you."

"Oh dear, Fitz, we're awfully sorry."

The clear, steady blue eyes, the smashing smile, the face that belonged in a garden party in the London suburbs. She started to say more but stopped herself at some vague sign from Douglas.

"You won't be by yourself," he said. "I'll be going with you."

"A tough business, and risky, I know," Barrett chimed in. "You won't, of course, be expected to cover all the Nuba, just as much as you can in a fortnight. That would give us a picture of the whole. The board's given me the okay to offer you five thousand U.S."

Fitzhugh shook his head.

"Not enough?" asked Diana, frowning.

"Oh, no. Fine and dandy. Much more than the UN would have paid for a fortnight's work. But you see—" He broke off, silently questioning Malachy's assessment of Diana as a woman whose head wasn't a hatchery for mad schemes. Maybe she didn't hatch this one, but she sure was part of it. His glance moving to the window and the trellis outside, with its cascades of red and purple bougainvillea, he recalled that he'd read or heard somewhere that the air in the Kenyan highlands had caused the early European settlers to lose their senses, filling them up with grandiose visions. Evidently it had not lost its power to addle the white mind.

"The Nuba is a thousand kilometers from Loki," he said, starting over. "How do we get in there, and what's more, out?"

Diana gave him a quizzical look. "We've chartered Tara Whitcomb. She's not averse, if the occasion demands it, to fly on the dark side. And she knows Sudan better than any pilot in Africa. She'll fly you and Douglas in, same as she did John. You know Tara, don't you? At least heard of her?"

He nodded.

"To reduce the risk of the wrong people finding out where you're going, she will file a false flight plan," Diana continued, a sudden chill in her voice. "As she did with John."

"And we didn't have a wink of trouble," Barrett added by way of assuring him. "Khartoum makes a lot of threats, but they haven't got the means to carry the half of them out."

Fitzhugh wanted to say that it was the other half that concerned him, but he kept silent on that point, going straight to the crux of the issue and of his confusion. As far as he knew, there were no landing fields in the Nuba mountains capable of handling cargo planes. How, then, did the well-meaning Canadians of International People's Aid propose to deliver tons of aid to the Nuban people? Were they going to build airstrips? Use airdrops? With Arab raiders on the ground and government planes in the sky? He asked these questions one after the other, *bim, bam, boom,* not so much to elicit answers as to show how crazy and impossible the entire enterprise sounded to him.

"It's going to work this way," Douglas answered. "I've incorporated an air charter company, Knight Air Services. All the red tape's been taken care of. Like I said, all I need is an airplane."

"An essential piece of equipment, I'd say," Fitzhugh remarked drily.

"I'll get one, and once I do, IPA is going to be my first client. I won't be playing Mother May I? with Khartoum. It'll be nothing but flying on the dark side."

"Running the blockade," Fitzhugh murmured. An excitement, tinged with fear, spread through his chest.

The American's eyebrows lifted and dropped, quickly.

"While you're doing what you've got to do, I'll be looking for drop zones for airdrops, I'll be looking for suitable sites for landing strips. We're going to need more than the one Tara landed at. Good hard ground, room for bigger planes to land and take off. And yeah, we'll get them built. I *know* we can do this. It's a place where a few people can make a big difference."

Fitzhugh didn't share his confidence; he was all but certain that they could not do it. The plan had the quality of a behind-enemy-lines operation that seemed to call for commandos, not a cargo pilot and an aid worker with a bum knee. Astonishing himself, he stuck out his hand and told Douglas and the others that they could count him in. He wondered if the heady highlands atmosphere had affected the vulnerable Caucasian part of his brain, for at that moment he had a sensation of being split in two. His dark-skinned half, skeptical, sober, wise, stood off to the side, as it were, and frowned at his light-skinned half, shaking hands and announcing that he could be counted in. *Sleep on it, think it over, you might regret this,* the dark warned the light, but the light had the upper hand. Much later the clarifying beam of hindsight would show that it wasn't any hundred-proof air that had undermined his better judgment; it was Douglas and Douglas's remark: "*It's a place where a few people can make a big difference.*" Fitzhugh wasn't immune to the desire that's in most people to spray graffiti on the cold rock of the world and say "I was here and what I did counted for something." For someone of his temperament, the mere notion of undertaking a dangerous endeavor on behalf of a desperate people held an irresistible appeal. But there was still more to it: He felt that he would have disappointed Douglas if he'd said no. He could have said it to Barrett or Diana but not to him. He didn't know why. There was something about the American that made you not want to let him down.

He wasn't, however, so drunk on the idea that he was ready to pack his bags then and there and fly off blindly into the unknown. "You are sure that this lieutenant colonel—what was his name?"

"Goraende. Michael Archangelo Goraende."

"You are sure he will provide us with security?"

"He'll have a detachment of his best lads to look out for you," Barrett assured him. "Should give you some comfort. Michael the Archangel is the patron saint of warriors, the Roman Catholic version of Mars."

Fitzhugh said he would be grateful for any help he and Douglas could get.

"Would you be a Catholic yourself?" asked Barrett, in as friendly a manner as he'd shown all afternoon. "Malachy tells me you've a bit of Irish in you."

"Only a bit."

"But enough to put the smile in that voice of yours. Comes from the Irish, make no mistake about it."

Mustang

"Good mornin' and jambo, *rafiki*."

He showed his pass with a quick flip of his wallet, a pointless formality; none of the askaris at Wilson Field ever looked at the damned thing. That one was no exception, waving him through without a glance, his bored expression as fixed as a mask.

The ancient Volvo's engine rattled as he eased the clutch and followed the line of pickup trucks through the gate. He parked beside his copilot's car while the trucks proceeded across the tarmac toward the Gulfstream. In the morning twilight its dingy white fuselage reminded him of a seagull in need of a bath. Must've been a right smart thing in her day, when she ferried CEOs to big important meetings. No frequent-flyer first-class-upgrade bullshit for those boys, no sir, no way.

Feeling a bit old—a resistance in his joints not alarming in itself so much as in its portent—Wesley Dare got out of the car, leaned against the door, and finished the lukewarm coffee in his Thermos. He swallowed half, spit out the rest. How in the hell can it be, he asked himself, that in a country where such fine coffee gets grown, no one can brew a pot that doesn't taste like it's been filtered through a secretary's pantyhose after a ten-hour day? Out on the tarmac the boys were unloading the trucks. A tally-man, a big guy, heaved the fifty-pound bags off the asphalt and held them up by the hook of a hand scale, squinting to read the weights. He called them out to Nimrod, who was Dare's loadmaster, bookkeeper, and fixer, all wrapped up in a squat package of somber conscientiousness and honesty, or what served as a reasonable facsimile of honesty in Kenya. "Twenty kilos . . . twenty-one . . . twenty-two . . ." chanted the tally-man, while Nimrod totaled up on a pocket calculator.

Dare lit a cigarette, one of the five he allowed himself each day, and watched Tony Bollichek, his Australian first officer, do his walk-around, checking the belly of the aircraft, the landing gear, the props for dings and pings. A fine, careful pilot, in contrast to Dare, who was a fine pilot but not a particularly careful one—the casualness of his maintenance and preflight checks were legendary in the bush pilot fraternity. Tony's girlfriend walked beside him, the Canadian, Something-Anne, or Anne-Something. Anne-Louise? Anne-Marie? Jane-Anne? In addition to her name, Dare had forgotten that she would be flying with them today. She'd spent the last three months copiloting UN Buffalos on airdrops over Sudan, and now her contract had expired and she was looking to get checked out on the G1. He suspected that she and Tony hoped he would offer her a job.

Not much chance of that. He couldn't afford another flier on the payroll. Besides, he was wary when it came to women; wary about them in general—a guardedness not surprising in a man who had survived four marital crashes—and especially about flying with them. It wasn't that he thought women were less competent; it was the streak of superstitiousness in him, which all his experience and technical training had never eradicated. A female in the cockpit, like a female aboard ship, was bad luck, and Dare believed in luck. It was one of the three things he did believe in, the other two being his ability to fly any airplane anywhere in any kind of weather, and loyalty to his fellow aviators. Those were the pillars of the personal philosophy Dare had constructed: a jerry-built structure, he would be the first to admit, but it suited his vagrant life and had seen him safely through twenty thousand hours of flying in dodgy places from Laos to Nicaragua to the Persian Gulf to Yemen. A Pathet Lao bullet, piercing the skin of an Air America C-47 somewhere over the Meo highlands in 1970, had nipped off half his right big toe, and he'd suffered a broken collarbone after an emergency landing in Honduras carried his plane off the runway into the jungle. Aside from the financial and emotional wounds of four divorces, that was all the injury his career had done him, and he reckoned that was because he was damned good and damned lucky. Lucky because he was good. If someone ever built a temple dedicated to fortune and skill, he'd worship there every Sunday. He could not picture himself in any other sort of church, hadn't set foot in one since he was thirteen. The past twenty-five years had taught him that it wasn't avarice that filled the public squares with corpses; it wasn't envy that pulled the triggers of the world's firing squads, nor lust that set the timers to the terrorist's bombs; it was faith in some particular creed, sect, ideology, cause, or crusade. Having seen what true believers were capable of, Wesley Dare had turned disbelief into a kind of belief in itself. It wasn't an attitude he put on when circumstances required it, like a parka in winter; it was part of his nature, lodged in his cells, a built-in antibody against the virus that led to zealotry and fanaticism at the one extreme, to disillusionment at the other. His life, so much of which had been spent in places that ran on bribery, theft, and fraud, had likewise immunized him to the conviction, widely held by otherwise intelligent people, that human beings are fundamentally decent. As a rule he had found it useful as well as prudent to trust his fellow man to do the right thing only when the wrong thing failed to present itself. Consequently he was seldom disgusted by corrupt officials who had their hands out; seldom did he feel angry, betrayed, or disappointed when someone tried to cheat or screw him in any way. To expect anything more of most people was as pointless as waiting for the lion to eat straw with the ox. This outlook had made Dare a jovial cynic. To his eye, the human comedy really was comical.

Her name was Anne-Marie.

He ground the cigarette underfoot, then did a deep-knee bend to reassure himself that the stiffness in his limbs was the benign variety natural to a man of fifty-three and not the beginning of the acute rheumatoid arthritis that had crippled his father, who'd closed out his life in a wheelchair, fingers curled like talons. A rotten end for a guy who had barnstormed on the West Texas plains before the big war, flown P-51 Mustangs during it, and done a little bit of everything after it—crop dusting, instructing, air mail deliveries. Mustang. The word came from the Mexicans, *mestengo,* stray. And that was the old man, a wild one. There was no one Dare had admired more. The proudest moment of his life came when he was sixteen and soloed for the first time. He landed the 1941 Piper Cub with barely a bump, climbed out, and did his best to affect a veteran's saunter—not entirely a contrivance, as he had flown alongside his father since he was eleven and had landed planes before he'd learned to parallel park a car. Jack McIntyre, Dad's partner in the little flight school outside Fort Stockton, pumped his hand and said, "Damn near a greaser, Wes. You're rolled of the same makin's as the old man." It had been all Dare could do to keep his composure.

Now, taking a deep breath, he transferred some of his gut to his chest, where all of it had been not too many years ago, and ambled across the tarmac, greeting truck drivers and ground crew with a broad but synthetic grin. (He didn't much care for these city-bred Africans, saving his admiration for the regal Masai and Turkana.) "Hi, y'all! Good mornin'! One helluva fine day for movin' a little dope, ain't it?" Those who knew him grinned back and said, "*Jambo, Bwana* Wes." (He got a chuckle out of that, *Bwana* Wes.) Those who did not know him merely looked with silent curiosity at the beefy, cheerful *mzungu* with lamb's-wool hair like theirs, except that it was rusty red instead of black, big ears that stuck out, and a pug nose spread between narrow brown eyes and a wide mouth.

"Hey, Nimrod. *Hujambo.*"

"*Sijambo, asante,* Captain Wes," the small Kikuyu said, focusing on his calculations. Dare was an even six-one, but standing beside Nimrod always made him feel like a center for the L.A. Lakers. He glanced at the calculator, its numbers aglow in the dim light, and then at the sacks still to be weighed. Here and there, sprigs of *mirra* poked shyly through the throats of poorly tied bags or through the burlap weave.

"Not so good today." Nimrod tapped the "plus" key.

Twelve hundred and twenty-five kilos so far. The Somalis paid a bonus for any load of two tons or more. Dare would need around six hundred kilos more to make that, and he did not see six hundred remaining on the trucks. Nowhere near. Four at best.

"Well," he said with a philosophical shrug, "win some, lose some."

"And some are rained on," Nimrod said, finishing one of Dare's favorite sayings.

"*Out,* rafiki. Some are rained *out.*" He turned to Tony, who was murmuring relevant facts about the G1 to Anne-Marie. Cruising speed and altitude, fuel capacity and range. Did that pass as romantic conversation between two fliers? "How about that pump?"

"No ruckin' furries, or so I'm told," Bollichek said, indicating the hangar with a movement of his head. "We'll see."

He meant that the mechanics *said* they had repaired the pump, a claim whose veracity would be impeached if the amber warning light flashed during preflight. It had gone on yesterday, as he and Tony were taxiing to the runway for their afternoon run. Although Dare relished and even cultivated his reputation as an aerial cowboy, he turned around immediately, not about to take off with a malfunctioning pump. It fed a water-methanol mixture to the Rolls-Royce engine, increasing horsepower. Wilson Field was a mile high, and the plane needed the extra boost in the thinner air.

"So did they say what was wrong?"

"Buggered rotor. They replaced it."

Dare nodded, pulled his baseball cap from his hip pocket, put it on, and watched a chain of workers passing the sacks into the aircraft, its seats removed long ago and replaced with folding web jumpseats to make cargo space.

"Looks like we'll be ready for boarding right quick. Passengers needing assistance and with small children will board first by row numbers. How are you doin', Anne-Marie? Y'all ready to smuggle drugs into deepest, darkest Somalia?"

A doubtful smile fluttered across her lips, then faded.

"I was just kiddin'," he said, laughing. "Mirra, also known as *khat*, ain't really a drug. Like coke or grass, I mean. And we ain't really smugglin', because it's legal here. Grown like coffee on Mount Kenya's fer-tile slopes. Legal in Somalia, too. Of course, everything's legal in Somalia, since there ain't any law there."

"I know that," she said, bristling at the assumption that she was naïve about such matters. "It's Mary."

He hesitated for a beat, gazing at her. With her wavy, dark blond hair and hazel eyes, she reminded him a little of his first wife, Margo, mother of his only child and the only one of his spouses his mother had ever cared for. *"You would do well to hang on to her, Wesley. You got your daddy's looks, y'know. Ugly as home-grown sin."* That was Mom, not a strong one when it came to building her offspring's self-esteem.

"Well, shee-hit, and I could've sworn it was Anne-Marie," Dare said. "Now where did I get that idea? Tell you where. Because you're from Canada. Anne-Marie sounds sorta French, doesn't it?"

"I'm from Manitoba, not Quebec. Mary English. Can't get much more un-French than that, can you?"

"Hell, no! All right, Mary English"—dipping into his shirt pocket for a spare pair of gold-embossed epaulets—"wear these. We'll be gettin' off the aircraft while they off-load, and these'll identify you as crew. Just in case."

She unbuttoned the shoulder flaps on her khaki shirt, put the epaulets on, and asked, "In case of what?"

"In case of anything," Dare said. "Somalia, darlin'."

The sun rose without any gradual color-splashed ascent, just an abrupt burst of equatorial light. The ground crew finished loading, fifteen hundred and fifty kilos of bagged mirra piled on the floor secured with canvas straps tied to D-rings. Aside from Mary and Nimrod, the only passengers were the stockily built dealer, representing the big man behind the opera-tion, and the dealer's wife, gowned, veiled, her hands and arms displaying henna tattoos. Dare and Tony had flown together long enough to dispense with most preflight formalities; normally they gave the instruments, flaps, and rudder a quick check, fired the engines, and took off. This time, in the interests of providing Mary English with a proper introduction to the Gulfstream, they ran through the entire litany with the diligence of a com-mercial airline crew. She sat in the jumpseat directly behind the pedestal, looking earnest and attentive. Probably one of those girls who always lis-tened in class and got her homework in on time.

"Generator on," said Tony into his headset's microphone. Dare started number-two engine, and they all three watched the prop blades paddle slowly for a couple of revolutions, then spin into invisibility except for the black tips that merged to draw a blurred, stationary circle in the air.

"Clear one."

The other engine barked and revved up to a throbbing whine, and the plane shuddered as if she were excited, anticipating her release.

Dare got his taxi clearance from the tower—a UN-chartered Antonov would be ahead of them for takeoff.

"Let's roll," he said, feeling a mild impatience. "There's money to be made."

Mary asked how much, and he told her: thirty-five hundred U.S., plus six free drums of fuel, donated by the warlord in whose territory they would be doing business. The money had come not from the small fry in back but from his boss, a guy named Hassan Adid. He released the brakes and trailed the AN-28 toward the runway, past rows of idle aircraft, most beyond their prime. Sometimes Wilson Field looked like an airshow for used-up planes.

"Busy place, ain't it, Margo?"

"Mary."

"I mean Mary." He gestured out his side window. "Yeah, one busy airport, and all do-gooders, too. See that Cessna yonder? The red and white one? Those folks are goin' to save the elephant. And that other one, the old Fokker—they're goin' to save the rhino. And that Polish Let out at the end is another UN plane, so I reckon they're goin' to save people. Winston Churchill said that the UN isn't here to bring paradise on earth, but to prevent everything from goin' to hell entirely. But I ain't sure it's doin' even that."

"When did Churchill say that?"

"Hell, I don't know, but he said it."

Ahead, the Antonov swung off the taxiway, stood poised for a moment while her skipper throttled up, then lurched forward, an overbuilt assembly of collective-factory steel riveted together in the now-extinct Soviet Union. Dare turned into position and pushed the throttle levers forward and watched the RPM needles wind up, the engines protesting the restraint of the brakes. Tony's voice crackled in his earpieces. Flaps and rudders set . . . RPM normal . . .

"No light on the pumps," Bollichek added. "Reckon the blokes did what they said, miracle of miracles."

"You can bet Nimrod got on their asses."

"The hope of Africa, Nimrod."

"There ain't any hope."

"Wilson Tower, this is Five Yankee Alpha Charlie Sierra, ready for take-off," Dare said.

"Five Yankee Alpha Charlie Sierra, you are clear," the controller said in his accented English, then gave the wind speed and direction and temperature. A fine cool morning. Fast takeoff, use up less fuel.

"Thanks. See y'all for lunch."

He took his feet off the brakes again and went to full throttle. The Gulfstream lunged down the lumpy asphalt. The unkempt meadows alongside, vestiges from the days when Wilson was the grassy platform from which Beryl Markham flew west with the night and Finch-Hatton soared off for Tsavo and its elephant herds, sped by at sixty knots, eighty, ninety, one oh five . . . Dare pulled back on the yoke and the plane gathered herself like a high jumper, lurched, and was airborne, a free thing now, and he was free with her, liberated from gravity and the sordid earth. Gear up. Nairobi shrank below, the skyscrapers of the city center, the tidy red rooftops of Karen and Langata, the sheet-metal slums metastasizing on the outskirts. How many times had he done this since the first time with his father in a Steerman crop-duster, sagebrush and mesquite plains falling away and only sky ahead, where cloud flotillas sailed the stratosphere? How many? Four thousand? Five, six? He wondered if he would ever tire of it, the thrill of takeoff, the joy of flight. Aloft, he felt at home and somehow complete, as if in the exile of terrestrial life he were estranged from himself, a divided man.

At twenty-five hundred feet he turned, picked up his easterly bearing, and climbed over the highlands before leveling off at twenty-one thousand, where faint ribbons of vapor trailed from the wingtips and the bright sun, mitigated slightly by his polarized glasses, sliced through the windshield. Airspeed two hundred twenty-five knots. He throttled back to conserve fuel and crossed into the eastern savannahs and over the Tana river, shimmering golden brown between its gallery forests, the plains beyond a mottle of red and khaki that vanished into the haze at the horizon. Barely a cloud in the sky, a dry-season sky. The radar screen was blank, as if they were flying into a vacuum, which in one sense they were. From here on, control towers and beacons would be as rare as whiskey in a Shiite's living room. No ground radar to cross-check his altimeter reading, and not a soul to tell him about the weather and wind conditions at his destination, a small airstrip on the beach south of Mogadishu. Except for the GPS, he would have nothing more to guide him there than Finch-Hatton and Markham had had. All dead reckoning, and pray you reckon right, the penalty for being wrong pretty severe in Somalia. Fly into the wrong fiefdom, and you risked a shoulder-fired missile or some hothead shooting at you with a 12.7-millimeter antiaircraft gun.

"Fly the unfriendly skies of Somalia," he said, thinking aloud.

"Tony was saying."

Mary craned her head forward between the seats, an anticipatory look on her face. Tell me a story, Daddy.

"Airdrops got to be right boring, right, Marie?"

"Mary. Maaa-reee."

"Wesley's got a sure-fire cure for the airdrop blues." Dare switched on the autopilot and turned partway around, feeling the warmth from her cheek radiating into the cool cabin air. "Once upon a time I had to go to Djbouti for an Eyetalian NGO that was drillin' water wells over on the Somali side. That country used to be called the Territory of the Afars and Issas, but then they changed it to the name of the capital, so it's Djbouti, Djbouti, the place so nice they named it twice. Flew in some hardware, then over into Somalia to pick up one of their drillin' teams. Landed on a patch of dirt, and what do I see but three white guys runnin' for the plane like hell wouldn't have it and a mob of clansmen runnin' after 'em. Shootin' at 'em. I had both engines still runnin', which was damned fortunate. Got the Eyetalians on board, and weren't they just one squeeze away from shittin' their britches, which I don't blame them, because those clansmen were still firin' away with their AKs and I was about to shit mine. Cranked up and took off, but not before they shot my right prop all to hell, as I was climbin'. Now Djbouti, Djbouti, ain't so nice that it's got anyplace where you can fix the prop to a Hawker-Siddley. Had to go all the way to Cairo to get it fixed, and on the way, after the Eyetalians got settled down, I asked them, 'Who in the hell did you piss off and why?' "

" 'Wrong clan,' one of 'em says to me. 'Wrong clan work for us.' What he meant was, the boys shootin' at him and his buddies was a rival clan to the one they'd hired to do their well-diggin'. I asked him why they did that, and he said that if they'd hired *that* clan, then the one they *had* hired would've been the ones doin' the shootin'. That's when I realized how things are in Somalia. No matter which clan they'd hired, it would've been the wrong one. That was my first dealin' with the Somalis, and let me tell you, Margo, they're the meanest, baddest sonsabitches in East Africa. Just ask them Army Rangers they dragged through the streets of Mogadishu. It's how come I like flyin' mirra to the Somalis so much."

"All right, I give up," Mary said after a brief silence.

"Mirra does this to the libido"—Dare lowered a palm toward the floor—"so I figure the more of it I can bring in for them to chew, the less Somalis there's gonna be, and the world will be a better place. See, I'm a do-gooder, too."

She started to laugh but checked herself. A woman with a liberal social and political conscience, he could see that plainly, and as was his habit when he outraged someone's sensibilities, he decided to push the outrageousness a little further.

"Well, that's a lot more humane than nuking the black bastards, which is what we should of done after they dragged those Rangers through the streets in front of the TV cameras."

"Jesus, Wes—"

"Aw, you ain't thinkin' I'm a racist, are you?"

"You do have a reputation," she remarked guardedly. Her conscience notwithstanding, there was no percentage in getting into an argument with the man she hoped to ask for a job.

"Don't listen to my fan club," he said. "They like to flatter me, tellin' everyone that Wesley Dare is a cowboy pilot and a racist and a sexist and every other kind of 'ist.' In all humility, I gotta admit ain't none of it is true. Take the Masai, the Turkana, the Samburu. They're not exactly *white*, are they? But if it was up to me, I'd be flyin' aphrodisiacs into them so there would be more of them. And you've got to admit, the Somalis didn't put their best foot forward when me and them first met. They haven't done a thing since to change my first impression, but I'll be sure to keep an open mind."

A short time later he switched off the autopilot and dropped to twelve thousand, cruising at that altitude until he crossed the coastline, where he descended further, banking sharply as he did to fly due north, parallel to the shore and about three miles out. The Gulfstream cast a shadow on the Indian Ocean, which looked like a vast bolt of ruffled satin in the light southerly breeze. His principal concern now was to make sure he stayed well clear of Mogadishu; the clans in control of the city were especially trigger-happy and jealous of their airspace.

"We're lookin' for an abandoned oil refinery," he informed Mary. "That's where we'll turn inland on our base leg."

They flew on, and then it appeared, its rusty stacks rising from behind the barrier of coastal dunes and bluffs. He made a tight turn, over the breakers rolling ashore, the dunes, and the refinery, then brought the plane in on final, winging above expanses of scrub-speckled sand. Flaps down, gear down and locked. Flocks of goats, mud-walled huts, shacks built of corrugated iron appeared and disappeared. Altitude five hundred feet, airspeed one hundred twenty knots. The starboard wing's shadow passed over a group of black-clad women clustered around a well. A right biblical scene, women at the well, Dare thought as a Sunday school lesson came back to him, blurred by the distance of four decades. Four and then some. Rachel, wasn't it? No, Rebecca. Airspeed one hundred and five. Dead level. The G1 touched down, rubber softly biting hard-packed sand. Dare reached behind the throttles for the fine-pitch lever, tilting the prop blades to create drag to slow the plane. She rolled as smoothly as if he'd landed her on a freshly paved runway in L.A. or Chicago instead of a beach airstrip at the edge of Africa.

"Slick," Mary said. Buttering me up, thought Dare as she added jauntily, "Couldn't have done better myself."

"There's not many could have." He spun the plane around to idle toward the opposite end of the airstrip. "Put wings and a prop on it, darlin', and I'll fly you a brick shithouse anywhere you want to go."

"Mary," she said. "Not Margo, not Marie, and definitely not 'darlin'.' Or 'honey.' I'm a pilot, not a waitress. You don't mind, Wes."

"Not atall," he muttered, and spun the plane again, putting her nose into the wind in case he had to take off in a hurry.

After shutting the engines down, he pulled his holstered Beretta from under his seat, loaded a clip, and strapped it on.

"What's that for?" Mary looked, well, not alarmed exactly. Concerned.

"For show mostly. Somalis respect a man with a gun, but the truth is, if it came to a fight, the only thing this would be good for is committin' suicide."

Nimrod opened the forward door and dropped the ladder. Dare, Tony, and Mary climbed out into the midmorning heat. Dare was dismayed to see a mini-Minolta hanging from Mary's wrist by a cord. He took off the windbreaker he'd worn in flight—the heat had been turned off to keep the mirra fresh—and watched a convoy of Technicals bump down the dirt road leading from the town to the airstrip, each vehicle mounting a machine gun on the cab and carrying its complement of gunmen: boys who were boys in age only, assault rifles strapped across their backs and a menace in their expressionless faces and dead eyes. Shoot you down point-blank with no more feeling than if they'd squashed a bug. The trucks wheeled up and the gunmen jumped out, while Nimrod opened the rear door and porters began to off-load amid a lot of yelling and shouting. Hawkers and peddlers materialized out of thin air and turned the place into an open-air bazaar, barking offers for watches, jewelry, TVs, VCRs, cassette players, CD players, kitchen blenders—name it and they were likely to have it in one of their makeshift warehouses, brand-new stuff still in the shipping boxes that had been pilfered off the docks in Aden and Dubai and smuggled to Somalia on dhows.

"Take a look at this," Dare said to Mary. "Pure Somalia, a Wall Street stockbroker's wet dream, capitalism completely off the leash, and you got a license to shoot the competition. Y'all want to buy somethin' cheap and duty-free, now's the time and here's the place to do it."

"Not in a shopping mood, thanks."

The noisy jostle appeared to make her wary, and he didn't blame her. A current of instability and incipient violence buzzed through the carnival-like atmosphere like the hum from high-voltage power lines. The scene could turn ugly at any moment. Dare sensed it—he always did—and was pleased with Mary for sensing it as well. Her receptiveness to that hum of danger, a hum felt rather than heard, compensated for the camera, telling him that she wasn't some goddamned tourist, like a lot of the kids who came out to Africa with their pilot's licenses and the hope of obtaining adventure and a paycheck at the same time, never believing anything could happen to them because they were young, because Africa was the-ater to them and they were the audience. They didn't realize that the spec-tacle could spill off the stage right into their laps before they had a chance to run for the exit.

"Like to try some of what we brought in?" he asked her.

"Tastes like dried horseshit mixed with sour limes and rotten spinach," Tony said. "And you can get more of a jolt off a six-pack of Diet Coke."

"What a sales pitch," said Mary brightly. "I'd love some."

Ambling past a tribal elder carrying a bronze-bladed spear, Dare went to one of the trucks and plucked a handful of the dark green leaves from a bag.

"Damn! This old airplane once upon a time flew executive big-wigs for Kellogg's Corn Flakes, and now it's flyin' this shit into Somalia," he said, passing the leaves to Mary. "Kinda like me. Once upon a time I was the official pilot for the governor of Texas. Did you know that?"

She shook her head.

"Wad it up and chew it like bubble gum," he instructed.

She did this, grimaced, and spat the wad in disgust.

"Told you, love," said Tony.

The elder, a traditionalist in apparel as well as armament—he wore sandals instead of sneakers, a robe instead of jeans—grinned and told her that she should have brewed it as tea.

"Khat make a very fine tea, lady," he said.

"I can't believe these people like this stuff."

"Like it?" Dare said. "Hell, Mary, they love it. I've seen a roomful of guys chewin' on it like bunnies in a cabbage patch. When your religion won't allow you a taste of whiskey, you got to have somethin' to get you through the day."

She laughed very hard, and he said he didn't think he had been *that* funny.

"No. It was the way you said, 'Hell, Mary.' *Hail*, Mary. Like Wesley Dare, the big bad cowboy pilot was addressing the Virgin."

"I take it that wouldn't of been the case?"

"I'll bet Mary wasn't either," Mary said, with a provocative flip of her honey-blond hair. The kind of woman not to permit a man much sleep, oh, my, no.

"Good thing there's Muslims here, you're talkin' that blasphemeous trash."

She raised her arm and wriggled the wrist with the dangling Minolta. "All right?"

"Don't go too far and stick close to Tony, and if some guy says you got to pay to take his picture, don't do it," Dare advised.

Looking at them walk off side by side, Mary's bottom curving sweetly under her snug khakis, he felt an emotion he did not want to call desire or jealousy; a longing, rather. He tried to banish the feeling by reminding himself that she was twenty-odd years younger and would not have been interested in him even if he weren't as ugly as home-grown sin. The attempt wasn't successful. Another reason they're bad luck, he thought. Just when you think you've got yourself on an even keel, you meet one like her and realize you've been kidding yourself.

"Now finish."

It was the dealer, gesturing at the trucks, the last one of which was being loaded.

"Shukran, my friend," said Dare as he was handed three bundles of hundred-dollar bills, bound with rubber bands. They made him feel a little better about things, and stuffing them into his windbreaker pocket, he reflected on the odd ways that governed life in this part of the world. You could get killed here for no reason whatever, yet you could also stand in a crowd of heavily armed thugs with thirty-five hundred in cash in your pocket and feel as safe as if you were in the vault at Chase Manhattan. It was greed that protected you. Rip off the pilot who flew the stuff in, and there went your profitable trade. Thank the Lord for implanting greed in the hearts of men; if these clansmen were fighting for their faith instead of loot, it would be a different story altogether.

As the trucks drove off, trailing funnels of dust and sand, a dozen people queued alongside the airplane: two kids, three men, and seven women, clutching cloth valises and cardboard suitcases lashed with rope. Dare sometimes took paying passengers on the return legs of his mirra runs; dead-heading home with an empty, unprofitable aircraft was against his principles. While Nimrod collected the modest fare and checked passports—Kenya immigration could come down real hard if you flew in undocumented aliens—two Somalis topped off the G1's tanks with the drums of gratis fuel. One stood by the blue plastic barrels, cranking by hand; the other stood by the wing on a folding ladder and held the hose, which was patched with duct and electrical tape. They had emptied half the drums and had just begun the fourth when the man on the ladder yelled to his companion, who stopped cranking; under pressure, one of the patches had burst and several gallons of Jet-A1 splashed over the wing. The man climbed onto it, pulled off his T-shirt, and commenced to wipe up the spillage.

"Hey, y'all!" Dare shouted. "Don't walk on it! It's a wing, not a welcome mat!"

The Somali stood looking down at him, puzzled.

"Get the hell off there with those dirty boots!" Dare motioned at the ladder.

The Somali climbed down, muttering in Arabic. Cussing, apologizing, Dare couldn't tell which and didn't care.

After fetching rags and a roll of duct tape from a storage locker aft of the cockpit, he took off his shoes, climbed onto the wing and, on his knees, cleaned the footprints, the film of fuel, stinking of paraffin. That done, he repaired the ruptured hose with the duct tape, then turned and told the man beside the drums to start cranking again. From the top of the ladder, his eyes twelve feet off the ground, he spotted a thin, reddish-beige pall some distance off, in the direction of Mogadishu. At first he thought it was the tail end of the departing convoy, until he remembered that it had driven to the west, not the north. Besides, the dust cloud was moving *toward* the airstrip. Squinting into the glare, he saw a dark object top a high ridge-crest a mile away. In a moment, magnified by the mirage shimmering on the horizon, it revealed itself as a truck or a four-wheel-drive vehicle, and the heavy machine gun mounted on the roof was silhouetted against the pale sky. The truck went on down the ridge, another behind it, a third behind that, then a fourth, all moving fast, or as fast as they could, off road in the rock-strewn desert.

In a crisis, Wes Dare had the capacity for quick, effective action most often found in people lacking reflective minds and vivid imaginations. In the span of half a minute, he got the Somali to stop pumping, pulled the hose from the fuel-fill, screwed the cap down tight, ordered Nimrod to move the passengers clear of the propellers because he was going to start the engines, then stood atop the wing and called to Tony and Mary to run back and get aboard. They were only fifty, sixty yards away, across a swath of bare ground between the airstrip and the town, but they were surrounded by people and did not hear him. Mary was intent on posing Tony with the spear-carrying elder. Dare called again, waving his arms like a football ref signaling a missed field goal. His copilot turned to face him. In the same instant, the crowd knotted around the couple unraveled; people scattered in all directions as a squad of clansmen, assault rifles in hand, dashed across the field to take up firing positions. Evidently someone in town had also seen the approaching column and sounded the alarm. For a fraction of a second, Tony looked around in bewilderment; then he seized Mary's hand and broke for the plane.

"Nimrod! Get in, now!" Dare hollered, and leaped to the ground. His knees almost cracked from the shock. "The second they're aboard, secure the door!"

He scrambled into the cockpit without his shoes—no time to retrieve them now—and fired up the right engine, opposite the side the forward door was on. Bollichek, who was built like a rugby wing, boosted Mary onto the boarding ladder, all but threw her into the plane, and then got into his seat and began to flip switches—radios, pumps, hydraulic controls. Dare started the second engine, rammed the throttles to full, and released the brake. The G1 bolted forward and gathered speed. Ahead, near the end of the runway, geysers of sand and dirt flew up—big rounds, probably from a twelve-seven. Another three-round burst struck within yards of the nose, spattering bits of gravel into the windshield with a sound like hailstones. Tony ducked, but Dare, who had been here before, held his eyes on the runway. As soon as he felt the gear leave the ground, he put the plane into a steep climb, then into a tight turn, the wingtip clearing the high barrier dunes by a few yards at most. He leveled off and skimmed over the water, masked from the cannon fire, and flew out to sea, the blue swells racing less than a hundred feet below. When he figured they were out of range, he pulled back and climbed to five thousand feet.

No damage that he or Tony could see; the controls were responding well. Nevertheless he sent Nimrod aft to check for bullet holes. None, Nimrod reported. A miracle. Dare silently gave the miraculous powers their due and awarded the rest to himself. The altimeter turned. Ten thousand, fifteen, twenty—he felt that he could not get high enough, that he would fly her into orbit if only she were capable. He pictured himself up there, isolated and self-contained in the airless black of space, a human star untouched by the lunatic world he circled without end. Altitude twenty-one thousand feet. Airspeed two four zero. A tail wind aloft. He banked and set a westward course for Nairobi.

THE SKY WAS clear all around, an eggshell of blue.

"Well now, that was like what that Yogi Berra guy said—déjà vu all over again. At least they didn't get my prop this time. Pair of shoes is all." Switching to autopilot, Dare lit a cigarette. He figured recent events entitled him to increase his ration. "Goddamn! If I could figure a way to refuel in midair every day, I'd stay up here."

"What happened?" Mary's face was flushed, her voice a little breathless, but not in a way that suggested fear. She belonged to the breed who was stimulated by being shot at and missed. There was a quickness about her, a tense alertness in her eyes that he recognized; he had seen both in the crack special operations teams he had dropped over Laos, way back when Mary English was a toddler.

"Got no idea what that was all about," he said in answer to her question. "Some clan feud. Maybe a few thugs from Mogadishu out for a Sunday drive in their Technicals. Got bored, decided to raise a little hell."

"Abdul cheated Abdullah on a business deal, that's my guess," Tony said. "Or Abdullah cheated Abdul. Or Abdul caught Abdullah making eyes at one of his three hundred sheilas. Or was it Abdullah's sheilas Abdul was making eyes at? Crazy Somali bastards."

He motioned at the pockmarked windshield, and because the unsteadiness in his hand was obvious, Dare could not help but observe the difference between his copilot's reaction to the experience and Mary's. Tony had done damned well, and he made the observation without judgment, though the mere making of it might have been a kind of judgment in itself.

"So you guys don't think it was us they were after?" Mary asked.

"Ever roll a ball in front of a cat and see what it does?" Dare said. "One of those firefights gets to goin', and they'll shoot at anything that moves just 'cause it's movin', and we were the biggest thing in motion out there. Four legs and claws, two legs with a gun, a predator is a predator."

A puzzled frown from Mary, as if she wasn't sure what to think about this bleak assessment of the human animal. She changed the subject slightly, complimenting him on his flying. Pretty fancy work, the way he'd cleared the dunes, then dropped down below them.

"Defilade, it's called," Dare explained, surprised to discover that he enjoyed being flattered by her. "Learned it contour flyin' in Laos. Clip the treetops, put a ridge, a hill, anything you can between you and the bad guys."

"Bum one?" She gestured at his cigarette.

"Didn't know you smoked."

"I decided just this second to say yes to nicotine."

"After today I'll bet you're gonna sign up for another hitch of milk-run airdrops."

He turned partway around to give her a light. She held the cigarette awkwardly between puckered lips, blew out the smoke without inhaling, her mouth a perfect little O.

"Not likely. Not *bloody* likely, as Tony would say. If I wanted to play it safe, I would have stayed in Canada, flying sportsmen to wilderness lodges."

"Aw hell, don't tell me y'all came here for the adventure."

"Sure. Partly. Mostly it's the money. I can make three times what I could back home."

"That's a whole lot better. I trust folks who do things for the money."

"And we'll be making a pile in less than a month," Tony said, referring to the six-month contract Dare had signed recently to fly Laurent Kabila and his people in the Congo. "Can't come soon enough, far as I'm concerned."

"Yup, African Charter Services is gonna be the official airline of the Congolese rebels."

"The Congo's pretty dicey," Mary said.

"Right. Not like good old safe Somalia."

Dare conducted a brief debate with himself. Had she brought them bad luck or good this morning? Bad they had been shot at, good they hadn't been hit. Maybe the god of fortune had been neutral about her presence. He'd started the argument because he was considering hiring her. She and Tony could fly the G1 on some runs, giving him a break. Mary's nerves were certainly right for working the Congo. That left three things to be resolved: her flying abilities, his ability to afford her, and his troubling attraction to her, which could, under the right circumstances, undermine his loyalty to his copilot and lead him to do something he would regret. Taking the last problem first, he recalled that he had worked closely with a woman only once in his career, the year he flew deliveries for Federal Express. His first officer, Sally McCabe, had been smart, fairly good-looking, and single, but he discovered that the closeness of their association and the routine practicalities of flying a 727 together dissolved her feminine mystery, which had the same effect on his romantic impulses as he hoped khat did on the Somalis' sex drive. Sally became one of the boys in a female body. It could go the same way with Mary; of course it also could go the other way; was it worth the risk?

Tabling that question for the moment, he calculated that he could pay her seven thousand a month for the six months. It was only a bite out of the seven hundred thousand he figured to gross. Then he decided to test her skills. He took his headset off, got out of his seat, and maneuvered his bulky frame out of the cockpit, telling Tony to take over as captain.

"Mary, you're first officer. Let's see how well you do."

And she did fairly well, considering her unfamiliarity with the plane. The G1 being a more supple, responsive aircraft than the Buffalos she was accustomed to, she tended to horse it a bit, a little too much rudder here, a little too much yoke there. They reached the Tana river and commenced their descent, encountering turbulence. Mary handled it with ease. Approaching Nairobi, Dare cautioned her to steer clear of the hills to the south, far beyond which he caught the faint white blaze of Kilimanjaro's peaks. That old legend about the dead leopard found up there—what was it doing, nineteen thousand feet above sea level, in the ice and snow? Getting away from the bullshit on the ground, that's what.

Tony took over for the landing. Overall Mary's performance wasn't stylish—workmanlike, he judged—but workmanlike would do for now. He would have to sit down with Nimrod, go over the books and the numbers before making any commitments. And then sit down with himself and argue that other business through.

Tony parked in front of the hangar and shut down. Nimrod took his clipboard and flight reports and went to the office in back, Dare to his car for the old pair of sneakers that had been lying in the trunk for weeks. Reshod, he took Tony and Mary to the Aero Club for lunch. She had never seen the inside of that shrine to early African aviation, and the venerable atmosphere captivated her. Old wood, wainscot, varnish. She dawdled by the antique Spitfire engine mounted on a pedestal in the hall as if it were a museum exhibit and gazed at the black-and-white photos of long-dead fliers standing beside long obsolete planes, at the wooden propeller hung over the bar, and was it the same bar where Beryl Markham had drunk her gin?

"Think so," Dare said. "She died only about ten years ago. Eighty-odd years old. Probably still be alive, if she didn't like that gin so much."

He was charmed by Mary's wonder, like she was a kid at Disneyland, but her sightseeing annoyed Tony.

"C'mon, love, we'll do the tour later," he said. "We're hungry, and we've got another trip this afternoon."

They passed through the serving line, Kenyan girls in starched dresses dishing out spicy beef stew from chafing dishes, and sat next to a table occupied by a Russian crew, one of whom saluted Dare with a raised beer glass.

"Vesley! How are you? Good trip?"

"A daisy, comrade."

"Think I've seen him out at Loki," Mary said, and blew on a spoonful of stew. "Know him?"

"Name's Alexei somethin' or other. Antonov pilot."

"Bloke blasted us with prop wash couple of months ago," said Tony. "Wes gave him what for, he walked over to our plane, I guess to make something out of it. Wes told him, 'You all step under the wing of my airplane, I'll hit you so hard it'll hurt your mama in Moscow.'" Tony had done his best to mimic Dare's accent. "Bloke didn't understand Texas English, stepped under the wing. Wes decked him. They've been best of mates ever since."

"On account of we rescued his sorry ass a couple of weeks after that little incident," Dare elaborated. "He pranged up in Somalia, flyin' medicine to Baidoa for World Vision. Same place, same do-gooders we'll be flyin' for this afternoon. Them Russians are always crashin'. Good pilots, but their planes are about held together with Krazy Glue and thumbtacks." He chewed, swallowed, washed the food down with iced tea, and added in an undertone: "Tell you another thing the Russians do. They sign up for three-month contracts, flyin' hu-manitarian aid. Get a month off in between hitches. Know where some of 'em go on their vacations? Khartoum, to fly Antonovs for the Sudan air force. I'm talkin' the Antonovs that have been converted to bombers. They stack the suckers in the cargo bay and just roll 'em out when they're over the target. One day it's bread, next day it's bombs. It's kind of a—what's the word? Somethin' that stands for somethin' else."

"Metaphor?" Mary ventured after thinking for a moment.

"Right. Now I ain't sure what that metaphor stands for, bread and bombs, but a metaphor it is, sure as hell."

Nimrod came in, frown lines layered on his forehead—cat scratches on ebony. A real worrier, Nimrod was.

"Bad news, Captain Wes. World Vision canceled this afternoon. There is fighting in Baidoa again."

"Fine by me. One firefight per day is my limit. So is that all? Lookin' at you, I think your mama died."

"My mother died some time ago," Nimrod said formally. "There is a man from DCA wishes to speak with you. He's in the office."

Dare set his fork down, feeling a sudden loss of appetite. A personal visit from the Department of Civil Aviation—*that* was the bad news. Or could be.

"Who and what about, or didn't he say?"

Nimrod, reading from the man's business card, said his name was William Gichui. He had not disclosed the purpose of his call; that was to be made to Dare himself.

"What do you think? The boss wants more cookies?"

"That would be my best guess, Captain Wes. I don't understand—" Nimrod did not finish the thought, shaking his head with a look of distress.

"Well, we ain't gonna find out what he wants sittin' here," Dare muttered, rising. Then to Tony and Mary: " 'Scuse me, y'all. Got the feelin' we worked for taxes today."

The tin-walled shed that he rented as an office, mostly so he could say to clients, "Call me at my office," and thus claim their trust and respect, was attached to the rear of the hangar, like a shabby afterthought. Inside, two small desks, one for him and one for Nimrod, faced each other across a lane barely wide enough for someone to walk through. A phone, a fax, a laptop, a typewriter for use when the power went out, as it now did every day—another symptom of the country's slow disintegration. Vinyl-bound volumes of Jepps aviation maps were scattered on the desktops. Hanging askew from one wall was a schedule board smeared with grease-pencil scrawl. Observing the expression on Gichui's face made Dare embarrassed. The appearance of the place declared that African Charter Services was a fly-by-night operation, of no importance to anyone; that is, it could not be relied upon as a source of further under-the-table cash. Dare knew he would have to change that impression.

"Hey, Mr. Gucci! *Habari ya mchana. Hujambo?*" he said, extending his hand. Lay on the Swahili, let him know I'm not a baby who got here day before yesterday. "*Jina langu ni* Captain Dare."

"It's Gichui," said Gichui, a pleasant-looking middle-aged man with a plump waist and a pompadour that reminded Dare of James Brown's. "*Sijambo asante. Wewe je?*"

"*Nzuri*," Dare replied, taking a moment to size the man up. White shirt, frayed but immaculate. Gray trousers, shiny from wear but neatly pressed. Cheap tie but with a Windsor knot. The most middling of midlevel civil servants, underpaid yet concerned about appearances and maintaining a certain dignity and decorum. A bagman who would not appreciate the blunt approach. "Yeah, I'm doin' right well for a man about got shot out of the sky this mornin'. Business has been good, and it's gonna get better. Have a seat, *tafadhali*." He rolled his own swivel chair from behind the desk.

Gichui declined, stating that his business would not take too long—a polite way of saying that he had the leverage and was not about to sit while Dare remained on his feet.

"So what is your business? How can I help you?"

"By clearing up a few details." Gichui withdrew a folder from his brief-case and glanced at one of the papers inside. "Just to make sure, you are the operator of a certain aircraft, a Gulfstream One, identification number Five-Y-ACS?"

"Owner and operator."

Gichui lay the folder on Nimrod's desk and put on a little stage business, thumbing through the documents. "It seems we have no record of issuing an AOC to you," he said, and raised his eyes to regard Dare with an expression of studied neutrality. "Perhaps that is our fault. You have a copy you could show me?"

Dare leaned against the door, reached for a cigarette, remembered his rule, and pulled out his sunglasses instead. Twirling them to give his hands something to do, he glanced sidelong at Nimrod, who had taken the chair and looked like a suspect undergoing an interrogation. Dare was not encouraged.

"The problem of the air operator's certificate was resolved with the director some time ago," Nimrod said with a confidence he did not feel, judging from the way he was nervously fidgeting with a pen. "I saw to it myself."

"With the former director?" asked Gichui.

"And with the present one," said Nimrod. "I made sure to call on her after she took over. To inform her of—arrangements we made with her predecessor. She is very fond of cookies."

"Yes. Chocolate chip, I believe?"

"She asked me to bring her some peanut butter cookies. There is a kind made in the United States that she likes very much."

"And of course you did."

"Of course," Nimrod affirmed, seeming now to feel surer ground beneath him. "A large box of peanut butter cookies to, you understand, welcome her to her new post."

"A gesture," Gichui said.

"The very thing. She appreciated it. I think if you speak to her, she will tell you what you need to know about the AOC."

Gichui replied, without a crack in his bland look, "I would not be here if I had not spoken to her first."

Nimrod said nothing for several moments; then, his newly won assurance crumbling, he asked what the upshot of that conversation had been.

"Precisely what I stated," Gichui said. "Captain Dare is an air operator without a valid AOC, according to our records. So once again, if our records are incomplete, you could perhaps show me a copy?"

The nature of the game was becoming clear, though not as clear as Dare would have liked. He shook his head, both to tell Gichui that he did not have a certificate, valid or invalid, and to signal his weariness with the way things were done in Kenya. Though he had never expected even a semblance of integrity from the country's officials, it did not necessarily follow that he had ceased to believe, or hope, that there was an end to their double, triple, and quadruple dealing. Most places you paid your bribe, and that was that. Not here, where bribery came on the installment plan.

"Captain, the penalties for—" Gichui began.

"Yeah, I know." Dare pushed away from the door to sit on a corner of the desk, sunglasses spinning in his hand. "Anybody ever tell you you look like James Brown?" He was stalling for time and trying to put Gichui off balance. "The soul singer? Y'all look like him. The way you wear your hair."

"I don't know this James Brown."

"I flew James Brown on tour for a spell. Had a company back in the States, flew big-name rock-and-roll acts. Brown. Stevie Ray Vaughan. Now there was my main man! Stevie Ray Vaughan and the Double Trouble band."

"I know none of these people."

"Stevie Ray autographed a couple of old-time vinyl albums for me. He died on tour. Plane crash. Not my plane, of course."

"I have no idea what you are talking about."

"No?" Dare gave him a crocodile's grin. "Well, I've got a good idea what you're talkin' about. You're about to tell me that you do have a record of an AOC issued to a Kenyan guy, Joseph Nakima. Right?"

"I don't know him, either."

"Oh, sure you don't. Like you don't know that he used to be with Kenya Airways, been a businessman for the past few years. Aviation mostly, but construction, real estate, import-export, most of it aircraft parts. Like you don't know he's my silent partner. Silent and invisible. Seen him but once the past two years. He's got wires into all sorts of places, and I was told that it would be a good idea to take on a Kenyan partner when I got here, and that Joe was a good bet. He helped me incorporate this outfit. Fact is, he's the president. I'm telling you in case you don't know that either. Would of taken me forever and three days if I'd tried to go through channels. That left the AOC. Well, it would of taken another forever and three days to get one on my own, so we made a little arrangement. That I would fly under his certificate, which I've been doing, and the director knows about it, and last I checked, it was all right with her. Or is that another thing you don't know?"

Gichui sat on the opposite corner of the desk, and the two men faced each other, like bookends.

"That is highly irregular." Long practice had given him the ability to feign shock with a good deal of credibility.

"Sure is. And I reckon it's irregular that every month, my friend Nimrod here sends a share of our gross profits to Joe. We're leasing his AOC, you might say, twenty cents per mile, a commission sort of. It ain't cheap, but it's cheaper than scratchin' all the backs I would of had to scratch and greasin' all the palms I would've greased if I was to try for an operator's certificate on my own. Anyway, it was all set up, so what's the problem?"

Gichui's brows knit. The slang—scratching backs, greasing palms— appeared to confuse him.

"I'll put the question a different way. What does the director want me to do?"

"To show that you have a valid certificate. If you cannot, then you will not be permitted to operate an aircraft in our country."

He had dropped the pose of pleasant impartiality, becoming deliberately, maddeningly obtuse, as if to tease Dare for his own amusement. How could he be made to reveal what the demand was?

"All right, fine, then I reckon I'll have to operate it in some other country," Dare said, playing the only card he had, and it wasn't much. "Which is what I'm fixin' to do in just about three weeks."

"How would you do that, captain?"

"By flyin' the goddamned thing out of *this* sorry-ass country, that's how. We've got a contract for—"

Experiencing a flood of sudden and painful light, he stopped himself, sprang from his seat, squatted in front of the safe, opened it, and pulled out the Gulfstream's certificate of registration and ownership.

"That's a Sierra Leone registry," he said, waving the document in Gichui's face. "You'll notice that my name's on it."

"Yes, I see that."

"Y'all mind if I take a look at what you've got in that file?"

"I mind very much," Gichui said. "It's an official file."

"Right. Y'all don't have a Freedom of Information Act over here. But hell, I don't need to see it to tell you that's there's two pieces of paper in there, one de-registering the plane in Sierra Leone, and another one re-registering it in Kenya—under the name of Joseph Nakima. What do you say? Right or wrong?"

Dare's seeming clairvoyance upset Gichui's equilibrium, and he stammered that he had not looked through the entire file, so he couldn't say one way or the other.

"Why don't you take a peek, then? Go on."

"That won't be necessary." Recovering himself, Gichui slipped the folder back into his briefcase. "The plane's registration is not what my business is about."

"You oughtn't to have asked me that, how was I gonna fly the plane in another country. That question did this." Dare brought two fingers to his temple and mimicked turning on a light switch.

Gichui shrugged and, tucking his case under his arm, stood to leave, warning Dare that he would be prohibited from flying in Kenya. Written notification to that effect would be forthcoming from the DCA.

"Thanks. I'm gonna treasure that piece of paper. Y'know, I've always been dumb, but I must be gettin' downright ignorant in my old age. Should of figured out from the get-go that y'all came here wearin' two hats."

"Pardon?"

"The DCA might of sent you here, but you're really representing Joe Nakima."

"I don't work for any Mr. Nakima." Gichui's offended tone was almost believable. "I told you I don't even know any such man."

"That's insultin' my intelligence, William, so either you kiss my ass or get yours the hell out of here."

The human comedy, Dare thought, *and right now I'm the butt of the joke.* He fell into his chair, at a loss as to what his next move should be. He wasn't sure if he even had a next move. Nimrod was of no help, sitting in a silent, sorrowful daze. The hope of Africa? Trouble was, there was all of Africa and only one of Nimrod.

"Been one helluva day so far, and it's hardly half over."

Nimrod said nothing.

"Stop lookin' like that," Dare told him.

"Like what?"

"Like someone just shot you with a stun gun. It's making me more depressed than I already am. It ain't your fault."

He was being diplomatic because he felt sorry for Nimrod, who prided himself on his talent for getting things done, solving problems, removing or finding ways around obstacles; a talent owed to his keen eye for spotting the straightest, quickest, and least expensive paths through Kenya's larcenous bureaucracies and kleptocratic ministries, in particular the Department of Civil Aviation. Nimrod was smart that way, but he wasn't clever. He thought that the deals he cut were solemn contracts to be honored, instead of shady provisional arrangements that could be discarded in an instant. His weakness was an inability to see all the treacherous moves on the board, and so he could not defend against them.

"Way back when, Joe took all the paperwork—maintenance records, airworthiness certificate, all of it—including the bill of sale and the registration. Said he needed it for the incorporation papers, and I said go ahead," Dare continued. "So it's my fault. Should of seen that he was thinkin' way ahead. All right, Joe knows we're gonna be takin' the airplane out of the country in a little while, so what he must of done was make copies of all that documentation, then took it to an airplane broker. Any broker in the world will de-register a plane for you in one country and register it in another one. Costs you about thirty grand. A crook might charge another ten for forging the registration. Then I reckon he cut the DCA in on what he was doin', he'd want her on his side in case of a problem. Figure he paid her a thousand, and what he's paying William wouldn't even be walkin'-around money. Half-a-million-dollar airplane, four-fifty pure profit. Pretty good for a day's work."

"You think he wants it to sell it?" Nimrod asked. "Not take over our business?"

"Our business ain't worth it. Hell yes, he's gonna sell it. Probably needs to raise cash quick, and this is the quickest way he can think of. Sellin' assets, even if they ain't his."

"And so he sent Gichui, number one, to put you on official notice and make sure the plane goes nowhere. Number two—"

"A fishin' expedition," said Dare, completing the thought, "to see if we've got anything, any damn thing at all, to make a case in case we go to court. He's got to figure on that contingency. And that's what we're gonna do, rafiki."

"Go to court?" Nimrod scoffed, as if that were the most ridiculous course of action possible. "He will have the judge paid."

"I know that. I just want to get into the courts to tie things up for a while, buy a little time for us to come up with a better idea. I'll shoot that son of a bitch before I let him walk away with my airplane. It's all I've got."

Man of All Races

THEY WERE BY the pool, drinking beer and talking while Turkana women passed down the dry riverbed in front of them, beyond the barbed-wire fence. The tribeswomen wore long skirts of brown cloth or cowhide and bead necklaces stacked to their chins. Fitzhugh enjoyed watching them, striding boldly, balancing bundled sticks on their shaved heads, their backs so straight they looked like exclamation points in motion, their gazes fixed on the path ahead, as if they couldn't stand to look at the tents, warehouses, and bungalows sprawling alongside the riverbed. An eyesore crowded with pink-faced strangers.

Tara Whitcomb's compound, where Fitzhugh and Douglas were staying, occupied one small corner of the vast encampment, and a cushy neighborhood it was, its guest tukuls built to resemble Turkana dwellings, with amenities no Turkana could have dreamed of, like electricity and running water and concrete floors swept daily by maids in starched outfits. The place looked like a luxury safari camp. Its occupants were doctors from Médicins sans Frontières, aircrews from Douglas's former employer, PanAfrik, volunteer aid workers from religious NGOs, most of whom were American evangelicals whose homogenous wholesomeness made them look more or less identical, like soldiers in uniform. Last night, sitting outside the tukul he shared with Douglas, Fitzhugh overheard a few of these pilgrims reading scripture aloud in the neighboring hut, after which they beseeched God to bless and protect their Sudanese brethren. He was touched by their fervor, their heartfelt expressions of solidarity.

It seemed to him that he needed some of what they had—the calm of an abiding conviction. He wasn't getting cold feet, but he felt a slight chill down there in his soles. Lacking religious impulses, he knew he couldn't undergo a sudden conversion. If not faith, then what? An outlook? A philosophy? An attitude? At any rate, some sort of inner resource that he could draw on. He had gotten out ahead of himself, enlisting in Barrett's cause in a moment of enthusiasm before he'd had time to prepare himself, psychologically and emotionally, for the trial ahead. Tara had painted a picture of the Nuba for Douglas and him at least as grim as Diana and Barrett's. The war had made it a wilderness once more or, more accurately, a wasteland, as near a thing to a terra incognita as you were likely to find this late in the twentieth century.

"I'm actually hoping for bad weather, though we're not likely to get it this time of year," she was saying now, sitting erectly at the head of the table, sunglasses cocked over her forehead, reading glasses, hung from a cord around her neck, resting on the top button of her white captain's shirt. "Tail end of the wet when I flew John in. Better that than this"—she motioned at the cloudless sky—"and it's like this now in the Nuba."

Douglas questioned her with a look.

"There's a government garrison here, and another here," she answered, pointing at the map spread in front of her. "And here's Zulu One, the airstrip."

An understanding nod from Douglas. There was between him and Tara the special bond that made bush pilots seem like members of a secret society who could speak volumes to each other with a few words.

"Do you mind explaining why you want the weather to be bad?" Fitzhugh asked. To him, small planes and thunderstorms weren't a desirable combination.

"Our course takes us between the garrisons." Tara gave him the indulgent smile a kindly teacher bestows on a slow learner. "In clear weather, it will be easier for the troops to . . ."

"Shoot at us?"

"I'm not too worried about that. We'll be flying out of small arms range. I'm more worried they'll send patrols to find out where we've landed. If that happens, Zulu One will be compromised, and then I shall have a jolly time coming in to pick you up, won't I? Zulu One is it for the Nuba, although by the time you're ready to be taken out, I hope Douglas will have found a couple of alternatives."

She looked at Douglas expectantly, but he only turned his head, his attention drawn by the birds flitting in the branches of a nearby tree. Flashes of dark blue, iridescent blue, russet.

"Beautiful, aren't they?" he remarked, with an irritating irrelevance and a seeming indifference to what Tara had said. An indifference underscored by his posture: slumped low in his chair, ankles crossed, fingers clasped behind his head. "As common as robins back in the States, but I never get tired of looking at them."

"Which? The superb starlings or the rollers?"

"Both."

"Are you a birder? You don't look like one."

"How is a birder supposed to look?"

"Oh, owlish, I guess." Tara grimaced as if in disapproval of her own pun. Like Diana Briggs, she was a woman of a certain age who looked much younger. The same clear English complexion, somehow preserved from the effects of time and African suns; the same startling blue eyes, the same blond hair, though hers was a darker blond and cut shorter than Diana's. The two women could have been sisters. Close cousins anyway. Tara was taller at five-eight or -nine, and broader boned, with a strong, square face and an aloof, self-contained air that came from years of flying solo over wild and dangerous country. Not unfriendly, but certainly a woman who would prefer a handshake to a kiss on the cheek, no matter how long she'd known you. "I flew lots of birders into Tsavo in the old days, and they all looked owlish to me. Glasses like this"—circling her eyes with thumbs and forefingers—"thick in the middle, skinny legs. They were always in a sweat to see carmine bee-eaters."

"That's an incredible bird!" Douglas popped out of his slouch in a burst of enthusiasm, the first time Fitzhugh had seen him shuck off his cloak of studied cool. "I saw a few down there myself last year. Got pictures of them."

"Ah! So you *are* a birder."

"Not the one my mother is. If it's got feathers and it flies, she can identify it, tell you where it winters and summers, and maybe imitate its call. She came over to go to Tsavo with me. Maybe I ought to say I went with her. She's been around half the world with her binoculars and bird books, and when she isn't gallivanting, she's out on the San Pedro or Sonoita Creek. Nature preserves near Tucson."

"That's in the West, correct?" asked Tara as Fitzhugh thought, *A mother who can afford to come all the way to Africa just to look at birds?*

"Arizona," Douglas informed her. "And that's north of Mexico, south of Colorado, east of California."

"A geography lesson. Splendid. Now I shall give one. As far as anyone in Loki is concerned, we're flying to Kakuma tomorrow," she said, referring to a mission station and refugee camp a short hop south of Loki. "And in fact we will be going there, to give ourselves a cover in case anyone gets nosy. We will pick up supplies for a hospital in the Nuba. It's run by German Emergency Doctors, the only NGO Khartoum allows to operate up there. Of course, the hospital is not supposed to be receiving supplies from outside Sudan, but it's been in a fix lately, short of everything. We will leave for the Nuba, and when I get back, I will tell everyone I was delayed in Kakuma by mechanical trouble. I cannot stress enough the need for discretion. I prefer that to 'secrecy,' don't you? After all, we're not spies."

Douglas shrugged to say that he was neutral about semantics.

"But Khartoum has its spies around here," Tara went on. "Let's say they have a controller or two at Loki tower on the payroll. He finds out where we're bound, we are in a fix."

"But we're flying with Tara Whitcomb, the legend, the modern-day Beryl Markham," Douglas said with utmost sincerity. His eyes fastened onto her, and Fitzhugh suddenly felt shut out of the conversation; felt moreover that he had disappeared as far as Douglas was concerned.

"I am fifty-five years old." Tara, with a laugh, gave her head a stiff, controlled toss backward. "Quite beyond flattery."

"I wasn't flattering. I heard about you almost from the day I got here. How some missionary was sick in a no-fly area. The mission radioed Loki for an evac. UN flight ops told them they would have to wait until they negotiated with Khartoum for clearance to land."

Tara nodded, adding that someone in flight operations sent a message to the mission, urging them to evacuate the dying man by road, a ridiculous idea, as it was the middle of the rainy season and the road to Loki impassable, or nearly so, not to mention the chance of ambush by Turkana or Tuposa bandits.

"So you got him. You said, 'Fuck all this chickenshit red tape,' and went in and got him."

"I didn't use that sort of language, Doug."

"You had to fly through a helluva storm, I heard. You called the mission and told them to have the guy at the airstrip at such-and-such a time and you'd be there."

"Three twenty-five," she said.

"And they were there at three twenty-five and so were you. Right on the money."

"Oh, really." With a small movement of her head and a quick shrug, she signaled that the accolades were beginning to embarrass her. Then, pushing back from the table, she clasped her hands over her crossed knees and gave Douglas the same direct, penetrating look he was giving her. "There's quite a lot of stories floating around here about you, you know. You've gotten quite the reputation."

The remark appeared to catch him off guard. His back stiffened.

"What sort of reputation?"

"Depends on who you're speaking to. To some people, you're a hero. Others . . . to them you're an air pirate, or the next thing to it."

"*What?*"

"They say that what you did came this close"—holding her forefinger next to her thumb—"to a hijacking."

He said nothing and, with a shift of his glance, invited Fitzhugh back into the conversation, though Fitzhugh had no idea what to say. Ever since meeting him, he'd been eager to learn what had caused Douglas's departure from PanAfrik and put him on the UN's shit list; but when he had asked, on the flight to Loki yesterday, the American had answered with a blank-faced silence, as if he liked playing the mystery man. In the past forty-eight hours, all he'd revealed about himself was that he was thirty-one years old, hailed from Tucson, Arizona, and had flown for the U.S. Air Force in the Persian Gulf War, a spare autobiography that was the source of some anxiety for Fitzhugh. He didn't relish the notion of tramping through the Nuba mountains with a man about whom he knew almost nothing.

"Who in the hell accused me of hijacking?" Douglas asked, in a tone more wounded than angry.

"No one's really accused you," answered Tara.

"I can make a good guess. That Dutchman in flight operations, Timmerman. That's the kind of thing he'd say. Fact is, he did say it to me after I got sacked. A hijacking. Jesus H. Christ. I was the first officer. How can anyone say that I hijacked my own flight?"

"Doug, if I'd known it was going to upset you—"

"Hey, Tara, if you found out a story like that was going around about you, it wouldn't upset you?"

"Of course it would. But if you will allow me to . . . I mean to say, if you were first officer, then it wasn't *your* flight, strictly speaking."

Douglas frowned, half-cocking one ear toward her. "I don't believe you said that."

He came out of his chair, suddenly enough to startle her and Fitzhugh. His lips parted, but he appeared to have second thoughts about whatever he intended to say and, muttering that he had better give his gear one last check, walked off.

"Oh dear, I'm afraid that wasn't very diplomatic of me." Tara turned to watch him, striding down the path toward his tukul. "Now I shall have to make amends."

Fitzhugh asked, "What happened? What is this about a hijacking?"

Tara shook her head. "I had better apologize straight away." But she hadn't gotten across the pool terrace before Douglas returned, chin tucked in, eyes level, arms swinging at his sides. He seized her elbow and towed her back to her chair, then dropped into his.

"It *was* my flight," he said. "Estrada got sick. Dysentery. He couldn't fly. Turned the plane over to me. T. J. Estrada, stocky Filipino guy, forty-five, maybe fifty? Crew cut? Flew Hercs for the Filipino Air Force?"

"I—I may have seen him around," she said, a little stunned by the way he'd manhandled her.

"He got sick. It was a check-out flight for me, and he was the captain and my check pilot. Routine airdrop out near Ayod. Sixteen tons of maize. Poor guy was on the deck behind the flight engineer, doubled up, shitting all over himself. He'd been complaining about a bad stomach, but it really hit him right before we got the call to divert and pick up those people in Ajiep. He gave me the con, so it was my flight, if that makes any difference."

"Yes, you said that, but I think you're going a bit fast." She nodded in Fitzhugh's direction. "He doesn't know any of it."

The American stopped and rewound his narrative, beginning it again at the moment of the drop. Having told Fitzhugh nothing, he now seemed intent on telling him everything, his tongue loosened by the need to defend his reputation. He didn't discriminate between relevant and irrelevant facts, informing his listeners that the cockpit was decorated with photos of bare-breasted Filipina pinup girls, that the weather over Sudan was unsettled that day, the sky dotted with compact squalls, and that he remembered the smell of rain coming in through the auxiliary vents as the engineer depressurized the cabin on the descent toward the drop zone. Estrada had flown the plane from Loki, but as it neared the DZ, the captain turned the controls over to him.

"This is when he got sick?" Fitzhugh asked.

"No!" Douglas answered with a swat of his hand. "Told you, it was a check-out flight. He was checking me out, evaluating me. He gave me the controls but not command of the plane. That came later."

He passed his test. The captain gave him a B-plus and said he'd make it an A-minus if Douglas took the plane back to Loki. "Musta caught a bug. Feels like termites are eating my guts."

Douglas climbed toward cruising altitude. The plane wasn't halfway there when the captain got out of his seat and went for the head, bent at the waist, sweating. He didn't make it. A stench filled the cabin, and he fell onto the deck, knees drawn into his chest.

"A Herc is fairly easy to fly, but I wasn't wild about the idea of taking it back to Loki single-handed, with a captain in the shape he was in. How about another beer?"

Tara signaled a waiter and told him to bring two Tuskers and a Coke. Douglas picked up the thread of his story, saying that only minutes after Estrada was stricken, an urgent call came in from flight operations Loki, ordering the Hercules to change course for Ajiep, almost two hundred miles to the west; the town was under threat of attack by government militia; the supervisor of the UN compound there had requested an emergency evacuation for him and his staff, fifty-odd people all together.

The waiter came and set the bottles, sweating in the afternoon heat, on the table. Douglas wiped his with the tail of his shirt, took a drink, and sat silently for a few moments, holding the bottle by the neck.

"I plugged Ajiep's numbers into the GPS and did a one-eighty and told the engineer to clue Estrada in—Estrada had his headset off, remember, and hadn't heard any of it. Had to hand it to the old guy. Pulled himself together. Got into his seat, said he'd do what he could. The plane was mine, but he'd do whatever he could. Yeah, had to hand it to him. He was feverish and stinking like hell, Jesus, the whole cabin smelled like a horse stall. One of the loadmasters got the first-aid kit and gave him a bunch of pills, Imodium, I think, which was pretty much like putting a Band-Aid on a sucking chest wound."

They flew on for an hour, crossing vast swamps, then descended over arid scrub stretched to the horizon. The Jur river lay ahead, a glinting cord in the stark landscape. Beyond it pillars of smoke leaned in the wind, and Douglas knew by the looks of them that they were not from seasonal fires set by slash-and-burn farmers. He raised the UN outpost on the radio. The supervisor—Douglas recalled that he spoke with a French or Belgian accent—told him the town had been shelled half an hour ago.

"We are afraid there are Arab horsemen approaching," the man said. "If they are here before you, I will shoot myself. Better to shoot myself."

Like everyone else in Sudan, Douglas had heard stories about the mounted warriors who served as the government's irregular cavalry. They called themselves by their tribal names, Messiriya, Humr, Hawazma, Rizeygat, but were collectively known as *murahaleen*, holy warriors. The stuff of nightmares for white man and black man alike, they attacked without warning, materializing out of the desert like the jinns of their own mythology, five hundred to a thousand men robed in white, Koranic talismans fluttering from saddle blankets, a reincarnate terror from another time, with only their assault rifles to testify that they were coming on in the here and now.

Douglas followed the Jur like a radio beacon, coming in over the town and the dust-reddened tents of the aid agency compounds.

"The runway there is metaled and long enough for a Herc, but just long enough," he said and, like every pilot in history, illustrated with his hands. "I wanted to give myself every foot of roll I could." He skimmed a palm over the tabletop, then slammed it down. "Dropped her, like you do on a wet runway. Bang! We stopped with maybe a hundred and fifty feet to spare. I turned her around for takeoff. Keep the engines running, get the people aboard, and the hell out."

A pickup truck and a couple of Land Rovers were parked beside the runway. The loadmasters went to the rear, the ramp was lowered. The aid workers, men and women bent under hastily packed rucksacks, piled out of the vehicles and jogged toward the plane. That was when Douglas saw the townspeople, sitting or standing in the grass and thornbush groves nearby: women in pink and white pinafores, children, a few old people. A fountain of brown smoke rose through the trees a kilometer or two away; a sound like a heavy steel door slamming shut, muted by the engines. The crowd did not stir. They were all very still, staring at the Hercules, their only hope for deliverance from the evil gathering itself, out there in the desert.

"What got to me was how calm they were. Some of them were standing in line, like they were at an airport. I don't mean resigned. Accepting, I guess. That's what got to me. It was tough to see them, waiting like that. Waiting to find out if we'd take them or not."

The loadmaster called him on the intercom. The aid workers were on board. And then: "There's a Sudanese guy here says he needs to talk to the captain."

Douglas turned to Estrada, who told him to see what the man wanted, but to be quick about it.

The Sudanese was nearly seven feet tall and immensely dignified. With a formality out of phase with the circumstances, he introduced himself as Gabriel, the chairman, but did not say what he was chairman of. A handful of SPLA guerrillas stood behind him, Kalashnikovs slung across their backs, and a girl lay on a litter at their feet, wild-eyed, breathing heavily. She looked to be fifteen or sixteen and was naked from the waist up, her belly enormous. An older woman in an orange smock—mother?

midwife?—was beside her, holding a reed basket and skin waterbag in either hand.

"Do you suppose you could take her, captain?" asked Gabriel. "I know your regulations, but she is very close to her time."

"What was I supposed to tell the guy?" Douglas asked his listeners rhetorically. " 'If you know the regs, dude, then you know that we're authorized only to evacuate civilians who've been wounded in the fighting. And snakebite, that's okay, too. Otherwise, tough shit.' Was I supposed to tell him that?"

Two rebel soldiers lifted the litter and carried the girl into the plane, the older woman following. Another shell exploded, near to where the first had struck. With a languid movement of one huge hand, Gabriel gestured at the people waiting in the distance and pleaded with Douglas to take them as well.

"*All* of them?"

"It's a very big plane and they are not many," Gabriel said, speaking with great composure. "If the murahaleen come, you know what will happen—" Another shell, bursting somewhat closer, interrupted him. Douglas noticed a movement in the crowd, a rippling as of grass in the wind, and he thought or imagined the people made a sound, a kind of collective sigh, as of wind moving through grass.

He took a headset from one of the loadmasters and told Estrada what was going on.

"I'm hurting, man, really hurting" was all the captain said. "C'mon, get up here and let's go."

"Call Loki. Ask them to authorize."

"Forget it! They're not going to let us bring half the town into Kenya. Get on up here before we get blown off this runway!"

"Is it still my plane or what?"

"*Get your ass up here now.*"

Douglas felt a flashing envy for people who dwelled in the peaceful nooks of the world, where there was time to ponder before making difficult moral choices.

"All right, but get them aboard in a hurry," he said to Gabriel, then returned to the cockpit, stepping over the pregnant girl, while the aid workers, strapped into their web jumpseats, looked at him, bewildered.

If Estrada had not been so sick, he might have taken a swing at his copilot. He called the loadmasters on the intercom and ordered them to raise the ramp. They said they couldn't; there were people on it. Then kick 'em off, Estrada said. The loadmasters couldn't do that either because there were too many, sixty, seventy at least, and what was more, men with guns standing outside the door.

"All right, Yankee boy, you caused the problem, you fix it. Turn those people around. Tell 'em big mistake. This isn't American Airlines."

At Douglas's refusal, the captain rose from his seat and turned to go to the rear of the plane. Just then, another wave of dysentery bound his guts, and he doubled over again. Seeing his chance, Douglas strapped himself in and told the loadmasters to continue boarding the refugees. A few moments later, when the DOOR OPEN light went dark, he pushed the throttles, let go the brakes, and started his roll.

"Good thing there weren't any weapons on board. I think Estrada would've put a pistol to my head."

"Yes, I think I might have, too," Tara said with a sternness that chipped the armor of Douglas's self-assurance.

His gaze wandered for a moment; he drummed the table with his fingers. "Listen, I found out later that what the French or Belgian guy was afraid would happen did happen. Five, six hundred Arabs on horseback overran the airfield less than half an hour after we got out of there. The big guy, Gabriel, got killed, I heard, and whoever was left in town either got killed or was hauled off into slave camp."

"Yes. I think you did the wrong thing for all the right reasons."

He drew back, as if Tara had raised a hand to slap him.

"You *did* commandeer the aircraft. And I say that in the spirit of constructive criticism."

But he did not take it that way. He looked insulted and incredulous, as if he were convinced that his actions had been so manifestly right that only a blind, stupid, or morally corrupt person could think they'd been otherwise.

"All right, I've heard the criticism, what's the construction? Clue me in."

The combination of petulance and flippancy made her wince. For his part, Fitzhugh had fallen in love. The American was a spiritual brother, with a zeal and daring he could only wish were his own. He decided to give Douglas a little support. To put everything on the line to save a few strangers of no importance to anyone, he told Tara, had been a triumph of conscience over self-interest.

"I did say it was for the best of reasons, didn't I?" An adamantine varnish seemed to flood her eyes, and their hard blue glare unsettled him.

"But from what I heard, the story didn't have a happy ending. Immigration incarcerated those people, then packed them off, back to where they'd come from."

"A better ending than the one that could have been," Douglas observed.

"I can't argue with that, but—"

"You will anyway."

"Sudan being what it is," Tara said, "one has to wonder if you spared them from their fate or merely postponed it."

"Hey, I made my call. I stood by it. I stand by it now. Okay?"

"Fair enough. Do you know what happened to the pregnant girl?"

"You just said it. Sudan being what it is. The things that happen there break your heart when they don't turn your stomach."

"Either she died or the baby or both."

"The kid." Douglas nodded. "It happened on the plane, when we were only an hour from Loki. The loadmasters told me about it after we landed. I saw the girl holding the kid in a blanket, a piece of cowhide really. She wasn't crying. Like she expected it." He paused just long enough to highlight the next statement: "Maybe I should have, too."

A lilt in his voice turned it into a question, and Tara, her expression softening, told him he could not have possibly expected any such thing and shouldn't blame himself. Biting his lip, Douglas nodded to accept her reassurance, which could have been what he sought; the appeal for solace implicit in the way he'd spoken those final five words seemed intentionally to draw her sympathies toward him and his feelings, as if they and not the girl's tragedy were what mattered in the end. That was Fitzhugh's impression, but being in love, he immediately dismissed it as a figment of his imagination, telling himself he was making too much of a mere phrase, a tone of voice.

"Didn't mean to sound like such a scold," Tara was saying. They were getting used to her quirk of being brutally candid, then apologizing for it. "You already got your paddling in the headmaster's office. You don't need another from the likes of me."

"Two paddlings," said Douglas. "First PanAfrik's boss told me that if he had anything to say about it, I'd never fly anything for anybody ever again. And then the flight coordinator, that Dutchman, told me I was no better than a common hijacker. That son of a bitch. Can you imagine that coming from him? Every day he has to fax Khartoum a list of every destination the UN is flying to and ask permission to land. How can he look at himself in the mirror? So I told him he was on the wrong side, he was on Khartoum's side, and he said the UN wasn't on anyone's side, that the situation was so complicated that if it did take sides, it would quote turn a disaster into a calamity unquote."

"You don't think he had a point?" Tara asked, meaning that she thought so.

"C'mon, Tara." He presented his most engaging smile and leaned over to lay his palm lightly on her wrist. He had an instinct for knowing where and how to touch someone he wanted to win over, but the instinct failed him in this instance, Tara sitting with cool rigidity, demanding that he respond, and not with pretty smiles and intimate touches. His hand rose to her elbow, then lighted on her shoulder, and finally dropped in defeat. "All right, here's what I think. I told that dude that sometimes people make things more complicated than they have to be so they don't have to get off their asses and take a stand. Sometimes neutrality is just another word for cowardice."

"And how did he react to *that*?"

"Oh, he got cute and said that 'neutrality is another word for cowardice' sounded like one of those bumper stickers Americans are so fond of."

Tara laughed. "Well, it does, doesn't it? Let me tell you about something that happened a couple of years before you got to this part of the world."

Tara then related the tale, with which Fitzhugh was familiar, about the conflict that arose between Riek Machar, second in command of the SPLA, and John Garang, the commander in chief. Machar and one of his deputies attempted a coup to remove Garang from power. Irreconcilable differences over war aims were the stated reasons—Machar wanted an independent southern Sudan, Garang a united, secular Sudan.

"But that was rubbish," Tara went on. "It was tribal. You do know, don't you, that Machar is a Nuer and Garang a Dinka?"

"Yeah, yeah," Douglas muttered.

"So the Nuer and the Dinka are rather like the Serbs and the Croats. Hated each other ever since, oh, the big bang. The Nuer, most anyway, decided to follow Machar, and the Dinka lined up with Garang, and the next thing you know, there is no longer one SPLA but two. Machar's men attacked Bor—that's Garang's hometown—and slaughtered two thousand people. Tied children up and executed them. Hung old people from trees. They disemboweled women, whether after they'd shot them or before, I don't know. After, one hopes. The rest, thousands of them, fled into the swamps, and a lot of them died of starvation and malaria. I evacuated some of the victims, by the way. I *saw* it, Douglas. Garang's troops retaliated in kind, and it goes on to this day."

"Okay, proving what exactly?"

Tara looked surprised by the question, its answer was so plain. "Well, Machar and Garang both hold doctoral degrees, so to get philosophical about it, I suppose it proves that education is no vaccine against savagery, even though many people persist in thinking otherwise. More to the point, it proves that one cannot take sides. You're on the side of the southern Sudanese? But which southern Sudanese? The Nuer or the Dinka? And what of all the smaller tribes, some allied with the Nuer, some with the Dinka, some with their own armies? The southerners are their own worst enemy, and—"

"The fanatics in Khartoum are their worst enemy," Douglas interrupted.

"Oh, have it your way, then. I must say all this chatter makes me glad I fly planes instead of make policy."

"Fly planes instead of make policy? Hey, what are we? Bus drivers? It's our responsibility, yours, mine, Fitz's, everybody here"—he made a wide sweep of his arm—"to think about what we're doing, and if it's the wrong thing, make it right. Otherwise, we might as well pack our trash and go home. There's things we can do, big things, and Fitz and I are going to start doing one of them tomorrow, and you're going to be part of it, even if you think all you're doing is driving the bus. Sorry if I sound like I'm lecturing."

"Oh, I suppose it's good for the middle-aged soul to be lectured by the young now and then. My children, and there are four of them, do it all the time."

"I haven't spent the last couple years out here just playing Herc jockey," Douglas carried on, as if he hadn't heard her. "I've read a lot about Sudan's history. How the Brits divided the country, just about built a great wall of China between the north and south, and when they left, way back before I was born, told the Arabs and blacks that now it was up to them to figure out how to get along."

"Oh God, don't remind me that nineteen fifty-six was *way* before you were born," Tara said, with another restrained, backward toss of her head. "I remember when we—when the British left. I was one of the ones doing the leaving."

They each gave her a questioning look.

"I was raised in Sudan, you know. My father was an engineer, in charge of a postwar development project. A sort of social experiment. Provide land and income to tribesmen without either."

"Then you know better than anybody what I'm talking about."

"Actually, no." Tara smiled, but the stern look, returning to her eyes, nullified it. "I'm not defending colonialism, but I rather think the argument that it's to blame for Africa's problems has worn a bit thin. Something else is going on. As far as Sudan goes, I think it's up to the southerners to sort themselves out."

"And up to us to pitch in and help them do the sorting."

"You don't make a good carpenter by building his house for him," she said.

"Right. You give him a hammer, show him how to use it. But then you don't stand back and feel real good about yourself and say *tsk-tsk* when he bends a nail or whacks his thumb. Sometimes your arm has to get sore with his. Sometimes your sweat has to drip on the ground with his. Sometimes you have to swing the hammer with him, and yeah, sometimes you have to swing it *for* him, not sit in the air-conditioning like Timmerman with maps and pins and fax machines."

"And you don't eat Danish ham and drink French wine while the other guy gets by on his porridge and bad water," Fitzhugh added, his own fervor rising with the fervor in Douglas's voice. "And when the job's done, you leave with the shirt on your back, not a hundred thousand in back pay."

Douglas made a fist and rapped him on the shoulder. They were at that moment like two wires, feeding off the same current.

"I'm impressed with your passion, and I mean that." Tara's body canted forward to emphasize her sincerity. "But Sudan, it's a vast place, and there's something about it—" She hesitated, searching for words; she was a pilot, accustomed to expressing herself in the language of action. "Something bigger than its size. All that distance is inspiring, it gives you the impression that anything is possible, but then it deals you a nasty setback, and you think nothing is. That's the physics of Sudan. For every emotion there is an equal and opposite emotion." A slight, uncertain smile—she was pleased with the turn of phrase but unsure if it made any sense. "My father's project didn't come to much. He knew our time in Sudan was coming to a close, he wanted to leave a legacy. Toward the end he saw nothing of the sort was going to happen. Dad left a disappointed man, wondering if all he'd accomplished for all those years was to draw a paycheck and provide an interesting life for himself and his family.

Oh dear, listen to me! Nattering on. I'm afraid I'm not doing a good job, getting my point across." She stood abruptly, straightened her shirt, and tugged at her jeans, a little too tight for her figure. "So I'd best shut up. My vocal cords aren't used to all this talking. See you tomorrow, then? Wheels up at eight. I'll have a driver come round to pick you up. Half past seven."

They watched her walk off, her steps quick and short, her honey-blond hair bouncing over the back of her upturned collar.

"My goodness, looking at her from behind, you would think she was thirty," Fitzhugh observed. "Her and that Diana."

"Yeah," Douglas drawled, stretching with a long, languid movement. "What do you figure all that was about?"

"Some advice from an old hand?"

"More to it than that, it seemed to me."

Tara was by now out of sight, but Douglas continued to look after her, as if following her movements in his imagination.

"Pretty nice operation she's got going here." His head turned in a slow arc to take in the stone-walled tukuls, the bar and pool, the grounds-keepers raking the dirt pathways bordered by whitewashed rocks, the gardens that scented the dry air. It was more of an examination than a casual survey, as if the place were for sale and he a prospective buyer. "Has her own airline and her own hotel. Yeah, pretty nice. It's a safe bet that when she leaves, it won't be with just the shirt on her back."

Fitzhugh's own words, but he didn't care for the inference—if, that is, Douglas was making one.

"What are you getting at?"

"Ask you something? Do you think she's on our side?"

"Of course she is!" The question shocked Fitzhugh. He rather liked Tara. "Would she be taking a big risk for us if she wasn't? I think maybe you're rankled by some of the things she said to you."

"Doesn't pull her punches, for sure. But I admire her for that."

Fitzhugh finished his now-warm beer, put the back of his hand to his mouth, and belched.

"Now let me ask you something. Of all the sides in this war, which one do you think *is* ours?"

A GAME OF *bau* was in progress under a tamarind, men in homespun robes and bark skullcaps gathered with their treasuries of stones around egg-shaped holes scooped out of the ground in double rows. Tara's driver braked as a goat with prominent ribs ambled across the main road, toward a market where women cloaked against the chill were buying and selling charcoal. Its smell mingled with the smells of woodsmoke and dung, the scent of backcountry Africa. Beyond the town the cliffs of the Mogilla range looked like copper battlements in the new light, the crests of the ridges like copper roofs. In the pickup's cab, with Douglas wedged between him and the driver, Fitzhugh smoked his second cigarette of the day. The feeling that he was a twig in a current was still with him. He glanced at the plastic bags and cardboard boxes drifted alongside the rutted streets—the detritus of modern life had come to Loki without its blessings—at the rundown shops with signs that were reductively simple—TAILOR—or pretentious—MADAME'S EUROPEAN BEAUTY SALON—or baffling—GOD DOES NOT FORGET YOU, YOU FORGET HIM—and for a slivered moment regretted leaving this tumbledown, fly-plagued, rubbish-strewn crossroads. It would seem like the heart of civilization after a few days in the Nuba.

Douglas reached across his lap and swatted the smoke out the window. "How did a big-time soccer player get hooked on those damned things?"

They were passing the aid agency camps now. Brown storage tents as big as barns. Stacks of blue fuel drums. Razor wire. Radio antennae soaring.

"After eight years of keeping in training, I felt that I needed a vice," Fitzhugh grumbled, annoyed at Douglas, not for criticizing his habit but for making them late.

This morning, after taking a long shower, shaving, and combing his hair, he decided he could not appear in the same shirt he'd worn yesterday, as if anyone would notice or care. Finding the one he wanted—a pale blue denim—involved unpacking and then repacking his rucksack and wasted a good ten minutes. In the mess, he lingered over his eggs and bacon and was pouring himself a third cup of coffee when Fitzhugh, patience at an end, tapped his watch and reminded him that they were to have met Tara's driver five minutes ago. Douglas shrugged and said that no one was going anywhere without them.

A Turkana askari swung open the gate to the airfield, where a PanAfrik Hercules was taxiing for takeoff on the morning run. Tara's aviation company was headquartered near the western end of the landing strip. Four white Cessna Caravans and two Andovers, each with a maroon stripe and the word PATHWAYS above it in back-slanting letters, were parked on the apron. A wave of reassurance washed over Fitzhugh, calming his fears of flying in small planes. One look at Tara's, so immaculate they appeared to be made of bone china, told him they weren't going to suffer engine failure because of careless maintenance. She was in the small terminal, conferring with one of her pilots, an Ethiopian with a chiseled burnt-umber face. Static and distant voices crackled through the high-frequency radio on the varnished counter against which she leaned on her freckled forearms. Flight plans on clipboards hung from the wall behind her, between a tapestry of aviation maps and a chalkboard containing remarks on conditions at various airstrips. All the order and cleanliness of her domain spoke of something deeper than mere efficiency. She herself looked as put-together as her surroundings—khaki trousers with a military crease, starched white shirt set off by captain's epaulets, hair brushed and makeup on just so.

"I suppose I should be cross," she said when she finished up with the pilot. "Wheels up at eight, and here you are at ten past."

Douglas apologized, but some devil in him did not allow him to leave it at that. He explained that they had taken extra time to give their gear a last-minute check, and with a look he asked Fitzhugh not to betray the outright lie.

"No harm done," said Tara. "I had to go over a flight plan with the chap who just left, George, my senior pilot."

"Your *senior* pilot? How many have you got?"

"Twenty."

Douglas whistled appreciatively.

She packed an insulated cloth case with sandwiches, a Thermos of coffee, bottled water. "Shall we, then?" she said, and slung the case over a shoulder and tucked her sleeping bag under the opposite arm, declining Douglas's offer to carry one or the other for her.

They crossed the apron to one of the Caravans, Douglas lagging a little, studying the other planes as he had the grounds and buildings in the compound yesterday afternoon—with a covetous, appraising look. Noticing his interest, Tara volunteered that Pathways flew fourteen airplanes, ten out of here, two in Somalia, and two more out of Nairobi.

"I own the Caravans. Lease the rest," she said, and opened the baggage compartment under the rear door.

Another whistle from Douglas as he stowed his rucksack. What was she going to do if things were ever settled in Sudan? Not that that was likely anytime soon, but what if?

She was standing under a wing, her hand on the strut. "Are you implying something?"

"Nope."

"That I hope the mess is never settled because it keeps me in business?"

A ground crewman kicked the blocks from under the wheels. There was a silence several seconds long; then Douglas, with outspread hands, appealed to her to believe that his question had been innocent curiosity, nothing more. She opened the door and, with a jerk of her head, told him to climb in.

He strapped into the copilot's seat, Fitzhugh into the seat behind him.

"Sorry for snapping at you," Tara said, donning her sunglasses and headset.

"Hey, I'm cool if you are," Douglas said. "Let's fly."

Loki tower—a frame cabin atop a wooden derrick—then hangars and forklifts feeding pallets of sorghum into a cargo plane's innards shot by before the Caravan left the ground. It seemed to float effortlessly aloft, like a hot-air balloon. Holding her altitude to three thousand feet, Tara followed the Lokichokio-Lodwar highway. It was nearly devoid of traffic, so heavily ambushed by Turkana bandits that only armed convoys dared to travel it. Fifteen minutes after takeoff, she commenced her descent. The town appeared on the sun-blasted, khaki plain that stretched into eternity: a twin-spired mission church, huts fenced by thornbush *bomas*, the depressing geometry of the refugee camp, rank upon rank of tin-roofed barracks laid out on a grid of dusty streets.

"See the church?" Tara motioned as she made her approach. "Some time ago I fell madly in love with the priest, Father Tony O'Mara. Terrifically handsome in a dark Irish way, but true to his vows, and I know because I did my best to get him to break them. So every time I flew near Kakuma, I buzzed the church to say hello and remind him I was around. In case he had a change of heart."

She let out a wicked laugh that rang like wind chimes, and her two passengers saw, as faint as a ghost on a negative, an image of the wild girl she must have been. It was hard to reconcile that picture with the contained, middle-aged woman she was now.

The former temptress of a priest, the daredevil who buzzed churches, was quickly all business again, working rudder pedals and flap levers to make a smooth landing on a strip that wasn't much more than a graded gravel road. Without switching off the engine, she climbed out and directed a couple of Kenyans to begin loading the medical supplies— boxes of surgical gloves, antibiotics, syringes, bandages—into the back of the plane. Two people, faces turned from the whirling dust, approached the aircraft—a short white man and a white woman wearing a wide-brimmed straw hat, which she held tightly to her head with one hand. She and Tara embraced and started talking. Diana. The man with her was Barrett. She stepped under the wing and gestured to open the door.

"Fitz! Doug! Hello!" she shouted over the engine. "John and I had business here, so we thought we'd meet the plane and wish you bon voyage!"

Fitzhugh nodded his thanks, his heart arrested by her smile, the bright hair as yellow as her hat. The Kenyan was loading the boxes into the cart.

"Do give our best to Gerhard," Diana said.

"Gerhard?"

"All that stuff in back is for him," Barrett said. "Sort of a sample to show him the things we could do for him once we get the operation rollin'."

"Who is this Gerhard?"

"Gerhard Manfred." Diana again. "The doctor who runs the hospital up there."

"And a dedicated one he is. A bit daft and difficult, but be diplomatic with him. He could be of great help to us. He'll be happy with those supplies." Barrett extended his hand. "Best of luck to you. Michael the Archangel will meet you at Zulu One with an armed escort. Godspeed!"

Tara returned to her seat, Douglas latched the door, and Barrett and Diana stood back and waved as the plane taxied away, the cargo stacked under a cargo net. Fitzhugh pressed his face to the window, jumped by strange emotions. A titled lady almost old enough to be his mother, and here he was, wondering if she might be divorced from Mr. Briggs or his widow. He hadn't noticed a wedding ring.

In a short while they were over the stark Lolikipi plain, veined with dry watercourses, then crossed the northern tip of the Mogillas, fissured and barren. Tara scribbled notes for her log on a pad strapped to her thigh. She spoke into her headset microphone, but Fitzhugh couldn't hear, he could only see her lips moving. Ending the message, she pushed the mike aside and said they were now in Sudanese airspace and would observe radio silence from here on, emergencies excepted.

The uplands of Eastern Equatoria passed monotonously below in their drab dry-season colors. Seen from twelve thousand feet, the landscape looked as level as a football pitch. You could dribble a soccer ball for a hundred miles and not hit anything but a termite mound, Fitzhugh thought. Farther north, the immense marshes spreading away from the Nile tributaries in smears of somber green relieved the arid desolation with a desolate lushness. Primeval cradles of malaria haunted by venomous snakes and crocodiles. Miles and miles of bloody Africa—the hackneyed phrase seemed apt. Such emptiness.

Looking at it, Tara became nostalgic. She turned on the autopilot, unpacked the sandwiches and Thermos, and over lunch reminisced about her early days, when she flew hunters into Sudan and stayed in their camps, listening to lions call in the darkness. She described an Africa recent in history yet as remote as the continent of Stanley and Livingston: antelope migrating in dust-shrouded rivers of flesh, hooves, and horn, elephants journeying by the hundreds across their native range. Almost all gone now, she said, as much the victims of war and famine as the people who'd slaughtered the antelope for meat, the elephants for the ivory that bought guns and bullets. *That* Africa ended her idyll. Ever since all she'd done was fly on the light side for the UN, on the dark side for renegade relief agencies. Food here, medical supplies there, priests to beleaguered mission stations. Answering summonses to pick up the victims of snake-bite, of malaria, of an accidental blow from a panga or mattock, or any one of the thousand and one mishaps the southern Sudanese suffered whether there was peace or war. Often a few wounded guerrillas would be waiting at the airstrip with the sick or injured civilians. She would take them on board and deliver them to the Red Cross hospital near Loki, her nostrils stuffed with Vick's camphor rub against the reek of gangrene.

"I'm not really supposed to do that, evacuate rebel casualties, but it would be damned difficult to leave them there."

"Yeah?" Douglas said. "Well then maybe you understand why I—"

"Oh, I do, Doug. Believe me." She scanned the skies, glanced at the instruments, and said: "The one thing I haven't done is run guns for the SPLA. Been asked to, but I won't."

"Too risky?"

"In more ways than one. There's a—how shall I put it? A moral risk. And I know what you're thinking, the both of you. How much moral difference is there between putting a gun in a man's hands and flying him to hospital when he's been wounded so he'll be patched up to fight and kill again?"

Douglas was silent. Fitzhugh said that a thought like that had passed through his mind.

"The difference might not be all that great," she said, "but it's there all the same. Not to sound high and mighty, but I want to have as much to do as I can with saving lives, nothing to do with taking them."

"We all want that," said Douglas. He was looking at her, she at him, the expressions in their eyes cloaked by their sunglasses. "Wouldn't be in this business if we didn't. But I don't know that it's so easy to split things that fine."

"Directly or indirectly, you'll get some blood on your hands? Perhaps. But that shouldn't give you the green light to dip your hands into it." A keenness had entered her voice. "You have to draw the line somewhere. How did you get into this business, by the way?"

He replied that he would have to give it some thought. Apparently a lot of thought, Fitzhugh surmised after a couple of minutes passed in silence. Tara asked if he'd like to take the controls, to get a feel for the plane.

"Been waiting to hear that," Douglas said.

She switched off the autopilot, and he gripped the yoke.

"Three one zero and no loop the loops or chandelles."

"Hey, there's old pilots and bold pilots—"

"But no old bold pilots," she said, finishing the hoary adage. "And I am an old pilot, dammit."

The Nile appeared ahead, the great umbilical of the continent, the giver-taker, provider of flood and fertility, of commerce and bilharzia. It looked only a yard wide from this height, its banks stitched by slender threads of grass and marsh. Beyond it lay a sea of clay plains. Tara spread a chart on her lap, checked the GPS and compass, and declared they were dead on course, cutting the river midway between Kodok and Malakal.

"I don't know how to put it without sounding like I'm, you know, a Joe Goodguy," Douglas said abruptly, and they realized in a moment that he was answering the question put to him a quarter of an hour ago.

"Don't be shy," Tara teased. "We'll forgive you."

"After I got out of the air force, I thought I wanted to go commercial," he said, his wrists resting on the yoke. "But pretty quick I realized I wanted to do something more with it, with flying, I mean. Something more than . . . well . . . went to Alaska, flew there for a while. A twin Otter. Delivered mail and stuff to Eskimo settlements hundreds of miles from any road. A lot of school supplies. Computers. It was something to see the look on the teachers' faces, the kids' faces when I brought the first computers in. Like I was Santa Claus or an angel. So when I found out the UN was looking for people to fly in Sudan . . . so here I am."

He left off at that, palpably uncomfortable with talking about himself in this way. Fitzhugh, who'd expected a further insight into what made Douglas Douglas, felt a little let down. Later, he would learn that his friend belonged to the breed of American male who dislikes revealing his innermost self, not because he's shy or ashamed of what's there but because he abhors introspection and prefers to act, without giving much thought as to why.

Soon Tara took the controls again, descended to ten thousand, and leveled off above a Mars-scape with trees. She pointed to a long line of distant mountains, shimmering blue-gray in the noonday haze. The Nuba.

"Keep your eyes open for Antonovs. They patrol here fairly regularly."

"They could shoot at us?" Fitzhugh heard the rise in his voice and wished he'd done a better job of masking his alarm.

"No," said Tara. "They're either bombers or recce aircraft. But they could track us and radio their chums on the ground."

"This is the kind of thing that makes it hard to feel neutral. Okay, I'll watch the right. Fitz, take the left."

Douglas did not sound alarmed or tense or anything but stimulated. Fitzhugh shifted to the left-hand seat and looked out the window, alert for any movement in the bright heavens. His imagination got the better of him, transforming a speck on the Plexiglas into a far-off plane. Later he was about to call Tara's attention to a dark object, soaring between them and the ground, when he realized it was a large bird. They were over the mountains now. The Caravan leaped and fell suddenly, his heart with it. An updraft, Tara explained. Hot air gyring off the mountains. The altimeter needle wound downward, the plane shuddering and bouncing. Fitzhugh was distracted from his observational duties by the terror turbulence always induced in him, and by the wild architecture reeling below. Finger pinnacles, rocky spires and pyramids, boulders and ravines and scree-covered slopes. They swooped over a plateau where the cylindrical huts of a Nuban village clustered between two baobab trees as old as time. Beyond was a valley of dead yellow grass. Tara flew down the length of it, toward a serpentine of scraggly trees that defined a watercourse, winding at the foot of a low, bare escarpment, golden rocks scattered across it like immense nuggets.

Craning her neck, she pointed and said, "There it is, Zulu One," but Fitzhugh saw nothing that looked like a landing field, only the trees and the riverbed and the meadows. She flew over the escarpment, made a wide turn, and cautioned her passengers to be sure they were buckled up. Fitzhugh tightened his seatbelt. A second later his organs slid into his throat as the plane dived steeply, spiraling as it plunged so that he caught alternating glimpses of ground and sky. He was almost sure that something had gone horribly wrong, that Tara had lost control, but everything was happening too quickly for him to feel anything but nausea. He choked, turned aside, and vomited on the seat beside him, the plane pulling out of the corkscrewing dive at the same instant to shoot over the trees, nearly clipping their flat tops. The landing gear hit the ground. The Caravan bounced, rocked to one side, straightened, touched down again, and made a bumpy roll. A stack of fuel drums went by. Tara braked to a stop and killed the engine.

The silence was eerie after the wind-rushing roar of the dive, but Fitzhugh thanked God that he was alive and on earth again and no longer in motion. Tara turned around and wrinkled her nose at his mess.

"Good thing I've got my Vicks with me." She pulled a rag from under her seat and handed it to him, and he wiped the seat. "Fault's all mine. Ought to have given you better warning. A precaution, landing in dodgy areas. Coming in like that makes you a difficult target, in case there's any-one below with a mind to take a shot at you."

"So that was deliberate? I wasn't sure."

Douglas laughed, patted his shoulder.

"First time in the Nuba, and you hurl lunch."

"Breakfast, too."

Just then a procession of men emerged from the scrub, men as tall as Dinka but more powerfully built and almost naked. The best clad wore patched shorts, the rest strips of cloth or animal hide tied to braided waist cords or leather belts. Behind them came more giants, gowned in white *jelibiyas* and leading a string of donkeys toward the plane.

"Give me a hand," said Tara, motioning at the cargo.

She flipped up the top half of the rear door, then swung open the bot-tom half. The half-naked men were outside, formed up in a human chain, and the sight of them close up momentarily arrested Fitzhugh and Doug-las. One man had cut horizontal bands into his hair so that he seemed to be wearing a striped stocking cap, and another had painted a white streak down the middle of his skull. There were half a dozen more, each pro-claiming his individuality with one sort of ornamentation or another: gold hoop earrings and nose rings, feathered ankle bracelets, armbands encircling thick biceps, bead necklaces on muscular necks, bare ebony chests decorated with tribal scarring in the forms of antelope and lizards and leopards.

"They're quite something, aren't they?" Tara said.

Douglas pronounced them "incredible" and then, deciding that the adjective was inadequate, "beautiful, magnificent."

Fitzhugh felt as if he were looking into the face of an Africa that hadn't changed in a thousand years. The Nuban at the head of the line, making movements with his immense hands, shook him and Douglas out of their trance. Time to do some work. They and Tara pitched the boxes outside, to be tossed down the chain to the giants in white, who wrapped them in hide blankets and lashed the bundles to the donkeys' backs.

The job done, Tara stood in the doorway and looked around, making a visor with her hand.

"Ah, here he is," she said, and climbed out, her two passengers following her into a heat aggravated rather than relieved by the sear wind hissing through the trees, the desiccated grass. A man approached them, consuming six feet or more in a stride. His jelibiya, which would have been ankle-length on someone of ordinary height, reached only a few inches past his knees and made a startling contrast with his jet-black skin. He looked like a three-dimensional shadow dressed up as a ghost.

"Goraende?" Fitzhugh asked.

She shook her head.

"Tara! And pleased to see you once again!" the man said in almost perfect English. The top of his skull not far below the Caravan's overhead wing, he made Fitzhugh and Douglas look short and shrunk Tara to the stature of a child. "Always welcome and good day to you. These are our gentlemen?"

Nodding, she introduced them. The man's name was Suleiman, and he shook hands by gripping the fingertips and then moving his own fingers rapidly, creating a tickling sensation. Fitzhugh blinked at the peculiar greeting and Suleiman grinned.

"Our way of saying hello! Which of you is the one to look for good landing places?"

"That would be me," Douglas said.

"We will be working together. I know the Nuba, top to bottom, and I know airstrips, I am your man," Suleiman declared. "And please for you both to follow me."

They reached for their rucksacks. Suleiman shook his head and called to one of the half-clothed men in a Nuban dialect. He came up, slipped each fifty-pound ruck over a shoulder with ease, and lugged them to where the donkeys waited in the shade, under their loads.

"We can hump our own gear," Douglas said.

Suleiman looked puzzled.

"We can carry our packs ourselves."

"I am sure you can, but why do it when there are donkeys to carry them for you?"

Airtight logic, Fitzhugh thought.

"I'll be going as soon as I top off the tanks," Tara said as two men rolled fuel drums across the runway. "If you can, call me on Michael's radio the day before you're ready to come out. That way, I'll be sure to have a plane ready. Whatever, I'll be here."

"On the money?" asked Douglas, clasping her hand.

"On the money," she said, and they turned and followed Suleiman, striding into the trees.

Maroor

"Do you suppose war to be here what wars are elsewhere?" Stopping in midstride, Gerhard Manfred flung one thick arm at a Nuban hospital aide sterilizing surgical instruments over a campfire. "Do you suppose that it is an event, with a discrete beginning that will proceed to a discrete middle *und so weiter* on to a discrete end? No! It is a condition of life, like drought. There is war in Sudan because there is war."

"Like Vietnam?" Douglas murmured. "We're here because we're here because we're here."

Manfred's gaze passed from the American's face to his boots, then back up again.

"I have no idea what you are talking about." His English bore only a whiff of Teutonic accent; otherwise he sounded like a Cambridge don. He was a man of fifty or so, judging from the white invading his blond hair, and powerfully built in a way that wasn't threatening; his square, compact body looked more adapted to withstanding punishment than to dishing it out. "What has Vietnam to do with this?" He jerked his cleft chin at the aide, whose surgical smock rode up his long legs as he bent over, stoking the fire to make thin flames lap the soot-streaked sides of the sterilizer. "Did you Americans experience this in Vietnam? The coils shorted out one month ago, and of course I have not a technician to fix it, nor has a replacement been sent, so now this is how I sterilize my instruments. And why? Because there is war. Why is there war? Because there is. Ha! Make note of that, my friend—" He addressed Fitzhugh, who had his pocket notebook out. "Write that down, please."

Fitzhugh stood silently for a moment, feeling light-headed. Yesterday, with Michael Goraende, Suleiman, the porters, and a rebel escort of twenty men, he and Douglas had walked for hours from Zulu One over a rough, rocky track and under a punishing sun until the drone of an enemy Antonov forced them to hide in a dense acacia grove. There, with the pack animals tethered to the trees, they waited until dark before setting off again, the path illuminated by a gibbous moon. They made a cold camp under a giant baobab at midnight and, without so much as a cup of tea, resumed their march at four this morning, tramped on through a ruby dawn, and came to a hilltop village, from which they could see the hospital on a lower hill a kilometer away: two long, mud-walled bungalows joined by a breezeway, umbrellas of solar panels gleaming incongruously on its thatch roofs. Crossing the narrow valley between the two hills, they arrived at Manfred's compound just as the heat was making itself felt and the doctor was beginning his day of treating people for fever, goiter, snakebite, broken bones.

Straight away the man seemed intent on making himself as unpleasant as possible. He inspected the medical supplies without a word of gratitude to anyone for delivering them, shook hands with Douglas and Fitzhugh as if they were inconsequential tourists, and then, instructing them to remain, told Michael to vacate the premises with his men. The hospital was neutral ground, and Manfred intended to keep it that way. Suleiman and the porters, being unarmed, could stay, but not the guerrillas; if it became known that he'd welcomed rebel soldiers to his compound—and the bush telegraph would be sure to carry the news to the government garrisons scattered throughout the mountains—the army would have a perfect excuse to bomb or shell the place. Fitzhugh wasn't entirely confident that an army that felt no restraints about bombing schools and missions needed an excuse to blow up a hospital. Twenty men with automatic rifles would be no defense against a high-flying plane; all the same, their presence was reassuring, and he hoped the guerrilla commander would tell the doctor to kindly leave matters of security to him. Michael was an imposing man, six and a half feet tall, but he was as deferential toward Manfred as a schoolboy toward a teacher and made only a mild protest, explaining that Douglas and Fitzhugh were under his protection. Manfred insisted; they would be safe with him. Michael gave in and led his men back to the village.

"You want me to write down what?" Fitzhugh asked.

"That we need a new sterilizer, what do you think? Also diesel fuel for our auxiliary generator, for use when the solar power is lost. Also . . . everything else. Yes! Everything is needed now in the Nuba, which makes your task of assessing our needs an easy one. This place should be called the Needa. Ha! Need a what? Need a whatever you can think of. Come along, I will show you."

It seemed Manfred needed a tranquilizer. Well, Barrett had warned that he was a bit daft, so maybe his rudeness wasn't intentional, but a symptom of that peculiar form of daftness summed up in the word *bushed.* The simmering anger, the lack of simple civility—Fitzhugh had seen it all before, in aid workers isolated too long, working sixteen hours a day because more than a few hours' rest seemed an unjustifiable indulgence in the face of colossal suffering. That, and Barrett's caution to be diplomatic, inclined him to humor the doctor's idiosyncrasies.

He led them around the back of the hospital to a neat stone bungalow, picturesquely situated in ficus shade, overlooked by a soaring butte. A former British rest house, Manfred said, which he'd restored as a residence for himself. There was a lemon grove behind it, and a vegetable garden tilled by a young Nuban with a makeshift hoe. The doctor called to him in some local dialect, and the young man trotted toward them, a harlequin figure in patched denim shorts and a red and white T-shirt stamped with a faded legend PROPERTY OF OHIO STATE ATHLETIC DEPARTMENT. Manfred seized the hoe by its thick handle and, as if to test Fitzhugh's forbearance, thrust the blade at him with such violence that he had to step back to avoid being hit in the face.

"Do you know what this is?"

"I believe it's a hoe."

"No! This! What is this?"

Manfred brushed the dirt off the blade, revealing a couple of yellow cyrillic letters painted on the olive drab metal. Fitzhugh squinted at the writing and shrugged.

"It's shrapnel from a Russian bomb," Douglas said.

"Precisely! More precisely, a Russian cluster bomb, one of the four that fell on the mission six months ago."

"That would be St. Andrew's?" asked Fitzhugh.

"Twenty-seven people killed, sixteen of them children. Thirty-one injured. I know the precise number because I was summoned there to stitch the wounded back together. I did not entirely succeed." He handed the implement back to the gardener, who returned to his labors. "So after the funerals, after the proprieties were observed—the Nubans set great store by the proprieties of death, they believe in the immortality of the soul, yes, they fear that if they neglect their obligations to the dead, the dead will neglect their obligations to the living and perhaps bring calamities, although one wonders what calamities could be worse than cluster bombs."

Frowning, Manfred went suddenly silent. He appeared to have lost his original train of thought.

"You were saying, after the funerals?" Douglas reminded him.

"The funerals, yes. After the funerals, local farmers returned to the mission and collected the bomb fragments and from them made hoes. So that shows you how little we have here. The war has taken almost everything away, but sometimes it gives a little back. Swords into plowshares, bombs into hoes. Write that down in your little book. We need hoes so we don't have to wait for another bombing to get new ones. Ah! This is all so silly."

"*Silly?*" Douglas made a show of wriggling a finger in his ear, as if he hadn't heard right. "What's silly?"

"What is not?"

Turning sharply on his heel, Manfred stomped off. His two visitors didn't realize they were supposed to follow until he looked over his shoulder and gave them a jerky wave. He brought them to a tukul identical to those in the village. Manfred flipped a light switch, and they beheld a spotless X-ray machine that rested on the dirt floor.

"A Siemens, my young friends. It was flown to Khartoum from Germany more than a year ago, then on to Abu Gubeiha and delivered from there by lorry. A fine instrument, not so?" He stroked the padded table and the smooth steel arm of the camera as if they were living things. "My X-ray technician is an Arab fellow, quite competent, trained in the U.K. Only one thing is missing. Can you guess what it is?"

Another riddle. Fitzhugh yearned for a smoke and a long nap.

"Film!" the doctor shouted into their silence and then laughed. "I have no film! I have not had any for six months! I have made several requests by radio for film to be sent, I have been assured it has been sent, but it never gets here. I have no idea what happens to it, though I have my suspicions. The Sudan military confiscates it for their own use. What do I do when someone comes to me with a broken bone? I poke, I prod, I guess. When someone comes to me with a persistent pain here or here or here"—he touched his liver, his stomach, his back—"and I suspect cancer? I cut them open and have a look. Exploratory surgery, performed with instruments sterilized over an open fire. I return to medicine as it was practiced a hundred and fifty years ago. Ha! Longer ago! I could be a surgeon in the Roman army. Silly, silly, *nicht wahr?*"

"Criminal is what it is," Douglas said.

"Criminal? Are you a prosecutor? And whom will you prosecute?" Manfred faced the machine while words tumbled from his mouth like rocks in an avalanche, and his pale blue irises shot back and forth as if they were looking for a way to fly out of his head. "*Absurd.* Yes, that is the better word than *silly.* This entire century has made friends with the absurd, and none are better friends with it than the Sudanese. A war whose beginning no one can remember, whose end no one can see, whose purpose no one knows. Yes, they are best of friends with the absurd."

Thinking, *Count on a German to go abstract on you,* Fitzhugh wrote "X-ray film, sterilizer, hoes, diesel" in his notebook.

Probably the man hadn't had anyone's ear for weeks. There were two other Europeans at the hospital, a German nurse and an Italian logistician, but Fitzhugh would bet that they'd listened to their boss's rants once too often and had made his silence on certain issues a condition of their continued service.

Manfred turned off the light with a swat—there was a savagery in almost all his movements—and ushered his visitors outside.

"And this mission you two are on is absurd also. I hope you realize that."

The remark struck them like a backhanded slap.

"If that's what we thought, we wouldn't be on it, would we?" Douglas said.

"I shall enlighten you, then. Even if you find places to land big planes and even if those planes are not shot down, how do you propose to get what you deliver to the people who need it? There are hardly any roads to speak of, and the only vehicle I know of is my Land Rover, which I need if I am called away and which can't carry very much in any case. So tens of porters will be needed. What a tempting target a column of porters will make to some Sudanese pilot. He will not be able to resist. The first time such a procession is strafed, you will find it difficult to recruit others for the job."

"Let us worry about that problem." Douglas's expression had gone blank, and Fitzhugh now knew him well enough to recognize that studied blandness as a sign of anger.

"I fully intend to," Manfred stated. "I have too many problems of my own."

Half of them probably self-inflicted, Fitzhugh thought, following him into the U-shaped courtyard formed by the breezeway and the two long buildings. Infants in their laps, several women were sitting against a wall, some wearing the sorts of dresses collected by church groups in the West, while two were nearly naked, rows of bright beads girding their waists. Their bellies were ornamented with ritual tattoos, the raised scars on dark brown flesh resembling rivets in leather. The women sat with the listless postures and lifeless expressions Fitzhugh had seen everywhere in southern Sudan, the faraway stares and slumped shoulders and bent heads forming their own kind of ritual tattoos, marking all, regardless of native tribe, as members of the single tribe the aid agencies called "affected populations." Manfred, squatting down, read the notations written on the strip of surgical tape plastered to each mother's forehead. He spoke to each gently, patted the infants' heads, even sang a few bars of what must have been a Nuban lullaby. It somehow pleased Fitzhugh to see that his personality had another, more attractive dimension.

"The little ones are going to be vaccinated, and they're afraid, the mothers," he explained, rising. "It is the unknown. They have been told their babies should be vaccinated, but of course they have no idea what is involved, so I explain it to them in a way they can understand."

He spoke to them again, and the women stood and filed inside, the half-nude females displaying on their backs and buttocks, brown as burnt cork, round as bubbles, the same intricate patterns as were stitched into their stomachs.

"They're from a part of the Nuba where the old customs haven't died out," the doctor said, noticing Fitzhugh's stare. "They believe that certain tattoos prevent disease, and that is not pure superstition. It is done like so. First, a small cut with a knife, then the flesh is lifted with a thorn. Germs enter the cuts, and the system develops antibodies, creating immunities. Not that the Nubans know anything about antibodies and immunities, they only know what works. So that is how I explained vaccinating to these women. Their babies will be pricked by a special thorn filled with healing spirits that will make their babies strong against sickness. Those two walked here from their village, by the way. Four days."

An infant's cry came from inside.

"There, the first one. They think of us, the Nubans, as powerful *kujurs*—their word for witch doctors. I told the women that the healing spirits in the thorn were brought by you two from the sky."

"You didn't really," Douglas said.

"Of course I did. As a favor to you. It will help you make a favorable impression on these people."

"That's incredibly condescending." Douglas had found a way to retaliate for the doctor's earlier remark. "These people aren't children."

"Certainly not. But what do you know about them? You've been in the Nuba all of what? Twenty-four hours?"

"Long enough to know that they aren't children who need to be told that we brought spirits out of the sky. I'd think they know what an airplane is."

"Most certainly! They have been bombed by airplanes, but you, my young friend, don't know anything to make such a cheeky comment as you just now made to me."

Douglas started to reply; Fitzhugh nudged him to keep quiet.

"Condescending indeed," Manfred carried on, arms crossed over his chest. With another movement of his divided chin, he pointed at the breezeway's screen, through which they saw one of the tattooed women, in all her six-foot beauty, standing in front of the nurse's table while a Sudanese aide daubed her infant's arm with cotton. "Look there. You have had a taste of what it's like to walk in these mountains. Now imagine please walking in your bare feet, carrying a child for four days. I try to imagine some fat cow in my country—*eine grosse Kuh,* it sounds more like what it is in the German, *nicht wahr?* I try to imagine the *grosse Kuh* walking barefoot from Bonn to Berlin to have her child vaccinated, and I cannot imagine it. Condescending? I have for these women nothing but admiration, but I overlook your comment. I think you are perhaps too tired from your journey to remember your manners."

Fitzhugh winced, fully expecting Douglas to say that Manfred was no one to lecture about manners. Instead, he switched on his charm, as quickly and effortlessly as someone turning an ignition key. The broad, guileless smile, the touch, the sincere gray eyes framing the doctor like a portrait lens, so that he, like everyone else upon whom Douglas bestowed that unique look, felt that he was the only one in the picture.

"You're right. That was a stupid thing to say, and I'm damned sorry I said it." This in his slow, calm drawl, the smile turning ever so slightly abashed as he let go of Manfred's forearm and extended his hand. "I'll feel like hell all day if you don't accept my apology."

"Not necessary. I said I overlook what you said."

"If you don't mind. I won't feel right otherwise."

"Very well."

Douglas cupped his left hand over their clasped rights, as if sealing a solemn agreement.

"And you're right about another thing." His gaze held the other man as firmly as his grip. "I don't know anything, except two things—how to fly planes, and that you're gonna get your X-ray film and your fuel and your new sterilizer. The farmers will get their hoes. And anything else you need or they need. I'm gonna see to it. Don't mean I'll try. I mean I *will* see to it, count on it."

An effective little touch, Fitzhugh thought, that folksy, cowboy *gonna* instead of *going to.*

"So this is American confidence?"

"Doesn't have a nationality. This mission will work."

"Ah, that." His hand now free, Manfred slapped the air. "That was a stupid thing to say also. So you will please accept *my* apology."

"No problem. Okay, Suleiman and I—" gesturing at Suleiman and the porters, resting in the shade of silver-barked trees—"are going to start scouting today for a place we can turn into an airstrip, closer to here than Zulu One, so it won't take a day to get the stuff here."

"Not too close. An airfield would be a tempting target also." Manfred looked off into the middle distance. "It will be a risk for me, to be supplied without Khartoum's sanction."

Douglas clutched the doctor's shoulders, and he didn't object to the familiarity; he was under the Braithwaite spell.

"You already took that risk."

"This one time, yes, but flights coming in here, once, twice a week, every week—"

"If you want the stuff, I don't see that you've got much choice," Douglas said, tucking into the statement a tone of regret, as though he wished Manfred had more options. "Got a favor to ask. Okay if I send one of the porters over to the village to ask Michael for a couple of his men to come back here? That wouldn't be breaking your rule too much, would it? Suleiman and I are going to need some security."

"I suppose that would be—"

"Hey, thanks. We'll be out of here in no time. While we're gone, it would be good if you sat down with Fitz, drew up a detailed shopping list. What you need, how much, what's priority."

Manfred nodded and said Fitzhugh could join him on his morning rounds; they could make the list then.

"Okay, I'll get rolling." Douglas strode off to speak to Suleiman, who woke one of the sleeping porters. In a moment the man was on his feet, loping toward the village.

Looking at the American, the doctor pronounced him "an interesting fellow," a statement Fitzhugh interpreted as a tribute to the masterful way the younger man had subdued him and taken control without trying to do either.

UNDER SPUTTERING FLUORESCENTS and bare bulbs of middling wattage, the ward looked like a dimly lit cavern. A fine dust blew through the wire window grates and powdered the beds, the night tables, and the steel poles from which IV bags hung like transparent cocoons, plastic tubes trailing from their undersides into the veins of the famished, the fevered, the wounded. With his eyes shut, Fitzhugh would have known he was in a bush hospital by the smell—the indefinable odor of sickness crowded in with the musk of unwashed bodies lying on unwashed linen in unwashed clothes. Manfred said, apologetically, that circumstances had forced him to compromise his standards of hygiene. He wished he could keep the infernal dust out with proper windows, but one might as well try to import ice cream as panes of glass into the Nuba; they could never survive the journey over the rough roads. He would prefer a tin roof to the one he had. Snakes and spiders nested in the thatch, and what trouble it was, keeping them out. Yes, corrugated tin—he could use that. Franco, his logistics man, could tell Fitzhugh how many square meters were needed. And the bed linen! Of course it should be laundered and changed daily; of course that was impossible. In the Nuban dry season, there was nothing so rare as water, and Khartoum's recent military activities had made it rarer still. Arab raiders had destroyed a lot of wells. Poisoning a well was forbidden by the Koran, but the holy book was silent about plastic explosive, so that was what the murahaleen used. A charming distinction. There was only one well for the hospital, and it didn't produce near what was needed. The rest was delivered by lorry in fifty-liter drums during the dry season when the track to Abu Gubeiha was passable; but this year, the deliveries had become sporadic.

Manfred paused to study the chart of a middle-aged patient, fabulously tall, his feet thrust between the bedstead's metal posts. "This is the game. This hospital has for Khartoum a propaganda value. Somebody like Amnesty International reports that the government denies aid to the Nuba, the government points to us and says, 'Wrong, and there is the proof, a fine one-hundred-twenty-bed hospital run by the most efficient Germans.' But we are also a little problem. The government wants the Nubans to go to its so-called peace camps for medical attention. Once they are in, very hard to get out."

"And you're a problem because you give them someplace else to go," Fitzhugh said.

"Precisely. We are here a little sanctuary. So Khartoum needs us on the one hand, but we on the other hand make it more difficult for them to subdue the Nubans. Therefore it makes things a little more difficult for us. Our water supplies?" Manfred turned an imaginary tap. "Enough to survive, nothing more, and I dare not protest. Water. Before everything else, water. Do you suppose it's good for the soul to devote so much of one's energy to obtaining something so basic as that? Do you suppose it teaches the value of simple things?"

Fitzhugh didn't want to get into metaphysics and asked how much water was needed. Check with Franco, the doctor replied. Franco could tell him, down to the barrel. Franco was very precise—a northern Italian, you know.

Manfred leaned over the bed and conversed with his patient, who turned his head aside, exposing a round pink scar on his neck. The doctor examined it and said:

"Goiter. I removed it yesterday. A lack of iodized salt in the diet. The Nubans used to trade with Arab merchants for salt, but that is so much more difficult now. There is your priority number two. Salt."

He moved on to the next bed, occupied by a strapping youth with the chest and arms of a Greek statue, wearing a gold earring in the style of Nuban males; it hung from the top of his left ear rather than from the lobe. A long horizontal scar, crisscrossed by recent stitches, ran around his side, just under his ribs, and he lay in a stupor induced by an IV drip of Demerol. A woman who could have been anywhere between forty and sixty sat at his bedside, on a dirty floor mat. She raised weary, bloodshot eyes toward Manfred, he muttered a few words to her, and she responded in a voice as tired as her eyes.

"A beautiful specimen of Nuban manhood, not so?" Manfred said after checking the young man's chart. "A *kadouma* in his village, a wrestler. He and his mother came here last week. He had a bad pain in his side. They thought he'd been injured in a match. I suspected amoebic liver abscess, but when I cut him open to drain the abscess, I discovered a tumor. With the X-ray, I could have found it beforehand and spared him the surgery. The tumor is inoperable. Now we wait for him to die. He's nineteen years old."

They went from the surgical ward to the medical ward, the two divided by a plywood partition, then into pediatrics in the next building. Fitzhugh, making occasional notes, felt he was being guided through an exhibition of half the injuries, infirmities, and pathologies to which human flesh is prone. Dysentery and gastroenteritis declared themselves by the stench; dry coughs announced tuberculosis; febrile brows and shivering bodies testified to malaria; skeletal limbs whispered starvation; blood and pus oozing through gauze dressings rumored bullet and shrapnel wounds; amputated limbs screamed gangrene. He was able to look on the adult cases with detachment; he had seen their like before, his heart had grown the necessary carapace, thinner than the impenetrable callus that made some people incapable of feeling a thing yet thick enough to allow him to gaze on the worst sights without crippling his sanity; but in the children's ward he realized that his prolonged leave from relief work, bringing sweet reminders of what normal life was like, had opened cracks in his emotional armor. An infant with a belly bloated by severe malnutrition being fed intravenously because the terror of a bombing had dried up his mother's breasts; a young woman clutching a month-old daughter born, said Manfred, ten minutes after her twin had emerged dead from the mortar fragment that had pierced the woman's stomach: those were sights Fitzhugh couldn't bear.

He fled outside, with a pressure in his chest like the onset of a coronary. What a war this was that offered no sanctuary anywhere. A soldier in any one of its armies and militias was probably safer than a child in the womb. Jesus, aborted on the threshold of life by a hot steel sliver propelled by the random physics of a shell burst. He wished he knew where that particular projectile had been assembled, and the identities of the workers who'd packed the explosive and installed the fuse and detonator; he would like to show them what the products of their labor did. Not that imparting such information would make any difference. Those workers wouldn't walk off the job in moral disgust. They had mouths to feed. It seemed that in the struggle between mercy and cruelty, cruelty would always have the upper hand. What weapons were there in the arsenals of mercy to equal the simple effectiveness of explosive, fuse, detonator, much less the complex electronics that guided a missile or fired a gunship's rockets? Did mercy's armies possess a bomb capable of restoring a village incinerated by napalm? Could they ever be anything but outnumbered and outgunned by the armies with howitzers and tanks?

"Too much for you?"

Manfred came down the path, the bright coin of his stethoscope's gauge bouncing against his stomach.

Fitzhugh lit a cigarette, held out the pack to the doctor.

He took one and bowed to the proffered lighter. "I try to look at it as the mother does. She told us that her ancestors' spirits had decreed that the one should be sacrificed so she and the other could live. Some truth in that, you know. Had its body not absorbed the fragment, the mother's kidney would have been pierced and all three would have died."

"And it helps you to look at it that way?"

"Provided I don't think about certain things."

"Such as what?"

"Such as what the Nuba was like the first time I came here, twenty-two years ago. I have worked also in Rwanda and the Balkans, and when I returned here, I never expected to see the things I saw in those places. But I think you have perhaps heard enough from me? You would wish a word with Franco?"

"I could use a nap first."

"Yes! Of course! There is a spare bedroom in my house. You are welcome to it. I'll have someone wake you . . . When?"

"A couple of hours." He glanced at his watch. "Two o'clock, since you like precision."

Franco was a lean man with a saturnine face perfectly suited to his surly disposition; he was, however, as exacting as advertised, and within an hour of waking from his nap, Fitzhugh had filled several pages of his notebook with a wish list of needed items and their quantities. All through the conversation, a jangling melody of squawks, bleeps, and what sounded like birdcalls came from the cottage next door to Franco's. Ulrika, the nurse, a broad-boned woman on the frontier of middle age, was addicted to computer games and played them whenever she had a spare moment. Franco said it drove him half nuts. *"Basta! Basta!"* he'd shouted through the window, adding suggestions that Ulrika take up reading or meditation, anything that didn't cause so much noise.

"Go to hell, you sorrowful pus!" she called back in a thickly accented English.

"Sourpuss, that's the correct phrase, *cretina*!"

There was in this exchange a note of lovers who'd had a falling out. The racket went on.

Around five he, Franco, and the nurse convened for drinks on Manfred's *mustaba,* a raised platform of sun-baked mud behind his house, overlooking the lemon grove and vegetable garden: a pleasing view, Fitzhugh thought, sitting in a canvas chair with a cold beer from the refrigerator where the plasma was stored. He sensed that the cocktail hour was a daily affair at the hospital, one of those rituals whites followed faithfully in the bush as a prophylaxis against going crazy. Ulrika was delighted with his presence: someone new to talk to, a visitor from the outer world. He found her interest flattering. She peppered him with questions about himself and Douglas, asked how things were these days in Loki and Nairobi, and about Barrett and Diana, and would he *please* tell them when he got back to *please* send her some decent shampoo. "This dust! This goddamned dust!" she said, tugging at her long, pinned-up hair. She shot a questioning glance at Manfred, who nodded.

"Herr Doktor does not wish luxury things to take up space in the airplanes that could be used for the medical things," she explained. "But the shampoo is okay. So you will please ask John to send?"

He took out his notebook and jotted a reminder, pleased to perform this little service for her.

"Speaking of John, there is one thing about his plans I don't understand," Manfred said. A table had been set for dinner on the mustaba, and he sat at its head, the pater of this small, isolate familia. "This notion he has to rebuild the mission. What is the sense of that? As you have now seen, we have more urgent needs than churches."

They were joined for dinner by the rest of the staff—the X-ray technician, the lab technician, and Ulrika's assistant, a light-skinned woman from an Arab part of the Nuba—and finally by Michael. Good diplomacy demanded that he be included; Manfred did not want to offend the rebels any more than he did the government; the proprieties of neutrality had to be observed, however, and the messenger who'd gone to the village with the invitation informed Michael to come without his uniform, pistol, or bodyguard.

He complied, arriving accompanied by only one of his troops, who was armed with nothing more deadly than a musical instrument—some kind of homemade lyre. Michael's shaved head was bare of its usual red beret, and he'd exchanged his camouflage for a borrowed jelibiya, as white as an egret's wing and pinched at the waist by a cord, accentuating the spread of his chest and shoulders. At thirty-five, he was still as hard-muscled as the wrestler he'd been in his youth. Ulrika and her aide locked on to him the instant he appeared, magnetized by his stature, the almost perfect oval of his face, with its deep-set eyes, its vaguely smiling lips and small ears, a gold earring in one. This whole photogenic ensemble rested on a neck that appeared to have been hewn from an athlete's thigh, its dark musculature set off by a strand of white beads.

"I think it's customary in the West to bring a gift when you're asked to dinner," he said, tilting his head at the musician. "All Nubans love to make music, but this guy is the best."

The last phrase betrayed the time Michael had spent in the United States, taking military training at Fort Benning. He sat down at the end of the table opposite Manfred while the musician perched on the edge of the mustaba and tuned his instrument, a curious-looking thing consisting of three sticks tied into a triangle, the two longer pieces attached to a calabash with a leather membrane stretched over it to hold the strings.

"We usually play opera at dinner," Manfred stated, pointing at a cassette player on the floor. "It was to be Verdi today, but live music is best. Thank you, colonel."

Addressing the guerrilla commander by his rank, Fitzhugh assumed, was the doctor's way of making up for his earlier brusqueness.

"But where is the American, Douglas?" Michael pronounced it *Douglass*. "I expected them back by now."

"I told him not too close to the hospital, for reasons I think you can appreciate. Perhaps they took me too much at my word?"

"If they did, that guy Douglas is with, Suleiman, will see to it that it's far enough," Michael said. "No one can walk like him. Fifty kilometers a day he can do without a problem."

Dinner—canned turkey, beans and tomatoes from the garden, with bitter Sudanese beer to drink in tall brown bottles—was nothing like the elegant feasts Fitzhugh had seen laid out in some aid compounds in the south. Manfred prided himself on the austerity of the fare and mocked his counterparts in Médicins sans Frontières. He and his staff ate *doura* for breakfast, doura and maybe some beans or groundnuts for lunch, like the Nubans, but those froggies, ha, they could not do without their croissants, their fine Bordeaux, their cheeses. Not serious people.

Mouth inches from the plate, his fork darting like a hungry hawk's beak, Michael ate with single-minded haste, as you would expect from a guerrilla fighter who spent most of his time on the move. Ulrika looked at him, politely aghast, her first impression of the striking lieutenant colonel undergoing some revision. Finished before everyone else was halfway through, he leaned back and closed his eyes and softy joined the musician in a chantlike song that floated with the lyre's notes above the multilingual hum of hospital shop talk. Listening to the melody, Fitzhugh noticed again a quality he'd observed in Michael yesterday, a quality defined as much by the absence as by the presence of something. He lacked the harshness and arrogance seen in many SPLA officers: those swaggering Dinka and Nuer warlords, reared to lives of violence, taught from childhood that they are the lords of all men, trained to the courage that puts fear of death to flight and also breeds the ferocity to inflict death, if not with eagerness then without reluctance. Michael had to be as brave—he'd been wounded three times—and it had been obvious on the march from the airstrip that he had a gift for command; yet his martial virtues seemed grafted onto an essentially peaceable nature. There was a softness in his expression and voice and manner entirely out of phase with the personal history he'd disclosed to Douglas and Fitzhugh when they were hiding from the bomber, waiting for dark.

He'd begun his military career as an enlisted man in the Sudanese army, won a commission as a lieutenant, been sent to America for further training, and shortly after his return, deserted to join the rebels when his commanding officer told him he would have to convert to Islam and adopt a Muslim name if he expected to rise in rank. He'd been fighting ever since. If all that combat had brutalized him, as it had brutalized just about everyone else in Sudan (*"Even your mother, give her a bullet! Even your father, give him a bullet!"* Fitzhugh had once heard SPLA recruits chanting. *"Your rifle is your mother! Your rifle is your father! Your rifle is your wife!"*), he hid it well. He gave the clear impression that the mellow, muted ballad he was singing now was much more in keeping with who he was.

"I believe you can ease your mind, colonel," Manfred said abruptly, and squinting under a visor made with his hand, he pointed toward the savannah that lay between a mountain range to the west and the hill occupied by the hospital compound.

Michael and Fitzhugh stood and looked, the low sun almost directly in their eyes, and made out five figures, moving single file across the plain. In the liquid light of Africa's magic hour, they seemed to be walking on the bottom of a translucent copper sea.

"I think someone's been hurt," Fitzhugh said; as the figures drew closer, he'd seen that two, lagging well behind the others, were carrying what appeared to be a litter.

"But who? I sent three men to guard the American and Suleiman, and I count five men out there."

"Yes, five," Manfred confirmed. "But we'd better see if something's wrong."

Instructing Ulrika to prepare a bed in case one was needed, he set off with Fitzhugh and Michael, following a footpath around the garden and down the hill. The sun dipped below the western range and a wind sprang up and the grass on the hillside danced in the wind, as if rejoicing in its release from the heat that had baked it dry as paper. When they were about halfway down, they met Suleiman and two of the guards, both shirtless. Michael fell into an incomprehensible conversation with them, Suleiman gesturing at the third guard and Douglas, laboring up the hill with the litter.

Fitzhugh called out and started toward them with Manfred. Douglas and the soldier set the litter down. It had been made with a pair of crooked poles, between which the guards' shirts had been stretched, tied down by the sleeves. On it lay what at first looked like a heap of rags but on closer inspection revealed itself to be the emaciated body of an old man.

"Hey, Fitz"—he gave a tired wave—"glad to see you. We could use a hand the rest of the way."

"And damned glad to see you. But what is this?"

He looked at the body, lying motionless on its back, more bone than flesh, and the black flesh shriveled and the hair on its head sparse, grizzled, and white.

"Found him about three miles back, in a riverbed," said Douglas, his face raw from sunburn, his shirt drenched clear through.

"But why carry him all that way? He's dead, isn't he?"

"That's what we thought when we found him."

Manfred kneeled beside the litter on one knee and looked for a pulse. As he did this, the man's eyes half opened, his lips parted, and he made a dry sound, half gasp, half whisper. Fitzhugh felt a small chill; it really was like seeing a corpse come to life.

"Three miles that way, in a riverbed, you say?" the doctor asked. "You saw a village near there?"

Douglas shook his head.

"Well, there is one. Not very big. Perhaps you didn't notice it. He must have come from there." The grass all around had grown pale in the twilight and the distant mountains turned gray, and in the gloom and steady breeze, the man's hair moved as a cobweb moves when a door swings open in a room. "I suspect he'd been in that riverbed for a day or two."

"Wouldn't know. I spotted him under a tree. First glance, I didn't think it was a human being, and then, maybe a few seconds later, it hit me, and I said to Suleiman, 'That was a body back there,' and he said that, yeah, he knew and that he was dead. I wasn't so sure, so I went to check. He opened his eyes and made a sound, like the one he just made now. Tried to get him to drink from my water bottle, but he spit it up. I told them we had to get him to the hospital before it got dark."

"But of course your companions told you to leave him where he was."

Douglas glanced at his fellow litter-bearer, who seemed to be listening with great concentration, as if he could understand what was being said through sheer effort. A few pale stars had come out, signaling the end of the brief equatorial dusk.

"How did you know that?"

"Never mind. Go on."

There was no way Douglas was going to abandon a starving old man in the bush. He took a guard's panga and cut some poles, then tied his own shirt between them. It wasn't long enough to accommodate the man's body, so he turned to the soldiers and asked them to contribute their shirts. The demonstration of his resolve appeared to shame them, and they stripped. The litter was assembled, the man laid on it, but he didn't seem to realize that he was being rescued; he marshaled some hidden reserve of strength, rolled himself off, and tried to crawl away. He hadn't gone a yard when he collapsed. Unconscious, he was placed back on the litter.

"Quite remarkable of you, convincing those men to bring him such a long way when they knew it was pointless."

"How do you mean, pointless?"

"You did a fine thing, your good deed for the day. But tell me, you found your airstrip?"

"Yeah. And it's not too close. What was pointless?"

"Really, it was remarkable. A testament to your powers of moral persuasion. I commend you."

"I'm not looking for any commendations. Anyone would have done the same thing."

"I commend your modesty as well. I, for example, would *not* have done the same thing." Manfred rested his palm lightly on Douglas's shoulder. "Your companions were right. There is nothing to be done for him. He isn't dying of starvation or thirst or a sickness. He is dying of living too long."

The American scowled in confusion.

"When Nubans get to be very old, they often choose to go off somewhere to die."

"And they're just *left*?"

"Their relatives usually know where they've gone. They keep a watch, and when the person dies, then come the proprieties. I imagine this fellow's people will be looking for him in the morning, and they'll wonder what became of him. They'll be worried that he was dragged off by a leopard or some other wild beast. They will be very anxious to find his body so the proprieties can be observed and his spirit not become meddlesome."

Douglas rubbed his forehead with a thumb, seeming to massage his brain into puzzling out how his actions could produce effects he'd never intended.

"So what the hell do we do now? Bring him back to where we found him?"

"Impractical, now that it's dark. Also, you've brought him here, he is still alive, and I have my own proprieties to observe. I am required to do what I can, which I think will be to make him as comfortable as possible for the night. If he dies, he dies. If not, then not. Either way, we'll send word to the village where he is."

"And that's all?"

"Douglas! Listen to me, please. Can't you see why he tried to crawl away from you? Come on. You must be famished. I will see to it that he is brought up to a bed."

"I'll give a hand," Fitzhugh said.

As he bent down to pick up the litter, the man looked up at him, and he fancied that he saw a plea—no, a demand—in those yellowed eyes in their cavernous sockets. A part of him, the part that was heir to his African ancestors' wisdom, felt obliged to obey that silent imperative; but the rest of Fitzhugh Martin did not belong to his ancestors' world; it dwelled in Douglas's and Manfred's and Ulrika's world, which had imperatives and obligations of its own.

SOMETHING HAD PUT a rat in Fitzhugh's belly, and it began to chew its way out after midnight, waking him from a deep sleep. Flinging his mosquito net aside, he grabbed his flashlight from the night table and, keeping it pointed at the floor to avoid waking Douglas, fled out of the room for Manfred's front door. The rat took a breather, allowing him to leave the house and cross the compound without too much pain. He was dismayed to discover padlocks on the doors to both pit latrines. How Germanic to padlock a latrine. How un-Germanic to fail to tell one's visitors where the key was kept. The gnawing in his gut began again. There was nothing for it now but to bolt for the bushes. Just then he spotted the small circle of a penlight bobbing toward him. His own light revealed the nurse, clad in a shift, with an object gleaming between her breasts like a pendant. The key! He could tell by her walk that her need wasn't half as urgent as his.

"Ulrika! Give that to me! Now, please!"

She hesitated a beat, startled by his assault; then she took the key from around her neck and handed it to him.

He quickly opened the padlock and, slamming the door behind him, squatted over the hole. With deep gratitude for Ulrika's fortuitous appearance, he commenced to evict the rat. There was a click outside as the nurse pulled the key from the lock—he'd had the presence of mind to leave it there for her.

"Is the Sudan beer," she said. "I never drink it. Pfooey! God knows what is in it."

The beer? He'd never known any brand of beer to have an effect like this. Finished with her business in the adjacent enclosure, Ulrika gave him a knock.

"Fitz, you are all right?"

He came out, feeling embarrassed, although there was no reason to; a bush nurse wasn't likely to attach any opprobrium to the most disgusting functions or dysfunctions of the body. During his emergency, he'd failed to notice that she'd taken her hair down for the night. He noticed it now, cascading over her shoulders, lending a little flair to her sturdy, peasant looks.

"In case it wasn't the beer, something more serious, do you have any pills?"

"What a stupid question. This is hospital."

In the dispensary, she rummaged in a cabinet filled with boxes and bottles while he stood behind her holding the light. The back of her hair, an extravagance of waves and curls, shone with a brightness that reminded him of Diana.

"Cipro." She slapped a foil-wrapped packet in his hand. "Good for many things. One a day."

They headed back to the living quarters, he in his undershorts, she in her shapeless shift, past the sleeping forms of patients' relatives camped out on the hospital grounds. A breeze fanned the ashes of their dead cooking fires and a faint aroma of smoke tinged the night air.

"How do you say 'thanks' in German?"

"*Gedanke*," she answered, and leaned a little further forward, neither innocently nor with seductive intent but with a lack of self-consciousness that meant she was completely comfortable in his presence. And that amounted to a seduction.

"*Gedanke*," he repeated.

They returned the way they'd come, past the sleeping people, down a footpath bordered by rocks. Out here the night sky was almost intimidating in its clarity; the numberless stars seemed to assault you. Fitzhugh and Ulrika walked straight to her cottage and went inside without a request or invitation being spoken. She sat down on the edge of her bed and peeled off his shorts as if she were undressing a patient; then she pulled her shift over her head and held the mosquito net aside, motioning to him to get in first.

Less than half an hour later, with a friendly pat on the ass, she asked him to leave; she couldn't risk his staying the night. Herr Doktor wasn't a puritan, but he expected discretion, she said, although Fitzhugh suspected she was more worried that he would be seen by Franco.

He felt a little ridiculous, tiptoeing into Herr Doktor's house like a kid who has violated a parental curfew. He crept into the room and saw that Douglas was still asleep. Returning to his bed, Fitzhugh was nagged by the guilt that always assailed him when he'd indulged his appetites. The guilt, however, was mitigated by the fact that he hadn't enjoyed himself very much. Something had blocked his climax, despite Ulrika's skillful manipulations and sexual choreography. Maybe they were what blocked him—a bit too skillful, too clinical, too, well, nurselike. She touched him everywhere the way she would tap his knee to test his involuntary reflexes. What finally brought him off was a fantasy. Shutting his eyes, he pretended it was Diana grinding away beneath him, Diana's lips nibbling his ear, her breasts offered to his mouth.

In the morning, after he and Douglas had finished washing up, there was a commotion at the hospital. They saw a knot of people clustered around the door to the medical ward and went to have a look. Inside, the old man lay on his side on the floor, his eyes open and still. The bedsheets were still wrapped tightly around him from his shoulders to his feet, which didn't make him look like a mummy so much as like a giant larva with a human head. Whether he'd fallen out of bed or had deliberately thrown himself to the floor, it was impossible to say.

Ulrika, dressed in her uniform, stood over him, speaking quietly to Manfred in German. The doctor nodded, instructed a couple of Nuban aides to remove the corpse, and came outside.

"So, gentlemen, *gut schlafen*?" He rubbed his beard with his knuckles; the nurse must have summoned him before he'd had time to shave. "You slept well?"

They said they had.

"He will be taken in the Land Rover to the village near where you found him." Manfred cocked his head at the aides, lugging the body through the door. "We will hope that is where he came from, so we don't have to search all over for his people. We also hope"—he sent a stern look at Douglas—"that some true emergency requiring the vehicle does not arise while it's gone. What a pity if someone were to die who doesn't need to because of this. I trust that the next time, if there is one, that you find someone lying in the bush, you will go on."

"Don't think so," Douglas said after a silence. "I understand what you're telling me, but I don't think I'd be able to do that."

The response didn't surprise Fitzhugh in the least.

A BIG *MAROOR*, Suleiman called their journey. *Maroor* meant "trek" in Sudanese Arabic, but "trek" suggested an organized migration from point A to point B and did not describe the circuitous wanderings upon which Michael Goraende led them for the next twelve days, westward into ranges called the Heibans, the Moros, the Limons, then north, east, south, north, and west again across unpeopled plains, up and over rock-strewn trails steep as staircases. They paused for a day's rest at Michael's headquarters, secreted within an isolated valley, and then made a short hike to New Tourom and St. Andrew's mission.

Throughout the trek they traveled at night as much as possible to escape the crushing midday sun and the government Antonovs, ceaselessly prowling the unblemished skies. In the mornings, while Douglas and Suleiman surveyed for landing strip sites, Fitzhugh interviewed shopkeepers in the village marketplaces, asking how much they had sold in the past and how much they were selling now, and made careful notes of the dwindling stocks of soap and salt and cooking oil. He inspected household granaries where winnowed grain was stored in clay jugs. He went into the fields where men threshed grain by beating it with long, heavy wooden paddles, and he made more notes as they spoke about lack of rainfall and this year's poor harvest and the raids that had driven them from valleys, forcing them to sow their crops on the stony mountainsides. They pleaded for seed and oil presses and implements. They complained of headache, bellyache and, Fitzhugh suspected, purely imaginary ailments and asked for medicine. He borrowed scales from village merchants and weighed small children and took their heights with his tape measure to determine if they were suffering from malnutrition. All in all, assessing the Nubans' needs wasn't difficult: they needed almost everything.

He slept through the blazing afternoons, and when the sun set, Michael would rouse him and Douglas and they would set off to the next town. They drank tepid water flavored with the iodine of their purification tablets. They ate doura and more doura and Fitzhugh notched up his belt until he ran out of notches. Maroor, trek? It was more an ordeal, never more so than on the night of the thirteenth day, when they pressed on to

Kologi, the chief village of Suleiman's tribe. They'd left a town called Kauda just before sundown, following an old road through an undulating plain. Michael set a murderous pace, hoping to reach a mountain named Jebel Gedir and its surrounding hills by daybreak.

A full moon rose, bright enough to turn the night into a colorless imitation of day. The scattered acacia cast distinct shadows on the whitened grass. Venus was pinned above the horizon, spreading thin petals of light so that it earned its Arabic name, El Zohar, the flower. Sometime after midnight Fitzhugh's old injury woke up; it felt as if someone were injecting a scalding liquid into his knee. His legs went numb, and he pitched forward with each step, as if he were stumbling downhill. An hour or so later, when the Jebel's rim appeared outlined against the lesser blackness of the sky, he was for all practical purposes walking in his sleep. The ash-daubed bodies of the Nuban porters gave off a pale glow in the moonlight, like phosphorescence. Suleiman's white jelibiya seemed to be floating in midair beside them, and Fitzhugh hallucinated that he was looking at a ghost shepherding a flock of dimmer specters. He managed one conscious, rational thought: *Why am I doing this to myself?*

They reached the mountain shortly after dawn. Douglas, also reeling from exhaustion, checked his GPS and said they'd covered thirty miles in twelve hours. He and Fitzhugh didn't bother to fetch their sleeping bags from the donkeys but collapsed on the spot and blacked out, until awakened by the heat and flies of late morning.

He ached in every muscle and bone. His marrow ached. Why *was* he doing this to himself? What strange magnetism had pulled him back to this country?

Sitting against a smooth rock slab, he looked up at the cave mouth gaping in the splintered face of the mountain. It was, said Suleiman, the cave where the Divinely Guided One had prayed and fasted day and night, steeling his soul for the great task before him.

"Truly, this is where the Mahidiya began. On this mountain, in that cave, the Mahdi saw that he must unite all Sudan behind him to get rid of the British and the Egyptians. And that is what he did!"

Yes, the Mahdi, thought Fitzhugh. A brilliant general and also an early Muslim fundamentalist. Today he would be a terrorist. What was it about this place that it created visionaries of all kinds, warrior-prophets and warrior-saints, messiahs true and false, Sufi mystics, dervishes dancing in the desert? Was Tara right in saying that Sudan's distances conjure up mirages of the mind, its boundless horizons inspiring men to imagine that anything is possible? Do its skies, so threatening in their vastness and vacancy, foster feelings of insignificance that force men to turn to God for solace and validation of their existence? And does the silence that greets them when they turn—the unbearable silence of Sudan's immense spaces—cause them to hear voices in their own heads and trick them into thinking that what they hear is the voice of God, commanding them to sacred missions? And what is it about this place that even as it molds true believers out of its native clay, it also draws true believers from elsewhere? General Gordon, the Christian mystic, tugged to Sudan by his own messianic vision: to abolish the slave trade, and how he tried, with his band of zealots. But the law of unintended consequences operates here like nowhere else.

"The father of my grandfather fought with the Mahdi when they defeated the General Gordon at Khartoum," Suleiman was saying. "He saw the head of the Gordon placed on a stick. *Shuu!* What I tell you is true. His sword was honored with English and Egyptian blood. I have it still, in my house in Kologi, and when we get there, *inshallah,* I will show it to you."

A curious fellow, Suleiman. He didn't carry a rifle. He was a kind of pacifist, for all his talk about swords honored with enemy blood. His tribe, the Kowahla, were Nubans who had been converted to Islam, but he stressed that they were Sufi Muslims. Earlier in the journey he'd told a story about a day, two years ago, when he was in a Khartoum *souk* buying a pair of work boots. (He'd driven a bulldozer for the Ministry of Civil Aviation; hence his knowledge of airstrips.) While he was haggling with the merchant, a detachment of police and soldiers arrived in army lorries. They leaped out and began rounding up young men for conscription into the militia. An officer came up to him, demanding his identification. He showed his card, confident that his status as a government employee would exempt him, and if that didn't, his age—thirty-five—would. He was stunned when the officer told him that a tall, strong fellow like him had to fight in the jihad in the south, and ordered him into a vehicle loaded with twenty others, all of whom wore the look of men sentenced to hang. It was common knowledge that the militia suffered dreadful casualties. Suleiman turned and fled through the marketplace crowds, soldiers and policemen in pursuit. His long legs saved him. After hiding out with friends for several days, he hitched rides from southward-bound lorry drivers and then made his way on foot back into the sanctuary of his native mountains.

"Isn't it hard for you, a Muslim, to be fighting against other Muslims?" asked Douglas, sitting opposite Suleiman.

Fitzhugh had been wondering the same thing but couldn't think how to pose the question diplomatically. Douglas had got around all that simply by coming right out with it, like a child, his innocent candor avoiding any suggestion that Suleiman suffered from divided loyalties.

"I am not a fighter."

"You know what I mean. You're part of the struggle."

"See my skin." He pinched his forearm. "I am not an Arab. I am Nuban, Kowahla. Not a true Muslim, the government thinks. Because we believe in the Islam of the heart, not the Islam of the Kalashnikov. We Sufis believe the Holy Koran when it says there shall be no violence in matters of religion."

Douglas nodded, and then, his attention diverted by a circling bird, fished a pair of binoculars from the case on his belt.

"An eagle," Michael said, squinting up at the gyring bird.

"Nope. An augur buzzard."

"Come, my friends," Michael said, standing. "Kologi isn't far." He glanced at Fitzhugh, getting to his feet like a man of eighty. "You have to put up with this for just two more days. Tomorrow we will return to the airfield."

Fitzhugh drew a laugh when he said, "*Al-hamduillah*—praise be to Allah."

Kologi was an isolated place of tall round huts and boxy market shacks marooned on a range of low hills rising from clay plains and flat acacia forests that vanished into a shimmering horizon. Upon their arrival, Douglas and Suleiman, displaying a stamina Fitzhugh found amazing, went off on another excursion in search of landing fields. He toured the souk with the tribal chief, called a *nazir,* a stout, gray-haired man with a gray beard like a chin strap. Later on he and the nazir rode out on donkeys, accompanied by Michael and a couple of his soldiers striding on foot. They crossed a red, rolling plateau trenched by flash-floods, the donkeys' hooves raising talcumlike puffs in the loose, dry soil. It was a windy day, and the wind blew dust into their faces and dust-devils whirled across their path. The land angled gradually downward into a shallow bowl, where a tobacco plot's orderly holes, resembling the cups in an egg carton, pitted the ground near a draw-well and stalks of chopped sorghum rattled in the wind. If any trees had ever grown here, they'd long since been felled for houses and firewood. The one exception was a *tulla* grove, in whose shade the nazir assembled some twenty or thirty farmers and introduced "His Excellency, Mister Fuzzyew, who will bring assistance to you." The men should make their needs known, he commanded, and they did, half of them speaking at once.

The clamor stopped suddenly. Freezing in their various postures, the farmers fell into a silence that seemed tangible. The nazir and Michael and the soldiers squatted, their heads cocked. Fitzhugh's senses were dull, his reactions slow; he looked around in bewilderment until Michael wrapped a wrestler's arm around his knees and, with one tug, jerked him off his feet. He fell like a sack on all fours. Only then was he conscious of a distant droning in the sky, growing louder.

"Remember what I told you," Michael whispered, as though the plane might hear him. "The bombs will make a noise. A hum. If you hear that, fall flat on your face and cover your head."

The hum. Yes, he remembered. It was made by the tail rotor in the bomb. He held his breath, afraid the sound of it would muffle the hum just enough to make a fatal difference. To his eyes, the red-barked branches above appeared to have gaps yards wide, and that made him feel as visible as a man wearing Day-Glo orange.

The throb of the turboprop engines was distinct now. Still on his hands and knees, not daring to move, he looked at the farmers, also motionless except for their lips, mouthing silent prayers. Ever so slowly, heads turned to the right. Fitzhugh's turned with them, and he saw a silver dart in the spotless sky. It was winging northward, six or seven thousand feet up, far lower than Antonovs dared fly in the south, Michael murmured. The pilots knew that the rebels in the Nuba had no antiaircraft guns or missiles. He shaded his eyes with a hand and observed that the rear cargo doors were closed. At least they appeared to be. He hoped so.

"They push the bombs out the back, you know. There is no aiming. There is no address for the bombs. They are addressed, To Whom It May Concern."

The drone faded, then grew louder. A second plane? No, the same one, circling around. Michael told everyone to lie still. Fitzhugh pressed himself into the earth, so that he felt every pebble. From the sound of it, the Antonov was going to come in right over them. Fitzhugh listened with his whole body, with his skin, each pore becoming a microscopic ear, opened for the whirr of a tail rotor, spinning downward, though he knew that if he heard the sound now, with the plane directly above, it would be not a warning but merely an announcement that his death was seconds away. What did it feel like to be blown apart?

He wasn't aware that the Antonov had flown on until Michael shook him. He stood up. If he'd ever felt this relieved before, he couldn't remember it. How splendid the clear sky looked, how beautiful the vivid tulla trees. He had an almost overpowering urge to laugh, to clap each man on

the back and shake his hand, as though they'd accomplished some difficult task together. He didn't know the name of even one, yet a rush of
affection flooded through him, and of something more than affection, of
solidarity. An old man, white-robed, shuffled up to him and spoke with
angry shakes of the cane. He said his cotton field had been bombed and
burned several months before and that he wished to inform His Excellency of a particular need he had. He stated what it was. After the rest
made their petitions Fitzhugh and the nazir remounted the donkeys and
rode back to the village.

He returned to Suleiman's compound, where an underfed goat greeted
him in the little courtyard formed by a ring of five tukuls. Everything
seemed oddly normal and domestic. Two of Suleiman's wives were
preparing a pot of doura in the cooking hut. The third wife, a beauty of
eighteen or nineteen, her plaited hair trailing to her waist, stood in the
doorway of the women's quarters, nursing a baby. She offered Fitzhugh a
dazzling smile.

In the hut that was Suleiman's exclusive domain, Douglas sat stripped
to the waist on a worn leopard skin while Suleiman attempted to tweeze
out a tick embedded in his side. Their quest had been unsuccessful, Douglas said. They'd found plenty of good level ground, but a few pokes with
Suleiman's stick revealed that it was all soft black-cotton soil under a fragile crust incapable of bearing an airplane's weight.

"Speaking of planes . . ."

"Saw it," Douglas said.

"A wonder it didn't bomb the town."

"Oh, they do not try to destroy us," Suleiman remarked airily. "Only to
make our lives a misery so we come over to their side."

How unnaturally pale the American's skin looked, contrasted with
the black of Suleiman's hand, carefully manipulating the tweezers. Fitzhugh took a seat on a crudely carved chair, against the wall on which the
curved sword of Suleiman's great-grandfather hung in a cracked leather
scabbard.

"They told me the thing they need the most is for the war to end," he
said. "It's what one old man said to me. We can bring in all the tools and
seed and clothes we want, but it will mean nothing if the war goes on."

"What did you say?" Douglas asked.

"Nothing. What can you say to that?"

"I have got him, all of him, and the head, too," Suleiman exclaimed, his
left eye twitching as he held up the tweezers to display the blood-gorged
trophy.

Fitzhugh opened his notebook on his lap and began to rough out the report he would present to Barrett. Figures for the number of malnourished children, for this year's crop yield. He drew up columns for the items and commodities that were in short supply and jotted a reminder to tell Barrett that a shipment of Unimix would be needed to supplement the children's diets. The feeling that had dogged him since before leaving Loki, of being a twig in a current, was dissolving. He felt strong, purposeful. This was his work, the only work he knew how to do, and he stopped wondering why he was doing it. Did his father wonder what was the point of managing a hotel for tourists? The point was obvious—it won bread for his table. At least Fitzhugh's work possessed a moral dimension that his father's lacked. It wasn't only for himself; it won bread for the other man's table as well as for his own. But was it worth the sort of danger that had brushed him today? The sort of hardship he'd endured two nights ago?

AFTER ANOTHER MEAL of doura, the nazir came around to tell Their Excellencies that a dance was to be held that night in their honor. The Kowahla hadn't had much cause to celebrate in the past year. Douglas and Fitzhugh's visit had given them one.

They were delighted to find out that Suleiman's hut had a shower: a perforated calabash hanging from a peg in an alcove, with a pull-cord attached. One of Suleiman's younger sons, a boy of eight or so, filled the calabash from a rusty jerry can. Douglas stepped in, the boy staring at him, wonder-struck by the sight of a naked white man.

"All yours, Your Excellency," Douglas said when he was finished.

Fitzhugh bowed. "Thank you, Your Excellency."

The kid refilled the calabash. It held less than a gallon and succeeded only in turning five days' accumulated grime into a silty film, but he gloried in the cool water splashing on his overheated skull, trickling down his chest and arms. He shaved in a pocket mirror, combed his thinning hair, changed into his spare T-shirt and shorts, and with his similarly spiffed-up partner, went into the courtyard to wait. Suleiman and the rest of his family were gone, and Fitzhugh noticed that the sword was missing from the scabbard on the wall. A distance away, a crowd was gathering in the twilight on a broad pitch, where wood had been stacked for a bonfire and drummers were tuning up, loosing staccato bursts.

In a fresh jelibiya, the nazir appeared, preceded by a man holding a paraffin lantern, followed by a retinue of tribal elders, and flanked by two sword-bearers, one of whom was Suleiman, the polished blade once honored by British and Egyptian blood held vertically in front of his face. The nazir motioned to his guests to join the procession. Everyone looked so solemn that if he didn't know better, Fitzhugh would have thought they were going to an execution. They marched to the pitch. Two chairs had been set out for them, a table with clay jars on it to one side, the musicians to the other—half a dozen drummers sitting cross-legged on the ground, one man standing behind a crude xylophone made of hollow wooden tubes. The moon had risen, a pale fruit with a sliver sliced off one side. Four or five hundred people ringed the pitch, the bonfire rose high in the middle of the circle, and the oiled limbs of twenty young dancers, ten men and ten women, gleamed in its light.

Setting his lamp on the table, the lantern-carrier passed a jar each to Fitzhugh, Douglas, and the nazir, who sat on a mat beside Suleiman and the other sword-bearer. The nazir drank. Douglas raised his jar, then hesitated, looking sidelong at Fitzhugh, who took a healthy swig to assure him that the thick, white liquid was safe to drink. The American sampled it, licked his lips, and frowned.

"What *is* this?"

"Fermented sorghum. *Marissa,* it's called."

The female dancers had lined up at one end of the pitch, the men at the other, and the musicians broke into a fast, thrilling rhythm, the quick heartbeat of Africa itself, a sound that reached back to the first ages of the human race. Straight-backed, their breasts thrust forward, the women moved toward the men with a foot-stomping strut. Wound into hundreds of plaits, their long hair swished back and forth, their bead and coin necklaces rattled and jingled, their feathered skirts swung with their hips to make a rustling sound. They danced past the fire, then stopped and stood, swaying to the beat, and with graceful gestures of their hands and arms, they beckoned to the men, who advanced on them, pounding their feet on the ground in time to the drums. The two lines met, separated, and moved away from each other, and then the pattern was repeated. As the women stood swaying near the fire a second time, the whole crowd began to sway with them and took up a chant, male voices singing a chorus, female answering with a high, lilting refrain that ended in a short, shrill ululation, like the warbling of a thousand birds, before the men responded with another chorus. The dancers met once more and parted to begin the cycle anew. It went on for ten or fifteen minutes without stopping. Fitzhugh took another drink. His flesh tingled as voice, drum, and choreography fused into a harmonious whole that summoned him out of his separate self, called to him to unite himself with it, and his pulse quickening to match the pulse of the drums, he swayed with the people all around him. They had become one thing, a single being proclaiming in the union of sound and movement concordant joy in a divided, joyless land. The human spirit will endure, cried this being composed of many beings drawn into a circle; war and suffering will pass away.

The music abruptly stopped. The male dancers fled the stage. The xylophone played a rill of light, swift notes, and the drums began again, sending flurries of wild, syncopated throbs across the circle, stirring the women into a new dance. They snaked around the fire twice, and a third time, and then wound toward Fitzhugh and Douglas, strutting as before. The spectators broke into another communal chant, and in that flickering, enclosed world, its effect was almost hypnotic. The women drew closer and closer till they were barely a yard away from where Fitzhugh and Douglas sat with the nazir. Suddenly one girl leaped in front of the old man and, with a violent toss of her head, flung her braided hair over his head. He jumped up, wrapped one arm around her waist, and pressed his cheek to her forehead. His legs briefly recovered their youth as he danced with her in that posture; then he raised his free hand, snapped his fingers, and sat down again. Fitzhugh realized that this was a demonstration of what to do, for in a second one of the dancers came to him and covered his face with her hair while another did the same to Douglas. The American got into the spirit of the thing; he was on his feet and dancing. Fitzhugh remained in his chair. The woman paused in her movements and looked at him as if he'd insulted her. His heart rapped against his ribs, whether from ecstasy or fear or a little of both he couldn't tell. His partner was Suleiman's junior wife, and he didn't know if dancing such a sensuous dance with her would provoke a fit of jealous rage. Suleiman had that sword at his feet.

The nazir appeared to sense his quandary. He grinned and told him, "*Shuu!* Your friend, do as he is!"

Douglas couldn't quite get the beat or the steps, but he was trying, whirling and stomping like an American Indian, to the crowd's delight. Fitzhugh knew he could do better. He'd been a good dancer in the tourist discos of Mombasa. Of course, he wasn't in Mombasa and this wasn't a disco, but when Suleiman's wife again threw the canopy of waist-length braids over him, he was out of his chair, all self-consciousness gone. The drumming took control of his limbs as he embraced her slim, taut waist with his left arm and lay his cheek to her forehead, the musk of her sweat and of the oil that made her legs and arms gleam intoxicating him as all the marissa in the village could not have done. He danced till he was breathless, then raised his right hand above her head, clicked his fingers, and let her go. She gifted him with that smile of hers, and he heard the throng laughing and cheering its approval. He was relieved to see Suleiman laughing and cheering right along with them.

Douglas and Fitzhugh tried their hand on the drums, then danced some more, caught up in the jubilant atmosphere. The celebration was an act of rebellion, no less than firing a shot; it rebuked the dour, violent ascetics who ruled this country. After the fire had burned down to embers, Michael emerged from the crowd to remind Their Excellencies to get some sleep; he intended to start for the airfield well before dawn. Suleiman picked up his sword and escorted them home.

In a state of happy weariness, Fitzhugh flopped onto his sleeping bag and smoked a last cigarette. "I think the old man was wrong," he said to Douglas.

"What old man?"

"The one who told me that if the war doesn't end, it won't make any difference how much stuff we bring in here. He's wrong."

"There's my man."

Douglas

It is the day after his fifteenth birthday, and he is in his room with a pencil and spiral notebook, writing down six goals he is to achieve in the coming year. This exercise has been ordered by his father to sharpen his mental discipline and give him a sense of direction. He did poorly in his freshman year at the public high school he attended here in Tucson; next month he will be packed off to a rigorous boarding school a continent away—Milton Academy, his father's alma mater. Dad had to pull strings to get him in, but he is being admitted on condition that he repeat ninth grade, an experience Douglas is not looking forward to.

It's the middle of August, the rainy season in Arizona. There was a downpour last night, and the scent of the desert after a rain has seeped in through the air-conditioning vents—a tang of creosote bush. The cacti have bloomed, and summer poppies spill down the hillsides and through the forests of saguaro, spiny arms pointed skyward. The beauty outside his bedroom window distracts him. So does Pink Floyd, piped through the earphones plugged into his cassette player. So do the model planes that surround him. Prop planes and jets, fighters, bombers, and airliners climb and bank on plastic pedestals; they hang from the ceiling on slender wires, stirred into an imitation of actual flight by the air conditioner and the paddle fan twirling overhead. He pictures himself in a cockpit, alone, in complete control, answerable to no one.

Why six goals and not five or ten or some other number that makes sense?

He forces himself to concentrate and, when he's finished, goes down a long corridor to the study, where his father is studying blueprints. Weldon Braithwaite, a tall man with the fleshy but still powerful physique of the aging athlete, is CEO of Web-Mar Associates, a development firm that has covered vast swaths of Arizona with strip malls, fairways, and retirement communities bearing faux Spanish names like "Rio Vista Estates." Douglas announces himself with a cough. Weldon looks up. His son says, "Here it is," and hands him the sheet of looseleaf.

1. TO GET A "B" AVERAGE AT LEAST.
2. TO WATCH MY TONGUE (DON'T TALK BACK TO TEACHERS).
3. TO GO OUT FOR A SPORT AND STICK WITH IT.
4. TO DO SOMETHING FOR THE POOR, LIKE WORK IN A SOUP KITCHEN ON XMAS VACATION.
5. TO LEARN ABOUT THE BIRDS IN MASSACHUSSETTS.
6. TO TAKE FLYING LESSONS & GET A PILOT'S LICENSE.

Weldon knows his son well enough to see that he's telling his parents what he thinks they want to hear. Except for number six. That's for the kid himself. Wanted to fly ever since he knew what an airplane was. One and two are intended to please Mom and Dad both, three to please Dad, four and five go to Mom, the family do-gooder. Weldon feels a twinge of resentment that two goals have been tailored to Lucy's tastes, only one to his. The emotion troubles him. He would have thought himself too large-minded for such petty jealousy, though he knows that he and Lucy have been wrestling for years for possession of Douglas, the youngest of their three children and their only son.

Lucy had wanted a boy as much as he, and Weldon figures that's one reason why they have waged a kind of custody battle for the greater share of Douglas's love and loyalty. Then there are the differences between him and his wife. She's a westerner, born in Flagstaff; he's from New England, like every generation of Braithwaites going back to 1640; he was raised Presbyterian, she's a Mormon, a lapsed one who nonetheless exhibits, in her crusades for the rights of Native Americans and Mexican immigrants, the self-sacrificial, and sometimes self-righteous, spirit of her proselytizing forebears. Weldon is all for helping the disadvantaged, but to his mind that's best done with charitable contributions, preferably tax deductible, not by spending time away from your family teaching English in barrios or on Indian reservations.

He looks at the paper and then at his boy, so scrawny now, having grown four inches in as many months without gaining the weight to go with the height; scrawny and awkward, his brain unable to figure out how to communicate with the suddenly longer limbs. He is fidgeting, and Weldon guesses what he's thinking: "The old man wants me to set an 'A' average as a goal; he'll say he wants me to get a real job over Christmas vacation, not dish out soup to derelicts." But that's not what the old man is going to say. He's had a flash of insight. What's the kid really telling me with this list? That he doesn't want to be the prize in a war between Mom and Dad. That he wants to please both of us because he belongs to us both.

"You misspelled 'Massachussetts,'" Weldon says. "Look it up."

"Okay."

"Make you a deal. If you really do one through five, you'll get six next summer."

"Don't say that if you don't mean it," Douglas pleads after several moments of silence.

"Solemn promise. You'll be in the air when you're sixteen."

Douglas is there already.

Redeemer

WHILE THEY WAITED for a boat to be brought up, in a heat like none she'd known back home, even on the stillest, muggiest days her mother called "dog days" (Quinette in her childhood wondering what hot weather and dogs had to do with each other), she remembered how wide the Mississippi had looked the first time she saw it from the Dubuque levee, near the foot of the bridge arching like a steel rainbow into another state, the trees on the Illinois side and the hills beyond appearing so distant she felt as if she were looking across a lake rather than a river, her idea of a river being the Cedar or the Shell Rock or the Little Cedar, slender enough that two people on opposite banks could talk to each other.

The Mississippi lived up to the way she'd pictured it in sixth-grade geography period. Mrs. Hoge told the class that Mississippi was an Indian word meaning "Father of Waters," because it was the longest river in North America. Not, however, the longest in the world. That honor belonged to the Nile, she said, moving her pointer to the world map pulled down over the blackboard like a window shade: more than four thousand miles from here—the rubber tip stabbed at a country called Uganda—to here in Egypt—the tip moving to the river's mouth, opening onto the Mediterranean Sea.

As Mrs. Hoge went on, Quinette recalled the story of Moses from Sunday school—how he had drifted in a reed basket coated with pitch until he was found by Pharaoh's daughter and spared from her father's cruel edict to have all firstborn Hebrew boys killed. Her thoughts ran from there to an old movie she'd seen about Moses, starring Charlton Heston. Because the subject matter met with her mother's approval (unlike her father, who'd gone to church only at Christmas and Easter, her mother was a devout Lutheran), she allowed Quinette to stay up late to watch it on TV. Nicole and Kristen weren't interested and went upstairs to listen to Kristen's new Pat Benatar tape. How small and vulnerable Moses' basket looked, how miraculous that it stayed afloat on the immense river. Her mother, sitting beside Quinette on the old sofa with its brown and gold pattern like late autumn leaves, looked at her out of the corner of her eye and smiled gently, the smile telling her that there was good in everyone, even in heathen Egyptian women, and that God's hand was everywhere. He had guided the basket into the arms of Pharaoh's daughter so the baby inside could grow up to be Charlton Heston and lead his people out of bondage.

All those memories, of Mrs. Hoge's class, of the day on the levee, and of the Nile as it appeared in the movie, rushed at Quinette as she sat with her companions under a wide-spreading tree, hot sunlight slivering through the branches as through pinpricks in a worn awning, and gazed at the real Nile. Colored like mud mixed with wet cement, and sluggish and less than half as wide as the Mississippi, it was not the mighty, awesome river that had surged in her imagination, and she felt cheated. She usually did when things turned out to be less beautiful or exciting or inspiring than she'd hoped—as if she were the victim of an intentional fraud.

It had been that way when she was born again. Most of the congregation at Family Evangelical Church had described their salvation as a rapturous experience—the Holy Spirit moving through them like a wind, and nothing the same afterward. Like they were all Saint Paul on the road to Damascus. Quinette had been stopped at a red light, on the road from work to her night-school computer class at the University of Northern Iowa, when she accepted Jesus Christ as her personal lord and savior. She immediately recited the sinner's prayer, as her minister had advised her to do. "Jesus, I admit to you that I am a sinner, in need of savior." The light turned green, but she continued. "I repent of my sins." The driver behind her honked his horn, she waved to him to go around. "I believe that you died on the cross and rose from the dead as a substitute for our sins, and accept that you have come into my life, amen."

Her words were as honest as any she'd ever spoken, but the woman who drove on was still the same Quinette Hardin, twenty-four years of age, a saleswoman at The Gap in the Cedar Falls mall, a recent divorcée temporarily living with her elder sister and her brother-in-law on Hyacinth Street, in a new subdivision across from a cornfield. Passing the UNI-Dome, lit up for a night basketball game with Illinois Wesleyan, she found herself, just as she always did, looking forward to going out for a drink after class, hoping to meet a cute, intelligent guy tall enough to date a woman who stood six foot one in her bare feet. If she'd been saved, and she was sure she had been, why was she eager for the taste of a bourbon and Coke and an encounter with some dude in a bar? She was as disappointed as she was baffled. The moment that was supposed to change her life forever had been no more thrilling or transforming than when she'd grasped how to do square roots in freshman algebra. She pulled into an Amoco to call Pastor Tom Cullen on the pay phone. When he answered, she told him that Jesus had come into her life. (Tom had asked her to call, no matter what the hour.) In his staccato voice, he said he was very happy for her, this was as joyous an event for him as it was for her. Picturing him in his old frame house, his narrow head, topped by a peninsula of flaxen hair, leaning into the phone, Quinette didn't have the heart to tell him that she did not feel joyful or different, so she pretended that the experience had been like everyone else's, laid it on with a trowel, affecting a breathless voice as she told him that the Holy Spirit had swept her into a whole new life of the soul. She felt a little the way she had faking orgasms with her ex, part of her hoping that the real thing would somehow, some way arise out of the deception, if it were done well enough, disgusted with herself afterward, angry at life for denying her what it gave to other women (unless they were *all* lying). It was kind of like that, and it wasn't fair.

"I thought it would be bigger than this," she said to Jim Prewitt, sitting next to her, his forehead spangled with sweat.

He looked at her questioningly. She pointed at the river.

Jim took off the short-brimmed hat and ran a bandanna through his damp hair: sparse strands of brittle gray, like the bristles on an old paintbrush.

"You should see the Jordan," he said. "First time I did, oh, it must've been twenty-five years ago, I was really expecting something. All those stories in Joshua, all those hymns. Turned out to be not much more than a muddy creek. We crossed it by way of the Allenby Bridge. Took about five seconds. We'd gone over Jordan, and everybody on the bus looked at each other and you could tell we were all thinking the same thing—Is that *it*?"

Jim was also a reverend. At one time he'd led tour groups on trips to the Holy Land. Now he was chairman of overseas missions for a family of ministries in California.

"Know what you mean," she said, and then told him about the first time she'd laid eyes on the Mississippi.

Well, things always look bigger to you when you're a kid, Jim remarked, as if she didn't know that, then informed her that the river before them was the Upper Nile, the White (as if she didn't know that either). After it joined the Blue in Khartoum, it got bigger, and by the time it made it down to Egypt, he would bet it was as broad as the Mississippi. He'd seen it there more than once, leading his pilgrim tourists.

He spoke slowly, with an undertone of condescension that made

Quinette bristle. Talking to her like she was still a kid in Mrs. Hoge's geography period. Okay, she wasn't the brightest bulb in the chandelier, but she wasn't stupid, and she hated it when people talked down to her. Maybe the heat was making her irritable—it must have been a hundred degrees—and she stood and fanned herself with her hat and blew down into her shirt. She had to watch her temper, anger being a sin she fell into fairly often. That had been true since the day when she was fourteen and yelled curses at the people bidding for her father's tractor, the John Deere she used to ride on with him when she was little; vile curses hurled at the top of her lungs, and then she hurled something more tangible at the auctioneer—a rock. Threw it as hard as she could, almost knocked him cold, and she didn't feel sorry about it for a long time.

Remaining on her feet, swiping her hat past her face, she allowed her thoughts to return to the river, pushing slowly past its reed-choked banks. Papyrus reeds, she believed, like the kind Moses' basket was made of as it floated into the saving arms of Pharaoh's daughter upriver, no, *downriver* in Egypt. Somehow, she couldn't get used to thinking of north as down, south as up. *"And then Pharaoh's daughter went down to the water"*—the old hymn sang faintly in her memory—*"went down to the water so blue."*

Out from under the tree, where the light was better for filming, the CNN reporter was interviewing Ken Eismont. He had the look of a strict high school principal—round rimless glasses, hollow cheeks, a sharp chin, short brown hair. The man in charge, executive director of the WorldWide Christian Union. Also its chief fundraiser and PR man. It was Ken who got the CNN team to report on his latest mission into Sudan. The reporter's name was Phyllis something, a scrawny, auburn-haired woman with the gravelly voice of someone who smoked and drank too much, though Quinette had yet to see her with a cigarette and of course there was nothing to drink out here, except tepid water. The Kenyan camera crew, two young men who didn't smile much and wore worried looks, moved around, changing angles on Ken, and when Phyllis was done with him, she turned to Mike and Jean, the Canadian couple who were taking their vacation time to help Ken redeem the slaves. Not redeem them in the spiritual sense, but to buy them back from their masters and then set them free.

In the meantime, making jerky movements with his hands, Ken was asking Santino to find out why it was taking so long to find a boat to ferry everyone across the Nile. Santino was a heavyset Sudanese with the blackest skin imaginable and short knotty hair matched to his complexion, so that he looked bald from far away. Ken called him his "banker." He carried the cash that bought the slaves their liberty: on this trip, more than ten thousand dollars in hundred-dollar denominations, stuffed into a blue and white airline bag. Quinette watched him hand it over to Ken, then walk off toward the village of mud-walled huts clustered on a low hill above the river. Ten thousand dollars was more than half what she would earn this year at The Gap, and Ken stood with the bag slung over his shoulder, out here in a war zone in the middle of nowhere, as nonchalantly as if it contained spare socks and underwear.

In a few minutes Santino reappeared, flanked by the two SPLA soldiers who had been searching for someone with a boat. The three men came down the path leading from the village, the huts behind them crowned by thatch roofs layered like wedding cakes, the soldiers wearing floppy green hats and camouflage uniforms, assault rifles swinging at their sides and ammunition belts draped over their chests, the bullets gleaming in the late morning light. Two more guerrillas lounged nearby, beneath a tree rising out of the reeds on a trunk pale green as a stalk of early corn—a fever tree, someone had told her. She was glad to have the four soldiers on her side; they were scary-looking guys, each over six and a half feet tall, with tribal scars etched into his forehead in shallow V's and his bottom front teeth missing. A custom, Santino had informed her an hour ago, when the soldiers appeared at the airstrip and grinned their hellos, the jagged gaps in their teeth startling her. They were Dinka tribesmen, and it was customary among the Dinka to have their bottom front teeth chopped out when they were ten years old. Santino didn't know why, not being Dinka himself. That was the way they did things.

He was conferring again with Ken, in low tones. Ken set the airline bag down and pointed toward the river. Suddenly Quinette's knees felt rubbery, and people and objects wavered before her eyes, as though a translucent curtain had dropped between her and them. Thinking she was about to faint, she sat down and leaned her head against the tree trunk and took in deep breaths, her heart beating as if it were trying to get out of her chest.

"Are you all right?" Jim Prewitt asked.

She nodded.

"You look white as a sheet."

"Got woozy for a second. I'm okay."

"It's the heat," Jim said, wiping his brow for emphasis. "Jet lag, too, I'll bet. Maybe that malaria medicine. That can do it, too."

She nodded again, although she knew, now that the vertigo was gone and her heart rate was returning to normal, that it wasn't the heat, the malaria pills, or jet lag. It was the airline bag, stuffed with ten thousand dollars and Ken standing there so casually with it at his feet. It was the rebel soldiers with their fierce, scarred foreheads and missing teeth and the trees with green trunks instead of brown and the knowledge that she'd been plunked down in a place without electricity, telephones, highways, cars, TVs, or a single familiar thing. She'd left home only three days ago. Actually, she wasn't sure if it had been three days. She'd lost track of time, flying from the small airport in Waterloo to Chicago O'Hare, from O'Hare all the way to Geneva, Ken and Jim meeting her there, then whisking her off to a connecting flight to Nairobi, where she'd tried to sleep but couldn't, and then at dawn this morning winging on to Lokichokio in a twin-engine plane, stepping off it into the single-engine Cessna that had delivered her to this nameless place on the White Nile. Her mind and senses had been in suspended animation until that dizzying instant, moments ago, when they were awakened to the foreignness of her surroundings and to the reality of the incredible turn her life had taken. She who had been out of Iowa only a few times, never for very long and seldom very far, and who'd never done anything exceptional in her life, unless you counted the mess she'd been making of it until recently (and you really couldn't because it had been an unexceptional mess—"trailer park trash, that's what you've turned into," her mother had scolded her, as if the commonness of her bad behavior was what made it offensive), had journeyed to a country at war in the heart of Africa, on a mission to liberate two hundred and nine black people from captivity. She felt inadequate to the task and completely out of place and a fleeting but intense longing to be home again, amid its everyday routines.

"Looks like we might be here for a while longer, so I might as well take advantage and do you two." It was Phyllis, with her cameramen. She was done up in a Jungle Jane outfit—short-sleeve safari jacket with lots of pockets and green, lightweight pants and a wide hat over her long hair.

Phyllis motioned for her and Jim to come out into the light.

"I'll start with you." She indicated Quinette with a movement of her head. "You're the reason I'm here. You're the story."

Quinette flinched and gave Phyllis a puzzled look. True, Ken had invited her to go on this particular mission and paid her travel expenses to draw attention to his cause, but she didn't think of *herself* as the story.

"It's the kids. They're the story," she began.

"Right. Sunday school kids from the American heartland, that's the spin," said Phyllis in her rough voice. "But you organized the campaign, right?"

"No. I helped out, but I—"

"Let's make sure I've got your name right." She took out a notebook from a side pocket of her Jungle Jane jacket and spelled out Quinette's first and last names, and Quinette nodded that she had it right, and then was asked her age and what she did for a living and if she was married and had children, the reporter jotting down her responses in the flip-up notebook. At a gesture from Phyllis, the man holding the video camera on his shoulder zoomed in on Quinette.

"Do you mind if I brush my hair first?" she pleaded, with a sidelong glance at her rucksack, where her hairbrush was.

"This is an interview, not an audition. Better if you look a little rough. You're in Africa, the bush."

"Okay, but there's one other thing."

"What's that?"

"I didn't organize it. Our minister and the two Bible study teachers did, Alice and Terry. I worked on it, sure, but they put it together. The only reason they're not here is because they're, you know, middle-aged and married, with kids to take care of."

"Are you saying you're here instead of them because you're expendable?" Phyllis asked, in a jokey sort of way that wasn't entirely jokey. Quinette felt that the woman was trying to put words in her mouth.

"No!" she answered. "It's just that it is dangerous out here, and—"

The reporter raised her hand like a crossing guard stopping traffic.

"I'll be sure to get your role in this right. I'll say that you were *one* of the organizers, how's that? So let's get started. Are you rolling?" she asked the cameraman. He nodded. In a twinkling, Phyllis's posture and demeanor changed. She struck a pose, putting one foot forward and straightening her shoulders. Even her voice changed, no more gravel, just a smooth, formal, oh-so-clear TV-reporter voice, asking: "Your campaign is called CLASS. What does that stand for?"

Quinette hesitated, rosettes of sweat blossoming on her shirt. During the fundraising drive, she'd been interviewed by the *Des Moines Register* and by a cable TV station out of Iowa City, becoming a local celebrity for a brief time. It had been exciting to have perfect strangers come up to her in the mall to say that they recognized her, but that hadn't made her a media veteran. This was CNN. Her face, her voice would be broadcast all over the country, maybe the world.

"Did you understand the question?" asked Phyllis.

Quinette said she did, then explained that CLASS was an acronym standing for Christian Love Against Slavery in Sudan.

"And of course it also refers to a Sunday school class. It was the children who thought up the idea. Could you tell us about that? How it got started?"

Quinette didn't know where to begin. She wished she would stop sweating, but how could she, standing in the sun? Phyllis, though, looked dry as a pressed leaf. Kristen once kept a whole book of them—oak and maple and cottonwood leaves flattened between thin sheets of paper and all so crinkly they would crumble into fragments if you didn't pick them up by the stems.

"The kids were studying about the captivity," Quinette said, "the Babylonian Captivity. A girl in the class, a thirteen-year-old, raised her hand and said she'd read a newspaper story about how black Christians were being captured and put into bondage by Muslims, you know, like the ancient Israelites had been by the Babylonians. Well, that was news to everyone, not just the kids, but the teachers too, Alice and Terry. It was news to them."

"They were shocked that this sort of thing is going on today?" Phyllis asked.

"Sure, of course they were. The girl had cut the story out and brought it to the class and showed it to, I think it was Alice, and Alice read it out loud and the kids heard about Ken and the WorldWide Christian Union, over in Switzerland. How it sent people into Sudan to buy back slaves with money that was donated by, you know, church groups and ministries like Jim's here. The kids decided they had to do something to help. To raise money and send it to Ken. Alice and Terry figured out how to do it, but like you said, the idea came from the kids."

"How much money and how did they raise it?" was Phyllis's next question.

The goal was twenty-five hundred dollars, enough to purchase liberty for fifty people. They did it by selling T-shirts and running bake sales in the church basement. A special collection was taken up at services one Sunday, donations were solicited by telephone and by going door-to-door in Cedar Falls and in neighboring towns like Waterloo and Waverly, and the response was overwhelming, it was just so gratifying. When the drive ended, three months later, it had collected five thousand dollars.

"So half the people who are going to be freed on this trip will owe their freedom to these children from Iowa, who probably never heard of Sudan before. That's pretty impressive."

Quinette couldn't tell if it was a question or a statement, and there was a canned, faked quality to the emotion Phyllis had thrown into her voice, like she was trying to tell her viewers what to feel when she didn't feel it herself.

"Tell us, Quinette, what led you to get involved?"

She hesitated. The rosettes were spreading, their petals touching at the tips. Another five minutes of this, and she would look like she was in a wet T-shirt contest. People would see her bra line, strangers in their living rooms all over the U.S.A. Where the hell were those guys with the god-damned boat? *Forgive me, Lord.*

"That's kind of personal," she said.

"In what way?" Phyllis persisted.

Quinette paused, images reeling through her mind of the Sunday morning service in the church that didn't look like a regular church, with pews and stained-glass windows, but more like an auditorium, with lots of flowers on the carpeted stage and the choir in pale blue robes at the back and the band on one side, warming everyone up with the hymn "I Want to Be a Christian," before Pastor Tom got up and led off with Isaiah— " 'The Spirit of the Lord God is upon me; because the Lord has anointed me to preach good tidings unto the meek; he hath sent me to bind up the broken-hearted, to proclaim liberty to the captives, and the opening of the prison to them that are bound' "—pausing to let Isaiah's words sink in, then describing the wonderful thing that had happened in the Sunday school the week before, how the Holy Spirit had touched the children's hearts, so they could hear and answer the cry for deliverance that was coming from across the ocean. And it's coming to us, too! Tom thundered, his voice ringing off the walls. He was really fired up, it was one of his best sermons ever, holding four or five hundred people spellbound. *"And we must heed it. . . . Our brothers and sisters in faith are being persecuted over there in Africa. . . . Our children are giving us a lesson in Christian duty, and we cannot let them down!"* He stood without speaking for a while, his hands on the lectern, his glance sweeping over the congregation so that he seemed to meet each pair of eyes. The kids were going to need a big hand from adults, organizing the drive and making sure it ran smoothly, he said, his tone cooler now and more matter-of-fact. Alice and Terry were busy women, with families to watch after, and couldn't manage everything by themselves. Anyone who wanted to volunteer to assist them should check in at the church office after the service. Then he announced the special collection and called on everybody to contribute, to get the drive off to a running start. Ushers started down the aisles, passing polished offertory plates from row to row, and as Quinette watched men reaching for their wallets, women opening their purses, she heard a voice. It was her own voice, but it was coming from outside of herself, telling her that here was what she had been seeking ever since she'd been saved: a real purpose, a cause she could devote herself to, and this as well: a channel for the restless energies that tempted her to backslide. She didn't wait for Pastor Tom to return to his office but approached him at the church door, as he was saying good-bye to his flock. He looked at her and said, "I knew you'd be the first, you're just who I had in mind when I asked for volunteers."

How could she sum up all that in a soundbite?

"It was the right thing to do," she replied to Phyllis's question. "I'm a Christian, these people here are Christians—"

"Not all of them, maybe not even most of them," Phyllis interrupted.

"Excuse me?"

"Some of them practice their traditional religions. Nature-worshippers, ancestor-worshippers, old-fashioned pagans. You didn't know that? Did the kids in your Sunday school know that?"

There was a slight, scornful curl to the reporter's thin lips, a vague hint of ridicule in the way she'd spoken.

Flustered, Quinette didn't know what to say. She and everyone in the congregation assumed the slaves were Christians, because that's what the newspaper had said—the story the girl had brought to class.

"If you had known that, and all the people who contributed to your drive, do you think it would have made a difference?" Phyllis asked into her silence. "Would you still have raised five thousand dollars?"

A dislike of Phyllis rose, a hot little flame. The woman had made her feel dumb and look dumb.

"Slavery is a violation of human rights, and last we checked, these people are human beings," Ken Eismont declared in the hard, no-nonsense voice he could put on when he needed to. He'd been standing a little ways behind Quinette all the time, and she could have kissed him for rescuing her.

He gave the reporter a brief lecture about how the Arabs had raided Dinkaland for centuries, stealing cattle, capturing women and children, making concubines out of the women, and forcing the children to gather firewood and tend livestock. It was like a tradition, so much so that the Arab word for Dinka—for all black people—was *abid,* slave. Slavery had been abolished in Sudan seventy-odd years ago, he said, but then the new Islamist government revived it, for political reasons. It supplied the Arab tribes with horses and modern weapons, it ordered them where to raid and when.

Quinette listened, rapt. Ken was a smart, tough-minded guy who'd had a good deal of experience dealing with the media and had testified before Congress and the UN Human Rights Commission. She had watched videotapes of his testimony in Nairobi, and it was almost like observing a fine athlete in action, the way he fielded questions from congressmen and commissioners, giving quick, sharp answers, and he didn't act as if he was grateful they'd invited him to testify, but as if they should be grateful to him for accepting. A man with an attitude, all right, more than a match for the acidic Phyllis.

"So what concerns us is that Khartoum deliberately violates human rights," he was saying. "The religious beliefs of the victims are beside the point."

"I take it you would agree with that?" Phyllis turned to Jim, the cameraman turning with her, like they were one person with two heads.

"This is my third time out with Ken," Jim replied, sweat dripping from his long nose like raindrops from a gutter spout. "So sure I agree. But I, we—the ministries I represent—we do hope these people will be more receptive to the gospels, once they learn that Christian people have helped them gain their freedom."

"So for you this is missionary work?"

"I believe Miss Hardin stated it perfectly," answered Jim, Quinette swelling with pride. "It's the right thing to do."

Phyllis cut the interview when Santino announced that the boats were here at last.

Heads turned toward the riverbank. The two vessels were long dugout canoes, wider in the front than in the back, each with two paddlers, Dinka boys with twisty muscles, as if there were ropes under their skin. They stood in the shallows beside their vessels, leaning on their paddles.

Quinette and the others hoisted their rucksacks and filed down the muddy path through the tall papyrus reeds. Now that she was beside it, the Nile looked bigger, the current more powerful. Gobs of dirty foam bobbed downstream, a tree branch with the leaves sticking up sailed by, at the speed of a man walking fast.

"Let's pray first," Jim said. "All of you, if you please. Pray with me."

He knelt down, and Quinette knelt beside him, there in the mud at the river's edge. The others hesitated for a beat. They were anxious to get on across and start walking, to make sure they got to the town well before dusk. It didn't seem an appropriate moment for prayer, but then Jean and Mike dropped to their knees, and Santino followed. Ken was the last. He wasn't the praying kind, even though he worked for a religious organization, but Phyllis had signaled her crew to start filming, and Ken must have figured it would look bad on TV if he was on his feet while everyone else was kneeling.

"Heavenly Father, we call upon you to guide and protect us on our journey," Jim intoned in a booming voice. He'd done some radio evangelizing on the Christian Broadcast Service. Head bowed, Quinette could feel the camera trained on her and the little band of redeemers. "Bless all who have come so far in your holy name and for your holy work." Jim's head wasn't lowered, and he wasn't looking up at the sky either; he was staring straight into the Nile, as though the Heavenly Father dwelled in its murky depths. "Bless our brothers Ken, Santino, and Mike, bless our sisters Quinette and Jean." Quinette was trying to focus on God, but she was distracted by the self-consciousness the camera aroused in her. Did she look all right? It was hard to keep your mind on prayer with a TV crew videotaping you from only a few yards away. "Bestow your blessing, Heavenly Father, on the captives we seek to set free. Hold your hand over them as you held it over your children in captive Israel. We ask this in Jesus' name, amen."

"Amen," Quinette murmured with the others, then stood and brushed her knees. Her baggy safari shorts dropped over them. Not the kind of thing she would have chosen for herself, loving as she did bright figure-flattering clothes to offset her drab brown hair and a face that was a little like Iowa, neither pretty nor ugly. Back in Nairobi, Ken had taken her to a camping store on Biashara Street and made her buy the shorts and the olive drab shirts to go with them. He'd objected to the outfits she'd brought from the States: a kaleidoscope of canary yellows, teal greens, salmon pinks. It was the dry season in Sudan, Ken had told her. Government planes could be flying, militia might be patrolling the countryside. Making herself so obvious could prove dangerous, to her and her companions.

They took off their hiking boots and sandals and waded in, the water warm as bathwater, and with the paddlers holding the unstable craft steady, got on board: Phyllis, her crew, Mike and Jean in one with two of the soldiers, Quinette, Ken, Santino, and Jim in the other with the remaining soldiers. They sat on the gunwales, three to a side, their gear between them. With sign language, one of the soldiers cautioned them to sit very still. A pod of hippopotami wallowed a little ways downstream, their gray-black backs humped out of the water. Quinette had never seen a hippopotamus before, except in one of those *National Geographic* specials Jake Mueller, her brother-in-law, liked to watch. The most dangerous beast in Africa, Ken had informed her on the flight from Loki. Killed more people every year than all the lions and leopards put together.

The stern paddler launched the dugout with a strong shove, then hopped in so nimbly that it barely rocked. Just then Quinette spied a crocodile basking on a mud bank toward the far side of the river, stationary as a log, its long head tilted slightly, like someone with his chin in the air, its plated back silvery green in the sunlight. Ken had given her some information about crocs as well—if hippos got the gold medal for killing people, crocs got the silver. They usually nabbed native women, washing clothes by the riverbank, dragged them in and rolled them over until they drowned, then devoured them. The thought of such a death stirred a primal dread in Quinette. Back home you tossed dirty clothes into the Maytag and forgot about them; here doing your laundry could have gruesome consequences. She could only trust that the Heavenly Father had listened to Jim's petitions.

Eddies creased the surface of the dark Nile, little whirlpools formed and vanished and re-formed. Angling upstream to make up for the river pushing the dugout in the opposite direction, the paddlers dug in hard, their ropy muscles writhing. They were a beautiful people, these Dinka, so tall and lithe, with big, oval, slightly slanted eyes and skin so dark it looked as if God had cut bolts out of the midnight sky and made human beings from them.

The croc slipped off the mud bank with a leisurely sweep of its tail and disappeared. She pictured it cruising through the half-light below and felt vulnerable, sitting on the edge of the canoe. The soldier across from her must have seen the look on her face because he made a reassuring movement with his hand, then patted his automatic rifle. *Yeah,* she thought, *a lot of good that'll do you if you end up in the drink with the rest of us.*

The paddlers in the second boat, lagging a little, quickened their strokes and pulled up parallel to the one she was in, allowing the cameraman to film it broadside as it crossed. The camera's glass eye stared straight at Quinette from five yards away, and she stared back at it and forgot her fears as she imagined everyone she knew looking at her on TV. It was a little like sneaking into a room full of people viewing a home video of yourself. You saw them and your own screen image at the same time; you were both the observer and the observed. Her mother, Kristen, Nicole and Jake and her nephew Danny, Pastor Tom, Mrs. Hoge, Alice, Terry, and the pupils from Sunday school—she saw them all watching her, sitting in a dugout paddled by bare-chested tribesmen, with a croc-infested river in the background and an African rebel beside her, wearing his ferocious scars and garland of ammunition. The Quinette in that inner picture did not appear as out of her element as the real Quinette felt; nor did the papyrus reeds and fever trees and soldiers' faces, framed by the flickering rectangle in her mind's eye, look as foreign and weird as they did to the eyes in her head. Visualizing the scene as it would appear on TV, before all those familiar people, had somehow domesticated it. An odd and wonderful thing happened when she turned away from the camera's hypnotic stare to gaze at the world around her: the mental image dissolved, yet its feeling of familiarity lingered. The soldiers' faces had lost their exotic menace, appearing no more peculiar or frightening than the faces of punked-out kids back home, with their pierced tongues and noses and spiked, tinted hair. The strangeness of her surroundings and this whole experience, which had nearly made her faint, had dissolved completely, and the sense that she was a stranger here dissolved with it. The thing she was doing no longer struck her as bizarre but seemed perfectly natural, something she was meant to do. A gusher of joy sprang from her stomach into her throat, and for a second she thought it would fly right out of her mouth in a birdlike cry, like lyrics that made you so happy you could not contain them inside yourself but had to sing them out loud. All that kept her silent, as the boats drew close to shore, was the knowledge that she was to be here for a short time only—five days, that was how long Ken figured it would take. Then she would begin the journey home, back to the routines she had longed for barely half an hour ago and now, suddenly, dreaded.

They entered a cove where the water was only knee deep. The soldiers and paddlers got out and walked the dugouts ashore, swinging them parallel to the bank so the passengers could disembark without getting their feet wet again. There was a large tree atop the bank, and from beneath the umbrella of its branches, another squad of four guerrillas stood up suddenly, surprising Quinette as she was lacing up her hiking boots. Where had they come from? Who were they? Dinka, she observed, noticing the same chevrons slashing across foreheads, as if they'd been clawed by an animal with a sense of precision. The same gap-toothed grins. Not just a cruel custom, she thought, but a tragic one, because the Dinkas' teeth were as white as their skin was black; if they were allowed to keep them all, they could blind you with their smiles.

"Quite a bodyguard. Expecting trouble?" Phyllis said to Ken.

"Expecting it? No. Ready for it if it comes, yeah," he replied. "But we'll try to avoid making you a war correspondent," he added in a patronizing tone of voice.

"Sarajevo, the intifada, Afghanistan. Been there done that, so it would be no problem," Phyllis shot back, and you could tell it wasn't just bravado.

The guerrillas collected the team's rucksacks and shouldered them. Jim Prewitt blew out his cheeks, relieved that he wouldn't have to carry his tent and sleeping bag the rest of the way. The leader issued commands in Dinka, and half the men jogged out in front, rifles clattering. The rest brought up the rear, and then the column filed through the reeds. The air was still, thick, and rank with the odors of mud and decaying vegetation. A mosquito sang in Quinette's ear, another bit her on the forearm. She slapped it, smearing her skin with blood, then got bug repellent from her fanny pack and sprayed herself liberally.

They followed the trail up out of the marshes and onto the savannah and trooped down a narrow, rutted laterite road that cut through high grass the color of hay. This part of deepest, darkest Africa wasn't dark at all, but light light light, as flat as Iowa it seemed, and almost as open, with the acacia trees wide apart. An arid wind blew across the vastness, relieving the heat but raising dust from the road that powdered everyone's sweaty skin. Clouds sailed on the wind, like scattered blimps. The band of redeemers and guards walked on through the heat and dust, Jim, the oldest of the bunch, barely keeping up and the Kenyan cameramen, softened by life in Nairobi, sweating buckets as they took turns lugging the video camera. Quinette had expected Phyllis to be their weakest link; despite her war correspondent's résumé, she looked too thin and citified to withstand a long tramp through the bush, but she was holding up pretty well, swinging along in her jaunty hat and safari jacket. Santino wasn't having any trouble either, nor Ken, nor Mike and Jean, even though both were on the short side and had to take two steps for every one the rebel soldiers took, their legs nearly as long as the two Canadians were tall.

"I can't figure out how the Arabs make slaves out of these people," Quinette remarked, walking alongside Ken. She pointed at the soldiers in front of them.

"Don't know how or don't know why?" Ken asked. He'd clipped polarized lenses to his glasses and now looked like a blind man.

"It's the same question, isn't it?"

"Not exactly. You heard me tell Phyllis why."

"Government policy. But Ken, these guys, they're like a professional basketball team with assault rifles. Who would want to mess with them? Santino told me they're as tough and mean as they look."

"They are." He was looking not at her but dead ahead, his wrists resting on his two army-style belt canteens.

"Dinka boys learn to fight with sticks and how to wrestle, and when they get their teeth chopped out, they're not allowed to cry or make a sound, that's what Santino said. Doesn't make sense how Arab pipsqueaks can attack guys like that and steal their cattle and their kids and their wives. You'd think the Dinka would just kick their butts right into the middle of next month."

Ken gave a short, dry laugh, but she couldn't tell if he laughed because the phrase amused him or because he thought she'd said something stupid. She would be mortified if that was his opinion. She respected him for his dedication to his work and for his knowledge of this part of the world, and she wanted him to respect her. His approval seemed a thing to be coveted if you didn't have it, cherished if you did. Maybe she should have explained the choice of clothing she'd brought from home. Taking part in the liberation of two hundred and nine people was a joyous event in her book, and she'd wanted to proclaim her joy by dressing in vibrant outfits. Nothing shallow or frivolous about that, was there? You didn't go to a wedding dressed for a funeral, did you?

"Horses and Islam," Ken said.

She quizzed him with a look.

"That's why the Arabs are able to do what they do."

"Because of horses?"

"And Islam."

"All right. Horses and Islam. So?"

"Think about it."

"I hate riddles," she said.

Ken was silent.

Her thin canvas hat barely softened the rap of the sun's knuckles against her skull. Despite the steady breeze, flies swarmed around her face.

"The Dinka don't have horses," Ken said. She guessed he was giving her a hint. "North of here is desert and Arab territory. When the wet season comes, this part of the country is loaded with tsetse flies. A horse wouldn't live a week, but the Arabs can take theirs north, into the desert, and then come back down here in the dry season. That's when most of their raids take place."

She conjured up an image of mounted Arabs galloping over the sun-dazed plain, a tide of horseflesh and man-flesh washing over whatever stood in its way. "Okay, I get the horses part. I don't get what the Arabs' religion has to do with anything."

"It unites them," answered Ken. Quinette swiped at the flies, hoping they weren't the tsetse kind. "No matter what tribe they're from, they're fighting for the same idea. It gives them the go-ahead to kill infidels or to capture them and force them to convert, at gunpoint if need be. You could say the Arabs are evangelists and their Kalashnikovs do the preaching. They really believe they're doing it for Allah. Not all of them, but enough to make the difference."

"It's holy work to them, in other words? They think *they're* doing what Jim said *we're* doing?"

"We're not killing people or forcing anyone to believe in anything," Ken said flatly.

"I didn't mean that!" Her face flushed.

"I know." He squeezed her arm in a fatherly way, which appeared to be as demonstrative as Ken ever got. "And listen, Quinette. I'm grateful to you and Jim. Every dollar was raised by you two, but don't make more out of this than what it is. It's necessary work, but holy? I wouldn't call it that."

"That isn't real inspiring," she stated, hoping she didn't offend him. An expression of gratitude from him was a rare and precious coin, not to be squandered.

"I don't trust inspiration," he said, "or enthusiasm. They don't last. I've been doing human rights work for twenty years, and the big lesson I've learned is that burnout is an occupational hazard. People get into it fired up, thinking they're going to change things overnight. Work their hearts out for a while, find out they haven't made much of a dent, get discouraged and worn out, and quit."

"I'm not the quitting kind," she said. "If I were, I would've quit on myself a long time ago. I almost did, but in the end I didn't."

Quinette's psyche had not lost all its baby fat; she was still young enough to find herself fascinating and to think that the story of her journey from darkness into the light of grace was unusual, if not unique. She was inviting Ken to ask her to tell it, but he said nothing.

"The Lord wouldn't let me quit, I guess." Trying a different approach. "A lot of people were praying for me, and they wouldn't let me either. I wouldn't be here otherwise."

It was hard to interpret the movement Ken made with his head. A nod encouraging her to go on? But there was an impatience in the motion, suggesting that, whatever her story, it was one he'd heard before and didn't care to hear again.

The red road ran on, hard underfoot and cracked everywhere, as if it had been paved with broken bricks. Termite mounds and anthills made of the same sun-baked clay rose out of the grass to heights of five feet or more, some resembling obelisks, some eroded sand castles, with wind-worn towers and turrets. Quinette marveled at the industry of the insects and wondered how many ant and termite generations it had taken to build those structures. She thought of the stonemasons who'd built the cathedrals in medieval Europe—fathers, sons, and grandsons working on the same project and not a one living to see it completed.

They passed near a village: conical-roofed huts perched on stilts to discourage rats and snakes from coming inside, cattle byres that looked like pyramids made of sticks, forests of stakes driven into the ground for tethering cows and calves, and the smell of smoke and manure heavy in the overheated air. A man in shorts came by, walking in the opposite direction on legs so thin they didn't look capable of supporting his weight, much less the weight of the bundled grass he carried on his shoulders in a sheaf maybe two feet thick and six long. A young woman wearing bead ankle bracelets and big hoop earrings sat in front of a hut, nursing a baby that looked too old to still be breastfeeding. In fact, the kid was standing up, as if he were at a drinking fountain. He stopped suckling, and as he turned to look at the strangers parading by, flies lighted on the dried milk smeared around his lips. Quinette had an almost overpowering urge to wipe his mouth and to scold the mother for not doing so herself. And yet the primitiveness of the village appealed to Quinette at some basic level, and she was drawn to the austerity of the landscape, with its thorn-bristling trees and earthy tones of beige, brown, rusty red. Life stripped down to its essentials. Two women came up the road, one behind the other, the first wearing a dark, saronglike gown and a five-gallon water can on her head, like a plastic top hat. The second was in a sundress that must have been donated by a mission or the UN, and carried on her head a woven basket of ground maize, with a rolled-up mat atop it. The women barely glanced at the soldiers and cameramen but shot a long look at Phyllis and stopped to stare at Quinette with an expression of startled curiosity in their dark Nilotic eyes.

"Hello," she said, offering a tentative wave.

They didn't speak or smile or do anything except continue to stare as she walked on by, and she looked back at them over her shoulder, trying to figure out why she was the object of their attention.

"They're not used to seeing white people out here," Ken explained, without being asked. "Especially white women on foot, and a white woman as tall as they are is a real novelty."

They stopped for a break at midafternoon, the hottest part of the day, and rested in the shade of tamarind and ebony trees around a dry water hole, its banks dimpled with the hoofprints of the cattle that had watered there during the rains. Seedpods hanging like brown tongues from the tamarinds rattled in the wind, and brilliant birds ornamented the branches—birds with golden breasts, or black heads and iridescent purple wings, or feathers that were palettes of pale green, turquoise, and lilac.

"I told myself the last time that it was going to be the last time, " Jim Prewitt said, leaning into the trunk of a tree. "I'm too old for this, but here I am."

"And we're all here with you," Ken stated. He took a GPS from his pocket and tapped the buttons. "Five K's. Three miles. You can make that."

"I'll have to." Jim smiled wanly. "But I don't like walking around like this in broad daylight." He gestured at the whitened sky. At first Quinette thought he meant the heat; then she realized he was indicating the danger of enemy planes.

"Can't be helped," Ken said. "Too easy to lose somebody at night. Wouldn't want one of my team snatched by a lion."

"There's lions out here?"

The idea that there were simultaneously frightened and excited her; it made her feel like a true African adventurer.

"Supposed to be a few left. I was just kidding about them snatching a person. Mostly they prey on cattle. Everything else has been killed off. Drought, the war."

"It doesn't really look like there's a war on here," Quinette remarked, though she did not have a clear picture of a battlefield's landscape, except for remembered images from her father's photographs of Vietnam, a TV documentary she'd seen about that war.

"It's a fluid sort of war," Ken said. "Moves around a lot. A year ago this area was a real hot spot and we couldn't be doing what we are now. And it could get hot again, practically overnight."

She had emptied one of her water bottles. Standing, she looked around and started toward a bush she could hide behind.

"Where are you going?"

"Do I have to raise my hand and ask permission?"

"Oh, that. Be careful."

"Lions?"

"Snakes. Spitting cobras. Puff adders," Ken said.

She made a thorough search of the ground and stabbed at the thorn-bush with a long stick. When nothing hissed, puffed, or spit, she pulled down her shorts and underpants and squatted, listening to the stream splash against the hard-packed earth beneath her. An urgency came to her bowels, and she did that too, her own stink rising, and she cleaned herself with the roll of toilet paper in her fanny pack. Good thing Dad had taken her along on his deer and pheasant hunts—she'd learned not to be shy about relieving herself in the outdoors. He'd turned her into something of a tomboy, a stand-in for the son he would never have, teaching her to shoot and track and to look for antler rubbings on the trees. The last two autumns of his life. Walking beside him down the rows of mown corn, with Jenny, his springer spaniel ranging out ahead. Huddling with him in a deer blind in the chill gray of a November dawn, falling asleep and waking with her head on his shoulder, feeling the warmth of his body coming through the thick pile of his camouflage coat. Teddy Bear, everyone called him for his first name and size and gentle temperament. He was gone by the following fall—a rare blood cancer that the doctor said had been caused by his exposure to Agent Orange. "So that goddamned war got him after all," his younger brother Gene had murmured at the funeral.

Oh, there are depths to grief no one can imagine until she has plumbed them herself.

She'd forgotten to take pictures! The autofocus camera Pastor Tom loaned her was in her rucksack, with a dozen rolls of film and her journal. Tom wanted her to give a talk and slide presentation at the church when she got back. She hadn't exposed a single frame or made a single note, a situation she had better start rectifying right away.

"Excuse me, I have to get into my pack," she said to the young soldier who'd been carrying it and was now using it as a pillow as he lay on his back, legs crossed at the knee.

She removed the camera from a side compartment, turned it on, and checked the frame counter on the lit-up display panel.

"Okay if I take your picture?"

The soldier pointed to himself, raising his almost invisible eyebrows.

She was pleased to see a silver crucifix hanging from his neck by a silver chain. "Yes. You."

He stood, his stick limbs unfolding with movements that suggested the extension of a carpenter's ruler, and posed as if for a guerrilla recruiting poster, a warrior's scowl on his teenage face, his shoulders stiffened, rifle held crosswise over his front.

She flipped to the back pages of her journal and wrote "Roll 1" at the top and the number 1 at the side, and beside the number "SPLA soldier" and the date. Ken, Jim, and Santino were her next subjects. Taking the photographs, identifying them by frame number, was very satisfying. She was no longer a mere passenger on the expedition but someone with a real, active role to play. Already, she was starting to think about what she would say at her presentation and how she would say it. The thought of addressing a large crowd did not intimidate her. She had shone as a public speaker during her otherwise dismal high school career, never nervous when called on to recite in class. Her strong, rich voice, with its slightly masculine timbre, caught people's attention. It made her feel poised and attractive, blurring the picture she had of herself as a rawboned girl with eyes set too far apart alongside a nose too long above lips too thin.

The group resumed its journey. Women at a well, one cranks the pump handle, a jet-black breast showing above the polka-dot robe knotted over the opposite breast. *Click.* Another woman farther down the road grinds grain by pounding it with a pestle the size of an oar in a wooden mortar. *Click.* Quinette would bring to them, those midwestern farmers and small-town folks, images from a world they'd never seen and probably never would, not even people like the Formillers, who owned something like six or seven thousand acres of corn and soybeans in Black Hawk and Grundy counties and had money to burn and had gone to Europe on vacation and taken cruises to the Caribbean. They would never cross the Nile in a dugout canoe or look upon Dinka boys herding belled oxen—*click*—or tribesmen squatting under a baobab—*click*.

"Sister, you would like to ride on my bike?"

He had come up from behind, a soldier, although he wore no uniform, only dark blue shorts and a ratty striped shirt. A Kalashnikov with a folding metal stock was slung across his back. He pedaled alongside her for a few yards, the front wheel jerking side to side because he was going so slowly; then he stopped to stand straddling the seat, and he was so tall that there were several inches of daylight between the seat and the V of his legs. He asked her name and she told him, and he said his was Matthew Deng.

"Bye-bye, Kinnit."

"Bye-bye?"

"He means hello," Ken called out. "A lot of times they'll say bye-bye when they mean hello."

"A woman should not be walking," Matthew declared gallantly. He had buck teeth; or maybe he just looked as if he did because his lower lip was drawn in by the cavity where his bottom teeth had been. "You are doing so much for us, I must do something for you. I can take you the rest of the way. You'll get there before everyone else."

She looked at him and the vintage one-gear bike, with its rust-pitted rims and wide bald tires. "And just how do you know where we're going?"

"Bush telegraph," said Ken. "It's faster than e-mail and you don't need a modem."

He told her it would be all right if she accepted the offer—the town was less than two miles away and this was a liberated area, firmly under SPLA control.

Matthew stripped off his shirt, folded it, and lay it on the carrier over the rear fender. She climbed on and sat with her hands on the carrier for balance, her legs thrust out to keep her feet off the ground. They rode past fields of harvested sorghum; the strewn brown leaves and chopped stalks brought to mind her father's lost acres, the memory causing her old grief to jab her with a keenness that caught her off guard; then the needle withdrew and the hurt passed from her. Trees bordering a stream, some tributary of a tributary, spun a filament of green across the sere grasslands. There were women bathing in the stream, skirts hiked up and knotted around their thighs, and they stopped and stared at the bike in shock, then doubled over in laughter.

"They have never seen before a lady on a bike," Matthew explained.

"Dinka girls don't ride bikes?"

"Oh my, no," he said, as if she'd mentioned some inviolable taboo.

Standing up on the pedals, Matthew pumped hard to get over a gentle rise. The back side was steeper than the front, and they coasted down with alarming speed. He locked the brakes, the rear wheel slewed to one side, and Quinette flew off, landing on her rear end, clutching the camera close to her tummy, like a mother protecting an infant.

"Oh! Kinnet! You are all right?"

"No bones broken," she said, and laughed, and the Dinka laughed with her.

"Please hold on to me the rest of the way," he said, retrieving his shirt from where it had fallen and putting it back on the carrier.

She did as he asked, though she couldn't see what good it would do if he lost control again. There was no fat on him. Holding him below the ribs, Quinette felt that she could have squeezed his narrow trunk like a toothpaste tube if not for the hard, tensile stomach muscles, moving under her fingers. His back, coated with sweat, had the sheen of a black lacquer table, and he gave off a strong but not unpleasant musk. She felt a stirring she knew she shouldn't and let go of his waist and returned her hands to the carrier.

They entered the town. Well-swept dirt yards, pavement smooth and shrouded by mahogany trees faced each other across a street that was more like a cowpath, full of potholes and deep, meandering ruts made, she guessed, by rainwater sluicing through in the wet season. Some tukuls had religious petitions painted on their clay walls—"God Bless All Within,"

"Christ Jesus Bless this House." What was Phyllis talking about, saying that most of these people were heathen ancestor-worshippers? The bike ride ended in the marketplace. From stalls made of woven branches and sheet metal and roofed by plastic tarpaulins, men and women sat selling cigarettes, canned goods, amber bricks of soap, spices in small burlap sacks. There wasn't a whole lot more—a few cotton dresses hanging from a door on wire hangers, hand towels, and flour in cloth bags stamped with a drawing of a white hand shaking a black one and a stars-and-stripes shield and the word USAID. She wondered how even those meager goods had found their way to such a remote place, and she thought of the mall where she worked, with more bounty in one square foot than in this whole market.

Matthew led her by the hand to one of the stalls and offered her a wooden stool to sit on and asked if she would like a cup of tea. She preferred coffee to give her a lift, for she was light-headed from exhaustion, but this didn't look like the place to get picky. Matthew spoke to the woman sitting inside, in a darkness that would have been like a closet's but for a kerosene lamp and the light infiltrating through the latticework of the twig-and-branch walls. In a few minutes, she set a small china pot and two cups on the counter, and Quinette's chauffeur filled them and dipped a spoon into a bowl of brown crystalline sugar, asking how many she wanted. She said one.

"Your tea, mah-dam," the Dinka said with a mock bow. "I was one time a waiter in the hotel in Wau."

"Wow?"

The cup looked pretty dirty, but she decided to drink from it, to be polite.

"A big town to the south. Far away. Government town. I cannot go there now." He swung the Kalashnikov from behind his back and slapped it. "SPLA! They would shoot me down!" His glance lifted quickly, toward a pair of men outside a stall across the way. They were watching Quinette and Matthew. Both wore turbans and long white robes, like bedsheets, and they weren't Dinka, even she could see that, noticing their cherrywood complexions and noses like eagles' beaks. One had a short beard, the other was clean shaven.

"*Salaam aleikum,*" said Matthew, his hand fluttering past chin, nose, forehead before it swept outward with a comically exaggerated flourish.

"*Aleikum as-salaam,*" said the bearded one. A knife in a hide scabbard was strapped to his upper arm, and he didn't appear to be amused by the Dinka's theatrics. He jerked his pointy chin at Quinette, in a kind of contemptuous way and said something in a language she didn't recognize, though she could tell that he was asking a question. Matthew answered, and the man grunted without expression; then he and his friend walked off, robes swirling around their brown ankles.

"Messiriya," Matthew said.

She cocked an ear.

"Those fellows. They are from the Messiriya tribe. Arabs."

"What are they doing here?"

"That is what they asked me about you."

"I thought the Dinka were at war with the Arabs."

"We are, yes."

"Then what are they doing here?"

"We are not at war with all Arabs."

"You mean, with their tribe? You're not fighting this Miserya tribe?"

"Messiriya. We are fighting them all the time. The Messiriya and Dinka—" He made fists and knocked them together, knuckle to knuckle.

She gave him a long, searching look. "I'm confused."

"Oh, yes. The war makes a big confusion. Sometimes I am confused by it." He gazed down the street in the direction the Arabs had gone. "The *omodiya* of those fellows is not at war with us. For now. A few months from now—" Matthew twitched his shoulders to indicate the unpredictability of future events.

"The *omo* what?" Quinette asked.

"Omodiya. It is like a very big family. How in English? A very big family?"

"Clan?"

"Yes! The clan of those fellows has made peace with the Dinka for now because they need to graze their cattle on Dinka land and also to come to Dinka towns to buy things. Soap. Sugar. Tea. Also to sell slaves. That is what those fellow are here to do. They go about in the north, buying slaves from the people who own them, and when they have so many, they bring them here to sell them back to their families for cows or goats, sometimes for money."

Trading cows and goats for human beings? Her brain was swimming.

"Three cows for one person," Matthew continued. "But many Dinka don't have three cows to give. That is why you, your friends are so very welcome. You have the money for buying them, return them to their families."

Looking past him, she observed that several women and children had gathered on the street to gawk at her with fixed, quizzical stares. Well, she was probably as conspicuous here as one of these Dinka females would be in Cedar Falls.

"Was anyone from your family taken?"

"My sister. Two years ago. I have heard she will be among those to be given freedom, so I got the permission from my commander to come here and bring her home."

The small crowd edged closer, approaching as if she might be dangerous.

"Hello, bye-bye," said Quinette, raising a hand.

A young woman in a long black skirt and Chicago Bulls T-shirt turned her face aside shyly and giggled.

"Ha-lo. Bye-bye," replied another woman with two small kids at her side, a girl in a ragged dress, a younger, naked boy. The woman touched Quinette's forearm, the way you would touch an iron to test its heat, and then spoke in a soft, musical voice.

"She is saying that you are her sister," Matthew translated.

She liked the sound of it. It persuaded her that she'd read the glances of the two women down the road accurately.

"Tell her that I'm honored to be her sister," she said.

She reached down and lifted the naked boy into her lap, a gesture that brought a murmur of approval from the crowd. She loved kids and occasionally regretted that she and her ex hadn't had any (though she was more often not the least bit sorry, knowing that she would now be a single mother working two jobs, battling for child support, and probably not getting any, because Steve was an odd-job handyman five days a week, a guitarist in a tenth-rate country music band on weekends, imprisoned by the futile hope that he would be discovered and asked to come to Nashville).

Ken and Jim came parading in with the others, surrounded by a welcoming mob.

"See you've made friends," Ken said to Quinette. "Our ambassador of good will." He gave the boy's head a knuckle rub. The movement was stiff and awkward. "C'mon. Let's get settled in. Big day tomorrow."

She joined the procession, holding each kid by the hand, their mother walking alongside on bare, dust-reddened feet and chattering away.

"This woman," Matthew translated, "she wants for you to stay in her house this night."

Quinette hesitated, looking to Ken. He shook his head and said the local commander already had designated places for them to stay. He wanted them all together, for security reasons.

She was disappointed—it would be interesting to see how a Dinka woman lived—yet her heart beat quickly with a secret excitement. Here she was, a stranger, and the woman had invited her under her roof with hardly a word exchanged between them. Why was that? Now that she thought about it, why had Matthew offered her a ride and not Phyllis and Jean? A spontaneous harmony seemed to develop between her and these towering coal-black people.

The parade ended at a compound enclosed by a straw and branch fence. The soldiers wouldn't let the townspeople inside. Quinette let go of the children's hands and followed Ken and Jim through a rickety gate. The soothing shadows of fruit trees striped the bare ground and climbed low tukul walls to spread a tracery of leaves and branches on the grassy slopes of the roofs. Fallen mangoes lay here and there like big ochre eggs, giving off a sharp, ripe odor just short of rotten. The place would have had the sad, romantic atmosphere of a neglected orchard if it had been uninhabited, but there were quite a few people around: a couple of soldiers stirring a blackened pot over a fire, a few more playing some sort of game with stones, two others raising on makeshift poles a canvas enclosure about the size of a phone booth—"that'll be the ladies' room," Jean said in her singsongy Canadian accent. An SPLA officer in a red beret and a civilian wearing a baseball cap sat at a table in front of a small whitewashed bungalow, with a sign over the door reading SOUTH SUDAN RELIEF AND REHA-BILITATION AGENCY, the name of the indigenous NGO that cooperated with Ken on his missions.

The soldiers who had been carrying the rucksacks went off to drop their burdens at the doors of the tukuls, and Quinette noticed, with a sinking feeling, that she and Phyllis were going to be roommates. Ken and Jim approached the table. The two men seated there stood up and shook hands with the Americans. Ken introduced Quinette, and when he mentioned that she had raised half the money, the civilian in the baseball cap, whose name was Manute, enveloped her hand in both of his and thanked her "on behalf of the people of southern Sudan." She knew it was just a phrase; all the same, she felt a tingling in her chest, picturing a forest of bony black arms lifted up in gratitude.

During the flight from Loki, Ken had briefed her and Phyllis on the procedures for redeeming captives. The retrievers—the men who had bought the slaves back from their owners—were to be paid in Sudanese pounds, which were supplied by the SRRA. Now it was time for a currency exchange. Manute went inside the bungalow and came out with a metal file box, from which he drew bundles of crisp multicolored bills. He made some calculations on a pocket calculator, then turned it around so Ken could read the numbers.

"What rate did you use?" Ken asked.

"The one our Loki office gave me. I called them on the radio just this morning."

Santino, in the meantime, began counting the Sudanese money, the airline bag with the dollars at his feet.

"It's not what the bank quoted in Nairobi," Ken declared. "Look, the retrievers will be expecting twenty-nine thousand four hundred a head." He paused to tap the calculator keys. "Six million one forty-four total. I'll be coming up fifty-seven thousand short with the rate you're using. Fifty-seven thousand buys two people. What do I do? Pick out two and tell them, sorry, better luck next time? Do I pay for them out of my own pocket?"

"Of course not! I will make up the difference if it comes to that." Manute pulled out his wallet for emphasis. "But it won't. The retrievers will use the same rate like me. If they insist on the other, we can tell them, 'Take it or leave it.' They will take it. You know what they pay the owners for the captives. Nine, ten thousand for one. At the most fifteen. So a lot of profit for them. They will take it."

Ken chewed his lip. "If they don't, I'll hold you to your promise," he said.

Manute made a movement with his head; it might have been a nod, it might have been a reflexive twitch caused by the flies, which were everywhere.

Santino hefted the airline bag onto the table. Out came the American currency in one-hundred-dollar denominations; in went the Sudanese pounds while Manute and the officer flipped through the greenbacks, then stacked them side by side to make sure they were the same height. Quinette focused her camera on the men's hands and the piled bills—*click*—and wondered what she would say about this picture when she gave her presentation. She hadn't considered the economic practicalities of God's holy work; they made it seem less than holy. All of Manute's talk—*"nine or ten thousand for one . . . a big profit"*—like he was discussing cattle prices.

After Manute and the officer left, Quinette observed Ken throw a brusque, sidelong glance at Phyllis, who looked back at him with her quick green eyes. She straddled the bench across the table from him and drew her notebook from her pocket as if it were a gun.

"A little bush-league currency arbitrage?" she asked.

Ken said nothing. A couple of dozen flies made tiny polka dots on the back of his shirt.

Phyllis had taken her hat off, and the light slicing through a gap in the trees exposed the gray streaks in her reddish hair and the whisker-thin wrinkles etched into her papery skin. The woman might have owned a certain pale, gaunt beauty when she was younger, but now, with the honed planes of her high cheekbones raked alongside the blade of her nose and her chin tapering sharply below taut lips, her face had so many points and edges that Quinette imagined it could cut you anywhere you kissed it.

She stood aside and listened, somewhat baffled by the conversation that followed. Phyllis said, "So they'll take the ten grand and exchange it at the Nairobi rate and pocket the fifty-seven thousand difference," and Ken replied, "Fifty-seven thousand pounds comes to about a hundred bucks."

"A hundred bucks goes a long way in a country with a per capita income of about five hundred. And if these guys from the SRRA do skim a hundred or two every time you come out, then they're making themselves, oh, say about a grand a year."

"Think I'll grab something to eat and set up my tent before it's dark. Hate doing that job by flashlight."

This from Jim, rising stiffly.

"Good advice for everybody," Ken said. "Unless you're interviewing me, Phyllis, and if you are, just what is the question?"

"Do you think you're getting ripped off, and if you do, how do you feel about it?"

"We're talking human lives here, human rights, and you're talking petty change, even if what you're insinuating is true, which I don't think it is."

"Not what I heard in Nairobi."

"What did you hear in Nairobi?"

"Rumors that this slave redemption program is a cash cow for some people."

"From skimming nickels and dimes off a currency exchange?" Ken shook his head to highlight the absurdity of Phyllis's suspicions.

"Then how about the redemption money?" she asked, unfazed. "What happens to the dollars after you turn it over to them? What do they do with it? A total of a hundred grand so far, isn't that what you told me on the plane? So let's forget their skimming the cream and talk about the whole pail of milk. A hundred grand isn't nickels and dimes, is it, Mr. Eismont?"

Ken flinched—he'd picked up on her change to his last name.

"It goes back into the SRRA's accounts, to repay for the withdrawals of Sudanese pounds for the redemptions."

"You're sure about that? In Nairobi I've seen movers and shakers from the SRRA in new suits, driving new cars."

"Better follow Jim's example. Get your tents set up. You know how it is in this neck of the African woods. Not much twilight. It's light, then it's dark."

"We're staying in a hut. We don't need tents."

"All kinds of critters in these roofs. Spiders, snakes. They drop down at night. You wouldn't want them crawling all over you. Or would you?"

Phyllis snapped her notebook shut, picked up her hat by its chin strap, and swung it onto her head, tucking her hair underneath. "Don't take things so personally, Ken. Only doing my job."

"YOU SLIP THE poles through the sleeves, then fit the ends into the bottom pockets and the thing pops right up, like this."

In the tukul's dim interior, Phyllis demonstrated the technique, Quinette mortified that she, a country girl, couldn't figure out how to erect her tent. Phyllis had hers up in half a minute and went outside. Quinette assembled the sections of the poles and felt a sense of accomplishment when the shapeless folds of mesh and cloth ballooned into a dome, just big enough to accommodate one person. Like Phyllis's, hers wasn't exactly a tent but a mosquito net with a sewn-in ground sheet. Side by side the two shelters resembled giant soap bubbles, risen out of the hard-packed dirt floor. She dragged her sleeping bag and air mattress into the bubble. Probably she wouldn't need the sleeping bag—the air inside the windowless tukul, smelling like damp hay too long in the barn, was stagnant and hot. She lay down for a moment and, looking up through the mesh, searched for snakes and spiders in the thatch ceiling. Her head began to swim again; she felt herself teetering on the brink of sleep, the desire to fall into it checked by the grumbling in her stomach. She rummaged in her pack for a PowerBar and a bag of trail mix and went out with the food and her water bottle. Phyllis was sitting on a camp stool, her back bent as she gazed into a hand mirror propped against a rock at her feet and rubbed her face with cleansing cream.

"Thinking of entering a beauty contest?" Quinette said, peeling the wrapper off the half-melted PowerBar.

"In my business, every goddamned day is a beauty contest." Phyllis's eyes peered through a white mask. "Got to keep the crone at bay. A lot of cute patooties about your age would love to have my job. Think they want it, anyway. One day like today, walking ten miles in hundred-degree heat, sleeping in some native shithole, and those darlings would be whining to be sent back to the air-conditioned studio."

She was speaking again in her natural voice, stone grinding on stone. Quinette held out the bag of trail mix.

"Thanks. I'll be dining on my own delicious stuff in a minute."

Phyllis pointed at a can under the camp stool. Quinette was dismayed to see that it was a can of beans.

"Like some tea with your gourmet granola?"

"Sure. Okay."

The reporter set the jar of cream aside and looked toward the soldiers, squatting in a circle around the steaming pot on the campfire. Holding two fingers in a V she called out, *"Tungependa mbili chai, tafahadli."*

The soldiers turned toward her with blank faces. Matthew was with them.

"Forgot, these characters don't know Swahili," Phyllis muttered, then called out again, *"Ideenee etnayan shi, minfadlik.* And if you don't understand Arabic either, I'd like two cups of tea, pah-leese."

"This is not safari, you know, and we are not camp boys," Matthew said, the smile on his lips absent from his voice.

"But you are gentlemen, aren't you?" Phyllis shot back. "And I did say 'please,' in three languages."

Quinette asked, "So what is your job that all those cuties want it?"

Phyllis looked at her askance. "Hello? Where have you been all day? I'm a foreign correspondent for CNN, Nairobi bureau chief."

" 'Only doing my job,' you said to Ken. That's what I meant. I didn't think you were being fair, digging at him like that. So is that your job?"

"If you saw me when I'm in a mood to be unfair, then you'd know I was being anything but." Phyllis contemplated herself in the mirror, turning her head one side to the other. With a tissue she carefully wiped off the excess cream from her forehead, her nose, the arrowhead of her chin. "Varnish removal, that's my job," she said, facing Quinette. "People put a high gloss on things, layers of it. I rub it off, get down to the bare wood, because nothing is ever what it appears to be, and nobody is what they make themselves out to be."

"Wait a minute. Are you saying you think Ken . . ."

"Nah. Your Ken . . ."

"He's not mine," Quinette interrupted. "What did you suppose, that I'm fucking him?"

Phyllis drew back, in a burlesque of shock. "Doesn't sound like language from a good Christian girl."

"I wasn't always."

"Bad girl gone good? Listen, don't be so damned defensive. That's the last thing I'd think, you and him in the sack. I was going to say that he strikes me as straight and earnest as they come. A true believer in what he's doing, and maybe that plays into the agendas of some of the people he deals with."

"He doesn't seem like the kind of guy people could take advantage of. Seems pretty smart to me."

"He is, but you know how it is with true believers."

"No. How is it?"

"Their belief gets in the way of their brains."

"If you believe in something, then you're stupid?" A sudden wind blew through Quinette, and it wasn't the wind of the Holy Spirit but the Enemy's wind, rousing her to anger. Realizing that she was being tested, she silently beseeched God to help her contain her temper and to feel, if not a little Christian love for this harsh woman, then at least a little Christian forbearance.

"Not stupid, no—" Phyllis began.

"Madame."

It was Matthew, looking sullen as he held a calabash of hot water and two tea bags. He dropped the bags into two cups the women had retrieved from their bags, then filled the cups from the calabash.

"*Asante sana, shukran,* and thank you," Phyllis said.

Matthew turned on his heel and went back to his comrades. The smoke from their campfire rose in a pale gray pillar that leaned to cross a band of sunlight, shooting almost horizontally over the tukul's roof. Phyllis picked up where she'd left off.

"Not stupid. Belief is a virus, and once it gets into you, its first order of business is to preserve itself, and the way it preserves itself is to keep you from having any doubts, and the way it keeps you from doubting is to blind you to the way things really are. Evidence contrary to the belief can be staring you straight in the face, and you won't see it. No, not stupid. True believers just don't see things the way they are, because if they did, they wouldn't be true believers anymore."

The Lord answered if you called on Him with an honest and contrite heart. Belief a virus, faith a disease that blinded you? Awful words, yet Quinette was able to listen to them without the least bit of anger.

"So you don't believe in anything, not even in God?" she asked, not completely sure she wanted to hear the answer. She'd known sinful people in her trailer trash period, but she'd never met a real atheist before, at least not an atheist willing to admit he was one.

"Read much of Ernest Hemingway?"

The reporter raised one knee and clasped her hands around it. From up in the trees, where the campfire smoke split into delicate tendrils, a bird sang a soft, plaintive note, while off in the distance somewhere cowbells rang.

"In high school," Quinette said. "We read a couple of his short stories."

"He once said that a writer needs a built-in, shock-proof bullshit detector. That goes double for a news correspondent, triple for a news correspondent working in Africa. I guess I believe in that. In skepticism. When you're in the varnish-removal business, that's the active ingredient. My apologies if that offends you, but you asked."

"No offense taken. I think I feel sorry for you, and I'm going to pray for you," Quinette said with brittle calm.

"Make it from the Old Testament. I'm Jewish."

She didn't know any Old Testament prayers. *How did you pray for a Jew anyway?* she asked herself, taking her Bible from her rucksack. She walked to the edge of the compound, and there, with the wide yellow plain stretched out before her, she opened her Bible. It was small, designed for travelers, and difficult to read in low light. Straining, her eyes fell on Psalm 115: "Wherefore should the heathen say, Where now is their God? But our God is in the heavens.... Their idols are silver and gold, the work of men's hands." The answer was right there—her hand must have been guided to it. Phyllis was a kind of idol-worshipper, and her idol was her skepticism. Quinette closed the book and asked God to show Phyllis the falseness of her beliefs, prayed for help in learning to love Phyllis the sinner while hating her sin. Oh, she could feel the love beginning to course through her, as if she'd been transfused with warm honey. The wonderful thing about being saved was that it made you feel better about other people because it made you feel better about yourself. You couldn't love your neighbor if you didn't love yourself first, the way God loved you, without condition. That was how a father was supposed to love his children. Her own father had loved her like that, even when she was bad, and how she missed his all-forgiving embraces and the way he would call her "Quinny" while holding her in his lap as he drove the John Deere through the hayfield, the mower tossing golden dust into the air and the rows of chopped grass waiting to be bundled into the cylindrical bales that looked so lovely, like huge butternut cakes, in the autumn meadows.

The liquid light of the dying sun poured that same color across the savannah. And was that another reason she felt at home here? Dinka boys in tattered robes tied over one shoulder were herding cattle toward a byre, the cattle with horns shaped like crescent moons and the boys striding so effortlessly on their wiry legs, they seemed to float over the plain. She watched them tie the calves to tethering pegs and start a fire, its smoke turning a faint peach in the sunset. Some of the boys were singing, a few others laughed while the cows bellowed for their bound calves and the calves lowed for their mothers and the bells on the oxen chimed. As the red sun vanished, the birds in the tree above her began to chorus, as if to celebrate dusk's commutation of the sun's sentence. From somewhere back in the town, a drum call sounded, slow and rhythmic, like the heartbeat of a man asleep, and birdsong and man-song, laughter, drum, bell, bleat, and bellow merged into a whole as harmonious as a symphony: Africa's natural orchestra, and it was playing just for her.

Twilight was a brief intermission between day and night. Just as Ken had said, it was light and then it was dark. The stars began to show themselves, sharp and clear in the moonless sky. She searched for the Southern Cross, which she'd read about in the guidebook she'd bought in Nairobi, and found it: not so much a cross as a diamond. The Dipper was there, but much closer to the horizon than it was at home. The birds had fallen silent, the cattle had settled down. Soon crickets filled the silence, so many chirping at once that they made a single high-pitched cry, like locusts in late summer. Frogs croaked in the green corridors along the stream forming the town's northern border. They also made one unbroken chorus, the croak of each individual lost in the din of countless throbbing throats. Quinette felt the racket of insect and amphibian more than she heard it; it seemed to penetrate her skin and vibrate inside her, becoming one with the rush of blood through her veins; then in an instant her flesh became like the smoke from the herdsmen's fire, all sense of herself as a separate being evaporating as her soul, set free, dissolved into an ecstatic union with frog song and cricket screech and the vast dark plain lying under the stars of an alien hemisphere. It was like nothing she'd ever experienced before, and when she came back to herself just seconds later (though she felt as though she'd been gone for hours), she tried to make sense of it. There was no drug or drink on earth that could have produced such a sensation, such an intense joy. Starting back toward her tukul, her head as buoyant as a balloon, her limbs tingling, she remembered something Pastor Tom had read to her in one of the counseling sessions she attended when she joined his church. *That is happiness; to be dissolved into something complete and great.* That was the transcendent emotion she'd sought but hadn't found in her spiritual rebirth. She'd discovered it here. More than ever she wished she could remain. In this immense, unknown country she could begin her life anew.

IN THE MORNING, with the smells of woodsmoke and dung fires lingering in the air, a small army mustered to escort the redemption team to where the slaves had been brought during the night. Two dozen soldiers, a few armed only with spears, lined up in front of the bungalow. Shellacked in dried sweat and dirt, Quinette felt in need of a shower and also a few more hours' sleep. Phyllis's snoring and pungent bean farts had kept her awake till past midnight. She'd tried to read herself to sleep with a Christian romance novel, holding a penlight between her teeth. When that didn't work, she got her diary, propped it against her upraised legs, and attempted to describe her out-of-body experience, but it was impossible to find the words. Finally, a wave of exhaustion washed her into unconsciousness, but soft thuds above her head woke her up. She flicked on the light and saw spiders and beetles dropping out of the thatch ceiling onto her mosquito net, crawling down the sides with a scratching of busy legs. A bat darted through the flashlight's beam, quick as an apparition. She lay wide-eyed and cringing until dawn. Two cups of freeze-dried coffee barely cleared her head, but now the scented air and the soldiers standing at attention and the early light glinting off rifle barrels and spear points quickened her senses.

The walk was a short one down a footpath through the dun grass, past a dried-up water hole ringed by palm trees, a background against which the spear-carrying soldiers made a picturesque sight—*click.* They came to a small homestead, with a beehive hut where two Arabs waited, sitting on bamboo chairs—the same two she'd seen in the marketplace yesterday, the one bearded, the other clean-shaven. The retrievers. We are the redeemers, they are the retrievers. She heard Ken call the one with the beard by name, Bashir, but the other remained anonymous. They'd put on their Sunday best for the occasion—fresh robes and turbans, leather shoes instead of sandals, rings on their fingers, dressy watches on their wrists. The soldiers fanned out to encircle the homestead and an enormous mahogany tree nearby. It cast its branches out for fifty feet in all directions, the lower branches hanging almost to the ground to form a tent of leaves. The Arabs stood and greeted Ken and Jim and Manute. There was a bit of conversation, then the retrievers led everyone to the tree; the one called Bashir parted the branches and held them aside. Ducking her head,

Quinette followed Jim into the shaded circle, and there the slaves huddled in the cool red dust, faces blending with the shadows so that all she saw at first were four hundred eyes, shining white and lifeless, like fragments of clamshells set in lumps of mud. They were all women and kids and teenagers, barefoot, dressed in rags, in shorts, in what looked like feed sacks with armholes. Her vision adjusting to the dimness, she saw a naked chest ridged with scars, and the absence of pattern told her that they were not the decorative marks with which some Dinka ornamented their bodies. No one spoke, even the babies were silent, lying limp in their mothers' laps, hair reddened and tiny bellies bloated from malnutrition. The only sound was the hum of flies, the only movement the flutter of bony hands brushing the flies away, and one adolescent boy did not have a hand, swatting with the puckered stump of his wrist. Another, sitting with his legs spread-eagled and a crude crutch at his side, was missing a foot.

Jean and Mike began a head count. Quinette volunteered to help, because she wanted to do more than gawk at these wretched souls as if they were a sideshow attraction.

"Okay, take the bunch on the right, we'll take the ones on the left," Mike said. "Count 'em twice to make sure."

Quinette moved in closer, her finger wagging left to right, right to left. *These are people, these are human beings,* she said to herself, for the slaves sat so passively, so devoid of emotion that she felt as if she were making an inventory of inanimate objects. Swaddled in unlaundered clothes, bodies that hadn't known soap and water for weeks or months threw off a dense, sour, salty stench. People, human beings who'd been whipped, who'd had a hand or a foot lopped off because they tried to escape. Making her second count, she noticed a small, deep scar gouged into many faces, beneath the left eye. Wondering what the marks signified, she lowered her gaze, squinting at an emaciated woman with a stained blue scarf on her head. She tried not to make her curiosity obvious, but the woman noticed and hissed. Quinette looked away, a little ashamed. The woman hissed again, pointed at the scar, and stabbed the air with a fist. *Hssss.*

"She's trying to tell you that she was branded," Jean said matter-of-factly. Jean was a nurse back in Canada, a pert woman with curly chestnut hair and a bowed mouth. "That's what most of the owners do, brand them with the same brands they use on their cattle. It's always under the left eye. If you look closely, you'll see the brands are different. That way each owner knows who belongs to who. How many?"

"Fifty-eight."

Quinette backed away, trying to imagine what that felt like. A branding iron in your face. She wasn't ready for this.

"Takes some getting used to," said Jean, giving her a maternal pat on the arm. "But you don't ever want to get *too* used to it."

She and Mike had counted a hundred and fifty-one, so that made two hundred and nine all together. The Arabs had "delivered the merchandise," as Mike indelicately phrased it. He was a paramedic, with a wrestler's torso and a streetwise toughness about him, and Quinette wondered if his wife was thinking of him when she warned about getting "too used to it."

Now it was time to pay the retrievers. Ken passed the bricks of Sudanese pounds to the Arabs, who licked their thumbs and counted, slowly, carefully. When Phyllis's crew moved in for a close-up, they stopped, the clean-shaven one ducking behind a pair of windowpane sunglasses, Bashir masking himself with a length of his turban. Mike, who was standing just behind them, lit a cigarette. Both men flinched and whirled around, wadded bills falling from their laps.

"Jumpy as long-tailed cats in a room full of rocking chairs, that's what my dad would've said," Quinette murmured to Ken. "What's the matter with them?"

Ken laughed his cold, enigmatic laugh and said they must have mistaken the click of Mike's lighter for the cocking of a pistol.

"They're worried we're going to rip them off?"

"No. They're playing a dicey game. If the government found out they're dealing with us, they'd be shot or thrown into a ghost house. That's what they call the jails in Khartoum, and for damned good reason."

Phyllis jumped in, practically hitting Ken in the teeth with a thrust of her microphone. She looked rough and disheveled, swollen half-moons beneath her eyes.

"It's a dicey game that pays pretty well, isn't it?"

A note of distaste was folded into the question, and for once Quinette found herself sharing the reporter's sentiments. The gold rings, the watches, the sheen of greed on the retrievers' lips as they counted the money and stuffed it into canvas sacks stirred feelings of shame and taint, as if she were watching something she was not supposed to see. She wished this part would end; it had the trappings of a drug deal.

"If I understand the economics right, your retrievers pay around fifteen bucks a head, and you pay them more than three times that," Phyllis went on. "Pretty hefty markup."

"They take big risks, rounding up these people, so I have to pay them a risk premium."

"That's what you call it?"

"You've got ideas for a better word, put it in the suggestion box. Look, I don't particularly like these guys. They're a necessary evil, and maybe not an evil. The Dinka respect them. Without them—"

"Right, right," Phyllis said impatiently. "But my information is that if this slave trade were left to—to—ah . . . market forces, it would just disappear. Goes like this. The Arabs who own them have to feed them, house them somewhere. It's trouble and expense. And if the owners want to sell them back to their families or to some other Arabs, what they would get out of the deal is a few bucks at most, a couple of goats, a cow. Not worth the trouble of capturing them in the first place."

"The question, Phyllis? Oh, hell, you don't have to ask it. You've talked to the UN people in Kenya, right? They don't like what we're doing any more than Khartoum does. Just leave the slave trade alone, and it'll go away—that's the UN party line. By buying freedom for these people, are we promoting the trade instead of ending it? That's the question?"

"It's the UN's criticism. What's your response?"

He turned on her, a quick snap of his head, and snatched the mike from out of her spindly fingers and held it close to his mouth, like he was about to sing a tune.

"Bullshit!" He handed the mike back to her. "See if that gets on the air."

"Think you could explain your response?"

"I already told you," he said, a weariness in his anger. "This is politics. Economics has nothing to do with it. You're making me sorry I asked you along."

"I'm a newswoman," Phyllis flashed out. "You want a PR agency, hire one."

"I'm tempted to leave you. A few weeks out here might do you some good. You might learn something."

Jim stepped up and, resting his hand on Ken's shoulder, said, "Easy now, my friend. You're on candid camera."

Ken turned aside.

"You start early in the varnish-removal business," Quinette whispered to Phyllis. Looking at her blowsy hair and baggy eyes, and having listened to her snores and intestinal rumblings half the night, she didn't find the woman quite as intimidating as before.

"Ya, Eismont. *Tiyib*," Bashir said, rising with brown hand extended.

She gathered that *tiyib* meant that everything was okay. Ken shook hands and said thank you in Arabic—*shukran*. The Arabs, each holding a sack of money, went down the footpath, their white-clad figures growing smaller in the oceanic expanse of grass and trees.

"Do they just walk home, across all that, with all that money on them?" Quinette said, thinking out loud.

"Not something you'd try in L.A. or New York, is it?" Jim remarked with a shrug. He studied his feet, mopped his forehead with his fingers. "I don't like it either, this end of it."

"OUR HEARTS ARE heavy with your sufferings." Ken stood making a speech before the assembled slaves, pausing between phrases to let Manute translate, his flat American voice and Manute's sonorous bass alternating with chantlike rhythm. "Many people who care about what you have endured. . . . Donations from people in America. . . . I am happy to tell you that you are now free."

The flies hummed, leaves rustled in a breeze, the people sat in a slack-jawed, dull-eyed silence. Quinette's hands rested on the camera, loaded with a fresh roll for the photographs that she hoped would match those already printed in her imagination—the emancipated captives singing and dancing, embracing their liberators. Thinking ahead, she saw the pictures projected on a screen whose light reflected the rapt faces of worshippers filling every seat in Family Evangelical; she saw herself at the podium, describing the scene and her own exalted emotions as grateful arms encircled her. It would be the high point of her presentation. Everyone who'd worked so hard would be thrilled to see images of the happiness and thanksgiving their efforts had brought. But what could she tell them now? That the people just sat and stared when they heard they were free? She didn't feel cheated this time; irritated, rather. Ken's delivery was all wrong. The people knew they were free, but they didn't feel it because they didn't hear any passion in Ken's voice. The man who'd testified before Congress and the Human Rights Commission with such conviction sounded as if he were reciting a speech he'd given once too often.

Jim did a little better; in the cadences of a radio evangelist he told the story of Jesus, sowing the seeds he hoped would sprout into a whole new crop of souls. People had given money, he said, but in the end it was Christ's love that had broken their chains. Still, the crowd barely stirred. Maybe they already knew the story of Jesus. When Jim was finished, he asked Quinette if she would like to add a few words.

"Wha—what should I say?"

"Whatever comes to mind. Maybe you could tell them about the kids."

She hesitated, a mild terror streaking through her. Nothing whatsoever came to mind; then she recalled Pastor Tom's sermon that one Sunday and tugged her fanny pack around to her front, unzipped it, and pulled her travel Bible from between the bug spray bottle and the squashed roll of toilet paper.

"I want to read you something from one of our prophets. He told about the coming of Jesus, the Messiah."

She turned to Isaiah, chapter 61, and began, " 'The Spirit of the Lord is upon me,' " and waited for Manute. Coming from him, Isaiah sounded more like the word of God, even in Dinka; his deep and solemn voice could make a recipe like the word of God. " 'He sent me to bind up the broken-hearted' "—pause—" 'to proclaim liberty to the captives' "—pause—" 'and the opening of the prison to them that are bound.' " She was determined to coax a response from her listeners and repeated that last ringing verse. Pastor Tom did that sometimes, recited a biblical phrase three, even four times over, stressing different words with each repetition, building a rhythm that lifted people out of their seats to cry out, "Praise Jesus! Praise His name!"

When Manute was finished, she raised the Bible up over her head—one of Pastor Tom's patent gestures. "Praise God. Praise Him for sending His only son, Jesus Christ, to save us all." Two hundred pairs of eyes looked up at the book. When she lowered it, they fastened on her, clinging with an almost tactile pressure that evaporated her terror and summoned out of hiding the confident girl who years ago stood to recite and didn't beg or call for her classmates' attention but seized it effortlessly. "Jesus Christ proclaims your liberty"—pause—"He has opened your prison." She told them that the river of Christ's abiding love had flowed into the hearts of schoolchildren on the other side of the world; it made them care about the sufferings of people they had never seen, moved them to bring those sufferings to an end. She didn't have to search for the words or think about them, but heard them with her inner ear and then uttered them, as though she were reading from a teleprompter scrolling in her brain. A rapture filled her. She felt powerful and commanding and absolutely sure that every word was right.

"That will never happen to you again." She pointed at an adolescent boy with scars balled up into an ugly knot on one shoulder; and as Manute converted her declaration into Dinka, she waded into the crowd without a second's forethought, lifted the boy by the arm, and led him to the front so all could see. Somehow she knew that this too was right, exactly the right move to make. "This will never happen to any of you again"—pause—

"That's what it means to be free." Taking a step forward, she picked up the woman in the blue scarf, the one who had hissed, and turned her around to face the assemblage. "And this will never happen to any of you, ever again." She laid her finger on the mark beneath the woman's eye. "You will never be beaten, ever again. You will never be branded, ever again. You will never be made to tend the Arabs' cattle, ever again." She was really cooking now, an electric current surging through her and out of her, seeming to sweep over her audience. "You women will never be raped, ever again. You boys will not have your hands and feet cut off, ever again." Manute, struggling to keep pace with her outpouring, seemed to catch her fervor and threw up his arms with the last repetitions of "ever again."

"You are free!" Quinette cried out, and spread her own arms wide.

Someone made a soft clicking noise. It was echoed by another, and another, and in a moment, every tongue was making it so that it became like the crickets and frogs she'd heard last night, a single sheet of sound.

"The Dinka way of saying they like what they have heard," Manute explained, grinning from beneath the bill of his baseball cap.

Applause! And it sounded to her ears like a standing ovation. A woman began to sing; high clear notes rose out of the chorus of clicks. The other women answered in unison, and the boys took up a contrapuntal melody and beat their hands against their thighs, all swaying to the rhythm. It was a jubilant song but not a lively one, with an undertone of sorrow, and it was haunting and lovely, that slow beat, that smooth, rich flow of voices, there under the mahogany tree. Quinette never imagined she could touch people as she just had, breaking the seal to the rejoicing she'd known was in them, setting it free.

"What is it you do for a living?" Jim asked, and his voice had the same effect as an alarm clock.

"The Gap. Salesperson."

She almost grimaced, it sounded so banal.

"Missed your calling."

Ten minutes ago she would have feasted on the compliment, but it seemed meager fare after the banquet of approval laid out for her by all those people. Yet it wasn't their approval that satisfied her most, but her ability to bring them some measure of joy. Looking at the faces before her, listening to their song, she felt the craftsman's gratification, beholding his creation; and that was a pleasure she'd never experienced in her daily life, retailing commodities she'd had no hand in making.

*   *   *

My name is Aluet Akuoc Wiere. I am twenty-five years old. I was captured four years ago. The Arabs attacked our village in the early morning—

"Manute, her village," Ken interrupted. He was sitting with his laptop in the chair previously occupied by Bashir. It and the other chair, in which the people being interviewed sat, had been moved under the tree. The sun was well up now, so white it looked like a gigantic light fixture.

"The village of Aramwer," Manute said, and spelled it, Ken typing with sparse brown eyebrows knit, lips pursed. He was a hunt-and-pecker, and his fingers were turning a tedious process into a torturous one.

On every mission Ken collected stories from the former slaves, for inclusion in the reports he sent to the WorldWide Christian Union's board of advisers and the Human Rights Commission. He needed specifics—the names of the villages the people came from and of the places they were brought to, the names of their captors and the masters to whom they were sold, the dates when they were captured and details about the raids and how their masters treated them. *An Oral History of a Crime Against Humanity,* that was what Ken called it. Quinette's job was to hold a microphone between Manute and whoever was being interviewed, so it could pick up both voices, and to keep an eye on the battery light and flip the cassettes in Ken's tape recorder, a big old-fashioned thing gloved in vinyl.

They came on horseback, many, many of them . . . The woman called Aluet Akuoc resumed her tale. With her oblong face and narrow mouth, the upper lip curled to perpetually bare two front teeth, Aluet was not as pretty as some of the other women. She wore a shapeless striped shift, pulled down over one shoulder so her baby, a boy of perhaps two, could suckle her breast. . . .

Some wore white jelibiyas. Some in light brown uniforms. Some rode two on a horse. One to guide the horse, one to shoot. They shot the men and the old people.

Ken raised a hand, asking Manute to give him time to catch up.

"I think I could do that a lot faster," Quinette ventured.

Ken looked at her.

"I took a typing and dictation course in high school," she said, and thought she sounded as if she were applying for a job.

"No end to your talents, is there?"

Another of his hard-to-read remarks. Something he just tossed off, or did he think she was being presumptuous? Whatever, he got up and took over on the tape recorder. She sat in his place, settling the keyboard on her lap, tilting the screen forward a little, to keep the light that speared through the branches from bleaching the contrast. Unlike the tape recorder, the computer was brand-new, state of the art, and a long cable snaked from the DC outlet and across the scalloped circle of tree shade to a small, collapsible solar panel.

My father was running away. He didn't go far. The Arabs were on horse-back. They shot my father. They shot my husband. His name was Kuel. He tried to defend us, but he had only his shield and fighting stick. The Arabs' bullets went through his shield. I saw him shot down in front of me. Every-one started running, but the Arabs shot anyone who ran, so I stopped run-ning. They caught me and tied me to a long rope with twenty other women. I was separated from my little daughter. I have not seen her since.

Aluet's was the fifth—or was it the sixth?—story Quinette had heard, and although Ken chose his subjects at random, each story seemed worse than the one before, a chapter in a narrative building toward some unbearable climax of atrocity.

They made a zariba in the forest and put us in it. It was a bad night for all the women. Three men raped me. I was then three months pregnant. That night I had a miscarriage. We had to walk seven days, seven nights to the Jur river. A woman and a child died on this journey of thirst. We rested at the Jur and then walked three days more to the river Kir. There I was given to a man called Abdullai. I worked for him and his wife, Nyangok. My job was to grind sorghum. I did this from morning till night for no pay. At first they treated me harshly. Abdullai put a branding iron to my face so I could be identified if I ran away. Nyangok beat me with a bamboo stick if I did not grind the sorghum fast enough to suit her. Sometimes she beat me for no reason and called me jengei.

"That means 'nigger' in Sudanese Arabic," Ken interjected dispassion-ately. "Put that in parentheses, Quinette. Put 'nigger' in parentheses."

The soft tap of the keys. (Nigger.)

But I was lucky. Nyangok's mother was Dinka and lived with Nyangok and Abdullai. She told Nyangok to stop beating me and calling me jengei. "Would you call me, your own mother, jengei also?" was what she said to Nyangok, and the beatings stopped. Things were not so bad after that, except when Abdullai's brother, Iskander, came to the house. He would come to the house when no one was there and force me to have relations with him. That's how I got pregnant and gave birth to Hussein.

Quinette looked up from the screen and saw Aluet stroke Hussein's head.

Then the Arab called Bashir came to Abdullai's house. They had a long talk and reached an agreement. I was sold to Bashir for some money and Bashir brought me here. I hope I will find my daughter. She will be nine years old now.

Ken thanked her, and Aluet rose and walked over to the homestead to stand with the others. They were lined up behind Manute's Land Rover, parked beside the tukul with its rear doors open and a row of jerry cans inside. Soldiers were pouring water out of the cans into tin cups and giving each person a drink. While they stood waiting, Jean listened to their heartbeats with a stethoscope and Mike took their pulses and temperatures and made notes on a clipboard. The people then filed off to where more soldiers were cooking porridge over an open fire. The soldiers ladled the porridge out of a big cast-iron pot into wooden bowls, and the liberated slaves found whatever shade they could and sat down to eat with wooden spoons that looked like ice cream scoops. Phyllis's cameramen were shooting the scene. They had filmed the first three people Ken interviewed but seemed to get bored with the repetitious accounts of rape and murder and forced labor and went off to get some videotape of the slaves' picnic.

A boy sat down with his arms resting on the bamboo arms of the chair. Black on light brown. Quinette recognized him.

My name is Atem Amet. I am sixteen. I was captured in the same raid as my cousin, Aluet Akuoc Wiere. I was given to a man named Osman Mekki. He had many slaves, working in his fields and cattle camps. One day, a year after I was captured, I lost one of his best bulls. Osman was very angry. He said that if I didn't bring the bull back, he would cut off my hand. I didn't know where the bull was and couldn't bring it back. Because of my failure, Osman tied me down and cut off my hand with a panga.

So that was how it happened. Not for trying to escape but for losing a bull. Quinette was stunned that the boy described his amputation as if it were not out of the ordinary. All these people talked about their torments that way, and their tales expanded her conception of what human beings were capable of, in the way of both enduring cruelty and inflicting it. The joy she'd felt only a while ago fled her heart, pushed out by pity, and the pity fertilized an egg of rage.

A woman thirty-three years old. *Then my master, Hamad, said I had to become Muslim. A woman came to his house. She told me that I had to have my genitals cut to be a proper Muslim woman. I resisted. Other women were called to hold me down. The woman gave me an injection and then cut me with a scissors. It didn't hurt at first, but after a while, it became very painful.*

Quinette shuddered, and the little egg grew, its cells swiftly dividing to form fetal arms and legs, a froglike head, slitty little eyes, rudimentary ears.

A twelve-year-old boy.

Everyone from our camp who wasn't killed was tied to a long rope. I saw the Arabs kill four older boys who tried to flee. They tied them together and chopped their heads off with pangas. The Arabs said we would be killed in the same way if we tried to escape.

A woman of fifty-five.

The Arabs raped me over and over. It was too much for me. I am an old woman, and it was so long since I thought of sexual relations with a man. It was too much. I fainted.

The thing inside Quinette had a heartbeat now.

Ayuang Bol, Malang Agok, Ahol Akol Teng, Nyanut Ngor Mayar thirty years old twelve years old twenty-three fifteen eighteen twenty

the Arabs stole all our cattle and goats carried looted oil on my head for eight days they came on horseback and on foot khaki uniforms white jelibiyas shouting Allahu akhbar

that means God is great in Arabic, Quinette, put it in parentheses

a twelve-year-old girl raped beside me that night her screams more than I could bear Muhammad beat me with a stick and broke my nose we were brought to a camp and made to study the Koran and those who were slow in learning were denied food and water five girls tied to horses I slept outside with the cattle my bed was cattle dung every night for three years.

It turned over and kicked. It grew and grew, leaving no room for any other emotion.

A twenty-six-year-old woman, Atem Deng.

And because I would not allow my genitals to be cut, Ahmed's wife called me jengei and filthy infidel. I was very angry and struck her. She beat me with a horsewhip and told Ahmed when he came home that I had struck her. Ahmed said he would punish me in a special way. That night, he took me to a zariba

(That's a pen made of thornbushes, put it in parentheses, Quinette)

and stripped me naked and held me down with my face in the dirt. He told me he would show me what happened to women without the genitals of a good Muslim woman. And he did that thing to me and it was very painful.

Atem Deng fell silent. Ken asked if she had anything more to say. She did, and each word was as sharp and distinct as the crack of a bullet, the sense so clear that Manute's translation was almost unnecessary.

I wish I was a man so I could carry a rifle. I would find Ahmed and kill him. I would kill his wife and all his children. I would massacre them all.

There was a kind of beauty, an appealing purity in the woman's longing for retribution. It was even refreshing, after listening to the others recite the outrages they'd suffered with such forbearance. Quinette typed,

I would massacre them all,

and the crisp black letters seemed to leap from the glowing screen and enter her, feeling like a midwife's hands, drawing out her own incubated rage. The infant's red eyes were open, and through them she saw herself standing alongside Atem Deng, cutting down the man called Ahmed and his wife, and the man called Abdullai, and Ibrahim and Iskander and all the nameless raiders who had thundered into the lives of these violated people, who could never be truly free because they would be forever chained to the memories of what had been done to them. The fantasy had the terrifying clarity of a hallucination, and she blinked and shook her head as if to physically eject it from her mind.

"Getting tired?" Ken asked.

"Are there any more?"

"Two, maybe three. I try to get twenty to twenty-five each time out."

She stood and set the laptop down on the chair. "You'd better finish up, then."

"Two or three, then we're done."

"You finish up."

She started to walk off, toward the homestead. Maybe she could help out there, serve the porridge, write down temperatures and pulse rates for Mike.

"Quinette."

"You finish up. I really don't like feeling the way I do now."

"Like what?"

"Like I could do what she wants to."

Ken studied her for a moment. "That's natural. You'd have to be made of stone not to feel angry. First time I did this, I thought, 'They must be making this stuff up.' But they're not. Too much of a pattern."

"Jean told me it takes some getting used to but that you don't want to get too used to it."

"She's right. It's a trick, though."

"I'll try to get the hang of it."

Mike and Jean didn't need her help; nor did the soldiers at the outdoor soup kitchen. Matthew was among them, and he offered her a bowl of the porridge.

"They need it more than I do," Quinette said. "Your sister?"

"There she is. Amin Madit."

He gestured at a handsome bare-breasted girl of eighteen or nineteen, wearing necklaces of blue beads and shells and brass bangles on her wrists. A pile of cold ashes from the cooking fire lay at her feet, and she sat polishing her teeth with a finger dipped in the ashes while an older woman shaved her head with a razor, sculpting a skullcap of hair at the crown.

"I brought those pretty things for her to wear, and now her hair is being cut and she will look like a fine Dinka girl when I bring her home."

Amin Madit would never tell her family about whatever defilement she'd undergone in captivity. Quinette was certain of that, so she was relieved that the girl had not been among those interviewed; it would have been too awful to know her secrets and have to keep them from her brother.

"She's very beautiful. I'm happy you found her."

Matthew pushed the bowl toward her.

"Please eat. It's made from doura," he said, as if doura were a rare delight, like caviar.

The porridge had the color and texture of raw dough, but she took it anyway and went off by herself, sitting in the one shred of shade that had not been appropriated. One spoonful was all she could take, not because she disliked the taste—a little like grits without the butter—but because it seemed wrong to eat in the company of people who probably hadn't had a decent meal in months. Quinette felt wrong just being here, a woman whose flesh was ignorant of rape and the lash and the circumciser's blade. How stupid she'd been to think she had touched these people with her impromptu sermon, that her words had given breath to their stifled happiness. The chasm between her and them was wider than the one between America and Africa, between black and white; they had suffered greatly, she had not. It troubled her to feel so separated from them, the women most of all. She stared at the thornbush beside her, barbed with spikes as long as her thumb. It beckoned her to throw herself into its bristling arms, to make herself bleed and hurt and bind herself to the Dinka women in a sisterhood of pain.

Fear of the very pain she desired restrained her; fear and the knowledge that it would be sinful. And what about her anger, that little monster she'd spawned minutes ago? Ken said it was natural, but was it? And if it was, so what? All sin was natural. Quinette's thoughts now turned to the state of her own soul, a subject that always commanded her attention. Pastor Tom had counseled her that not all anger was sinful. There was righteous wrath, like the Lord's when He cast the moneychangers out of the temple, and the ire inspired by the Devil, like the kind that had come over her when she'd thrown a rock at the auctioneer. So what was this that had caused her to see herself, so clearly, as an avenging angel? Righteous wrath or the devil's ire? The Lord said that if you commit adultery in your heart, then you've committed adultery period. She couldn't recall if He'd said anything about committing murder in your heart.

She watched Ken unplug the laptop and fold up the solar panel. Lugging both, he came over and sat next to her.

"Feeling any better?"

"I guess."

"It hits me sometimes. Like this is an evil that just screams to be crushed." He scuffed the dirt and was silent for a time. Then in his abrupt way he said he was considering creating a new job, because managing his program from his headquarters in Geneva was getting to be difficult. He could use a representative on the scene.

"It would be a job with more than one hat," he went on. "Based in Loki. Someone with computer skills, because I want to build a complete database of liberated captives. Then there would be coordinating with people like Manute to set up dates and places for redemptions, and making sure aircraft are chartered to fly our team in, and as if that wouldn't be enough, I'd want someone to establish relations with the foreign media in Nairobi, you know, to get as much exposure as possible." He scuffed the ground again. "I'm thinking you could be who I'm looking for."

Quinette said nothing.

"Jim and I are impressed by the way you've handled yourself out here. That speech you gave, it was something. You're pretty good on that laptop, you didn't complain once about the heat, the dirt, the flies, and you were fairly poised in front of the camera. So what are your thoughts?"

"I—I have no idea what to think. Or say."

"Responsibilities back home?"

"If you mean a husband, children, no. Not much of a job either. But I—God, I don't know. I mean, I couldn't just pick up right now and—"

He laughed his dry laugh. "It wouldn't be for right now. I have to work out a lot of details first, take a couple of months at least. Are you interested?"

"At the moment, I'm a little . . . stunned?" She paused. That wasn't the right answer, so she seized his hand and shook it.

"Good," he said. "Expect to hear from me after you get back to the States."

The Partnership

FITZHUGH PRODUCED THE needs assessment for John Barrett, who declared it excellent and paid him his five-thousand-dollar fee. A man of moderate habits could have made the sum last a long time in Kenya, but Fitzhugh's inner tyrant regained power and renewed its demands, *I want, I want, I want,* and he rid himself of more than half of it within two months. One of the things he wanted—to see Diana Briggs again—would not have cost him anything in monetary terms; it would, however, strain his emotional resources. She often infiltrated his thoughts, the picture of her in her loose, flowing linen trousers teasing him. Her voice, crisp yet musical, had impressed itself into the grooves of his memory. He considered calling on her but could not think of a plausible excuse and was glad he could not, sensing that if he spent an hour alone with her, his would become a captive soul. This attraction to a woman who was at least sixteen years older baffled and frightened him. Differences in age aside, there was the question of her marital status, and there were the barriers of race and class, which counted for a great deal in Kenya. No rich white woman was going to surrender herself to an unemployed brown-skinned man.

Staring into a future vacant of all prospects except the doorman job his father had offered, which appalled him as much as ever, he visited several soccer clubs, asking if they needed an assistant coach. A few years ago they would have hired the Ambler on the spot; his athletic stardom, however, was now as faded as the newspaper clips in his scrapbook, and he was turned down. Despite his dwindling bank account, he was relieved, no more able to picture himself as a coach than as a hotel doorman. The intensity of his experiences in the Nuba, he realized, had rendered him incapable of adjusting to the routine of a regular job or to anything resembling ordinary life. When Tara's Cessna had picked him and Douglas up at the Zulu One airstrip, he'd been delighted to get out of the bush; now he found himself missing those distant mountains, their hardships, their dangers, the communion with the Nubans he'd felt that night of the dance in Kologi. Above all else, he missed having a sense of purpose and relevance. He was one more jobless, superfluous human being among Nairobi's millions.

Douglas rescued him. The American tracked him down to the flat he was sharing with an old university classmate to tell him that Knight Air Services would soon be in business. Douglas had an airplane, a Gulfstream One-C, under lease with an option to buy, and had hired an out-of-work pilot as his first officer, an Australian named Tony Bollichek. Barrett's report on the situation in the Nuba mountains had been favorably received by the board of International People's Aid. The first shipments would be arriving within a month, and Barrett had contracted Knight Air to be IPA's exclusive carrier.

"I think you should throw in with us," Douglas announced. "You'll be our operations manager."

Fitzhugh protested that he knew nothing about managing airline operations. Douglas dismissed his reservations with an airy, "There's nothing to it."

Two weeks later they took off for Loki from Wilson Field with office furniture, a high-frequency radio, a satellite phone, a Cretaceous-era desktop, a generator, and two boxes of T-shirts and baseball caps in the Gulfstream's cargo bay. The shirts and hats, in Knight Air's colors of green and white, with the company logo affixed—a lance-wielding knight astride an airplane—were to be worn by present and future employees. The G1C also had been repainted, a bold green stripe streaking down the center of the fuselage, the company's name above it, the flying knight emblazoned on the nose. "When she sees this plane, Tara Whitcomb is going to realize that she's got competition," Douglas proclaimed as Nairobi's skyscrapers fell below.

Barrett had a lorry waiting for them at the airfield. They unloaded the furniture and moved into Knight Air's new office, a bungalow in a compound that some fan of classic American rock had named Hotel California. There was nothing of California in its five dusty acres. It resembled an army camp wed to an African village: tukuls, mud-brick cottages, green wall tents pitched on concrete slabs under makuti-roofed shelters. It was headquarters for International People's Aid and several other agencies that operated independently of the UN. Fitzhugh's first task as operations manager was to find a secretary and a flight mechanic; until he did, he would do the clerical work and Tony Bollichek, who had been to aircraft mechanics school, would be in charge of maintaining the plane.

The presence of a competitor did not trouble Tara. She even seemed to welcome it, generously allowing Fitzhugh to lean on her manager, a white

Kenyan named Pamela Smyth, to teach him about flight operations. There was considerably more than nothing to it.

Another two weeks passed before IPA's first shipment was ready: sheet-metal roofing for Manfred's hospital, drums of drinking water, boxes of salt, all manner of medical supplies. Some ten tons altogether. As the G1C could carry only four tons, three trips, at eight thousand dollars per flight, would be required to deliver it all. "My man, if we can keep this up, we'll gross a hundred grand in our first month," said Douglas, in a way that made the conditional sound more like a prediction. He invited Fitzhugh to come along on the inaugural flight—"a historic occasion," he called it.

Two uneventful hours later they landed at Zulu Two, one of the new airstrips built on a site Douglas and Suleiman had discovered during the trek through the Nuba. A mass of female porters and SPLA guerrillas surged onto the runway. The unloading began, Douglas, Tony, and Fitzhugh pitching the boxes and the roofing panels out the aft cargo door, the porters packing the lighter stuff into baskets, the soldiers lashing the tin panels to the backs of camels. When the offload was finished, Fitzhugh's heart attached itself to the column of people and pack animals, filing off, in radiant dust, across the undulating yellow hills toward the hospital, twenty kilometers away. "Dudes, there it is," Douglas said, jaw cocked, raptor's nose raised, a distance in the gray eyes, as if they beheld something beyond the swaying camels, the women trudging under their laden baskets. "There you see what we're here for."

Inspired by a renewed sense of purpose, Fitzhugh worked hard to convince the other independent agencies to join in the effort. The need in the Nuba was too great to be met by IPA alone. He called on the Irish, the Belgians, and the Dutch and was turned down by all except one: the Friends of the Frontline, a band of evangelical American military veterans whose speciality was ministering to beleaguered Christians in war zones. Along with the usual material aid, they delivered Bibles and schoolbooks. They sent in missionary teams to help local preachers spread the gospel. They made documentaries and distributed them to their membership to raise funds to rebuild churches and schools.

Fitzhugh, a confirmed secularist, was comfortable in the company of worldly clerics like Malachy Delaney, but people of intense religious convictions, whether Christian or Muslim or something else, always made him ill at ease. So it was with the Friends of the Frontline's two representatives in Loki. Garbed in quasi-military outfits—trousers with cargo pockets, shirts with button-down shoulder flaps, starched and pressed as if for an inspection—they were exceedingly polite and soft-spoken and wore an air of disquieting serenity that Fitzhugh had come to recognize as the calm of people absolutely sure they are on the side of the angels. One was a Vietnam veteran, Tim Fancher, a dark-haired man of fifty-odd with a long, grave face; the other, Rob Handy, had served in the Persian Gulf War and had a boxer's physique and clear, steady green eyes that one could imagine squinting through the scope of a sniper's rifle.

To them, Fitzhugh made his appeal. They were interested in what he had to say, particularly in John Barrett's plans to restore St. Andrew's mission. Like Barrett, Fancher had been ordained as a minister of the Evangelical Episcopal Church of Sudan. He mentioned that he and Handy had often discussed establishing a ministry in the Nuba mountains—"an island of Christianity in a sea of Islam" was how he described it. Perhaps Fitzhugh's proposal was a sign that they should stop talking and start doing. They promised to get back to him.

Which they did, more quickly than Fitzhugh had expected. Appearing at Knight Air's office one morning, they announced that they had spoken to Barrett and agreed to work with International People's Aid, and yes, they would be pleased to sign a contract with Knight Air. This inclined Fitzhugh to think that the pair of Christian soldiers weren't such strange fellows after all, and it delighted Douglas. "My man, you've really come through," he said, and offered to make Fitzhugh a junior partner, entitling him to a five percent share of the company's net profits in addition to his salary. Fitzhugh Martin had become something he'd never imagined: an entrepreneur.

Knight Air's business doubled. It could now afford additional employees. Fitzhugh lured a flight mechanic away from the UN, a black-bearded South African named VanRensberg, and hired a Kikuyu woman, Rachel Njiru, as secretary and bookkeeper. But Douglas and Tony were flying five to six missions a week, a schedule that put a strain on them and on the airplane. "What we need," Douglas declared, "is another airplane and the crew to fly it."

WESLEY DARE'S CAMPAIGN to stop Joe Nakima from seizing—stealing—his old Gulfstream One had succeeded, though the price for that triumph was the loss of the plane to a legal limbo. The day after he was visited by the man from the Department of Civil Aviation, Dare hired a lawyer and filed suit against Nakima, alleging fraud. Nakima countersued. The judge hearing the case slapped an injunction on both litigants, prohibiting each from claiming the aircraft until its ownership could be decided. There followed a perfect carnival of delays and postponements, some requested by Dare's attorneys, some by Nakima's.

The day after he filed suit, Dare began a desperate hunt for another airplane so he could fulfill his contract with Laurent Kabila, on the march against Mobuto Sese Seko in the Congo. After two weeks of scouring aviation trade publications and contacting airplane brokers, he ran into Keith Cheswick at the Aero Club in Nairobi. Cheswick, a pilot of fortune, was an old friend; they'd flown together in Sierra Leone for Blackbridge Services, a mercenary outfit that provided security forces for diamond and copper mines, weapons for warlords who wanted to seize the mines, bodyguards for African dictators, and military advisers to rebels trying to overthrow the dictators—a perfect closed loop. Over lunch he told Cheswick about his dilemma. Cheswick, who was still with Blackbridge, replied that maybe they could help each other out, because he was looking to unload one of the firm's aircraft, a Hawker-Siddley 748. She was a bit long in the tooth but in good shape overall. How much? Dare asked. Three hundred thousand U.S. He didn't have that kind of money, but Cheswick said he might be able to come up with an alternative—in the spirit of friendship, eh, old boy?

Three days later he phoned and asked Dare to meet him for dinner at the New Stanley. When Dare arrived, Cheswick handed him a slender sheaf of papers, faxed from Blackbridge's Cape Town headquarters.

"Here's the deal, and it's take it or leave it, Wes. We lease the plane to you for a dollar a month, but you assign your contract to us. We own net profits. At the end of the job, the Hawker's yours. She's your bonus."

"That contract is worth at least seven hundred fifty. So you make a total of twice what it's worth, leavin' me plane rich and money poor. Do I get gas money to fly her out of the Congo? Who picks up the salary for my first officer?"

Cheswick had been an RAF fighter pilot, and he looked like one: a martial gray mustache, thin lips that smiled thinly.

"*You* are going to be *my* first officer," he said. He did some things with his face, trying to give it a warm, affectionate expression. "You can't expect the firm to let an airplane go on trust, can you?"

Dare's glance sidestepped across the dining room. White linen, soft lights, wainscot buffed to a gloss, tourists babbling about their photo safaris to the Masai-Mara. "I'd be tempted to leave the airplane there, take the money and run. You're going to be my adult supervision."

Six months later, after ferrying Kabila and his staff from one jungle redoubt to another, Dare was back in Nairobi, owner of a three-hundred-thousand-dollar airplane with not much more than walking-around money in his pocket. There had been no progress in his lawsuit. The G1, its engines and cockpit windows covered in canvas, sat orphaned in a part of Wilson Field reserved for derelict planes. Looking at it amid those stripped hulks gave Dare an almost physical pain, but he derived a compensatory satisfaction from knowing that he'd kept it out of Nakima's larcenous hands, and he hoped the bastard ground his teeth in frustration every time he saw it, parked out there beyond his grasp.

He dipped into his piggy bank to present the director of civil aviation with her favorite American cookies; she returned the kindness by issuing him a valid air operator's certificate. He then sought to hire out his services but found no takers. One Saturday afternoon, on the advice of a logistician he knew at Catholic Relief Services, he called on a small aid agency he'd never heard of before, International People's Aid. It sounded like a Communist front. It was based in Lokichokio, but the guy in charge lived in Nairobi, out on the Langata road—an intense, talkative little Irishman married to a towering Sudanese. Dare could not picture the pallid, undersize man making love to that statuesque woman, but it must have happened: three brown brats were running noisily around the small stone-walled house when she let Dare in.

Barrett was sitting in a vinyl chair with tape over the rips in its arms. Dare declined the offer of a soft drink and stated his business, but the little man didn't want to talk business. As a breeze passed through the jalousie windows behind him, teasing the fine hair banded above his ears, he made a long, impassioned speech about the plight of the southern Sudanese, the cruelty of the Khartoum government, the obligation of the world's privileged nations to help, but not as the UN was helping, oh no, make no mistake about it, we cannot be neutral, for the southerners were fighting *our* battle against militant Islam, so the hand we lend them must be the hand of an *ally*.

To Dare, this was all bullshit, but his pressing need to help himself opened up reserves of patience he hadn't known were in him. He listened without a peep. Likewise, he suspended his policy of zero tolerance for children, forbearing the brats' shrieks as they ran into and out of the room, paying absolutely no attention to their mother's commands, delivered in a lazy, unconvincing voice, to settle down. A size ten in the ass is what they need, he thought, pretending to be delighted by their rumpus-room antics, which had at least one beneficial effect: They caused Barrett to lose his train of thought, and while he fumbled around for it, Dare was able to get in a word. He made the sales pitch that he now could just about recite in his sleep. With his Hawker-Siddley, he would deliver people, cargo, or both anywhere in Sudan or Somalia for less than anyone else Barrett cared to name. The Irish shrimp replied that his agency was pleased with the company they had under contract, Knight Air. What kind of planes did they fly? Dare asked. They had only one airplane, a Gulfstream One-C.

Dare put on an expression of disbelief and distress. "Have y'all ever considered the possibility that that G2 might have mechanical problems? Or that it might prang up somewheres? What do you do then?"

"We would—"

"Never mind," Dare interrupted. "Listen, a G1C cruises at two-eighty. That's forty knots faster than a Hawker, but the Gulfstream has a capacity of four and a quarter tons. I oughta know, I flew a Gulfstream for years, got one in mothballs right now. So that airplane is gonna make a thousand miles about forty-five minutes faster'n my Hawker. It'll save you a little over twelve hundred bucks. But I want you to think about the difference in cargo capacity. The Hawker carries five and a half tons, round figures. For twelve hundred bucks more, or"—he took a notepad and calculator out of his briefcase, scribble, scribble, press, press—"sixteen percent more money, I'm deliverin' you one and a quarter tons, or *thirty percent* more cargo. Still with me, Mr. Barrett? So let's say, for the sake of argument, y'all need to send twenty-five tons of cargo. The G1C will cost you, round figures again, thirty-four grand. The Hawker does it for twenty-nine thousand five hundred, a total savings of"—scribble, press—"forty-five hundred. Hell, you can't argue with those numbers."

Dare flashed the figure-blackened notepad, thinking, Christ almighty, I sound like some telemarketer, plugging a great new long-distance plan.

"And a wizard with numbers you are, and I'll not be arguin' with them or with you." Dare's pulse rate rose, like a telemarketer when he's closed a sale. "But I will ask you to put 'em all in writing and fax me a proposal, and I'll ring you up soon."

The call came a little over a week later, but it wasn't from Barrett. Dare was lying on the sofabed in his apartment on Milimani Road, reading a month-old copy of *Shotgun News,* when the phone rang. The voice announced a name that sounded kind of British, but it was a distinctly American voice, in which Dare detected southwestern inflections subtler, softer than the steel-guitar *wa-wa* of his own West Texas. Douglas Braithwaite further identified himself as managing director of Knight Air, and Dare asked if that was supposed to mean something to him.

"You were talking to John Barrett not too long ago, right? He mentioned us."

Braithwaite sounded peeved, so Dare decided to strike first.

"Yeah, the name of your outfit slipped my mind. So what about it? Y'all gonna tell me to lay off tryin' to steal your business? Got news for you, buddy boy. That's how free enterprise works."

"I don't need lessons on capitalism," Braithwaite said after a silence. "I think we can work together. We're in town the next couple of days. If you're interested, let's talk."

At Dare's suggestion, they met at the Red Bull in central Nairobi. It was done up like some Swiss chalet, but it served steaks that didn't taste like warmed-over racehorse. He deliberately showed up ten minutes late. The restaurant wasn't crowded, and the two men were easy to spot: a big Kenyan guy going prematurely bald and a slim young American wearing a starched khaki shirt, pressed Levi's, and brown western boots—cheap Tony Lama's, Dare noticed when he sat down. Shoving his chair away from the table, he flung one leg over the other to better display his own pair of Rio of Mercedes, custom made in Fort Worth of python skin.

There was the usual let's-get-acquainted small talk, and then they ate, the Kenyan devouring his steak like a starving lion. Halfway through the meal, he said in a stage whisper that he and Braithwaite would appreciate it if Dare kept their conversation to himself. Flying aid into the Nuba was a risky business.

"What we're doing is not for public consumption, yes?" he added.

Braithwaite said, "We've been at it a few months. The Nuba is really hurting. Fitz and I saw for ourselves. Spent nearly three weeks on the ground in those hills. We saw guys making hoes out of bomb fragments, rubbing sticks together to light their cigarettes—"

"Listen," Dare interrupted, "I've got a bleeding heart too, and it mostly bleeds for myself. I'd be obliged if y'all would come to the point, if you've got one."

Braithwaite, clasping his hands on the tablecloth, looked at him with such attentiveness that Dare temporarily lost awareness of everyone else in the room.

"We need you," he said with an undertone of entreaty.

"What for?"

"We need another pilot and another plane, and if everything we've heard is accurate, you're it."

"Barrett showed you that stuff I faxed him?"

"Yeah. But it was a couple of people who've flown with you who convinced us. Tony Bollichek and Mary English. Tony's been with us from day one, and we hired Mary last week. They've been alternating as my first officer."

"Yeah. I guess where Tony goes, Mary is sure to follow," Dare said.

"They told us you're one helluva pilot," Braithwaite said. "Last month we did twenty-one turnarounds. It's hard on the airplane and on us, so here we are, talking to you."

"Y'all gonna offer me fringe benefits? A good dental plan? Hey, I run my own show. I don't wage-ape for anyone." Dare censored himself from adding, *Especially for a kid who hadn't got his first hard-on when I was flying gooney birds over Laos.*

"I'm talking partnership, Mr. Dare. We run the show together, split the net down the middle."

"I like the sound of that a whole lot better. Okay, facts and figures."

Braithwaite took a moment to compose himself, or rather, to transform himself from bleeding heart into managing director.

"Bottom line is, thirty to thirty-five net. Fifteen to seventeen-five per month for each of us."

"I just finished up a contract in the Congo. Seven hundred fifty thousand in six months," Dare said, shading the truth. "You're talkin' chump change, you'll excuse my sayin' so."

"We're planning to step up operations, planning to expand."

"Planning or hoping?"

"Planning, Mr. Dare. Planning to start flying routes into southern Sudan beside the Nuba. I'm talking the no-go zones, for independent NGOs."

"You've got contracts with these NGOs or are you betting on the come?"

"We're going to get them," Braithwaite said in the tone of card-counter who knew, just *knew,* he was going to hit blackjack on the next deal.

"Lemme have one of those," Dare said to the Kenyan, who'd pulled out a pack of Embassies.

"I was about to offer," he said, shaking a cigarette loose.

"You were bein' too leisurely about it." Then, turning back to Braithwaite, Dare said, "Still sounds like it's on the come."

"Mr. Dare"—Dare considered telling Braithwaite to call him by his first name but decided he preferred the deferential sound of *Mr.*—"in two years, Knight Air is going to be as big as Pathways and maybe bigger."

"What's Pathways?"

"Our competition. It's run by a woman named Tara Whitcomb."

"Yeah. Think I've heard her name around."

"We're offering you a shot at getting in on the ground floor, and in the process, you'd be doing a helluva lot of good for a helluva lot of people."

To avoid wincing, which might have offended Braithwaite's sensibilities, Dare canted his head back and blew smoke at the ceiling.

"The part I like best is thumbin' your nose at Khartoum. I like that part. I never did care for askin' for permission."

"I can't say we *like* it," Braithwaite said solemnly. "It's something that has to be done. I expect you'll want to think things over?"

"Sure will," Dare declared.

"We'll be at Barrett's place till noon tomorrow. It's hard to get hold of us in Loki, so—"

"Let you know tomorrow morning."

Double Trouble was singing to him as he pulled through the gate into his apartment compound and parked under a bottlebrush tree, between a rust-pitted van and a hibiscus bush whose blossoms looked plastic in the parking-lot lights. Double Trouble—"DeeTee" for short—was Dare's pet canary; he'd named it after Stevie Ray Vaughan's band. DeeTee lived in his head, and it warbled infallible warnings whenever something or someone did not look, sound, smell, or feel quite right. Its senses were capable of detecting the faintest trace elements of falsehood or fraud, the slimmest cracks in a man or woman's character, the smallest potential for danger or disaster in any given situation. DeeTee's acuity, coupled to its absolute loyalty to its master—it never, ever lied to him—had made it indispensable. It was the partner of Dare's luck. Without DeeTee, he reckoned he would now be dead, languishing in some third-world prison or putting up his feet in a homeless shelter. Conversely, if he'd listened to DeeTee every time it sang a premonitory song, he would now be living out his dream as a gentleman rancher in the sweet Texas hill country, driving around in a new Cadillac convertible, as LBJ used to do along the Perdenales, and basking in the warm assurance of a peaceful and prosperous old age. He listened most times, but now and then one of his many vices or flaws caused him to pay no heed to the faithful bird.

Lust. DeeTee had tipped him off that his first wife was going to make him miserable before he married her, but Margo's tits, which approached

Dolly Parton's in shape and volume and were besides the first pair of white tits he'd set eyes on after years of gazing at tits of color in Laos, flipped his canary override switch. Over the next three years Dare was stunned by the accuracy of the bird's forecast, and a very traditional divorce toted up the cost of ignoring it.

Greed. When Joe Nakima had asked for the papers for the G1, DeeTee chittered loudly, "Don't let him get his hands on them!" But with a contract to run mirra into Somalia at stake—nine to ten grand gross a week!—Dare plugged his ears. He was still living with the consequences of that willful deafness, and they had produced other consequences, in a kind of ripple effect, and the ripples had washed him into the Red Bull tonight.

So what was the vice this time? *Pride.* He hated the position he now found himself in, peddling his services door to door like an encyclopedia salesman, begging his lawyer to give him another week or another month to pay his fees, suffering bouts of acid reflux when he looked at his bank statements. It was undignified, it offended his sense of who and what he was. Becoming partners with a Gen-X crusader didn't exactly fit his self-image either, but he couldn't see an alternative.

The problem was, DeeTee was sending negative signals about the fair-haired managing director of Knight Air Services Limited: "There's something wrong with the guy, and no good will come from getting mixed up with him."

"So what's wrong with him?" Dare asked, crossing the lot to his door. Sometimes, when he was alone, he spoke out loud to the canary. "You're gonna have to be more specific."

He entered his apartment—it was furnished in the minimalist style of a man used to clearing out of places in a hurry—pulled a Tusker out of the refrigerator, and sat on the sofabed, staring at a blank wall like a nursing-home patient at a TV during a power blackout.

"Start with the way he was dressed," DeeTee said. "That starched shirt, those creased Levi's. You gotta watch out for guys who put creases into their blue jeans."

"Still ain't good enough. Nowhere near."

"If it comes to a choice between leaving somebody in the lurch and saving his own ass, guess which way he'll jump?" DeeTee twittered. "And how about that look he gave us? So frank, so open, so empathetic. And that high-flown speech he made, that crap about you doing a whole lot of good for a whole lot of people."

"You're sayin' he didn't believe a word of it. He's a phony."

"I'm saying he believed every word."

"Gotcha." He gulped the can dry and went to the fridge for another. "How about the business end of things? Bullshit too? He sure can talk the talk, sure sounds like he knows what he's doin'."

"He was giving you the straight skinny, that's my judgment. If we could take him out of the picture, look at this purely as a business venture, it's okay, the best you're likely to find under present circumstances. But we can't take him out of the picture, can we? He *does* know what he's doing. A true believer and a smart businessman at the same time. Double Trouble says that's double trouble."

Dare crunched the empty, shot a three-pointer into the wastebasket, opened the new can, and leaned against the refrigerator, looking at the floor with the same expression he'd fixed on the wall.

"Think Pat Robertson," chirped DeeTee. "Think Jim Bakker and any other televangelist you can name. Just oozing sanctimonious sincerity, one eye on the Bible and the other on the bottom line, and twenty-twenty vision in both. Praise the Lord and pass the collection plate, brothers and sisters!"

"I'll be sure to have everything in writing, every *i* dotted, every *t* crossed."

"You know what paper is good for over here."

"Goddamn it, you said yourself it's the best I'm likely to find."

"All right," DeeTee warbled wearily. "Your mind's made up. But do me one favor? Keep the Hawker in your name. Don't go fifty-fifty on that. You know what happens when you don't listen, so listen to me on this one little point, please?"

When Dare phoned the next morning to accept the offer, Braithwaite sounded like an excited boy. "That's great!" he said, and in short order offered to buy a half share in the Hawker and to incorporate it into what he grandiosely called Knight Air's "fleet." Dare kept his promise to DeeTee and replied, "No deal. I lease the plane to the company."

"But Wes," said his new partner, dropping the *Mr.,* "we're supposed to be equal partners."

"Y'all want that plane and me, those are the terms," Dare said.

"All right," Braithwaite said, disappointment in his voice. "I'll have a contract drawn up."

"Another part of the deal. There's a loadmaster worked for me, name of Nimrod, Kenyan fella. He comes with me, 'cause I don't trust anybody else to load my planes."

"Okay again. Expect to see you and the Hawker in Loki—when?"

"Give me a week."

In fact, it took only five days for him to clear out of his apartment with his meager belongings, to inform his lawyer of his new address, to sell his clapped-out Mercedes and buy a used motorcycle—more practical than a car for getting around in Lokichokio—and to ferry the plane and Nimrod to their new place of work.

The disturbing emotions that Mary English stirred in him were fresh in his memory. After he got settled in, he told Braithwaite that he wanted Tony to be his first officer, but his partner insisted on keeping the Australian. Mary would be Dare's copilot, and that was that.

She didn't know the first thing about a Hawker-Siddley, so his first order of business was familiarizing her with the plane. He began the day after his arrival. After she harnessed herself into the second seat, he briefed her on the controls and the instrument cluster. Arranged in a classic T, free of most electronic frills, it possessed the simplicity of a true workhorse aircraft, the kind he was used to. Looking at the array of clean analog gauges was like looking at the dashboard of a well-kept 1956 Chevy pickup: it stirred a feeling of cozy familiarity marbled with nostalgia.

"I love this old airplane," he said. "A Hawker seven-four-eight is kinda like me, it's a child of the sixties."

Mary laughed. "I don't see you as a child of the sixties. Can't imagine you in bell-bottoms and a tie-dyed shirt, smoking a bong and groovin' on the Beatles."

"I did smoke, and unlike the asshole currently occupying the Oval Office, I did inhale, but I was a Rolling Stones man. I had sympathy for the Devil."

"Oh yeah, I'll bet you did," she said, with a teasing flip of her honey-colored hair. He knew then that he was in for more trouble than he'd imagined.

Douglas

"He thinks they're patsies. The slang isn't au courant*"—she comically exaggerates the French to show that she isn't being pretentious, she hates pretense—"but you get what I mean."*

She sits in the passenger seat of her abused Cherokee, binoculars not much bigger than opera glasses strung from her tanned neck by a vinyl cord tucked into the cleavage of the bosom she tries to conceal by wearing a shirt that would fit his father. She does this because she doesn't want people to take her for some babe with big tits instead of the serious woman she believes herself to be. The serious woman she is. Lucille Braithwaite has a sense of humor and a natural enthusiasm, but both are restrained by the lessons of her Mormon girlhood, which she's never forgotten. Life is no gag, and we are here to merit the Celestial Kingdom.

"Yeah, I get it," Douglas says, feeling grown up because he's driving. Indeed, chauffeuring his mother makes him feel more adult than soloing in the Beechcraft in flight school.

"What's more, he thinks his family has a history of being patsies. Not exactly the kind who get roped in by pyramid schemes, but dopes who let their principles get in the way of their self-interest."

The inflection in her voice makes it clear that she, on the other hand, approves of such people.

"Like for example."

"Like for example, some great-grandfather or great-great-uncle—I forget which—had a friend who was starting a chewing gum business in Chicago. He needed investors, you know, seed money, and asked the great-whatever to kick in and get in on the ground floor. He was a real old-timey Boston Yankee. Thought chewing gum was a disgusting habit, so he turned his friend down, who happened to be named P. K. Wrigley."

"Like in Wrigley's Spearmint?" Douglas asks, impressed.

"Like that. Disapproving of gum chewing isn't what I'd call a moral principle, but maybe it was to a Boston blueblood."

As she speaks, she looks out the side window, scanning phone wires, mesquite and palo verde trees, and the tall, prickly candles of saguaro. The back of her head faces Douglas, so that all he sees out the corner of his eye is the long, thick, naturally blond hair that very much contributes to the babe look she works so hard to hide with her baggy shirts and minimal makeup and sensible shoes. Too hard sometimes, so that the attempts to camouflage her physical attractions, by their very obviousness, call attention to them. That's all right with Douglas; he's proud that his mother doesn't look her age and fits no one's image of a mother.

"I think your dad thinks there's a funny gene in his family, the patsy gene," she goes on. "That's why he came out West when he wasn't much older than you are now."

"On account of this gene?" asks Douglas, baffled.

"Because of, honey. 'On account of' sounds like some hick cowboy."

"Okay, Mom."

"He needed to get away from his family, I mean all of them, that whole clan, that tribe. He wanted to start with a clean slate. A nineteen-year-old ought to have a clean slate to begin with, but he felt that his family and all that history of theirs had scribbled on his slate and that, willy-nilly, he'd become whatever they wanted him to become. So it was 'Go West, young man' for him. What's the West for? What's it always been for? It's where you go to invent yourself, or reinvent yourself, depending on how much life you've lived."

Much of this is going over Douglas's seventeen-year-old head, though he has an inkling of what she means about Dad's family. His uncle Tim, Dad's younger brother, and aunt Betsy, who live in Amherst, visit him often at Milton and have become almost surrogate parents. A month ago, at the end of the second term, they scooped him up and brought him to the family compound on the coast of Maine to meet some of his relations. The big old house, big as a hotel, had a weird name, Mingulay—a Scottish name, someone told him—and oil paintings and brownish old photographs of Braithwaites going back several generations hanging on the board-and-batten walls. The place teemed with around forty aunts and uncles, great-aunts and great-uncles, first, second, and even third cousins, with whom he sailed and canoed in Blue Hill bay, played tennis, hiked in the piney woods, and ate dinner in the baronial dining room, where all males over sixteen were required to wear jackets and ties and all females over the same age had to wear dresses and everyone engaged in brilliant, witty conversations he had a hard time following. Tim and Betsy showed him a family tree that was periodically updated, like the U.S. census. He saw his own name and where he fit into that consanguineous universe and learned that he was directly descended from two people who'd come to America not long after the Mayflower. His father had never once mentioned that. In the library one evening his aunt and uncle paged through photo albums with him, and he saw his father as a kid, back in the early fifties, and his grandfather and great-grandfather in their youths. On the bookshelves were family histories and self-published biographies and autobiographies of various ancestors, and he got the idea that Braithwaites were proud of their past and the high-minded, noble things family members had done, putting their principles above their self-interest, like the Boston doctor who could have made a pile treating rich patients but started a charity hospital instead, like the woman who'd been arrested in a demonstration to give women the right to vote, like the naval officer who'd left the quarterdeck during a sea battle in the War of 1812 to save his wounded captain and got court-martialed for abandoning his post. To a kid from the West, where people's roots didn't go down very far, unless you were an Indian or a Mexican, all the ancient family lore was fascinating; yet it was also kind of smothering. He too was proud that he came from such fine people; at the same time, he felt an eerie pressure from his dead relations, as if they were telling him that he had to live up to their self-sacrificial ideals, whether he wanted to or not, while the presence of so many living relatives made him feel that he was losing his individual identity, that he was being absorbed into their collective life, like a drop of water into a sponge. He'd had a lot of fun, but a week was enough, and he was relieved to be by himself after Tim and Betsy dropped him off at Boston Logan and he boarded the plane for Tucson.

So he can understand why Dad wanted to get away and be his own man, but he can't fathom what that has to do with the reason his mother started this discussion about his father.

"He dropped out of Princeton and transferred to the University of Arizona," she is saying now. "Can you imagine? Trading Princeton for the U of A?"

She snorts, suggesting that she thinks that move was as dumb as the great-whatever passing up a chance to get in on the ground floor of Wrigley's Spearmint.

"If he didn't, he wouldn't have met you," Douglas says in its defense.

"True."

"And then I wouldn't be here."

"Also true."

"And neither would Megan and Lisa."

"Ditto."

"So we're real glad he dropped out of Princeton," he adds, reaching for a lighthearted tone.

She senses that it's not genuine, a pretty wrapper in which he's trying to smuggle a not-very-pretty question.

Turning from the window, she says:

"I am, too. You're all three the most precious things in the world to me. Don't worry. I know it sounded bad last night, but it's not as bad as it sounded. How many times have you and your sisters heard us quarrel?"

"Mom, that wasn't a quarrel."

"Fight, then. How many times?"

"Not many."

"Drop the *m* and you've got it."

"Okay, first time. But it was—it scared us."

"I lost my temper. There was no earthly reason for him to do what he did. He's one of the most successful men in town, in the whole state. The governor—the governor, for Christ's sake—calls him by his first name." *She was getting worked up again.* "And we've got that house and those cars and you in a fancy-dancy eastern prep school, and a portfolio to die for. There was just no good reason."

"Hey, Mom? I've learned something at the fancy-dancy school. Trial by jury? Innocent till proven guilty?"

She sighs and fiddles with the binoculars, her lower lip curling into the pout she assumes whenever she has to say something she doesn't want to say.

"Honey, your dad admits to doing everything the people who are suing him say he did. Well, almost everything, and the houses are right there to prove it. He's just saying, and the hotshot Phoenix lawyers are saying, that he had a legal right to do it."

"What do you say?"

"I don't like getting into the legalities, I'm not a lawyer, thank God. It wasn't necessary, that's what I say. He knew he was pushing the edge of the envelope, knew he was taking a big risk of getting sued and maybe worse, but he went right ahead with it. So now his reputation is on the line, his future, our future could be in jeopardy, and for what? The whole thing, legal or not, was kind of sleazy. Your dad always prided himself on being a class act, so that when you saw the Web-Mar logo on a development, you knew it was top of the line and on the up and up. This—this was the kind of thing some fly-by-nighter would do. Pull over, Doug."

She's spotted something, and he slows down and steers to the shoulder of the road. She tells him to back up, which he does, twisting and craning his neck to see over the stacks of boxes that partly block the rear window.

"Here. Stop."

She lowers her window, the scorching June air smacking Douglas like a hot hand. *His mother freezes the binoculars on several birds, perched on a roadside wire above a dry wash, and after looking for half a minute, she hands the glasses to him.*

"Time for one of Mom's pop quizzes. Identify them."

Leaning over, he focuses on the stocky birds, a few drab females and two males with royal blue crowns and breasts and black eye-rings like masks. He isn't sure what they are, and it's hard to concentrate, what with his heart still fluttering from that remark she'd made about their future being in jeopardy.

"The females look like cowbirds, but the males like indigo buntings."

"Close doesn't count. Can you see the male's wings?"

"They're facing head on."

"Which means, honey, that you have to get out and change the angle."

From ten yards up the road, amid the heat and unearthly desert silence, he spots the rufous wing bars. She's unbelievable, he thinks. How did she see them, going by at sixty miles an hour?

"Blue grosbeak," he calls, and she sticks her hand out the window, bends thumb and forefinger to form a circle, then waves him back.

They drive on in silence for several minutes, crossing the boundary into the reservation, where she is going to deliver the stuff in back: notebooks, textbooks, pencils, used electric typewriters. Most of it was donated by one of the charitable organizations she belongs to. She bought the rest out of her own pocket, following the maxim that she repeats to her children every chance she gets: Much is expected from those to whom much is given.

The land on both sides of the two-lane asphalt rolls away, meeting, toward the south, the blue, hazy wall of the Baboquivari mountains. Dwelling place of the Papago Indian gods, his mother has told him, cautioning him to refer to the Indians by the name they have for themselves, Tohono O'odham.

"No good reason for him to do it, but there is a reason," she says, picking up where she left off. "Your dad has this need to think of himself as a tough-minded, hard-nosed guy without a sentimental bone in his body, who never lets an opportunity pass him by and never lets anything stand in the way of him getting what he wants. Why am I telling you this? Same reason I tell it to myself. So I can understand him better. He's just got to prove that he isn't like the rest of his family. He wouldn't have loaned P. K. Wrigley a few bucks, he would have made himself his partner and then taken over the whole she-bang."

She pauses in this analysis to glance at a settlement of squalid adobe shacks, in front of which dark-skinned children play in the dust and the inevitable pickup trucks squat on deflated tires. Douglas, who has never been on this reservation before, feels vaguely uneasy, as if they've crossed the border into Mexico.

"And all the deed restrictions and covenants and conservation easements that old woman put into the contract were in his way," Lucille resumes. "Stopped him from building a high-density development at double, triple the profit. So he got those Phoenix lawyers to change the contract and they somehow got the old lady to agree to the changes. How, I don't know, maybe I don't want to know."

"Mom, the paper said the woman's heirs, her kids and all? It said they said she didn't agree."

His mother shrugs.

"They told the paper they might do more than sue. That they might go to—to—"

"The attorney general. Criminal fraud. Maybe they will, but I don't think it would stick."

"He didn't do that, fraud, you're saying?"

"I told you, I don't like to get into the legalities."

This is not the answer Douglas hoped to hear.

PART TWO

Warlord

THE RAINS HAD been sparse throughout the wet season and were falling but once or twice a week as the season drew to a close. Conditions were good for a raid, and Colonel Ahmar ordered Ibrahim Idris to lead one into the Nuba hills, where the infidel's forces were becoming a nuisance and foreign airplanes were bringing in contraband, in defiance of the government's decrees. He was to teach the Nubans and the foreigners a lesson by destroying a town and a smuggler's airfield about two days' ride from Kadugli. Ibrahim Idris studied the colonel's maps and hired guides—good Nubans loyal to the regime—and then mustered his men, pulling them out of their fields and pastures—a very big nuisance, for they were busy bringing in this year's millet harvest and gathering their herds for the annual journey to the southern grasslands. Still, as he'd answered Colonel Ahmar's call, so did the Brothers answer his. They said farewell to their families, saddled their horses, and with Kalashnikovs strapped across their backs and magazine belts full, they rode out from Babanusa town and across the wadis Ghallah and al-Azraq to Kadugli— two hundred kilometers through hard country in a little over three days. There they waited for a company of militia from the Kadugli garrison to join them. The rest was welcome. The horses were worn out, and so were the men, and so was Ibrahim. How he ached. He guessed he was getting old, he *was* old, forty-five, possibly forty-six or -seven.

A woman should now be massaging my legs with liquid butter, he thought, sitting in the shade of an ebony tree. Yes, the woman Miriam, with butter churned in a calabash and warmed over coals, not this nephew, who rubs my calves with the smelly stuff from that chemist's shop in the souk at Babanusa. A balm, excellent for the sore muscles, the Lebanese chemist had said. Half price to you, omda. For the jihad. Ibrahim smiled a sarcastic smile, thinking about the plump chemist, pretending that he was making a sacrifice by peddling his smelly balm for half price. The Lebanese knew how to turn a profit, and that one probably had charged double. He would wager that he was not even Muslim but some

Greek born in Lebanon who did not give a damn for jihad or know the meaning of the word. Proud, like all his tribesmen, of his ability to do without, contemptuous of full-bellied townsmen like the chemist, Ibrahim was working himself into one of his fits of rage. I should have told him, "Take off your shirt and pants, fat-ass, and put on a jelibiya and come with us if you want to do something for jihad. Don't sit here on your fat ass and lie to me, telling me you're charging half price."

"Where does this stuff come from?" he asked Abbas.

"Why, we bought it in Babanusa, don't you remember, uncle?"

Abbas was not as clever as Ibrahim Idris wished.

"My meaning was, where is it made?"

"The chemist said in China."

"Perhaps it works best if you're Chinese."

"It isn't working?"

"It burns and it stinks."

Abbas rolled his calves vigorously between his palms, gave each calf a parting slap, and then wiped his hands on his jelibiya, declaring that the burn signified that the balm was working.

"When I was your age, I could spend one month in the saddle and not feel this that I do now. Ya Allah! On our migrations to the south."

These words evoked an image of himself as a lithe-limbed young man mounted on a white gelding, herding his father's cattle that flowed like a river through the woodlands, and the image evoked some envy for his nephew, in full possession of the youth that he had lost.

" 'Mesarna 'izz al Ataya,' " Abbas said, quoting from the poem.

"Our migration is the glory of the Ataya," his uncle repeated.

"But now we have the glory of jihad." For emphasis, Abbas smacked the stock of his Kalashnikov. He would have been a handsome lad if not for his nose, bent sideways by the fall he'd taken from a horse when he was a boy. "Tell me, uncle, which is the greater glory, the glory of our migrations or the glory of jihad?"

An odd question, but then Abbas was in the habit of asking odd questions. Why the devil doesn't he ask something sensible, like what qualities to look for in a breed bull or a riding bull, like which grasses are best for cows? Ibrahim looked around, at the men brewing tea and resting in the shade of the trees, at the horses with noses buried in the feed bales that the militiamen had delivered this morning. He drew in the odors of hot horseflesh and saddle leather and smoke. It all looked and smelled like cattle camp, except of course that no cattle were in sight, nor tents, nor kraals nor hearths nor one *angereyb* of wood, rope, and leather. Oh, what he would give for one of those portable beds now.

"They're two different things. The one is a glory of this world. It means, as I've told you before, that we Humr together with the Rizeygat and Hawazma and Messiriya taste to the full the fruits of the cattleman's wandering life. That among all the Baggara Arabs, we are the best. The other is a glory of the world to come. The martyr's paradise."

Pleased with this answer—it sounded wise, as if spoken by a mullah—he leaned forward, grunting at the stiffness in his back, removed the copper pot from the warm ashes of the fire, and filled his tea glass. The *chay* was overbrewed, bitter and strong, and his thoughts turned suddenly bitter, recalling the tea Miriam had made for him. Light and sweet and just right, the best he'd drunk. Surely she must have loved him to take such care with his tea, surely there had been love in her hands as she massaged his legs in the evenings.

"I wonder if I will become *shaheed* tomorrow," Abbas said, drawing Ibrahim's thoughts away from the girl, though not completely. "As you say, uncle, to be a martyr for the faith is the greatest glory."

"That's not exactly what I said."

Abbas looked at him with a puzzled squint. "What is, then?"

The older man took out his tobacco pouch and paper and rolled a cigarette, licked it lengthwise, and lit it off a twig pulled from the fire. He smoked for a while, calculating how best to answer. Days ago, as he was preparing for this raid, his sister-in-law had begged him to look out for Abbas; she'd pleaded with him to restrain the young man's zeal, and that was a commission he'd been happy to accept. Having sacrificed one of his own sons to the jihad nearly four years ago, he had no stomach for losing the nephew whom he'd raised like a son after his brother, Abbas's father, died of fever. He thought the desire for martyrdom, which the government and the mullahs were drumming into the heads of so many young men, was mistaken, but he dared not say that to his nephew, a pious youth who had been a favorite among his teachers at the *madrassah* in Khartoum. How strange that he, a rich man honored and admired throughout the House of Humr, needed to be so cautious in speaking to a callow boy not yet twenty. He resented it, but that's how things were these days, with the National Islamic Front so firmly in power. Everyone had to watch his words in matters of religion, even in private conversations, and leaders such as himself had to be doubly careful. His office—*omda* of the Salamat, one of the ten omodiyas of the Humr tribe—was a government appointment, and this government required its officials to be men of strong faith, or at the least, men who made a convincing show of faith. If he didn't try hard enough to dissuade his nephew from martyrdom, Abbas was likely to attain it by taking a foolish chance; if, on the other hand, he tried too hard, Abbas could begin to gossip among the other young men that his uncle was growing weak, his belief in the jihad wavering. Such gossip would spread quickly to the ears of his rivals and enemies, who would use it to intrigue against him. It was well known that Ibrahim had set his sights on being appointed nazir over all the Humr, for the present nazir was very ill and expected to die. So his dilemma was to make good on his pledge to his nephew's mother while saying nothing that might undermine his present position and threaten his future.

"The greatest glory is submission to God's will," he replied at last.

That all his uncle's pondering should produce so obvious a truth appeared to disappoint Abbas.

"If God wills you to become *shaheed,* you will, if not, you won't. In any case, He will favor you if you accept His will. There is no shame in not attaining martyrdom if that's what God wishes."

"Before the last raid, when I caught the fever and could not go, oh, my mother and sisters were so happy! I couldn't understand it. I asked my mother, for why you are so happy? Now for sure you will not be *umma'l shaheed.*"

"And she said what?"

"That it was all right if she was not the mother of a martyr. I couldn't believe my own hearing, and I was ashamed, uncle. It is my hope to see my cousin Ganis in Paradise, to sit beside him."

He was getting tired of talking to this kid, but he saw that he hadn't gone far enough toward fulfilling his promise.

"It pains me to hear Ganis's name mentioned. Listen, what does the Holy Koran say about those who fight for the faith?" He motioned at his saddle and bags, lying a few meters away. "My book is in there. Let's see how much you learned at the madrassah."

Abbas fetched the Koran and paged through it, his black eyebrows pursed.

"Is it this? 'God has indeed promised everyone Paradise, but God has preferred those who fight for the faith before those who sit still, by adding unto them a great reward, by degrees of honor conferred on them from him, and by granting them forgiveness and mercy; for God is indulgent and merciful.'"

"What say you to the meaning of that?"

"Why, that verse is clear. Those who are martyred for the faith are forgiven their sins and go to Paradise straight away."

"Read what it says, nephew. It doesn't say those who *die* for the faith but those who *fight* for it."

"Yes."

"So you see, merely by fighting in the jihad one earns mercy and honor. You will see Ganis even if you are one hundred years when you die."

"But the mullahs would say that by dying in the fight he earned a higher place."

"Then you can look *up* from your place and see him," the older man said, his patience nearly at an end. "Ya, Abbas! Explain something to your uncle. He's getting old, see the gray." He stroked his short beard. "His mind isn't as keen as it once was. There are things he doesn't understand."

Abbas assumed a mature, dignified air, raising his chin while squaring his turban. His skewed nose spoiled the effect and made him look a little silly.

"You've laid claim to Nanayi, and you've told her father that you hope to return from the raid with cattle for a bride-price, even though I have offered to loan you the cattle."

"My refusal wasn't meant to insult you."

"I know that! You believe that presenting Nunayi's father with cows you captured in a raid brings you more renown than cows loaned to you. My question is, how will you seize these cattle if you're martyred? How will you marry Nunayi if you're dead?"

"The Prophet, blessed be his name, teaches that those who die for God are not dead."

"Don't play these games with me, Abbas. You see the contradiction, don't you?"

"Of course, uncle. Martyrdom is my chief desire, but if God wills it not to be so, my next desire is to capture some cattle and marry her."

"I understand you now. *Esmah*, Abbas! Stay close to me, and I'll lead you to the cattle, I'll show you which are the best and those will be yours."

"Yes, uncle."

"See to the horses, yours and mine. It's another two days' ride to the airfield, and I think Barakat has a sore foreleg, the right. Give him some of that stinking Chinese stuff. Maybe it will work for him."

"And you?"

Miriam, Miriam, she was there again, her hands digging deep into his legs.

"It doesn't burn anymore, and yes, I feel better, so maybe that fat Lebanese knew what he was talking about. I still prefer butter."

As his nephew walked off, he poured a little water out of his goatskin flask and rinsed his glass, recalling the days, not very long ago, when young men left Dar Humr only to work for wages so they could save up to buy a cow and start a herd. Quite a few still did, but there were too many like Abbas who went away to madrassahs and government training camps, from which they emerged impatient to die for the faith, to the point that nothing else mattered. They had no interest in cattle, nor in the sweet things that owning them brought to a man—women, prestige, power. They could tell you what the Prophet had to say about this subject or that subject, but nothing about which grasses grew in what kind of soil and where and in what seasons they grew there. Why trouble yourself, acquiring such skills and knowledge, when your purpose was to die? Why yearn for prestige and position when your true yearning was for the martyr's grave?

Ibrahim Idris couldn't understand it. The old saying was true; cattle were *fadd umm suf*—silver with hair—yet they were more than that. His attachment to his own considerable herd was almost mystical. Everything he had and everything he was he owed to cattle, and he owed his cattle to God, from whom all blessings flow; to God, yes, but also to his own shrewdness, for the proverb states that the owner's eye brings increase; to his industriousness, for the proverb states that wealth lies between the upper and lower millstones; and to his pastoral skills, the sharp bargains he'd driven with his daughter's suitors, and the years of self-denial that had given him the resources to add to his herds. Today more than eight hundred head bore his brand. Rarely did he sell his stock for cash, but when he did, the proceeds were more than enough to keep his wives in tea, sugar, soaps, and perfumes. To each he'd provided one riding bull and several milk cows, so each could churn butter for sale and thus keep herself in good blue cloth and gold earrings and other luxuries.

Wealth had brought him power; power, responsibilities. His poorer kinsmen came to him for milk and millet. He provided calves to nephews, nieces, and cousins as well as to his own children. Guests from all over were drawn to his tent, and to them he extended lavish hospitality. His advice was sought on various matters, from stockbreeding to politics to clan disputes over property and women, which he arbitrated with fairness and wisdom. Although Ibrahim had achieved fame among the Salamat for his physical courage, his generosity was what had made his name. The minstrels sang in praise of his liberality, not only in the camps of the Salamat but in the camps of the other omodiyas as well.

Nevertheless, slanderous campaigns continued to be mounted by factions determined to unseat him. He fought them off successfully, thanks be to God and to his relationship with the nazir, cemented by the marriage of his eldest daughter to the nazir's youngest son. Despite his cares, he was sometimes able to enjoy the fruits of all his effort. Whether in the dry-season camps in the south or in the wet-season camps amid the millet fields and ebony trees of the north, he would sit or lie beneath the Men's Tree, drinking the tea and eating the meals his wives brought to him, talking to guests who honored him with their presence and whom he honored with bowls of sour milk and with a slaughtered sheep from the flocks his cattle wealth had enabled him to establish.

The hours would pass in ease and comfort, and before he knew it, evening would come, and that was the sweetest time, with the heat gone and the smoke rising from the wood and dung fires his servants had built and his sons and kinsmen returning with the cattle, bawling and lowing as they milled into the kraals. It was a pleasure to walk among them, inspecting them for ticks or signs of disease, smelling them, rubbing their humps and dewlaps and bellies, filled with the best graze his sons had been able to find. A pleasure too to watch the calves released for milking. Sometimes, as one wife sprinkled his tent with scent, he would milk a cow himself, and another wife would churn liquid butter from the milk and massage his legs with the butter before he entered his fragrant tent to sleep contentedly until awakened by the sound of someone churning the morning's milk outside his door.

Such days were rare, and after the coup that brought the National Islamic Front to power, they all but vanished from his life. News of the coup reached the Humr quickly, but few paid much attention to it at first; far removed from Khartoum, the Humr and the other Bagarra tribes were seldom affected by changes in government. But this coup was different, it was a revolution, and like the *haboub,* the cold wind from the northern deserts, it soon blew into the tribal lands, bringing changes. The provincial governor was removed from office for displaying insufficient zeal for the new regime's policies, and replaced by a man of Khartoum's choosing; in the towns, civil officials, police officers, and military commanders were purged for the same reason, and it was rumored that some had been imprisoned or executed. The tribal leaders were left alone; even this militant new government was afraid of infringing on the rights and privileges of the fiercely independent nomads. Still, it was clear to Ibrahim, and to all the others, that their wealth and popularity among their people would no longer guarantee their appointments; from now on they would also have to prove their fitness by displaying loyalty to the regime and that other virtue, piety, the virtue in which Ibrahim had always been deficient. Fearful that his laxity would provide new ammunition to his enemies, he made sure to behave properly. He would break off conversations with his guests or negotiations with disputing parties and bow to Mecca, trusting that his devoutness would be noticed and remarked on. Fortunately, those who witnessed these exhibitions couldn't see that his thoughts were usually far from God, dwelling on some quarrel he'd been asked to arbitrate, or on the sale of a bull calf, or—oh, he'd hoped he wouldn't burn in hell for this—making love to one of his younger wives.

Beyond the new emphasis on religion, life among the Humr didn't change much for about a year after the coup. The harvest came in, the millet was stacked and threshed. The cool winds of the early dry season turned warm, then hot, and the Humr moved south with their herds. No matter what passed in the affairs of men and government, cattle had to heed the call of the green grass. They stayed in the south till the air grew heavy and still and thunderstorms filled the wadis and insects began to swarm, sending the Humr northward again, there to plant a new millet crop and let their herds graze on the stubble of last year's fields. The big rains came and went, the skies grew miserly once more, announcing the advent of another harvest, and as the mown grain rose high on the drying platforms, the wind spun around to the north and the herdsmen began to muster their stock for the next migration to the southern pastures.

But that migration was to be like no other that Ibrahim Idris could remember. A short time before it began, army officers arrived in the Humr camps to call for young men to fight in the war. Ibrahim's was visited by a major and a captain, who came one afternoon in a Land Rover accompanied by a lorry filled with soldiers in tan uniforms. The officers, Humr themselves, declined Ibrahim's offer to stay for a feast of roast mutton, pleading that they had to see another omda before the day was done. As they relaxed under the Men's Tree, the major told him—in case he hadn't heard—that a *fatwa* had been issued in Khartoum declaring that the war was now a jihad. Ibrahim Idris nodded. And it was high time, the major said, sweating through his uniform. The way the previous government waged the war was a disgrace. So many defeats, so many soldiers deserting, so many officers tearing off their epaulets when ordered to the south. All that had changed. The army had been purged of cowards and traitors and reorganized into battalions of Islamic warriors trained by the Iranians. The major gestured at the soldiers in the lorry, some of whom wore scarves around their heads, printed with the profession of the faith, *La Allah ill Allah wah Muhammad rasoul Allah.* Already these warriors had won important triumphs, the major went on, sweating even more from the excitement he'd worked up. More were to come, inshallah, until the whole of the south was claimed for Islam. And now it was time for the nomads to join the holy cause.

He wiped his forehead and hands with a rag and pulled a piece of paper from his shirt pocket.

"First, I wish to read to you some words from the fatwa—"

"I can read," said Ibrahim, gesturing for the paper.

The major told him to pay attention to the words at the bottom, which said: "All Muslims who deal with the rebels or who raise doubts about the legality of jihad are hypocrites and dissenters and apostates to the faith, and shall suffer torture in hell for all eternity."

The major looked at him intently.

"One thing it doesn't say is that such dissidents and apostates will suffer tortures on this earth as well."

"Perhaps my honored guest will tell me what he means?"

"Ya, Ibrahim! Esmah!" His hand went to his heart to sign his sincerity. "I am Humr, and I know that our people have made friends with many Dinka and other abid. I know that we are in the custom of making arrangements with them to allow our cattle to graze in their pastures in the south. That is the kind of thing that must now stop. That is the kind of dealing the fatwa forbids."

"Tell me, does the fatwa say how, then, we are to graze our cattle?"

"Yes."

"I don't see it here," he said, scowling at the smudged paper.

The major smiled a broad smile. "Ya, Ibrahim! Has it ever made sense to you that abid should have such fine pastures as they do? Has it ever made sense that we should bargain with them for grazing rights, when grass such as theirs rightfully is ours?"

He replied that, no, it didn't make sense; nevertheless that was how things were.

"No longer."

At a nod from the major, the captain drew out a map from the case he carried, spread it on the ground, and pinned its corners with rocks.

"We're clearing the blacks out, from here to here." Joining three fingers, the major swiped a vast corridor of land. "It will be, inshallah, a land without a people. And all the Baggara tribes will help make it so, and their reward will be all that pasture. It will be theirs alone."

Ibrahim stared at the map, his heart racing at the vision of those lush, immense savannahs, there for the taking. But how, he asked, would the Baggara help make that so?

"The army asks for each omda to furnish a certain number of men, as many as can be spared," the major said, wiping his brow once again. "The omdas will choose the men themselves. These murahaleen will be our cavalry."

Each fighter would be provided with a modern rifle, an enlistment bonus of fifty thousand pounds, and a horse if he didn't have a mount of his own. The army would give the recruits a fortnight's training, to learn military discipline and how to use Kalashnikov rifles. From time to time during the dry season, or whenever conditions were suitable for mounted operations, the murahaleen would be ordered to make raids on southern villages and towns. Sometimes they might be commanded to escort government trains and convoys, to protect them from rebel ambushes. And of course anyone who was killed in this sacred struggle would be honored as a martyr, and his family would be paid a pension for life.

"The murahaleen will be under the command of my commander, Colonel Ahmar," the major said. "Colonel Ahmar knows the army is asking a lot of you. With so many men away on operations, who will look after livestock? Who will tend the fields? So he has authorized me to tell you omdas that the taking of captives on the raids is permitted. Those old laws forbidding it are lifted. Those laws were imposed by the English." He spat. "The government encourages you to seize as many captives as you wish, to do the work the fighters would be doing. After all, these blacks are not called abid for nothing. They are slaves. Why pay for labor when you can get it for nothing?"

It wasn't difficult to find recruits. Some were zealots, but many were from the poorest of the Salamat. The ownership of a horse made each of them a knight, at least in his own eyes; the fifty thousand pounds was more than enough to buy a cow, and what stock it didn't buy could be got on raids, so that the most destitute had a chance of accumulating a bride-price. And so the herds trekked south that season watched over by children and graybeards while Ibrahim Idris and two hundred men of fighting age went north to an army training ground to learn how to maneuver their horses in battle and to fire the Kalashnikov rifle. The Humr had not practiced the arts of war for a long time, not since the slave- and cattle-raiding days of their grandfathers' time, but war was in their blood and the men learned quickly. When they were through, mullahs blessed them and presented each fighter with a booklet of sayings from the Koran and with a key that would open the gates of Paradise if he was martyred. The men hung the keys around their necks by leather thongs—keys of different shapes, sizes, and colors, some, like the one given to Ibrahim, attached to plastic tabs with mysterious writing and numbers on them. Curious about what they said, he asked several Brothers if they could interpret the message. None could. The major who'd recruited him cleared up the mystery, explaining that the words were in English and that they said "Khartoum Intercontinental." With an incredulous laugh, Ibrahim Idris asked, "I am to unlock the gates of Paradise with a hotel key?" The major smiled his broad smile. "Put it away, omda. These are things for the young men, to inspire them."

The day before they left on their first operations was marked by a great rally on the field where they had practiced mounted drills. It was attended by a general and the provincial governor himself, who arrived on a military airplane. Horsemen came from all the Baggara tribes mustered. A battalion of militia was there as well, drawn up in formation in their light-brown uniforms. Tall, black-bearded Colonel Ahmar stood on a reviewing stand with the generals, and one, a short, big-bellied man from Khartoum, made a speech promising victory. At the end of it the colonel stepped up to the microphone and reminded the murahaleen of their heritage—they were descendants of the warriors who had followed the Divinely Guided One to triumph over the infidel General Gordon. He held a Koran high over his head in one hand and a Kalashnikov in the other and declared:

"With these we will conquer the south! The rebels who resist us are enemies of God, and they will find the murahaleen are God's scourge upon them! *Allahu akhbar! Allah ma'ana!*"

Like the sere wind that ruffled the horses' manes and the riders' white jelibiyas, the colonel's voice, strong and deep, swept through the ranks, stirring hearts and souls, and to the crash of rifles fired in the air and the crack of braided whips, a thousand throats hurled the words back at him: "Allahu akhbar! Allah ma'ana! God is great! God is with us!"

Ibrahim Idris, who always considered himself a man with a cold eye and a calculating head, was surprised to feel his own heart rising and to hear that same cry fly from his lips as he snapped his whip overhead. The order to march past the reviewing stand was given. The militiamen went first, stomping their feet in time to a drumbeat, then the Messiriya, and then the Humr. Riding at the head of his brothers, the men singing, "Carry the rifle whose fire burns the liver and sears the heart, for I need a slave-boy from the country of the blacks," Ibrahim Idris seemed to be borne along not by Barakat, his chestnut stallion, but by some invisible force that was outside and within him at the same time. For once he gave not a thought to his cattle, his wives, possessions, and responsibilities. He was, at least in that transcendent moment, no longer omda of the Salamat but a captain of holy warriors, and as massed riders surged through the roiling dust shouting and singing, he knew with certain knowledge that this was what it had been like to be with the Mahdi or with the True Believers who had first carried the faith with sword and fire to the far corners of the earth. Yet some part of his eye stayed cold, and through it he saw that the jihad offered an opportunity to distinguish himself in battle, as Humr men had done in the old days, and that with luck and the help of God, he might rise further than he'd ever dreamed.

That was five years and a century ago, and though he had won honor in several skirmishes, though his men had seized more than their share of cattle and captives, though they had obeyed to the letter the mullahs' calls to kill infidels wherever they found them, his ardor for the jihad was indeed fading, leaking, drop by drop, out the hole that Ganis's death had torn in his heart and that nothing could repair—not the honor bestowed on a martyr's father, nor the songs praising his son's valor, nor the mullahs' assurances that Ganis had earned a favored place in the garden where rivers flowed, nor the revenge that Ibrahim Idris had taken. That was something he'd had to do—no Humr man could retain his self-respect and the respect of his wives and kinsmen if he failed to avenge the loss of a favored son—but he hadn't done it only because it was demanded of him. He'd thirsted for it from the moment he'd beheld Ganis's body, shredded by the hot steel claws of a rebel mortar bomb. He had five more sons, but Ganis had been the one most like him, with ambition and an eye for judging stock and a knowledge of soil and grasses that most men didn't acquire till they were much older.

On the next raid Ibrahim Idris left his Kalashnikov behind and carried a spear instead. That was the proper instrument for exacting retribution. The power of an automatic rifle was in the rifle, but a spear's was in the heart of the man who hurled it; it was an extension of his sinew and bone, flying from his own hand, not a gun barrel. With it he killed an infidel soldier, a Dinka, in personal combat. Youth for youth, blood for blood, he thought, then tied a rope he used for binding captives to the corpse's ankles and dragged it behind Barakat, calling out to the Brothers that Ganis had been avenged.

His thirst was slaked, but the tear in his heart was a wound beyond healing. Nor had jihad made the land of the abid a land without a people; clear them out, and they flowed right back in. One might as well try sweeping water from a swamp with a broom. Though a man his age could retire from the fighting without disgrace, he stayed in it because he didn't trust anyone else to lead his men. His first duty now was to preserve as many Salamat lives as he could, so as to preserve the Salamat. Each man's loss diminished the next generation. Half his men would now be dead if it weren't for him, for he'd shown as much skill as courage in battle. When there was resistance, he attacked from the rear, or from the flank, and if a frontal charge was unavoidable, he made sure to come at the enemy when the sun was in their eyes. In recent months he had made separate truces with some Dinka commanders, promising to avoid attacking them if they refrained from attacking him and allowed Salamat cattle to graze on their land. It was forbidden by the fatwa, but so many omdas had returned to that practice that the government would have to arrest them all to stop it. As for Ibrahim Idris himself, no one dared to denounce him; he was the father of a martyr.

He continued to make war on those abid who refused the hand of his friendship, but now the stench of burned villages and corpses seemed ingrained in his nostrils; he could smell those smells when there wasn't a flaming house or a dead body within a day's walk. And he could not get out of his head the cries of the women his Brothers raped as they were brought to the slave markets or to the government's peace camps. He'd tried to get them to stop, telling them that the jihad didn't license rape, that rape was indeed *haram*, forbidden, but the Brothers seemed to think it was their right, and so he'd stopped trying. A jinn was loose in the land, making men crazy.

Miriam. Once more she rose to the forefront of his consciousness. He saw her, in the blue cloth he'd bought her, walking toward him with sinuous grace to bring him the sweet tea she made, felt her strong fingers rubbing the liquid butter into his calves, heard her say "I am here" when he came to her at night; and the memory of the way she pleasured him now caused him to long for her with an unbearable longing. To remember the first time he saw her . . .

"I've heard that the abid here go without clothes, and now I see that it's true," the militia captain had said scornfully. His company of infantry had been attached to the murahaleen for the operation, the first the murahaleen had run in the Nuba hills.

He passed his binoculars to Ibrahim Idris. The village on the opposite hill appeared so close that Ibrahim could see the little gardens planted alongside the tall, round houses, the lines made by the layers of grass thatch on the roofs. The men threshing grain in the field between the hills looked to be only a few meters away. Some wore shorts, but the rest nothing more than wide leather belts.

"Shameful, isn't it?" whispered the captain, a young man wearing a green headband with the profession inscribed on it in white. "People like that deserve what we're going to give them."

"Would you not give it to them if they were clothed?" Ibrahim asked.

"What do you think?"

"Then you see, we're giving it to them because these Nubans support the rebels, not because they're naked."

Ibrahim scanned the countryside, looking for armed men, and stopped when the lenses brought into plain view a girl grinding grain or nuts on a stone at the edge of the village. She was kneeling, ankles crossed to anchor her, and had not a stitch on except for a white bead belt and a red bead necklace that swung between her breasts as she rocked back and forth, pressing the stone in her hands against the grinding stone at her knees. Her black skin sparkled with sweat, and when she pressed down, the muscles in her arms and along her ribs stood out, like those in a slightly underfed leopard. Her braided hair trailed to her shoulders and was slathered with ochre and oil so that it glistened like her flesh. He doubted he could have taken his eyes off her if he wanted to. She brushed the ground-up grain or nuts into a basket and stood, looking, it seemed, straight at him, and when she stretched her tired arms overhead, it was as though she were displaying herself for him alone. Her long legs, the mounds of her breasts, the flat belly that told him she had not yet borne a child—all of this stunned and captivated him. He caught the gleam of the gold ring in her nose, but the binoculars weren't strong enough to reveal her features; still, he sensed that her face was as beautiful as the rest of her, and he nearly groaned with desire as she turned and walked toward a house, her back straight, her high, lean buttocks switching under the white girdle of beads. He returned the binoculars to the captain and pointed the girl out to him and declared, his voice thick: "I'm claiming her now."

"That's no girl for an old man," the captain remarked. At least he had a sense of humor.

"Listen," said Ibrahim in case his companion wasn't joking, "you tell your men, I'll tell mine, that anyone who seizes a girl with a long red necklace brings her to me unharmed."

Yamila—that was her name in her tongue. His claim on her had spared her from the Brothers that day of the raid. In his camp he'd spared her from the abuse of his wives, jealous of her beauty and the attentions he paid her; and when the time came to have her genitals cut, he'd spared her from that as well. Though she was a concubine, he treated her like a wife and perhaps better. Bought her the blue cloth to cover her nakedness, gave her a tent of her own so she did not have to sleep in the kraals and goat pens like his other slaves, and when she became pregnant, told her that by the laws of the Humr all children she bore him would be freeborn, full members of his lineage, and that he would lavish wealth upon them so they would have plenty to take good care of her after he was summoned to Paradise.

In spite of his kindness, she'd run away at the first opportunity, fleeing back to the Nuba. She'd taken their infant with her, and the loss of him had widened the hole in Ibrahim's heart. It tortured him to think of the boy, growing up among savages, never learning all the things a father could teach about cattle and soil and grasses. What did he look like? Was he well and strong, or sick, and if sick, who among those heathens with their kujurs and silly superstitions could heal him?

What had he done to earn this torment? Ya Allah! He knew. He'd sinned, bribing the woman who was to circumcise Yamila not to do it but to pretend she had, and then bribing her further to ensure her silence. It was then that he'd bestowed the name Miriam on Yamila, proclaiming to his kinsmen that the concubine was now a Muslim, and he supposed that public falsehood had aggravated his offense. His thoughts were turning bitter again, his longing congealing into anger. You would think that Miriam would have shown some appreciation and gratitude; he'd damned his own soul for her sake. It was she who'd begged him not to allow her to be cut, though he'd granted her wish for his own sake, too. Circumcision would prevent her from taking pleasure in the sexual act, and the pleasure she got from it had heightened his own, so much so that he'd begun to neglect his wives. Abruptly, his emotions swung back to longing. Oh, the way she would whisper "I am here," and then turn over on the sleeping mat and arch her back, presenting herself like a lioness in heat, and then make sounds in her throat and move against him, the little stifled cries and the thrusts of her buttocks restoring the powers of his youth. Surely she could not have taken such delight from him if she didn't love him. Surely she could not have been deceiving all that time. Everything was in God's hands. Perhaps God had willed Miriam to escape with their son to punish him for his sins. If that were so, then he had to submit himself to God's will, but he was incapable of such resignation.

"Ya, uncle. It was a thorn."

"What?"

"In Barakat's leg." Abbas showed him the thorn, long as a man's thumb. "It was in very deep. I pulled it out with my teeth," he said, baring his teeth, which were strong and white and straight.

"Barakat can be bad tempered. You're lucky he didn't kick you in the head."

"God told him I was trying to help him, and so he was quiet."

"You see the hand of God in every little thing."

"I see it because it's there."

Ibrahim Idris again motioned at his saddlebags. "I wish to further test what you learned. Read to me what the book says about the coveting of women, if you can find the verses."

"I think I can." Abbas sat down with the Koran opened in his lap, his lips moving as his finger moved across the pages. "Yes, here it is. The twenty-third *sura*. It says a man may know only his wife and the captives he possesses. If he covets any woman beyond these, he is a transgressor."

"So it's not a sin to covet a captive woman?"

"The verse is very clear."

Then Ibrahim spotted Kammin, his chief servant, and called to him. "Make fresh tea and tell my guests I'm ready to receive them."

Kammin, a good Dinka who'd converted to the faith, jerked his head in acknowledgment, removed the pot from the fire, and went off.

"Ya, Abbas! Have you cleaned your rifle yet?"

"Of course, uncle. It's the first thing I do every morning."

"Go somewhere and clean it again. I wish to speak to my guests in private."

Led by Kammin, the Messiriya trader Bashir approached with his companion. They sat down, folding their legs, and Kammin poured them each a glass of tea and they exchanged greetings with their host, who asked if they'd slept well. They looked tired. Bashir scratched his beard and replied that the hospitality of Ibrahim Idris made the hardest ground as soft as a bed.

"A new acquisition?" he asked, gesturing at Bashir's wristwatch. "It looks very dear."

"It is. A Rolex. Entirely of gold."

Bashir took it off and passed it over for his inspection and admiration. The watch was heavy for so small an object and the band gleamed and there were two small dials within the big dial, which, Bashir explained, gave the date and the day of the week. He handed the watch back to the trader.

"So business must be good for you to afford such a watch that does all those things."

He leaned against his saddle and waited for Bashir to say something. He had little respect for men who bought and sold for a living—it wasn't man's work, like raising cattle—and he especially disliked Bashir. Dealing with him was a tiresome chore but a necessary one. The government provided horses to the men but not feed, saddles, and bridles; they were expected to furnish those themselves, and because many could not afford such items, the cost came out of Ibrahim Idris's pocket. The fifty-thousand enlistment bonus had been for one time only; the government did not pay the murahaleen wages for the time they spent away from their herds, and that was another expense he had to bear. For all practical purposes, he was a privateer, and the jihad had been draining his treasury before his path crossed with Bashir's, during the last dry season. God be praised for causing their paths to cross! He'd come upon Bashir and his associate, making their way home from the south with bags of money, a great deal of money, and after he persuaded them to reveal how they had acquired so much treasure, he proposed that they enter into an arrangement of mutual benefit. Bashir could not refuse. He traded with foreigners and infidels who stood in enmity to the regime and to the jihad, and knew full well that Ibrahim Idris had the power to shoot him on the spot, or to turn him over to the military authorities, who would shoot him later. His life and the liberty to continue doing business—those were what he would get out of the arrangement while Ibrahim got income to defray his expenses.

"This trip wasn't as profitable as my previous ones," the trader now said. "As I'm sure you know, we were able to collect only ninety-two this time."

Bashir reached under his jelibiya and produced his machine and pressed the buttons and turned the machine around to show the figure. The machine fascinated Ibrahim Idris. So small it fit into the hand, yet it could make calculations faster than any man could speak the numbers.

"There is what comes to you. The machine doesn't lie," Bashir said, tilting his jaw.

"Only if the one who uses it doesn't lie." Ibrahim motioned at his saddlebags and said, "I'll count it later."

One of the other men removed the bound bills from a pouch slung over his shoulder and leaned over and stuffed them into the saddlebags. It wasn't necessary to remind Bashir that he and his companion were to remain his guests until the money was counted.

"This business would be much more simple and quick if you accompanied me with the murahaleen." Ibrahim was voicing a thought that had been on his mind for some time. "As soon as I have the captives rounded up, I sell them to you on the spot, then you bring them to your foreigners and they pay you. *Halas.*" Wiping one hand with the other. "It's finished with."

Bashir did not appear enthusiastic.

"It would spare you from going from owner to owner, buying one here, two there," Ibrahim added. "It would spare me the trouble of bringing a lot of people to the markets."

"Ya, my friend! It's not so simple. With what money would I buy them from you on the spot? To pay you, I need first to be paid by the foreigners. They come here only a few times a year. What would I do with all the captives in the meantime? Also, the foreigners ask the captives to tell their stories. They record their stories, word for word. If we made an arrangement as you propose, the abid would say they were sold to me by you on the very day you seized them and the foreigners would see what we're doing and stop dealing with me." Bashir cupped his knees with his hands, as if to push himself to his feet. "You could count it now, Ibrahim? We have a long way to go."

"Moment, moment." Motioning to the trader not to be so anxious. "How often do your travels take you here to the Nuba?"

"Why do you wish to know?"

"A Nuban girl, a *serraya*, escaped from me some time ago, with our small son. One of my wives, the youngest, arranged for their flight in secret."

"Jealous, was she?" Bashir asked with a knowing leer. "You know the proverb, 'Beat your wife each morning—if you don't know the reason for it, she will'? Ya, with a wife who did that, you would both know the reason. And I would divorce her after beating her."

"What I did is no concern of yours. This serraya's name is Miriam, but her Nuban name is Yamila. The boy is called Abdullah. The girl is perhaps eighteen years. Tall and very good-looking, with two lines of marks across her forehead, like this"—he traced his finger over his brow—"and more marks on her belly, in the shape of bird's wings, and still more marks around her upper arms, like bracelets. Also—"

The trader rather impolitely stopped his speech by raising an open palm. "You wish her returned to you."

"I do."

"Ya, Ibrahim! It's not our trade to take captives or to retake them when they get away."

"It isn't necessary to tell me what your trade is. Esmah! You must see and hear a great deal in your journeys. The blacks speak freely to you. They consider you a brother, while I'm their enemy and all our conversing is with guns. Should you hear of her or, inshallah, discover where she is, I ask you to report it to me. If I am then able to get her back, I'll extend to you the hand of brotherhood."

"Brotherhood with you—a thing to value highly," Bashir said, kissing the tips of his own fingers. "But may I say that I would wish there to be something else in the hand you extend?"

"Provided your information is accurate and the girl once again with my house, there will be."

"How badly do you wish for that?"

"One hundred thousand."

The trader gazed at his associate, who offered no expression with voice or face, and then he picked up a stick and made marks in the dirt.

"That's four times what the foreigners pay for each captive," Ibrahim Idris reminded him.

"A little less four times. Twenty-nine thousand per head they pay. But that's for any abid, young, old, strong, weak, beautiful, ugly, man, or woman. A serraya such as you described is extraordinary, worth ten to one, I would judge. In addition, there is the son. Your own blood, omda."

"I'm not offering to buy them. I'm offering to buy information."

"But in this case, the information would be the same as buying. Without it, you have nothing. Three hundred."

"That's outrageous."

"For a young and beautiful woman? For your own blood?"

"I'm not going to bargain for them as I would for cows."

"Very well then, don't bargain." Bashir, in the time-honored custom, made a show of anger and disgust, flinging the stick aside, rising suddenly. "You have a lot of spies and good ones, too. They certainly know what I'm up to, day to day."

"Yes. Those spies are to help you resist the temptation to make off with your income without paying my percentage."

"Ask them to find her."

"I have, but they have not been successful."

Bashir tsked in contempt, and as he turned, pretending to leave, Ibrahim Idris offered one-fifty.

"Two-fifty," the trader countered. "What you're asking won't be easy. It would take a lot of time, and if I ask too many questions, the abid would become suspicious. Two-fifty, no less."

"Who do you think you're dealing with?" Ibrahim Idris stood to his full height and willed a glint to enter his eyes. When it came to shows of anger, he took second place to no one, and in this instance, it was not entirely a show. "I'll tell you who. The omda of the Salamat, the owner of eight hundred head, a captain of murahaleen, the father of a martyr! A man about whom songs are sung!"

"I've heard them," Bashir said calmly. "And most are in praise of your generosity."

He paused. The remark had pricked his pride in his reputation.

"Two then. Two hundred thousand and no more."

Again Bashir glanced at his companion, who gave a quick nod.

Bashir said, "Done."

Redeemer

MORNING LIGHT INFILTRATED through the mesh windows and the cracks in the zippered tent flaps so that she now could see the canopy of her mosquito net and the dark blots made by the dormant flies clinging to it. Mosquitoes were not abundant in Loki this almost rainless rainy season, but flies made up for the deficiency. *Was it darkness or the cooler temperatures at night that put them to sleep?* she wondered. In the two beds to the right of hers, Anne and Lily, the Irish girls from Concern, lay cocooned within their nets, Anne snoring lightly, but Quinette had been awake since before dawn, taut with anticipation. She'd tried reading herself back to sleep, first with Scripture and then with a Christian romance, but neither the novelist's stilted prose nor the dull prescriptions of Leviticus quelled her excitement.

Almost everything in Africa excited her. The most common scenes of everyday life—boys playing bau under a tree, a Turkana man striding down the road with his walking stick and wooden headrest, a flock of goats bleating along a dry riverbed—thrilled her because they weren't mere tourist backdrop but part of her daily life. She was the WorldWide Christian Union's field representative in Loki. She had a real place here and real work to do, and it was hers to do for as long as she wanted and for as long as she could put up with the privations, and she was sure she could because she didn't regard living in a tent with two other women and outdoor privies and taking showers under a canvas bucket as privations; nor were the heat, dust, mud, and bugs, the isolation and the hazards of flying into Sudan in small planes. These were minor trials, the small price she had to pay for fulfilling what she'd always known would be her destiny— to live an extraordinary life. She was doing something difficult, unusual, and dangerous in a difficult, unusual, and dangerous part of the world. Best of all, it was righteous work.

Since her return to Africa two months ago, there had been times when she felt lonely and homesick, when the heat, dust, and bugs got on her nerves, when a desperate boredom seized her because there was absolutely nothing to do after working hours except to hang out in the compound bars with the aid workers and pilots. Bandits roamed beyond the compound's fences, making it inadvisable to venture out, even in a group. Besides, there was nowhere to go, Loki being just about the most wretched town on earth—a bunch of filthy tukuls and mud-walled shops with corrugated iron roofs and streets adrift with trash and stinking of shit. Goat shit, cow shit, human shit.

When the spells of loneliness or boredom came over her, she bucked up her spirits by reflecting on the torments and hardships the early Christians endured for their faith. Not that Quinette believed there was any equivalence between those and the inconveniences she faced. It was the lesson the first Christians provided: they embraced their sufferings as gifts flowing from God's love and favor, for He reserved a special place in His heart for those who suffered in His name.

God loved her, and Jesus was her friend. She was more sure of that than ever. If He didn't love her, if He didn't see her as exceptional and suited for the job, He would not have hired her. Sometimes she saw Him not as an Abrahamic patriarch in long white robe and long white beard but as a celestial executive, the CEO of the universe, sitting behind an enormous desk in a smart Armani suit, poring through thousands and thousands of résumés, rejecting ninety-nine point ninety-nine percent, looking for one that stood out. The résumé of a chosen one. She imagined Him selecting hers from the pile and remarking upon it favorably and then, through some mysterious means of divine communication, directing Ken Eismont to make good on his promise to hire her.

After returning to the States from Sudan, she'd waited a long time to hear from Ken. She feared he'd forgotten his offer, or had given the job to someone else, and grew desperately unhappy and backslid a couple of times—a night in a bar, a one-night stand with a guy in her computer class. God forgave her, after she vowed to improve. But it was hard. The excitement of her homecoming had worn off, the attention she'd received after her slide presentation at Family Evangelical—it had been a terrific success—had faded. She felt a little like Cinderella after midnight, slipping back into the drab clothing of her old life and self: Quinette Hardin, shopgirl. When six weeks passed without a word from Ken, she considered moving out of her sister and brother-in-law's house, feeling hemmed in and tired of playing the poor relation who's been taken in, but she continued to hope that escape was at hand.

The letter arrived on a Saturday morning. Sorting through the mail, Nicole said, "This one is for you." In Nicole's commonplace kitchen, the letter looked as out of place as Waterford crystal would have on the Formica table. The pale blue envelope bordered by diagonal stripes, with the words *Par Avion* printed below the Swiss stamps, larger and more artistic than American stamps, and the postmark that said *Genève* instead of Geneva, exhaled a foreign glamour, and so did the return address, the street number coming after the name, beneath the words, "WorldWide Christian Union—International Headquarters."

"I'm saved," she murmured when she finished reading.

"Since when did they start notifying you by mail that you're saved?"

"Not that kind of saved," Quinette said, and gave the letter to her sister to read. She hadn't told Nicole, or anyone, about Ken's offer.

"Omigod, Quinny, you don't mean you're going to take it, do you?"

That voice, its pleading whine marbled with the snappiness of a scold, was so like their mother's. At twenty-eight, Nicole was beginning to look as well as sound like Ardele. Flab was robbing her chin of definition, her hips and bosom were growing ponderous. The first thing that had struck Quinette when she came back from Africa was how fat people in her hometown were. Women with upper arms like kneaded dough, men with gourdlike bellies hiding their belts—that rural midwestern lumpiness resulting from a tradition of heavy eating passed on by grandparents and great-grandparents who'd hauled water from draw-wells and chopped firewood and plowed with mules and horses. Not that everyone had put on twenty pounds in the time Quinette had been away. They hadn't changed; she had, noticing their thick, coarse bodies because of the contrast they made with the slender Dinka. Over there all was subtraction, over here addition, and lots of it.

"You bet I am," she said to Nicole.

"They want you to sign a two-year contract. You might, you know, give it ten seconds of thought?"

"Don't need to. Ever since I got back all I've thought about is going back."

"To *Africa*? And for not a whole lot more than you're making now?"

"Twenty-five there is like a hundred here, and it's not for the money anyway."

And then her older sister teared up and embraced her in her squishy arms.

"Oh, Quinny! It's so far. And two years! It scares me. Like if you go, you'll never come back to us."

Quinette said nothing. The prospect of never coming back wasn't disagreeable.

There were sobs from her mother as well, and then an attitude of sullen disappointment. Her troublesome, unpredictable middle daughter was letting her down again. One cockeyed thing after another. Why, even when she mended her ways, she didn't return to the solid Lutheranism she'd been raised in, but to some evangelical sect of hand-clapping holy rollers. Why couldn't Quinette get married to a decent guy with a decent job and start giving her grandchildren, like Nicole? Kristen phoned from Minneapolis to tell her that she was making a dumb move. What kind of future could there possibly be in working in some African shithole for a bunch of starry-eyed do-gooders? Just the argument she expected from Kristen, the pick of the litter in the brains department, winner of a scholarship to Iowa State and now in her first year of graduate business school at the University of Minnesota. Even Pastor Tom questioned if she was ready for the hardships, the commitment.

As it happened, Quinette discovered that breaking away wasn't as easy as she thought. She'd typed her acceptance and was going to fax it to Ken, but she carried it around for two days. Small-town midwestern caution, that don't-stick-your-neck-out-someone-might-cut-your-head-off conservatism, was a gravitational force that bound people to the land of flat horizons generation after generation. It made them afraid of breaking away, and the insidious thing was the way it pulled you from the inside as well as from the outside. Quinette could feel that fear tugging at her guts. Her father and some other family farmers, she reflected, had taken a risk when the Farm Bureau advised them to "get big or get out." Disaster was what Dad got when prices fell in the eighties and he couldn't keep up his payments, and the only blessing was the cancer that spared him from seeing the farm, in the Hardin family for four generations, go on the block.

Troubled by self-doubt, she drove out to the old place, barely recognizing it because the corporation that had snapped it up at auction had replaced the barn and outbuildings and the house where she and her sisters had grown up with industrial pens occupied by thousands of hogs whose excreta made her eyes water. The stench and the sight of those steel-roofed sheds, all of it managed by some guy who had no more of his heart in the land than a foreman did in a factory, stirred up her hatred of the invisible, intangible, indifferent forces that had robbed her family of its legacy and ruined its happiness.

She spoke to her father as she stood at the roadside, the barbed-wire fences singing in the wind, and asked him to help her make the right decision. Then she closed her eyes and pictured the L-shaped white frame house that had once stood in the shade of cottonwood windbreaks. She saw her twelve-year-old face in the window of the bedroom she and Kristen shared, with its two maple beds on either side, under an angled ceiling so low that you had to watch your head when you sat up. It was a bleak November morning and she was dressing for school when a movement outside caught her eye. She looked past the barn and silo toward the cornfield sloping down to the trees lining the Little Cedar River. A flight of starlings, bunched into a dense, dark ball, then drawn out into a whirling funnel, then squeezed to a ball again, rose and dipped above the khaki stubble, their perfectly synchronized movements making them look like a smoky kite that changed shape instant by instant. It was almost hypnotic, watching them. Ardele called her to breakfast, but she didn't respond. *I'm not going to be like her,* she thought, soaring and dipping with the starlings in her imagination. *I'm not going to be like any of them, I'm going to be different.* It was so weird, in a nice way, how the words came from out of nowhere, sounding in her head not like the expression of a desire or hope but like a declaration of her fate. She accepted it happily. Would she marry a rock star and tour the country? Would she become rich and live in a great city like Chicago or New York? Who could tell? The important and marvelous thing was knowing that she was destined to live a bigger life in a bigger world and would never ever be like the woman her mother was now and her sisters and friends would grow up to be. Farm wives, housewives, beauticians, bank tellers, schoolteachers, check-out clerks in a convenience store. She knew that was what would happen to them, even if they didn't. She could see it in them. Something in their eyes, in the way they carried themselves, in the clothes they wore, in their voices, as plain as the land they'd been born to and would be buried in, marked them for ordinariness. Quinette felt sorry for them, even as she rejoiced in her exemption, and she smiled to herself, looking out at the barn and fields and the Little Cedar, sliding under the distant trees.

It was as if life had made a pledge to her, a pledge it withdrew after her father died. It seemed she'd been wrong, it seemed Kristen was the blessed one, her brains boosting her out and away. Every day of Quinette's life had been a handful of commonplace dirt, thrown on that thrilling moment of childhood promise, interring it under so many layers for so long that she'd all but forgotten it. Now Ken's letter was offering her a chance to repossess it, a lawful inheritance denied to her all these years. She was being called to Africa to do no small thing. She drove back to the Mailboxes outlet in town and sent the fax.

*   *   *

"JESUS MARY AND JOSEPH, what the hell time is it?"

"Seven-thirty," Quinette said, pulling her dress over her head—a Dinka woman's ceremonial dress, bright yellow with brown and gold swirls. She'd bought it at a market on her most recent trip into Sudan.

"Half seven of a Sunday morning, and you're up and about?" asked Lily Hanrahan. Quinette loved her accent and her quaint way of phrasing things. "Did you ever consider that some people might want to be sleeping in?"

"I have to meet Father Delaney at the Red Cross hospital."

"In that?" Lily poked a finger into her mosquito net to indicate Quinette's dress, over which she now draped a green and white bead necklace. "What've you got, a *date* with the old goat? Going to show him what he's been missing all these celibate years?"

Quinette hung her small gold crucifix over the necklace. "He's taking me on his rounds of the Turkana villages. Guess I'll be going to church in a way—so, my Sunday best."

"Would you two kindly shut up? I'd like to sleep," Anne Derby grumbled in the far bed.

Lily pushed her net aside and sat up. She was a short, broadshouldered woman with lank brown hair and an almost-pretty face. Wearing a snug singlet and panties, she sat the way a man would sit, her squat legs spread apart. A few pubic hairs peered out from the crotch of her underwear.

"I know you know that the bloody Turkana killed four people just three days ago," she said. "Shot 'em dead and left their wallets and money and took their shoes and clothes, and you're going to go on a tour of their villages?"

"Malachy said I'll be perfectly safe with him. They respect him. I mean, he's been out here since before any of us were born, and he ain't dead yet."

"Who do we write if you don't come back?" Anne asked. She swung out of bed, a wraithlike figure in her cotton nightdress, swigged from a bottle of Evian at her bedside, gargled, and then unzipped the front flap and spat noisily. "Mouth feels like the army marched through it in their socks."

"Which army?" asked Lily.

"The bloody army. Who cares which one?" Anne took another drink. " 'Let us have wine and women, mirth and laughter, sermons and soda water the day after.' Byron."

"Why, thank you. Should be 'wine and men' for us, but that doesn't scan right, does it? How about this? 'Heaven has sent us soda water as a torment for our crimes.' G. K. Chesterton."

"Happy hour the crime, a bad mouth and headache the torment. He was a cute one, that pilot with the guitar. Not a bad voice either."

"My ex could sing twice as good and he was tenth rate," Quinette said, slipping into her flip-flops. They didn't go with the dress but were an improvement over sneakers or hiking boots.

"As a husband or singer?" Lily asked.

"Singer. As a husband, no rating, none, zero, zip," Quinette answered in a tough, worldly voice. As a divorcée, she had a certain status in the eyes of her better-educated but never-married companions, and she tried to sound like a woman who'd been around whenever she had the chance.

She grabbed her minicamera and went out, hearing Anne call from behind her, "Ta! Say a prayer for us, will you?"

It looked as if the rains would fail again today. The sky was cloudless, and dust swirled and sparkled in the thin light air, reminding her of the soap flakes in those glass bubbles that are turned upside down to create an illusion of snowfall. Farm life had fine-tuned Quinette's sensitivities to weather, and she knew that if she were a Turkana, she would curse this brilliant sky. "Their cows and goats are perishing by the dozen," Malachy had said last Thursday, after news of the ambush spread from compound to compound. The bandit gang had waylaid four aid workers, two Kenyans and two white guys, as they were driving out to drill a bore hole. "What a bitter irony," the priest intoned in his deep Irish voice, "that they should kill those trying to help them survive." Quinette reckoned it was, though she didn't understand how killing people for their clothes and shoes would fill a stomach or help anyone get through a drought.

She strode toward Hotel California's mess hall, imitating the super-erect bearing of a Dinka female. Back home she habitually slouched or crooked her knees to make herself look shorter, especially when she was around men of average height, but here she felt free to stretch herself to the max. "White Dinka Woman"—that's what the people in Sudan had taken to calling her, and she cherished the nickname.

"Hey-ull, if that airstrip doesn't have foxholes dug in it, I'll land on the goddamned thing."

It was the Texan, and he was sitting with four other people at one end of the dining room, which wasn't a room really but a broad patio surrounded by a low stone wall under a vaulted grass roof with wooden poles running down from its center. There were Fitz Martin, Knight Air's operation chief, and the woman who flew as the Texan's copilot, and two people Quinette didn't recognize—a short, bald guy and an older woman with dyed blond hair. They stopped talking the second she walked in. She wanted to believe that they'd been struck dumb by her outfit and regal carriage but sensed by the suddenness of their silence that she'd intruded on a private conversation. Not surprising. The bunch from Knight Air were secretive and standoffish. At mealtimes they sat by themselves, speaking in low tones, like a clique in a high school cafeteria. Quinette herself hadn't had any contact with them, except for a brief, inconsequential exchange with Fitz a couple of weeks ago on the compound's volleyball court. The girls' team was playing the boys', and she was at net opposite Fitz because she was tall and had played intramural volleyball in high school and was pretty good at spiking. Afterward Fitz complimented her on her play and then, patting his belly, said something about needing to get exercise to lose weight.

She glided up to the service counter, where two Kenyans stood behind steam tables and a propane stove, and asked for an omelet. As she waited for the eggs to cook, the Texan said, "Damn, girl, in that getup, all you've got to do is slap a little shoe polish on your face and y'all could pass." Quinette turned and saw his copilot give an exaggerated eye roll. He pulled back an empty chair and boomed, "C'mon over and join us. We're pretty damned bored with each other."

"Sure I'm not interrupting anything?" she asked after she got her breakfast.

"Hey-ull no."

He slapped the chair, but she elected to sit next to Fitz, finding him as appealing as the cowboy was obnoxious. His skin was a lovely shade of burnt sienna—the longer she was in Africa, the more unaesthetic she found white skin, her own excepted—and she remembered liking his boyish voice and the way his black eyes had seemed to undress her without offending her or making her uncomfortable. He had the sexiness of a man who loved women. Not that she had any intention of encouraging him.

"What gets you up so early on a Sunday?" he asked, pouring her a cup of coffee from the Thermos on the table.

She told him and explained that Malachy wanted to show her that the Turkana weren't as bad as their image.

"Ah, those people should pay Malachy a salary for all his advocacy," the bald man said.

"We haven't met. Quinette Hardin."

"John Barrett. Malachy and I go back a long way."

The older woman introduced herself as Diana Briggs, extending a hand that confessed to the age her tinted hair and makeup tried to conceal. Quinette recalled the reporter from her first trip, smearing on facial cream, and she thought of Tara Whitcomb, arranging her hair and freshening up her lipstick before she flew Ken and the team into Sudan. These middle-aged babes at war with the clock. It was kind of pathetic. When the time came for her to get old, she would just let herself get old, as God intended.

"Are you working with Malachy in some capacity?" Diana asked with a stiff formality, accentuated by her Anglo-Kenyan accent.

Quinette shook her head and asked, "So what gets all of you up so early?"

There was just the slightest pause, just the briefest exchange of glances, before the Texan replied.

"Got us a load of goodies to bring into Chukudum," he said. Chukudum was a Sudanese town not far over the border. "For that hospital the Norwegians built over there. Can't bring the stuff in by road, so they called on us, old Fly-by-Knight."

Quinette bit into her slightly burned omelet. She surmised that Chukudum was not his final destination, if he was going there at all. Everyone knew that the people from Knight Air were flying into the Nuba mountains, which was supposed to be very dangerous. A halo of danger and outlawry glimmered around these people, and it piqued her curiosity.

"I don't see your partner. What's your name again? "

"Wes Dare," the Texan replied, his glance slipping sideways as if he were ashamed of it. "Doug's in Nairobi with Tony, leavin' me and Mary to do the grunt work." His arm went around the young woman's shoulders, then dropped. "I like that name you've got. Shows your mama had some imagination."

"It was my dad thought of it. Quinette was his grandmother's name."

"Knew it!" Wesley Dare's eyes again skidded off to the side. He had jug-handle ears and a squashed nose and curly hair colored the distressing red of rust streaks in an old bathtub. "It's been my experience that women don't have much imagination, and y'all can really see that when it comes to naming their kids. One year everybody gets named Jennifer and Tim, next year it's Matt and Margaret."

Mary looked at Quinette, pleading silently to forgive Wes, as if he were some idiot child who couldn't be held responsible for the things he said. That certainly had been a stupid observation, but it described Quinette's mother to a T. Ardele never could imagine a life other than the one she had. For some reason, alternatives never occurred to her. If they did, she never acted on them. She was only forty-four when she was widowed, but she never remarried. She was Ted Hardin's widow; nothing else was possible.

"So who named you?" she asked Wes.

"My mama, who else? Wesley ain't very imaginative. If it had been up to my old man, I would've been named Quanah."

That drew a little shriek from Mary. His glance shot to her, then ricocheted back to Quinette.

"On account of my great-grandma was a full-blood Comanche, back when their big chief was Quanah Parker."

Quinette squinted skeptically.

Wes pulled out his wallet and produced a laminated card, with his photo on it, testifying to his enrollment in the Comanche Nation. "Where do y'all think these come from?" He thrust his head toward her, prying his eyes into circles with his thumbs and forefingers to better display his chocolate-brown pupils. "I'm like Fitz. A genuine mongrel. This here"— he tugged at a lock of his hair—"comes from the man great-grandma married. Not the color, the curl. He was a storekeeper on the reservation. Part white, part Comanch, and part black. His grandma was an escaped slave." Wes hesitated for half a breath, and his tone of voice changed, taking on an edge. "Now I reckon that oughta give you a nice warm glow."

"I'm afraid not. Should it?"

"You being in the business of freeing slaves, I figured it would."

"It isn't a business."

"There's some might say it is."

She saw that he'd been setting her up with his genealogical discussion, and that she'd walked right into it.

"I've got you pegged," she replied, whetting her own voice to cut back at him. "You like to jerk people's chains to see which way they'll jump. Your technique needs work."

Fitz laughed, slapping the table, and Wes picked up his sunglasses and gave them a quick twirl. "And here I thought you were a sweet young idealist."

"Guilty to the last two. The last time I remember being sweet, I was in eighth grade and even then I had to work at it."

Wes said, "Would you bet that I was once an idealist?"

"I don't gamble."

"I was. Fresh out of Texas A and M with a degree in aero engineering in the late sixties. I think I smoked too much bad dope back then, because I decided to teach math to underprivileged Messican kids in El Paso. Did that till it come to me, like a light, that I hated kids of any creed or color. So I signed up with Air America to fly in Indochina, doin' my bit to fight Communism. My mama wrote and asked me, 'Wes, what are y'all doin' over there?' I wrote her back, 'Mama, I'm flyin' good to the good and bad to the bad.' Ten years later I'm flyin' guns into the Nicaraguan Contras for Southern Air, and I told Mama that I was flyin' good to the good and bad to the bad, but it was sometimes right hard to tell which was which. Few more years go by, and I'm flyin' photo-recon missions for the Royal Saudi Air Force, so we could liberate those useless Kuwaitis from those scum-suckin' Eye-Raquis, and I wrote to Mama and said I was flyin' good to the good and bad to the bad, but there wasn't any difference. And now that I'm flyin' in Africa, I tell her that I'm flyin' bad to the bad because they're all bad over here."

The monologue pummeled everyone into a few moments' silence. Then Mary said, "Jesus, did you sugar your cereal with cocaine this morning or what?"

Quinette looked at her watch and stood up suddenly. "Hate to leave this brilliant conversation, but I'll be late. I'm meeting Malachy at the Red Cross hospital."

"Do you have a car?" Diana asked.

Quinette shook her head.

"You intended to walk there?"

"Sure. It isn't far."

"Don't be silly," Diana said in a motherly tone. "Really, I'm surprised at Malachy, asking you to meet him there instead of his picking you up here. He ought to know better."

"Some of his parishioners are in the hospital, and he—"

"Come along now."

Diana and Barrett led her to a Toyota pickup, painted utilitarian gray, with the red and white logo of International People's Aid on the doors.

"So that's your connection with Wes and Fitz? You're with IPA?" Quinette asked, climbing into the middle of the bench seat. It was immediately obvious that she was too long-legged to avoid being kneecapped by the floor shift, so Diana traded places with her.

"I am," John replied, steering through the gate with a cheery "*Jambo!*" to the askaris. "Field coordinator for its Sudan operations. Diana is one of our benefactors."

"A rich bitch buying her way out of white liberal guilt is how Wes would put it," Diana said. "How he *has* put it. Quite the character, isn't he?"

"He would be if he didn't work so hard at trying to be one," Quinette observed, pleased that she drew a laugh from both people.

"Bloody good pilot, though," John said, as if that forgave everything.

"If what I hear is true, I guess he has to be."

"There are a lot of rumors in Loki, and one needs to be careful about the things one hears."

"More careful about the things one says," Diana added, looking at Quinette sidelong. "Loose lips sink ships—and crash planes as well."

Quinette kept silent, considering herself warned not to press them about where Wesley Dare was headed today.

They went past the compounds of Norwegian People's Aid and Doctors Without Borders. If the UN's base, with its neighborhoods of white and blue bungalows and offices, was the city, the camps of the independent agencies were the suburbs, though the organizational flags flying above them and the armed guards at the gates lent them the look of military outposts, an image Quinette preferred, as she preferred to think of the people inside not as aid workers but as warriors enlisted in the battle against hunger and disease and conquest. A Hercules thundered overhead, bearing westward. The four engines, sending tremors through the air and through her skin, shook her back into the excited happiness she'd felt when she woke up; and the antiquated throb of propellers caused a remote in her brain to click and bleed all color from the scene, so she saw it in the documentary black and white of the History Channel, the plane becoming, briefly, a World War II bomber, soaring away to pulverize the enemy. The Herc was going to drop sacks of grain, not high explosives, but food was a weapon in this war. So was breaking the chains of the enslaved. Her grandfathers had liberated people in France. She was carrying on in their tradition. Maybe thirty or forty years from now, this crusade would be on the History Channel, and she would be able to tell her grandchildren that she'd been in it, been part of something altogether noble and so much bigger than herself.

The hospital, in a village near Loki called Lopiding, appeared unexpectedly. There were mud-and-wattle huts and little congregations of goats lazing under tall tamarind trees, then suddenly a high gate with the usual complement of askaris, and beyond it whitewashed buildings and white tents as big as barns, the Red Cross emblem on their roofs, and people swarming everywhere: doctors and nurses in surgical smocks, ambulatory patients wearing light brown hospital gowns. Almost all were Sudanese men and boys wounded in the war, legs in casts or braces, arms in slings, heads bandaged, hands wrapped in dressings like prizefighters. One young man on crutches was trying to kick a soccer ball with his good leg. She recognized on some faces the V-shaped cicatrix of Dinka, the horizontal lines of Nuer—she was learning the various tribal marks—but most of the other tattoos were strange to her, and some were not tribal markings at all but scars left by bullets and bomb fragments and landmine shrapnel.

"Here you are," John said, stopping in front of the admissions building. "A pleasure meetin' you. Be sure to tell Malachy that I expect him to watch out for you."

Several Dinka sat around flattened boxes spread on the ground, playing cards. As she waited, she was conscious of their glances; admiring glances, she hoped, though she didn't rule out the possibility that a white woman dressed like one of theirs presented a curious figure, even a ridiculous one. It was impossible to tell what they were thinking. Their expressions revealed nothing, the famed Dinka mask made more opaque by the dead, blank look acquired by men who'd been in battle. She'd seen it on her father's face, in a photograph of him and his buddies in Vietnam. The thousand-yard stare, he'd called it.

When ten minutes passed without Malachy, she went looking for him, peeking into the cavernous tents, catching glimpses of men with limbs in traction, of a woman sitting beside a bed occupied by a child with its face and arms burned from black to a shocking suppurating pink. Such a variety of injuries, so much suffering, more than she could grasp. From inside a tin-roofed building came the screech of a band saw, a belt sander's rough hum, and when the noise stopped, Malachy's voice—"I'll pay you out of my own bloody pocket"—and another voice, speaking English in some sort of European accent—"I am sorry I must ask you, but those are the regulations." She stepped in and saw, through a light mist of sawdust, a row of leg braces with metal clamps attached, and also dozens of prosthetic legs—knee-length and full-length, shiny and flesh-toned, standing on shelves or piled up in bins, as if some psycho had dismembered a store full of manikins. Several Kenyan workmen in coveralls stood around wielding power tools, another placed an artificial limb on a conveyor belt and fed it into what appeared to be an oven. A middle-aged Turkana sat on a chair, half of one leg sticking out like a thin stovepipe. A teenage Sudanese, missing a leg, stood on his crutches while a technician took the length of his right with a measuring tape. At one end of the room, beside rows of canvas sacks filled with coils of brightly colored rope, Malachy was deep in conversation with a crew-cut young white man. In olive shorts, a white cotton shirt, and Teva sandals, the priest looked emphatically unclerical. He spotted her in the doorway, looked at his watch, and bumped his forehead with the heel of his hand.

"Oh, Lord! How long have you been waiting?"

"Not long. What are you doing here? What is this place?"

"Orthopedic workshop!" the other man shouted, as the band saw started again. "We make here the prosthetic limbs! Who are you?"

She didn't answer, a little nonplussed by his enthusiasm.

Malachy waved her to come on in. "Sorry for keeping you. This poor sod, one of my parishioners"—he motioned at the Turkana—"gangrene. He's in here to get fitted—"

"From this!" the ebullient European said. He dipped a hand into the rope and pulled out a ball of red and blue and green strands tangled up like multicolored spaghetti. "Polyprop! We melt it down and from it make new legs for those who have not theirs!"

"And it's free if you're Sudanese, but if you're a local, the Red Cross charges you," the priest said. "I'll be but a minute, and then we're off."

"I'll wait outside," she said as the workman with the belt sander started up again, putting the finishing touches on a well-shaped calf.

Orthopedic workshop! she thought, her nostrils twitching from the polypropylene dust. Kind of like Santa's workshop? With the happy elves making new legs as stocking stuffers? The young Sudanese came out, swinging on his crutches, went past her, and then pivoted so quickly he nearly fell.

"Sister! Sister Kinnet!"

She narrowed her eyes, as if looking at him in dim light. *Kinnet.* She faintly remembered someone calling her that.

"You don't remember me? Because of this?" He tapped the stump of his upper thigh, over which his trouser leg was folded and pinned with safety pins.

"My God! Matthew? You gave me a ride on your bike?"

He beamed in affirmation.

"But how . . . what happened?"

He'd been wounded, not in a battle but while herding cows; one of the animals stepped on a landmine. It was killed outright, and shrapnel pierced Matthew just above his left knee—not a serious wound, he said, but it became infected, and by the time he was evacuated, it was too late to save his leg.

"I am so sorry, Matthew."

"I will soon have a new one," he declared, with such absence of rancor and sadness that she wondered if he was still in shock. "But did you see them, Kinnet? They're *white*. I think I will have to paint mine black, or I will be a Dinka with the leg of a *hawaga*!"

"Your sister. I remember she was one of the ones set free that day. Is she all right?"

"Very much. She got married. To SPLA commander, an important man, a captain."

Moved by his stalwart optimism, she cried out, "Oh, Matthew!" and embraced him.

He seemed not to know what to make of this expression, to be slightly embarrassed by her clinging to him, so she let him go.

"It's not so bad, sister," he said, then lowered his voice. "I have been fighting for a long time, Now I won't have to anymore. But with the new leg I can herd cows. I will be able to sing to my ox all day, with no fighting."

"I hope so. How I hope so."

"Amin Madit speaks of you," he said.

"Amin Madit?"

"My sister."

"Oh, yes. She remembers me?"

"Very much and speaks of you. About the hawaga lady who made such fine words to make her happy."

"Not really?"

"Yes, yes. All the captives spoke of you. They liked your words very much."

The pleasure of hearing this instantly pumped in a warm transfusion of pride, for which she pardoned herself.

"And I think Amin Madit would like very much your dress also."

"Oh? And what do you think?"

"Very much," Matthew said as Malachy emerged from the workshop, wiping his glasses with a handkerchief. "Sister, can you find for me the black paint? The kind in the can with the button? Like this." He mimicked a spraying motion. "They don't have it here."

"I don't know. I'll try. Promise."

"You know that lad?" the priest asked as they walked toward his Land Rover.

She told him how she and Matthew had met and how he'd lost his leg and that sometimes she felt such fury toward the Sudanese Arabs, it frightened her.

"They do a lot to make one furious, don't they now? But *Iram est brevem insaniam*. So said Seneca, quoting Horace. 'Anger is a temporary madness.'"

Nothing caused her more embarrassment than moments like this, when the paucity of her education was made plain. Who was Seneca? Who was Horace?

"I'll confess to feeling a touch of the temporary madness a few minutes ago," Malachy said, pulling out of the hospital gate. "A lad like your Sudanese friend gets treated gratis. But a Turkana has to pay a hundred shillings just to be seen by a doctor. Where on earth is a Turkana to come up with a hundred shillings? Any wonder they turn to banditry?"

He stopped in front of a tukul and beeped the horn. A man in Western clothes came out, Catholic missal in hand, and climbed into the backseat. Malachy introduced him as his deacon and said that he spoke English and would help Quinette follow the morning's services.

They headed down an excuse of a road paralleling a dry watercourse, its banks hedged by shrubs and thornbushes. Without the dashboard compass, Quinette never would have known they were traveling southwest. Her sense of direction wasn't all that developed, and the country offered no landmarks: a featureless pan of pale brown, with only a few acacias, spread like umbrellas, to relieve the desolation. Some places lacked even those sparse trees, and she looked out at flat expanses devoid not only of life but, it seemed, of the hope of life. This was her first close look at the world that lapped the compound's perimeters, and she wondered aloud how people lived in it.

"With great difficulty." The priest flapped a hand, indicating a herd of camels swaying along in the distance. The Turkana walking behind looked like a dark reed in motion. "There are settlements all up and down these riverbeds. Don't you worry." He patted her knee. "I know where I'm going. Blazed this track we're on myself, thirty years ago. No GPS then, didn't even have a compass. Dragged a log behind my truck each time I came out, and eventually I had a road. Put a few turns in it to give it an Irish twist."

"John said to tell you that he expected you to look out for me."

"John Barrett? You saw him?"

"This morning at breakfast. Gave me a lift to the hospital."

"Haven't seen him in weeks. What sort of trouble is he causing now?"

"You'd know more about that than me. He said you two go back a long way."

"We do." Malachy slowed down to ease over a washtub-size bump. Several yards away, like blackened tarps, lay the rotted hides of dead cattle. "But Johnny doesn't keep me abreast of all he's up to."

"Since priests never lie, I'll take your word."

He looked at her, silently asking what she meant.

"There are all these stories that IPA and Knight Air are flying into the Nuba mountains, but they won't say so," Quinette said. "Why the big secret? We fly into places that are off limits and we're not shy about admitting it. We don't advertise where we're going, but when we get back, we put out newsletters about where we've been. We put it on the Internet. Why do those people act, you know, like they're on some CIA mission?"

"And why are you so intrigued about what they're doing?" he asked, giving her a quick look, then as quickly returning his eyes to the road.

Quinette shrugged. She wasn't sure why. It was more than mere curiosity. Fitz, Wes, and the others formed a kind of club, and it bothered her to be left out. True, they barred everyone in the compound from their tight little circle; nevertheless, because she wasn't like everyone else, she thought she was entitled to be let in.

"To answer your question," Malachy said, "if I were flying stuff into the Nuba, I would want it known only by the people who need to know. Your organization goes into no-fly zones, sure it does, but you have to understand that even though the Nubans are as black as the Dinka, their mountains belong to northern Sudan. In the south you can get away with some things because the south is much more in the public eye. Khartoum absolutely loathes the spotlight you people have put on the slave trade, they would love to stop you, and they probably could, but they don't because Sudan already has a reputation as a rogue country. But the Nuba, it's so very isolated, and the government has a free hand to do as it chooses. It could blow an aid flight out of the sky and the world wouldn't know, and probably not care if it did. Is it necessary to say more?"

There were more carcasses on the desert now, some recent and bloated, swarming with maggots, others old and mummified. A horned skull with birds' nests in its eye sockets, a ribcage, and fragments of leg bone lay at the foot of a termite mound like the remnants of an animal sacrifice at an altar. A cow's backbone, white in the sun, writhed alongside the road. At last they arrived at the settlement. Turkana women wearing stacked necklaces that looked like colorful neck braces stood around a well, pumping water into calabashes and waterskins. Malachy parked near a stick-and-thornbush boma ten feet high, got out of the car, and stretched, his white hair ruffled by the wind, an aggressive wind that seemed to suck the moisture out of Quinette's skin. Missal in hand, the deacon went out among the tukuls, calling the people to come to church, which appeared to be the ring formed by the boma. People began filing inside, women in their long drab dresses, men in striped and checkered robes knotted over their knobby shoulders, walking sticks and braided stock whips in hand.

"Look at that fella over there." Malachy's hand fell heavily on her shoulder, and he turned her partway around to face a tall, wiry man who looked to be about fifty and wore an ostrich feather in his bark skullcap and ivory bracelets on his arms. "Can you see the scars on his chest, like a row of beads?"

She cocked her head forward, squinting, and said she couldn't.

"You will in a moment, when we're inside. He's the senior elder here, more or less the boss. Each one of those marks represents a man he's killed in battle. Toposa probably, and I'll wager they weren't all killed in self-defense. It's a hard, hard place, this, and it breeds hard people, and my mission is to make it a little less hard so as to make them a little less hard. More Christian. I see to it that wells are dug for them, that they get medical care, that they get fed in times of drought."

Looping her camera's cord around her wrist, Quinette followed him into the boma, where the whole settlement had gathered, cramming themselves into a circle not thirty feet in diameter, the men on one side, elders in front, women and kids on the other, sheltering under a tall tree that broke the torrent of direct sunlight. People who barely had water to drink had none for bathing, and the smell of so many bodies in so small a space was powerful—not sour or rank, just strong. The deacon motioned for Quinette to sit on a flat rock. He gave her permission to take pictures, and she boxed the priest in the viewfinder as he turned to the elders and uttered a single word in a booming voice. They answered in unison.

"Father Malachy has addressed the elders," the deacon translated, "and they have said, 'Apoloreng, we are here!' That is what we call him. Father of the Red Ox."

Turning to the women, Malachy called out to them, and they responded with a rhythmic chant.

"Now Father Malachy says that he is glad to see all the Turkana here, and the women say, 'We are here.' "

Then a melodious litany was sung, the priest leading, the women answering him first, the men coming in, high voices blending with low, rising, falling in a slow tempo. The African cadences pierced her to the depths.

"We are here to call on God," Malachy sang in his baritone.

"Oh, yes!" the congregation sang in response. "We are here. We are here calling on God."

"God of Abraham . . ."

"Yes!"

"God of Saint John . . ."

"Yes!"

"God of Mary . . ."

"Yes!"

"All you people are calling on God."

"Oh, yes! We are calling on Him."

"God of Matthew . . ."

"We call on him!"

"God of Mark . . ."

"We call on him!"

"God of Luke . . ."

"We call on him!"

"God of John . . ."

"We call on him!"

"All you people are calling on God."

"Oh, yes! We are calling on Him."

It was beautiful, elemental, bewitching, and Quinette's eyes flooded. She wished she knew Turkana so she could join in, although there was a whiff of paganism in the ceremony that made her a little uneasy: the chanting worshippers assembled in a circle under a tree, Malachy presiding over them like a white witch doctor rather than a minister of Our Lord. When the litany ended, the deacon rose and preached a homily. With no one to translate, Quinette had no idea what his message was. He spoke with a great deal of fervor, now stabbing the air with a finger, now tearing at the missal's pages to read a passage aloud, pacing back and forth as he read, the people shouting "Eh-yay!" whenever he made a point they particularly approved of. Feeling out of things, she looked at the ostrich-plumed elder and tried to count the scars beneath his left shoulder. How strange and thrilling to be in a church—if this could be called a church—with a man whose chest bore the record of the blood he'd shed. Endeavoring to be unobtrusive, she balanced the camera on her knees, swiveled her legs to point directly at him, and pressed the button.

She noticed that a young woman sitting beside her was wearing what appeared to be a calculator as a pendant, its buttons and display window giving off an anomalous plastic gleam among the bright beads half covering her breasts. Quinette leaned over for a closer look and made out the words TEXAS INSTRUMENTS. She raised the camera, snapped a picture, and began to mentally compose the letter that would accompany the photographs when she sent them home. She'd been debating with herself whether to tell her family about the ambush: Why worry them unnecessarily? Now she decided she would, then go on to say that she had ventured out only a few days after the aid workers were killed, with no more protection than an unarmed priest and deacon, and taken photographs of the fierce Turkana without them harming a hair on her head. She would make some witty remark about the woman wearing a Texas Instruments calculator as jewelry, and explain the meaning of the marks on the man's chest, making sure to adopt an offhanded tone to show that she didn't consider it any big deal. She wasn't sure how Kristen would react, but Ardele and Nicole would freak out, and in a corner of herself, the same dark nook where her wild impulses once flourished, prompting her to do things guaranteed to outrage her family, she relished the thought of upsetting those two timid, domesticated females with a tale of her daring—and with pictures to back it up.

The deacon finished his sermon and sat alongside her again as the congregation broke into a hymn—a hymn in praise of Father Malachy, the deacon said. "Apoloreng remembers us," the crowd sang. Malachy stood grinning against the background of bare sticks and thornbush, his hair brightened by an arrow of late morning sun piercing the branches fanned over his head. He seemed to bask in his parishioners' adoration, which didn't appear quite right to Quinette. Shouldn't he tell them to offer their thanks and praise to Our Lord instead? At the same time she envied his communion with them. He'd opened his heart to this parched corner of Africa, and it had taken him into its heart. Maybe one day she would experience the same reciprocity. She loved Africa and wanted it to love her back.

"Hey, you Turkana!" the priest called out as the last trilling ululations died away. "Let us pray for rain!"

"Eh-yay!"

"May all you people be blessed!"

"Eh-yay!"

"May you elders be blessed!"

"Eh-yay!"

"God of Saint John!"

"Give us rain!"

"God of Mary!"

"Give us rain!"

Two hundred pairs of dark arms and one pair of pale arms rose toward the cruel blue sky, and Malachy seemed more than ever the tribal shaman.

"We call upon the one God to bring rain and our animals to come back from death. Make us fat! Give us oil and food! The one God, make us happy!"

"Eh-yay!"

"May all cattle thieving go away!"

"Eh-yay!"

"May peace come down on you and the Toposa!"

"Eh-yay!"

"Goodness come down!" He raised his hands high, lowering them, palms facing the ground. "All evil, go away!" He thrust his hands to one side, as if casting an object over the top of the boma. "Goodness come down! May all you people be blessed!"

The appeals went on, voices rising to such an emotional pitch that Quinette would not have been surprised if the heavens clouded over and thunder cracked that very minute. She felt herself caught up in the steam-locomotive rhythms, the football-cheer repetitions, the movements of arms, swinging up, swinging down. It was hard to restrain herself from tossing her own arms into the air, and she probably would have if the service—no, rite—had gone on much longer, but it ended in another burst of keen ululations that made the enclosure sound like an aviary. Breathless, sweating under her arms, she watched the people begin to file out, greeting Malachy at the entrance, just as churchgoers did back home when church was through.

"So what did you think?" the priest asked Quinette. Cheeks flushed, the tails of his sweat-blotched shirt hanging out of his shorts, he was standing beside the senior elder.

"It was . . . interesting? Actually, beautiful," she added, deciding that *interesting* sounded too wishy-washy. "It wasn't . . . It was strange? I mean . . ."

"Not quite Christian is what you mean. The Vatican has the same opinion."

"Mind if I take your picture?"

"Surely I don't."

"With him."

Malachy spoke to the Turkana chief, who grasped the priest's hand and then said something to Quinette.

"He's telling you that he and I are of the same brand, meaning that we're brothers."

She framed the two faces—a white square one and a black oblong one side by side.

"Turkana identify themselves by their cattle brands," Malachy said, as Quinette stepped forward for a closer shot. "That's why saying you're of the same brand means you're brothers."

She flicked her head to acknowledge this snippet of ethnological information and took the photo.

"And I *am* his brother," the priest carried on. "The secret to working with these people is that you bring yourself to them and become one of them without ever, ever forgetting who and what you really are. It's a bit of a high-wire act."

"Could you get my picture with him?"

She posed with her shoulder touching the Turkana's, the print developed in her mind before the shutter clicked. She saw it laid out with the other photos on her mother's kitchen table, the ancient white steel table with a border of thin black stripes that Ardele had salvaged from the auction because no one would buy the ugly old thing. She and Nicole were sitting at it, looking at Quinette in her long, golden Dinka dress and at the African beside her, his robe slashing diagonally across his chest, his ritual scars bared. They would show the picture to their friends, and the story of Quinette's experience would spread, as stories do in small towns, and soon everyone would know that the distance she'd traveled from Cedar Falls could not be measured in miles alone.

A Clash of Cultures

"Radio and avionics on, Captain Quanah. *Quanah.* I love it. Was that an inspiration of the moment?"

"It's one of my established routines," Dare said.

Mary flipped black toggle switches. "GPS on and checked. How about the reservation card? Quanah Dare, the certified Comanche? Where'd you get that?"

"Beyond top secret. If I told you, I'd have to kill you *and* your dog. Throttles and control levers are set. Ditto hydraulics."

"It didn't convince her. She's smarter than she looks. Fuel quantity—"

"I can see we're topped off," he said, gesturing at the fuel gauges.

"The sheet says that it's the FO's responsibility to check fuel quantity. I thought we agreed to do things by the book."

"This ain't a goddamned library. You think she looks dumb?"

Mary shook her head—a flow of blond waves that broke his heart. "A little wonder-struck, kind of how I looked when I first got here. An innocent abroad."

"That one ain't all that innocent."

"That dress!" Mary did one of her patented eye rolls. "Who does she think she is? The honky princess of Zanzibar? Wish I had her legs, though. They don't *stop.*"

"She's a long drink of water, all right, but your legs look just fine," he said, and patted a denim-sheathed thigh and allowed his hand to linger a little longer than he should have, to see how she'd react. She didn't react one way or the other, as if it weren't there. "We're done with pre-start, Marian the Librarian, unless you want me to verify that the parking brake is set, which as you can see for your own self it is." He motioned at the brake status light on the upper panel, then slid the side window open and looked at Nimrod, standing beyond the wingtip, a wheel block in each honest hand. "All clear down there, rafiki?"

Nimrod gave him a thumbs-up. Starter-motor whine, the prop making a couple of slow turns before the engine fired. He revved it up, checking the gauges, listening for flaws in the smooth turboprop snarl, then fired the other engine. A pair of Rolls-Royce Darts, each delivering eighteen hundred and eighty horsepower, and every one of those would be needed on this run. The plane was fully loaded with eleven thousand eight hundred pounds of cargo destined for the Nuba mountains. Here comes Santa in his Hawker-Siddley sleigh.

He got his clearance from Loki tower and eased down the taxiway toward the airfield's western edge, where heat shimmers danced off the asphalt.

Forklifts were stuffing two UN Buffalos full of sorghum. The flight crews stood around in their corporate jumpsuits. Dare couldn't make up his mind what they looked like: garage mechanics, janitors, or delivery truck drivers. Employees whatever the case, wage-apes. He laughed silently—contempt always gave his spirits a lift—and thanked the fates for sparing him the disgrace of ending up on someone's payroll. He hadn't warmed up to Douglas and knew he never would—besides being a bleeding heart and a humorless workaholic, Douglas came from a millionaire family with a social pedigree to go with the money, and the self-assurance that was a legacy of his privilege sometimes stirred in Dare's hardscrabble heart a desire to bust his nose for no reason except to watch him bleed. But he had to admit that his partner so far had done nothing to support DeeTee's fears and reservations. He appeared to be a straight shooter, raising the unsettling possibility that the canary had been wrong for the first time in its existence.

He tested the flaps, rudder, and elevators and called that he was ready to go. The tower gave the barometric reading. Mary adjusted the altimeter.

"Clear for takeoff, standard point delta departure," the voice in his earphones continued. "Temperature three zero Celsius. Be advised Pathways Four Bravo tracking inbound, bearing oh niner five at level seven, forty miles out."

That would be Tara Whitcomb, returning from one of her solitary runs. Dare aligned the nose, advanced the power levers, and took off. He switched to Knight Air's company frequency and called Fitz.

"Read you loud and clear," answered his cheerful voice. Even when he was miserable, that guy sounded like it was Christmas morning.

"We're on the way. Estimate arrival in two hours. Call you then." If the tower was monitoring the company radio frequency—which Dare trusted they were not—they would know from that last transmission that his flight plan was a work of fiction. The listed destination, Chukudum, was seventy-five miles away, a distance the Hawker could cover in a little over twenty minutes.

"You can take it from here, darlin'," he said to Mary.

She gave the exaggerated shrug, shoulders almost touching her ears, that signaled anger or exasperation. Flying with her four to five days a week for the past three months had given him a marital familiarity with her tics and mannerisms. "Wes," she said, "your social skills are way behind your flying skills. For the hundredth time, please knock that darlin' shit *off*."

"Take it from here, First Officer English, ma'am. How'm I doin' in the social skills department now?"

"You can knock that off too. It's M-A-R-Y."

WHAT IS THE mother of desire?

What causes a man rich in cattle, honored in war, blessed with sons, endowed with wives, and granted fame to awaken each morning with his thoughts possessed by an infidel girl?

In what womb of heart or mind is this obsessive longing conceived, what milk does it drink that it should grow so strong as to clutch heart and mind with an unbreakable grip?

What is the price of desire?

For now, Bashir and I have set it at two hundred thousand pounds, but it will cost more in the end, and not in currency alone.

Astride Barakat, leaning lightly against the saddle's backrest, reins in one hand, the other hanging loose at his side, Ibrahim Idris silently vowed that if Allah, the all-merciful, the all-loving-kind, returned Miriam to him, he would atone for his sins by making the pilgrimage. He would see to it that she was made a proper Muslim. He would divorce Howah, the jealous one who had arranged her escape, and take her to wife in Howah's place.

And if her return was not God's will?

Then I must, Ibrahim said to himself, submit to God's will. I must learn resignation. I must not allow this desire to master me. Jihad is also struggle with oneself, it is above all struggle with oneself. Yet "war is enjoined you against the infidels, but this is hateful unto you." So spoke the Prophet in Sura of the Cow. "Yet perchance you hate a thing which is better for you, and perchance you love a thing which is worse for you— but God knows and you know not."

Behind him flowed more than five hundred men and nearly that many horses, murahaleen in white, militiamen in tan, some riding double with the horsemen, some afoot. Alongside him, walking, were his two Nuban guides and Kammin, and, riding, his lieutenant, Hamdan, and the militia commander, the same one who had been with him when he first saw Miriam kneeling at her grindstone. He was still a captain, but not quite so zealous as he was then. The captain had been wounded, which, Ibrahim had observed, often sobered a man. Saddle creak, soft jiggle of bits, bridles and rifle slings, tramp of feet, hoof-clop. Sounds of war as much as gunfire and mortar bursts. Sounds that had become hateful to him, and was it possible that this that he had grown to hate was better for his soul while that which he loved and desired was the worse for him? "War is enjoined you against the infidels." To wage jihad was, then, an act of faith; therefore to hate jihad was to hate the faith. Perhaps that—an apostasy of sorts— was also a sin to be added to the others.

In a ragged double column, the raiders crossed a plain plastered with the dried mud of a recent rain. Low hills made a brown barrier to the north; to the east, the direction in which the column was headed, rose an escarpment crowned by big oblong boulders that resembled resting elephants. His objectives, the Nuban village and the airfield used by the foreign contrabanders, lay on the plateau atop the escarpment. Good Nubans at peace with the government had reported that bad Nubans in the village harbored infidel soldiers who guarded the airfield. Ibrahim's mission was to wipe out the rebel force, kill or capture everyone in the village, burn it to the ground, and then wait while a squad of militia engineers from the Kadugli garrison, trained in their arts by Iranian and Afghani brethren, destroyed it. He wasn't reluctant to engage the infidels in battle—it was honorable to fight men capable of fighting back—but the rest of the business, the killing and capturing of the villagers, the burning of their houses, had become hateful to him. Five days ago, before departing from Babanusa town, he'd had a talk with a mullah. Was it not haram to kill people, even infidels, who offered no resistance? The wise man shook his head, saying it wasn't necessary for them to resist actively to be considered enemies. They were deserving of death if they sympathized with the rebels, if they disobeyed government orders to move to a peace camp, if they failed to report rebel activities in their neighborhoods. "From the Fourth Sura," the mullah said, and then recited the verse from memory. " 'You shall find others who desire security with you and at the same time to preserve security with their own people: so often as they return to sedition, they shall be subverted therein, and if they depart not from you, nor offer you peace, nor restrain their hands from warring against you, take them and kill them wheresoever you find them. Against these we have granted you manifest power.' "

Ibrahim Idris memorized the passage, and had recited it to himself before going to sleep, as a charm against the evil dreams. The dreams came regardless, and old men fell with gushing wounds before his sleeping eyes, flaming roofs crackled like heavy rifle fire, women being raped cried out to him to save them.

Back in the column, a handful of murahaleen were singing to relieve the monotony of the ride, perhaps to stir their fighting spirits, for the attack would come today.

> The tailed one that lows
> When she strays she is not soon found
> A fine lad plants his sand-ridge to the edge of the plain
> A fine lad is ready to die by the spear.

An old droving song. It made him nostalgic for the days of his youth, when a fine lad stood ready to die by the spear not in a jihad but in defense of herds against cattle thieves, lions, leopards, hyenas. There didn't seem to be as many lions, leopards, and hyenas as before. The war must have gotten rid of many of them, which didn't cause him any grief; and yet the absence of their roars and shrieks was a sign of how much the war had changed things, maybe forever, certainly for what remained of his lifetime. Sometimes his own land seemed a foreign place, and during those times he yearned for old, familiar things, even things he feared and despised, like cattle-killing lions.

Barakat's leg was much improved. The stallion was stepping over the hard, uneven ground with his former lightness and sureness of gait. The removal of the thorn and the Chinese balm had done the trick. The balm was more effective on horses than on men; Ibrahim was still sore and stiff.

Southward a long way cloud mountains rose, and one appeared to rest on the leaning black pillar of a heavy downpour. If the storm moved this way, it would fill the wadis and turn the ground to glue and make the going very difficult, but he saw that it was sweeping toward the west. He was grateful for the rain that had fallen here a few days ago. The mud had dried to a mortar, and that kept the dust down and thus lessened the chances of the column being spotted from any great distance. Ibrahim preferred to move at night and attack at dawn, but unfamiliar with this part of the Nuba, and uncertain as to how reliable his Nuban guides were, he'd decided to approach in daylight.

Once his force was up on the plateau, he was going to divide it: half his men and the militia would assault the airfield under cover of a mortar bombardment, while the other half swooped down on the village, a couple of kilometers away. They would then rejoin the first group at the landing strip. After its destruction was complete, they would return to Kadugli town, there to sell the slaves and cattle the men didn't want to keep for themselves. Simple battle plans were the best battle plans. War might have become hateful to Ibrahim, but he was good at it.

Suddenly one of his foul moods fell over him. Where did these spells come from? It felt as if a gusher of dark blood were spilling through his arteries. He was powerless to contain it.

"Ya, Kammin."

"Ya, Ibrahim," his servant answered.

"Find Abbas. Tell him to come up here."

Abbas rode up alongside. "Yes, uncle."

His nephew's posture, round-shouldered, too far forward in the saddle, did nothing to brighten his spirits. Dusty jelibiya bunched at the waist by a belt of frayed, sun-faded magazine pouches, Kalash slung aslant across his back, Abbas was wearing a grave expression. *He probably thinks I'm going to give him a special mission that will better his chances of martyring himself,* Ibrahim thought.

"Didn't I tell you to stay close to me?"

"When the action begins—"

"You'll stay here now. I don't think you'll be needing this today."

He leaned over and hooked a finger in the leather cord holding Abbas's key to Paradise: room 420 in the Grand Hotel Sudan.

"And straighten your shoulders. Sit your horse like a Humr man." The dark blood thickened. He was cold inside. For no reason, he felt like slapping this kid. Perhaps what Bashir had said of a wife—beat her every morning, if you don't know why, she will—applied to a nephew as well. But he would not beat him with his hand; with his tongue instead.

"What is this stuff?" He motioned at the ground.

The thick eyebrows crawled together, and Abbas looked at his uncle as if he were crazy.

"Why, it's dirt."

Kammin and the others laughed out loud.

"What kind of dirt, you foolish boy? I taught you a long time ago.

You've forgotten? Look at the short grasses, how few bushes and trees there are. Look at how the soil isn't cracked. Look how there are in places rain pools with water still in them."

Abbas's brows parted and came together again and parted again.

"Oh, I've forgotten the name. I know it's good for nothing."

"*Naga'a.* We call it naga'a. It's the clay that doesn't crack, and so the rains don't soak into it, and so little grass grows in it. Yet it is good for something. You saw there was more grass and more trees where we camped last night. I'll help you with the riddle. Those were red acacia trees."

Abbas was silent.

"Ya, Ganis could have solved that riddle when he was a child. You can sing verses from the Koran. Sing to me now from the book of grasses, the book of soils. Or can't you read them?"

The boy's shoulders slumped again as he seemed to shrink under his uncle's scorn, and his diminishment excited Ibrahim to humiliate him further.

"You wish to marry Nanayi. You wish today to capture cattle for a bride-price, but you don't know the first thing about cattle. I dare say none of you do," he snarled, turning to face the young men riding directly behind him; then, turning back to Abbas: "Not the first thing about where to find water and good grass for them. How do you intend to keep your bride-to-be in good cloth, in tea and sugar?"

"*Allah karim,*" Abbas answered in a small voice.

"God is generous indeed, to those deserving of his generosity. Do you expect Allah to provide even if you do nothing? Esmah! Move into town with your bride, become a mullah, earn your bread preaching in the mosques."

He knew he was going too far; knew also that he was making everyone in earshot feel embarrassed by speaking thus so publicly, but he couldn't stop himself. The dark blood had to run its course.

"Do any of *you* know what the soil is called where we camped last night?" Turning once more to the young men at his rear. "Do any of you know why grass and trees are abundant there and not here? One day this war will end, inshallah, and what are you going to do then? You youngsters don't listen to tradition in anything, but especially in the matter of cattle. So will you become farmers? But you don't know enough even for that. Maybe you'll all leave Dar Humr to work for pay in town."

They and Abbas had seen him like this before and knew better than to speak when one of his black spells was upon him; but he believed their voices were muted more by ignorance than by fear. And their silence, like the nights empty of lion roar and hyena cry, was yet another sign of how greatly life had changed, how unlikely its chances of returning to the way it used to be. He took so many pains and precautions to spare the lives of his men so the Humr would continue to exist and, God willing, be strong. Yet what was the good of that if none knew the things a Humr should know to call himself a Humr? All our traditions rest on cattle, he thought. Without them, the Humr won't be Humr, and there will be no more cattle if no one knows how to breed and raise them. When I was young, I knew not to graze cows too long in the north because the grasses there are salt-less; I knew when to move them to graze on the salty grasses of the sand ridges farther south. Does Abbas know that? Do any of them? Do they know, as I did when their age and even younger, that the succulent grasses in Bahr el Ghazal, when eaten down to stubble, will spring up again and can be grazed a second time?

"You had better capture a lot of abid today, boys," he said to no one particular. "Ha! You're going to need them to do the work you can't do!"

With a snap of the reins, Abbas turned his horse to bump Barakat and get his uncle's attention. The stallion, intolerant of such cheeky behavior, tossed his head and tried to bite Abbas's horse, which shied sideways, almost dumping its rider.

"Ya! Uncle! We don't capture these blacks because we need them but because it's warranted. Because it's commanded!" His temerity surprised Ibrahim and gratified him at the same time. The boy's got some spirit, at least. "The soil where we camped is the cracking black clay called *talha*! Grass and the red acacia grow there because the water from the naga'a runs off like rain from an iron roof and flows down to the talha, which captures it in the cracks!"

"And short grass grows in the red clay that doesn't crack in the south!" a voice behind him shouted.

"We plant millet on the sand ridges, as the song says!" another voice cried out. "A fine lad plants the sand ridges to edge of the plain!"

"The grass named *liseyg* is fine grazing, but too much of it bloats cat-tle!" a third voice called.

The tension had been relieved. Hamdan, riding on Abbas's left, burst out laughing. "Listen to them, Ibrahim, my friend. They'll make fine cat-tlemen yet!"

"God willing," Ibrahim said, and the clotted dark blood broke up in the wadis of his body, and he joined in Hamdan's laughter.

*   *   *

> Well, it's floodin' down in Texas
> And all the telephone lines are down . . .

Whipper Layton, banging out a slow blues beat on the drums. Long, mean riffs, mean but sad at the same time, poured from Stevie Ray's guitar, notes running like muddy water over rocks, and Dare pictured a windowless cinder-block roadhouse with its complement of pickup trucks in the dirt parking lot and enough secondhand smoke inside to give you instant lung cancer, urban cowgirls grinding up against their urban cowboys never rode a horse cuz they don't know how.

> And I been tryin' to call my baby
> And Lord I can't get a single sound . . .
> Dark clouds are rollin'
> Man, I'm standin' out in the rain . . .
> Yes, flood waters keep on rollin'
> Mine's about to drive poor me insane.

He tuned down the cassette player and pulled out the chart wedged between his seat and the pedestal, checked the course directions greasepenciled on the acetate cover, and then his dead-reckoning against the coordinates flashing on the GPS.

"Should be comin' up on it in just a few minutes," he said.

Mary, flying the plane, nodded. They were into their descent, the Hawker bobbing in the turbulent columns of hot air whirling up from the jumbled landscape below: grassy flats wedged between scattered beige hills; long narrow ridges of exposed rock smooth as the overturned hulls of ships, Nuban villages perched atop them. Suleiman had told him that the Nubans built their houses on hills and ridgetops for defense and because the air on the heights was healthier than in the hollows, advantages that had been nullified by the Sudanese air force. Easy targets for Antonovs and helicopter gunships, the villages were neither defensible nor healthy places to be. Some had been blasted back into their component dust, some were abandoned, makuti roofs rotted away so that, from above, the cylindrical huts looked like giant gopher holes.

The next tune drove hard, like a runaway train, echoes of Chuck Berry in the high, fast wails of Stevie Ray's electric Fender.

Well, I'm a love-struck baby, I must confess . . .

Dare's theme song. But how ridiculous for the veteran of four divorces, a man who suspected that all women were terrorists of the heart, to have his own kidnapped by someone who'd been, let's see, in seventh grade when he was the age she was now. Was this what they called midlife crisis? That millions of men suffered the same emotional insanity didn't comfort him; it made him feel worse about himself, because it meant he was no different from every other potbellied fiftyish male, and he'd never seen himself as a guy who ran with any herd.

"Visibility sure is rotten up here today," she said, squinting into the brassy haze.

Not the slightest sign, not the vaguest blip, acknowledging that she sensed his attraction to her. That meant one of three things: she wasn't very perceptive, she was pretending not to notice, in the interest of keeping their relationship strictly professional, or—the explanation he preferred—he'd done a very good job of masking his feelings, in the interest of maintaining his masculine pride.

He'd hoped that the shared routine of piloting the Hawker would have the same effect on his perception of her as it had on his perception of Sally McCabe, his copilot back when he was flying a 727 for Federal Express. That hope failed, he'd come to realize, because it hadn't been the workaday association with Sally that had made her androgynous; it was Sally herself, a Miss Six o'Clock in the figure department, who never wore makeup and kept her hair cut boyishly short and was kind of boring, too. Not much amperage in Sally, whereas Mary had more than a twenty-four-volt battery and would need to wear a dropcloth to hide the virtues of her body. He liked the smart remarks that crackled from her mouth as much as he liked its shape. And those cascades of blond hair—well, Stevie Ray was singing now what that did to him.

Every time I see you, I feel so fine
My blood is runnin' wild.

Her only interest in him, far as he could tell, was in his role as her mentor. She was competitive and ambitious. She admired Tara Whitcomb and was envious of her at the same time for establishing a feminine beachhead on one of the last male-held islands in the world. Commercial airlines, fearful of lawsuits alleging sex discrimination, courted female pilots, but there was no affirmative action program in the bush-pilot fraternity; a woman had to prove herself, and Mary was determined to do just that, eager to learn the tricks and techniques that would turn her from an average flier into a polished ace like Tara. The fine points that would shave minutes off the time it took her to reach cruising altitude, to save fuel costs. Things like that. He was just as eager to teach her, though he did so with conflicting hopes. Hope A was that his skills and knowledge would overwhelm her into falling in love with him; Hope B was that nothing of the sort would happen, sparing him, her, and Tony from entrapment in the awkward geometry of a love triangle. It was the more realistic hope by far, because his age, bulging gut, Dumbo the Elephant ears, and obnoxious ways were liabilities that outweighed his assets by a considerable margin. Hope B, however, dissolved in a stormy fusion of jealousy, heartache, and bug-eyed lust whenever he saw Mary and Tony walking hand in hand into the tent they shared. Hope A then would get the better of him, and he would give serious thought to putting a big move on her when her boyfriend was away, just to see what would happen. But he never got beyond the thinking stage. He behaved impeccably. No advances or innuendos; no invitations to meet him for a drink at the bar. Although he liked to think that his self-restraint evidenced a certain nobility in his character, proving that he treasured loyalty to his former first officer above all else, he knew it was due only to his fear of making a fool of himself.

"Dead ahead. The envy of every guy, lust-object of every size queen."

Mary pointed through the windshield at the landmark, a red rock pillar, rounded at the tip, rising in the haze-dimmed light from between a pair of low testicular hills. A couple of months ago, when Dare took him up for an aerial tour of Nuba landing strips, Suleiman had dubbed this formation "The Mahdi's Penis" in tribute to his hero's manhood.

"You'll make a shallow turn when we're over it," Dare instructed Mary. "Bearing three one zero. Michael's boys are supposed to light a fire when they hear us, give us the wind direction by the smoke, but don't count on it."

> She's my sweet little thing
> She's my pride and joy
> She's my sweet little baby
> And I'm her little lover boy.

"Wes, think we could conclude our program of in-flight entertainment? It's distracting."

He switched the cassette player off as she banked into the turn and commenced to descend, shooting over Manfred's hospital, its new tin roof and the solar panels atop it glinting off the starboard wing. She dropped to two thousand feet, which became fifteen hundred when the land ascended to the plateau west of the hospital. A thousand feet now, eight hundred, coming in on her base leg. Zulu Two appeared in the distance, a red scar showing through the acacia trees.

Dare lowered the wheels.

"Gear down and locked. No smoke yet, like I figured."

"I'll make a pass. We can assess the wind ourselves. We don't need no stinking smoke."

"Flaps down."

She reduced power to approach range and decreased altitude to five hundred feet, then two hundred, and now they could see Manfred's cream-colored Land Rover, a Red Cross painted on its roof. (Dare thought it would make a fine aiming point for a Sudanese pilot.) Women porters, scores of them, waited near the airstrip, their dresses a kaleidoscope of colors amid the pale green scrub. Mary flew along the right edge of the runway, allowing Dare to visually inspect its condition. He saw a long strip of white cloth flying from a pole as a windsock. Suleiman would have thought of that in lieu of the smoke. A good man was Sul-ee-man.

"Got a little bit of a crosswind out of the southeast. We'll have to come in at the rough end," Dare said, referring to the corrugations, like the washboards in a gravel road, at the north end of the runway.

Mary circled around to bring the Hawker in on final, and as the plane was halfway through the turn, Dare caught something in his peripheral vision—movement of some kind, flickers of white in the dense forests that covered the western side of the plateau all the way out to where it fell steeply to another plain. He tried for a better look, but then Mary completed her maneuver and his side window was facing the opposite direction and the view out of hers was blocked by her head.

WHEN IBRAHIM HEARD it in the distance, he thought it was an Air Force Antonov. The sound grew louder. He couldn't see the airplane, the forest here being thick, the trees too high, but he knew it must be flying low; most times the Antonovs, which in his opinion were flown by cowards, stayed up so far they made barely a whisper. He reined up to listen. Louder still, then faint, then loud again. Suddenly he didn't hear it at all. Thinking it must have flown on out of earshot, he nudged Barakat forward; an instant later, realizing that the plane had landed and shut down its motors, he stopped again.

"Allah karim!" he muttered under his breath, for God was presenting him with an opportunity. He told Hamdan and the militia captain that the plan had changed; he wasn't going to split his force. They would attack the airfield as one.

Hamdan balked, baffled by this order, and asked the reason for it. That was the Brothers' way. They weren't disciplined soldiers, like the captain's men, trained to obey without questioning. The Brothers preferred discussion, and so he took a few moments, precious moments, to explain that the village wasn't important; it would be nearly empty because most of the abid, maybe all, would be at the airfield unloading the plane, which was not an Antonov but a smuggler's plane. It was now on the ground. That was why the sound had stopped so suddenly.

"If we move fast, we can capture everything that's in it and destroy it before it takes off!" he went on, underscoring his urgency with extravagant gestures. "And take many abid captive besides!"

Hamdan's confusion vanished, and an excited expression came to his face. The government had posted a standing reward of five hundred thousand pounds to any murahaleen commander who destroyed a smuggler's airplane, and Hamdan knew that Ibrahim, the generous one, would share the reward. He also knew that the contraband cargo could be sold at fine prices in the marketplaces, in addition to whatever the captives fetched. This could be a very lucrative expedition. As for Ibrahim himself, he hoped for profits beyond the material. So far no commander had seized a plane. He would present Colonel Ahmar with a piece of this one as proof of his achievement; luster would be added to his fame, and the nazirship could be his for the asking. He was feeling much better about the jihad now. He gave Barakat his heels and rode on at a trot—the crowded trees wouldn't allow anything faster—and the mass of horsemen wheeled to follow him.

"Wo IST ES?"

When he was agitated, which in Dare's experience was pretty near all the time, Gerhard Manfred reverted to his native language.

"Wo is what?"

"X-ray film! Where?"

It had taken less than fifteen minutes on the ground to turn the

Hawker's interior into a microwave, and the doctor was hemorrhaging sweat as he pawed through the stuff piled up in the forward end like a frantic shopper at a rummage sale.

"Should be right where you're lookin'," Dare said from the rear, where he was working up a dense sweat of his own, helping a couple of Nubans with the offloading. Cartons of surgical masks, surgical gloves, surgical instruments, syringes, and pills, plastic jerry cans of water, white sacks of sorghum and seed, farm and garden implements bound together with duct tape, bags of salt, boxes of soap and cooking oil, pots and pans in net bags, bundled T-shirts, shorts, and dresses collected by small-town church groups out on the Canadian steppes, wheelbarrows, and several bales of snow fence (Dare would love to see what use they would be put to) were tossed out the rear door into the hands of strapping SPLA guys, who hauled it across the runway and stacked it up and then came back for more while the female porters wrapped the supplies in shawls and blankets or stuffed them into baskets that they would transport on their heads, some to their villages, some to the hospital, half a day's march away. Men seldom served as porters in these hills. Dare reckoned that would make a swell feminist issue if these people ever got enough of a break from war and hunger to think about feminist issues.

"Hey, y'all," he called to a six-foot-six-inch bruiser carrying one small box. "This would go a lot faster if you put a bunch of those in one of those wheelbarrows and made one trip instead of a dozen."

The man walked on.

"Hey! The wheelbarrow!"

"They don't understand English, you fool!" Manfred snapped. His face was the scarlet of imminent stroke. "Why can't I find this film? You are sure you brought it? I have three patients in urgent need of X-ray!"

Fucking kraut.

Dare went forward, caught his foot on a corner of the cargo net, and almost fell face-down onto a steel-banded box stenciled with a description of its contents.

"Here you go, Adolf Eichmann. Reckon you can't *read* English."

Manfred gazed down at the container reproachfully, as if it were a dog that hadn't come when called. "That was a crude and insensitive remark you made just now to me."

"Callin' a man a fool ain't my idea of sensitive." On their first meeting, about two months ago, Dare had taken a deep and instantaneous dislike to the doctor, which Manfred never failed to nurture.

"But in your case, 'fool' is more accurate than referring to me as Adolf Eichmann," he said.

"Hey, rafiki. I ain't clever with my mouth, so I'll tell you what. Call me a fool once more, and I'll drop-kick you straight back to your butcher shop."

Manfred regarded him for a moment, assessing the seriousness of Dare's words. A warning or a promise? "You must understand how much stress I am having. More fighting now, and so more patients than ever. My logistics man Franco is sick with the diarrhea, so I had to leave my patients to drive myself to here."

It wasn't an apology, but the tone was less belligerent, confirming Dare's belief that physical violence, or the threat of it, remained a useful tool in promoting civil behavior.

"My life of course is stress free," he said, not yet willing to let things go. "Yup. One fun thing after another, like flyin' five hundred miles across a war zone just to bring this stuff to you."

"And I do thank you for it," Manfred said, though with difficulty.

"Thank you? Did you say thank you? Well, holy shit. You're welcome. So to show my appreciation, I'm gonna bring in some camo netting for you next trip, so y'all can cover up those solar panels and that shiny roof if you need to. You can see 'em for about a hundred miles."

"The government continues to respect the hospital's neutrality," the doctor affirmed, sounding as if he were responding to a question at a press conference.

"I'll bring it anyway. In case they get a change of heart."

In Nuban, Manfred summoned one of the men from the rear of the plane, then climbed down the boarding stairs and crossed the runway to his Land Rover with the motions of a windup toy wound too tight, the Nuban following with the box of X-ray plates on his shoulder.

Dare noticed Suleiman stacking more of the medical supplies on the vehicle's roof-rack. Mary, in the snug khakis that so flattered her ass, its delectable curve visible from fifty yards away, was photographing him. She took pictures compulsively; she had a film record of every mission they'd flown. He found this endearing.

He went into the cockpit and fetched two sandwiches and two Cokes from an insulated bag. Outside, the gift of the breeze was nullified by the full force of the afternoon sun, thumping his skull like an L.A. cop's nightstick.

"I'm takin' you to lunch, First Officer English." He handed her a Coke and sandwich.

She unwrapped it and cautiously, as if something might jump out at her, parted the slices of bread to examine the contents. Finding them acceptable, she bit down as the wind raised her hair into a coxcomb. It was all he could do to restrain himself from smoothing the unruly strands, and he stepped away, munching on his baloney and cheese, and called out, "*Ma'salame!*" to Suleiman, who was lashing a tarp over the roof-rack.

"Ha-llo, Captain Wes. And how are you?"

"Pretty good. I'd be better if the offload speeded up. These boys don't understand me when I tell 'em it'll go faster if they put those wheelbarrows to use. Y'all mind tellin' 'em for me? I'd like to be out of here before midnight."

"Straight away, Captain Wes."

After Suleiman got the work crews organized into a human conveyor belt, men pushing empty wheelbarrows to the plane and full ones from it, he said good-bye and levered his long frame into the Land Rover beside the doctor. The two drove off slowly down a rutted path not much wider than a city sidewalk. Guarded by a few SPLA soldiers, two dozen porters followed on foot, loads on their heads, their arched backs exaggerating the thrust of their breasts, the protrusion of their high, bubble-shaped butts.

"Y'know, lookin' at them," Dare remarked to Mary, "reminds me that my Baptist mama would've killed me, she ever found *Playboy* in the house. So I used to read *National Geographic* to look at the pictures of the nekked native women. I was in college before I realized that white women had tits, too."

"Another charming commentary. I have to pee. Don't leave without me."

He lit his first cigarette of the day, pleased with himself for holding out this long, and returned to the Hawker to check on the offload's progress. Ten, fifteen minutes more, he judged, then sat in the shade of a wing to finish his cigarette. Mary would scold him for smoking this close to the airplane. A dust-devil tripped across the runway. Some distance to the south, a great sheet of dust raised by some freak gust formed a scintillating curtain that blurred a far-off range of hills. Douglas and Fitzhugh had a romance going with the Nuba—Douglas called it the "real" Africa, as if the rest of the continent were an illusion—but it ranked high on Dare's list of desolate places, and it took some doing for a place to qualify as desolate in the eyes of a man born and raised in West Texas. Another gang of porters was filing off into the scrub, flanked by their guards. He watched them, perplexed and amazed; several women were carrying loaded wheelbarrows on their heads.

Mary emerged from behind her privy bush and approached the plane with her sporty walk, a kind of straight-shouldered bounce. He turned aside, took a last puff, and snubbed the cigarette underfoot. A cold pain bolted through his chest; then he felt a frantic thudding against his breast-bone and ribs. If he hadn't experienced this unpleasant sensation before, he would have mistaken it for a coronary.

He waved to Mary to hurry up. When she got to him, he told her he was going to help finish the off-loading; she was to get the plane checked through for takeoff, so that all that would need doing when he took his seat was to start the engines. "I want to be ready to go the second the last box is off this airplane."

"Sure." She offered a Girl Scout salute in response to his Schwarzkopf-in-the-Persian-Gulf tone of voice. "What's up?"

There was no way to tell her that he was experiencing a thoracic turbu-lence caused by an imaginary bird inside him that beat its wings furiously whenever he was in imminent danger. Even if Mary were to accept this feathered guardian angel as an actual being, she would want to know, What danger? And he would have to answer that he didn't know because the canary's warnings, like a watchdog's bark in the night, alerted him to a threat without revealing its precise nature.

In the cargo bay, he dragged two sacks of sorghum across the floor and dumped them outside.

The dust cloud.

He'd noticed that it hadn't moved when he turned to take a final drag of his smoke. If it had been raised by a high wind, it would have blown away, but it was hovering right where he'd glimpsed it a minute earlier, off to the south and low over the trees, which is what dust would do if it were stirred up, on a day of light airs, by movement on the ground. A lot of movement, judging from the amount of dust. And what was moving? Whatever it was he'd glimpsed when they were coming in for a landing, and he now realized what that was. He leaped from the plane and told the men unloading it, "Finished now! All done!" He waved his arms like a ref-eree, then like someone shooing unruly kids out of a house. "You people have got to get going, now. Go on. Get going. Get a move on."

He jogged to the side of the airstrip where the cargo was piled and grabbed a young woman by the arm and shoved her, pointing in the direc-tion he wanted her to go, then back over his shoulder. "Get moving! Arabs!"

She gave him a fierce look. A couple of SPLA interposed themselves between her and Dare, and one pushed him backward with the flat of his rifle.

"You assholes! I ain't your problem! Set up a firing line over there! Give these people a chance to get the hell out of here!" He snatched the soldier's collar and spun him around, motioning at the dust in the distance. "Arabs! See!"

The scowling soldier poked him in the chest with the gun barrel. What a time for a failure in communication! He wished Suleiman and Manfred had stuck around a little longer. *The Arabs are coming, the Arabs are coming.* He was Paul Revere in the Nuba mountains, and no one could understand what he was trying to tell them.

"YA, IBRAHIM! You didn't need to hit him. It's worked out for the best. *Allah ma'ana.*"

The captain of militia carefully folded his scarf and retied it to his forehead. Behind him, atop the gentle rise on which he and Ibrahim Idris sat, the captain's artillerymen were setting up the mortars, three of them, each leaning on two metal legs, the bombs stacked neatly on the ground.

Bombs, like the kind that killed Ganis.

"The trees here are not so many as in there," the captain said, gesturing at the acacia forest they had passed through. "It would have been hard to find a place in there to fire the mortars, but here, not so many trees to get in the way, and from this little hill, I can see the target and adjust my fire immediately." He pointed at the airfield, two, perhaps three kilometers to the north. The foreigners' airplane was clearly visible to the unaided eye. "So you see," the captain continued, "it has been for the best that these niggers got us lost. Perhaps God directed them to do that."

One of the two Nuban guides sat nearby in sullen silence; the other, lying on his back and looking as though he had a large mango stuck in the side of his mouth, would be silent for a few days to come. A couple of minutes ago Ibrahim had broken his jaw with the butt of his Kalashnikov. The savages had cost them a great deal of time, stumbling in the woodlands. Instead of leading them straight to the airfield, the two had brought them here, well south of it, and as the country south of the airfield was more open than that to the west, it would be more difficult to achieve surprise. A look through the binoculars had also revealed a great many women leaving with things that had been unloaded from the plane. Far ahead of them, Ibrahim had observed the rolling dust of what he assumed was a motorcar or a lorry, and it was doubtlessly taking more things away. He concluded that the guides had got lost on purpose, delaying the mura-

haleen so their fellow Nubans could make off with the booty he regarded
as belonging to him and the Brothers, while at the same time forcing him
to attack from a disadvantageous direction. In a flare of temper, he
ordered them to be executed as traitors, but the captain intervened, calming him by pointing out that the two abid weren't smart enough to have
devised such a ruse, besides which, the guides might be needed on the
return journey. Ibrahim saw the sense in the captain's advice, but his fury
had to be appeased, and so he dismounted and struck the man with his
rifle. *If I don't know the reason why, you will.*

Now he stood beside Barakat as all around the murahaleen assembled
for the attack. Their leaders commanded them in conversational voices—
he'd adjured them to be as quiet as possible, as sound carried far in this
flat, open country. The horses wheeled and snorted and pawed the ground
and kicked up a lot of dust, more than Ibrahim Idris liked. A cloudburst
would have been welcome, but God was not so with the murahaleen as to
gray this blue, blue sky. The plan was to advance at a trot in two long lines,
single-mounted warriors in the first rank, double-mounted in the second;
at his signal—three rifle shots—the Brothers would charge at full gallop
and, inshallah, overrun the infidel defenders, who did not appear to be
many.

The maneuvering into position was going too slowly, and in his anxiety to attack, he disobeyed his own order for quiet and yelled, "Quickly,
Brothers!" It would be impossible to catch up with the motorcar, but the
porters could be overtaken easily by men on horseback—he would send a
detachment in pursuit. His concern now was that all this delay would rob
him of the airplane. There it sat with silent motors, so vulnerable. Grasping it with his eyes, actually seeing its size, shape, and color, had heightened his hunger to grasp it with his hands. A prize of war. His, *his.* God
willing, he would also capture the foreigners who'd flown it. Perhaps that
would bring an extra reward.

He saw that the first rank had got itself organized—three hundred
murahaleen extending in a line nearly a half kilometer long—but the second was suffering from some confusion, which he intended to cure immediately. He jammed a booted foot into the stirrup and swung into the
saddle.

"Watch us through your glasses," he said, looking down at the captain.
"When you judge us halfway there, begin firing. Move the fire back from
the near end of the airfield to the far. I don't want my men blown up by
yours."

"Don't worry." The captain raised a fist. *"Allahu akhbar."*

"Yes, of course. Allahu akhbar," Ibrahim replied, for the form of it.

He pushed in among the jostling horses, whacking some with his whip, jabbing riders with the whip handle and calling out, "Quickly, you idiots, get yourselves straightened out!" Barakat's nostrils flared and a wild look came to his eyes, and he shook and reared his head against the bit as Ibrahim held him to a slow walk. The men in the second rank were still having difficulties; the mounts weren't accustomed to carrying two riders and were balky. He couldn't wait any longer. Spurring Barakat, he trotted along the front line, a tall, bearded man in white on a chestnut Arabian, a ribbon of his turban streaming behind him. "Forward at a quick walk when I command it! Charge at my signal, three shots!" Repeating the order, he rode on. The acrid stink of sweating horseflesh and sweaty saddle leather was strong, his nose seemed so keen that he could distinguish the scent of his elephant-hide reins from those other smells. The hard sun sparked off rifle barrels and the trees glittered, greener than they were only minutes ago, and the ache in his joints had dissolved, and with it the reluctance he'd been feeling these past several days. The strange intoxication of battle's prelude was the balm his body and spirit needed; would he be able to go back to herding cattle, would he return contented to the sweet, easy life he dreamed of nearly every day, or would he be restless, longing for these moments when his senses grew sharp and the quick, corsair's blood leaped within him, and five hundred quick-blooded men on quick-blooded mounts waited to ride into combat at his word? He came to the end of the rank, turned, and cantered out to the front, where he halted. Standing in the stirrups, leaning well forward, he stuck his backside up in the air, looked back over his shoulder, and gave the command he was known for, the one the men loved to hear: "Follow my ass, Brothers! Follow my ass!"

A BLOSSOM OF smoke and a hard, flat, crunching explosion became Dare's translator. The SPLA soldiers swung their weapons off their shoulders and ran for cover, hollering to one another. Crying out, the women sprinted away, a human herd in a blind animal panic. Lots of places to run out here, nowhere to hide, and there was nothing he could do for them now. The shell had burst toward the far end of the airstrip, but a good hundred yards to the east of it, a ranging round. He dashed for the plane and heard the whine and growl of the starboard engine starting up, then the port. *Bless her, I'd fly to Mars with her.* He ran up the steps and dogged the cargo door shut. *Ca-rump.* A second shell struck somewhere west of the airfield. The next would split the difference between the first two, and if the mortarmen knew what they were doing, they wouldn't need another to have the runway zeroed in. His capacity for fast thinking and effective action in a crisis, the gift of his unreflective, pragmatic brain, went to work, bits and bytes of information flashing through his mental microcircuitry. *Mortars firing from the south, that end of the runway pointing right at them, or almost. They're going to walk their fire down the runway to try to hit the plane. Roll now, we'll be moving into their fire, and it's always harder for mortarmen to shorten their range than to lengthen it, so if we time it right, if we're real fucking lucky, they'll be elevating their tubes and we'll be airborne.* He rammed the throttles forward, praying to the God he didn't believe in. The Hawker bounced and squealed and rattled down the rough strip. She seemed, this insentient piece of metal, rubber, and rivets, to be conscious of the danger she was in. Dare didn't say a word. Mary didn't say a word. A gray-black flower bloomed fifty yards ahead and a little to the left. Plane and shrapnel sped toward each other, colliding in a splattering like the crackle of hail on a tin roof. One piece, or a rock thrown up the blast, struck a glancing blow at the side window behind Dare's head. He couldn't turn around to see if it had shattered. One-fifteen now. Rotation speed. He pulled back hard, the Hawker's prop blades dug into the air, her nose tilted, and she was aloft, two shells exploding not far in front of her and fifty feet below, close enough for her to buck and shudder in the blast waves, as she would in a wind shear. Dare was sure her undercarriage had gotten peppered, how badly there was no way to know. She skimmed the trees beyond the runway's end. Dead ahead was a sight that he knew would be engraved in his memory for as long as he had one. It looked like a rodeo stampede with all the cowboys dressed in bedsheets: a horde of robed horsemen galloping across the tree-spotted plateau. They were going to go through the scattered SPLA defenders like a semi-trailer through a snake-rail fence. The women wouldn't have a chance.

At five hundred feet he made a hard left turn and saw riders swarming all over the plateau; saw, with the acuity that comes to human vision in situations of extreme stress, that several horsemen had halted and were firing at the Hawker. Trusting they would miss, shooting as they were from the saddle at a high, fast-flying target, he climbed away and called for the flaps. Mary acknowledged, and he called for gear, and Mary uttered the aviator's favorite four-letter word, as useful in moments of mere annoyance as it is in moments of mortal danger, and quite often the last word recorded on the black box when a pilot runs out of altitude and ideas at the same time: "Shit!"

The gear light was still green, indicating that the wheels remained down and locked.

She pulled the knobbed lever once more, but the light stayed green. The absence of the thunk and thud of retracting gear and the Hawker's vibrations declared that the problem wasn't a faulty light switch.

"Shrapnel must have severed a hydraulic hose."

She pointed at the annunciator light for leaking fluid; it was dark.

"Maybe we got a damaged circuit, too."

They were making a hundred and sixty knots a thousand feet above the plain that lay like a waterless sea between the hospital and the Kologi hills.

"One more time."

She pulled the lever again and said "Shit" again.

He glanced at her. Her complexion had the color of an oyster shell. "There is nothing so stimulating as to be shot at without effect." So said Winston Churchill. Mary had been stimulated by that flap back in Somalia last year, but this was different. If he was right about the shell fragments, they'd been shot at *with effect*, the effects of which were yet to be determined.

"Shit is the watchword of the day," he said, leveling off.

Mary asked what airspeed they had to maintain to avoid ripping the gear off the plane.

"What we're doin' now," Dare answered. "One sixty. One sixty indicated will give us a true airspeed of two twenty at twenty thousand. Trouble is, with the gear down, the drag is gonna increase our fuel consumption a lot, and we might have nothin' but fumes to land on if we try to make Loki."

How much brighter their prospects would be in the civilized world. Call the tower, state the problem, request emergency vehicles, and while ground crews foam the runway, circle the airport, dumping fuel, and then come on in. He could think of only one advantage to this situation: it prevented him and Mary from dwelling on what had almost happened to them and on what was happening to the people they'd left behind. No way he could have saved them. Still, he felt that he'd abandoned them. He felt, despite the heart that bled solely for himself, that he'd incurred a debt.

Dare thought their best bet would be to land at the big UN airfield at Malakal, on the Nile. It was only a hundred and forty miles away, so they would have plenty of gas to get there. Plus, Malakal had fuel and a flight mechanic. If they needed parts for the repairs, he could radio Douglas to fly them in on the G1C.

"You work out a course. I'll find us a way through that shit up ahead."

He gestured out the windshield at a bastion of dark anvil-cumulus looming in the south. At the moment, he could not see an opening in them, nor in their image on the radar screen—a line of red ellipses welded end to end.

THE WOMEN WERE in a pit, sending up doleful cries, arms raised, faces turned toward Ibrahim, standing far above. Their arms grew longer and longer, reaching for him with wriggling fingers, like a nest of rising serpents with worms for heads. They clasped his ankles, twined around his legs and chest, crushing the breath out of him.

With a strangled yell, he woke up, his heart thudding, flesh clammy and hot at the same time. Ribbons of smoke curled around him. He could see no stars, no light of any kind, except for a few red circles glowing demonically in a darkness doubled by the smoke that scorched his lungs. *And the companions of the left hand shall dwell amidst burning winds and scalding water, under the shade of a black smoke, neither cool nor agreeable.* He tried to stand, to rise above the smoke and breathe clean, cool air, but his legs wouldn't move. Now, overcome by terror, he understood that he was in the pit, pinned down by the abid women, a captive of his captives. He couldn't see them, yet he felt the pressure of their fingers, the coil of their arms. They no longer called to him for mercy, and he knew why: those appeals had been false; a trick to draw him to the edge of the pit so they could seize him and plunge him into eternal anguish. False! False! He'd mistaken the thing they were pleading for. They wanted his soul! *On the day of resurrection some faces shall become white, and other faces shall become black. And unto them whose faces shall become black, God will say, Have you returned unto your unbelief, after you have believed? Therefore taste the punishment. . . . As for the unbelievers . . . they shall be the companions of hell fire. . . .* His sins had made him like an unbeliever, deserving the infidel's chastisements in hell, and the only cry he heard now was his own prolonged howl.

Suddenly he was free. He sat up, again with thudding heart and hot, wet skin; again his lungs and nostrils burned, again he saw fuzzy, scarlet circles shining through vaporous ribbons, but when he looked up, he beheld the lights of heaven and realized that the smoke and red light were from the fires the Brothers had lighted to keep insects out of camp. His previous awakening had been an illusion, a passage from one dream into another. Now he was truly awake. Delighting in the real-world scent of Barakat's sweat, impregnated in the saddle blanket, in the tingle of this world's smoke in his nose, he wanted to shout for joy. Only a dream! No ordinary dream, though. In its clarity, in its *reality,* it had seemed like a revelation, such as a prophet would receive. He rearranged his goat-hair blanket, lay down on his back, and tried to interpret the meaning.

While he pondered, he once more heard cries, sobs, groans. How could this be? Was he going mad that he should hear those lamentations when he was not asleep? Or had the women become jinns, determined to pursue and afflict him in his waking hours as well as in his dreams? Or was he still dreaming after all? Had he awakened from one into another, thence into a third? A thick ball of smoke rolled over him, and he coughed and returned to his senses. He wasn't mad, wasn't dreaming, and the captive women were not jinns.

Some of his men had invaded the zariba where the abid were being held and were taking women out to satisfy their carnal appetites. Ibrahim was exhausted, having fought a battle and ridden all day, the last hour in the late-season downpour, and the screams and wails were stripping off what bark remained on the branches of his nerves. *Damn those men!* he thought. He had issued express orders that no one was to touch the women captives. Most of those taken in the raid were young, and though their youth didn't guarantee that they were virgins—Nubans were licentious, and it wasn't uncommon for unmarried females to have had sexual relations—it did make virginity more likely. Virgins were coveted as concubines, bringing better prices from the traders than tampered merchandise. So it made sound business as well as moral sense to leave them alone. Yet there was the moral issue, and that was the reason for his dream. Through it God had shown him the torments that he would suffer if he failed to stop his men from sinning. To allow them to continue with what they now were doing would be the same as committing rape himself.

Picking up his rifle, he buckled on his ammunition belt, jammed his whip into the belt, and with his torso pitched forward and his head tucked into his shoulders, he struck off toward the zariba. Horses stood tethered to the trees, men lay snoring, barely visible in the darkness. He tripped over someone. The man cursed and said, "Watch where you step." Ibrahim Idris cursed him back and said, "Watch where you lie down!"

Foul with the reek of bodies and shit and piss—couldn't these people control themselves till morning, when they knew they would be allowed to relieve themselves?—he smelled the zariba before he saw it. When he got to the enclosure, a ring of sticks and thornbushes, he was shocked to find it unguarded. Not a single sentry in sight, and he'd commanded a double watch posted, both to enforce his order and to prevent escapes. The sentries were absent because it was they who'd raided the very thing they were guarding: plunged in, selected their victims, and made off with them, like hyenas raiding a stock pen. Ibrahim's anger blew up into an exalted rage.

In today's attack he'd lost only two men and five horses while slaying more than twenty abid soldiers. The airfield had been destroyed by the militia engineers. One hundred and fifty captives, more than Ibrahim had ever taken in a single action, had been seized, along with goods worth tens of thousands of pounds: clothes, implements, food, and medical supplies. All in all a successful mission, except for the airplane, and to Ibrahim that was no small exception. He could still see it, soaring so low above his head it seemed he could snatch it from the sky with his bare hands; so low it seemed impossible that he and his men could not shoot it down. They filled the air with bullets, and yet it flew on, and his hopes for rewards and honors went with it. The prizes he did take compensated somewhat for losing the one he coveted most. Now the miscreant sentries, thinking with their penises, had put it all at risk. A good thing the captives still inside the zariba were so frightened—they might try to flee otherwise. A fine job that would make, gathering them up in the middle of the night.

He caught voices and stifled cries coming from somewhere off to his left.

He came to a clear space in the woods and stopped at its edge, the shadows of the trees concealing him. A few meters away the long, skinny legs of a girl, flung down on her back, glistened in a fire's embers. Her arms were pulled back past her shaved head and were held at the wrists by one man, while another, his jelibiya rolled up around his waist, knelt between her splayed limbs and ravished her with the spastic thrusts of a dog mounting a bitch. Finished in seconds, he got to his feet and traded places with his companion. It was like a dance, so fluid and practiced were their movements. Several more of these criminal couplings were taking place, farther from the fire. Ibrahim couldn't tell how many, nor identify the culprits—a mere cuticle of a moon was shining—but he was able to observe that the girl in front of him was quite young. The sentries had taken the most valuable. Ibrahim was appalled by their disobedience, their carelessness, their lack of self-control. Had he raped Miriam after capturing her? He'd had no relations with her till he'd returned to his camp and brought her into his house as his formal serraya. Self-denial, self-restraint were marks of Humr manliness. These Brothers were not manly but slaves to their impulses. And yet he did nothing, said nothing, held in mute arrest by the lurid, captivating choreography of white-clad men, wreathed in smoke tinged red by the embers, leaping onto black bodies, lying so still he would have mistaken them for dead if not for their muffled sobs. The two murahaleen closest to him were finished with their victim and called to a third, and in the instant before the man fell on her, Ibrahim saw her fully from the side, her young belly flat and her small breasts flattened also by the pull of her outstretched arms, her face turned aside so that she seemed to be looking straight at him with a look such as he'd seen on the faces in his dream. *False! False!* he thought. He fancied he saw an entice-ment in her eyes, a beckoning that spilled the pollutant of desire into the fine, pure waters of his rage. He was surprised that he should feel such lust—he expected better of himself; so when he lunged out of the shad-ows, in two big strides, the rifle in his left hand, the whip in his right, and laid a hard stroke across the man's back, Ibrahim was lashing out at him-self as well.

The recipient of the blow yelped and threw himself off the girl. Ibrahim hit him a second time, and he fell and rolled in the dirt, covering his head with his hands against the cut of the braided hide. A third stroke tore the sleeve of his jelibiya, a fourth made his knuckles bleed. The man lay doubled up. A floret of red blossomed on his back. Someone grabbed Ibrahim to stop him, but he broke free, pushed the fellow aside, and immediately gave the one lying at his feet another whack.

"Stop, please! I beg you, stop!"

In disbelief, Ibrahim stood for a moment, the whip poised; then he lowered it and, planting a boot in his nephew's ribs, he shoved him onto his back.

"What are you doing? Practicing for your wedding night?"

Mistaking the cold sarcasm for calm, Abbas risked standing up, confu-sion and fear on his face.

"Answer me! Are you practicing for Nanayi with this—" He jiggled the whip over the girl, who was sitting up now, shaking as if from cold. Two brass disks were pinned to the sides of her nose, and their barbaric gleam disgusted him and made him bring the whip down across her thighs. She screamed. *Why did I strike her?* "This whore?" She bent over her slashed legs, and he gave her one across the back, raising a red welt from her shoulders to her hips, like a second spine, and she screamed again. *Why do I hit her?* He felt possessed by someone other than himself, prodding him to do things he didn't intend to do, some jinn or demon that dwelled in these mountains, this *bilad al Kufr,* land of unbelievers, beyond the sight of God, the all-merciful, all-loving-kind. "You know my orders, Abbas! All of you! You all knew my orders, and yet you . . . with these . . ." And the whip, seemingly of his own will, striped her again. She accepted it with barely a sound. Oh, that he could fly, fly right now back to Dar Humr, to Dar al Islam, House of the Faithful. "Answer me, Abbas! Answer some one of you! You are instructed to do one thing, and you do the other. You desert your posts to practice fucking with these abid whores." The next stroke, laid crosswise to the one preceding, sent the girl sprawling.

Abbas backed away, his arms outspread, his bloodied knuckles facing Ibrahim. "Please, uncle . . ."

"Please, what? Please to stop beating your whore? Then shall I beat you again instead?" He stepped forward, the whip raised. Dropping it and his rifle as Abbas turned to run, he snatched his nephew by one arm, and with a strength that amazed himself as much as it did Abbas, he flung the boy down atop the girl. Ibrahim pinned him there, a knee in the small of his back, a hand on the back of his neck. *I don't understand what I'm doing.* "Practice now. I'll give you another chance for practice." *I must get out of here.*

"Oh uncle, please . . . Oh God . . ."

"Oh God? Esmah, you pious hypocrite! Had I told Ganis to stand watch over the captives and not to touch them, he would have stood his watch and not touched them. Not you. You had to practice. Therefore, practice."

He pressed down on Abbas's neck, pushing his face into the girl's shoulder. Her face blended in with the darkness, so her eyes seemed suspended in space, two disembodied ovals glaring up, as empty of expression as the disks fastened to her nose. She made some animal-like croaking sound.

"Please" came his nephew's voice.

"What? They didn't teach you this at the madrassah? What would your teachers say if they saw you as I saw you?"

His nephew should have looked out for his interests, his nephew should have restrained the others, not shown contempt for his uncle by joining them. The uncle who had been as a father to him. He knew why he was doing this. It no longer had anything to do with his dream or obedience to orders. He was doing this to Abbas for betraying and humiliating him, for being a hypocrite, for being stupid, for having an ugly crooked nose, for not being like Ganis, for breathing the living air while Ganis occupied a grave. "Let's see you fuck her now." He dug hard with his knee, driving his nephew's loins into the girl's.

Two men seized him from behind by the straps of his ammunition belt. With a single powerful jerk, they pulled him off.

"Ya, Ibrahim! Enough! Have you gone crazy?"

He recognized the voice of his lieutenant. Someone must have summoned him. Just as Ibrahim turned to face Hamdan, Abbas, feeling the weight lifted from him, leaped to his feet and whirled, his right hand darting to the opposite shoulder. Like most young murahaleen, he had a short dagger strapped to his upper left arm, and this he drew, faster than any eye could follow, and slashed at his uncle's throat. Ibrahim Idris had just enough time to draw away, so the blade cut across his chest, tearing through his jelibiya. Abbas lurched forward, carried on by the violence of his thrust, tripped over the prone girl and fell; fell very hard face-down. He grunted, then pushing himself up with his left arm, he drew one knee into his belly and attempted to stand. His arm gave way, and he dropped again, halfway onto his side, the dagger's handle protruding from his ribs, just below his heart.

"MIGHT AS WELL tell me what the matter is."

"Nothing."

Draped in the folds of the mosquito net, she was sitting on the edge of the cot, facing a mildewed wall, its single window covered by a screen and shuttered by two scrap-lumber boards. This was their second night in Malakal, where the Hawker was undergoing repairs. The base manager had assigned them two empty bungalows, side by side, and a little over an hour ago Mary had knocked at his door. When he opened it, she said, "I just wanted to tell you that yesterday? The way you got us out of that fix, and the way you handled the plane in those storms . . . Ah hell, that's not what I want to say, this is what I want to say." And clasping the back of his neck in both hands, she gave him the most thrilling kiss of his life.

Now from the Malakal riverfront came the sound of a Nile boat's diesel, the laborious whine suggesting that it was pushing a barge up-current. Dare's finger explored Mary's spine, from her pale neck down to the smooth rise of her splendid hips.

"Well, you ain't said word one for what I reckon is two minutes."

"Nothing's the matter."

"It's been my experience that when a woman gives that answer to that question, she means just the opposite."

"Listen to the old man of the mountain, gone through more women than most men have socks."

His finger retraced its route, sliding over her damp skin, the sweet little bumps of her vertebrae. "Any man who says he knows the first thing about the female gender is a fool or a liar and maybe both."

Her hair made the faintest whisper as she turned to look down at him, her chin nestled into her shoulder. Beads of sweat on her forehead and upper lip sparkled in the glow of the kerosene lamp, its mantle filmed with soot. She pressed Dare's nose as if it were a doorbell.

"You didn't have to ask. You know damned well what the matter is."

"Yeah, all right."

"I always go home with the guy who brought me to the dance, so I've got some self-image issues to deal with."

"Me too. Me and him flew together for two years."

"Except I started things, didn't I?"

"Yeah, you did."

And lying on his side, admiring the sculpture of her ribs, the line and curve of her arm, and the breast it partly concealed, he was very glad she did. He considered himself the most fortunate man alive.

"Of course you know what we're doing, confessing how guilty we feel. We're justifying ourselves. We're saying to ourselves, 'Well, we did what we wanted, but we don't feel exactly right about it, and that means we're decent people after all.' It's a license to cheat, sort of."

"Mary quite contrary, don't go psychological on me."

"Anyway, Tony is only the half of it."

"The other half bein' what?"

"Here's a girl who just fucked her boss. What's worse, she would like to fuck him again."

"The boss would like that too, but the boss is fifty-four and he won't be up to it till mornin'. Pun intended."

She thought about this for a while. "That's a theory, not a fact, and with the boss's permission, I'm going to test it."

She made little legs with two fingers and walked them over the plateau of his chest, up the hill of his belly, and down into the bristling valley below his navel, from which, with manipulations tender and skillful, she caused a stalk to sprout, much to Dare's amazement. Upon this stalk, straddling him, she impaled herself and proceeded to demonstrate, once again, how wrong he'd been to think that *lusty* and *Canadian* were an adjective and noun that didn't go together. She made love like a woman who wanted to get pregnant—an event he hoped would not come to pass—and climaxed first, burying her face in the pillow to muffle her delighted squeal. She lay like that for a few moments; then, feeling him still hard within her, sat up straight so that they formed an upside-down T in violent motion, Dare thrusting, Mary grinding her hips with a mechanical professionalism that, strangely, excited him more than her previous abandon had done. She brought him off and rocked forward, pinning his shoulders with her hands.

"Oh yes, I can!" she said with wicked laughter.

He wasn't sure if she was speaking for him or for her ability to stir him to such an accomplishment, as if she were a director who'd coaxed a brilliant performance from a washed-up actor.

She gave his nose another touch. "Some old man you are. It's a good thing you're ugly and a Neanderthal attitude-wise. If you weren't . . ." She left the comment hanging.

"Sounds like a backhanded compliment, but I'll take it." He reached for his cigarettes, on the packing crate that served as a night table, and lit one for each of them. "I reckon, then, if you had to sleep with the boss, the one you slept with is safer than the other one."

"Doug?" she asked, spitting smoke to stress her incredulity.

"Good looking, says all the right things, not a Neanderthal, attitude-wise."

"He's sexless. Looks like a catalog model for L.L. Bean."

She slipped off the cot, snatched her clothes from the floor, and got dressed. "So what do we do now, Wes? How the hell do we handle this?"

Leaning against a wall in the lantern light, the cigarette between her fingers, all she needed was a dress with padded shoulders to look like a film-noir femme fatale. And this was neither a pose on her part nor an illusion created by bad lighting. She was a throwback to rogue dames like Jane Greer and Barbara Stanwyck, with their mixture of toughness and vulnerability, their guilt, their dangerous allure.

"I can tell you how we're not gonna handle this. We're not gonna go makin' any confessions and get down on our knees and beg Tony to forgive us."

He'd used the plural for diplomacy's sake. He'd meant her.

"That wasn't even on my radar screen," she replied with a flash of pique.

Oh, a part of him hoped this one-night stand would not go any further. She would be difficult and demanding and not allow him to get away with anything.

He got up and, as he dressed, felt painfully self-conscious about his middle-aged body, of which only his arms and shoulders retained their youthful form. Was Mary averting her gaze? Did his anatomy repel her, now that she saw him clearly rather than through the fog of whatever randy impulses had led her to come to him? Was she asking herself, *What possessed me to jump in the sack with this flabby old dude?* He was disturbed that this possibility disturbed him as deeply as it did.

"We're gonna put tonight into the 'It was just one of those things' compartment," he stated, with a certain paternal finality. He imagined she wanted this from him, the voice of wisdom and experience. "It happened on account of the unusual circumstances. We had a right full day yesterday."

She crushed the cigarette in an old tuna fish tin and regarded him contemptuously. "The eroticism of danger? Two people have a close call that makes them itchy, and then they scratch it and go on like nothing happened?"

"Don't know I'd put it that way, but that's the idea."

"It's stuffy in here. I need some air."

At this time of year, close to the Nile, the air outside was almost as still, cloying, and sultry as it was inside. A mosquito sang a high C in Dare's ear. He took a spray bottle out of his shirt pocket and lacquered his neck and hands with the stuff, eighty percent Deet, pure poison, but it could keep a thirsty vampire bat off of you. He'd had malaria twice, and though both cases were mild, the sweats and chills and crazy dreams weren't anything he cared to repeat. Mary slapped her arm, and he handed the repellent to her. The tents and huts of the UN compound showed in silhouette, kerosene and Coleman lanterns burned here and there, the generators having been shut off for the night to conserve fuel. The tail of a C-130 loomed above the warehouse tents at the airstrip. The Hawker, out of sight, was parked on an apron, awaiting the further ministrations of the British mechanic who had confirmed Dare's first suspicions about the landing gear: shrapnel had punctured the hydraulic lines, bled them dry. Why the warning light had failed remained a mystery.

"Must've damaged the sensors when it hit the lines," Dare mumbled, thinking out loud.

"What are you talking about?"

"The plane. Can't figure out why we didn't get a light, losing all that fluid."

"Do not try to change the subject."

"It's just that I understand airplanes a whole lot better," he said after a pause.

"None of that right-stuff crap. You always know what to do next. So what do we do next about this?"

The question came in an uncharacteristically querulous tone. It was also, he realized, a challenge, one he didn't feel up to accepting.

"Already said what."

She let out a sigh and placed her hands on her cocked hips, and this petulant stance was likewise out of character; it was as if, in this strange new emotional territory, she were reverting to the mannerisms of adolescence.

"You are pathetic if you think that we can really can go on flying and working together and pretend nothing's happened."

"Then we split up. Me and Tony, you with Doug."

"I have no intentions of flying with Doug. He's not half the pilot you are."

Dare said nothing and looked up at the stars of the southern latitudes, the ones he'd used, in the days before GPS, to tell him where he was and thus where to go. Antares and Arcturus, Canopus and Spica and Rigel Kent. All perfectly useless in these circumstances.

"And you are further pathetic," Mary carried on, "if you think that tonight was just some bitch who got horny because she"—her voice went mock-dramatic—"*had a brush with death.* Jesus, what rubbish. You mean to tell me that you haven't been able to see how I feel about you?"

With his internal organs tumbling as if they were inside a clothes dryer—his goddamned pancreas was doing flips—he looked at her, trying, in the weak light of the slivered moon, to parse the grammar of her facial expression and see if it agreed with the meaning of her speech.

"It's been pretty obvious to me how you feel," she said.

"Thought I'd hid it pretty well. You sure did, right up till tonight."

"It astonishes me how obtuse men can be. I *had* to hide it. Okay, I don't want you to think that what happened tonight was all glandular, so." She drew his face to hers and gave him another kiss.

He stood there in a state of terrified joy, astounded that this woman actually cared for him, desired him, maybe even for Christ's sake loved him; yet he sensed a certain restraint on his happiness, heard a cautionary warbling in his head. Remember your mama, feeding the old man when his arthritic fingers couldn't hold a fork? That's not Mary English, DeeTee warned. You two might be flying a sophisticated piece of technology together, but her attraction to you goes back to the cave. You've gotten her through some perilous moments, and she respects you for your powers. Get it? Hope A has been fulfilled. Your competence has overcome all your deficiencies in other areas and won her to you, but that comes with an attached rider: you'll lose her affections if ever you lose your competence, and the day is coming, Wes, you know it's coming, when your joints will stiffen—they're stiffening even now, aren't they?—and your nerve and instincts will fail and your skills desert you; the day is coming when you won't know what to do next, and that's the day she'll be gone, not because she's cruel or selfish or shallow but because she isn't built to be with any man weaker than herself.

And with those thoughts echoing in his brain, he kissed her back, as ardently as she had him, though with less grace.

"Well, goddamn," he said, holding her by the waist.

"That's all you got to say?"

"For now, yeah."

"So how do we handle it?"

"That depends on how you feel about Tony. I mean, if you've felt like you say you do all this time, what in the hell have you been doin' with him?"

"Fair enough. Tony and I drifted into a relationship, and we've been drifting ever since, and I suppose one day we'll drift out of it. That's how I'd like it to happen anyway, but I don't think it will now. I'm looking for some advice on damage control."

"No, you're not. What y'all are lookin' for is how to dodge the consequences."

She tossed her head to one side, her hair swirling across her face, and laughed. "Bingo!"

"Never happen, darlin'. Never happen."

Man of All Races

IT WAS A disastrous rainy season that year in Sudan. Each afternoon cumulus would tower on the horizon and distant thunder would sound false rumors of relief. As the dry season approached, pastures darkened to burnt brown, water holes turned into bowls of cracked clay, and doura stalks took on the color of dried tobacco, growing no higher than a child's head. The cattle began to show their ribs and shoulder blades. The drought was most severe in Bahr el Ghazal. Fitzhugh heard about what was happening from aid workers sent to that distant province to access the catastrophe. The Dinka had turned to the Masters of the Spear, who could speak to the ancestors, and through them, to the ancient tribal deity, Nialichi. The Masters of the Spear ordered white bulls to be brought to the sacred byres for sacrifice. The bulls' horns were sharpened, for battle against the hostile spirits that had caused the drought; their throats were slashed and men and women danced around the carcasses, dipping spears into the bulls' blood while the magic-men called to the ancestors, "Tell Nialichi that our lives have never been so hard, our children are dying. Tell him we must have rain."

It seemed, however, that Nialichi had other matters to attend to, and his heedlessness sent some people to mission churches to implore the God of the gospels for deliverance; but it seemed that he also had other things on his agenda. Or perhaps he'd reverted to his Old Testament self, for in the hiss of the parching wind, the people heard the harsh pronouncement of his prophet Isaiah, "*Woe to the land shadowing with wings beyond the rivers of Ethiopia.*"

The elders conferred about what to do. They spoke to their chiefs, who sent urgent messages for food to the hawaga, the white men who flew the blue and white airplanes that had saved the Dinka from starvation in the past. The hawaga answered that relief would soon come, but first the people had to clear fields and mark them so the airplanes would know where to drop the sacks of grain and the tins of powdered milk. This was done.

Now the villagers and the herdsmen in their cattle camps scanned the skies not for clouds and rain but for the blue and white airplanes—which never came. It appeared the hawaga too had more important things on their minds. The people in those isolated settlements had no way of knowing that the white men were prepared to help but couldn't because the government forbade it. They had no way of knowing that the regime far to the north had seen an opportunity in their catastrophe to break the will of the infidels' resistance in Bahr el Ghazal. They didn't hear the mullahs preaching in the mosques of Khartoum that Allah had withheld the rains from the land of the gazelle expressly for that purpose. To fail to take advantage of such a providential event would be an offense to heaven, and so the government ordered the expulsion of the UN teams established in Bahr el Ghazal and decreed that the aid embargo, previously restricted to those parts held by the rebels, would be imposed on the entire province. The only planes that showed up were those sent to evacuate UN workers.

Yet rumors flew that the white men had established big camps, called feeding centers, in certain provincial towns. In their desperation, driven by a hunger that had long since passed from their bellies into their very cells, the people began to walk to the towns, some traveling as far as sixty or seventy miles under a tyrannical sun. The roads Fitzhugh heard, were as he had seen them in the previous famine: filled with emaciated men; with mothers whose breasts had run dry carrying infants with swollen bellies and heads that looked too big for their necks; with the aged and the sick, who sat in the scant shade of shriveled trees to wait for death. Unlike Nialichi and the hawaga and the God of the gospels, it did not keep them waiting for very long.

While the Masters of the Spear had been praying for rain, Fitzhugh had to face the inescapable truth that his own fortunes were now inversely proportional to the fortunes of the southern Sudanese. He was a junior partner in an enterprise that was as much a business as it was a cause (and maybe more the former than the latter). The calamity in Bahr el Ghazal—a sharp spike in the ongoing calamity that was Sudan—was the best thing that could have happened to Knight Air and thus to him.

The UN's compliance with the embargo left relief entirely in the hands of the independent agencies. Tara Whitcomb's airline, despite its fleet of fourteen planes, wasn't able to handle the volume of business. Logisticians from various NGOs began to call on Fitzhugh, asking to charter the G1C and the Hawker. The company's invoicing doubled and then tripled. One plane would fly out in the morning, the other in the afternoon. If that kept up, Fitzhugh's five percent share of net profits would come to more than he'd earned in his four years with the UN. Those prospects brought him a joy that outweighed his pity for the starving victims, which shocked him, as a devoted son would be shocked to find his sorrow over the untimely death of a beloved father lightened by the discovery that he'd inherited a small fortune.

In six weeks Knight Air flew sixty-one missions, grossing almost half a million dollars. Rachel Njiru, the secretary and bookkeeper, deducted for expenses and salaries and declared that the company had netted two hundred thousand. The next day Fitzhugh flew to Nairobi to personally present a check to the South African from whom the G1C was being leased. Knight Air now owned the airplane free and clear.

In the meantime UN officials in Kenya pleaded with Khartoum to lift the embargo. After resisting for a time, the fanatics relented. UN Hercules and Buffalos began to make daily airdrops. Tara's company was contracted to deliver smaller shipments, but Knight Air was left out because of an obscure regulation: to carry UN cargoes, an independent airline had to possess a UN radio call-sign. Douglas got a meeting with base officials and, deploying his persuasive charms, convinced them that in the present emergency, one should be issued to Knight Air.

Fitzhugh, Douglas, and Dare waited for a rush of new clients, but none came. The UN agencies continued to send their business to Pathways.

"Don't have to think too hard to figure out what's going on there," Douglas declared one morning, after he'd returned from a flight. He and Fitzhugh were in the office. Douglas, polishing off a six-pack of Coke, seemed drawn to a high, fine edge, each gray eye cupped by a shadowy crescent as he twisted a pencil through his fingers. "She's not sleeping with agency logisticians, so that leaves the alternative. She's got them on her payroll. Ten percent of each flight's charges goes back to them."

"You don't have any proof, and besides, I can't picture Tara giving kickbacks to anyone."

Douglas braced the pencil over his two middle fingers, hooking one around each end, as if he meant to break it in two. "That woman's got everybody sold on the idea that she's some sort of nun. The flying nun, but hey, you don't get where she's gotten without marking a few cards in the deck." He pulled off his baseball cap and gave it a Frisbee toss across the room. "Talk to those people. You know them. Talk to 'em, see if you can get them to throw some business our way. Give 'em the sales pitch. Tara can't do it all, and what she can do for nine thousand, we can do for eight."

"I'll try," Fitzhugh said. "But you know, we don't have the aircraft to handle much more than we do now."

"Tony and I will do two turnarounds a day if we have to, and so will Wes and Mary."

This was a different Douglas Braithwaite from the one Fitzhugh had met in Diana Briggs's house last year. He was harder somehow, annealed by the pressures that had been on him, transforming Knight Air from an idea into a going concern, flying mission after mission in dangerous skies. In the process the old Douglas had not so much vanished as been over-shadowed by another side to his personality, which displayed the defects of his virtues. Lately his resolve, passion, and drive manifested themselves in an obsessive quest to surpass Tara Whitcomb. "We're playing Avis to her Hertz, but not forever," he'd said, and more than once. Reversing that equation had become the focus of his energies. Tara had done nothing to earn the animosity he'd worked up for her. Was there some strand of hostile competitiveness woven into his American DNA that wouldn't allow him to be content with second place?

"As far as equipment goes, I'm working on that," he said now. "There's a Russian guy in Nairobi looking to lease an Antonov-thirty-two. Tony found out about him. The deal comes complete with a five-man crew. Five-fifty an hour, with a sixty-hour-per-month minimum. The Russian pays the crew and insurance, we pay the rest."

"So"—Fitzhugh took a calculator out of the desk drawer—"if it does just twenty turnarounds a month, we—"

"Gross about one-sixty," Douglas cut in. He'd already done the arithmetic. "After lease fees, fuel, and operating costs, net seventy and change. But here's the sweet thing. An Antonov carries seven and a half tons and cruises at two-twenty. That's three tons more than one of Pathways' Andovers and reduces block time by a factor of forty miles an hour. We deliver seven-odd tons, at a buck-thirty a kilo, she delivers four at a little over two bucks. Less for more. We'd be irresistible to any logistics guy trying to stay in budget. I'll be talking to this Russian or whatever he is in a couple of days." Douglas spread his arms out wide. "We've got the big mo, and if I learned anything from my dad, it's that when you've got the big mo, you keep it rolling."

"The big what?"

"Momentum." He paused. "Try *hard*, Fitz, with those logisticians."

Fitzhugh caught the subtext—he was being given the green light to offer commissions. Thinking, *This is how we speak now, this is the language of the aid entrepreneur,* he plopped himself down on the edge of the big steel desk. "Block time. Block speed. Per kilo rates. Lease fees. Momentum," he said. "And commissions—kickbacks. Is this what we're all about? Is this what we came here to do?"

Douglas frowned and made more weaving movements with the pencil. "Nope. It's what we *have* to do to keep doing what we came here to do." He got up suddenly and clutched Fitzhugh by both shoulders. That need of his to press the flesh, as though his words might not be heard without the amplification of his touch. "Fitz, my man! We're not a nonprofit organization. If we weren't in business, those Dinka in Bahr el Ghazal would be dying, the Nubans would still be rubbing sticks together to light their fires, that German doctor would still be slicing people open to find out what's wrong with them. Did we cause the drought? We're not firemen who turned arsonist to give themselves a paycheck. We're fighting a fire someone else started."

Douglas let him go and stood looking at the schedule board, with its grease pen notations on airstrip conditions. "Okay, assuming we get our hands on the Antonov, we'll have a fleet with a total capacity of—" With the grease pen, he wrote "17" on the board. "And we can deliver those seventeen tons faster than Pathways, and faster means cheaper, and cheaper means the agencies come to us first."

Tara again. All conversational roads led back to her.

"The Sudanese get food, they get their lives back, and the agencies save money, and we make it and stay in the game," Douglas went on in an over-caffeinated rush. "Everybody benefits. It's win-win, Fitz. Win-win all around."

Steering Knight Air's company car, a Toyota pickup with worn shocks and a pitted windshield, down a Loki side road, Fitzhugh felt a tad splenetic. *Fitz, my man.* Well, he was Douglas's man, wasn't he? The brown boy running an errand for the white boy, the Bahss. To keep the lid on his bubbling resentment, he reminded himself that the American, like it or not, was the Bahss and that it was part of his job as operations manager to negotiate agreements with NGO logisticians.

A few enterprising Turkana were peddling handicrafts outside the UN compound's bright blue fence of corrugated steel. Wedging the pickup between two uniformly white Land Cruisers, he got out, conscious of the bulge in his midriff. He'd come back from the Nuba as lean and hard as he'd been in his soccer days, but the tailor of his appetites had since altered the Ambler into the man nearly everyone in Loki called "Big Bear." I should have walked here, he thought. I should walk a mile every day and play more volleyball.

Well, he'd been doing his share of legwork today. There were forty agencies enlisted under the UN banner, and he intended to visit as many as he could. Going up a lane fenced by whitewashed rocks, past signs bearing inspiring slogans—DEFEAT AIDS, LET'S CONQUER POLIO IN SUDAN—he recalled that his old boss, the one who'd told him he possessed an insufferably Hebraic soul, had once termed the situation in Sudan "a permanent crisis." The base's appearance underlined the accuracy of that near-oxymoron. Everything here suggested perpetuity: buildings instead of tents, streets instead of paths, even street signs. The recolonization of Africa by the imperialism of good intentions.

He strode into the office of a small Dutch NGO, confident and commanding, dressed for the occasion in pressed khaki trousers instead of rumpled shorts, shoes instead of sandals, and in place of his usual T-shirt, a dark green polo displaying Knight Air's name and emblem over his heart.

Appearances weren't enough to persuade the Dutch to switch carriers; nor was his sales pitch. He also failed with CARE, Catholic Relief Services, World Vision, and the Adventist Development and Relief Agency. It appeared that Knight Air wasn't so irresistible after all, but he pressed on, agency to agency, extolling the virtues of the G1C and the Hawker over Tara's sluggish Andovers. He made no offer of commissions, hoping to persuade his prospective clients through force of personality and the promised quality and economy of his company's services. As he rattled on about block times and block speeds and per kilo rates, his tongue on automatic, his spleen bubbled up again. He bore Tara no ill will, and so long as he earned a decent living, he could not have cared less if Knight Air played Avis to Pathways's Hertz till the end of time. Why, then, was he talking himself hoarse to help Douglas realize his ambition? Because he couldn't let him down, that was why. As much as he might resent his role as Man Friday, he realized that it was perfect casting. There was something in his character that suited him for the work of the deputy, the same something that made his father an effective hotelier. He was born to oblige, to cater to others' wishes, to be of service.

His next stop was a group bearing the cumbersome and redundant name of Global International Aid Services. It employed a multiracial, multinational staff that served to veil, somewhat, its Washington origins and the identity of its principal donor, the U.S. Agency for International Development, which some people believed was an arm of the CIA. Global's logistics chief was a dour Belgian known as the Flemish Phlegm, a sobriquet whose shortened version, "Flemmy," was used so often that the man's real name had been forgotten. He had been Fitzhugh's main informant during his private investigation into the UN's practice of destroying surplus food. Though he'd scrupulously kept the source of his information secret, Flemmy had suggested afterward that Fitzhugh owed him something more than the protection of his anonymity.

After he'd listened, patiently and without expression, to Fitzhugh's spiel, he presented the bill.

Chewing on an unlit pipe, Flemmy complimented him for landing on his feet after his dismissal from the World Food Program's staff. "But," he added, "you seem to be still learning the nuances of your new job. You haven't convinced me to make any changes in our present arrangements. You need to—the American phrase is 'toot your own horn'— a little more . . . loudly? No. Not loud. More sweetly. Has anyone else pointed that out to you?"

"No, you're the first," he answered. That Flemmy had not flatly turned him down and had taken the time to point out the deficiency in his proposals represented progress of a sort; but he elected to say nothing more. He would feel better about himself if he left it to the other man to make the proposition.

"We have a lot of stuff to move, and you with only two airplanes—" He wagged a hand scornfully. "Why, that could delay a shipment for days, whereas your competitor has the means to deliver it right away." Flemmy paused and tapped his thumbnail with the pipestem. "On the other hand, we aren't contractually bound to Pathways, and you make a good case that we could save a thousand dollars per flight with you. I think I could see my way clear to . . . oh, you know, every third delivery, perhaps every other delivery."

Fitzhugh heard the emphasis on "think" and listened to the irritating *tap-tap*. "Whatever you feel comfortable with," he said.

"That depends upon what you feel comfortable with," the Belgian said softly. "Just to be sure we're clear on that." He wrote on a piece of paper and passed it across the desk for Fitzhugh's inspection. "I believe that follows established custom?"

Aware that he wasn't acting under duress of circumstance, that he was making a clear, conscious choice and a compromise that could lead to further compromises, he nodded.

Flemmy tore the paper into quarters and tossed the fragments into the wastebasket. "Of course we don't need to shake hands."

"Of course."

"Excellent. I'll be in touch soon. In the meantime, may I suggest that you need not be shy about offering the full . . . the full range of your company's services to whomever else you speak to. I think you'll get better results."

Fitzhugh followed that advice, and the results were more favorable. By the end of the day he'd made arrangements with three NGOs similar to the one he made with Flemmy. He might have gotten more if his discomfort hadn't been so obvious. During the proceedings, his mind became a kind of TV split-screen; a scene from the famine was projected on one half—skeletal kids grubbing in the dirt for spilled kernels of airdropped grain—and a picture of himself negotiating sleazy deals was projected on the other. The two dissonant images produced a physical sensation, as if he were coated in some sticky substance that had drawn ants to his body. Watching him squirm and grimace, it was apparent to the logisticians that he was disgusted with himself and with them and the whole business. Fitzhugh could tell that they could tell he was acting contrary to his scruples, which caused them to wonder if he would be stricken with an attack of those scruples later on and renege on his promises. They sent him on his way. He found that success came when he told himself that he was doing a small wrong thing in order to do a big right thing—a version of Douglas's statement "We're doing what we have to do so we can keep doing what we came here to do." Those words banished the sticky, crawly sensation, and he would feel more confident and sound more convincing when he proposed to his customers that they would personally benefit from an association with Knight Air Limited.

He reported the outcome to Douglas that night in the Hotel California bar. It was the beginning of their transformation into co-conspirators, for they spoke in conspiratorial tones—three other customers were sitting at a nearby table, Quinette and her Irish roommates.

"You came through, knew you would," Douglas said.

The compliment brought a delight that momentarily overcame Fitzhugh's doubts about his actions, while the delight, like a pretty yacht towing a garbage barge, dragged into the harbor of his self-esteem a mortifying awareness that his friend's opinion of him had a direct effect on his opinion of himself.

"I had to offer incentives," he confessed reluctantly. "I tried to think of it as a marketing tool, yes?"

"That's exactly what it is."

"I'm not sure how to tell Rachel how to handle these arrangements on the books."

"I'll take care of that." With his Coke glass, he clinked Fitzhugh's can of Tusker. "To the big mo."

Three days later Douglas concluded the lease agreement with the owner of the Antonov-32. Soon afterward, with a decal of a green knight straddling an airplane pasted to her nose, she flew her first delivery into Bahr el Ghazal.

As that cruel dry season advanced, misfortune continued to be Knight Air's ally. A very bad piece of bad luck was suffered by the crew of a Pathways Andover, flying sorghum and Unimix to a village near the Jur river. SPLA guerrillas surrounded the plane at the airstrip and began to offload its cargo onto lorries while the villagers watched helplessly. It was the third or fourth incident of rebel army theft since the famine struck, and the Andover's captain—it was Tara's senior pilot, the Ethiopian named George Tafari—was fed up. He told the rebel officer in charge that if his men didn't turn over the food to the civilians, he was going to report the banditry to UN authorities. In the account that would later be given by the copilot, the officer replied that his troops were starving too and couldn't be expected to fight on empty bellies. George persisted. The overstrung commander then drew his pistol and instructed George to speak not one word more and to clear out immediately.

The Andover wasn't five hundred feet off the ground when the guerrillas opened fire with assault rifles and machine guns. A bullet through the head killed George instantly, and a Kenyan relief worker on board was wounded in the arm. The copilot, a devout Somali, would later say that the hand of Allah saved the plane from crashing; the hand of Allah kept his hands on the controls and gave him the strength and presence of mind to fly the crippled aircraft a thousand kilometers back to Loki, with the relief worker screaming in the back, the pilot-side windows blown out (making it impossible to pressurize the cockpit so that he had to fly the entire distance at six thousand feet), and with blood and brain matter sprayed all over the instrument panel.

Fitzhugh had monitored the distress calls on his own radio, and when he heard the Andover coming in, he went to the Pathways terminal to see if he could be of any help. He was inclined to believe the story of divine intervention after the Somali, bleeding from the fragments of George's skull embedded in his cheek and temple, described what had happened. It also seemed miraculous that the man hadn't taken leave of his senses.

Tara lost her composure when a Red Cross ambulance crew pulled George's body from the cockpit. To see that iron woman fall to both knees beside the stretcher and weep would have moved Fitzhugh to tears himself if he hadn't been struggling so hard against a wave of nausea.

Tara declared she was suspending Pathways flights into the stricken province until the SPLA high command assured her that George's murderers would be found and punished and that every measure was being taken to prevent a similar incident.

Sudan, Sudan, Sudan, Fitzhugh thought as all this unfolded. Woe to the land beyond the rivers of Ethiopia. The rebels were the best friends Khartoum could ask for.

Knight Air, having the field entirely to itself, was still flying. Clinging to the belief that the quality of one's actions was affected by the quality of one's motives, Fitzhugh struggled to stop thinking about what this would mean for the company's revenues, and he was aided in this endeavor by the return of the old Douglas, defiant and impassioned. It appeared that events had summoned him out of hiding. At breakfast, on the morning after Tara announced her decision, he told Dare and Fitzhugh that he was going to try to talk her out of it.

Dare sopped up egg yolk with a piece of toast. "That makes a helluva lot of sense. The woman hands you a blank check and you want to give it back."

"There's a quarter of a million people out there starving to death. I think that takes precedence." Douglas let a faint sigh slip, as if relieved to discover that he could still make a statement like that without a false note. "With only three airplanes, we can't handle the volume."

Asking Fitzhugh to come along, Douglas met Tara at her tukul in the Pathways compound, that sanctuary of floral-scented order. She was in her garden, pruning a rosebush with the single-minded concentration people devote to simple physical tasks to distract themselves from emotional turmoil. Her hair was unkempt, her makeup was off, and she was wearing, instead of her usual starched captain's shirt and creased trousers, a dirty T-shirt and a pair of shorts that exposed her varicose veins. They judged her appearance a measure of her grief. Cordial as always, she offered tea, which they declined, and then listened attentively as Douglas pleaded with her to change her mind. He was unable to resist touching her arm as she stood there, holding the pruning shears in one gloved hand.

Tara let him know that she didn't care for the physical contact by drawing back about a yard, to lean against the bicycle she pedaled to and from the terminal each day to keep fit. "Not one of my planes is going into Bahr el Ghazal until I get assurances from Garang himself that he's going to crack down on those bloody renegades."

Denied contact with another's flesh, Douglas's hands seemed not to know what to do with themselves. "Tara, people, thousands of people, are going to—"

"Do you suppose I haven't considered that?" Her lips stretched and her jaw tightened. "But I have just spent the past two days arranging for George's body to be shipped back to Ethiopia. I have written a letter to his wife. I do not wish to repeat that experience. I've got twenty other people flying for me, and my first responsibility is to them. And to their families."

"But they know the risks, same as we all do."

"Which are quite enough without the SPLA adding to them. The people who are supposed to be on our side." She shook her head. "No, I would no more send one of my crews out there than I'd let them take off in a faulty airplane. Not until I get those assurances, and I will get them." She seemed to close the discussion by stepping forward to clip an unruly stem. "George was with me from the very beginning. He and I flew the first relief missions out of here together. He wasn't just an employee but a friend. When his daughter was born, he asked me to be her godmother."

"Can I say something?"

"If you're asking for forgiveness in advance for whatever it is you want to say, you don't necessarily have it."

"Okay, fine. I think the best way for you to pay tribute to George would be to keep your planes in the air. I think that's what he'd want. I think you're letting one bad incident get the better of you."

"Douglas," she said with a cold smile, "the day you see one of your pilots with half his head blown off and his brains splattered all over the cockpit is the day when you shall have earned the right to make a comment like that. Thanks very much, but I'd like to get on with my roses."

"I guess that means I'm not forgiven," Douglas muttered as they drove out of the compound. "Can you believe her? One guy gets killed, and she throws in the towel."

"She's not exactly throwing in the towel. I don't think we're in a position to judge her."

"The hell we're not." Turning onto the main road, he popped the clutch, jammed the accelerator, and made gravel fly. "What does she expect? This is a war, for fuck's sake."

Fitzhugh kept silent. In his delight with its return, he'd forgotten that the old-model Douglas came equipped with some unattractive features.

His prettier parts were on display that night, when he and Dare convened a meeting of Knight Air's staff. Along with Fitzhugh, Tony, Mary, Rachel, Nimrod, and the flight mechanic, VanRensberg, the Antonov's crew—whose roster read like the cast of characters in a Russian novel, Alexei, Sergei, Leonid, Vladimir, and Mikhail—shoehorned themselves into the tiny office. Dedicated smokers, the Russians joined with Fitzhugh to turn the room into a gas chamber. Whether it was to escape the smoke or to make himself appear more commanding, Douglas stood on the desk and, while Dare leaned back in the chair and pretended to be studying the shine in his snakeskin boots, presented his idea, summed up his meeting with Tara, and made his a-quarter-of-a-million-people-will-starve-to-death-if-someone-doesn't-do-something speech.

"And right now, that's us. It's up to us." He brushed a lock of hair from his eye, with a casual diffidence that offset his imposing stance. "But I sure as hell wouldn't want what happened to George Tafari to happen to any of you. I can't ask you to risk your necks any more than you are already. So it's your call. We've got other places that need us, like the Nuba, although you know that's no piece of cake either."

"Me and Mary sure do," Dare muttered, referring to their narrow escape, which had become legend in Loki.

Douglas then turned to Tony Bollichek, who said, "If you're asking for volunteers, mate, I'm one."

"Great. That's great. Mary, what about you?"

"I'd rather be here than in Manitoba."

"All right! So we've heard from Australia and Canada. Alexei," he said to the Antonov's captain, "what's the word from Russia?"

There was a murmuring of Slavic consonants as Alexei, a short apple-cheeked man, conferred with his crew.

"Sure. Why not?" he answered with a fatalistic shrug.

"All right! All right! Old Fly-by-Knight is a team! So listen up, we'll all be working our butts to the bone. Not just the aircrews but all of you. Wes and I decided that everyone gets a bonus at the end of the month. How much depends on how much we take in, but if we have to, we'll forgo what we pay ourselves to make that promise good. I'll see everyone at the bar. Drinks are on us."

"And y'all can bet that last part was Dougie's idea, not mine," Wesley drawled to laughter.

As Douglas climbed down, Alexei applauded. Half a second later everyone but Dare joined in, and Fitzhugh could tell by the enthusiasm of the ovation that they were going to do whatever they had to not for the sake of a bonus, or even for the sake of the suffering multitudes hundreds of miles away, but for Douglas Braithwaite's sake. No one wanted to let him down.

The Antonov made food drops, sometimes two a day, leaving Loki at dawn, returning by noon to refuel and take on another shipment, then departing once more and coming back at dusk. Wes and Mary in the

Hawker, Doug and Tony in the G1C, flew daily for twenty-two days straight. They were often dangerously overloaded, and, the lifting of the embargo notwithstanding, there was the ever-present menace of ground fire or an encounter with a Sudanese MIG or helicopter gunship. Each flight was an act of faith, in Providence, in luck, in the *rightness* of the mission, and because self-dramatization is necessary if one is to continue taking such risks, the exhausted crews began to look upon themselves as embodiments of the company's logo: airborne knights, rescuing the peasants from the twin dragons of starvation and war.

Fitzhugh, busy with flight schedules, invoices, and other minutiae, wasn't able to cast any such chivalric light upon himself. The distasteful part of his job—taking care of the ten percenters—made him feel like a bagman, which brought on a relapse of the sensation that he was coated in a sticky substance swarming with ants.

The incantation "We do what we have to so we can keep doing what we came here to do" no longer was sufficient to exorcise this feeling. He needed to break out of the isolation imposed by his administrative duties and reconnect himself with the wretched humanity in whose name the pilots gambled with their lives and he compromised his principles. On two occasions he flew with Alexei and the Russians on airdrops over the parched immensities beyond the Jur. With Dare and Mary he landed at a place called Atukuel, where what looked like the population of a small concentration camp greeted them. All he saw was sharp angles— protruding ribs and collarbones, shoulder blades like wings, cheekbones, knee bones, thigh bones with a mere appliqué of flesh. Gangs of the living dead approached the plane, dragging plastic sheets and canvas tarps. Fitzhugh pitched in with the off-load. It felt good to sweat honest sweat, to use his muscles again, and to see a light switch on in the glassy eyes looking up at him. What was it but the light of hope? Hope in a twenty-five-kilo bag of sorghum. Hope. The human capacity for it astonished him. Hope and the will to go on, even when going on seemed pointless. If those people could have seen their futures as clearly as they did their present circumstances, they probably would have laid down on the spot and allowed themselves to starve to death. He watched the men on the ground drag the sacks into the sheets and tarps, which were fashioned into carriers by twisting each end into a makeshift rope. Two men would sling the ends over their shoulders and lug the loads to the edge of the airstrip. It amazed him that those skeletons, who looked barely capable of carrying their own shadows, could haul a hundred pounds any distance at all. He and the tall

Norwegian working alongside him heaved out bag upon bag, and jerry cans of water and boxes of evaporated milk. More than five tons' worth. He got careless once, giving one sack too hard a toss. It split open, its contents spilled out, and a vision from his mental split-screen became a reality as a crowd of kids, their hair hennaed by starvation, rushed forward to scoop the sorghum into wooden calabashes. They picked each grain up, like a flock of birds. Relief work—what a bland phrase, as if it were merely another form of labor. But it wasn't. It reaffirmed the human bond. It was the marshaling of resources to organize compassion into effective action, for without action, compassion degenerated into a useless pity. It was what he'd come to do, and if to do it he had to trim a few moral corners, then he would trim them. In the face of so much misery, self-recrimination seemed a self-indulgence. Guilt was a worthless currency out here.

Toward the end of that month Tara received a message asking her to come to the Nairobi office of the Sudanese People's Liberation Movement, the rebellion's political arm. There she was shown a copy of an order issued to all commands promising swift punishment to anyone who hijacked a relief plane's cargo. Also documents recording the court-martial of the soldiers who'd shot at George Tafari's Andover. Also photographs of the execution by firing squad of their commanding officer. She returned to Loki shaken by the photographs. She hadn't expected an execution. It was a case of, Beware of what you ask for, you may get it.

But she had the assurances she'd sought, and she put her planes back into the operation. By that time many of her former customers, satisfied with its performance as well as with its under-the-table fringe benefits, decided to stick with Knight Air. If the company had had a larger fleet, it would have taken more of her business.

"We need to expand, big-time," Douglas said one evening, drinking with Dare and Fitzhugh in the compound bar. "We need at least one more airplane, three or four if we can get them."

"Maybe I got a solution," Dare said. He had just returned from Nairobi, where he'd conferred with his lawyer about his lawsuit, in the hopes of breaking the legal deadlock and reclaiming his G1, still in mothballs at Wilson Field. "My hearing is way back on the docket, and even if the judge rules in my favor, he's got to let Nakima have his day in court and rule on his countersuit, and then maybe, maybe the plane's all mine again. Trouble is, the judge is in Nakima's pocket, the idea being to keep delayin' the thing till I wear out and quit. So I figured, as long as I was down there, to pay me a call on Hassan. He knows half the MPs and judges in this sorry-ass excuse of a country. Reckoned he might take the one on my case out to lunch, say a few words on old Wesley's behalf."

"Who the hell is Hassan?" Douglas asked.

Dare blew the foam off his beer. "I used to fly mirra for him."

"What about helping you out with the G1? We could use that airplane, Wes."

"Watch the 'we,' rafiki. I get the plane, we have the same arrangement with it as we got with my Hawker. I lease it to the company."

Douglas frowned. "About time for you to develop a little trust, isn't it?"

"Don't take it personal. Half the time I don't even trust myself. Anyhow, me and Hassan got to shootin' the shit, he asked me what I was up to these days. I told him, and he said he'd like to talk to us."

Fitzhugh swiped a finger across his damp forehead. "What does your court case have to do with us?"

"Not a damned thing, but I got the idea he might like to put some money into Knight Air. Kind of a venture capital thing."

Douglas, who'd been bird-watching the hour before dinner, fanned the pages of the book lying on the table, *Birds of East Africa*—a show of disinterest that meant he was interested. "And he's got the capital?"

"I think that Somali would need one of them supercomputers to count his money."

"He's a Somali?"

Dare's glance made one of its sidelong, downward casts, as if he were embarrassed, though it was hard to imagine him embarrassed by anything. "I wouldn't call a man a Somali if he wasn't one. He's not from Somalia. He's what they call here an ethnic Somali, from eastern Kenya. Same difference, but he's about the only Somali I care to deal with."

"He's someone you do trust?" Fitzhugh asked.

"Hell, no"—pulling the word *hell* like it was made of taffy. "Put it like this. He won't stab you in the back, he'll stab you in front with one hand and be shakin' your hand with the other, and he'll do it so quick, y'all won't know you've been stabbed till you see the blood. I trust him in that sense."

"What're you saying, Wes? That we shouldn't talk to him? We should? What?"

"He might be more disposed to go to bat for me if we did. I sure as hell would like to get that airplane back."

They took a Kenya Airways commuter to Nairobi. On the way down

Dare offered an informal background briefing on Hassan Adid, whom he described, with his usual disregard for Fitzhugh's origins and sensibilities, as "way above, light-years away from your average bush-baby African hustler." A one-man conglomerate, the cultivation and exportation of mirra was just one of his many enterprises, which included mining precious stones like tanzanite and tsavorite, construction, and cattle, Adid having inherited from his father one-third ownership of the Tana ranch—a million and a half acres of grazing land near Tsavo National Park. "A kind of African cowboy, you might say."

In the 1970s and 1980s the Adid family had tripled its fortune in the illegal ivory trade. Somali poaching gangs had been trespassing on the ranch for years, using it as a base for their raids on the park's elephant herds. Unable to keep the poachers off their sprawling property, the elder Adid and his two Arab partners decided to employ them and to turn their disorganized forays into an efficient industry.

"They brought Hassan into it after he got out of school. He got a fleet of trucks to haul out the ivory instead of havin' it carried out on foot," Dare said, standing in the aisle beside Douglas and Fitzhugh's seats, his head bent under the small plane's ceiling. "Must've needed the trucks to haul the money out. Those days ivory was goin' for six thousand U.S. a kilo. Shoot one big bull carryin' forty, fifty kilos in each tusk, and you've grossed half a mil to six hundred thousand and change, and those boys they had workin' for 'em was shootin' dozens, hundreds. Wouldn't have been one elephant left if it wasn't for Dick Leakey, y'know, the son of that famous scientist, some sort of ologist."

"Paleontologist," Douglas offered helpfully.

"Yeah, it was his son, Dick Leakey, who put a crimp in their operations when he got put in charge of the Kenya Wildlife Service. He formed up those antipoaching commando teams, and they and the gangs had them a regular war goin' on down there in Tsavo. Then Leakey lobbies for a worldwide ban on ivory, and he gets it, and pretty soon the Adids are back in the cattle business. I met Dick once. He was a pilot, y'know—"

Fitzhugh interrupted, saying that yes, he knew, and that one day Leakey's plane developed mechanical trouble in midair and crashed, and some said it was no accident.

"Yup. Crippled up Dick Leakey for life. He had him a helluva lot of enemies, and the Adids were at the top of the list. Anyhow, the old man sent Hassan to graduate school in the U.S. Hassan got him an MBA from—the University of Florida, I think it was—and after the poaching party was over with, he went legit, bought a couple hundred thousand acres near Mount Kenya, and went into the mirra trade, ivory to dope, and then he got into everything else."

Adid's degree was from the University of Miami, not the University of Florida. He must have been proud of it; it was the sole object on the wall behind his desk, positioned to catch the light from the window overlooking traffic-fumed Kenyatta Avenue. It appeared that he treasured his privacy and liked to keep a low profile. A simple plastic sign reading THE TANA GROUP hung on the door to a spare reception room, where a stout woman announced the three visitors on an intercom, then led them through two doors with electronic locks and into Adid's private office, which was smaller and more modestly furnished than the lavishly appointed acreage Fitzhugh had pictured. The man himself, studiously casual in open-neck shirt and raw silk sport jacket, looked to be in his early forties. He was a little under six feet tall, with coat-hanger shoulders, a slender, almost delicate frame, a small head, and very dark, very piercing eyes—miniature black holes that took everything in and let nothing out.

He was an ardent soccer fan, and when he learned that Fitzhugh was *the* Fitzhugh Martin, he spent several minutes tossing him bouquets of praise and reminiscing about the Ambler's glory days on the Harambe Stars.

"It's an honor to meet you, truly it is."

Fitzhugh squirmed in his seat and made a dismissive gesture.

"But I see I must be embarrassing you. You're a man who is humble about his achievements. Would it embarrass you more if I asked for your autograph? I would like to give it to my son. He plays with a club."

Fitzhugh replied no, it would not embarrass him, for it wasn't the laudatory comments that made him uncomfortable but Adid's gaze, which seemed to bore through his skin. There was a weird disconnect between it and what he was saying. While the tongue flattered, the eyes studied, and Fitzhugh got the disconcerting impression that Adid knew everything about him, or at least as much as he needed to know. He'd been sized up.

A pen and notepad were pushed across the desk. He wrote, "To Hassan Adid, My Very Best Wishes," and signed his name, adding "The Ambler" as a flourish.

"Thank you, my son will be thrilled," Adid said in his low, adenoidal voice, then turned his attention to Douglas and apologized for wasting time. "You didn't come all this way to listen to us talk about soccer," he said, and spread his hands on the desktop, his long fingers like the ribs of a fan. "So I think I could be of some benefit to you, and of course you to me. I'm always looking to diversify." He gestured at the photographs on a side wall, showing the many facets of the Tana Group: an office building under construction, a mining operation, a sloping field abloom with mirra. "And lately I've taken an interest in aviation. Actually, it's an old interest of mine. I took some flying lessons when I was in the U.S. There are some excellent flight schools in Florida. Where did you learn, Mr. Braithwaite?"

"The U.S. Air Force."

"You can't ask for a better school than that. What did you fly? Were you a"—he mimed a pilot jockeying a joystick—"top gun?"

"Not quite. I flew A-tens. Warthogs."

Dare did a theatrical double-take and said, "All this time and you never mentioned you were a Hog jockey." It was also the first time Fitzhugh had heard anything specific about Douglas's military career.

Responding to Adid's puzzled frown and looking pleased to display his technical knowledge, Dare explained that a Warthog was a ground attack plane. "It's used mostly to bust up tanks and armored vehicles."

Adid turned back to Douglas. "And did you, ah, 'bust up' any tanks?"

"Yeah. In the Persian Gulf. Iraqi convoys, too. The last day of the war, when the Iraqis were pulling out of Kuwait—they were in commandeered taxis, city buses, dump trucks, private cars, anything that had wheels and gas in the tank, making off with the stuff they'd looted—my squadron blew the shit out of them. There were guys on fire running out of the vehicles, and we strafed them with cannon fire. They never had a chance. Sometimes I think that's why I got into what I'm doing now, flying humanitarian aid. We weren't shooting up an army but a rabble, and it wasn't war, it was bloody murder. It made me sick."

This speech—which sounded more like something that would be said in a bar after one too many, and which was so off the point and so unlike Douglas, who hardly ever revealed anything about his past—left everyone speechless.

Leaning over to slap Douglas's knee, Dare broke the silence. "My partner's got him a bleeding heart, Hassan. It had been me, I'd have shot the shit out of those Eye-raqis and gone lookin' for more."

Adid said nothing, perplexed by the outburst. So was Fitzhugh. Why pick such an inappropriate moment and setting to tell a stranger what you'd withheld from your friends? He thought Douglas had disclosed more about himself than he should have, for all the while, Adid was subjecting the American to his CAT scan gaze, as if he were making exposures of his psychic interior, pinpointing his strengths and weaknesses, the places where he was sound, the places where he was unsound, soft, vulnerable. Douglas too was being sized up. Someone who'd cut his baby teeth in the world of commerce by selling contraband ivory must have learned how to make quick judgments about other people, and make them accurately.

"Perhaps we should turn to what you're doing now," Adid said finally. "I have a few questions."

"This ought to tell you what you need to know."

Douglas removed from his briefcase a financial statement that Rachel had typed up on the desktop. The one-man conglomerate read it carefully, a finger moving down the columns of assets and liabilities, and said that he hadn't expected so thorough an accounting of Knight Air's condition.

"I guess I learned a few things from my father," Douglas said with a shrug of modesty. "I worked for him a couple of summers in college. He was my business school."

"So was mine. What does your father do, Mr. Braithwaite?"

"It's what he *did,* and make that Douglas or Doug. He died when I was in college. Heart attack. He was a developer. Golf courses, condominiums, that kind of thing."

"Did your father teach you about business plans?" Adid asked. "One thing I don't find in here is a business plan. I assume you have one?"

"Sure. It's to stay in business."

A pause.

"If that's it, you won't," Adid warned, sharply. "Grow or die, the fundamental axiom. The most valuable lesson I took from there." He motioned at his degree. "So you could perhaps tell me the prospects for growing, the impediments? Do you have competition, and who are they, and what's their share of the market, and what's yours? Do you have a vision of where you'd like your company to be in two or three years? My thought is to invest in it, but naturally I need some idea of what the prospects for a return are. I'm not a charity."

"We aren't either."

"Yes. You fly for charitable organizations."

"I wouldn't call it that. We're not just any old cargo haulers. There's a point to what we're doing. Beyond just making a few bucks is what I'm saying."

"Of course. *Of course.* But could you tell me please something about the making of the few bucks?"

Business plans. Grow or die. Market share. Whatever Hassan Adid had learned from his ivory-poaching father, it wasn't this. This argot had come straight from his graduate school days in the United States. Fitzhugh, feeling that he and Dare were more eavesdroppers than participants, listened to Douglas describe Knight Air's prospects for growth, its present share of the market, and his vision of its golden future: a fleet of twenty planes, flying aid not only into Sudan but to Somalia and the Congo and other African basket cases as well. It would provide a shuttle service for relief workers traveling between Nairobi and Lokichokio; and in the unlikely event that the Sudanese civil war ended, it would be on hand to deliver materials and workers for the country's reconstruction.

Adid occasionally jotted on a legal tablet, his round chin in his free hand, his expression betraying nothing of his thoughts. Suddenly he grimaced and, throwing his head backward, pinched the bridge of his nose. Douglas fell silent.

"Forgive me," Adid pleaded as he removed a bottle of nasal spray from a desk drawer. He squeezed it into both nostrils. "A sinus condition. Please, continue."

Douglas did, and when he was finished, Adid solemnly shook hands and suggested they reconvene at dinner that evening. "How does the Tamarind sound? The best seafood in town. If you like seafood."

"I'm a brown food man," Dare said, "but I'll go along."

Under a thin layer of gunmetal clouds, they walked back to the Norfolk Hotel. Douglas had insisted they stay there, despite the rates, or rather because of them. He didn't want Adid to think they were required to accept budget accommodations. He asked Dare what he thought—the one-man conglomerate was a hard guy to read.

"Sure is. Askin' us to dinner, that's a good sign. But count on it, if he does bet on us, it won't be a helluva lot. Hassan's got it to burn, but that doesn't mean he likes to burn it. He's no gambler, strictly a percentage player."

They crossed Kenyatta toward Muindi Mbingu. Sooty pythons coiled from buses, cars, garishly painted matatus, and secondhand London taxis to slither through the palms lining the middle of the boulevard. Toxic as it was, mile-high Nairobi's air felt bracing after Loki's empyrean noons.

"If you ask me, I think we should stay away from him," Fitzhugh said, pausing to contribute to a band of village kids who were singing and drumming, their begging bowls set out. J. M. Kariuki, the great Kenyan socialist, had predicted this years ago—a country of ten millionaires and ten million beggars. "I don't like him."

"What don't you like?"

"He's what we used to call a *wabenzi*. That was a word for fat-cat prof-iteers who drove Mercedes-Benzes."

"Who the hell cares what he drives?" Dare said.

"He's out of our league, yes?"

"The idea is, he helps us get out of the league we're in." Erect, confi-dent, ball cap pulled low over his forehead, Douglas strode through the crowds swarming around the pungent city market: an English lord in nineteenth-century Bombay, a Roman in some provincial Gallic town. "With an outside investor backing us, we can expand a lot faster than we ever could out of cash flow. Another lesson from my dad. Never do with your own money what you can do with someone else's."

"*Kwenda huto!*" In Texas-accented Swahili, Dare dismissed a hustler who was after their money, although what he was offering in exchange wasn't exactly clear. The phrase was repeated several times as they passed the Jeevanjee Gardens, where AIDS orphans popped out of bushes reek-ing of human excrement to pluck at the sleeves of the two mzungu and their darker-skinned companion. A sprint across University Way brought them to Harry Thuku Road, separating the central police station from the University of Nairobi campus. Fitzhugh had always believed the place-ment wasn't accidental: the university, generator of political dissent; the police right across the street, poised to quell student demonstrations.

At the entrance to the Norfolk, that relic of empire, its Tudor facade some nostalgic colonial's re-creation of an English country house, safari vehicles were dropping off or picking up passengers weighted down with camera gear and dressed up like *Out of Africa* extras in multipocketed bush jackets and wide-brimmed hats with fake leopard-skin bands. More tourists, along with a few expatriates, were lunching on the Delamere Ter-race, the same wood-beamed platform from which long-vanished sahibs and memsahibs, taking high tea, watched gazelle grazing on the plains—the view considerably altered now to one of smog-shrouded concrete and brick. The three entrepreneurs of aid found a free table, and just as he sat down to look at the menu, Fitzhugh was seized by a sudden longing, accompanied by a dread of spending the dinner hour in Adid's company. He declared that he was opting out of the evening's engagement, unless his presence was absolutely required, and he doubted it was.

Douglas twitched his head in surprise. "What would get you to turn down a free meal?"

"An old girlfriend," he lied.

"Right. I guess *that* would."

The longing persisted all through his lunch of fish and chips and beer.

He was surprised by how firmly it gripped him, but when he thought about it, it wasn't so surprising. She'd been dwelling in the back of his mind ever since he'd seen her, and he was always delighted to see her again, the rare times she showed up in Loki. The only cure was to act. Resolute, like a soldier, he went to his room, got his address book from his overnight bag, sat on the bed, and dialed. The housekeeper answered.

"*Halo, Bibi Di*—" he began, then cleared his throat, deciding on a more formal, businesslike approach. "*Nataka kusema na Lady Briggs tafadhali. Ni mimi Bwana Martin.*"

"*Bwana Martin*, okay. *Subiri kidogo.*"

He waited, long enough to feel his nerve failing him. Then:

"Fitz! So sorry to keep you. I'd just finished up in the ring."

"The ring?"

"My horse. Where are you?"

He told her, and she said he was moving up in the world. He pictured her in jodhpurs and boots, tousling her hair, matted by the riding hat she was holding by the strap.

"I'm here with Doug and Wes. Talking to some wabenzi who's interested in advancing us some capital."

"Marvelous. I was speaking to John the other day, and he rather feels you've been neglecting him. He's got, oh, *tons* of stuff waiting to go to the Nuba, and he can hardly get a plane scheduled."

"We've been so committed. That mess in Bahr el Ghazal, yes?"

"Dreadful."

"You heard what happened to Tara? To her pilot, I should say?"

"Ghastly."

He paused to gather himself and, in a voice scrubbed of any emotion, asked if she was free for dinner. The first part of her answer—"Delighted!"—came so quickly and was so positive that the second part—"On condition Wes keeps the obnoxious remarks to a minimum"—didn't register immediately. When it did, he hesitated.

"Are you there, Fitz?"

"Yes." His heart was stammering. "Wesley won't be there. Or Doug. *I'm* asking if you're free."

"I still am."

"It's a long way for you into town, and a woman alone ought not to be driving at night."

"Perfectly capable of taking care of myself."

"I know! I'd prefer a place out your way."

"There's the Horseman, which I don't like, and the Rusty Nail, which I do. I know the chef. I'll ring up for a table and meet you there. Now listen, Fitz, it's a frightfully expensive cab ride. Let me pick that up."

"I am perfectly capable of paying for myself." He raised his voice to a feminine treble, mimicking her accent. "See you there. Seven."

She laughed, and he heard her say, as if speaking to someone in the room with her, "My God, I believe I've been asked out on a *date*."

He knew the dim lighting flattered her, erasing every line; still, his throat tightened a little when he saw her, ravishing in a sleeveless dove-gray blouse with a scooped neckline, and a linen skirt that teased her knees, a silk shawl tossed over her bare shoulders, a choker throwing off emerald gleams from her throat, her hair champagne-gold. Though he'd showered, shaved, brushed his hair, and splashed on some Bay Rum, he felt grubby and underdressed. He also felt conspicuous. Apart from some of the help and one black couple, his was the darkest complexion in the place. Plus, he was in the company of an older white woman, who might or might not be married (he still wasn't sure) and who was obviously not dressed for a business meeting. He caught a few patrons stealing looks at the mismatched couple sitting at an intimate corner table, near a window. He tried to ignore them, reminding himself that he was now a junior, albeit very junior, partner in a successful young airline and belonged here as much as anyone else. Diana was perceptive enough to notice that he was failing to convince even himself.

"Do relax and don't mind them," she said, laying her hand on his. She seemed to deliberately leave it there as a waiter presented menus. "I know everybody here. It would be jolly fun to get some gossip going."

He didn't know what to make of the remark. There was some sort of encouragement in it, surely; but he didn't care to be a prop in some game of cheap social scandal.

She did know everybody, interrupting her study of the menu several times to flutter her fingers (still no wedding band, he observed) at this table and that table. When the owner, a gaunt, papery-skinned man with a long English jaw, stopped by to pay his respects and make recommenda-tions, Fitzhugh began to feel more at ease. Diana's standing was such that she probably could have walked in here arm in arm with a Masai chief in full tribal regalia and not done herself or the chief any harm: an aristocrat who could get away with things prohibited to a woman of the hoi polloi. She asked the owner to give her very best to Rick in the kitchen. In a few moments Rick-in-the-kitchen dispatched a waiter to tell her that he'd just received a shipment of fresh prawns from the coast and would be delighted to prepare them especially for her and her guest in a garlic, butter, and white wine sauce, to be preceded by his signature dish, capellini primavera.

"Brilliant!"

When the waiter handed her the wine list, Fitzhugh gave up all notions of exercising any masculine authority. He was in her world.

"I think a Montrachet would be nice, don't you?"

"Brilliant," he said.

Over Rick-in-the-kitchen's signature dish, he told her about the meeting with Adid, and that the man made him uncomfortable with his piercing look. He related his thoughts as he passed by the university, his memories of his unsuccessful stab at playing angry young man, when he'd led a protest march in honor of J. M. Kariuki, who'd been murdered by his political rivals. Those recollections had probably moved him to cancel out on Doug's dinner plans—

"Fitz, dear," she interrupted, and drew her face closer to whisper teasingly, "you are supposed to say that what moved you was an overwhelming desire for the pleasure of my company."

He didn't take it in the lighthearted spirit she'd meant it, and he protested that he *had* longed for the pleasure of her company, really, he had—but he couldn't deny that he'd also dreaded, with a dread equal to the longing, listening to more talk about business plans and market share. In recent weeks he'd sensed that he was drawing further and further away from the man he used to be, and the outraged nineteen-year-old who'd led a protest march now seemed so far away as to be someone else. One more hour in the wabenzi's presence would have made the distance feel all the greater. And yes, he added by way of epilogue, he was aware of the irony of his speaking this way in this place, sipping Montrachet and dining on capellini primavera with a beautiful woman.

Delivering the compliment caused his heart to stutter again, but Diana did not react. She only fixed him with her dark blue eyes—they looked indigo in the sconce's hooded light—and daubed her lips with her napkin as the plates were cleared away.

"I must sound like I'm in a psychiatrist's office," he said, fearful of her silence.

"Not at all." Again covering his hand, though in a more maternal way. "But if I can play amateur analyst, I'd say you suffer from a common delusion. You equate poverty with virtue, but it isn't virtue. It's just poverty."

He shrugged one shoulder, screwed up a corner of his mouth.

"Oh, yes. You could go to any bush village right now, find the smartest kid there, send him to school, and make him a success, and he won't be likely to turn out any better than anyone else, and maybe worse. You can bet he'll forget where he comes from and everyone there. He'll distance himself from the people who helped him on his way because he'll need to believe he did it all on his own."

"This sounds like the voice of experience."

"It damned well is." She sipped her wine. "But better that than to leave the kid there. And there's always the chance you'll find the one in a thousand who doesn't forget and who makes a difference."

"That's it, Diana! That's what I was saying. All I've wanted to do is to make a difference, not make money."

The prawns arrived, twice the size of a man's thumb, curled up pink in their shells.

"Fitz, there's more of that nineteen-year-old in you than you know. The one does not necessarily preclude the other."

She peeled one of the shellfish, stabbed it with her fork, and bit it in half; the sauce glistening on her lips made him want to bite them.

Searching for a lighter topic of conversation, he patted his midriff and joked that the expanding distance from his former inner self was being matched by an expansion of his outer self. Then, feeling that he was talking too much about himself, he asked what she'd been doing lately. The usual: scrounging after aid grants, visiting refugee camps, finding sponsors abroad, obtaining visas. Recently she'd befriended a young Kenyan craftsman who was trying to start his own shop. Lived in one of those corrugated iron shanties that line the Ngong road. No electricity or running water. She'd helped him find space where he could begin turning out tables and chairs for sale at the roadside.

"He's related in some way to my housekeeper, so I took him on." She sighed. "Wes would say, rich bitch with a guilty conscience."

Fitzhugh bowed his head, pretending to an interest in the dessert menu. "I have a confession to make. When I first saw your place, I thought something like that myself, yes? Not rich bitch. A daughter of colonials, making up for the sins of the fathers."

"Can't say I blame you—"

The waiter interrupted, asking if they'd decided. Just coffee, said Diana. Fitzhugh followed suit, in the interest of his waistline.

"But I really think I do what I do because I love this place," she resumed. "It is my country as much as it's yours or anyone else's. Oh, it was so exciting here, the first few years after independence, wasn't it? All that hope and promise."

Her tone was eulogistic. But now, she went on, Kenya, like the whole of black Africa, appeared to be devolving, not into the primitive conditions before European conquest but into chaos. The temptation to write it off as hopeless was irresistible, and she rather thought that much of the world had written it off. She hadn't because she couldn't, and she couldn't because she loved her country and her continent too much. Couldn't imagine herself living anywhere else, certainly not in the damp gloom of her ancestors' homeland. The hope and promise had not been entirely extinguished. She was trying, with small actions like assisting the young craftsman, to keep the fragile flame burning. And with larger actions as well, like the White Papers she wrote for foundations and governmental aid agencies, pleading with them to do their bit to arrest Africa's whirl to the bottom. She compared it to a family's intervention on behalf of a relative destroying himself with alcohol or drugs. You do it because he's your blood. Well, Africa was in everyone's blood, from America to China, wasn't it? This was where Lucy stood upright one gray dawn a million years ago and left in the mud of the Olduvai Gorge the footprints of the true Eve. The ribs and femurs and mandibles of her children were buried in African soil. Diana tilted her body forward; she seemed to be lit from within. If everyone turned their back on Africa, it would not merely fall further and further behind, it could very well lead the world into a dark and lawless tomorrow . . . then abruptly, she shook her head. "Goodness! Listen to me!"

He was, as attentively as ever he'd listened to anyone. How glad he was that he'd chosen to spend these hours with her.

"That was beautiful, Diana."

"But a bit too—too philosophical? Maybe pretentious?"

"No." She who'd claimed a portion of his heart from the moment he'd first seen her now owned it all, and she'd seized his mind with it. He surrendered. He would not try to argue himself out of the emotion roaring through him. It wasn't an emotion that had ever submitted to reason. The only thing left to do was to express it, if he could marshal the courage.

"Another confession," he said. "That day when Malachy . . . when you came to the door? Malachy had told me how old you were."

"Fifty-one last month," she said, in a neutral voice.

"When you came to the door, I was expecting—I wasn't expecting you to look the way you did, the way you do."

"Vitamins and lots of riding." She laughed. She didn't want the conversation to go where he was taking it. She stroked his forearm. "I'm sorry. I don't mean to make light of it. I believe you've said more lovely things to me than I've heard the past year."

"I wasn't intending to say lovely things. I was, am, well, you're as beautiful inside as you are outside." God, he thought, did I really say something that trite?

"Oh, bosh. I'm quite ordinary."

"No, no. Listen, today at lunch, all of a sudden I needed to see you. It came from nowhere, but maybe it didn't. I think I'm—" An icy pain bound his chest and trapped the words in his throat. She took advantage of his hesitation to keep them there.

"You're what, thirty-odd?" she asked, sounding almost prosecutorial.

"Thirty-four. Five in a few more months."

"My daughter, had she lived, would have been just a year younger."

Stunned by this revelation, he blinked, swallowed, stirred his coffee cup with his spoon. The cup was empty, and the metal made a nerve-wracking sound against the china.

"Daughter," he muttered after a long silence.

"Born dead."

"I'm sorry. So you're—"

"Yes."

"You don't wear a ring."

"No."

This was brutal. As her answer, delivered in a downward pitch, cut off further inquiry, he did not make any. He swept up the check before she could.

"I have an account here," Diana said. "That's completely unnecessary."

"I asked you to dinner. You could at least leave me that."

"Very well. But I insist on saving you the taxi fare and driving you back into town."

He was going to make one final attempt. "Diana."

Thinking that he was about to protest her offer, she turned partway around, patted the purse hanging from her chair, and said, "No rubbish about me driving myself back home alone. I have a friend who lives here, chap named Walther. I've been trained to use him, I practice with him about twice a month, and I wouldn't think twice about pulling the trigger on some thug."

Now he gave up and said, "I believe you wouldn't. I didn't realize I was in dangerous company."

"Hardly." She tossed her head in the self-deprecatory way that had so charmed him that afternoon in her foyer. "I've got to stop off at the loo. Meet you outside."

He interrogated himself as he stood by the door, looking at the parking lot and the long drive sloping down in the darkness toward the road. Why had she accepted his invitation, and why had she touched his hand with such tender pressure, and why had she made that remark about the pleasure of her company? Why had she dressed and made herself up so gorgeously if not to look pleasing to him? Was he being presumptuous? Women had always come so easily to him, he must have thought she would too, despite the manifest obstacles, the pressures of convention. He must have misread her entirely. But if he hadn't? Then she and her husband must be living under some sort of arrangement—You're free to fuck whomever you want so long as I am, too. Yes, that could be it. Long ago these white uplanders had established a reputation for adulterous hijinks, and he doubted they'd changed. It would be just the thing for a married middle-aged woman high up on the social ladder to have an adventure with a younger brown-skinned lover. Get some real gossip going, just for the thrill of it. A flash of pure rage brought sweat to his forehead. He shook out a cigarette, then tossed it unlit into the shrubbery. A new thought sprang up, calming him somewhat. She'd said she was going to drive herself back home, which didn't suggest that she intended to make him a toy in some game of infidelity. Or was she playing it coy? He'd never been so confused. Well, he could thank her for preventing him from declaring his love and making a complete idiot of himself.

"Shall we then?"

She'd freshened up, and her beauty instantly dissolved his turmoil. Love—that was the only word in his mind, the only thing he could feel.

She started across the lot with her sergeant major's stride, her heels clicking martially on the pavement. They came to her car, the same sedan he'd seen her drive more than a year ago.

"My daughter was not by my husband, nor by any previous husband," she announced without preamble. "My husband came later."

He decided to be chivalrous and held the door for her, even as he thought, I don't need or want to hear any of this. But as she climbed in, his eyes shot to her skirt, riding up to reveal her equestrienne's thighs. She tugged it down, and the rustle of cloth against nylon brought on a convulsion of raw lust. He circled to his side and got in and slammed the door. She didn't switch on the ignition. She looked at him with a peculiar intensity.

"David lives in the U.K. We've been separated for a very long time. For reasons that are—excuse me—none of your business, we've never divorced." *Money,* he thought. "But I haven't seen or heard from him in over ten years. So, this."

She held up her bare left hand.

"There are some reasons that are my business," he said coolly. "Why you're bothering to tell me all this."

"Frankly, I don't know."

What did he have to lose? He reached over with one arm and took her by the waist and kissed her—a hard, almost violent kiss, forcing her mouth open, his tongue darting in to lick the inside of her lips. He'd no idea what he was trying to express, love or anger or a little of both. She didn't resist, nor did she respond, her body limp.

"That was the reason, yes?"

She drew away, flung her head over the back of the seat, and said in an aggravated tone, "Oh, Christ!"

"Was that the reason, Diana?"

"I'm flattered, really I am," she replied, holding her gaze to the overhead light.

"I don't want to flatter you. I want to know if that was the reason."

Lowering her head to look out the windshield, she assumed the posture of a race car driver, gripping the wheel with extended arms.

"Yes."

"I don't know what's going on with you, Lady Briggs."

"Lady Briggs doesn't know either."

"Which is why you wouldn't let me say what I wanted to say?"

"What do you think? This isn't merely wrong, it's absurd." She hesitated. "I noticed the way you looked at me, the day Malachy brought you over for the meeting. I wonder if you noticed the way I looked at you."

"I think so, yes."

"And the times we've seen each other in Loki. The past several months, I've found you sneaking into my head like a bloody burglar, and I thought I must be mad or a randy hag looking to rob the cradle."

He could not have been more thrilled, hearing this. "You're no hag, and thirty-four going on -five is not the cradle."

Then he swooped down on her and kissed her again. If his was gentler than his first, hers was more ardent. She bit his lips lightly, pulled away, and lightly nipped one ear, then the other. His hand fell to her lap, parted her thighs and moved up under her skirt, searching for the band of her pantyhose. She gently pushed him back.

"For God's sake, not here."

"No," he said, smiling. "But you know, I'm still anxious about you driving home alone at night, no matter your little friend Walther."

"Ha! I don't know why I said that." She tidied her blouse, smoothed her skirt. "Walther is locked in a drawer at my bedside. The only thing in my purse is a can of Mace, so old it's rusty."

"Now I am more anxious than ever. I think you should ease my anxieties."

"I know about you, Fitz. More than you think. You're quite the swordsman from what I've heard. I've no interest in adding to your collection. Here's a black one, here's a white one, here's a young one, here's an old one. Thanks very much, but no thank you."

"I'm in love with you," he said, and felt greatly relieved, like a criminal admitting to his crime.

She looked up again, and speaking to some invisible personage, she repeated her exasperated "Oh Christ!" adding, "He's in love with me. Barely knows me and he's in love with me." She returned her eyes to him. "As to your anxieties, I have staff. They'd be scandalized, and they're terrible gossips."

"Then you should drive me to the Norfolk tonight and yourself home in the morning. Or would that scandalize them, too?"

"Not as much." The statement came in a wavering voice, the next in a tone of fierce resolve. "I'll ring them up and say I'm staying in town with a friend and not to worry."

Then she turned the key and put the car in gear.

Douglas

He's in the pod. The pod is his window unto the world, and the world he sees below is white, with shades of gray and black and blue-gray mixed in. The boom points at it, a long steel finger, fins at a forty-five-degree angle so he can read, on the left fin, the word ARIZ, and on the right, the letters ANG. Not thirty feet below, a dark F-15 floats like a manta ray. He could see the color of the pilot's eyes if the pilot raised his visor. The fighter plane rises slightly, fuel port open, seeking the boom, as the boom seeks it, the boom wavering in the frigid air, twenty thousand feet above snow, ice, rock. Lying on his stomach, Douglas maneuvers the boom to and fro with the joystick, and then the nozzle finds what it's looking for, just behind the F-15's cockpit bubble, and locks in place. Two planes are one now, traveling together at four hundred knots, over the craggy roof of Kurdistan.

"Engaged," Douglas says into his headset mike. Yes, engaged. Married. It's impossible not to think of sexual imagery, not to imagine the KC-135 tanker as a gigantic male dragonfly, penetrating its smaller mate, pumping her full.

The F-15 fighter-jock gives a two-fingered salute: two men, twenty-five feet apart, looking at each other through Plexiglas. "Appreciate it if you guys could top me off," the voice drawls. "Need about ten grand."

"Sorry," Douglas says. "Seven is all I can give you. Got four other customers." He gestures at the other fighters, lined up in echelon off the tanker's left wing.

Behind him pumps whirr, though he can't hear them through his earphones. This is a silent place, the pod is. Numbers flash on the digital dial, and when they reach seven thousand pounds, he disengages the boom, and the fighter-jock gives another salute and peels off, twin tailfins and swept wings bristling with missiles slicing through the thin blue skies. Douglas goes with him in his heart. He's where I should be, he thinks as the next F-15 lines up.

Finally the last one is refueled, slides away, and banks southward.

"*That's it, Bob,*" *he radios the tanker's pilot. Things are informal in the Arizona Air National Guard—a crew sergeant can call a captain by his first name.*

"*Okay, Doug. The Diamondheads are done for the day.*" *Diamondheads is the nickname of their outfit, the 171st Air Refueling Wing.* "*Saddam Hussein is contained once again! And it's back to another fun-filled night in magical Incirlik. C'mon up.*"

He crawls out of the pod and into the belly of the aircraft, past the rest of the crew—radar operators, mission specialists—and into the cockpit, where Bob Mendoza is commencing his turn back to Turkey. Lou Engleman, the copilot, is talking to flight operations in Incirlik.

"*War is hell,*" *Bob remarks, turning halfway around in his seat, his captain's bars two black stripes on his desert tan flight suit.* "*Three days and a wake-up and home to Phoenix. 'By the time I get to Phoenix, she'll be waiting,' *" *he sings.* "*She'll be horny too, I hope. Are we empty, Doug?*"

"*Not a drop left,*" *he replies, his glance falling covetously on the yoke in Bob's hands, on the throttles and the instrument array. Altitude thirty thousand. Airspeed four hundred eighty knots. Engine parameters normal. In a little while he'll be able to fly this airborne gas station, if the National Guard will let him, which it won't. He's well into commercial flight school back home and will soon have his multiengine rating.*

"*I got the scores from the tower,*" *Engleman says.* "*Cardinals lost again. Twenty to seven.*"

"*They shoulda stayed in St. Louis,*" *Bob declares, shaking his head.*

"*Triple A!*" *A voice screams into their headset.* "*Repeat! Triple A airburst!*" *A second voice:* "*You got 'em?*" *It was the fighter squadron they'd just refueled.* "*No! Whoa! SAM launch now. SAM missile launch!*" *Second voice:* "*Got 'em. Off to the right, right!*"

"*Holy shit, the real deal,*" *Bob says.* "*Doug, get on back, tell me if you see anything. This honey is a big flying target, a big ole X for Saddam's boys.*"

Douglas bounds out of the cockpit, too excited to be scared, and on through the crowded interior, nearly bowling over a lieutenant, and swings himself back into the pod, his window to the world. "*Another SAM!*" *one of the voices shouts.* "*More triple A!*" *And he sees, miles to the south, a black cloud of flak appear in the clear heavens, and another, and a third, blooming like an evil flower. A bright ball streaks upward, trailing vapor that fades. Two more, and the bug-size specks of the F-15s peel off to dive. Their missiles flash.*

"*How's it look, Doug?*" *Bob asks him.*

He doesn't answer right away. He's captivated. It's all somehow beautiful. The clear sky, the white mountains, the flashes and dark billows appearing and vanishing.

"Some flak, maybe three SAMs that I saw," he answers, trying to sound laconic and calm. "Didn't hit anything."

"Firing blind. Won't turn their radar on, or they'd get nailed before they pulled the triggers."

The radio goes silent. The skies are empty once again. It's over.

"Okay, folks," Bob announces to the crew. "A little antiaircraft, maybe five SAMs, all out of range. We're all right."

Douglas remains in the pod, face pressed to the glass, heart banging against the floor. He wants to see it all again. He doesn't want it to be over.

BOOK TWO

Flights to the Dark Side

PART ONE

Nuba Day!

WHEN HE WAS asked, the next morning at breakfast, how his date with the old girlfriend had gone, Fitzhugh replied that he wasn't the kind to kiss and tell. Douglas didn't press him—he had bigger things on his mind. He was ebullient to the point of giddiness and barely touched his bacon and eggs, hands flying with Mediterranean abandon as he described the *outstanding* results of last night's dinner with Adid. The one-man conglomerate had pledged to rescue Dare's G1 from legal no-man's-land—it would take no more than a phone call or two—and to make an initial investment of five hundred thousand dollars, with another half million to come. "A mil, Fitz! A cool mil!" Douglas gushed. "With that kind of money, we can buy two more planes, maybe three!" Adid had demanded quids for those quos—he was to participate in any major business decisions; he would not venture the second half of his investment until he saw a return on the first, along with a sound plan for expanding operations; finally, Dare could retain ownership of the Hawker 748 and continue leasing it to the company, but that cozy arrangement would not apply to the Gulfstream. If Dare wanted it out of hock, he had to agree to sell it to Knight Air, receiving in exchange company stock equal to its market value. Dare resisted at first, said he wanted twenty tons of cold metal in his hands, not pieces of paper. Adid argued that he couldn't be expected to risk his assets when one of the partners wasn't willing to risk his. If Dare was that skeptical about Knight Air's future, then perhaps he, Adid, would need to rethink his offer. With no alternative except to continue waging a hopeless court battle, Dare gave in.

Fitzhugh couldn't quite focus on the conversation or, rather, monologue; thoughts of the previous night distracted him. He'd been as nervous as a boy. Undressing her slowly, tentatively, he was fearful that Diana naked would not be half so attractive as she was clothed. He'd told himself that appearances shouldn't matter, if he truly loved her; nevertheless, they did matter. Fortunately, his concerns along those lines proved unfounded. He knew women his age who would have traded bodies with her; and he was happy to discover that the marks the years had made on it possessed a kind of charm, like a warrior's scars. He kissed the lines etched into her hands, the little belt of flab around her abdomen, the cellulite puckers on her thighs and hips; and he blessed her and loved her the more for the humor that overcame his awkwardness. Laughter in her eyes, she stroked his erection and said, "So glad I did this, Fitz. It would have been a waste of a natural resource if I didn't."

She'd left his room at six this morning, to make sure she wasn't discovered by Fitzhugh's companions. That bothered him—a woman like her ought not to be stealing out of a hotel in the predawn twilight. As Douglas rattled on—"Hassan suggested we market ourselves more aggressively, and that's what we're going to start doing the minute we're back in Loki"—he felt almost breathless. He was caught up in a love affair that had gone from zero to a hundred overnight, and he wondered where it was headed, if it was headed anywhere. Then Dare, unshaven and smacking his lips, came down and joined them for breakfast.

ADID WORKED HIS MAGIC, and the G1 was soon in service, in a new coat of green and white. Two more pilots were hired, another two to fly a used twin Beechcraft bought with a portion of Adid's investment to ferry aid workers to and from their assignments in Sudan. The company now had five aircraft—the two Gulfstreams, the Hawker, the Antonov, and the Beechcraft—and seventeen people on its payroll. Grow or die! Adid had proclaimed, but while Knight Air's fleet and payroll had grown, its revenues had moved in the opposite direction. The rule that what was bad for the southern Sudanese was good for the company and vice versa had taken effect, with the advent of a new wet season as generous as the previous one had been penurious. Bahr el Ghazal was delivered from famine, and with the easing of the crisis there, invoices declined sharply. Frantic to meet Adid's targets, Douglas hustled a contract with World Vision to deliver aid to Somalia. The G1 was taken to Nairobi to fly those missions. The Hawker and the G1C, meanwhile, continued to make runs into the Nuba mountains for IPA and the Friends of the Frontline, but not frequently enough to compensate for the shortfall. Douglas then decided to attempt once more to get the other independent agencies to commit to the Nuba. He devoted his not-inconsiderable mental energies to figuring out how to sell them on the idea and asked Fitzhugh to help him, but Fitzhugh wasn't of much help because he was preoccupied.

He was required to go to Nairobi once a month to deposit Knight Air's receipts and contrived reasons to send himself to the capital more often. He would arrive at Diana's Karen estate with a briefcase, pretending he was there on business, to avoid scandalizing her staff. They would talk and take tea in the room where he'd met Douglas and Barrett for the first time, the open windows admitting a perfume of frangipani, bougainvillea, and hibiscus that doubled the light-headed feeling her nearness induced in him. He was amazed and gratified, how comfortable they were in each other's company, talking about her work and his, about Africa's plight, about books and politics; but there was a tension in every conversation, for they were eager to touch and kiss but had to restrain themselves, what with the presence of the servant, the cook, the housekeeper, the gardener, the driver, the groom, the askaris at the gate, and the restraint heightened their need until it became almost unbearable. Diana got some relief by riding after their conversations. Poor Fitzhugh had no outlet as he stood by the steel fence and watched her, cantering around and around in boots and a jacket pinched at the waist, her legs sheathed in jodhpurs. It was more than he could stand, but he couldn't take his eyes off of her, thrilled by her mastery. When she took a jump, leaning forward in the saddle, her thighs and hips forming a delicious curve, woman and horse looked like one mythic being, poised in midair.

She wouldn't allow him into her bedroom, again in the interests of propriety, but put him up in the guest house. She came to him there after her staff had gone to bed. Diana made love with an intense but bridled passion, her legs flung over his shoulders, her back arching at her orgasm, her head thrown back and her gasps becoming one long, muted cry that fell off into a silence in which he swore he could hear his blood and hers, flowing through their veins. In the early morning, before dawn, she would leave him and creep back into her own room. He never felt so lonely and desolate as he did then, with her scent impregnated in the sheets and on the pillow. After his third visit he was sure they weren't fooling anyone, but it seemed the housekeeper, the cook, etc., would tolerate their mistress's liaison so long as she respected their sensibilities and kept up appearances. How he resented them, forcing him and Diana to sneak around like adulterers. He wanted to sleep beside her in a mutual bed and wake up with her in the morning. He wanted them to have dinner together without a lot of strained dissembling. The thought of marrying her had slipped into his mind, though he knew that was impossible; knew as well that not all the impediments to it arose from the conventions and prejudices of the society she lived in but from himself. He would like to be a father someday, and although Diana had not yet undergone the change, it couldn't be far off. Nor could he picture what a future with her would be like. When he reached her age, she would be seventy. Seventy! How would that work out? They couldn't give any serious thought to the future. Rowers in a tide too strong for their oars, they could only go where it took them, out to sea or to an unknown shore.

He returned from one of their trysts to discover that another odd love affair had caused a crisis. The day before, Tony had marched into the office to announce that if Douglas didn't get rid of Dare and Mary, he was going to quit. Said he'd rather starve than suffer the humiliation of being around those two—"a whore and a fat wanker," as he described them. After recovering from his shock, Douglas pointed out that he couldn't fire his partner and asked the reason for Tony's outburst. "Talk to your fucking partner" came the answer. Douglas did, and that provoked an argument between him and Dare. To the Texan's remark that what he did with his personal life was of no concern to anyone, Douglas replied that it damned well was when it affected business. "Because of this high school shit, I'm going to lose a damn fine first officer!" In the end, a way was found to keep Tony on the payroll: Douglas transferred him to Nairobi to skipper the G1 on the Somalia runs, at an increase in salary, and brought the plane's captain back to Loki to take Tony's place as copilot on the G1C.

"So that little romantic intrigue is going to cost us another grand a month," Douglas complained to Fitzhugh. "Dare and Mary, an item! Can you feature that? Talk about beauty and the beast. What the hell does she see in him?"

Involved as he was in his own intrigue, Fitzhugh elected not to speculate. The intricate equations that have bedeviled mathematicians for centuries were easier to solve than the riddles of the heart.

The problem in employee relations, combined with the financial stresses, made Douglas irritable and short-tempered. Once, in front of Fitzhugh and Rachel, he flung a pile of papers off the desk—they contained the business plan, which he was refining.

"I hate this!" he shouted. "You said it a while back, Fitz. Is this what we came here to do?"

"Yes, I did. But you see what's causing this? It's that wabenzi's promise of more money. Forget that, and you'll—"

"I'm not going to forget it, goddamn it! What the hell is the matter with you?" He paused and with a look directed the secretary to pick up the papers—Douglas wasn't inclined to clean up the messes he made. "We have got to find some way to get those agencies on board. It'll be good for us, it'll be good for the people in the Nuba."

"Win-win," Fitzhugh murmured. "And the big mo."

"There it is."

Yes, there it was, Fitzhugh thought. Douglas was a soul split down the middle, the entrepreneur and the idealist. If he could enlist those agencies in his crusade, he could reconcile the halves of his divided self and serve God and Mammon at the same time.

A memoir written by a long-dead colonial official—Douglas had found it in a Nairobi bookshop—gave him an inspiration.

In the days when the British ruled Sudan, after Gatling guns and lyddite howitzer shells had opened the Native's mind, disposing him to hear the missionary's word and the lessons served up by apostles of Advancement and Justice—young men in topees and khaki drill who appeared in out-of-the-way places with vaccination kits or lists of crop production quotas or a contingent of Native policemen—a ceremony called Governor's Day was held once a year. It provided a holiday for farmers and herdsmen, their chiefs with a venue to air their needs and gripes to His or Her Majesty's representative, and him with a chance to tell His or Her Majesty's subjects what the government would do for them and what it expected from them. The memoir contained a colorful account of a Governor's Day celebration in the Nuba mountains, which Douglas read to Fitzhugh and Rachel one humid morning. It sounded like a real show, mingling aspects of imperial pomp with those of a tribal festival. A regimental band tooting the airs of empire; native soldiers presenting arms; turbaned dignitaries greeting the governor-general and his retinue of district officers; lofty speeches and exciting dances (the sort of dances that both shocked and captivated the Victorian mind, while reinforcing the conviction that it was the mind of a far superior civilization); and wrestling matches staged between champions cloaked in animal skins and plumed in ostrich feathers, grappling and tossing, bashing each other with iron bracelets that spilled as much blood as a bare-knuckle prizefight.

"Nuba Day!" Douglas cried out, closing the book with a clap and so startling the secretary that she accidentally hit the delete key on the desktop and sent an hour's work into the ether.

"We must get a new computer. This one, you make one mistake and you lose everything and can't retrieve it," Rachel said.

"That's what we'll do! Nuba Day!"

Fitzhugh, working out flight schedules for the next day, looked up. He recognized from the tone of voice and the quick, mechanical pacing, like a sentry's at a memorial tomb—one two three four turn about one two three four turn about—that Douglas was in the throes of what he called a "cool idea." Cool ideas were not like ordinary ideas—he didn't have them, he experienced them, as an epileptic experiences seizures.

"So we'll do the same thing, only we'll call it Nuba Day!" he said, coming to a halt to face his audience of two, though he seemed to be talking mostly to himself.

Fitzhugh asked what the purpose of this event would be. To make the relief agencies aware of the Nubans' plight and convince them to send assistance—via Knight Air, Douglas answered, as if the purpose were so obvious it didn't need explaining. Pacing the room, he outlined a plan in staccato bursts, and Fitzhugh realized he was making it up as he went along.

A representative from each NGO would be flown to the mountains, to—where? To St. Andrew's mission, that would be the perfect setting . . . Michael Goraende would assemble tribal officials to describe what their people were going through and their needs . . . The agencies would hear it first hand . . . We'll need translators and sound equipment, and a generator for that, maybe solar panels if we can't get a generator . . . And Manfred! We'll bring the German in to talk about his hospital and the problems he's got, keeping it in operation . . . Okay, it shouldn't be all work . . . The Nubans would do a traditional dance for entertainment, and wrestling matches . . . Michael could set that up, too, that would be a sight to see . . . And maybe we could stretch it into two days, have those agency people spend a night in a Nuban village and see for themselves what things are like up there . . . Media! Christ, if we could round up a couple of reporters . . . Hey, I know—that woman who works for those slave redemption people, Quinette? They deal with the media all the time, maybe she would help us get some coverage. The Arabs are taking captives in the Nuba, same as they are in the south, that should get her group interested . . . Okay, I'll work with Michael and Manfred, setting things up at that end—Fitz, you'll be in charge at this end, lining up the NGOs, and tell 'em we'll fly 'em up there free of charge . . .

Douglas's enthusiasm was infectious, as always; yet Fitzhugh foresaw any number of problems, with communications, with timing and coordination and security. And if the scheme didn't work, providing nothing more than some amusement and an all-expenses-paid adventure for the aid workers, much time, effort, and money would have been wasted. He aired none of these thoughts. He knew from previous experience that it would do no good, when Douglas was gripped by a cool idea, to present the difficulties standing in the way of its realization and suggest they deal with them ahead of time. Something in his nature—the font of his confidence, his optimism, his immunity to self-doubt—prevented him from seeing obstacles to his plans until they confronted him directly. His misgivings aside, Fitzhugh thought the scheme could be made to work.

"I'll get on it as soon as I can," he said, then returned to the flight schedules. Finished with that task, he took a legal pad and ballpoint and began to list the things that would need doing to turn Douglas's cool idea into a reality. This was expected of him, the right-hand man. He expected it of himself.

THE PLANE SHUDDERED in wing-wagging leaps and sudden dips, and Quinette's delicate stomach felt each one. A week of Cipro and Imodium had tamed the dysentery but hadn't conquered it. As miserable as it had made her—it felt as if ground glass were in her belly—she'd welcomed the infection; it was part of her initiation into the sorority Lily Hanrahan and Anne Derby belonged to—the Honorable Order of Old Africa Hands, they called it. You couldn't be considered for membership until you'd survived at least one bout of amoebic and another of malaria. She'd dodged malaria so far but figured she'd catch it eventually and in a way looked forward to it. She envied Lily and Anne their sufferings. They'd passed a test.

Lily was suffering now. Her complexion matched her name as she sat on the canvas jumpseat, her rucksack clamped between her knees. Even the Kenyan cameramen on Lily's left appeared to be turning a shade of white tinged with green, and Phyllis Rappaport was holding a barf bag to her mouth. The reporter's distress caused a bubble of pleasure to rise in Quinette. Phyllis was the same acerbic woman she'd met last year. It was hard to tolerate her, much less embrace her with Christian love. This morning, as they were boarding the plane, was a good example. Because of Quinette's efforts, Phyllis had been included in the press pool, the first to go into the Nuba mountains. Did she say thanks? No. Attitude instead of gratitude, that's what Quinette got from her. "What are they doing here?" she'd asked, indicating the other two correspondents. "You told me I was getting an exclusive."

"I don't think I said that at all."

"I think you did." Phyllis took a step closer. "Look, Mr. and Mrs. Average Citizen aren't exactly glued to the TV, waiting to hear the latest news from Sudan. I sold the news desk on this story on the basis that it was a CNN exclusive. What do I say when they see it in *The New York Times* and on the AP wire? That I fell for your bullshit?"

Drawing a few words from the vocabulary she'd stopped using after she was saved, Quinette reminded Phyllis that the press release she'd sent to news bureaus in Nairobi had told everybody the same thing: a group of relief workers was going into the Nuba; there would be room on the plane for a limited number of media people; this was an exclusive opportunity to report from an arena of the war that had so far been uncovered. Exclusive opportunity didn't mean the same thing as *an* exclusive.

"That's cute," Phyllis said. "You're a real wordsmith. Okay, I'm here. Guess I'll make the most of it, but I'll thank you not to bullshit me again, *Mizz* Hardin."

As she climbed into the plane, it was all Quinette could do not to crack her on the back of her red-haired head. She'd worked so hard on drafting the message, striving to make it as enticing as possible without going overboard. Fitz had given her a little help, but most of the wording was hers. Yes, she had changed "unique opportunity" to "exclusive opportunity" because she'd become familiar enough with reporters and their wants to know that the word *exclusive* would pique their interest; but it wasn't as though she'd lied. She'd presented the final draft to Fitz for his approval. She was proud of her effort; proud too that the people at Knight Air had had enough confidence in her to admit her into their clubby circle and give her a role to play in one of their operations. Fitz had approached her, told her what he and Douglas were planning to do—they were removing the cloak of secrecy from their activities—and asked if she could help them get press coverage. She knew most of the correspondents in Nairobi—at one time or another, they'd gone with her and Ken and Jim Prewitt on redemption missions—and she gave him the names of two print reporters. What about TV? TV coverage was what they really needed. Quinette suggested CNN. Later, she contacted Ken in Switzerland, asking him to authorize her to go on the trip. It would be, she argued, a fact-finding mission to learn about the slave trade in the Nuba, though in truth her motives were more personal than professional. She was curious about that mysterious region; she wanted to see it.

Mary emerged from the cockpit, looking jauntily professional in her aviator's shirt and cocked baseball cap with earphones clamped over it. She leaned for support against the cargo pallets stacked in the middle of the airplane and, raising her voice above the engine noise and the cacophony of bangs, rattles, and bumps, apologized for the rough ride. "We'll be out of this soon and it'll be smooth sailing. We should have you back on Mother Earth in about an hour."

"An hour," Lily groaned as Mary returned to the cockpit. "A bloody hour of this, and I'll be ready for hospital."

Quinette looked out the porthole, streaked with quivering filaments of rain, and watched the wing knifing through dense, roiling clouds, vapor trailing from its tip. Her heart nearly stopped when lightning lit up the gloom. The plane shuddered. She felt it was her responsibility to pray for all. *Don't let any lightning hit us, Lord. Hold us in the hollow of your hand.* She couldn't imagine that a merciful God would send them on this mission, only to have them die pointlessly in a crash.

"HOW'S EVERYTHING BACK THERE?"

"Much longer in this shit, and we'll run out of barf bags," Mary answered, looking a little peaked herself. "Good thing I thought to bring them."

"Nuthin' like a woman's touch."

"Right. Next thing I'll hang curtains."

Dare laughed, keeping both hands firmly on the yoke. He never felt so at one with an aircraft as in a thunderstorm, a unity he compared to a champion rodeo-rider's with a bronc, anticipating each buck, jump, and twist so that he knew what the horse was going to do before the horse knew. Dropping his glance from the rain-webbed windshield to the altimeter and radar screen, he said, "A few more minutes, we'll be there."

"Wonder what our passengers would say if they knew they were guinea pigs in an experiment."

"This ain't an experiment."

"Wes, you've got a college degree, why do you insist on speaking like a rube?"

Mary, he'd come to find out, was big on proper grammar and syntax. "It's my way of stayin' in touch with my roots. Like I said, this ain't an experiment. I've done it dozens of times. What this is, it's part of your postgraduate education, darlin'." Now that they were officially lovers, she'd ceased her objections to that term of endearment. "We don't waste fuel goin' around thunderstorms, we fly into 'em and use 'em to get a free ride up. There's good pilots and then there's really good pilots, and really good pilots know how to get the most out of every drop of gas. Gas is money."

"Okay, professor."

His skills and knowledge—as long as he held on to them, he would hold on to her. The plane jumped, as if yanked by a string; then the string parted, and it fell. A few moments later it was out of the turbulence and in the aerial equivalent of a millpond. The altimeter began to tick upward without a change in altitude.

"We're in the elevator now," Dare said, meaning the shaft of warm air rising in the heart of the storm. The Hawker rose with it toward the anvil as effortlessly as a soaring bird riding a thermal. "No stops till the penthouse. It's rough goin' in, and it can be rough goin' out if the storm's big enough—y'all want a big storm because then the column of hot air is big enough for you to stay inside the shaft—but it sure is smooth once you're inside. Now we ease up on the gas pedal." He pulled the throttle levers back. "See? It's as easy as losin' your kid's child support money in Vegas."

"I wouldn't know about that. Heard from yours lately?"

"Me and Bobby mostly communicate by rumor," Dare quipped, masking a hurt that had never healed completely. "Last I heard—it was a year ago—he'd started University of Texas at Austin."

"How much do you reduce power?" Mary asked, returning to her lesson.

"Depends. One time—this was in Honduras—I rode one of these, and it spit us out at thirty-two thousand with both engines damned near on idle."

"My hero!" she said in a falsetto to make sure he didn't take her seriously. In case he didn't get the message, she turned to him and stuck out her tongue. A little innocent razzing mixed in, he judged, with some genuine resentment.

In the weeks following their romp in Malakal, she'd managed to duck the consequences by sleeping with both him and Tony; with Tony in the tent they shared in Loki, with Dare on a sleeping bag in the Hawker after they were finished with an offload—the aviator's version of getting laid in the backseat of a car, but with more room. He was surprised at Mary's capacity for compartmentalizing her emotions. They would finish up, she would dress and climb into her first officer's seat and be all business; and at the Hotel California mess, she would sit next to Tony and feign that everything was as it had been, feign so well that Dare began to entertain serious doubts about her. Her ability to pretend suggested a sociopathic personality, though he was doing a credible job of pretending himself. Sometimes he felt sorry for his former copilot, which made him all the more uneasy about his present copilot—if she could lie so convincingly to Tony, then she could lie to him, too. Still, he found the arrangement convenient if not altogether satisfactory. Like an affair with a married woman, it spared him from making a commitment that could draw him into another marriage. As much as he loved her, he didn't think he could take that drastic step ever again. He'd once heard a second marriage called "the triumph of hope over experience." By that standard, a fifth would be considered the triumph of sheer insanity. So he was content to let things go along in their sordid, furtive way. But Mary wasn't.

Whether her conscience got the better of her, or the tension got to her, he couldn't say. Whatever, she told him, one day on a short hop into eastern Sudan, that she was "sick of living a lie." She was going to break it off with Tony, as gently as she could. Dare's feelings were mixed. He was gratified she had found a bottom to her reservoir of pretense, but he was anxious. "Y'all don't have to tell him everything," he'd advised. "Just say your feelings have changed, you want to move out." That isn't what she told Tony. She didn't tell him anything. Her nerve failed her, and all she did was to stop making love to him, pleading the standard excuses from the female playbook. That he fell for this, not for a few days but for two full weeks, caused Dare's pity to sour into contempt. If the Aussie was that lunkheaded, he deserved to lose her. Finally, Tony confronted her, asking what the hell was going on, and she broke down and confessed. Confessed to it all and took the brunt of his anger, which included a backhanded crack that knocked her down and blackened her eye. She said she didn't mind the blow, she'd earned it and felt that it paid her debt in one installment. Dare wasn't so tolerant. He went to Tony's tent. "I'm the worst pig there is," he said, "but I ain't never laid a hand on a woman. You had best not even think of hurting her again." Tony was silent but not intimidated. "Y'all need to hit someone, here I am." Tony said, "In my own time, mate. You'll hear from me in my own time, my own way," and gave a look that Dare wouldn't forget soon, hurt, betrayal, and wrath congealing into a glare that could have frozen meat.

Mary was at first ecstatic with relief—as if she'd beaten cancer, she'd said—but after a time the reaction set in. She got to feeling guilty and remorseful, and through some kind of twisty feminine logic (an oxymoron if ever there was one, Dare thought) she decided that Dare was to blame for the whole sorry mess, as if he were a matinee idol who'd stolen her from the boy next door.

So here they were, lovers flying cargo together, like those boy-girl teams of long-haul truckers. The thermal lifted them into the anvil, where lightning flickered, then popped them out into the bright ultraviolet at twenty-eight-five, and there abandoned them. Dare nudged the throttles forward. They didn't need much to maintain cruising speed in the slender air.

He raised Douglas on the radio and asked for a report about conditions at Zulu Three, the airstrip nearest to the SPLA's Nuban headquarters and the town of New Tourom. Skies clear, light wind out of the southeast, visibility couldn't be better. A heavy rain last night had rendered the first fifty meters of the runway unusable, but the remaining eight hundred were in good shape. A rare pleasure, having a reliable source of information on the ground. In most cases he had to rely on local rebel commanders for assessments of landing conditions, and they inevitably exaggerated. Runways were always at least a hundred meters longer in their sunny reports than in reality, visibility infinite; strong crosswinds never blew, nor was there ever any fighting within fifty miles.

"How's the security situation?"

"No worries," came Douglas's disembodied voice. "The Archangel has men posted on all the high ground and around the landing field. Haven't seen a sign of the bad guys since we got here."

"They're all bad guys, rafiki, it's just that some are worse than others," Dare replied, and signed off.

Doug and Fitz had been in the mountains the past three days, shuttling tribal dignitaries to the mission from far-flung villages and setting up the stage and sound equipment for their extravaganza like a couple of rock concert impresarios. A real promoter, Doug was. If he laid off the high-minded speeches, Dare might begin to like him, but Doug the crusader lived side by side with Doug the promoter. He and Knight Air were going to be the Nubans' saviors. Lately Dare found himself looking at his partner and all the do-gooders in Loki not with his usual cynicism but with anthropological curiosity. They were almost a distinct subspecies, possessing an ability to breathe in, to thrive on, the molds and pollens of altruism that caused him to suffer severe allergic reactions. What made them the way they were? His best guess—and he knew it wasn't good enough—was that for one reason or another they needed to be needed.

He pushed the yoke, plunged back into the thunderstorm, and after another wild ride found smooth flying above fleets of stratocumulus that appeared motionless, as if tethered to the mat of grass and trees below. Silvery watercourses threaded the plain, and solitary massifs rose from it. Westward, distance merged two mountain ranges into one, creating the impression of a continental coastline. Dare turned toward it, descending as he turned until he could make out the old British road that led to the town of Kauda, which was held by the SPLA. There the road ended in a junction with another, running south toward Talodi and north toward Heiban, which were in government hands, with army garrisons in both. He never liked coming into Zulu Three. The distance between it and the garrisons—never more than twenty miles in either direction—was much less than he cared for.

"Sometimes I think you and me ought to quit this," he said, his glance flitting from the windshield to the instruments and back to the windshield, boxing the plain and the road and the blue mountains, drawing closer.

"And do what?" Mary asked, looking out the side window.

"I don't know. Something else."

She said nothing, squinting at something below. She reached behind her seat for the binoculars. "I'll be damned. A whole herd of ostrich. Is that right? Herd? A gaggle of ostrich? A flock?"

"How about a covey?" Dare said. "And how about some feedback? One thing I can always count on from you is feedback."

She put the binoculars down and sat primly erect, in a way that reminded him of a witness in a jury box. "I kind of like this work, y'know?"

"Wonderin' all the time if you're gonna get shot out of the sky or get mortared on the ground. You like that?"

"The work, I said. I like the work, and I like the money, and that other stuff goes with the territory. Got to take the shit with the sugar. I think we're there, Dad."

She jerked her head at the windshield to indicate Kauda, a cluster of tukuls and trees a few miles ahead and more than a mile below. Dare called for the flaps, and they came in on their base leg, swooping over rocky cornices and a bowl valley ringed by terraced hillsides. Dare spotted the airstrip, a long hashmark on the valley floor, and then white patches glinted through the camouflage netting thrown over Doug's G1C, parked in a clearing at the edge of the runway, near a grove of palm trees. Just in case his partner had been mistaken about the absence of bad guys, he put the plane into a one-hundred-eighty-degree turn, losing altitude at the same time so the Hawker dropped as if caught in a whirlpool. He reckoned the maneuver had his passengers reaching for their barf bags again.

Ten minutes later they were disembarking on wobbly legs into the cloying heat of a wet-season morning. A few looked ready to kiss the ground in gratitude. Two plus hours without a bathroom break sent a few more, that tall Bible-bouncer among them, scurrying for the bushes. They weren't likely to find much privacy; the usual mob greeted the Hawker's arrival. There were teenage rebels in ragged uniforms or in just plain rags, a few armed with spears, the rest with used and abused AK-47s. Men in shorts and ratty jelibiyas clambered into the dark, still-frigid cargo hold.

Women porters, clad in flowered dresses or wrapped in *kangas* topped by T-shirts bearing the names of famous beers, American football teams, and Canadian hockey teams, streamed down from the ridge and swarmed across the runway to descend like flies on the cargo the men were tossing onto the ground: South African sugar and Egyptian powdered milk, pharmaceuticals, soap, plastic jerry cans, washbasins, and sorghum seed in sacks stamped CANADA or USA, boxes of pencils and school notebooks and one crate of Arabic-language Bibles. Four Nuban Land Rovers—camels— knelt down with flapping lips amid the boys with the guns and spears and the women and the listless, orange-haired children clinging to their mothers' hips, tiny heads wobbling like the heads of puppets. Near Douglas's plane stood a detachment of SPLA guerrillas who presented a sharp contrast to their tattered adolescent comrades. They wore canvas boots instead of flip-flops or sandals cut from truck tires. Their weapons were in top shape, their uniforms uniform, and they had the look and carriage of crack troops: veterans of the southern battlefields who now served as Michael Goraende's bodyguard, although their job today would be to guard the tender bodies of the aid workers on the walk from the airstrip to New Tourom. It would be bad publicity for the cause if one or two of them were to get killed.

Douglas came up, his face sunburned, his jaw roughened by a three-day growth of sandy beard. "It's coming off, almost can't believe it myself."

"Yeah. If somebody ever wants to restage Woodstock, I'll give y'all a recommendation." Dare motioned at the G1C. "Know what that looked like when we were comin' in? Like a camouflaged airplane. You should get a few of these boys to stick some branches in that netting—that white fuselage shows up like bare tits in church."

Douglas turned to look at the plane. "Why don't you take care of that?" he asked in the harried voice of someone with more important things to do. "I'd better get everyone on the road. It's a two-hour hike."

Dare put the airfield sentries to work, and in about twenty minutes the plane was festooned with palm and acacia branches. By that time, the crowds had cleared out. A silence as oppressive as the heat fell over the airstrip. There was no sound except the wind, the rattle of palm leaves, and an occasional murmur from the pubescent sentries, lolling about in a manner that didn't inspire confidence. One tore a page out of a pilfered Bible and used it as rolling paper for a cigarette, which Dare figured would do the kid more good than reading it would have done. Standing at the back of the airplane, cleaning his fingernails with the blade of his Leatherman, he watched the processional of aid workers, guards, porters, and laden camels winding up the ridge, around slabs of rock leaning like abandoned idols. Mary, who'd begun to add video footage to her photographic archives, was filming their departure with her new camcorder.

"Ever wonder where the hell they go with all that stuff?" he said. "I mean look at this place. Where is it? It's nowhere. They pick it up in a nowhere place and take it to some other nowhere."

"Is something bothering you, baby?" He loved it when she called him that. "You don't seem quite yourself today."

"Bothering me? I don't know. Here's what I'm thinking right now. As far as the people at Loki tower know, this airplane isn't here. It's three hundred miles away—I'm gettin' right creative with those phony flight plans. And all that cargo those folks are carryin' off from no place to no place, none of it was registered with Kenya customs. That midget Barrett pays the customs people off to avoid the duties. In so many words, we fly cargo that doesn't officially exist on flights that don't officially exist to places that don't officially exist on anybody's map. If you and me pranged up and got killed, nobody would know we were dead because we don't officially exist. We're phantoms, we're the Flying Dutchman."

She rubbed his arm up and down sweetly. "You're thinking about flying those rock bands again, or the governor of Texas."

"This kinda work, it doesn't seem dignified for a man of my age and talents."

"Love you, Wes, but I'm sticking with it. I'm not your age."

"Stick with this, and you'll catch up in no time."

QUINETTE HAD NEVER FELT as far from home and all things familiar as she did out here, and this feeling pleased her. Resting with the others atop a promontory, she looked back at the way they'd come, the stony track winding downhill past a baobab, across a valley where huge rocks leaned into one another to form arches and tunnels, then up the western side of the ridge whose opposite slope faced the airstrip, the track vanishing in the flame-yellow grass near the ridge-crest, beyond which a savannah flung itself toward a far-off range that appeared to be an extension of the thunderclouds hovering above it. The Nuban landscape was more pleasing to the eye than the monotonous flatlands farther south, but it was tougher on the body. The scree was treacherous, ankles turned on the rocky trails, and the heat was intense despite the altitude. Sweat popped from every pore in Quinette's skin, blackening her shirt and cotton trousers. Her hair, when she passed her fingers through it, felt like a mat of seaweed.

"What in the bloody hell did we get ourselves into," said Lily, her fair cheeks and forehead reddened. "The Devil himself would need a cold pint in this place, and it's only ten!"

Quinette jerked her head at the girls who'd been roped into service to carry the aid workers' and reporters' rucksacks. They wore cloth circlets on their heads for bearing the loads. "Look at them. They're not complaining."

"They live here," Lily said emphatically. "I'd like to see how well they'd make out in a good cold Irish rain."

Quinette was grateful for the many long treks she'd made with Ken, and for her regimen of walking and biking every day in Loki. Weakened though she was by her illness, she was in much better shape than her companions, sprawled out as if they were on a death march—except for the indefatigable Phyllis, taking notes, and two fit men who hadn't allowed the porters to carry their packs and now stood with the packs on their backs as if to show off their physical superiority. One middle-aged, the other maybe thirty, both quiet and aloof, they were from California and belonged to the Friends of the Frontline.

"Everybody got their second wind?" Douglas Braithwaite called out, sounding as chipper as a scoutmaster on a hike. Lily was a little gaga over him and flirted with him, holding out her arm and asking him to help her to her feet. "Not much further," he said, all white-bread handsome and smiling and barely a blot of sweat on his shirt. "Twenty minutes, half an hour at the outside."

Single file, flanked by their SPLA escorts, the delegation of relief workers and correspondents trooped down from the promontory and made their way into New Tourom. The town lay on a plateau beneath bare crags and pinnacles resembling a fortress wall. Young women squatted in little gardens, pulling weeds, or went at the brute hard labor of pounding millet, mashing groundnuts on grindstones. A listless, melancholy air hung over the place. New Tourom had obviously once supported a much larger population. All around, crumbling tukuls stood amid farm fields and fruit orchards whose neat, domesticated ranks had been invaded by weeds and brambles. In the middle of town was the biggest church Quinette had so far seen in Sudan. Its tall windows had been blown out and gaped tragically in its brick walls, its domed tin roof was partly collapsed and full of holes. Among the outbuildings, one was undergoing repairs, but the others were wrecks: a long bungalow that looked as if it had been peppered from the blast of a giant shotgun; roofless, fire-blackened huts facing a dirt lane, two obliterated structures, nothing left but a few fragments of wall attached to cement-slab floors partly buried under shattered beams and chunks of concrete.

Douglas led his pilgrims to a dusty flat surrounded by low hills, forming a natural arena. It was thronged with people, assembled under fluttering flags, and here the atmosphere was festive.

"All right, folks, you're about to be greeted Nuban style," Douglas announced.

A weird noise split the air as a man sporting a pith helmet and sunglasses blew on an antelope horn with a long wooden tube fitted into one end. A mob of warriors, wearing loin cloths and feathered circlets tied to their arms and ankles, sprinted toward the visitors, waving spears longer than the men were tall, and they were quite tall, built like football players. Quinette saw Phyllis's cameraman heft his video camera to his shoulder, then lower it, as if he were afraid the onrushing wild men would mistake it for a weapon and turn him into a human pincushion. They peeled off and began to dance around and around the visitors, stomping their feet to a drum; around and around, loosing incomprehensible cries with a trance-like glassiness in their eyes until, with a leap and a single ear-splitting yell, the dance ended, the mass of bodies parted, and Quinette and her companions found themselves facing two uniformed giants.

In a bass voice, smiling a smile that could have advertised toothpaste, the one on the left welcomed them and introduced himself as Lieutenant Colonel Michael Goraende, the other as his adjutant, Major Kasli. At six feet five or six, Goraende was the shorter, but also broader, his shoulders and chest suggesting the solidity of a monument. He wore the badges of a high-ranking SPLA officer—scarlet beret, red and gold shoulder boards, carved walking stick, pistol—but the gold earrings that were pierced through the top of his left ear, the crucifix hanging from his throat, and the slight upturn to his full lips saved him from looking too stern and military. He shook everyone's hand. When he enveloped Quinette's, she had an urge to curtsy, his bearing was so dignified.

He brought them to a small wooden stand, shaded by a canvas tarp and facing a platform with a stand-up mike wired to a relic of a speaker wired to a solar panel. Quinette was surprised to see Diana Briggs and John Barrett sitting on the topmost bench. She almost didn't recognize them, out of their usual context. A third person was with them, a stocky, frowning man with flaxen hair. She waved hello and took a seat in the front row. The crowd of Nubans had moved off into the shade of the surrounding acacia trees. A few men in turbans and jelibiyas remained nearby, standing in a line alongside Douglas.

For two sweltering hours, the delegation listened to speeches. Barrett led off, talking about the work International People's Aid was doing in the Nuba, and pleading that it could not do it without help from other agencies. The stocky man followed, Gerhard Manfred, a doctor who ran a hospital in another part of the mountains. The gist of his address was that the government of Sudan made things difficult for him by stealing the supplies and equipment sent to him from Germany, forcing him to seek clandestine help from outside.

Then came the turbaned men, who were called *meks*. Like a master of ceremonies, Douglas introduced each by name. Their speeches took a long time, because they had to be translated from Nuban into Arabic by one man, then from Arabic into English by another. They told tales of bombings, raids, and abductions, of families driven off their farms and into concentration camps. That plucked a sympathetic chord in Quinette. Her family had not been exiled by bombs or raids, but she knew what it was like to lose your land and your place in the world, whether you were robbed of it by a violent tyranny or by the tyranny of banks and mortgages and big corporations.

The meks went on, and their stories added up to one long cry of need, one long appeal for the gears in the machinery of compassion to begin turning for them. The reporters and relief workers took notes during the first two or three speeches, but the litany of sorrows grew so repetitious that they stopped and just stared as if hypnotized. Until, after the last mek had said his piece, Michael Goraende mounted the platform with a stunning young woman six feet tall, with a kanga knotted over one shoulder, the top of her skull shaved, and the hair on the back of her head trailing in tight braids down past her shoulders. Her skin was as black as a panther's and she moved like one, and the look of proud ferocity on her strong square-jawed face, accentuated by the tribal scars stitched across her eyebrows, completed the picture of dangerous beauty.

Goraende said that her name was Yamila and that she'd been taken captive a while ago and sold into slavery. Now she wished to tell the distinguished guests what had happened to her. Quinette removed her tape recorder from her fanny pack and handed it to the Arabic-to-English translator, instructing him to speak into it. The young woman's fierce expression melted into one of fright as she stood awkwardly at the microphone and faced a score of strangers. The commander whispered to her, and she began in a halting monotone. Her story was one Quinette had by now heard hundreds of times, but it had one unusual twist: Yamila had escaped her Arab captor. One of his wives, jealous because Yamila had delivered a son whom the man doted on, helped her get away. With her child, she fled back into the mountains, found her home village a deserted ruin, and went on to a neighboring village, where she was given food and water. But the people there were from a different tribe and, fearing the Arabs would come after her, told her to leave. They directed her to New Tourom, where other refugees had settled. She arrived after a three-day journey on foot, but not before her breasts ran dry (from fear, exhaustion, lack of nourishment, Quinette surmised). Her son died on the night of the second day, and she carried his corpse the rest of the way and buried him in the mission cemetery.

Yamila stopped there, looking uncertainly at Goraende. Lily and a few other women in the stand choked up, but Quinette's eyes were dry. *"Takes some getting used to, but you don't want to get too used to it,"* Jean, the Canadian nurse, had advised her that first time in Sudan. She didn't think she'd become hardened, she was only being professional when, as Yamila was about to leave, she asked her when and where she was captured, and the name of her master and how he'd treated her. The translator passed the questions on. "It was in the Moro hills, south of here," the girl replied. "He was called Ibrahim Idris. He treated me not so bad." She hesitated. "Not so bad as some others, if I did what he wanted." She wouldn't say more, stepped down, and with her head and back erect, walked away, toward the long shadow of a tree.

The audience's bodies and emotions were given a break. A lunch of hard-boiled eggs, millet bread, and soda was served under a fly-tent lashed between two tall mahoganies. Quinette left the eggs alone and stuck to the millet, washing it down with a nearly boiling ginger ale.

Sitting on camp stools at two joined cafeteria tables, the group must have looked like one big safari party. Goraende was at the head, his adjutant to one side, eyes cloaked by opaque sunglasses. Fitz was giving an interview to the *Times* correspondent; Barrett, Diana, and the German had been cornered by Phyllis, while Douglas held court at the foot of the table, talking up his airline to Lily and a couple of other NGO representatives. Quinette had yet to form a firm opinion of him. Except for the squint lines at the corners of his pilot's eyes, he looked like the frat boys she used to see on the UNI campus, and he sometimes displayed a frat boy's cocksure, superior attitude. At the same time he had charm, a way of talking to you as if he considered you the most important person in the world, and his winsomeness was having an effect on Lily. She all but batted her eyelashes at him.

At the end of the meal Goraende rose to announce that his guests were to be treated to some traditional entertainment, wrestling matches.

Everyone returned to the field where the speeches had been made, once again alive with crowds gathered under their village banners, women in the background, men up front in a big circle. Wrestling, said John Barrett, who'd taken over from Douglas as master of ceremonies, was the Nubans' national sport. Wearing ratty shorts or skirts made from strips of cloth or wide leather belts to which eagle and ostrich wings had been attached, the contestants came out blowing tin whistles and making animal noises or bird cries, their bodies daubed in ash from burned acacia leaves—it was supposed to protect them from harm, so Barrett said. Two men would square off, watched by a referee wearing a red fez. The object was to toss your adversary onto his back. Most bouts didn't last more than fifteen or twenty seconds; several minutes if the wrestlers were evenly matched. They would go at it, locking arms, locking legs, bear-hugging each other. Sometimes two men would become so intertwined, with the ostrich or eagle wings flailing, that they looked like one eight-limbed being, part human, part bird. All the while, drums throbbed, antelope horns blew, the crowds yelled and cheered their favorites—a frenzy of noise, wild and breathtaking.

At the end of the last match the victor, a house of a man, was carried around by his fans. After they let him down, he strutted over to where Goraende and his adjutant were sitting, dropped to his knees, and made odd dancing movements with his hands and arms. At first Quinette thought he was dedicating his triumph to the SPLA commander. He looked amused by this demonstration, but when the wrestler raised his palms and lowered them, pressing them flat on the ground at his feet, Goraende's expression turned serious. He strode into the center of the ring, conferred with the referee, then snatched, from a man nearby, a long pole with a wooden triangle at its top and banged it on the ground several times. A cheer went up, rippled through the crowd, and swelled into a roar.

"Well now, you are about to see something interesting, an unscheduled event," Barrett explained to the bewildered visitors. "That fellow has challenged Michael to a match, and when one man challenges another like that, getting down on his knees, it can't be refused. Michael, you should know, was a champion in his day, never defeated, but of course it isn't his day anymore."

Michael. Quinette decided she preferred his given name. Sitting at the far edge of her row, she had a clear view of him, stripping his clothes off some distance away. Apparently he was so at ease in his own skin that he didn't mind baring it with a crowd of foreigners nearby. His one concession to modesty—if it was a concession and not merely an accident—was to stand facing away from them. Quinette averted her glance, but her own sense of decency wasn't equal to her curiosity, and she looked again, watching him squat over a mound of ash to scoop handfuls over his shaved head and chest while an assistant covered his back. The ritual took a few minutes. When he stood, an arm crooked to rub ash into the back of his neck, his strong legs, taut buttocks, and flaring back, every inch powdered gray, arrested her gaze. She thought he looked like Adam the moment after God molded him from the dust of the earth and breathed life into him.

He did a literal girding up of loins, wrapping a red sash around his midsection, tucking the end between his legs and tying it off. Walking into the arena, he seemed shut up in his own world. His opponent was shorter but younger, with a tree trunk of a chest. The two men crouched face to face, elbows on their knees, hands out, and circled each other, looking for an opening. The younger man's arm lashed out for Michael's ankle, but he saw it coming, shot both legs backward, and as the challenger stumbled forward from his own momentum, whirled and gripped him around the waist from behind. The SPLA soldiers in the crowd let out a yell. The challenger twisted free, and both combatants were head to head, hands clasping the backs of each other's necks. In that position they pushed, shoved, waltzed back and forth. Suddenly the challenger sidestepped, turning his immense torso at the same time. As his supporters bellowed, he hooked his left arm through Michael's right and drove him to his hands and knees. Dropping to his own knees, he attempted to flip Michael onto his back, but with one palm on the ground, Michael spun away and got up to face his adversary once again. The challenger lunged with both arms for Michael's head—a feint, for as Michael drew out of the crouch, raising his arms to block the move, the younger man ducked under his guard and clutched him in a bear hug. In that moment, their foreheads clashed with an audible crack. Michael wasn't cut, but blood was streaming into his adversary's eyes. Red blood on black skin, the coats of protective ash streaked with sweat—Quinette gasped at this exhibition, at the pure, raw maleness of it. Michael hooked one leg over the back of his opponent's and tried to trip him. He might as well have tried to trip a stone block. Straining, grunting, his face a mask of pain and effort, the half-blinded challenger lifted Michael off his feet and pressed forward. Michael began to topple backward but pulled the challenger down with him, breaking the bear hug; then, in a quick, fluid motion, he locked his adversary's arms in his, twisted sideways, and rolled him onto his back.

The defeated man lay there for a moment, panting. A couple of men rushed in to bind his wounded forehead with palm leaves. There was a delirium of shouts and yells as soldiers hoisted their champion onto their shoulders. Two women in Quinette's group, sitting just in back of her, complained that this had been a bit too brutal, a bit too much. Maybe it had been, but there had been a real passion in it, too, Quinette thought. She jumped up and applauded as Michael was paraded by.

A fascination had been awakened in her, but she couldn't admit that it was the reason she went to speak to him after he'd cleaned up and got back into his uniform. She persuaded herself that she needed more information about the slave trade in the Nuba. A few yards short of his circle of aides and bodyguards, a fit of shyness overcame her and she hesitated, lurking like someone who wants to join a cocktail party conversation but lacks the nerve. The adjutant spotted her.

"What is it?" he asked.

"Oh!" she said, startled. "I—I just wanted to say that we were all thrilled by the matches, and to congratulate the commander on his win."

Michael laughed a laugh that sounded the way velvet felt and said he was lucky. He shouldn't have accepted the challenge. The military commander of liberated Nuba had a certain dignity to uphold, and tussling in the dirt with a man ten years younger wasn't the way to do it.

"We were told you had no choice, that you couldn't turn him down."

"I could have," he said, twirling his walking stick in his long fingers. "I'm thirty-six years, and everyone knows that's too old to be wrestling. Pride made me do it, and I was taught that pride goes before the fall."

"Well, the other guy took the fall."

"Ha! Yes, he did! That guy is strong, but he's not very good, he only thinks he is. He was also tired from his previous match."

She drew closer. It was a tad awkward, talking to a man she'd glimpsed in the buff only an hour ago.

Michael tapped the stick's ivory handle in his palm. "And you are who?"

"Quinette Hardin."

"American, correct?"

"Correct."

"And you are with which agency?"

"It's not an agency exactly. A human rights group, the WorldWide Christian Union."

"Which does what?"

She told him and complimented his command of English.

"I see," Michael said. "So, Miss Hardin, what do you speak besides English?"

"Nothing. Unless you want to count two years of high school Spanish."

"I would be delighted to meet someday an American who speaks more than English. You Americans own the world now and you don't have to learn." There was no edge to the remark; he made it as if stating a mathematical fact. "But someday someone else will own the world, and then you'll have to learn their language. Who do you think it will be? The Russians? The Arabs? The Chinese?"

"Couldn't say. Never thought about it."

"I'll bet on the Chinese. The Arabs are too crazy to be masters of the world. The Russians are too drunk. But the Chinese, oh, they're so disciplined and hardworking, and there are so many of them!" With a languid movement, he pointed the stick toward the mission, hidden in the trees a few hundred yards off. "I learned there. The Englishman's English. The American English I learned taking military training at your Fort Benning in Georgia state. Do you know Georgia?"

"Not really. I'm from far away. Iowa."

"Where our commander in chief went to university."

"Yeah. Someone told me Garang went to Iowa State."

"Iowa State," Michael said distantly. "He studied agriculture, animal husbandry, I think. He's a Dinka, and the Dinka are like the Arabs. How they love cattle. Cattle are their lives. They're African cowboys, and the Arabs in Sudan are Arab cowboys. So this war, it's not cowboys and Indians, it's cowboys and cowboys."

"What is it you wish to speak to the commander about?" the adjutant growled, bootlegging into the question an impatience with the chatter.

"I'm sorry, I've forgotten your name," Quinette said.

"Major Muhammad Kasli."

You can't get more Muslim than Muhammad, she thought. Lord, you needed a program and a scorecard to keep track of who was on whose side in this war. To entice the major out of his dour attitude, she offered her hand and the wide, friendly smile that came naturally to a midwesterner (the tyrannical farmbelt grin, Kristen used to call it, because it announced that the one who wore it was so inoffensive that the one upon whom it was bestowed didn't dare to be otherwise). The pleasantries of the American heartland didn't apply out here. Major Kasli merely nodded, without so much as a pleased to meet you.

"The major, Miss Hardin, sees to it that my time isn't wasted," Michael added, with the faintest trace of sarcasm.

She took the cue and stated her business. What was the extent of the slavery problem in the mountains? Any estimates of how many people had been seized?

"I don't know much more than what I told you earlier," Michael said with a weary shrug. "How many have been taken?" Another shrug. "A few, like that young woman who spoke to you, escape and give us some names. We get some informations from people whose families have paid Arab traders to return them."

"We work a lot with a trader named Bashir. Is he one of them?"

"I have no idea."

"I know of this Bashir," Major Kasli interjected. "He's gotten rich selling slaves back to freedom."

Michael glanced at him sidelong, then said, "The taking of captives isn't our problem, it's the symptom of a problem." Looking away, he waved his stick at the red wafer of the sun, suspended on the rim of the far ranges. "There's the problem."

"I don't know what you mean," Quinette said.

"Those hills, and those over there, and those behind us. These mountains are so isolating. You have in one valley a village and you have in another valley another village and the people don't even speak the same language. This makes it easy for the Arabs to give rewards to one tribe if they will join with the government. Yes, I'm sorry to report that many Nubans have been bribed to fight against their own people. The old tactic, divide and conquer, and we do half the work for them by dividing ourselves. Tribalism is the problem here, in all Sudan, in all of Africa. Who brought the first African slaves to the slave ships? Other Africans."

He fell into a silence, looking at her as if he expected a response. She couldn't think of any. Her only thought was that he was a strikingly handsome man.

He turned from her to glance over his shoulder, toward the mission and its surrounding village. "I would like to show you something, Miss Hardin. If you care to see it."

"What?"

"What I hope will be a solution to the problem."

In the dusk that had dropped like a stage curtain, they walked a rutted lane, past tightly clustered huts, Michael presenting verbal snapshots of the town when it had been home to more than two thousand souls. The thriving marketplace, the harvest festivals, the church filled with congregants, the school with pupils, their voices and laughter ringing in the air when classes were over.

"And then Khartoum's bombers came, and then the raiders, and it became a village of ghosts," he said. "Only a few people escaped death or captivity. Those drifted back and discovered that the Arabs had failed to destroy the wells. Why, no one knows. News of this traveled, and in time refugees from elsewhere began to arrive. Because there was water. Water is hope. These new settlers began to rebuild the houses, to plant gardens and tobacco and sorghum fields." He stopped and motioned at a cooking fire, its glow illuminating the face of an old woman squatting before it. "She and her family are Moro tribesmen. And over there"—he walked further, toward the wink of a paraffin lamp—"are Nubans from the Tira hills. And there in those houses are Masakin Nuba."

Quinette nodded to be polite. None of the tribal names meant anything to her. Off in the distance, men and women were dancing, drums and chants providing a kind of background music to Michael's soliloquy.

"After I was given command of the SPLA forces in the Nuba and I saw what was happening here, I made my headquarters nearby. This is my main task—to unite the Nuba in a common cause. Very difficult, maybe impossible, but it begins here"—he stomped a foot—"because here the people have been uniting themselves. Without intending to, out of necessity, they've planted a seed. When you plant a garden, you build a fence around it. We fighters are the fence. Since we came, more people from all over the mountains have been settling in this refuge, and there have been no attacks. We now have almost half the original population, but from different tribes, learning one another's dialects and customs, discovering what they have in common. New Tourom belongs to no one tribe, it belongs to all. Out of destruction, the seed of a new society, with the old divisions and suspicions set aside. Now we must nurture it, help it grow into a fine big tree."

Darkness had fallen, a full moon had risen, and he stood in its light, a tall soldier speaking improbably like a visionary.

"Do you know what I think of when I see what's happening here?"

"N-no," she said, struck by the way his hands moved when he spoke; his fingers seemed to be plucking invisible harp strings in the air.

"My year in America, and the soldiers I trained with at Fort Benning.

White soldiers, black soldiers, brown ones. Soldiers with English names and Spanish names and Chinese names, all fighting for the same flag. I read about your history. You people began with one small colony, no bigger than this village. And it drew others like a magnet. A nation of immigrants, you call yourselves. Aren't these people here immigrants also? The relief organizations call them internally displaced persons, but I like to think of them as immigrants and of what's happening here as a . . . what is the word I want? An experiment? And I intend to make this experiment a success."

He led her to the mission, their legs swishing through knee-high grass. Michael stopped in front of the building that was under reconstruction, moved on to the long bungalow with flayed brick walls, then on to the row of roofless huts—living quarters for the teachers, he said—and from there to a shell that had been a clinic, to the carpentry and blacksmith shops, and finally to the church, crouched under the rock pinnacles. It had looked merely sad in the afternoon, but the moon transformed it and the damaged structures all around into something mysterious and romantic.

"For almost forty years this was here, not touched, till that day the Antonovs came."

He pointed to a plaque, bolted into a stone pedestal, over which a brass bell hung from a tripod of steel rails. CHURCH OF ST. ANDREW. 1957.

"Catholic?" she asked.

"Oh, no. ECS. The Episcopal Church of Sudan. Let me show you inside."

He opened the tall wooden door. Arrows of moonlight pierced the holes that bomb fragments had torn in the roof, and a diffuse beam fell through a gaping rip in the altar dome, illuminating the simple altar, some wooden pillars, and the halved logs that served as pews.

"I was baptized here," he said, the words echoing in the cavernous interior.

She didn't know why, but she was pleased to learn that he was Protestant.

"And the small man who spoke today, John Barrett, do you know him?"

"Yes."

"He preached here some years ago. He was once Catholic, a priest, but one of our local girls caused him to change his mind." Michael smiled. "Who could have thought then what would happen? That bombs would fall on a church?"

They went out and stood very near each other. In the cool night air she could feel the warmth coming off him and caught the rich, loamy scent of his skin, mingled with the sour odor of his unwashed uniform.

"When I was in school here"—looking directly at her—"the minister at the time taught us about doing certain things to show that we are true Christians. Acts of faith, he called them. To bring all this back would be an act of faith. Faith in the future. John's agency and one other are helping us to rebuild the school. With more help we can rebuild the clinic and train nurses and medical assistants. We'll rebuild the tailor shop and bring in sewing machines and teach women to use them. We'll rebuild the carpentry and blacksmith shops so the men can make useful things. We'll restore the church. It will be as it was, but better. All tribes living together in harmony. That's the tree I hope will grow from the seed, and perhaps the winds will scatter its seeds through all the Nuba, all of southern Sudan."

His voice seemed to set off vibrations that she could feel inside, like bass notes from an organ. She laid a hand on his forearm.

"What is it, Miss Hardin?"

"If you'd spoken like this today, all those other speeches would have been unnecessary. You should go back right now and tell everybody what you've just told me. You'll have them lined up, ready to give you whatever you need."

"Unfortunately, I've got to get back to my base." He jerked his head. "It's over that way." He stood quietly for a few moments, tapping the ground with the walking stick. "Perhaps you could speak to the others for me?"

She sensed that this was more than a request; a commission, rather. "I will. I will do that."

WITH OPEN EYES, she lay on her sleeping bag on a tukul's floor. It wasn't the long peals of thunder and the furious spatter of rain on the grass roof that kept her awake; it was the recordings of Michael's voice playing in her mind, the mental pictures of his smooth blue-black skin dusted in ash that produced a euphoric insomnia, a little like the crystal-meth highs she'd experienced in her bad-girl period. What a difference between him and other rebel commanders she'd met in her travels, with their narrow, foxhole views of things, their petty squabbles and conspiracies. Here was a big man with big ideas, and how privileged she felt that he'd chosen to share them with her. She'd carried out her commission and shared them with her colleagues at a lamplit dinner under the fly-tent. Lily had interrupted her at one point, asking, "Did he appoint you as his spokeswoman? Why doesn't he tell us what he'd like us to do himself?" Quinette told her why, but now she wondered if there might have been another reason for her appointment. She sat up and, peering at the prone forms of Lily and two other women, pondered the possibility that God was urging her to work on behalf of Michael's plans. God would give her a clear signal in His own good time.

Outside the wind picked up, the canvas covering the doorway billowed and sagged with a snap, and the temperature seemed to drop ten degrees in a few seconds. She wriggled into her sleeping bag and curled up, her arms between her legs. To muffle the racket of the rain against the roof, she pulled the sleeping bag over her head. In the darkness of that cocoon, she fell asleep to images of Michael's fingers, strumming invisible strings in the air.

Balm in Gilead

IN THE MORNING they discovered that Zulu Three's runway was one long slick of mud. With the cautious shuffle of someone walking a frozen river, Suleiman went up and down the length of it, stopping occasionally to probe with a long stick. He tapped bricks of muck from off his sandals and returned to the *doum* palm grove where Fitzhugh waited with Douglas. They'd arrived at the airstrip well ahead of time, to make sure it was usable after last night's thunderstorm. Barrett and Diana had come with them.

"Slippery, but this deep only," Suleiman reported, forking two fingers above the tip of the stick. "Very hard underneath. The naga'a clay. Rains run off it like it is cement."

Douglas clutched his arm and said, "Good man!" as though Suleiman were responsible for the runway's sound condition. "By the time our passengers get here, that surface gunk should be dry enough. Loki by lunchtime."

"And a proper bath and no more bloody ticks," Diana said, holding out a bare forearm blotched by two dime-size welts. Last night, before they'd made love, Fitzhugh had removed the ticks by the light of a paraffin lamp—a novel form of foreplay, she'd called it. He examined the bites now and in the morning glare noticed that four days and nights in the bush had left her skin looking shriveled and scaly. While this observation did not affect his feelings for her, the mere fact that he'd made it troubled him.

An eager grin cracking through his blond stubble, Douglas looked at Barrett, sitting cross-legged against the trunk of a palm tree.

"So what do you think? How did we do?"

"It all went much better than I expected. The wrestling was a big hit. I give the show four stars."

"I meant, do you think we won over any hearts and minds? It was hard to tell."

"Well, I'm not sure the matches and the dancing were a good idea,"

Diana said. "Everyone looked so fit and jolly that the aid workers must have questioned if things here are as bad as we say."

"Ah, but we may have a few converts—that Hardin woman, for one," said Barrett. "As for the rest"—he spread his hands—"we'll have to wait and see."

Douglas stood, brushed off the seat of his pants, and said he was going to radio Michael that the airfield was in good shape and to bring the passengers. As he went toward the airplane, which Suleiman and a work gang were divesting of its camouflage net and branches, Fitzhugh moved off into the bushes to take a leak. Barrett intercepted him on his way back.

"A quiet word?" He jammed his hands in his back pockets and shyly looked down, rocking back and forth on his heels. "Now then, Fitz, I want you to understand straight away that I'm the last one to moralize—"

"You're the most moralizing man I've ever met."

"Sure, when it comes to politics, but I'm not talkin' public morals in this instance." Barrett raised his eyes. "It's private behavior I'd never moralize about."

A bulbul sang plaintively. Fitzhugh knew it was a bulbul because Douglas had taught him to recognize its call. He shook out an Embassy, its tip yellow from his dried sweat.

"I figured she would have to confide in somebody sooner or later. I'm glad it was you."

"She didn't. I've suspected somethin' between you two for a while. It's been obvious, to me at least. The way you two look at each other. She's one of my dearest friends. A very capable woman, but she's got her vulnerabilities."

"I know what you're thinking," Fitzhugh said defensively. "About all I can do is swear to you that it isn't that. I really do love her."

"You'll understand why I find that strange?"

"Sure. So do I. So does she. Is this the place for this conversation?"

"No place is," Barrett said with another downward glance. "All right, I'll believe you that your feelings are genuine, but feelings change. Ah, she's goin' to be an old woman in ten years. I can't see what good can come out of a relationship like this."

"John, what good could come out of one between a five-and-a-half-foot white excommunicated priest and a six-foot African woman?"

"Sure and you've got me there," he said with a laugh. "I'm afraid of her gettin' hurt."

Fitzhugh was beginning to feel like a young suitor with a father's shotgun pointed at him. "She won't be."

"I hope so. I'd appreciate it if you wait till we're out of here to tell her about this little talk."

He readily agreed to the condition, although it made things a bit awkward when he again sat down next to Diana. Still, he was relieved to have the secret out. The clandestine trysts and the pretending that they were no more than friends in public were wearing him out. Maybe he should have announcements printed up for general distribution. Mr. Fitzhugh Martin and Lady Diana Briggs are pleased to announce that they are lovers. Mr. Martin wishes to declare that he's not after Lady Briggs's money. Better leave that last declaration out—it sounded like protesting too much.

The relief workers and the press contingent arrived about three hours later, accompanied by meks and villagers bidding them farewell. Watching the procession wind down the ridge, SPLA soldiers out in front and on the flanks, the church canon holding up a gold-plated crucifix before a couple of hundred hymn-singing men and women, Fitzhugh recalled Barrett's characterization of the war as a resumption of the Crusades.

"Let's get her ready to go," Douglas said.

They went to the airplane as strains of the hymn, sung to a drumbeat, lilted down from above. Fitzhugh strapped himself into the worn copilot's seat and slid the side window open to let some air into the stifling cockpit.

"Shall I read it off to you?" He picked up the clipboard that held the plastic-covered checklist. "It would make me feel useful and authentic."

"My man, I can do it in my sleep," Douglas boasted, his hands darting across the confusing array of switches, knobs, and instruments.

Only two days before flying into the Nuba, the G1C's copilot, an American farm boy of heroic size and with a heroic appetite for anything alcoholic, had got himself heroically drunk and fallen into a trash pit on his way to bed, breaking a leg. There had been no time to find another first officer. Douglas would have to fly the plane single-handed. He'd issued Fitzhugh a white shirt and epaulettes, instructing him to play the role of copilot but to please, for Christ's sake, *not touch one damned thing.*

Sweating, waiting for the air-conditioning to kick in before he shut the window, he watched the deacon emerge from the palm grove and lead the choir along the side of the runway to the solemn beat of the drum. The porters filed behind, and then came the passengers, shepherded by their armed escorts. The drum changed pitch: two flat, hollow thuds that sounded like warehouse doors banging shut. Douglas shouted, "Holy shit!" and pointed out the window on his side of the airplane. There was another, louder thud as a fountain of gray-black smoke shot up at the far end of the airfield.

The singing stopped, the drum fell silent, people scattered in several directions. Fitzhugh's senses were transmitting bits of information faster than his brain could sort them out.

Soldiers running.

People throwing themselves to the ground.

Five or six almost simultaneous explosions, rocks and dirt splattering with terrible velocity. The solitary figure of the deacon, marching down the middle of the runway, the crucifix held high.

Douglas yelled, "What the fuck is he doing?"

The man walked on, toward the dissipating smoke of the last mortar bursts, raising the bright cross higher, like an exorcist doing battle with demonic forces. Two soldiers tackled the lunatic and were dragging him away when thick vaporous arms enveloped all three and flung them through the air. Fitzhugh, pinned to his seat by shock as much as by the safety harness, stared at the broken bodies, one lying across another, a third sprawled several yards away. Diana! Where was Diana? Snapping out of his stunned state, he unbuckled the harness, rose from the seat, and fell back. It was only then that he realized that the plane was rolling.

"What're you doing? Diana's out there!"

Douglas seemed not to hear his cry, a deaf machine in control of another machine, canted forward in his seat, his eyes nailed to the runway ahead, one hand frozen to the yoke, the other ramming the throttles forward. The plane swerved in the still-slick surface mud, and Fitzhugh saw the ground falling away.

"You can't do this! Can't leave her—can't leave everybody—"

Douglas said nothing. He cranked a wheel in the pedestal, pulled a lever, and looked at the instruments or out the windshield with fierce concentration. He turned westward, leveled off at a thousand feet above the mission, then banked sharply and passed over the airfield, half obscured by torn veils of smoke and reddish dust. The Gulfstream flew on over the plain to the east and banked again. Douglas broke his silence.

"You didn't hear the gear retract, did you? I'm saving the airplane. Soon as the shelling lifts, I'll land and pick everybody up. Your job will be to get their asses on board in one hell of a hurry. Nobody's going to be left behind."

Fitzhugh wanted to rush to Diana's side and at the same time dreaded returning to the ground. The explosions, those compact maelstroms with their awful noise, a noise of things going out, of things rent and crushed, had unnerved him. Douglas circled the airfield again.

"Holy shit! There they are! There!" He pointed at a cone-shaped hill barely more than a mile away. "There! Dead ahead!"

Douglas changed the radio frequency and contacted Michael by his call sign, Archangel. There was no answer. He called again, and Michael's voice came through the static of his field radio.

"Archangel, I've got the mortars spotted! At the base of a hill southeast of the strip! Do you see it? Looks like a pyramid! Do you see it?"

"No! Give me an azimuth, give me the range!"

"Roger. Fitz, I'm gonna need you. Keep your eyes on this"—he motioned at the compass on the overhead panel—"and give me the bearing when I ask for it."

Turning again, they skimmed the ridgetop and sliced across the runway, the Gulfstream's nose aimed straight at the hill.

"Okay, now."

Fitzhugh squinted at the instrument, a strange dry taste in his mouth, as if he'd been sucking on the tip of a lead pencil, a quivering in his legs. He couldn't think.

"Give me the fucking bearing, goddamn it!"

The hill loomed larger in the windshield, a tall mound of jumbled rocks and grass the color of a lion's mane.

"One-fifty . . . one-fifty-five. Yes, one-fifty-five."

Douglas's glance flicked to the compass the moment before he hauled back on the yoke to clear the hill's peak. Something metallic glinted through sun-scorched trees fringing a wadi a few hundred feet below.

"Archangel, Archangel. Bearing one-five-five, range three thousand meters. Did you read that?"

Static.

"Archangel, do you read me? Bearing one-five-five, range three-zero-zero."

Michael answered and repeated the information.

"Fire a marking round, tell me when you've shot, and I'll try to adjust from up here," Douglas said, then made another turn, an airborne hairpin that brought a tug of G-forces.

"What's happening? What's going on?"

"We're in it, my man, that's what. We are in the goddamned war!"

Two minutes later, as they orbited the plain, they heard Michael report, "Shot out!"

They circled for ten seconds, fifteen, twenty . . .

Michael called, "Did you spot the round?"

"Negative. Give us one more."

A pause, then: "Shot out!"

Fitzhugh's heart leaped when he saw a geyser of dense white smoke somewhere between the hill and the airstrip.

"Archangel, you're way short!" Douglas said. "You're short five hundred! Add five hundred!"

Another geyser rose, well up on the slope.

"Too much! Drop two hundred!"

They flew on, banked, and with the Gulfstream tilted at a thirty-degree angle, the right side facing away from the target, Fitzhugh was blind to the next shot. Douglas's shout, blasting through his headset, hurt his eardrums.

"You're on 'em, Archangel! Fire for effect! They know you're on 'em, they're hauling ass! Fire for effect!"

As the plane completed its turn, Fitzhugh saw men running from out of the wadi. He saw them with a peculiar thrilling clarity—brown-clad figures scrambling and stumbling up the slope, some with what looked like sewer pipes on their shoulders. Shells from Michael's mortar battery burst in the wadi. The G1C sailed upward and looped around for another pass.

"Add one hundred! No, make that two hundred! Repeat fire for effect!"

Shells burst amid the fleeing figures. It was weird, not hearing the blasts, like watching a silent war movie. The leaden taste was gone from Fitzhugh's mouth. He felt a wild enthusiasm for the game, fancied himself and Douglas as film-land heroes, partners in daring. That the pathetically small creatures in panicky flight below had been the source of his terror seemed absurd. With godlike detachment, he saw a body tossed into the air. The hilltop passed below. The landscape beyond was empty and serene.

"Archangel, Archangel! You nailed 'em!"

"Very good," Michael replied. "I've sent some men in pursuit. Thank you, Doug-lass."

"My man, slap me five!" Douglas cracked his palm against Fitzhugh's, then landed the plane.

Fitzhugh sprinted across the runway. Nimble and swift, as if he were dribbling through an opposing team's defenders, he weaved through knots of dazed people, past soldiers carrying the wounded and the dead, and found her slumped in a culvert, her hands and the front of her blouse spattered in red. Her eyes were open, and she was breathing.

"Oh Christ, where are you hurt?" He fell to his knees beside her, pawing her to find the wound.

She sat up. "Fitz? God, am I glad to see you."

"Where are you hurt?"

"Nowhere. Not mine, his." She pointed at the body of a man, lying on his back in a puddle of blood, more blood than it seemed any one body could hold. "His femoral artery," Diana gasped. "Tried to—no good—came out like—" She flung her arms around him. "God, God, God, I am so glad to see you."

He embraced her. She felt very small. Her bloodsoaked shirt stuck to his.

"You're sure you're not hurt, darling?"

She nodded. "Never saw anything like it . . . came out of him like water from a hose."

"John?"

"I think he's all right. It's over? Tell me it's over."

"It is. We got them."

"What? Who did you get?"

"Later. Come on, we have to get you on the plane."

He helped her to her feet, this woman whom he loved now more than ever. She stared down at her blouse and then at the dead man and covered her mouth with the back of her hand.

"Come on. There's nothing to be done."

An arm around her waist, he walked her to the doum palm grove, in whose shade lay injured soldiers and villagers. More were coming in, some staggering under their own power, some carried in like sacks. Gerhard Manfred was performing triage, ordering this one to be placed here, that one there. He had pressed Quinette and Lily into service, tearing clothes into strips for bandages. Nearby Barrett, kneeling beside a soldier with a shrapnel-grated face, murmured prayers. The CNN reporter stood off to the side with her cameraman, filming the scene. Well, if she didn't have a story before, she had one now.

"Splendid, not so, Fitz?" Manfred said, waving a hand covered in gore. One man, supporting another who was hopping on one leg, came up to him. "There!" he commanded, pointing, then turned back to Fitzhugh and Diana. "Yes, things have come to a splendid conclusion."

Diana asked if there was anything she could do.

"There is. Help these girls make dressings with whatever cloth you can find."

"Start with mine," Fitzhugh said, stripping off his shirt, epaulettes and all.

"Splendid! Ha! Everyone is behaving splendidly."

Whatever the overwrought German meant by that remark, everyone *was* behaving, if not splendidly, then with greater calm than Fitzhugh expected after such an assault. A villager retrieved the canon's crucifix and planted it in the ground to make some sort of statement. People brought the casualties to the improvised aid station and went out to look for others with something like professional efficiency, as if they'd done it often in the past. Undoubtedly they had. Wails of mourning went up every so often, but the wounded bore their pain quietly—a moan was the loudest sound anyone made. Some were still in shock, but the Sudanese capacity to endure suffering probably accounted for their silent forbearance. In their world a mortar shelling was no more unusual than a drought, a flood, an outbreak of relapsing fever. Looking at their quiet, obsidian faces, he couldn't say he admired their stoicism, for there was an element of apathy or fatalism in it. He thought of a submissive dog that dumbly accepts its master's beatings, and the more accepting it is, the more beatings it gets. Did he pity these people then? Really, he had no idea what he felt about anything. His horror at the sight of terrible wounds was mixed up with his joy that Diana hadn't been hurt, a residue of his initial shock and fear with a druglike elevation, a kind of giddiness. He lit a cigarette and inhaled deeply, but it would take more than nicotine to guide him through this thicket of powerful conflicting emotions.

He stubbed the cigarette and went off to round up his passengers and to see if any had been injured. It took a while. The aid workers were scattered about, helping to collect the wounded and the dead, while the journalists were taking photographs. Finally he got them all together. Only one had been hit, a guy from Norwegian People's Aid with a superficial wound to his arm. The two Christian soldiers from the Friends of the Frontline had had a close call—a large mortar fragment had driven into a log they'd been hiding behind. They couldn't stop talking about it, how the shard, almost as big as a railroad spike, had struck with a thud *right between them* and sent wood splinters flying over their heads. A bilious resentment flooded into Fitzhugh. It was as if the perverse, malign spirit that ruled over this cursed land had decreed that only those with black skin would suffer death and serious injury.

After assembling the group in the palm grove, he boarded the plane and told Douglas everyone was ready to go. Manfred was in the cockpit with Douglas.

"Your passengers will be having in their travel plans a little change," the doctor said.

The Gulfstream was going to evacuate the casualties to his hospital, a mere twenty minutes away by air. Tara Whitcomb was coming in to pick up the reporters and aid workers.

"Tara?"

"I tried to get one of our planes, but they're all committed and too far away," Douglas explained. "Tara was near Malakal when she monitored my call. Only hitch is that she's in her Caravan. Fourteen is the most she can take and we've got sixteen. Your job, my man. Find two people who really like the scenery here."

"KEEP THE PRESSURE ON, don't relax," Lily said.

Quinette clamped the man's shoulder with her hand, her thumb pinching an artery to stanch the bleeding in his upper arm. The wound was a deep, almost surgical incision that went nearly all the way around his bicep, as if someone had tried to amputate his arm with razor-sharp hedge clippers. The man was conscious, but he didn't utter a sound, his eyes blinking erratically. There seemed to be a question in them, encrypted in the rapid blinks.

Michael was helping out, stretching a jelibiya taut between his out-spread hands so Lily could cut it into even strips with her pocketknife—a menial task for a commander, but the casualty was one of his best officers, a captain. Looping four strips over her arm, Lily handed a fifth to Quinette.

"Tie a tourniquet where your hand is," she said. "Not so tight you'll cut off his circulation. And be quick about it. He's lost enough blood as it is."

Then she folded two strips into thick compresses, knelt down, and held them to the wound, one on each side. When that temperamental Manfred had called for someone to give him a hand, Lily had stepped right up. It turned out that she'd been a trained paramedic in northern Ireland before she'd joined Concern, and had plenty of practice treating traumatic injuries on Belfast's bomb-blasted streets. Quinette had no experience along those lines, beyond a high school first-aid course, but she'd felt bound to help her friend in any way she could. Now, taking a deep breath to steady her nerves, she released her grip. With the relaxation in pressure, blood squirted from the wound, turning the compresses a vivid red. Fighting panic, Quinette bound the tourniquet snugly around the captain's shoulder and knotted it.

"That should do," said Lily, a compact bundle of competence as she wrapped the fourth strip around and around the compresses.

With the fifth, she fashioned a sling. The injured man groaned when she crooked his arm across the front of his chest and looped the sling over it and then around his neck. Wiping her hands on her trousers, she stood and looked down at her handiwork and said, "That will have to do."

Michael spoke softly to the captain in Nuban. The man's lips parted, but he didn't say anything. All he did was blink and wince, there in the shade of the palms, where fifteen other casualties awaited evacuation and where the dead, seventeen altogether, lay in a long row, some dismembered, some eviscerated, some full of small red holes that looked like measles or smallpox from a distance. The living hovered over them, waving off the flies, and sent up cries of grief and songs of mourning into the hot afternoon sky. The high-pitched lamentations pulled at Quinette's already overstrung nerves. Never in her life had she seen anyone die—her father had expired in the hospital at two in the morning—much less seen anyone die in the ways these people had. Their mangled bodies held a certain lurid fascination, like a grotesque highway accident, but she refused to look at them. The sight made her think things she shouldn't be thinking.

She must have been ten or eleven that winter Sunday morning when her father came down to the kitchen in his flannel bathrobe, his hair mussed and a stubble on his face. He went to the coffeepot—that old Farberware percolator Ardele loved for the aroma it gave off—and without a word poured a cup and stood looking out the window that faced the barn where the tractor and other machinery were kept in cold weather. The rest of the family, dressed for church, ate breakfast. They all four knew immediately that he'd had one of his war nightmares and had woken up reincarnated into the uncommunicative character her mother called "Remote Man" because he would seem so very far away when those spells came over him. It was an inner distancing, a kind of implosion, the man everyone knew compressed, under the pressure of his memories, down to a pinpoint until he almost vanished inside himself. Sometimes Quinette was scared that he would stay there and never talk to her again. It was almost impossible to get through to him when he fell into that black hole, and it was just as difficult for him to speak to anyone else, as though the things he saw in there and the things he felt were inexpressibly awful. But Ardele tried now and then to make contact. She'd tried that morning. *"Ted, there's still time for you to get ready for church. I do wish you'd come with us at least once in a while."* He said nothing. He stared out the window and drank his coffee. *"All right, just thought I'd ask."* He turned around suddenly. *"Why do you keep asking? You know I don't believe in that crap anymore. Maybe I never did."* Most times it didn't pay to contact Remote Man, because most times he was as angry as the real Ted Hardin was gentle. *"Ted, please, the girls."* *"Like, do you really believe you're going to heaven with all this churchgoing? Do you really honestly think we're going somewhere when this is all over?"* *"I won't ask again, promise."* *"Know that wall they've just put up in Washington? Fourteen of my buddies are on it. Three of them, you could've sent what was left of all three home in an eight-by-eleven manila envelope. Think they're somewhere right now, playing their harps?"* *"Please, Ted, don't talk like this in front of the girls."* *"A shovelful of dirt in your face if you've still got one and it's all over. End of story."* *"Not in front of the girls, I'm asking you, Ted."*

Quinette was shocked. How could the sweet man on whose ample lap she sat at hay-mowing time or during spring plowing amid the good smells of turned black earth not believe in God and the eternal rewards awaiting those who did? It meant she would not see him in heaven, and what kind of heaven would that be without him in it?

Now that she'd seen what he had in Vietnam, she understood why he'd uttered those bitter words. It was the fact of mutilation that caused her to think the inappropriate thought *There is no life after death.* The mortar shells had laid bodies open, seeming to expose a terrible truth—a human being is only skin, muscle, bone, blood, organs, and slimy viscera, no fit dwelling for an immortal soul. The randomness of those deaths troubled her just as deeply. Why had those particular seventeen people been killed? Pastor Tom would say that God had summoned them for His own good reasons, but as she'd lain in a ditch beside Lily, Quinette had perceived no selective process in the arbitrary explosions, in the chaotic flurries of hissing shrapnel, flying every which way above her head. It seemed that pure chance determined who died, who got hurt, who escaped unscathed. The deeper mystery, the one that vexed her most, was why God had permitted this to happen in the first place. How could he allow people to be killed and horribly maimed just as they were singing hymns in His praise? The moment before Lily had pulled her into the ditch (for she'd been standing up, in a paralysis of bewildered terror), she'd seen the canon marching down the runway with the crucifix raised high. It was a brave act of faith, and for it he'd gotten killed. Why would the author of all things good license such an evil? Unless it wasn't an evil but only appeared to be one to her limited human mind. Oh, these thoughts were so perplexing. Dangerous as well. They sowed doubt in the ordered garden of her belief, and

Pastor Tom had often preached, *"In matters of the spirit, there can be no room for doubt, for it is but a short journey from doubt to despair."*

"Done all we can," Lily said, intruding on her reverie, and a welcome intrusion it was. "Nothing for it but to wait. Looks like we'll be spending one more night in this godforsaken place," Lily added with a look at her watch. "Know the old soldier's advice, 'Never volunteer'? I'm wondering if we should've listened to it. It's my own bed I'd like for tonight."

Tara Whitcomb had departed an hour ago with their colleagues. A little before that Doug and Fitz had flown out for Manfred's hospital, with the most serious cases and a detachment of soldiers to help carry them off and into the Land Rovers. The plane should have been back by now. If its return was delayed much longer, it would be too late to evacuate the remaining casualties and make Loki before nightfall.

Quinette scanned the vacant sky and said, "They'll be showing up any minute."

"Here's hoping nothing's gone wrong," Lily said. "Did I say this place was godforsaken? God never considered it long enough to forsake it."

With his radio operator standing behind him, Michael knelt at the wounded captain's side and, cradling the man's head in one hand, tried to get him to drink from a calabash. It wasn't a suitable vessel; pouring out of the hole in the top, the water only dribbled down the captain's chin. Quinette squatted next to him, took out her water bottle, and inserted the nozzle between his lips. His Adam's apple bobbed as he sucked greedily.

"What's his name?" she asked.

"Captain Bala. He was one of the two who tried to stop that crazy canon from killing himself." Michael shook his head. "I don't know what that man thought he was doing. The people needed him."

"Do you wonder why he and the other man got killed and Captain Bala lived?" Quinette asked earnestly. "Do you ever wonder about things like that?"

"No."

"I guess what happened today is sort of routine to you."

"War is never routine. It's full of surprises, none of them good." He thought for a moment. "I suppose the answer is that it was God's will."

"And you believe that?"

"Of course."

"Do you think the canon is with God right now?"

"These are strange questions to be asking at this time."

"I know."

"We Nubans believe there is a world beyond this one, so of course he is now with God. Look at that." His fingers fanning like a magician's demonstrating a card trick, he gestured at a group of women making a pile of tree branches. "Those are from a special acacia. The ash of its burned leaves is sacred. It's used to anoint the bodies of the dead. If that and some other things aren't done, their spirits won't answer when you call on them. They might cause you trouble."

Her immediate thought was that this funeral custom wasn't fitting for people who claimed to be Christians, but recalling the words Malachy had spoken to her, that Sunday months ago in the Turkana village—"*You've got to meet them halfway*"—she refrained from voicing it. Indeed, these people, with their half-heathen, half-Christian beliefs, might even be a living reproof to her doubts. Their faith in the eternal life of the spirit had not been shaken; why, then, should hers? It must have been the Enemy who'd planted those questions in her mind. Once again her attention was diverted to herself and to the state of her own soul. She concluded that God was testing her. As the Enemy had tempted Christ in the desert, so was he now tempting her to cast off her faith and make the short journey into despair, in which she would be easy prey for his snares and wiles. She mustn't give in, she mustn't fail! If, as she'd thought last night, God was calling her to a new field of action, He would need to know some things about her first, like how strong was her faith.

"*Satan, get thee behind me.*" She felt stronger now, rerooted in the firm soil of certitude. "*Like a tree standing by the waters, I shall not be moved.*" She watched a woman borrow matches from a soldier and then set fire to the branches. In seconds the pile was ablaze, black smoke ascending pillar-straight into the windless air. Her gaze rose with it, and then she heard the drone of Douglas's plane.

The doctor had sent blankets back with him. The blankets were turned into makeshift stretchers, which made loading the second lot of casualties easier than the first. When it was finished, Michael and his radio operator climbed aboard and sat down at the forward end of the cabin, Captain Bala lying at his feet. As the engines revved to an urgent roar and the plane made a rough roll down the runway, Quinette was touched to see him clasp the officer's hand. He continued to hold it through the climb, the leveling off.

"You must be very close to him," she said.

"I would not be leaving my command post otherwise. But Major Kasli can handle things for a little while."

He bent down to speak to Captain Bala, who responded in a rasping whisper, and Michael folded the blanket he was lying on over his chest.

"He said he's cold. It must be the altitude, the loss of blood. Kasli is my second in command because of his rank, but this one I trust like a brother. We were in the army together."

It took a beat for the tense to register with Quinette.

"I don't understand, *were*."

"Sudan army. We deserted from the same garrison to join the SPLA. We've fought side by side from that day to this." He turned full face to her, and his smile, a bright crescent above his rounded chin, brought a flush to her cheeks. "So now you know you're sitting next to a fugitive and a deserter as well as a rebel, a man the government would hang without trial."

"I'm used to traveling in dangerous company," she said, affecting a jaunty tone.

"Three times I've been wounded," Michael said. "Bala not one time until today. Fighters stayed near him on operations. It was said a powerful kujur had given him a charm against bullets. I wonder if he began to believe that himself. I think that's why he did what he did, running after the crazy man."

The captain moaned, his good arm flopped over his waist, his hand slapping his side. Leaning forward, Quinette again fed him her water bottle. He gulped and spit up. She squeezed the bottle hard to squirt the liquid down his throat. He spit up again. *"There is a balm in Gilead to make the wounded whole."* The words to the old spiritual drifted into her mind—it had been sung at her father's memorial service in the church he would never enter when he was alive—and she hummed it now. *"There is a balm in Gilead to heal the sin-sick soul. Sometimes I get discouraged, and think my work's in vain. But then the Holy Spirit revives my soul again."*

A short time later she found herself at one more desolate bush airstrip, holding Captain Bala's wounded arm tight to his chest while Michael gripped a knotted end of the blanket, his radio operator the other. With great care, they passed him head first through the plane's door and lugged him toward a waiting Land Rover. The vehicle had been converted into an ambulance, the rear seats removed and a steel rack bolted halfway between the roof and the floor so six people could be carried at once, three on top, three on the bottom. A German nurse named Ulrika determined which six of the fifteen casualties were to be taken first. Wearing a blood-smeared smock, she made a quick examination of each one. "This one *ja*, this one also, this one *nein*," she said. The fateful litany went on. *Ja . . . ja . . . ja . . . nein.* The captain received a *"ja,"* and Michael and the radio-operator laid him inside, wedging him alongside two others on the top rack.

The sun was low on the serrate horizon. Doug said he couldn't make Loki before dark, even with luck and a tailwind, and elected to delay the return flight till morning.

"You and Lily might want some privacy, so you can sleep inside," he said while soldiers began erecting a tent of camouflage netting over the plane. "Fitz and I can bag out under a wing."

"Oh, I like the idea of sleeping out under the stars," Lily declared. She gave her dingy brown hair a coquettish flip.

"Might rain again tonight."

"I'll take the chance," she said. It appeared that the idea of spending one more night in the Nuba had suddenly become more agreeable to her.

Lily had just started to build her little nest under the wing when Ulrika bustled up, her bosom thrust forward, her rear end thrust backward for ballast. "You are the girl with nurse's training?"

"Nurse's?" Lily rolled out her air mattress. "I was a paramedic."

"*Ach!* Nurse. Paramedic. You think we care about such distinctions here? You must come."

"Come? Where?"

"With us to hospital, where do you think? Gerhard instructed me to bring you. We have so many, we need all the help we can find."

"You'll pardon me, sure, but I don't get paid for that, and I've got to be back in Loki by tomorrow to do what I do get paid for."

Ulrika drew back, as if she'd been insulted. "For what you get paid or not paid makes no difference! We have already lost three people and will lose more with your help or without it but more without than with." She collected herself and tried a less strident approach. "I appeal to you. I am not making a big opera, but this is life and death."

"Well, hell and bloody hell," Lily said, kicking the air mattress. "Never fucking volunteer." She glanced at Douglas and Fitz.

"Up to you," Doug said, "as long as you're back here between eight and nine. We want to take off before it gets too hot."

Quinette looked toward the Land Rover and saw Michael standing on the running board, looking back toward them. "I'll go with you, Lily, since they need help," she said.

They had to sit on the roof, enclosed by the roof-rack, which they clung to as the Land Rover rocked side to side or leaned at precarious angles when one set of wheels rolled along a ridge in the center of the road. On the running boards, clutching the braces of the sideview mirrors, Michael and his radio operator had the look of charioteers. The road was so badly ditched and potholed that the driver couldn't go much faster than ten miles an hour. In some places it became a series of evenly spaced heaves and dips, and Quinette watched the hood rise and fall like a boat's bow in a storm.

Up on her unstable perch, she felt daring and adventurous and reveled in the roughness of the ride, the dust blowing into her face. They possessed the glamour of hardship. She flew out of herself and pictured the scene as if it were a movie: the sky behind a shimmering rose, dusk gathering in the sky ahead, and the two vehicles filled with casualties of war plunging on through a strange landscape where rocky needles stabbed out of acacia forests and wind-carved boulders stood like fantastic sculptures. The image poured its drama into her, nourishing the conviction that she was where she belonged, living with the intensity that had always been meant for her.

At the hospital Lily was issued a surgical smock, mask, and latex gloves and shanghaied into the operating room, which was nothing more than a tukul set a little apart from one of the bungalows that served as wards. Quinette was relegated to helping a male nurse prepare the patients for surgery, cutting their clothes away from their wounds, sponging them with hot water and bacteriological soap. There weren't many beds open, so the injured had been placed on blankets on the ground, under an awning of plastic sheets propped up by crooked wooden poles. She and the nurse worked by a hissing high-pressure lantern that was a magnet for insects. He spoke only Arabic and a few words of German picked up from his boss, forcing him and Quinette to communicate mostly in an improvised sign language. She hadn't eaten since this morning and was dizzy with hunger, its pangs occasionally overcome by a swift, sharp cramp of dysentery. Her knees grew stiff from all the stooping and squatting, but she relished these afflictions; the thing she was doing wouldn't be worthwhile if it didn't hurt a little. And hunger and tummy cramps were next to nothing compared with the patients' sufferings. The fabric of their bodies gouged, slashed, and punctured, they appeared not to have been maimed so much as vandalized by some malicious delinquent.

Captain Bala was unconscious. He didn't flinch when the nurse, after replacing the makeshift tourniquet with a rubber tube tied below Bala's shoulder, ripped off the dressings. He motioned to Quinette, and she sponged the gash. The arm was swollen, and she feared septicemia had set in; and yet when she laid the back of her hand against the captain's forehead, his skin was cool to the touch, almost cold. If he had an infection, he would be running a fever, she knew that much. The nurse had meanwhile wrapped a blood-pressure cuff around Bala's good arm. He pumped the bulb, read the gauge, pumped again, and with a grave expression softly whispered, "*Ya Allah*—my God." Then, as he took Bala's pulse, his hand resting on the captain's midsection, he appeared to feel something strange, for he let go of the wrist and pulled up Bala's shirt, revealing a lemon-sized lump, with a red-rimmed pinhole in its center, just below the ribs on his right side. The nurse pressed it, and Bala awoke with a sudden jerk, a startling cry. A flurry of gestures told Quinette to fetch one of the stretchers leaning against the bungalow's wall.

The captain was Michael's size, well over two hundred pounds, and her back nearly popped as they lifted him onto the stretcher and carried him to the operating room. She was out of breath when they set him down outside. They waited. Bala lapsed back into unconsciousness. From somewhere behind the tukul, a generator throbbed. In a few minutes the door swung open and two orderlies passed through the rectangle of bright light, carrying a woman rolling her head from side to side, the stump of her right leg swaddled in bandages. Manfred and Ulrika followed behind, pulling off their masks. They cupped their hips in their hands and arched their backs and took deep breaths of the still night air before they each lit a cigarette. The lighter's flare illuminated Manfred's bloodshot eyes, the half-moon sags beneath them. His whole face looked like it was under the pull of a powerful gravity. The poor man had been bandaging and cutting and stitching and pulling metal out of people for the past eight hours. He and Ulrika smoked while the nurse apprised them of Captain Bala's condition. That's what Quinette assumed he was doing; she couldn't understand a word. The doctor motioned to bring the wounded man inside.

The operating room, with its baked mud walls and ceiling of corrugated tin, looked nothing like the ones on TV medical shows. Except for a breathing apparatus with a face mask hanging from it, there was no high-tech gadgetry flashing signals of life's functions. Overhead lights shone on a stainless-steel table covered by a stained foam mattress. Hot water steamed in pots on a propane stove. Lily was cleaning surgical instruments in one, dipping them with tongs.

The two strapping orderlies returned and laid Captain Bala on the table. Quinette stepped back toward the door but didn't leave with the male nurse. She had a special interest in this patient and figured that entitled her to stay and watch; however, her view of the operation was blocked by a wall of backs as Manfred and his assistants went to work. "I had better not put him under, his blood pressure is far too low," he murmured to Lily. "Let's see if we can make do with a local." Lily raised a bottle to the light and filled a syringe. Then the doctor called for a scalpel and forceps, and for several minutes there was complete silence, until he exclaimed, "Ah!" As he turned aside, pinching what looked like a fragment of a coat hanger between the forceps, Quinette saw the front of his smock spattered with a blackish fluid and Ulrika holding a compress to Bala's side. Manfred frowned when he spotted her, leaning against the door.

"You have a reason for being here?"

"I . . . no—I was just wondering . . . is he going to be all right?"

"You're not needed here, Miss Hardin."

She went out, feeling superfluous and embarrassed. She should return to her assigned duties but thought against all reason that if she remained close by, Captain Bala would be okay. Looking up at the stars, more stars than she'd ever seen back home, she prayed to God to deliver Michael's comrade from whatever danger he was in. Even as she did, she sensed that this petition wouldn't be granted; so she wasn't too surprised or saddened when, about a quarter of an hour later, the orderlies marched out with the stretcher between them and the captain on it, the blanket drawn over his face.

"I am sorry for kicking you out," Manfred said, emerging with Ulrika, Lily, and two other assistants. "I didn't know you and Miss Hanrahan worked so hard to save that man. The fifth one we lost today."

"We did a first-rate job, treating the wrong wound," Lily remarked caustically.

Manfred lit up again, bringing the two fingers holding the cigarette flat against his lips, pulling it out with a quick, nervous movement. "You could have done nothing with the right one."

"What happened?" Quinette asked.

"A thin piece of shrapnel this long"—he spread a thumb and forefinger about three inches—"pierced his liver, straight through to the inferior vena cava. This is the big artery from the heart to the liver. Not much bleeding on the outside—the piece was like a little cork—but a great deal of internal hemorrhaging. It is miraculous he lasted as long as he did."

"I'd better find Michael and tell him."

But at that inconvenient moment, a wave of nausea rolled through her. Hand to her mouth, she moved away and vomited.

Ulrika placed a matronly arm across her shoulders. "*Ach,* you are not used to this."

"Not that," Quinette sputtered. "I've got dysentery, and—"

"You have something for it?"

"Cipro."

"Then take one and get some rest. My little house, you can sleep there. I don't think I will be lying down for some hours yet."

Quinette shook her head. "As long as Lily is—"

"Do not with me play the heroine," Ulrika chided. "You have done your share. My little house. I will get someone to show you where it is."

Shining her penlight into the small room, she saw a box of matches on the nightstand and lit the paraffin lamp. Ulrika had asked her not to turn on the electric lights, to save juice in the solar batteries. The bed with its steel headboard looked like hospital surplus, its stern functional lines softened somewhat by the mosquito net that enclosed it. Figuring the invitation did not include use of the bed, Quinette propped her rucksack in a corner, unrolled her air mattress and sleeping bag, and placed them atop one of the floor mats. It was stuffy inside, and she opened the shutters, sat on a chair, and took off her boots and socks, wrinkling her nose at the smell. All of her clothes had a funky reek. Reckoning she did, too, she stripped and hung her clothes on a peg to air them out, then positioned the chair in the middle of the room, between the two windows, and washed her naked body in the night breezes.

She looked around at the floral print curtains on the windows, posters of German pop groups on the stone walls, a portable radio with built-in CD player on the desk, next to a laptop and a stack of computer-game software. She wasn't ready for sleep, though she'd been awake since dawn. What she felt instead of tiredness was an inner collapse. Everything she and Lily had done for Captain Bala, all for nothing. "*Sometimes I feel discouraged and think my work's in vain. But then the Holy Spirit revives my soul again.*" The Holy Spirit, however, seemed not to be in a revivalist mood as far as she was concerned, so she got her travel Bible from her rucksack and sat on the bed, holding the book under the lamp, and paged through it aimlessly, hoping to come upon some uplifting passage. Finding none, she lay down for a moment . . .

A knock at the door and the sound of someone calling her name woke her up. At first she thought she was dreaming, the voice and the rapping sounded so far away; but then she was sitting up and looking at her watch. Ten-thirty. She'd been asleep for maybe fifteen minutes, though it felt like hours. By the time her head cleared, Michael had given up and was walking away—she could hear his boots crunching on the gravel pathway. She called to him through the window.

"Miss Hardin? The nurse told me you were here. I woke you up?"

"What is it?"

He didn't answer. He didn't need to. She knew, instinctively knew, the reason for this visit and was thrilled he'd come to her.

"Wait a second. I'm not dressed," she said, and quickly put on her trousers and shirt and fluffed her hair. She was about to tell him to come in when she noticed that she'd left her bra and panties on the peg. That wouldn't look right, she thought, and stuffed them into her rucksack. Then she opened the door.

He had to duck as he entered; it was a low doorway—she herself had cleared it by only a couple of inches. He took off his beret and folded it under an epaulet and asked if he could sit down. She nodded, and he fell into the chair, looking stricken and exhausted. She placed the desk chair in front of him and sat down.

"I am so sorry," she said, covering his hand in her two. "I prayed for him, I did, but—"

"I didn't come here for the kind words." There was an equal measure of aggression and weariness in his tone. "Bala was a soldier and he died like one, and that's the end of it."

"You came because you needed to talk to somebody. And don't tell me I've got that wrong, because I know and I know because I lost someone close to me when I was fourteen. My dad. And afterward, after it finally sank into my teenage head that he was gone and never coming back, all I wanted to do was talk to people. To just about anyone who'd listen."

"But you *are* wrong," he said.

She released his hand and sat back, noticing how the lamplight lent a bronze cast to the cicatrix on his forehead.

In an undertone, his lips barely moving, he said, "You have no idea how sick I am of all this. I didn't come here to talk, but to listen to you talk. I want you to take me out of here for a little while. Talk to me about the Iowa state."

"Iowa?" she asked with a nervous laugh.

"Yes. I've heard Garang speak about his days at university there. He liked it very much. I wish to hear about it from you."

"There's not much I can say. I mean, it's kind of boring."

"Boring is good. The more boring the better. Because, as you've seen this day, Sudan can be so very interesting."

He cocked his chin as he stared at her, as if defying her to bore him, an unusual challenge that she did her best to meet, telling him that Iowa was very white, racially speaking, and very flat from the Mississippi in the east to the Missouri in the west, flat as a table except near the rivers, where it got hilly but not much, and owing to this flatness and the thick, rich, black soil, it was mostly farmland, corn and soybean fields and cow pastures, and nothing much ever happened there except during presidential election years, when candidates from all over descended on the state, vying for its citizens' votes because it was a big deal to win the state of Iowa, even though it didn't have a lot of people, like California or New York—*fat* people, she added, and described how heavy and ponderous everyone had looked to her when she'd returned home from her first visit to Sudan, why, your average Iowan could shed twenty pounds and give it to your average African and the Iowan would still be overweight and the African skinny, and was that boring enough for him?

"Delightfully boring," he answered. "But you're not fat."

It was hard to tell if he meant this as a compliment or as a mere statement of the obvious.

"I probably would be if I'd stayed. My older sister? The last time I saw her, she was getting like this." She made a circle with her arms. "She's not as tall as me—as I. I'm the tallest of three sisters. Take after my dad. He was six feet four."

"The father you lost," he murmured, and she could tell by the way he said it that he wondered how she'd come to lose him.

"He was a soldier, like you. In the Vietnam War. He got sick because he was exposed to a chemical they used over there. Agent Orange. You heard about it?"

"When I was at Fort Benning, yes. My father was also a soldier. In the British army. He fought with the British in the Second World War. Against the Italians in Ethiopia."

"You seem kind of young to have had a father in the Second World War," she remarked.

"He had three wives. I was a son of the youngest, a girl sixteen years old that he married when he was forty."

Three, she thought, and that brought a question, one she was reluctant to ask.

"But you haven't told me about your life in Iowa state," he said.

She laughed. "Now that would really bore you."

"I wish to hear about ordinary things."

She spun random, mundane anecdotes about Cedar Falls and the farm and the dull years in high school. Her life B.A.—Before Africa. A fear leaped within her that she was overdoing it, making it sound more commonplace than it had actually been. However much he wished to hear about ordinary things, she didn't wish Michael to see her as an ordinary woman, a desire that led her to carry on for several minutes about her sinful years and her eventual return to grace, a tale she thought sufficiently dramatic to balance out all the everyday stuff.

"And so you have come here to Sudan for what reason?"

"I told you. I work for the WorldWide Christian Union—"

"Yes, of course. But what are your own reasons? The reasons in your heart. Was your life in America too dull that you had to come here?"

The honest answer, she knew, was yes, but she didn't care for the sound of it: too personal, too selfish, and besides, it was not entirely true. "I think I was called here. I think I'm doing something God wants me to do. What about you?"

He smiled. "I'm here because I was born here, Miss Hardin."

"It's all right to call me Quinette. I meant, you said you're sick of all this. Why are you doing what you do?"

"There is a Nuban ballad, one for the modern times," he answered. "It says this:

> *The world becomes bad*
> *There is one man who doesn't want to go to war*
> *If you want me to fight, you must take me by a rope*
> *Around my neck and pull me there. I won't go.*

"Sometimes I wish I could be like the man in that song. To have the courage to say, 'I won't go.' But I don't have the choice. Some men fight because they love it. I fight because I hate it."

"I don't understand that."

"I fight in the hopes that if I fight hard enough, long enough, and with enough intelligence, I can make an end to fighting."

"I like that. It's beautiful," she said, and pulled her chair a little closer to his.

"It's necessary, not beautiful. I deserted the Sudan army for many reasons, but one was this—my commander told me I could never be promoted if I did not become Muslim and take a Muslim name. When I refused, I could not get paid because the commander said there was no one named Michael Goraende on the muster roll. But, he said, there was a man named Ahmed Goraende. All I had to do was report to the paymaster and say I was Ahmed Goraende. Still I refused. I had a wife and three children in New Tourom, and they suffered because of my stubbornness."

"Is . . ." Quinette hesitated. "Is your wife still there?"

"She was a teacher at the St. Andrew's school. She and two of my children, a son and daughter, were killed in the bombing. The third one, the oldest, a daughter, lived."

After taking a minute to absorb this revelation, Quinette told him how deeply sorry she was—and was appalled that it wasn't entirely the truth.

"I've seen a great deal of death," he said, "so much of it that even the sadness of losing a wife and two children did not last as long as it should have."

"Do you have another wife? Your father had three."

"No. No other." He was silent for a time. "Miss Hardin, will you be returning to the Nuba?"

"I don't know. It depends."

"On what?"

"If my boss decides there's work for us to do up here."

"There is. As I told you, a great many of our people have been taken captive."

"It's not that simple, it's a complicated process," she said. "We don't have any contacts up here. We would—"

"We could help you make these contacts. I would very much like it if—if you were to come back here."

She couldn't quite read that remark; his expression was likewise illegible in the wan lamplight. "May I ask why?"

"For selfish reasons. I enjoy talking to you."

"You'd like me to bore you some more."

With a tentative movement, he touched her knee and grinned. "Oh yes, bore me to death. No, no, of course not. It has been a long time since I've spoken to a woman as I do to you. My wife and I used to talk a lot. Like you, she was an educated woman."

Quinette stifled a yelp. "Educated? Educated doesn't describe me."

"Compared with the women here, you are. Many of them cannot read or write."

"By that standard, I've got a Ph.D.," she said.

"I should be going," he said abruptly.

"Do you have to? I enjoy talking to you."

"Another time. Tomorrow."

She leaned forward as he began to rise, intending to give him a chaste kiss good-bye; but she felt as if she'd fallen into some kind of magnetic field, for she kept leaning, her face drawn toward his, seemingly against her will. In the next moment she was on top of him, straddling his lap, clasping the back of his neck while he held her around the waist and they kissed; kissed without a pretense of tenderness, she biting the inside of his lips, his tongue darting for her throat.

They drew back from each other and into an awkward silence. To her, the surprising thing was that the kiss didn't surprise her. It had a quality of inevitability, of something foreordained from the moment she'd first seen him, yesterday morning.

He reached out and pulled her to him, and they kissed again. His mouth broke free and roamed over her face, until they heard someone walking outside. Ulrika! In a panic, Quinette leaped up, went to the window, and saw an orderly trudging toward the casualties' shelter, where the pressure lanterns flared.

"It's all right, it isn't her," she whispered.

Michael got out of the chair. "It will be next time. I must go."

"You could stay," she pleaded. "We could talk a while longer."

He silenced her with a subdued laugh. "I'm afraid that talking isn't what we would do."

That declaration made her feel wanted, even irresistible, but it was a poor consolation. She stood in the doorway and watched him stride across the hospital grounds, into the enveloping shadows. He didn't look back. She shut the door, afraid that if she left it open another second, she would succumb to a reckless impulse to run after him. She got into her sleeping bag. A faint growl of thunder sounded in the distance, rousing a hope that it would rain hard all night and wash out the airstrip and strand her here indefinitely. That wasn't likely, she couldn't rely on circumstance, she would have to find a way to return; and looking at the roof beams, she began to scheme how to do it.

"MY MAN! COFFEE'S ON!"

Sitting on his sleeping bag under the Gulfstream's wing, Fitzhugh ignored Douglas's cheerful summons, although he needed some caffeinating after a night of fractured sleep and fearful dreams inspired by the previous day's events. The contents of the nightmares had mercifully fled his mind as soon as he woke up, a quarter of an hour before sunrise. Terror lingered in him for a while longer but dissipated as the sun bulged out of the crenulated mountains, magnified to twice its high-noon size, its sharply slanting light heightening the shades of ochre and terra-cotta in the earth and rocks. Feeling like an astronaut who'd landed on some austerely beautiful planet, he gazed at the scene in blank-minded admiration until thoughts of Diana intruded and, so to speak, brought him back to earth.

The horror of seeing her covered in blood, the elation of discovering that it wasn't hers had shredded his notion to live their affair in the moment, shocked into an awareness of the depth of his love and into recognizing the truth that a serious romance cannot abide stasis; it must go in one direction or the other. Grow or die. Having no wish to allow the relationship to die, he would have to nurture its growth, which meant working toward marriage or some arrangement unsanctioned by law or clergy. The trouble was, the picture of them sharing a roof and bed was as fuzzy as ever; indeed, he couldn't see it at all, much as he wanted it. His desire for children was the biggest obstacle. That was curious; he hadn't given fatherhood much consideration before he'd become involved with Diana; it had been an abstraction. Now it had become a concrete issue, because to fulfill his love would be to foreclose on the possibility. He'd spoken about none of this to her. She was the one who seemed content with things as they were, happy to carry on in the present.

"Yo! Fitz! Get it while it's hot!"

He looked through the web of camouflage netting and across the runway toward Douglas, squatting beside a smoking campfire with Suleiman and the soldiers guarding the plane. There were times, and this was one, when his friend's sunny voice, his exuberance, got on Fitzhugh's nerves. Americans—now there was a people who managed to live in the future and in the here and now at the same time. To them, the future *was* the here and now.

He recalled a conversation he'd had with Malachy about Douglas's "cool idea" to save the Nuba. They concluded—somewhat reluctantly—that only an American could have come up with such a scheme, only an American could have had the confidence and enthusiasm to see it through. And so the discussion turned from Douglas to Americans in general. Malachy, who had relatives in the United States and visited there often, opined that they were an optimistic people with an almost childish faith in themselves and in the future because they lacked a tragic sense, not because America had never experienced tragedy but because Americans refused to admit that tragedy existed. Slavery and the Civil War and the Great Depression and the Vietnam War hadn't shaken their conviction that tomorrow would be better, and if it failed to deliver, the next day would. And why was that so? Fitzhugh inquired. Americans believed in a radiant tomorrow, Malachy replied, because they possessed an uncanny ability—it was a kind of self-induced amnesia combined with a deliberate blindness—to forget the bad things that had happened yesterday and to ignore the bad things that were happening today. He remembered being in the United States in the aftermath of Vietnam and the hostage crisis in Iran, the pall cast by those disasters darkened by a recession, inflation, the menacing shadow of the Soviet Union on the march in Afghanistan. What had America's president said to all this? What did that smiling movie actor tell his people? "It's morning in America!" And what did his people reply? "Why, yes it is!" Of course it wasn't morning in America, but Americans couldn't see that, dazzled by the illusory sunrise summoned up by the smiling actor. And look at where they are now! said Malachy. Richer than ever, victors in the cold war, the envy of all the world! Do you see, my old friend? It became morning in America because Americans willed it to be so.

"If Muhammad won't come to the coffee, then the coffee's got to come to Muhammad."

Holding a steaming tin mug in each hand, Douglas parted a flap in the netting and joined him under the wing. "Just the way you like it. Three sugars."

With the tip of his tongue, Fitzhugh tested the mug's rim for heat before he took a sip. "Two is how I like it."

"Lousy, isn't it? I got it from the compound's mess. You know what Wes always says about the coffee in Kenya."

" 'How come in a country where such fine coffee gets grown, the stuff tastes like it was filtered through a secretary's pantyhose after a ten-hour day?' " Fitzhugh said, attempting Dare's country-boy twang. "His figures of speech are very colorful. He said that once to Rachel in the office. She didn't appreciate it."

Douglas combed his days-old beard with his fingertips. It became him, maturing his undergraduate looks. "But he's right. You can't get a decent cup in Nairobi or anywhere. That gave me a really cool idea. I'm going to mention it to Hassan, see if he thinks it could fly. We open a coffee shop in Nairobi, kind of like a Starbucks back in the States. Serve cappuccino and espresso besides regular coffee. Cheap. If it goes over, we open another, build a local chain."

This early in the morning it was difficult to keep up with Douglas's inspirations.

"Diversify," he added. "We've got to do something with Knight Air's profits besides park them in a bank, so we put the money to work in another enterprise. Really good coffee at reasonable prices. Everyone benefits."

"Only you could find something socially redeeming about a chain of coffee shops."

"What is it, my man? You seem a little on edge. Look, I know you're thinking about what happened yesterday—"

"Actually, I was thinking about something else."

"I was thinking the same thing," Douglas carried on, not listening. "The NGOs will be scared of committing to the Nuba. Too dangerous. And that's what Khartoum wants them to think. Somebody tipped off the bad guys about what we were doing, so they figured to send a message, and a few dead relief workers would have been the way to send it, loud and clear."

"How do you know that?"

"I just know it." Then Douglas rested an encouraging hand on Fitzhugh's shoulder. "But I gave it some more thought this morning, and it came to me that things could work out just the opposite. Those people could be back in Loki right now, saying, 'We aren't going to be intimidated, things are really rough up in the Nuba, it needs all the aid we can send.' And if they're not saying that, that's how we should spin it when we get back. It's possible, I'm saying, that that mortar attack was the best thing that could have happened."

Pausing to absorb this remarkable statement, Fitzhugh lit a cigarette, his first of the day. "What you did yesterday impressed me, but you know, you make it hard for me or anyone to admire you completely. Because you have an unfortunate genius for saying things like you just now said."

He received in response the patented gaze, the disarming smile. "Hey, you don't really think I'm *happy* about these people getting killed and wounded, do you? All I'm saying is that some good might come out of it."

"Let's drop the subject. I was thinking about something else anyway. About Diana and me."

Douglas frowned. "Diana and you?"

"Barrett knows, so you might as well, too. We're involved."

"You're involved sex-wise?" Douglas asked, each word rising up the scale, the final one coming out in a high tenor of disbelief.

"I prefer love-wise. We're in love, and I was wondering where it'll lead to, if it can lead to anything."

In a parody of astonishment, Douglas slapped his forehead. "First Wes and Mary, now you and Diana. What the hell am I running? An airline or an odd-couple dating service?"

"Think of it as diversification," Fitzhugh remarked and, in an idle shift of his glance, noticed that Suleiman and the soldiers were standing in frozen postures, faces turned toward the sky. In a moment, Suleiman fell to his knees and scooped dirt onto the campfire to douse the smoke. He and Douglas heard it then—the low, uninflected growl of a high-flying Antonov.

The sound reduced everything else that was on their minds to triviality. They ran out from under the net and joined the soldiers in an apprehensive vigil, heads turning as they tracked the plane, a silvery cross in a powder-blue sky striated by cirrus clouds. It flew northward; then, with the leisured arrogance of an unchallenged bird of prey, it made a slow turn. The sound faded, but the plane was still visible as it overflew the hospital, several miles away, before turning again.

Douglas said, "I'm going to get Gerhard on the radio, tell him to start Michael and those girls back here right now."

Fitzhugh heard the growling noise once again. The plane had dropped in altitude. He fetched binoculars from his rucksack and saw the big, over-wing engine cells, the tailfins spread above the rear cargo door. The cargo door that doubled as a bomb bay. It was open. The soldiers had taken cover in the woods edging the airstrip, except for two, who'd leaped into a pit dug last night for their 12.7-millimeter machine gun, a weapon that had purely symbolic value against an aircraft flying at ten thousand feet.

It commenced another circle, descending farther as it headed eastward.

"Talked to the logistics dude, that Italian, Franco," Douglas called down from the cockpit window. "It flew right over them the first time around. Our people should be here—"

The muffled rumble of a bomb cut him off. In the distance a column of smoke roiled straight up and crowned out into a shape resembling a tree, one whose growth from sapling to full height was compressed into seconds, as in a time-lapse film. Fitzhugh felt a tremor beneath his feet as another tree rose, a third, a fourth, black and evil. Far above, flying slowly with its nose pitched up, the Antonov excreted the seeds.

"Jesus Christ, they're hitting the hospital!" Douglas hollered down. "I can't reach anybody!"

"Of course you can't if they're being bombed. Get out of there, Doug! We might be next!"

They sprinted into the woods and lay flat beside the soldiers, cradling their useless rifles. The pair in the gun pit crouched behind the twelve-seven, the barrel pointed skyward.

There was a brief silence, then another series of blasts, maybe half a dozen all together, the explosions and their echoes merging into a single thunderous roll. The earth vibrating under him, Fitzhugh could not imagine what it was like to be in the eye of that awful storm. Bombing a hospital, in the name of Allah, the most merciful, the most loving-kind. The difference between hearing about such barbarism and witnessing it was the difference between a vexatious rumor and a monstrous, undeniable fact. The one provoked distress, perhaps questions as to how humankind could pervert religion to such demonic ends; the other provoked purest outrage.

The last echoes of the last bomb died away, the plane flew on, and the morning's quiet was restored. The men emerged from the woods to see soot-colored shoals spread over the hills to the east and flames flashing intermittently in a dark funnel, whirling like a stationary tornado. They stared in silence. Fitzhugh thought of Ulrika and Gerhard, poor man, his illusion of the hospital's exemption blown to dust, and maybe he'd been, too; of Quinette, Lily, Michael, and all those wounded yesterday, delivered from one horror into another.

"Tell me what good you think will come of this," he said, pushing his face to within inches of Douglas's.

"Stay chilly, my man," the American said, then walked away and climbed back into the Gulfstream.

Remaining outside, Fitzhugh could hear him through the open cockpit window, trying to reach the hospital on the radio, the same words over and over.

IN A CLEFT between two large boulders, she lay with her face crushed into the dirt and her hands clamped to her ears and Michael's body pressing down on her.

"It's finished with," she heard him say through a high-pitched ringing, and felt his weight lifted from her as he stood up.

Finished with? The air raid had been so far beyond anything in her experience, beyond anything she could have imagined, that it would never be finished with, not to her. The ringing continued, shrill and unmodulated. The bombs had set it off, exploding with a noise that had penetrated her skin until it seemed to be coming from inside her.

"Quinette, you must get up."

She rose to her hands and knees. He helped her the rest of the way. A slight trembling passing through her legs, she leaned against one of the high rocks and stared, hardly blinking, at Michael and his radio operator, both men looking at her with expressions that asked, Are you all right? They meant, Is anything broken, are you bleeding, can you walk, can you see? That was what mattered to soldiers accustomed to war's terrors. Any other form of trauma was irrelevant. She understood this, so she said, "I'm okay."

Michael brushed the dirt from her face. "We must see if there's anything we can do."

She tried to spit the dirt from her mouth, but she didn't have any spit. "Can you give me a minute?"

"All right."

"Do you have a cigarette?"

He spoke to the radio man, who produced rolling papers and tobacco from a shirt pocket and rolled one. He struck a wooden match under his thumbnail and lit it, taking a drag before passing it to her. It was strong tobacco, and the first dizzying puff was like the first she'd ever taken, when she was thirteen—a Salem, she remembered. How odd that she could recall the brand, while her recollection of the past however-many-minutes-it-had-been (twenty? thirty? ten? five?) was like the recollection of a dream.

They'd gathered for breakfast at a table on a platform of baked mud behind Manfred's house, near a lemon grove—she remembered that much—and Michael saying "Antonov!" when the plane flew over the first time, and the doctor, bleary with exhaustion, for he'd been operating till two in the morning, telling him not to be alarmed, planes routinely flew over the compound. On its second pass the Antonov was much lower, and someone shouted, "Cover the solar panels!" and the guy called Franco came out of the radio room, calling to her, Lily, and Michael to get in a Land Rover and make for the airstrip. No. That wasn't the right sequence. Franco had spoken to them first, and then the plane came in. Lily had gone for her rucksack while Quinette, Michael, and the radio operator started toward the vehicle. That was when the first bombs struck a village across a narrow valley, maybe half a mile away. Michael seized her by one hand, the radio man by the other, and ran with her downhill, so fast her feet nearly left the ground. How they'd gotten here, into this crevasse in the rocks, she didn't know. Her only memory was of bomb bursts becoming one enormous eruption and of the ground shaking and metal falling from the sky, clattering against the rocks.

The next few puffs went down easier than the first. The tobacco stitched her nerves back together, tuned the ringing down. She heard the loud crackle of flames, smelled burning wood and rubber and diesel fuel and a stench she'd not smelled before but somehow knew was burning flesh.

"Lily! Did you see Lily?"

"I don't know," Michael answered. "Come, we've got to see what we can do."

She followed the two men up the hill, thinking that she ought to embrace them for saving her life, but for now it was all she could do to put one foot in front of the other. Reaching the top, they beheld a scene as arresting as a spectacular vista; it was as if horror and ugliness, when taken to this extreme, achieved a kind of beauty. Fuel drums for the hospital generators had burst, creating pools of fiery liquid; flames engulfed one of the Land Rovers, the other was flipped onto its roof, its tires four torches. Smoke twirled in plumes that wove together, forming a fog that turned the sun into a pale wafer. Through the smoke, people staggered blindly or crawled on all fours, some making inarticulate sounds, most stunned into silence. Ulrika's cottage had been obliterated; so had the adjoining cottage and radio room. The new tin roof of Manfred's house, a little distance away, had been peeled back and the breakfast table blasted into several pieces. Passing through the lemon orchard—the trees askew and stripped of leaves, shards of broken breakfast crockery littered everywhere—they came to the medical wards, or what had been the medical wards. Huge craters gaped in the courtyard once formed by the two long bungalows and the adjoining breezeway. All that remained were mounds of mangled tin, broken roof beams, charred mattresses, twisted metal bed frames, shining fragments of solar panel, and bodies and parts of bodies almost indistinguishable from the rubble. They found Ulrika, down on her knees, tearing at the wreckage bare-handed. Covered in soot, she ordered them to help her, there were people in there, Franco was in there, Franco had been covering up the panels when the bombs fell . . . Michael yanked her upright and told her that it was pointless, no one buried in that mess could be alive. After a few moments she said yes, they must save who could be saved, they must find the Herr Doktor. They went off, passing sights Quinette knew would provide the raw material for very bad dreams—and found Manfred at the pediatrics ward. It, the nearby dispensary, and the X-ray hut were the only structures to have escaped the high-explosive wrath, though shrapnel had flagellated the walls. A short distance away, in the encampment where the families of patients stayed, women ululated, and those trilling shrieks, mingling with the cries of children inside the ward, were almost more than Quinette could bear. "See what they do to us," Michael murmured, his jaw tightening, "see what they do."

Manfred, squatting down, was examining a woman who sat in the pediatrics doorway, holding an infant with blood running out of its ears. Its eardrums must have been broken by the explosions, but the doctor had his stethoscope on the child's knees. He listened attentively, then moved the instrument to its chest, its tummy, its forehead. He tapped its elbows and back before pressing the stethoscope to the mother's bosom and, after listening to her heartbeat for several seconds, told her that she was fine and so was her baby. He spoke in English. Quinette doubted the woman would have understood him in any language, for her ears were bleeding as well.

"I will give you something for that bleeding later," he went on, "but now I have a more serious case to attend to."

"Herr Doktor?" Ulrika said.

He turned, revealing a big purple lump on his temple, and looked up, presenting a peculiar smile. "Ah! Ulrika, Quinette. I am glad you have come. Don't worry about this mother and daughter. They are doing splendidly. But you can help me with Lily, a more serious case, but I believe I can save her."

"Gerhard, you have been hurt!"

He touched the lump and looked quizzically at his fingers, as if he hadn't been aware of his injury. "This? Nothing. I believe I knocked my head when I dove into the bomb crater. Ha! I saw it, and I knew no two bombs will strike the same place twice. Like lightning, *nicht wahr*? And so I ran for it. Run, run, I said to Lily. We ran together, but I was the faster." He scowled. "Lily, yes, the more serious case, but with your help, she can be saved. Come with me."

With a stiff mechanical gait, he went around the corner of the building and picked up, by the knees, a pair of short white legs severed raggedly at the thighs and, carrying one in each hand, walked off toward the X-ray hut. Quinette's head swam, an acidic bubble lodged in her throat.

Manfred shouldered the door open and dropped the limbs beside Lily's truncated corpse, lying face-up, staring with wide eyes of sightless green, her mouth open in a frozen scream, and two splintered ivory staves protruding from the stumps of her thighs.

Quinette choked as the bubble popped. The dead outside were strangers, but this was irreverent, competent Lily, brimming with life such a short time ago. Quinette knelt and brushed her palm over the still, startled eyes, closing them.

"You're so cold," she sobbed. "Aw, Lily, Lily . . ."

And do you still believe this icy, dismembered thing was the home of an immortal soul? the Enemy chuckled. *There is no soul, no heaven or hell for it to go to, no God.* She was being tested again, much harder than yesterday. She mustn't fail! *If you exist, then God does, too!* she shot back triumphantly.

"Stop that crying," Manfred said. "I need your help, Miss Hardin."

Dropping to his knees, he took Lily's left leg, joined its bone to the exposed bone in the stump, then pulled up the flaps of skin, making a seam that resembled a jagged cut. He did the same with the right leg, which took less time because it had been severed more cleanly. Everyone watched with morbid fascination, indulging him in his madness until he called for sutures and his surgical needle.

Letting loose in German—"Gerhard! *Herr Doktor! Mein Gott! Bitte!*"—Ulrika grabbed him by an arm. He shook free. From behind, she hooked him under the arms and tried to drag him away, but he resisted. She couldn't budge him.

"Michael, you must help me with this man."

A profound serenity coming over her, Quinette motioned to Michael to hold off. She knew what to do. It was like that time, which seemed a hundred years ago, when she spoke to the liberated slaves and somehow knew what to say. That kind of certainty.

"Leave him be," she said to the nurse.

Ulrika let him go and backed away and began to cry.

"Thank you, Miss Hardin. Now we can get to work! Suture! Needle!"

She passed him these imaginary items. Raising his hands, he mimed threading the needle, then, bent over, began to sew Lily back together. Stitch by stitch, he made every movement as if it were real filament and a real needle in his hands. He knotted off a suture and called for another of a different gauge. Quinette gave it to him, humming softly to him as he worked.

"What is that tune, Miss Hardin?"

"An American spiritual. Shall I sing it for you?"

Frowning in concentration, he pulled an invisible thread through the skin and tied it off. "Yes, if you please."

" 'There is a balm in Gilead to make the wounded whole,' " she crooned, thinking, *Yes, let's make Lily whole again, even if it's make-believe.*

" 'There is a balm in Gilead to heal the sin-sick soul.' " *God will overlook the deception when on that great gettin' up morning He shall raise Lily and all the righteous dead to walk, souls and bodies reunited, in perfect beauty.*

"How are the patient's vital signs?"

She pretended to look at a monitor and replied that the vital signs were normal.

"Excellent. I am almost finished with this leg."

And singing again, " 'Sometimes I get discouraged and think my work's in vain,' " Quinette rose and gripped Manfred under one arm. " 'But then the Holy Spirit revives my soul again.' " She pulled easily and, feeling no resistance from him, pulled with more force. He straightened his back and looked down at his patient.

"So you're finished with that one, Dr. Manfred?"

"Yes, I believe I am."

"You'll need a break before starting the next one. You don't want to make a mistake."

"Yes, of course. A little rest. In surgery like this, one must be very precise."

At a nod from Quinette, Ulrika took the doctor under his opposite arm. Together they lifted him to his feet and led him outside.

FITZHUGH SAT IN the cockpit, the voiceless wind in his earphones ominous and irritating. He looked fixedly at the radio as if through sheer concentration he could force it to give the response that Douglas's incantations had so far failed to produce. "Zulu Two Hotel, this is Foxtrot Twelve, do you read me, over." Pause and repeat the call. Switch from the hospital's frequency to Michael's. "Archangel, Archangel, this is Foxtrot Twelve, do you read me, over." Pause and repeat, but the answer was the same sibilant static.

It was seven-fifty, half an hour since the air strike. With his habitual pessimism, Fitzhugh feared no one was left alive to answer their calls.

Douglas pulled his headset off and said, "Okay, that's it. We go in for a look."

Fitzhugh was relieved; any form of action was preferable to waiting. He stuck his head out the window, calling down to Suleiman to remove the camouflage netting. Suleiman and the soldiers went to work while Douglas, with movements that reminded Fitzhugh of a pianist playing a complicated score, readied the plane for takeoff. Then came the jarring roll, the sensation of lightness as the wheels left the ground.

"I'll make the pass from the north, into the wind," Douglas said, pulling into a climb. "Two hundred feet at stall plus twenty, like an airdrop. You'll be my eyes. That low and that slow, I'll want to keep mine on the road."

On the approach, Douglas dipped the right wing to give Fitzhugh a better view. The destruction was worse than he'd feared. Through a thin canopy of smoke, bomb craters, pulverized buildings, and puddles of fire passed below. He caught the glint of twisted tin roof. The new tin Knight Air had delivered months ago to replace the makuti in which snakes and spiders nested. The shiny metal, combined with the solar panels, must have made highly visible targets. That would explain the air strike's accuracy. Thus the tin that had eliminated the danger of the patients suffering a bite had drawn the bombs that obliterated them in their beds. The law of unforeseen consequences was still in effect.

"See anybody moving around down there?" Douglas asked.

"Yes, but I couldn't tell how many or who."

"I'll come around lower."

They were above the savannah south of the hospital, the very one they had crossed on foot, in what seemed like another lifetime. Fitzhugh remembered that grueling night march and the festivities in Kowahla the following night. He remembered the bewitching moment when Suleiman's youngest wife had flung her braids over his face and how, after he'd danced with her, he felt that he'd made a commitment to her and, through her, to all the people in these war-stricken mountains.

Coming in at a hundred feet and straight on, he could make out bodies strewn everywhere, like so much blown trash. Douglas cursed the fanatics who'd committed this atrocity; Fitzhugh cursed right along with him. The two men were in tune once again. Climbing away, banking tightly, descending again, they buzzed the compound a third time and spotted someone near a cluster of intact buildings, waving his arms at the oncoming plane. It was Michael.

Douglas wagged the wings. A moment later the radio came to life: "*Foxtrot Twelve, this is Archangel.*"

"You are loud and clear, Archangel! We've been trying to contact you. What's the situation?"

Ghastly was what it was. Franco and Lily dead, Manfred slightly injured but in severe shock. Michael couldn't estimate how many others had been killed or severely injured. He was going to collect the survivors and the walking wounded and lead them to the airstrip on foot. Both Land Rovers had been destroyed, so those who couldn't walk would have to be left behind.

"We'll see about that," Douglas said, after pausing to absorb this information.

They arrived at a little past noon, faces plastered in dust and sweat: Michael trailed by Ulrika and Manfred, shoulders slumped, head held low, Quinette following with the radio operator and two orderlies, still clad in their smocks. They were carrying a body on a stretcher, covered by a blanket and attended by an assembly of eager flies whose buzzing was audible from several yards away. Lily's pale arms hung over the sides and flopped back and forth in a disturbingly lifelike way. After setting her down at the side of the runway, Quinette and her fellow stretcher-bearers hurried into the shade of the Gulfstream's wing. Her face was blanched. The water bottles in her fanny pack were drained. Fitzhugh passed his canteen to her. She nearly emptied it in one gulp, poured the rest over her head, and thanked him. He noticed that there was something different about her, a taut, drawn quality that accentuated the planes of her cheekbones. She lay down without a word. In two minutes, she was asleep.

Ulrika meanwhile attended to Manfred, sitting with his chin on his chest and his hands lying listlessly in his lap. Michael described what had happened to him. When he'd refused to leave the hospital and insisted on completing his "operation," the nurse fetched a tranquilizer and syringe from the dispensary and sedated him. As difficult as it was to like him, Fitzhugh would have given anything to see him restored to his voluble, irascible self.

Quinette stirred, making an unintelligible sound. A remarkable young woman, said Michael. (Fitzhugh traded glances with Douglas as Michael placed a hand on her forehead and then stroked her long brown hair.) She would not allow her friend's remains to be left behind. He had objected—carrying the body for ten kilometers would be exhausting—but Quinette prevailed, saying that she couldn't live with herself if she didn't try. Michael occasionally spelled his radio operator or one of the orderlies, but Quinette wouldn't accept relief. She clung to the stretcher pole for that entire punishing walk.

The survivors straggled into the airfield for the next half hour. There weren't many, and Michael said he would bring them to New Tourom, where they could either stay or make their way back to their home villages. Their injuries were slight enough to be treated by field medics from his headquarters. As for the badly wounded he'd been forced to abandon . . . he shrugged.

"They're going to be taken care of," Douglas said, and revealed that he and Fitzhugh had spent the past three hours organizing a medical evacuation by radio. Alexei and his crew would be arriving about an hour from now, with Knight Air's pickup truck in the cargo bay. The casualties would be shuttled from the hospital to the airstrip in the truck. Alexei would then fly them to the Norwegian People's Aid hospital in Chukudum, to avoid hassles with the Red Cross and Loki officialdom. It was all set up. Michael had only to order Suleiman and the soldiers to remain here to assist in the evacuation.

"You will need someone to make the triage," Ulrika interjected. "So I too will stay."

Quinette sat up abruptly and said she would as well.

"You will not!" Michael commanded.

She gave him a reproving look, and to soften his tone, he added half humorously, "After all, I am the military commander here. What I say goes, and I say you go back to Loki."

Douglas said, "All right, Ulrika, you'd better put the doctor on the plane with us and come along. We're going to have to get him to Nairobi."

Manfred broke his drugged silence and said in a slow, thick voice, "I am not going to Nairobi."

"Herr Doktor, you need rest." The redoubtable nurse turned to the American. "I will not go with you. I will stay here to make the triage and then go with Michael to New Tourom and continue as best as I am able. Perhaps, with some help, we can build someday there a new hospital. We must. Now the people have no choice but to go to the government's camps when they are sick."

"Yes. I think that was why the bastards committed this crime," Michael declared, "but what good will it do to build a new hospital?"

"*What good?*" Quinette asked rhetorically. "So the bastards don't get the satisfaction, that's what good it would do."

"Building a hospital is not the way to deny them the satisfaction." Michael leaned out from under the wing to glance at the mercilessly clear sky, then faced Douglas and Fitzhugh. "I thank you for everything you've done these months. All the Nuba thank you. The seed you have brought, the tools, the implements, the clothes, the oil presses, the medicines, the clean water—very nice. And I saw that you brought us some Bibles this time. Also very nice. The spirit must be taken care of, too. And all the things you delivered to Dr. Manfred, very, very nice. The X-ray film he needed, the malaria medicines, the fuel for his generators—"

"The tin for the roofs," Fitzhugh interrupted, just to get in a word.

"The tin. Yes, the tin roofs. But where is the tin now? What's happened to the X-ray film? Blown up, burned. Why? Because you cannot shoot down a bomber with a Bible or an oil press. You cannot destroy the airfield the bomber leaves from with a hoe or X-ray film. What is the point of bringing all those things to us if the government can do what it did today anytime it wishes?"

He conferred on the two men from Knight Air a solemn, inquisitive gaze, and Fitzhugh realized that the question he'd just asked wasn't the question on his mind.

"Twenty-five hundred meters, three thousand," he resumed. "The plane was no higher than that. With heavy antiaircraft guns or shoulder-fired missiles, we could have brought it down. But you see there—" gestured languidly at the machine gun—"the biggest gun we have got. Good for shooting the helicopters, but against the Antonov, the MIG, it's no better than a spear. And of course that's all some of my fighters have got. Spears. We fight an enemy who has got helicopter gunships and Antonovs and cluster bombs and we have spears! Whatever else we have is just enough to defend ourselves, and not even enough for that, as you have now seen this day."

Douglas extended his legs and leaned back on his hands, the relaxed posture out of phase with the attentive look on his face. Michael continued.

"You see, to Garang and the high command, the Nuba front is not the central front. It's a sideshow. They send us arms and equipment, but most of it, the best stuff, Garang keeps for himself and his Dinka commanders. But there is another difficulty." With his walking stick, he made some marks in the dirt. "Here is the Nuba, down here the Sudan border with Uganda. Most of the military assistance the SPLA receives comes through Uganda. The Uganda government is our ally, and the Sudan side of the border is firmly under SPLA control, but it is more than one thousand kilometers from the Nuba. So what few military supplies Garang does send to me must travel overland, and you can imagine what happens to them along the way. Local commanders help themselves, bandits steal it."

From its length and coherence, it was obvious that this speech wasn't entirely impromptu. These were thoughts he'd been considering for a while.

"You should tell them, Michael," Quinette interjected suddenly. "Why don't you just come right out with it and tell them?"

She was gazing off into the middle distance with an expression like an injured wildcat's—a ferocity mingled with pain, in which there was both an appeal for comfort and a warning that you might get bitten or scratched for your trouble. *This*, Fitzhugh thought, as if seeing her for the first time, *could be a dangerous woman.*

Michael gave her a reproving glance, then back at the two men. "We need your help. Can you give it?"

And Fitzhugh seemed to be seeing Michael for the first time. At any rate, he wasn't the same lyre-playing, ballad-singing man who'd presented himself on their first meeting nearly two years ago. He was more calculating. He'd been waiting for the right moment for his proposal to fall on receptive ears. He could not have asked for a better moment than now.

Douglas looked at Ulrika, who was within earshot. "Michael, Fitz, why don't we take a walk?"

They all three started down the airstrip, heat shimmers rising under the vertical sun, Michael tapping his walking stick. With each step Fitzhugh felt that he and Douglas were approaching a boundary, poorly marked but there all the same.

"I have to ask this," Douglas said. "Where would the money come from?"

"You are referring to the . . . shall we call them delivery charges?"

"Let's call them that."

Tap-tap-tap went the stick. "From the SPLA. We have representatives in Uganda. I would put you in contact with them. They would inform you of when and where the cargo is to be picked up, and pay the charges."

"I want you to know that after what I've seen, I'd do it for nothing if I could, but I can't."

"Charity isn't what I'm looking for," Michael said, paused, and pointed his stick at the plane. "Nothing at all can be done without that. Everything depends on what you decide to do, Doug-lass."

It was just the sort of comment to flatter the American's ego, his sense of himself as the essential man. He turned to Fitzhugh. "What do you think?"

Fitzhugh said nothing. It came to him that his old self would not have taken this walk, a short one in terms of distance, a long one in other terms; but the old Fitzhugh Martin had disappeared during the last twenty-four hours.

"For my part, yes," he said at last. "But other people would be involved."

"Yeah, I've got to talk this over with my partner before I decide anything," Douglas said, but Fitzhugh knew the decision was already made, the boundary crossed.

They heard then a distant droning in the sky. Alexei's green and white Antonov was approaching on its base leg. They quickly walked back to the Gulfstream. Quinette was standing under its nose, a question on her face. Michael nodded to her.

"Balm for Gilead," she said.

Mustang

DARE HAD COME to a conclusion about his partner: Doug was willing to do almost anything, but only after he persuaded himself that it was for the greater good of the human race. He was the kind of guy who would smuggle heroin, then tell you that heroin was a beneficial drug and expect you to believe that because he did. On the night of the day they returned to Loki, full of war stories, boiling over with moral outrage, Doug and Fitz huddled with Dare in Knight Air's office and filled him in on Michael Goraende's request. Marching from one end of the room to the other, Doug declared, in so many words, that running guns into the Nuba was a sacred duty. Humanitarian aid was no longer the solution to humanitarian problems. Antiaircraft guns and shoulder-fired missiles would transform the Nubans from victims into a people in full command of their destiny. He soared right into the rhetorical ionosphere, comparing them to free wild Indians and the people who hung around the UN feeding centers in the south to tame reservation Indians. "If I'd been around in the Old West," he said, "I would have armed Crazy Horse!"

Fitz, whom Dare had credited as being more sensible, was just as carried away. No doubt he would have been less inspired if the bombs had fallen on a military target instead of on a hospital. To Dare's mind, that didn't add up. Imposing rules on war—the Geneva Conventions and all that bullshit—was as silly as posting traffic signs at the Daytona Speedway. Once the bars were down, human beings were capable of any crime, and it was a waste of time to expect them to behave themselves. That was why the bars had been put up in the first place.

So he didn't share in his colleagues' indignation. The closest he could come to it was the feeling that he owed the Nubans something, for leaving them that day when the murahaleen attacked the airfield at Zulu Two. He said, "Enough of this shit. Let's get down to fundamentals. First off, who pays us and how much?"

"We've worked that out with Michael," Fitz answered, hooded in cigarette smoke. "The SPLA is the client, eighteen thousand per flight, that's twice what we get for flying nonlethal stuff."

"Okay, second off, where do we pick up the hardware?"

"It's funneled through the Ugandan Defense Ministry. Ugandans bring it to the border, then it's smuggled over to SPLA airstrips on the Sudan side. That's where we pick it up."

Doug opened the door and, waving his ball cap, tried to shoo the smoke outside. "Wes, we aren't telling you all this out of courtesy," he said. "We need you. Michael needs you."

"Well, ain't that nice. How so?"

"Garang just gives him leftovers. He needs his own suppliers. We thought you could help in that department."

"Reckon I could. There's a guy I flew with in Blackbridge Services. He could get Michael the heavy weapons he wants, and get them quicker, cheaper than anybody else."

"Outstanding!" Doug said, shutting the door. "That is *outstanding.*"

Before going any further, Dare was compelled to apprise his colleagues of certain realities. Number one—"and beg your pardon for talkin' to you like y'all are children, but when it comes to this, that's what you are"— both the UN and the Kenyan government winked at flying humanitarian aid into Sudan's no-go zones because it wasn't really "flying on the dark side but kind of the gray side." But smuggling weapons—now that was serious contraband, and if the UN found out about it, Knight Air would be banned from Loki in a heartbeat. As for the Kenyan government, well, it was sensitive about its relations with Khartoum. It would have to take action to prove its good intentions, and that would mean revoking the company's certificate and prohibiting it from flying anywhere in the country. "That's the best that could happen," Dare went on. "Worst case is, Kenya arrests us to make an example of us, confiscates the company's assets, and then boots us out of the country, and we end up with the hole in the doughnut."

"We've considered that, we're not that dumb," Doug said, and pushed away from the door to stand face to face with Dare. "So do we tell Adid about this? This qualifies as a major business decision."

"He won't go for it," Dare said.

"The guy was an ivory smuggler. Why would he object?"

"He wouldn't have any moral objections, on account of he doesn't have any morals. This would be too risky, business-wise. For all the reasons I just now told you."

"Right," Doug said. "There's another reason we need you. How do we minimize the risks? You've done this kind of thing. The Contras in Nicaragua, other places I'd suppose."

"You'd suppose right," Dare replied, and took a step back, giving himself room to breathe and to think. Running guns appealed to the outlaw in his nature, but he also saw how such an operation could win him financial independence and a ticket out of Africa. "First thing we'd have to do is form a shell company," he said, and paused, twirling his sunglasses, collecting his ideas. "Let's call it Yellowbird Air. We incorporate it in Uganda. President is me, the plane is my Hawker. It's in my name, doesn't belong to the company. That way, in case things go wrong and this operation gets found out, Knight Air's hands are clean. It's a way of providing y'all with what the CIA calls 'plausible deniability.' "

Doug asked, "What about you?"

"I would take the fall."

"Out of your devotion to the cause?"

"I'll be comin' to that."

"All right, so this Yellowbird would be flying out of Kampala?"

Dare shook his head. The Ugandan capital was twice as far from the Nuba as Loki. "We would leave from here with, let's say, a half load or a quarter load of nonlethal aid. You don't want an empty plane flying out of here, somebody's bound to notice and wonder what's going on. Then we pick up the hardware on the Uganda border and head for the Nuba."

And what about invoicing? Fitz wanted to know. How was that to be handled?

"Simple. Me and Mary keep half the eighteen thousand, deposit the other half in a bank account in Kampala, then that bank wire-transfers it to Knight Air's account in Nairobi."

"You and Mary," Doug said.

"Only two people will make the gun runs. Me and her, and only five are gonna know what Yellowbird is up to—me and her and Nimrod. Y'all and Fitz make it five."

As Dare had anticipated, Doug protested the first part of this provision. His partner wanted to fly the arms himself, maybe for the thrill of it, probably for other reasons.

"You don't want a direct hand in this operation," he cautioned. "You're too emotional about this. All that crap about it being your obligation, and the Nubans like wild Indians off the reservation, Christ almighty. No room in a thing like this for that. Anyhow, y'all want me in it, that's the deal, most of it."

"Most? What's the rest?"

"I'll fly these runs for a set period, say, no less than six months. When I'm done, I'm gonna quit. Quit it all. Quit Africa. I cash in those company shares I got for sellin' my old G1 to the company. Half a million bucks."

"Fair enough, you're entitled to—"

"Hold on," Dare interrupted. "Remember when I said I'd rather have twenty tons of cold metal in my hands than pieces of paper? There's always the chance those shares won't make good ass-wipe in six months' time. In case that happens, the company agrees to transfer ownership of the airplane back to me."

Doug went pale. "What are you talking about?"

"No matter what happens, I get one of two things when I'm done— half a million in cash or the G1. That's the rest of the deal. You and me are gonna see my lawyer and sign a contract to that effect, and that contract is gonna say that in case the Gulfstream cracks up between now and then, you pay me with the insurance money."

"What about Adid?" Doug asked. "How do we explain why the company is handing over an airplane to you?"

"Y'all are a creative guy," Dare said, smirking. "You've got six months to think of an explanation."

"I can't agree to that," Doug said.

"Then I can't either. Think it over, Dougie boy."

Two days later he appeared at Dare's tent and said, "Okay to every-thing." But he added a codicil—as an added layer of protection, Dare was to resign as co–managing director. He would retain his shares but would not be affiliated with Knight Air's management. That would make a plausible deniability more plausible, if one were needed. After mulling the proposal over, Dare agreed to submit his resignation.

"THERE'S WHY I love flying. Groundhogs don't see things like that."

The rainbow that would have presented itself as a conventional arch to someone on the ground appeared to Dare and Mary as a full circle in the sky. She was still young enough to be wonder-struck by such unusual sights, a girlish luster in her eyes, a breathlessness in her voice. He'd thought the days when a woman could make his heart do athletic tricks were well behind him; like an aging quarterback after one too many sacks, its joints were too stiff. She'd restored its agility. Loving her, he felt younger and more hopeful and found himself seeing things as she saw them. Without her he would have noticed the rainbow, but he would not have appreciated the glory of it, shimmering above Uganda's cloud-shrouded forests.

Dare had rediscovered happiness, and this felicitous state of mind had overcome his aversion to a fifth marriage. It had also moved him to change the ad hoc ways that had governed, or rather, misgoverned, his nomadic life for the past thirty years. He was finished with improvising, finished with the slapdash structuring of his days; he was making plans for the future, clear, concrete plans, and the vision of the life he and Mary were going to lead together was as much a source as it was a product of his happiness.

He hadn't proposed yet. That would come in due time, when she'd gotten her fill of living dangerously, and he reckoned a few months of arms smuggling ought to accomplish that. He wasn't so besotted that he considered her acceptance a sure thing. On the other hand, it would not be as unlikely as drawing an inside straight. Not too long ago she had gone on a riff about having children. She wasn't, it was true, talking about having children with *him,* she was speaking in a general way, but it would take a lot to convince Dare that she wasn't dropping hints. He'd been tempted to blurt, "I'll be the daddy!" but that sort of frankness wasn't his style. He played it cautiously and talked back to her in the same general way, telling her that she had plenty of time yet, hell, an aunt of his had given birth at forty-six, back in the days when most country women that age were thinking about grandchildren, if they didn't have them already. Anyway, he figured that when he said, "Let's you and me get married and have kids," the odds of a yes would be in his favor. That would mean he'd have to follow through, and following through would mean he'd have to learn to like children, or at least not hate them.

The private contract between him and Doug had been drawn up and signed. In six months he would have either five hundred thousand cash or an airplane worth that much. If it turned out to be the airplane, he would sell it and the Hawker, which would bring in a total of seven hundred and fifty to eight hundred thousand. Pooling that with whatever sum he and Mary earned with Yellowbird would give them enough to buy a corporate jet. Then he would tap his old contacts in the music business and go back to flying name acts on tour. He would give himself three years as a pop-music chauffeur of the air. By that time he would be approaching sixty, but Mary would still be young enough to have a kid. They could open a flight school together, or maybe retire to a ranch he'd always wanted in the Texas hill country—he wasn't too clear on that part, it was too far in the future.

His main concern now was not to let his newfound happiness fog his judgment, that was to say, not let it blur the keen vision of his cynical eye, nor dull the keen ear that picked up Double Trouble's warning chirps and tweets. He'd been in love before, or thought he was—it amounted to the same thing—and knew that when you were in love with one person, you tended to love everybody. If you loved them, you naturally trusted them, a bad idea in Africa. He would need to keep his rule of thumb in mind: people did the right thing only when the wrong thing failed to present itself. In this part of the world, the wrong thing never failed to present itself, and to complicate matters, it usually came disguised as the right thing.

Entebbe tower gave him the okay to start his descent. The Nile, under an armada of clouds sailing at ten thousand feet, made a fragmented serpentine of brassy brown amid green hills. It was said to have had a redder color when Idi Amin was feeding his real and imagined enemies to the crocodiles—another glorious moment in modern African history. Half a year, give or take, and I'll be the hell out of here with about a million. Dare's mind leaped ahead again, painting a picture of him and Mary at the controls of a state-of-the-art airplane, jet engines whispering in the cold, incorruptible realms of high altitude. Flipping on the autopilot, sharing a drink in a lushly appointed cabin with celebrity passengers. Staying at the best hotels instead of some makuti-roofed hut or a tent with a cement-slab floor. Landing at fine airports instead of on dirt strips scratched out of the bush. Front-row complimentary seats at the concerts. Lost in these images, he flinched when the tower cleared him for final approach. He eased into his turn. The Hawker's shadow flowed over the boat-specked, wave-ribbed glitter of Lake Victoria.

For the next couple of days Dare commuted on foot between the Speke Hotel, the central post office, and the government ministries he'd been directed to on Parliament Avenue. Within a week he had a postal box address for Yellowbird Air Services and the papers, with all seals and stamps affixed, attesting that it was a Uganda corporation. He took another walk down to the Barclay's on Kampala Avenue, where he opened a confidential account and left instructions for wire-transferring funds to Knight Air's bank in Nairobi. His final step was a meeting with the SPLA agents in Kampala. Michael had transmitted their names in a coded radio message. Payment arrangements were made, signals worked out. It almost made him nervous for things to go so smoothly.

In between business errands, he and Mary played tourist, she accosting strangers to take snapshots or videos of them in front of the Nakasero market or at the Kasubi Tombs. In the cool evening air, they drank on the rooftop bar at the Afrique, strolled to Fang Fang's to eat Chinese or to the City Bar and Grill for tandoori, and then made love on the big bed in their room overlooking Jubilee Park. Lying beside her, he decided not to ask himself what he'd done to be so lucky, because there was no answer.

On their last night in the city, after another vigorous tumble, Mary jumped out of bed and got dressed, declaring that she wanted to party at the two hottest spots in town, Al's Bar and a disco called the Half London. Dare wasn't about to drag his spent body on a tour of nightclubs; they had a big day tomorrow. After a lot of back and forth, Mary, with an angry pout and some comment about him being an old fart, went out alone. He couldn't believe she was being so rash. He knew about those two places, hangouts for Kampala's working girls. Any woman, white or black, who went in there unescorted was advertising. He lay in bed for half an hour. Finally, feeling a need to assert some masculine power, he got dressed and taxied to the Half London, where an Afro-pop band was entertaining a boisterous crowd of local yuppies, hookers, and expats. Mary was dancing on the open-air dance floor with a slim young guy. Watching her sensual movements in the smoke-veiled lights, Dare was hurt that she could be having such a good time without him. When the number ended, she went to the bar with her partner, who put an arm around her waist. Dare was pleased to see her pull it off, but that gesture did nothing to calm his jealousy. He approached them from behind, heard the guy say, "Oh, come on, sweet," in a British or Australian or South African accent, and then tapped him on the shoulder and said, "That's it, Nigel, last dance." The Brit, Aussie, or South African said, "Who the hell are you?" Mary let out a squeal of inebriated delight. "He's my boss!" Dare added that he was a helluva lot more than that. "Like what?" said the guy, squaring off. This was ridiculous! It wasn't dignified, a middle-aged man about to get into a bar fight over a woman. That was avoided when the band started up again and Mary pulled him onto the dance floor, where he felt awkward and out of place. "I just knew I'd get you out! " she said with a wicked sparkle in her eyes.

She wanted to stay until the set was over. He insisted they go back to the hotel and in the end practically carried her out to the taxi park down the street. They argued during the ride, the argument continuing in the lobby, in the corridor, and into their room, where it degenerated into a shouting match, Mary slapping him when he told her that she'd been behaving like a tramp. He said, "Lucky you're a woman, or you'd be taking an eight-count right now." With a fierce, challenging look, she said, "Don't let that stop you!" That scared him because it reminded him of Margo, who expected men to be violent and, when they failed to meet her expectations, egged them on until they were. Dare had never laid a hand on her, and he wasn't about to break that precedent now.

Things took their natural course. He and Mary resolved their differences with their bodies—the old fight-and-fuck syndrome. In the morning, as they packed for the trip to Murchison Falls, she was remorseful. He responded with his own apologies, though he wasn't sure what he was apologizing for. His happiness returned, but absent its former purity. A slender vein of doubt had come into it. There were drawbacks to love with a much younger woman.

They had one major mission at Murchison—to touch base with Dare's old associate from Blackbridge, Keith Cheswick—and one minor mission—to photograph, for Doug's benefit, a rare bird called the shoebill stork. Cheswick had chosen Murchison for their meeting place because he was doing business just over the border, in the Congo. They checked in at a lodge in Paraa, where a fax from Cheswick was waiting for them: "Enjoy the view and the pool. Meet me tomorrow eight-thirty sharp at the dock. A launch reserved for us exclusively. We can talk shop and you'll have a good chance of spotting your bird. Cheers, K.C."

Over two years had passed since he and Cheswick had flown together in the Congo. Cheswick still had the look of the RAF fighter-pilot who was aging well: the trim gray mustache, the flat stomach, the dry iron eyes squinting out of a tanned face; but the peculiar stresses of the mercenary's calling had begun to extract a toll. His movements weren't as supple as before, and his shoulders were slightly stooped, not so much from the weight of years as from the weight of too many unpleasant experiences.

The launch, piloted by a skinny Ugandan in shorts and a cast-off park ranger's shirt, was a wooden craft with an awning that aspired to the decrepitude of the *African Queen*. As it chugged upriver, Mary, a laminated photo of a shoebill stork that Doug had given her on her lap, swept the shores with her binoculars, and the two men sat in the stern and discussed the subject at hand.

"I made a promise that I could get the client the stuff he wanted faster, cheaper than anybody else," Dare said. "SAM-sevens or Stingers, fourteen-point-seven- or twenty-millimeter triple-A guns."

Cheswick leaned back against his clasped hands. "Who's the client?"

"The SPLA."

"They're the end user?"

"End user certificate should be made out to the Uganda Defense Ministry. They transfer the goodies to the SPLA."

"I've got some Israelis, private dealers but with solid channels to the government, who have an interest in doing what they can to make life difficult for the Muslim brethren in Khartoum." Cheswick glanced at a hippo, its yawning mouth a garage for a Volkswagen. "I can do the SAMs for ten thousand, the Stingers would be twelve. The triple-A five to seven and a half. The client is good for the money?"

"They are. They've got an arrangement with the Defense Ministry."

"Quantity?"

"Half a dozen missiles to start with, launchers and projectiles. Triple-A—"

He was interrupted by the launch pilot, who exclaimed, "Elephant!" and pointed at a solitary bull standing on a ridge above the shore marshes. Cheswick signaled his thanks for the excellent guide work.

"Figure one dozen triple-A."

Like a clerk filling out an order blank, Cheswick wrote down the items and their quantities in a notebook. Whirlpools spun in the current and convex lenses of smooth water swelled as the great river pushed over rocks and humps on the bottom. The falls ahead made a sound like a high wind blowing through tall pine trees.

Mary came back from the bow, the camera with its long lens swinging at her side. "If you're interested, there one is," she said, raising her arm at a large bird standing vigil in the shallows against a backdrop of papyrus reeds. It had a big ugly head and a bill that looked as wide as a water ski. "I got the picture. Mission accomplished. Won't Doug be happy."

"Doug is—" Cheswick started to ask.

"My partner," Dare said. "He's a bird nut."

"I see. So, anything else? Cut flowers and canned sardines?"

Dare shook his head. "For now, the missiles and triple-A are priority."

"Cut flowers?" Mary asked. "Canned sardines?"

"Assault rifles and ammunition," Dare explained.

"We call them cut flowers," Cheswick elaborated, jotting in his notebook, "because cut flowers are the gift that keeps on giving. If you've ever seen a steel small arms ammunition box, you'll understand why canned sardines. Did you know that your shoebill stork eats baby crocodiles?"

Mary shook her head.

"It does, but not if Mummy croc is around."

"Big things eat little things, the whole story of Africa right there," Dare proclaimed with a kind of rueful glee.

As the launch swept around a bend, they saw the falls before them, crashing through a narrow gorge, thundering into a cauldron of frothing water and mists. Raising his voice, Cheswick said, "The whole story everywhere. The Africans just aren't as good at hiding it."

Redeemer

SHE'D BECOME SOMETHING of a celebrity, a minor-league heroine, what with her media friends interviewing her about what happened in the Nuba mountains and relief workers from every agency in Lokichokio asking to hear the story firsthand. Quinette didn't think she'd done anything heroic—she'd survived, nothing more—but she obliged them. After a while she had the tale down to a routine, like a stump speech or a nightclub act, the narrative flowing seamlessly, with dramatic pauses thrown in at the right moments, until she could go through it without feeling a thing except hatred for the criminals who'd murdered her friend and dozens of people in their hospital beds. She asked Jesus to forgive her for disobeying His commandment to love her enemy (and those Muslims were her enemy, the bombing had made her a naturalized citizen of this war); she prayed to Him to show her if there was anything more she could do, for she felt a keen desire to do more than she was. Her work didn't seem to be enough. She wished to be called to take bold, direct action, as Doug and Fitz had been. If she could fly a plane, she would have joined them tomorrow and soared to the Nuba with rifles and rockets for Michael Goraende's army.

Her thoughts often turned toward him. How gallant he had been, throwing his body over hers as the bombs fell. She recalled little things as well, like the way his head leaned a little to one side when he smiled, and the memory of their kiss flooded her mind at random moments, with such vividness that it wasn't a memory but a reliving, a kind of poignant flashback. She didn't know what to make of that kiss. Was it nothing more than the brief cleaving together of two people in desperate conditions? Two people, from places and cultures so alien to each other that they might as well come from different planets. We are literally black and white, she thought, then heard her friends back home questioning her in the crudest terms. *You kissed a nigger?* She was appalled to feel a flash of shame, and to realize that she was really asking that question of herself. Quinette did not like to think she was narrow-minded, but you could not grow up as she had without absorbing some of the prejudices that still prevailed in the rural Midwest. To overcome that part of herself, to repudiate it and the world from which she'd come, she determined to nurture her nascent attraction to Michael.

One night she tried to communicate with him telepathically. Those mental transmissions proving unsatisfactory, she wrote him a letter by flashlight, confessing that she wanted to see him again. It would be difficult, she wrote, and suggested he could help by sending an official request for her presence. She could show it to her boss, who was coming to Kenya soon in preparation for another redemption mission to Sudan. There was no mail service to rebel-held territory. Her intention was to have the letter hand-delivered by the next Knight Air pilot flying to the New Tourom airstrip; but on the way to the airline's offices the next day, she had second thoughts, tore the letter up, and went to her office.

The compound where she worked, an oasis of cleanliness and order amid Loki's squalor, was a mile and a half down an unpaved road from the one where she lived. Behind a thornbush fence, under the green umbrellas of tamarind trees, two stone bungalows faced each other across a dirt yard brightened by rosebushes and raked daily by an old Turkana gardener who looked as thin as his implement. She rode there on a one-gear bike she'd bought from Tara Whitcomb for ten dollars. The tall mzunga who dressed like an African had become a familiar sight to the shopkeepers and townspeople. *"Jambo, missy!"* they called to her, and she called back, *"Jambo sana! Habari ya asubuhi?"* pleased to hear herself speaking Swahili so fluently.

The compound housed the offices of logisticians for several Catholic dioceses in Sudan and of the South Sudan Relief and Rehabilitation Agency. From the latter, Ken had sublet a small room for Quinette's use. With its wooden schoolteacher's desk, its wood swivel chair, its dented metal file drawers, black desk fan, and straw mats covering the cement floor, it possessed the chaste, ascetic appeal of a convent cell. The attraction that Africa had awakened in her, to the spare, the austere, the basic, had deepened, and so had her abhorrence for the world she'd left behind, consumed by consumption, choking on its own excesses. The only object from that world to invade her cloister was the IBM desktop Ken had furnished. Brand-new twenty months ago, it was probably now as obsolete as the manual typewriter she used when the generator conked out.

Ken had told her that the next mission would be "all-important to the continuation of our efforts." He was coming with an entourage worthy of a heavyweight champ: besides the usual team—Jim Prewitt and the two

Canadians, Jean and Mike—there would be TV crews from the BBC, French Television, and PBS, as well as reporters and photographers from the *L.A. Times*, the *Chicago Tribune*, and the *Guardian*. The reason Ken was bringing so much media had to do with the bad press he'd suffered several weeks ago, when the United Nations Children's Fund produced a report condemning the buying back of slaves as "absolutely intolerable" and demanded an end to it. The report said that slavery in Sudan wasn't nearly the big deal he made it out to be, and that only a comparative handful of people were seized in traditional tribal clashes, not thousands in government-sponsored terror raids. What made Ken livid was the implication, voiced by a UNICEF bureaucrat in an interview, that the World-Wide Christian Union was exaggerating the problem as a fundraising gimmick. He fought back, and the upcoming trip was part of his battle plan. Quinette had been kept busy obtaining travel permits for the correspondents and cameramen, arranging for accommodations in Loki and for flights into and out of Sudan. She'd chartered Knight Air, which had upset Tara, but Doug and Fitz had performed so courageously in the Nuba that Quinette felt she owed it to them to give them some business.

The day before Ken's arrival, her logistical work done, she turned to her main task—compiling the massive database of manumitted slaves that would provide the raw material for Ken's monumental tome, *The Record of a Crime Against Humanity*. Although it had been in the works long before UNICEF made its report public, he'd decided to use it to rebut that organization's claims. He intended to present it to the UN Commission on Human Rights and to the U.S. Congress, overwhelming them with proof that slavery in Sudan was as enormous as he claimed, and he instructed Quinette to get it done as quickly as possible. Her job, often the purest form of clerical drudgery, was to create a dossier for every person liberated since the program began: name, age, sex, tribe, home village, date of capture, and photograph, along with the captivity narratives collected on each field mission. Sometimes she was amazed that so much pain, suffering, and degradation could be compressed onto data disks the size of her palm; she half-expected them to melt from the outrages they contained. When she returned from the field, she transferred the narratives from the laptop to her desktop and later edited the tales down to manageable length. Ken said each one should be no more than two hundred fifty words. As if it were a contest—in two hundred fifty words or less, please tell us what it was like to be enslaved.

So far the WorldWide Christian Union's campaign had freed more than eleven thousand people. Quinette had completed dossiers for exactly eight thousand six hundred twenty-two. Once the database was finished, she hoped Ken would keep her on. The idea of going home was beyond depressing. She couldn't imagine it, not now.

She worked most of the day, compiling twenty more dossiers, and spent the last two hours on another task: keeping the rolls of captured people up to date. Their names were submitted regularly by the local authorities in southern Sudan to the SRRA, which then passed them on to her. After each mission the identities of the freed slaves were cross-checked against the register, and their names struck from the list. When she was finished, she noticed something odd: of the one hundred and sixty captives liberated on the last mission, the names of more than thirty had never been reported as captured. True, the identity of every single person wasn't known; often three or four in a particular group would not be listed on the register. But thirty? That was unheard of. She was pondering what could have caused the discrepancy when she was interrupted by a knock. At the door was the stocky red-cheeked Russian who flew for Knight Air, Alexei.

"I was asked to bring this to you," he said, passing her an envelope with the emblem of the SPLA in the left-hand corner.

She thanked him, shut the door, and tore the envelope open.

HEADQUARTERS, WAR ZONE TWO
SUDANESE PEOPLE'S LIBERATION ARMY
5TH NOVEMBER.

Miss Quinette Hardin
WORLDWIDE CHRISTIAN UNION
LOKICHOKIO, KENYA

1. During your previous visit here, you told me about the work your organization does in redeeming and repatriating abducted persons in south Sudan.

2. I would be grateful if you could fly here at a time of your convenience to discuss establishing a similar program in this zone. As you know, large numbers of Nuba citizens have been seized in government raids and have been sold into slavery or are being held in internment camps.

3. Upon your favorable reply to this request, I will contact the SPLA liaison officer in Nairobi to issue you the necessary travel documents.

LT. COL. MICHAEL A. GORAENDE
OFFICER COMMANDING

An excitement beat in her chest. This was astonishing. Michael had done the very thing she'd suggested in the letter she'd never sent; it was as though her telepathy had worked, her thoughts flying through invisible wires across hundreds of miles. She read his summons again, then stuffed it into her dress and pedaled back to the Hotel California before it got dark. That's when the bandits came out, like bats.

Two MILK-FED Canadians with hair the color of the boundless wheat-lands where they'd learned to fly took Ken's party on a route that Quinette now knew by heart, out over the brown Mogilla range into Sudan, skirting Kapoeta and the Didinga hills to bear northwestward above red plains polka-dotted with trees and cracked by dry riverbeds, the plains surren-dering to the wild As-Sudd, a swamp so vast it took the better part of an hour to cross it by air, the Bahr el Ghazal and the Mountain Nile appear-ing to lie upon the marshes like golden serpents on a dark green mat, and then over the savannahs beyond, fading to yellow in this, the transitional month between wet season and dry, the landscape's small details erased by altitude until, west of the Jur, the plane descended through broken clouds, and the beehive roofs of Dinka homesteads appeared, and cattle could be seen plodding out of smoky cattle camps, the animals scared into a trot by the plane's shadow breaking over a palm grove moments before the wheels thumped against the runway and the propellers raised dusty cyclones that made the people waiting on the ground crouch and cover their faces with their cloaks.

"Kinnet! Kinnet!" teenage girls cried out as she stepped off the plane into the hot sun. "White Dinka Woman!" She basked in their adulation and couldn't resist embracing them for the benefit of the television cam-eras. Ken got his entourage organized, and then they trooped down the same rutted road on which Matthew had given Quinette a bike ride on her first journey into these immense spaces. She wondered how he was faring. Was he nearby, hobbling on his artificial limb, singing praises to his song-ox while its bell collar chimed and buffalo-hair tassels waved from the tips of its curved horns? Was he happy, now that he didn't have to fight? Sudan's uncongenial soil didn't yield great harvests of happiness. As for herself, Quinette felt vital rather than happy, with the aromas of an African early morning in her nostrils, her eyes alertly scanning the sky for danger, her ears pricked for the sound of an approaching Antonov, and her train of young admirers capering alongside, giggling, rubbing her arms to bring out the black they were sure lay beneath the white.

The mission did not go well. As a means of vindicating Ken and the WorldWide Christian Union, it was a disaster. The day before leaving Loki, he'd spoken by radio with his liaison man, Manute, who told him that four hundred and twenty slaves would be assembled—the largest number freed in a single day in the campaign's history. Ken knew the media—get them to think they were in on something special—but he should have kept his mouth shut.

The first sign that things weren't right came when the sweating foreigners were introduced to Manute and several local councilmen. The men had trouble making eye contact. One took Ken, Jim Prewitt, and Quinette aside and whispered, "I am afraid we have only forty-eight captives for you to redeem." He sounded like a grocer apologizing to a customer for a shortage of bananas. Ken blinked behind his schoolmaster glasses. What had happened to the other three hundred and seventy-two? The councilman's glance slipped sideways, then up, then down, as if the absent people had merely been misplaced. He shrugged and said he didn't know.

Ken was furious, Ken was embarrassed, but in the end, all Ken could do was try to put the best face on things. Quinette cringed sympathetically, listening to him tell the correspondents that there had been a mix-up. He tried to buy a little time, speculating that the captives had been delayed—it happened sometimes, what with the distances they had to cover on foot. Maybe they would show up later in the day or tomorrow morning. Meanwhile there were forty-eight people to be given their freedom, and the press were welcome to observe the ceremony.

In many ways redemptions had become routine, more a scripted process than a ceremony. First a count was made; then Ken, Jim, and Quinette addressed the slaves, Jim doing a little proselytizing, Quinette delivering her set speech quoting Isaiah: "I have come to proclaim liberty to the captives, and the opening of the prison to them that are bound." She had never tired of giving it, nor of the reaction it always elicited: the joyful clicking of tongues that was the Dinka way of applauding. This time was an exception. The four dozen people seated in the dust before her didn't make a sound.

In step four, Ken's "banker," Santino, brought out his airline bag full of money and exchanged it for Sudanese pounds. For this trip, the twenty-one thousand dollars that was to have purchased liberty for four hundred and twenty people required two bags, but now he needed to open only one, from which he counted out twenty-four hundred dollars—the price for forty-eight people. And so things proceeded to step five—paying off the retriever, who in this case was an Arab Quinette had never seen before, a shabby-looking man with none of the ornaments displayed by traders like Bashir with his rings and gold Rolex and Italian loafers.

Recording the captivity narratives was the final step. Manute chose ten people at random while Ken set up his tape recorder and Quinette sat on a camp stool with her laptop. It wasn't easy, with the reporters circled all around, pointing cameras, jabbing with microphones. The interviews went on for an hour. The final one was a woman in her mid-thirties who told a lurid tale of being repeatedly whipped on the back for refusing to have sex with her master. A French TV correspondent interrupted, asking her to show her scars for the camera. It was just the sort of disgusting, shameless request Quinette had come to expect from the press. Manute passed it on to the woman. A frightened look clouded her face. She turned to Manute, making a mute appeal. He spoke sharply to her. She shook her head. Quinette was appalled when Ken, desperate to salvage some dramatic moment from this failed exercise, encouraged her to do as asked. Again she shook her head, muttering almost inaudibly.

"She will not," Manute explained. "The marks are very ugly. She is ashamed."

"Nice, Ken," Quinette remarked in an undertone, closing the laptop. "Like these people are in a freak show?"

Ten minutes later, while Jean and Mike were giving the former slaves medical exams, the French reporter came up to her and said, "She is not so ashamed now." He cocked his angular chin at the woman, standing with the back of her dress unbuttoned, while the nurse examined her with a stethoscope. "They do not always tell you the truth, these people?" the Frenchman asked. Suddenly Manute's furtive glances and the slaves' silent indifference to her speech made sense. So did the discrepancy she'd found in the records. Feeling vaguely sick and angry at the same time, she approached Ken, who was giving an interview to the *L.A. Times.* When he was finished, she said, "I need to talk to you. Not here, not now. When we get back to Loki."

On the return flight, she argued with herself which of the two topics on her agenda to bring up first. Should she lead off with her suspicions, or show him Michael's letter and ask for permission to go to the Nuba? God helped her make up her mind. The right thing to do was not to think of herself first but to show Ken that he was being taken advantage of. Not only was that right, it was smart—he would be so impressed with her detective work that he'd grant her wish. There was one thing she needed to do first, however. Leaving him to clean up and change clothes, she bicycled to her office, turned on the computer, and opened to the registry of abducted persons. They were organized chronologically and by location. Turning to the list of names from today's mission, she began to check them against those in the register. She was finished by the time Ken appeared, showered, shaved, and clad in a fresh khaki outfit that made him look like a tourist trying to look like a safari guide.

"All right, what's the top secret?"

She sat with her knees together and her hands folded in her lap and her back straight. "That woman who said she'd been whipped? Who wouldn't show her scars? There was a reason why not. She didn't have any. I saw her, and so did that French reporter. Not a mark on her."

"You're saying what?"

"I'll bet she never spent a minute in slavery. I'll bet none of those people did."

"Whoa, Quinette. *Whoa.*"

"Please, look at this." Ken leaned over her shoulder and peered at the screen. "Take this kid, Akol Yel. He says he comes from the town of Manyel and that he was taken in 1995. I checked the list of people reported to have been seized from Manyel that year. He's not on it. I checked ninety-four and ninety-six, just in case he got the year mixed up. Same thing. I've gone through all the people we redeemed today. Same thing again. No record of any of them being captured."

Ken stepped back. "That's happened before."

"Sure. Maybe a few here and there. Not this many."

He eased back another step and stood against the wall, arms crossed over his chest.

"I'm wondering if we've got people pretending to be slaves. And if they're getting paid for their acting work."

"By who?"

"My guess would be Manute, and he's in on it with the local councilmen. They've heard these captives tell their stories a thousand times. They rounded up these people and—"

"Told them what to say," Ken interrupted.

"Or maybe Manute was coaching them what to say while they gave their testimony. None of us speaks Dinka. We have no idea what he was saying to them. He'd known for weeks you were coming. He had the time. He and his buddies made themselves twenty-four hundred bucks, less whatever petty change they paid their make-believe slaves."

"Quinette, Qui-nette," he said in a singsong, as if she were a little touched. "They first told us, four hundred twenty. You don't really believe they actually had that many phonies lined up but that something went wrong and only forty-eight showed up? Strains credibility to say the least."

"I thought about that. Here's a possible scenario. They got word from a legitimate retriever that he was coming in with three hundred and seventy-two people, real captives, but all along they'd planned to salt the mine. They knew you wanted a lot of people, so they'd recruited forty-eight folks from nearby towns to pad the numbers and make themselves some money. Then for some reason, maybe a delay en route like you said, the real slaves didn't show up. That's what made Manute nervous. They must've figured it would be easier to hide their actors and actresses in a big crowd."

"And you're saying this happened because I put pressure on them?"

"No!" she replied with vigorous shakes of her head. She had to watch how she put things.

"Okay, Nancy Drew, what else have you got?"

She decided to ignore the Nancy Drew remark. "The other day I was catching up on our last mission. Thirty people whose names don't match. So there's another fifteen hundred dollars."

"I'd be careful, Quinette, about turning your speculations into fact," Ken said. "You're making an indictment on some very thin evidence. You're not being paid to be some kind of auditor, you know. Or a private eye."

This wasn't going at all as she'd expected. "Well, excuse me all to hell!" she said in a flash of temper. "Excuse me for taking the time to see if we're getting ripped off! If I'm right, don't you think it's pretty damned disgusting? Don't you want to do something about it?"

"I'll look into it." He stood there, while above his head, as bright as a jewel in the barred sunlight piercing the window grate, an orange lizard clung to the wall. "Have you mentioned this to anyone else?"

She shook her head.

"Someone at the UN or in the press could blow a thing like this way out of proportion," Ken said. "Like that bitch from CNN, Phyllis."

"I've got a reputation around here for being discreet."

"Don't do anything to ruin it. The possibility that there are a few cases of fraud out of thousands doesn't deny that there's a huge human rights issue here and that we're the only ones doing anything about it."

"Right."

"I know it's the principle of the thing, but the amounts that we might be talking about are really small."

The lizard had crept a couple of inches higher, its imperceptible movement creating the illusion that Ken had grown shorter.

"It would be terrible, *terrible*," he went on, "if someone like Phyllis Rappaport were to blow a small problem out of proportion and damage a program that's doing so much good."

The bitter seed of her disappointment in him flowered into contempt, a contempt she couldn't allow herself to show. She did need him, after all. "I'd never breathe a word to her or anyone. I'm a little surprised you think I would."

"I don't," he protested, then paused. "But I can see how I gave you that impression. Sorry."

Ken and contrition were a rare combination, which she could turn to her advantage, provided she didn't overdo things. "I wasn't looking for an apology," she said, and gave him some time to think about the comment. She could almost see his mental gears turning, notch by notch. After several silent moments she realized he needed a nudge, and striving for a tone half an octave below the resentful, she said, "I put a lot of effort into this that I didn't have to. I wasn't playing Nancy Drew because I was bored. I thought I was looking out for your interests, the organization's interests."

He got it, finally, and to cover up his chagrin, he made a comic show, hunching his shoulders, wincing, turning up his palms. "Okay. I get the same complaint in Geneva. I don't give my staff the credit they deserve. I stand corrected. You showed a lot of initiative and concern, and I'm grateful. I'll put you in for a bonus."

"You don't have to go that far," she stated, and while he was still feeling that he owed her something, she handed him Michael's letter.

"What's this?"

"It's in the initiative department."

"You don't have enough on your plate already?" he asked when he'd read it.

"Ken, this is a whole new area we could call attention to. I'd like to go up there and make an assessment."

"We sent you up there once to make an assessment and you damned near got yourself killed."

"I can't imagine anything like that would happen again. And the last time I was with a whole bunch of people. I hardly had a chance to talk to him. Didn't even scratch the surface."

"What would you get if you went back?"

"Facts, figures, an overview. What problems we'd have setting up a program there."

He set the letter down on the desk and looked at it pensively. "All right, but make it a brief visit. You've got plenty to do back here."

Brothers and Sisters in Arms

THEY MADE THREE flights in the first week, departing Loki at dawn with light loads of innocuous cargo, landing at an SPLA airstrip on the border to take on military hardware smuggled through Uganda in crates labeled "sewer pipes" (antiaircraft missiles), "insecticide" (triple-A machine guns), "fertilizer" (mortar shells), "typewriters" (mortar fuses), and "bulldozer parts" (mortar tubes), then flying on to the Nuba mountains for a quick off-load and a return to Loki in time for a late lunch. The second week was much the same. Mary videotaped and photographed these flights to the dark side. Dare indulged her hobby at first, then suggested that she leave her cameras behind in the future; keeping a pictorial record of their activities wasn't a smart idea. "The wrong eyes see that stuff, we've got big problems." And what about the videos she'd already shot? Did he want her to burn them? No, but it would be wise to buy a safe and lock them up. "All right," she said agreeably. "I don't need any more pictures. One mission is pretty much like another. Funny, isn't it, how even running guns can get to be routine."

Dare's canary warned him that a comment like that would not go unpunished. On their next mission, minutes before they were to take off from an airfield near Nimule, a deluge washed out the runway, stranding them for over two days. They drank river water filtered through a hand pump, painted themselves in Deet against the swarms of mosquitoes, and breathed through bandanna masks against the stench of the corpses littering the bush nearby. The bodies belonged to soldiers in the Lord's Resistance Army, an exceedingly violent band of crackpot Christians in rebellion against the Ugandan government. To retaliate for Uganda's support of the Sudanese rebels, Khartoum had overcome its abhorrence of infidels and armed the Lord's Resistance Army. A detachment of these lunatics, either on their own initiative or on orders from their Muslim allies, had crossed the border to seize the airfield. The SPLA defenders wiped them out and left them unburied to discourage further attempts.

"Africa sure is an interesting place," Dare said as they sat inside the airplane to get away from the stink. "Had enough of it yet?"

On the second day he figured the smell was more endurable than the Hawker's saunalike interior and went outside to check the runway's condition. After his inspection, he sat down for a smoke—and felt a dagger pierce his calf. In seconds an excruciating pain bolted up his leg. He hobbled back to the plane, flopped onto a cargo pallet, and groaned. Mary rolled up his pant leg, exposing a bulging red welt.

"Scorpion," she said. "You take it easy, baby. Mary will take care of it." She sharpened her jackknife, sterilized it with a cigarette lighter, and sliced the wound to bleed out the poison, then rubbed it with crystals of potassium permanganate from the first-aid kit.

Hours of throbbing misery followed. Dare's leg swelled up to the thigh. By morning the runway was usable, but he couldn't operate the rudder pedals well enough to fly. Mary said she would skipper the plane back to Loki—he needed a doctor. It was too risky to land there with a planeload of weapons, so she hustled some of the SPLA guards to take them off. With their roles reversed—she as captain, he as first officer—they made the trip without incident. She drove him to the Red Cross hospital, and as she helped him walk to admissions, he said, "I don't know what the hell I've done to deserve you, but I must of done it."

She kissed his cheek. "Nobody deserves what they get, good or bad."

While he recovered, Mary was summoned back to Canada by news that her father had pancreatic cancer and wasn't expected to make it through the month. Her departure forced Dare to revise his operational scheme and take Doug as copilot on the next flight. There were two others on Knight Air's roster more qualified to fly Hawkers, but he couldn't chance expanding the circle of the clued-in. Which was the reason why he was incredulous when Doug, before leaving on their second mission together, announced that they would be carrying a passenger—Quinette Hardin. She needed a lift to their final destination, Zulu Three. Before flying there, they were to put down at New Cush and pick up the latest shipment for Michael's forces—four eighty-two-millimeter tubes, two SAM-7 missiles, and three tons of ammunition.

"Are you nuts?" Dare said. "The slave queen? We can't let her see what we were doin'."

"Wes, she's known about it since the beginning. Before the beginning, when Michael first brought it up to Fitz and me. She'll keep her mouth shut."

Dare wasn't reassured. He recalled Mary's description of Quinette as "an innocent abroad" and his reply that he didn't think she was all that innocent. What if he was wrong? In his experience, an innocent caused trouble without meaning to, like a four-year-old playing with Dad's revolver.

"Dire Straits, a golden oldie from the eighties," she said from the jumpseat behind him and Doug. "Mary told me your in-flight entertainment is always Stevie Ray Vaughan."

Dare ignored her.

> I'm a soldier of freedom in the army of man
> We are the chosen, we're the partisan.

"It's my tape," Douglas said. "A guy I flew with in the Gulf War said the problem with real war is that there isn't any background music. So we provide our own."

> The cause it is noble and the cause it is just
> We are ready to pay with our lives if we must.

"Well, I guess it's appropriate," Quinette said.

"Sure, if y'all are ready to pay with your life, which I'm not with mine."

> Nothing gonna stop them as day follows night
> Right becomes wrong, the left becomes the right.

The song intruded on his thoughts of Mary. She'd been gone nine days and six hours to keep vigil at her dying father's bedside. She had never talked much about her family, and he hadn't asked her to. You didn't think of the nomad aviators in Loki as having families, or roots, or lives other than the ones they were living now. Cut off from their origins, it seemed as if, through some process of spontaneous creation, they'd sprung full grown into existence right here in Africa.

Quinette unbuckled her belt and stretched forward to look out the cockpit window. "This part looks so different. Like Africa the way I pictured it before I came here. Jungly."

"How about sittin' back down and strappin' in," Dare said in a rare display of safety consciousness. In the distance a thunderstorm was making up, a tightly wrapped, nasty-looking sucker, the cloud resting on a blue-black shaft of rain like a golf ball on a tee. He switched on the intercom and said, "Nimrod, wheels down in ten. Let's try for a quick load. Might rain, and I do not intend to get stuck again."

His loadmaster rogered him from the rear, in which a half ton of medical supplies were piled up under the cargo nets, destined for delivery to the clinic Ulrika had cobbled together in New Tourom, out of the stuff she'd salvaged from the hospital's wreckage.

Doug's tape wound on.

"Y'all like this shit?"

"Sure," Doug said, but offered to turn the cassette player off.

"That's okay. I like to keep my first officers happy. It's a fringe benefit of flyin' with Captain Wesley Dare. Flaps."

Doug lowered them, and they descended over bright green hills and valleys, laced with glittering streams. The New Cush airstrip, lying between two low ridgelines, resembled a fairway in need of serious maintenance. Dare radioed the SPLA on the ground, asking if the field was secure. Someone said it was, but there was tension in the voice, and Dee-Tee chirped an alert. Dare pulled his Beretta from under the seat and jammed it into his belt.

A strand of black smoke rose from one end of the runway, indicating a crosswind. He quartered into it, then touched down. As Nimrod opened the aft cargo door, a squad of SPLA soldiers popped out of the surrounding brush, led by an officer who looked ready for a parade: clean boots, a clean uniform, a polished shoulder-holster, and a silver-knobbed swagger stick, which he brought to the brim of his beret in jaunty salute.

"Good day, captain!" he called, standing below the cockpit.

Dare opened the side window. "And good day to you, rafiki. How y'all?"

"Quite well, thank you. May I have a word with you, sir?"

"Polite as hell, ain't he," Dare said in an undertone. "C'mon, Doug. I think we've got problems. Quinette, you stay inside."

"What kind of problems?" she asked.

"Soon as I find out, you'll be the first to know."

Outside, closely watched by the soldiers, a crew of civilians, barefoot and with prominent collarbones showing above their tattered undershirts, were lugging crates and containers out of the forest, toward the airplane.

With an amused expression, the officer glanced at the protruding butt of the Beretta.

"All Americans have a constitutional right to bear arms," Dare said.

"I know. My brother is in America. He recently got his green card. I and a few of my men will be accompanying you to Yei to make sure you arrive safely."

"You must of gotten some bad information, major. We're goin' to the Nuba, War Zone Two."

"You *were* going there. Your destination has changed. Your cargo is now needed more in Yei than in the Nuba."

Doug said, "We can't do it. Can't take you and your men. We'd be over-loaded."

The officer gave an abbreviated nod that more or less congratulated Doug for making a nice try. He then snapped an order to a couple of his men. Motioning with their rifles, they instructed the workers to put the weaponry on board.

"I don't believe this. You're hijacking cargo that's meant for someone fighting on the same side as you."

A quick, efficient smile—Doug's indignation appeared to amuse him as much as Dare's pistol.

"Know what, major?" Dare said. "When you started talking, I thought you were some kinda customs man. Like you only wanted to collect duty on imported goods."

The officer straightened his shoulders, bracing his swagger stick across his thighs. "Thank you for the promotion, but I'm a captain, not a major. Also a fighter, not a bureaucrat."

"I was only joking. But what would you figure the customs duties would be on all this stuff?"

"I have no idea." He spoke with firmness, but a wavering look came into his eyes. "Perhaps you do?"

He didn't slam the door, I can get to him, Dare thought. "I've got some-thing in the plane that will give me an idea. Y'all don't mind if I take a look at it?"

"Not at all."

With Douglas, he went into the cockpit. Quinette, occupying the pilot's seat, was looking out the window at the captain.

"I've been a good girl and stayed in my room, so tell me what's going on."

Dare reached into the seat pocket where he stowed flight manuals and charts and withdrew a vinyl purse, the kind shopkeepers use for carrying cash to the bank. It contained his emergency gratuities fund.

"What's goin' on is a lesson on why these blacks are never gonna win this war. Some commander over in Yei has decided he needs what we've got more than Michael does, and he sent that errand boy to collect."

She clasped his wrist tightly. "We can't let that happen."

"I'm tryin'," he said, counting out the fives and tens.

"If you need more, there's fifty in my rucksack," she said.

"Think this will do," Dare said, and wrapped the bills into a delectable bundle that he secured with a rubber band. Figuring the captain would want to conduct business in private, he called through the window, "If it's not inconvenient, could you join us up here?"

Douglas and Quinette stood outside the cabin door to make room for their guest.

"I calculate the duty fees come to this," Dare said quietly, and held the wad close to the man's face.

It probably was as much as a junior officer in the SPLA made in a year, yet the sight of it, the smell of it, the nearness of it, all in U.S. currency, did not have the desired effect. The captain looked over his shoulder, past Doug and Quinette into the rear of the plane, where Nimrod was supervising the loading.

"I am under orders," he said. "I have got to show something."

He proposed a compromise: Dare would leave half the military cargo here, fly the other half to Yei, then return to pick up what had been left behind and go on to the Nuba.

Dare reflected for a few moments. What difference would it make to him if one SPLA commander stole from another? He was getting paid eighteen thousand to make a delivery, to whom didn't matter.

While he pondered, Quinette said, "You people need medical supplies, don't you?"

The captain almost did a double-take, as if he were surprised that a woman would take part in the conversation. "Always," he said.

"We've got about half a ton, right there. Why don't you take that instead? You can tell whoever it is you need to tell that that was all we had on board."

Douglas looked at her with admiration. "It's a good idea, Wes."

"That stuff is for the German nurse. She's expecting it."

Doug said, "There are priorities here, and bandages and syringes don't make the top of the list."

"Well, listen to the two angels of mercy. Do-gooders gone bad."

"Gone bad?" Quinette said with anger. "Listen, I saw my friend with her legs blown off. One antiaircraft rocket would have saved her and a whole lot of other people. And since when did you start giving a damn about anything? You're the most cynical man I've ever met."

Which was why, Dare thought, he hadn't come up with the idea of trading syringes and bandages for weapons. It took an innocent's conviction to make that offer. He turned to the captain.

"Well?"

His face assumed a grave expression. "You understand, the man I report to might not believe that medical supplies were all you had. I would need to convince him, so I must ask for duties on the medicines in addition."

"I've got it right here," Quinette said, and bent down to open her rucksack.

She placed two twenties and a ten in the captain's hand, smugly, piously, like a parishioner dropping a big donation into the collection plate.

Nimrod was bewildered when Dare told him to offload the arms and wait at the airstrip with the workers until the plane returned. There were no problems at Yei. The captain's boss, a more senior captain, was in fact skeptical that the plane was carrying only medical aid, but a share of the wealth allayed his doubts.

They flew back to New Cush, got the shipment on board, and finally left for the mountains, Dare climbing quickly to cruising altitude to conserve fuel. The Hawker had a range of fifteen hundred miles, and the detour had consumed most of his reserve.

"So what are we gonna tell that Ulrika?" he asked.

Quinette said, "The truth."

"I'm kinda wonderin' what that is."

"That her stuff was confiscated by SPLA troops in Yei."

"I'd call that a half truth."

Douglas said, "Christ, Wes, our job is to get arms to the Nuba, not to every goddamned commander who gets a notion that he's entitled to them. We had to make a sacrifice. There's nothing to feel guilty about."

"Well, I'm gonna leave it to you two to explain to Ulrika why she's gonna have to send her patients to the witch doctors."

In the jumpseat Quinette had to speak to the back of Wes's head, its bald spot ringed by fine, tight reddish curls. "Ulrika will understand," she said.

She wasn't going to let Wes make her feel bad about herself. She was a citizen of the war, she had an obligation to do her bit, and she'd done it. Her idea had saved the day. Doug was right—there was nothing to feel guilty about. And if there was, she took comfort in the knowledge that God forgave all.

Behind her Nimrod lay asleep on a blanket, his head propped against a sack full of mortar shells. Could she ever describe this experience in one of her letters home? Who in that distant, drab, everyday world would believe that she was in a plane piloted by gun-runners? She hardly believed it herself. Had she ridden a rocket into orbit, she would not have felt farther away from all she'd come from.

Chin on her knuckles, she stared past the controls at the instrument panel, its dials as indecipherable as Chinese calligraphy. The only one she could read was the airspeed indicator. Two hundred and ten knots. It was over two hours to the Nuba. She wished she had the power to think herself there. She stretched out her legs, into the space between the bulkheads. Her legs were her best feature, but with bulky hiking boots reaching up to her ankles and baggy safari shorts down to her knees, their virtues weren't apparent. She frowned. She wanted to look as attractive as she could. Michael's last communication to her, delivered just three days ago, had been as dry and businesslike as the first, telling her he had compiled information she would find useful and had made arrangements that would ensure her a successful visit. The conclusion "I look forward to your arrival" was as personal as it got.

She dozed off, until a fullness in her ears woke her up. The plane was descending over blond hillsides and Nuba farmsteads, ringed by terraced fields stippled with sorghum.

"Zulu Three, this is Yankee Bravo approaching from the southwest," Dare called on the radio. When he received an acknowledgment, he asked if fuel was available. Yes, a voice replied.

An African truth, he thought when the top fell off a fuel drum as he, Nimrod, and Doug rolled it toward the plane. A mixture of Jet A1 and muddy water spilled out. Inspection of several other drums revealed that they too had been tampered with. Dare knew what had happened: villagers had siphoned fuel for their fires and lamps and topped off the drums with rain water to conceal their theft. While Michael's troops unloaded the plane, breaking open the crates like kids at Christmas, he radioed his problem to Fitz in Loki.

"Damn good thing we found out what was inside the drums," he said, trying to look on the bright side of his situation. "Been in a world of hurt if we'd pumped that shit into the tanks. Gonna need a fuel delivery soon as you can get me one."

Fitz told him to wait. When he came back on, some fifteen minutes later, he gave Dare the good news—Alexei would bring the Jet A1 in the Antonov—and the bad news—because of flight commitments, he couldn't make it for three days.

"There it is, Doug," he said with a shake of his head. "Y'know, I've always thought of myself as lucky, but lately it seems my good luck mostly consists of gettin' through the fixes my bad luck gets me into."

SHE STOOD AT the side of the runway, near the grove of doum palms where she had seen wounded and dead for the first time, but the sight of those trees evoked no dread or dark memories, only anticipation as Michael emerged, surrounded by his bodyguard.

"Miss Quinette Hardin, so very glad to see you again," he said, and took both her hands in his, his slowly spreading smile squeezing her like an embrace.

She would have preferred the other kind of embrace. She sensed—or was it hoped?—that he would have as well, but they stood an arm's length apart. This was one of the rare times when Quinette didn't place all her trust in feelings, because she wasn't sure what to call the emotion he awakened in her. She'd longed to see him, but now that she did, she was reminded anew of how different they were, how remote were the chances that anything could develop between them.

At the head of a column of soldiers and porters half a mile long, they climbed the path toward New Tourom but skirted the town, following a riverbed in which scattered pools, remnants from the wet season, lay in rocky basins, their surfaces creased by the wakes of aquatic insects. It was the hottest part of the day, and Wes, Doug, and Nimrod were soon very thirsty but didn't dare drink from the muddy, bug-infested pools. They hadn't expected to be on foot today and were unprepared for it. Quinette shared her water bottles with them and felt field-wise and competent when she paused at a pool to refill them with her filtration pump.

About a kilometer from town they came to a range of low hills and filed through a narrow passage into a broad bowl, with steep, tiered slopes on all sides. The effect was like passing through the entrance into a vast amphitheater. At the far end, three or four miles away, a line of trees trooped up a ridgeline, marking a watercourse. The place had the quality of a lost and isolated world, a kind of Shangri-la. It was anything but—gun emplacements picketed the hills.

They walked on, past men threshing grain with heavy wooden paddles, women balancing on their heads the inevitable baskets piled high with sorghum ears. As in Dinkaland, Quinette attracted a retinue of teenage girls, full of excitement and curiosity. They took turns carrying her rucksack, tousled her hair and twined it around their fingers, and touched her arms, chattering incomprehensibly.

Michael's garrison looked more like a Nuba village than a military base, except for the numbers of armed men moving about, the radio antenna sprouting from a nest of solar panels, and the SPLA flag flying over a mud-walled bungalow. Inside, several officers, among them the dour Major Kasli, stood at a table covered with maps. Another map, under a plastic sheet marked with arrows, circles, and rectangles, papered half of one wall. Wes, Doug, and Nimrod gathered with Michael around the radio, tucked in a corner atop a wooden crate. Wes called Lokichokio, and after a few minutes Fitz's voice, high pitched and chipper, broke through the barrage of static. Quinette sat down and waited while the two men talked. Once Kasli looked up from the maps to cast an unwelcoming glance her way. He was an unattractive man, with close-set bloodshot eyes and an exceptionally narrow head—a kind of squashed oval; his pointed chin accentuated by a goatee.

"Okay, Fitz knows we've arrived," Wes said, motioning to her to come to the radio. "Y'all better tell him to get a message to your boss, on account of you're gonna be a little late getting back to work. Fuel shortage in Loki. Now it's five days instead of three. Five at least."

She couldn't say that this news displeased her. Pulling the handset to her mouth, she gave Fitz Ken's number, told him exactly what to say, and promised to pay the sat-phone charges when she returned.

"It happened for a reason," she said to Michael as he walked her up a path. "Nothing happens without a reason."

"And what could that reason be, Quinette?"

She was glad to hear her first name. "I don't know, but I assume we'll find out."

Here at his base, his bodyguard wasn't compelled to shadow him everywhere, but they weren't quite alone. Her followers walked alongside, fussing with her hair.

"I've assembled several meks for you to talk to. They will give you numbers and names of people abducted from their villages. Also, that trader you mentioned on your last visit, Bashir."

"He's here?"

"Major Kasli located him. He knows where many of the captives are. You'll meet everyone tomorrow in New Tourom. I'll have a translator for you."

"You won't be there?"

"Very busy now. Planning an operation. We're going on it day after tomorrow."

"You'll be leaving?" she asked, disappointed. "What sort of operation?"

"Military secret," he answered. "This is where you'll be staying."

Ducking their heads, they passed through a low keyhole-shaped entrance into a courtyard formed by a ring of three tukuls, each joined to the other by a high wall.

"In here," Michael said, beckoning her to the center hut.

The dim, windowless room was hot. When her eyes adjusted, she saw geometric designs and primitive figures of people and animals painted in red and ochre, black and white on the clay walls, which threw off a dull bluish gleam, as if they had been varnished or rubbed to a shine. The air was filled with the strong aroma of the bunched herbs and dried bean pods hanging from pegs high up on the walls. A crude bed—sticks lashed together between four thick crooked posts, with a mosquito net overhead—was the only furniture, while a few straw mats did for carpeting.

"No TV or refrigerator," said Michael, grinning, "but you do have a shower." He pointed at a little alcove, where a flat boulder lay on the floor and a large calabash hung from a pair of cattle horns more than six feet above. "You fill this up and take this out"—he pulled a wooden plug from the bottom of the calabash—"but use the water with care. The dry season is here and water is like gold."

She loved its rough simplicity, and the gaiety and mystery of the wall paintings, and when they stepped outside into the courtyard, the feeling of cloister rendered by the encircled huts.

"This is my house," he said, "but of course I can't stay here with you."

"Of course."

"My daughter and her two cousins will be with you. Her name is Toddo, but you can call her Pearl because that's what it means in English. She and her friends will cook for you, look after you."

"It seems all the girls want to do around here is pull my hair," she said.

"They think it's disorderly. They want to braid it, like theirs. I must go. A conference with my staff."

Pearl, a pretty girl of fourteen, with Michael's rounded chin and soft eyes, had learned English from him and at school. There was a somberness about her—how could she be anything but somber after losing her mother and siblings?—but she had a lively curiosity and, as the other two girls ground sorghum with a wooden pestle, asked Quinette about America, where her father had learned to be a soldier. He'd told her that no one there ever went hungry, that there were black-skinned people in

America who'd once been slaves but now were as free as their former masters, and that farmers did not plant and harvest by hand but had machines to do the work for them.

Quinette didn't want to disillusion her, so she confirmed this idyllic picture. More or less to establish some common ground with Pearl, she mentioned that her father had been a farmer who'd grown corn and raised some cows, as Nuban men did; that he too had once been a soldier, that he'd died when she was fourteen, and that his death still made her sad.

"You are very high, like Nuba woman," Pearl said, raising her hand.

"The Dinka think so, too. Sometimes they call me the White Dinka Woman."

"No. You are not so skinny like a Dinka. You should be called White Nuba Woman."

"Well, you can call me that if you want."

"I don't like your hair."

"So your father told me."

"Can I fix it?"

Quinette hesitated, then said, "All right."

For the next hour she sat on the ground while Pearl changed her hairstyle.

"Your hair is too much skinny," the girl said, which Quinette interpreted to mean that it was finer than a Nuban woman's and difficult to weave into the tight plaits they favored. A bead was fastened to the tip of each strand. When she was finished, Pearl dipped her fingers into a clay jar of sesame oil and with it plastered the braids to Quinette's head. Then she leaned back to study her artistry. "Better now. I will show you."

She produced a small square mirror, with a corner missing and the backing so worn that the glass was almost as dull as tin. Quinette wasn't sure what to think of her new appearance. The braids on the top of her head were pulled straight back, making her forehead too prominent, and the oil that gave a Nuban woman's hair an appealing brilliance caused hers to appear greasy.

Pearl noticed her frown and assured her that she looked beautiful. "My father will like it."

Quinette felt a blush come to her cheeks. "I like you, Pearl," she said. "We're going to be great friends."

THE TICK BITES, inflicted on them almost the instant they lay down on their beds, itched like scabies, and it made Dare sick just to look at the mush a village girl brought to him, Doug, and Nimrod for lunch. The goddamned fuel problem had condemned them to a week of this. He'd rather spend a week in a Mexican jail, as in fact he'd done in his younger days. Noticing the three men clawing at their forearms and waists, the girl, with sign language, instructed them to drag their beds outside. That done, she whacked the posts with a stick to drive the insects out, and while they stomped on their tormentors, she poured boiling water on the posts to wipe out remaining pockets of resistance.

They carried the beds back inside the hut and turned toward the door when a voice boomed, "Hey, Doug!"

There, like a hallucination, stood a young American, short but powerfully built, carrying a video camera and wearing a high-and-tight buzz cut, basketball shoes, cammie trousers, and a sweat-stained Pepperdine University T-shirt. He had the look of I-don't-touch-alcohol-drugs-or-tobacco wholesomeness that Dare loathed. He'd seen the man before but couldn't place him. On his back was a rucksack, which he slipped off with a "Whew!" and a theatrical swipe at his brow.

"Rob," Doug said. "What the hell are you doing here?"

"You don't know? You're here to take me out, except you're four days early."

Doug gave him a look of incomprehension. Now Dare recalled who he was: Rob Handy, one of the Holy Rollers from the Friends of the Frontline.

"There's been a screw-up, hasn't there? Couple of days ago I radioed Fitz not to send a plane for me till the end of the week, when the show's over. You didn't get the word?" Handy met Doug's puzzled gaze with one of his own. "One of your crews flew me in here two weeks ago, with a load of tools and construction materials. Those Russians."

"That would've been Alexei," Doug said. "Sorry for the confusion, I don't keep up on the flight schedules. That's Fitz's job."

"You're not here to pick me up?"

"No."

"And you been here *two weeks*?" Dare asked.

"It's been terrific," Handy said. "I was just getting footage of the school we're rebuilding."

"You're making a film?" asked Doug.

"For our fundraising drive. It's unbelievable how many people back in the States have no idea what's going on here. The peril their fellow Christians are in. The fight they're putting up."

Lord, spare me from these people, Dare thought.

"Michael's given me the okay to film the operation he's got coming up," Handy burbled on. "I just got back from his staff conference. You know about the operation?"

Doug replied that they did not.

"You soon will. He wants to talk to you about it. It's going to be incredible, the climax of the film. Our contributors, they'll eat it up. Most of them are vets. But you know that. I was in the Gulf War myself. Fitz told me you were in that one, right?"

"Flew A-tens," Doug answered.

"No kidding," said Handy, dragging his rucksack inside to stand it against a wall. "I was with a Warthog squadron, too. Enlisted, though. What squadron were you with?"

Doug didn't answer. Glancing at the rucksack, he asked, "You're moving in? It's going to be crowded in here."

"It's the other way around," replied Handy. "You guys moved in on me. No problem. I sleep outside. It's cooler."

Dare sat on his fumigated bed and fumbled for a smoke. He was still holding himself to five a day, although he might need to increase his allotment now that he had a Christian soldier for a roommate.

Michael arrived later with Major Kasli. It was an official call. After asking how the guests found their accommodations—Dare chose not to answer—Michael sat down and inquired if Dare's sources could obtain 120-millimeter mortars and semtex.

"Reckon so. They're a one-stop shop. None of my business, I suppose, but why one-twenties and semtex?"

"You are correct," said Kasli. "It is not your business."

"I'll decide that, major," Michael said. "This dry season, I intend to carry the fight to the enemy. We are going to destroy an enemy airfield and sabotage the oil pipeline."

Doug let out a low whistle.

"That's ambitious," Dare commented. "How far is this airfield?"

"From here, a little more than a hundred kilometers. It's an oil company airfield, but Khartoum uses it as a base for its Antonovs. The plane that bombed Dr. Manfred's hospital left from it."

"A one-twenty mortar weighs a helluva lot," Dare pointed out. "How are y'all gonna move heavy mortars and the shells to go with them over a hundred kilometers? You'd need a camel caravan or a whole shitload of porters."

Major Kasli took off his wraparound sunglasses and smirked. "I see you are a tactician as well as a flier."

"Yeah, a goddamned Napoleon with a pilot's license."

"We are going to transport the mortars and the ammunition in lorries," Michael said. "And where do we find the lorries? We are going to seize them from the government." He smoothed the dirt with his palm and, with his finger, drew a map. "Here is Kologi. Douglas, you remember your visit there?"

"Sure. Suleiman's village. The Kowahla."

"Yes. We have learned from Suleiman that the government has made an offer to the nazir of the Kowahla. If he swears allegiance to Khartoum and its jihad, he will receive for himself a Land Rover and his people will get lorries to carry their cotton crops to market. If he does not, then the Kowahla will be considered infidels and will be treated accordingly."

Dare flexed his hand, working the stiffness out. "The old carrot and stick. Works every time."

"Not this time," said Michael, his almost feminine eyes going hard. "Here is where we are and here is Kologi." He made two dots in the dirt. "And here between us, near this road junction, is a Sudan army garrison. Two days ago the lorries arrived there, three of them with the Land Rover. Day after tomorrow we will attack the garrison and take them."

"Well, good luck is all I've got to say."

"I'm leaving as little to luck as I can," Michael said. "I've been training my men hard for a month. There will be more tomorrow afternoon. You're welcome to observe."

Dare clawed at a bite on his arm, hard enough to make it bleed. "It's better than gettin' bit."

HE RETURNED AT dusk, tired and preoccupied, and the scene that played out afterward was a peculiar version of a domestic evening in some 1950s American suburb. The man of the house, after a hard day at work, hangs up a pistol belt instead of an overcoat, then sits down to a family dinner, with the ground in place of a table and wooden bowls of doura and bean cakes in place of meatloaf and potatoes on china. At the end, completing the picture, he gives his teenage daughter permission to go to a dance with her friends. The intermingling of the familiar with the strange, of the ordinary with the extraordinary, beguiled Quinette. She recalled something Ken Eismont had said on one of their journeys—that the human race was born in Africa, so to come to Africa was to experience a kind of homecoming. That didn't square with what the Bible or Pastor Tom taught, but she was inclined, now, toward Ken's point of view. It was as good an explanation as any for the weird connectedness she felt to her present surroundings. The tukuls, the snug enclosure of the courtyard, seemed more like home than home. Looking at Michael, his face highlighted by the paraffin lamp, at the ground ribbed with the marks of the girls' twig brooms, and at the stars, like a million crystal rivets tacking a black velvet cloth to an immense cupola, she thought, *I could be happy here.*

"I like this," he said, passing a hand through her braids, the beads clattering softly.

"I was wondering when you'd notice."

"Oh, I noticed straight away," Michael said, then after the girls left, "Wesley told me, when we were walking here from the airfield, about what you did. That was quick thinking, and I'm grateful."

"It seemed like the right thing. I hope so."

"This is Sudan. The choice is never between the right thing and the wrong thing, but always between what is necessary and what isn't. And the supplies brought in today are necessary. Without them, I would be unable to carry off the operation."

"Is it still top secret?"

"For now, yes. I'm tired of thinking about it."

"It'll be dangerous?"

"Of course, but more dangerous for the men than for me."

"You'll be gone a long time?"

"If all goes well, it will be over in one day. But no more about it. I want to hear more about where you come from. Iowa."

"We pretty much exhausted that boring topic the last time."

"As I told you then, I like being bored. Boredom to me is a luxury."

"I had enough of that luxury to last me a while. A long while. Forever."

"Then tell me more about this work you do, this redeeming of captives."

She described the field missions, and the satisfaction she derived from seeing the joy on the former slaves' faces. It was the worthiest work she'd done, but, she was quick to add, the sights she'd seen in the Nuba had made it seem insufficient, awakening an urge and a will to do more. She thought she should be playing a larger role, though she didn't know what it could be. They fell into an intense discussion about the war, about the aid campaign, about restoring St. Andrew's mission and Michael's vision of creating a new Sudan, with the divisions of tribe and faith swept aside. Their shoulders occasionally touched as they talked, she watched the movement of his fabulously long fingers, and she smelled his sweat, but it was his voice and his ideas that generated the same magnetism that had drawn them into a kiss more than a month ago. She was sure he felt it, too, yet something restrained them now. Something like fear.

They lapsed into a silence, then he pointed at the cicatrix stitching his brows. "Do you know what these mean?"

"They're decorative aren't they?"

"Yes, but it is also believed that they improve eyesight."

"And do they?"

"My eyes saw you, didn't they? That day when all of you came to New Tourom, out of all the women with you, I noticed you first and then noticed no others."

This confession, coming so suddenly, left her momentarily breathless.

"I'm very plain. I know that."

"I don't think so. I looked at you and thought, 'She has legs like a gazelle.' "

"Every woman around here has legs like a gazelle." She paused. "All right, I'll tell you something. When I saw you getting ready for your wrestling match, covered in that ash, I thought you looked like Adam, the second after God made him. That sounds ridiculous, doesn't it?"

He brushed her plaits again. "How can I say it sounds ridiculous when you compare me to the father of the human race? You wouldn't be Eve, would you?"

From a distance, the sounds of drums, horn and whistle blasts, and singing spared her from answering.

"That's the dance?"

"There is dancing now almost every night. For the harvest. It is a ceremony we call *sibr*. Sibr is the name for sacred spirits and the ceremonies that honor them. This one is the Sibr of Fire. Would you like to see it?"

"Would you?"

"I've seen it a thousand times. I would rather be here, talking to you."

"You knew that's what I wanted to hear."

"I'm not a fool. But it's true all the same. If you want to hear music, I will make it for you."

He went into one of the huts and came out with a small handmade harp with three strings. Sitting again, he strummed and sang. She couldn't understand the words, but an undertone of sadness in the melody came through plainly enough. He finished the verse, then translated.

> *It is a big sibr, and they are happy*
> *They are celebrating because today is the sibr*

Of those who died long ago.
Because today is the day the spirits have said
We will celebrate the dead.

"Is it about her?" Quinette asked, and immediately wished she hadn't.

"No. It's only a song."

"I'm sorry. That was unfair of me," she said.

"I remember her and honor her," he said. "We always remember and honor our dead. We pray to their spirits for aid, but that is very different from loving them."

She wondered if he was being completely honest. No matter how much death he'd seen, how could his sorrow fade after only two years? And if he still grieved for her, was there love in his grief, breathing and beating still?

Then he kissed her forehead, and she almost wept when the carapace of his reserve broke and he clasped the back of her neck, pulling her mouth to his. She craved him more than she'd craved anyone, and yet was relieved when he drew away. There was another silence, and in that silence a distance grew, and filling the distance was the understanding that if they made love, it would change their lives in ways neither of them could foresee.

IN THE COOL of early morning she trekked to New Tourom with her personal bodyguard, a scrawny youth nicknamed Negev after the Israeli machine gun he carried, and a procession of students, children of Michael's soldiers. Pearl and her friends were among them, wearing white uniform dresses, gifts from the Friends of the Frontline.

In town workmen were roofing the new school, weaving makuti through the beams and rafters. There she was met by a teacher, Moses, a gaunt, middle-aged man in a white shirt who would be her translator. The meks, some of whom had come from villages as far as fifty miles away, were assembled inside St. Andrew's church. The retriever, Bashir, was with them, looking none too comfortable within Christian walls.

"Salaam aleikum," Quinette greeted, thus exhausting her Arabic.

"Aleikum as-salaam," Bashir replied, and sat on one of the halved logs that served as pews.

Breaking out her notebook and tape recorder, she took a seat alongside him. Some of the meks presented handwritten lists of abducted people; the others, illiterate, had committed the names to memory. Deciphering the scrawl, extracting detailed information like ages and dates of capture, was exceedingly tedious. The translations drew the business out even longer. The meks knew no English, each spoke a Nuban dialect different from Moses's. The only common language was Arabic, which few spoke well, requiring Moses to ask them, over and over, to repeat what they'd said. By midday Quinette had completed interviews with only two of the eight men and had not had a chance to speak to Bashir.

They broke for lunch, to resume in the afternoon. Moses invited her to eat with him and his wife. She might have turned him down had she known that he was also going to invite Ulrika.

They picked her up at her clinic, a square hut in front of which stood a queue of old folks and mothers with babies. Inside, a man sat handing out prescriptions through a window and writing in a cloth ledger that looked like an artifact from the nineteenth century. Ulrika was taking a child's temperature. When she came out, looking much thinner than when Quinette had last seen her, her face drawn, her long hair limp in the heat, she said that the child was suffering from severe diarrhea and that she had sufficient medicine to treat him for only two more days.

"After that I will be like a kujur and feed him the inside of a baobab gourd. That is supposed to cure the diarrhea, but if it doesn't, maybe he will die. I don't know."

She had heard that her supplies had been confiscated, and was that true? Her cheeks flushing, Quinette nodded.

"There was no way to stop them?"

"There were twenty, thirty of them with rifles."

Never a choice between right and wrong, only between what was necessary and what was not. She pleaded with God to not let the child die, trusting Him to understand that swapping the medicine for weapons could save the lives of many children.

They sat down outside Moses's tukul, in the shade of a mango tree. His wife had cooked a chicken that must have trained for the poultry Olympics, the meat was so stringy and tough. Quinette asked Ulrika about Dr. Manfred. The nurse had heard no word from him and very little about him, only that he'd returned to Germany and was recovering from his breakdown. "A temporary madness," she said in her brusque way, "but I don't think he is coming back for a long time, maybe never. He suffers from too much of Africa."

After lunch Quinette returned to the church and conferred with Bashir. Speaking in Arabic, he affirmed that he and his associates would be able to act as middlemen in the Nuba, as they did in Dinkaland. But travel in the mountains was more difficult and more dangerous, and therefore he would have to charge a higher "risk premium"—seventy-five dollars a head.

Outside a dog barked, the sound jarring in the scorched stillness of the afternoon. "I'll have to speak to Eismont about that," she said. "I don't think he'll agree to it."

"Sixty, then," Bashir countered.

She regarded him, with his Rolex and rings and spotless jelibiya. "I can't tell you how much you disgust me," she said, smiling.

Moses looked at her, alarmed. "Miss, do you wish me to translate?"

She said no and returned to interviewing the meks.

HANDY WARMED UP for his debut as a combat cameraman by filming the training exercise, a live-fire rehearsal for the attack on the garrison. It was conducted some distance from town, on an open plain where there weren't any people and the soldiers, thanks to the ammunition Dare had delivered, could practice with real bullets. They were a motley lot. Michael's bodyguard and assault troops wore uniforms; the rest were got up like they'd looted an army surplus store and maybe the used clothing bin at a Salvation Army depot. There were men in bathing trunks and shorts and T-shirts so full of holes they showed as much skin as they covered; men wearing camouflage trousers and brightly colored shirts that negated the camouflage. A couple of soldiers had donned skirts and petticoats so that they looked like armed cross-dressers. They wore sneakers, sandals, and shower shoes and covered their heads with World War II British officer hats and heirloom pith helmets passed on by grandfathers who'd served in colonial constabularies.

Dare had a low opinion of African fighting abilities, except for the Ethiopians and the Somalis—who'd shown their prowess at Mogadishu—but he looked past the sorry appearance of Michael's troops and observed that they moved well in the field, listened to their officers' commands, and handled their weapons as if they knew which end to point. The Archangel had taught them the lessons he'd learned at Fort Benning. With bundles of grass and tree branches tied to their belts, they advanced in choreographed rushes, one platoon sprinting forward while another laid down covering fire—short, disciplined bursts, not the unrestrained volleys of amateurs who liked to make noise.

Handy had come down with a slight fever and diarrhea, but he'd rallied after an overdose of Lomotil and now brimmed with enthusiasm, his camera trained on a mortar crew drilling with smoke rounds. He focused on the one who dropped the shells into the tube—he wore a shiny crucifix around his neck, a regular Crusader. "This will look terrific!"

"A few months ago these dudes were carrying spears," Doug said. "Now look at them."

Dare said, "From the bronze age to the twentieth century quick as a wink. Nothin' like progress."

SHE'D SPOKEN TO all the meks but two. They would have to wait until tomorrow. She was worn out, and so was Moses, practically hoarse from his translating work, and he still had teaching to do.

"An English class for some older students," he said. "Possibly you could assist me."

"Me?" Quinette said, her hand going to her chest. "I've never taught."

"This is only the English alphabet. Very easy."

"All right. You helped me, I'll help you."

The class was held outdoors, with a chalkboard propped against the trunk of a tree. There were ten students in their late teens or twenties, and among them was the woman of fierce beauty who'd spoken about her captivity on Nuba Day. Quinette couldn't recall her name, but her tale of escaping her master she hadn't forgotten. Moses spoke in Nuban, motioning at Quinette to introduce her. The young woman said something.

"Yamila says you have met before," Moses translated.

"Yes. Hello, Yamila."

"Ah-lo," Yamila replied without a smile.

Moses passed out the copybooks and pencils. No computers or visual aids here, no desks—the students sat on rocks or on empty cooking-oil tins—no nothing, not even a roof over their heads.

Moses wrote an *A* on the chalkboard. "What is the letter?"

The class, in unison: "Capital letter *A*!"

"Write, please."

Heads bowed over copybooks.

He wrote an *a*.

"Small letter *a*!"

It took half an hour to get to *z*. Moses checked the class's work. This was where Quinette was to give him a hand. It was difficult to read the students' scratchings. Yamila's were the most illegible of all; the letters looked like aimless scribbling. Quinette squatted, took a stick, and wrote an *A* in the ground.

"Ay," she said. "Capital letter ay." Motioning to Yamila to make the sound, stretching it out like she was pulling a rubber band. "Ayyy."

Silent, the young woman looked fixedly at her.

"Ayyy," Quinette repeated, and meeting with the same stare, she called Moses over. "I don't think she understands what's going on here."

"Oh, but she does," Moses said. "She wishes to learn to read and write, but she can be stubborn. Please try with her again."

Gesturing at the ground, Quinette encouraged her pupil to write the letter: "Ayyy." There was something intimidating about Yamila's expression, so untamed that the wonder was that anyone had been able to subdue and enslave her in the first place.

Yamila bent down and formed the letter and said "Ay," and turned to Quinette as if defying her to find fault with her writing or her pronunciation.

"Good. Now, bee."

She made an awkward but recognizable *B*.

"Now, cee."

"Cee."

They went on—dee, ee, ef, gee, aitch—with never a moment's softening in Yamila's countenance. Well, after what she'd been through, what else could she be but hard and full of rage? You couldn't expect her to grow mellow and tender just because a stranger was helping her learn the English alphabet.

Numbers were next, and then a spelling lesson, and by late afternoon the adult education class was over. The pupils stood, Moses leading them in prayer. "Father in heaven, watch over us. Do not kill us, do not allow us or our children to go hungry, do not make us sick. Father in heaven, bring peace to the Nuba, deliver us from war, deliver us from evil, Amen." This God wasn't the God Quinette prayed to. This was the God of Sudan, who had to be asked not to kill people, or starve them, or make them sick.

She walked back to the garrison with Negev. After they'd gone through the passage in the hills, she saw several figures dancing on a wide ledge atop a promontory.

"What are they doing?"

Negev replied vaguely that it was "for the sibr," and when she suggested they have a look, he shook his head. "Men are not allowed. Women only."

Now her curiosity was piqued. "Well, I'm a woman. Could I go by myself?"

"You are white lady, missy, and I don't know if it is permitted. If someone tells you to go away, please to do it."

She turned up a path, her approach masked by the ring of boulders that made a natural wall around the ledge. With the excitement of doing the forbidden, she hid behind one of the boulders and cautiously raised her head. High oblong rock formations leaned into one another at the back side of the ledge, like the poles to a teepee, and in the cave-like space between them, a pair of older women sat observing several girls, circling one another, holding long, supple branches or whips. They were naked, except for their beads and bracelets, and their bodies had been lacquered in oil. Three of the girls were Pearl and her cousins, Kiki and Nolli. Their white school dresses were laid out on a boulder. Pearl pirouetted, and as she did, her partner struck her hard across the back with a stick. She winced but made no sound; then her partner offered her back, and Pearl lashed her with a whip plaited of leather. Kiki, Nolli, and the remaining girls were similarly engaged, and they all bore the blows without a cry, only their faces registering pain. Soon blood began to flow, its color shocking against the lustrous black of their skin.

Flinching sympathetically with each crack of wood or leather but unable to turn away, Quinette wondered what she was witnessing. As the older women watched with critical eyes, the girls flailed one another several times more, their heads thrown back and eyes squeezed shut, the scarlet rivulets streaming over their buttocks and down their reed-thin legs. They seemed to be in a state beyond pain, a transcendent rapture, like the passion of saints. One of the women clapped her hands, and the witches' sabbath was over. Almost immediately the girls came out of their collective ecstasy and gathered around their mentors. The women wiped the blood with palm leaves, then dipped their hands into a mound of white ash and powdered the wounds. Quinette ducked down before she was discovered and rejoined Negev.

"They were beating each other," she said, short of breath, her heart fluttering. "Beating each other with whips and sticks. Why?"

He stood up, holding his machine gun by its carrying handle. "For the sibr," he replied—a flat declaration that closed off further inquiry.

She followed him home, confused less by what she had seen than by what it made her feel.

That evening, in response to her questions, Michael explained that the ritual was a rite both of initiation and of purification. The girls were beating the evil out of one another, in honor of the Fire Sibr, and at the same time subjecting themselves to a trial of their womanhood. No less than boys, who were tested in other ways, Nuban girls had to prove they possessed the bravery and strength to withstand the ordeals they would meet as adults. Those who failed suffered disgrace and scorn, which were worse than the sting of a whip. That was why Pearl and the others had not cried out under the blows.

"Was it wrong of me to watch? What would they have done if they'd seen me?"

"I don't know. Our customs don't say one way or the other what would happen if a strange woman observes the ceremony."

In the darkness he was all but invisible. It was good she couldn't see his face; otherwise she wouldn't have had the nerve to confess what she was about to confess.

"Watching them," she began hesitantly, "I felt . . . something."

"Shock? Disgust?" Michael prompted.

"Nothing like that. What I felt was . . . a longing. I envied them."

"But why?"

"I envied them for their pain, and the way they got beyond it."

He was quiet for a time. Then he said, "You already are a woman, Quinette. Your strength and bravery have been tested. I was there when they were, and you did not fail." After another, longer silence, he clasped her chin and turned her head to face him. "That is when I knew I loved you."

She sat inert, her heart pummeling her chest.

"There is no need for you to say anything."

"I can't. I—I don't know . . . Tomorrow? You will be careful, won't you?"

DIRE STRAITS PLAYED softly on Doug's cassette player. Dare was seriously considering stomping on it.

> *Through these fields of destruction*
> *Baptisms of fire*

"Can't believe this is happening," Handy groaned, stretched out on his air mattress. "Two weeks here, not a problem, and this hits me now."

"A hundred and three," Doug said, squinting at Handy's thermometer.

"They're leaving before daybreak." Handy kneaded his stomach. "They're going to make a night march to the garrison."

"You haven't thrown up, so it probably isn't amoebic," Doug said encouragingly. "You could be good to go."

He switched on his headlamp and occupied himself with a bird book—it went everywhere with him—while Nimrod poked at the remnants of his dinner and Dare carefully snubbed a half-smoked cigarette between his fingers and put it back in the pack. He had ten left, enough to last another three days with strict rationing. The prospect of being stuck here without the solace of tobacco wasn't one he relished. Besides the heat, the ticks, and wretched food, the boredom was beyond anything he'd experienced before. This afternoon, after the training exercise, he'd walked to the radio room, contacted Fitz, and asked if there was any change in the fuel situation. There wasn't.

As he left, he pilfered a few sheets of paper from the radio operator. Now, in the intervals between budgeted puffs on his cigarette, he composed by flashlight a letter to Mary. He missed her more than he thought possible; missed her smell, her sarcasm, the tuft of fine atavistic down at the base of her spine that he liked to tickle and that embarrassed her. Nights weren't the worst time; his ache for her was sharpest at dawn—the waking up without her beside him. He was reminded of something an old Air America jockey had told him years ago in a bar in Vientiane: "If you feel like hell when the sun goes down, you're all right—it's when you hate to see it come up that you know you're in trouble."

At the moment he was thinking selfish thoughts that her father get his dying over with and speed her back to Wesley Dare's arms and bed. There wasn't much chance she'd receive the letter before she returned to Africa, even if he mailed it the moment he set foot again in Loki; his only purpose, aside from the mental communion the writing offered, was to keep himself occupied so he wouldn't go insane.

"Heavenly Father, cure me of this sickness that I'll be able to film the operation." Handy was praying aloud. The only thing worse than having a Jesus freak for a roommate was having a sick Jesus freak for a roommate. "You know, Lord, that this footage will bring in the dollars to help your children fight the enemies of your son, Jesus Christ, Amen."

Dare left off his letter and relit the butt. Two things occurred to him: One, the Muslims in Khartoum were petitioning the same God to aid their fight against the followers of Jesus Christ, so did God ever get confused about which side he was on? Two, people like Handy had an exaggerated sense of their importance, thinking that a Supreme Being with a universe to manage would take time off to play doctor to a guy with the runs.

Handy suddenly popped up and scurried to the latrine—a pit enclosed by a grass fence. It appeared that the Divine Physician had other patients to attend to.

"Doug, do you know how to use a video camera?" Handy asked when he returned.

Doug said he did.

"If I'm not good to go—this is a lot to ask, the risks and all—could you take my place?"

At that Dare glanced at his partner and wasn't surprised to see the look of zest on his face.

Handy got his camera, a big Sony, then flopped onto the air mattress as if he'd just finished a long run.

"This is a professional's model," he said, then showed Douglas how to work it, paying special attention to the zoom. He would be shooting at a distance, and it was critical to use the zoom properly. Then something about light metering, the battery pack, and so on.

When the tutorial was finished, Dare took Doug aside. "What in the fuck do you think you're doin'?"

He had a logical explanation—he always had logical explanations for every illogical thing he did. The Friends of the Frontline were a client; therefore he would be doing nothing more than a favor for a client. Also, if Handy's film was successful, the increased contributions it raked in would ultimately translate into more business for Knight Air.

"Aren't you mixed up in this shit a little too much already that y'all have to risk your ass to help make a propaganda movie?"

"You're as mixed up in it as I am, and in some ways a little more."

"In some other ways, a little less. I mean to get unmixed up when the time comes. This isn't my war, and not yours either."

"Yeah, it is," Doug said with an affectless expression and a spooky tranquillity. "There are times when it's plain inhuman not to take sides."

"Me, I'm on Wes Dare's side. Take some advice from an older man. Tell that Bible-thumpin' propagandist y'all have changed your mind. You might get hurt, and old Wes doesn't want to see his partner get hurt, or worse."

"You're forgetting. I've been in combat."

"Goddamn it! This is gonna be *ground* combat, blue-collar combat, in your face and personal, not playin' computer games in an airplane."

"It'll be all right. It might even be fun."

Dare knew when to quit. Some kinds of ignorance were flat-out invincible.

The next morning, almost hallucinating from fatigue, his tongue swollen from thirst, his feet blistered, and every bone and joint aching, he called upon his sleep-deprived brain to produce one good reason for doing what he'd done. The brain offered a multiple choice: (a) Loyalty to fellow aviators being one of his pillars of wisdom, he'd decided to play the role of the experienced noncom to Douglas's young, impetuous officer; (b) corollary of (a) he'd realized he wouldn't be able to live with himself if, for lack of a restraining influence, his partner did something stupid and got himself killed; or (c) the boredom of hanging around camp was so colossal that anything was preferable to it. He chose (d), none of the above, because there was no good reason for subjecting himself to the ordeal of a forced march. He must have acted on blind impulse at three this morning, when, awakened by the sounds of the troops moving out, he saw Douglas shouldering the camera and said, "I'd best go with you." The younger man grinned and replied, "Knew you would." Nimrod saw them off with a face that said, "I hope to see you again."

Dare had almost collapsed, stumbling for hours down a stony track in darkness, his arthritic knees crackling like an echo of the boots, rubber sandals, and plastic slippers crunching the gravel underfoot. Doug had provisioned himself with a canteen of filtered water. It was empty before the march was half through. The troops didn't carry any water—apparently they didn't need it.

Now, as Dare lay on a hilltop overlooking the garrison about a kilometer away, his thoughts, hopes, and desires had reduced themselves to one: water. Water in all its tastes and textures. The satiny water of a woodland pond, the icy water of a glacial lake, the crisp water of a mountain stream; tap water with its hint of chlorine, well water with its hint of iron. He pictured fountains, fishtanks, swimming pools, bottles of Evian racked in a convenience-store fridge.

Doug lay on one side of him, cradling the camera in his elbows; Michael was on his right, with Suleiman and the radio operator, his radio wired to a car battery he'd carried on his head the whole way. Four heavy machine guns guarded by a platoon of riflemen were arrayed along the rim of the hill. Mortar crews stood behind them, the tubes elevated on the bipods, the shells laid side by side. Crouched low, barely more than moving silhouettes in the gray light, the assault troops picked their way down the hillside toward the dry riverbed from which they would launch the attack. A couple of hundred yards beyond, across broken ground strewn with boulders and picketed by thorn trees, was the government garrison: brown tents and grass-roofed huts clustered near a stone building, all of it surrounded by a dirt berm, with a bunker at each corner and a wide break in one side. A road led away from the opening and out across the savannah. A look through Michael's binoculars showed Dare a bulldozer, parked under a tree at the far end of the encampment. Beside it were the prizes—the Land Rover and three trucks.

He licked his parched lips, hoping for a swift victory—the garrison was bound to have a supply of water on hand. The radio crackled: Major Kasli reported that the assault force was in position. Michael called out, "Machine guns! Five hundred rounds each! Guns one and two, fire on the left bunker! Three and four, the right bunker! Mortars! Number one to fire smoke to mark the target! Two, three, four will fire for effect on my command!" The mortar squad leader gave the range and elevation to the first tube's crew, and the loader stood, poised to drop the marking round into the barrel. "Blast away!" Michael shouted, then looked through his field glasses, the deep, measured *dum-dum-dum* of the 12.7-millimeter machine guns and the crack of the mortar, sharp and definite, shredding the morning's peace.

With the target nearly a thousand yards away, the machine-gunners fired with more enthusiasm than accuracy. The bullets spattered into the berm and below it but nowhere near the corner bunkers. The mortar's marking round, spurting white as surf, fell between the riverbed and the garrison. "One hundred meters more!" Michael stood and ranged up and ran down the firing line, whacking the machine-gunners with his stick. "The bunkers! Damn you! Concentrate your fire on the bunkers!" The next fusillade was closer to the mark, the bullets kicking up dust around the sandbagged emplacements, but the second marking round exploded amid the vehicles. Lucky it was smoke instead of high explosive, or the trucks that were the whole point of this exercise would have been wrecked. "Shorter! Shorter by fifty meters!" The tube cracked again. Twenty seconds later the shell burst on the tents. "You have it! All guns, three rounds each! Fire!" Dare plugged his ears against the reports of the eighty-two millimeters. The salvos blasted the tents flat. A hut's grass roof caught fire. The garrison had been caught completely off guard. In the light of the risen sun, tiny figures could just be made out, running out of the tents and the stone building, from which a Sudanese flag flew, or rather hung—there was no wind. "Repeat fire for effect!" The projectiles made a dull, crunching sound that echoed across the clay plain below while Kasli's men, advancing by rushes, dodged and darted among the trees and boulders.

Waving his walking stick, Michael might have been a director, choreographing a war movie. Doug was the cinematographer, now filming close-ups of the gun crews, now zooming on the attack below. His face shone. He was in hog heaven. Rocket-propelled grenades crashed into the bunkers, dirt and debris flying out from the blasts. Government troops had taken up positions on the berm and were firing down on the attacking SPLA. Several men dropped, but it was difficult to tell if they'd been hit or were taking cover. The twelve-sevens, *dum-dum-dum,* raked the berm. Under their covering fire, half the assault force made a frontal attack on the eastern side; the other half peeled off in a flanking maneuver to charge the south side. Puffs of smoke squirted out of the ground. Dare thought he saw a few men fall. The advancing troops wavered, stopped, then turned and fled behind some rocks. The radio crackled again. Kasli, in a voice registering strain and panic, reported that they'd run into minefields.

"Calm down!" Michael bellowed into the handset, none too calm himself. "I will clear a lane for you with the mortars. You must rush behind them!" He dropped the handset and looked at Dare with a weak smile. "Let us hope my boys are good enough."

The defenders were trading sporadic bursts with Kasli's men. The twelve-sevens poured plunging fire on them and once again swept them off the berm. A garrison mortar went into action—the shell crunched into the hillside, about a hundred yards down. A second struck half that distance closer. Shrapnel pinged overhead, a sound like piano wires snapping in two.

"Got us spotted, Doug, walkin' it in, sixty-ones," he said, as if identifying the caliber made a difference.

While Michael's mortars ranged in on the minefield, the enemy's (Dare had to think of them as the enemy because it was his war now because he needed water and the trucks captured intact because he needed to ride back because another march like this morning's would kill him if he didn't die of thirst before then) dropped a shell on the machine gun at the far end of the line. The weapon clattered down the hill, and someone screamed.

The shrieks cued Doug to live out some fantasy of combat heroism. He dropped the camera and started to run to the wounded man's aid. Dare tackled him from behind, pinning him. "Dude, get off me!" Dare held him down. "You ain't goin' nowhere, you goddamned idiot!" SPLA mortars fired, the shells exploding in a series of rapid *ka-rumps*. With Doug squirming under him, Dare raised his head and saw the bug-size specks that were Kasli's troops sprinting into a pall of smoke. It enveloped them for a moment; then they reappeared, scrambling up the berm, with more men charging behind them, through the breach in the minefield opened by the barrage.

"Cease fire!" Michael called, and now the only sound, aside from the wounded man's cries, was the distant stammer of semiautomatic rifles. The assault force was shooting into the defenders, caught within their own four walls. It had to be like shooting cattle in a pen, although Kasli's troops had not blockaded the break in the embankment. They were leaving the militiamen a way out, not, Dare assumed, as a gallant courtesy but to make things easier on themselves. The trapped animal fights the hardest. Some government soldiers took to the escape route and fled down the road on foot. A few more followed in one of the trucks, and though they were supposed to capture it, Kasli's men couldn't resist the target the truck presented. An RPG burst under the vehicle, which tottered on two wheels, then rolled over onto its side, spilling its passengers. A second RPG slammed into its undercarriage, and the whole thing was engulfed in a ball of flame. A Hollywood volume of rifle fire, almost as seamless as the tearing of a large sheet of canvas, went on for a full minute, then fell off to scattered bursts, then to single shots, and finally the morning's peace returned, no more affected by the frenzied noise than a pond by the ripples of a thrown rock.

Michael the Archangel surveyed the destruction with his binoculars. "Let us go and see what we have got," he said, betraying no emotion.

Inside the garrison every sight, scent, and sound reminded Dare of some other war. The snap and smell of flaming thatch triggered memories of Laos and Vietnam. The corpse with the back of its head blown away and the pudding of brains quivering on the ground called to mind a Congolese rebel, head-shot in a fight over an airfield near the Rwandan border. The dead Sudanese soldier with his abdomen ripped open and his viscera coiling out like some sort of revolting toothpaste from a tube— he'd seen a Contra looking like that in Nicaragua.

"Our boys sure did make these ragheads sorry they joined the army, didn't they?" he said to Doug. "Don't forget to get some close-ups of these here bodies. Enemies of Jesus Christ, Handy said."

Water. He left his partner to go in search of it. Stepping around and over corpses and through the wreckage of the tent camp, cots, blankets, and shredded canvas strewn everywhere, he came to the stone building— the garrison headquarters. Inside, fingers of sunlight pierced the bullet holes in the tin roof and fell on several riddled jerry cans, lying helter-skelter in a puddle. He was thinking about licking the water off the floor when he spotted an undamaged container, upright in a corner. A Sudanese officer slumped against the wall beside it, but he was beyond all need of a drink. The five-liter plastic can was about half full. If he believed in miracles, Dare would have called its survival a miracle. Hoisting it in both hands, he tipped it to his lips. The water was warm and flat-tasting, and he gulped until his gut swelled.

He lugged the can outside and offered it to Doug, busy filming SPLA troops harvesting enemy weapons and loading them onto the two remaining trucks.

"I don't have any tablets," Doug said, setting the camera down. "Do you?"

"Sure don't."

Doug shrugged and drank with greedy swallows, water dribbling down his chin. "Goddamn, that's good." He wiped his mouth and guzzled more. "It's worth getting sick over."

Someone fired a shot from across the compound. There was another, and a third. Kasli, with a few other men, was kicking bodies and shooting any that showed signs of life.

"Y'all should get some footage of that, don't you think?"

"No need for that."

"Yeah. Handy's movie would get an R rating instead of PG-thirteen. 'The following film contains scenes of extreme violence and is not suitable for children.' Still and all"—he lifted the Sony off the ground and pointed it at Kasli and his cleanup crew—"I figure he'll want some realism to put those contributors of his in a giving mood." Dare focused on a khaki-clad militiaman with an arm blown off the shoulder. He was quite dead, but Kasli shot him in the head with a pistol anyway, and then one of his men bent down to pull off the dead man's boots. "Yup, they're gonna empty their wallets when they see this."

"All right, Wes, that's enough." Douglas grabbed for the camera. Dare let him take it. "They can barely take care of their wounded, so how can you expect them to take care of the enemy's? It's better than leaving them here to suffer."

"Kind of like a mercy killing?"

"Call it that if you want,"

"Mercy," Dare said. "Mercy, mercy, mercy."

MICHAEL'S THRILLING, ASTONISHING declaration had left her in no fit condition for work. After she'd finished up with the two remaining meks, she attempted to make a census of the abducted persons from their villages and the others', but she would count off only a few names before the words *That is when I knew I loved you* caused her to lose track. In her distraction, she wandered the mission grounds alone, asking herself how he could be so sure of his heart and if she loved him. She was learning that war has the same effect on human emotions as a gorge has on a placid river—it accelerates them. She was torn between a desire to be sensible and another to leap recklessly into the swift turbulence and surrender herself to its power.

She used an inflamed tick bite on her arm as an excuse to see Ulrika. Finding refuge from the sun under a tree, she waited until the nurse had seen to her patients. Then, stepping into the hut, hardly bigger than a storage closet, the shelves racked along all four walls making it appear smaller still, Quinette rolled up her sleeve, baring the welt above her wrist.

"You have had in your hands a chicken?"

Quinette nodded. Last night she'd helped Pearl pluck a chicken for dinner.

"*Ja*. These things come from the chickens. Whoever pulled out the tick left in the head and jaws. This is what causes the inflammation."

Pushing off one foot, Ulrika rolled herself to the table under the window and removed a scalpel and forceps from a drawer. Taking Quinette's arm in her thick strong hands, she daubed the bite with a cotton swab soaked in anesthetic. Then she sliced off a thin shred of skin, pulled out a black object the size of a pinhead with the forceps, squeezed ointment from a tube, and rubbed it in.

"I would give you this to take with you, but I have no more left. I have so little of everything. The child died, early this morning."

"Child?" asked Quinette, buttoning her sleeve.

"The child with the diarrhea." Ulrika's eyes, of a pale unearthly blue, gazed at her steadily. "The mother's milk, it no sooner goes in the mouth than out the other end it comes. The baby dies of the dehydration."

Quinette detected an accusatory glint in the woman's stare. No, her own imagination and her guilt had put it there; Ulrika couldn't know.

"Would you have saved him if you had more medicine?"

"Possibly."

The indefinite answer left Quinette unsure about her culpability.

"This is certain—if I am not soon resupplied, some other child will die," Ulrika said.

"As soon as Wes and Doug get back, I'm going to let them know how desperate you are," Quinette promised, figuring that this intention—the intention alone—would propitiate her conscience. "I'll tell them to make sure there's plenty on the next flight in. Give me a list of what you need and I'll see to it myself that you get it."

"What do you mean, when Wesley and Douglas get back? Where have they gone?"

"With Michael. On the operation. They went with Michael."

This was a good moment to change the subject, but she didn't know how to begin, nor even if she should begin. Wouldn't she be betraying Michael's confidence?

Ulrika looked at her quizzically. "There is something else I can help you with?"

"Could I talk to you? It's not a medical problem. It's about Michael."

"What about him?"

She was silent. With a scooping movement, the nurse prodded her to speak.

"Last night he—" Quinette laughed and rolled her eyes toward the ceiling. "Could you keep this to yourself?"

"If I knew what, I would."

"He told me that he was in love with me."

"This is not a surprise," Ulrika said without hesitation. "He speaks about you a great deal. And?"

"I guess I had to talk to someone about it, another woman."

"Because you don't know if with him you are in love."

Quinette said nothing.

"If you don't know, that means you aren't."

Count on Ulrika to be blunt, even brutal, Quinette thought. "It isn't that, it's—"

"It is this? If you do love him, you are afraid of what could come of it."

"Exactly. And I don't like to think of myself as being afraid of anything."

"You would be a fool if you were not afraid." Ulrika patted her arm.

"For this I have remedy, for that none. You must look to yourself for the remedy."

DARE HAD FALLEN asleep—passed out was more like it—his chin to his chest, head flopping side to side with the rocking motion of the truck. A jolt knocked his skull against the window frame and woke him. From the rear came the groan of a wounded man, one of several piled up like bloody sacks.

"Sorry about that," Douglas said.

"Talkin' to me or him?" Dare jerked his thumb at the back window.

Doug glanced at the odometer. A wonder he could read it, with the talcum-thick dust blowing through the windows. "At this rate, we'll make the last of it around moonrise."

They were in a dry riverbed, all six of the Russian army truck's wheels seeking purchase in the sand. In planning the operation, Michael had neglected to find out which of his men knew how to drive. It turned out none could, with the exception of Suleiman, Major Kasli, and Michael himself. Considering that the object had been to capture motor vehicles, Dare thought that a right strange oversight, but it did save him from leaving the comfort of his prejudices. Michael's diligent planning and efficient execution of the attack had almost forced him to change his opinions about Africans; now he didn't have to. No Vietnamese officer would have overlooked such a critical detail, hell no Arab, Honduran, or Nicaraguan would have. It was a very African thing to do.

So Michael had to take the wheel of one truck, with his second in command riding shotgun. Douglas and Dare took the other, and Suleiman, the ex-heavy-equipment operator for the Ministry of Aviation, drove the Land Rover. It was leading the column. Michael's truck followed, carrying the captured weapons and the dead (he'd lost seven men), then Dare's and Douglas's with the seriously wounded. The riverbed made a natural road, and the trees galleried along its banks helped to mask the convoy's movement from the air. It couldn't go much faster than a walking pace, so the troops tramping behind and alongside had no trouble keeping up.

"Let me know when you want me to spell you," Dare said, a sour taste in his mouth.

"Doing fine. Good to go all day. This has been an incredible experience."

"That's what you call it? An experience?"

His partner's face seemed to glow beneath the film of dust. "Seeing the difference we've made in action. Two, three months ago these guys couldn't have pulled off what they did today."

"Gives you that nice warm feeling, and the best part is, this experience ain't over yet."

They drove on, the riverbed narrowing as it rose toward its source in the mountains, wavering insubstantially in the heat shimmer, like an illusion of mountains. Half a mile farther on, the banks became miniature cliffs the height of the trucks' roofs, with not much more than a yard's space on either side. Suleiman stopped and climbed out of the Land Rover.

"We cannot go more this way. No room to pass. We must back up."

They did, and after Suleiman found a way up the bank, they proceeded along the river, weaving through the corridor of trees, until a steep-sided gully twenty feet deep blocked their path. Suleiman turned a hard right and followed the gully out into the rolling, open grasslands. He stuck out his hand, signaling for a halt, then got out again to range ahead on foot, looking for a way across.

"This keeps up," Dare grumbled, "it won't be moonrise, it'll be sunrise tomorrow."

Then he saw Suleiman running toward them, waving his long arms. "Heel-o-coptar!"

Dare flung his door open, leaped out, and cowered in the riverbed, Doug beside him with the video camera. All around, men were jumping in, taking up firing positions. The helicopter came on with a throaty growl, following the course of the river. Dare reckoned he had a good idea what it feels like to be a field mouse when a hawk shows up in the neighborhood. From somewhere up ahead Michael and Kasli yelled to the men to hold their fire until they got the order. Suleiman, sprawled flat under the opposite bank, was praying out loud—*Bismillah ar-rahman, ar-rahim*—and Doug lay on his back, the camera aimed toward the sky. Dare tore off his baseball cap and clapped it over the lens. "That thing will flash like a mirror, you goddamned—" He didn't get a chance to say what kind of a goddamned thing he was. The chopper passed directly overhead, its shadow broken by the trees: an old Soviet MI-24, the gunship that had raised holy hell in Afghanistan, a flying tank. It was five hundred feet above, drifting, almost hovering, its armored underside like the breast of some pterodactyl, bombs and rocket pods racked under its stubby wings, minigun barrels protruding from the nose. Quite a package. Suleiman's prayers grew frenzied, a garble of pleas in which Dare could distinguish only one word, *Allah*. The trucks and men remained hidden in the gallery forest, but the Land Rover was parked in the open. The chopper crew had to see it. Then some fool, tempted beyond endurance by the low, slow-flying gunship, opened fire. That gave everyone else the go-ahead, rifles and machine guns ripping through the trees, sending down flurries of shredded leaves. Stung but otherwise unhurt by the swarm of bullets, the helicopter swooped away. Kasli screamed at the soldier who'd shot first, smacked him in the face with his pistol, and kicked him, his lesson in military discipline cut short by the gunship, which looped around and let loose with its miniguns, firing so quickly—four thousand rounds a minute—that the three-second burst made a noise like a millsaw cutting a log. There was a loud *whump* as the Land Rover's fuel tank burst. Michael's troops were firing without restraint. Now a thousand feet up, the chopper wobbled—it had taken a solid hit—and flew off again.

Two men, one with a SAM-7, another with a spare launch tube and missile strapped to his back, sprinted into the open—the trees must have prevented them from taking their shot. Rising to a crouch, Dare peered over the bank. Ten yards in front of him the men lay, the SAM's launcher resting on a flat boulder. Flames engulfed the Land Rover; smoke funneled upward, a perfect aiming point for the gunship. And if it didn't serve, the missile-gunner's outfit would: He was one of the army's cross-dressers, garbed in a pink housedress.

A mile to two miles out, the MI-24 orbited the savannah. The last burst of ground fire had given the crew something to think about before trying another strafing run. The chopper finished its circle, started another. The missile-gunner got up, his outfit standing out amid the duns and greens, shouldered the launcher, and lined up the fore and rear sights but held his fire.

"Well shoot, for Christ's sake!" Dare shouted. The trucks had survived the first strafing; they wouldn't survive the next one. "They're in range! Shoot!"

Doug said, "What the hell's wrong?"

"The guy's dressed like a girl for one, and for another, he was carrying a spear two months ago, that's what. There's a two-stage trigger on a SAM. Pull it back once, a green light tells you you're locked on, the second pull fires the booster. Somebody must have put that thing in his hands with a set of instructions he couldn't read."

The gunship banked and came on, nose canted slightly downward, rotors flashing in the sun. Now everyone was yelling in Nuban and English—"Shoot! Shoot!" Doug bounded out of the riverbed, snatched the launcher from the gunner's hands, shouldered it, and aimed. There was a brief pause; then he fired. The booster rocket flamed and fell; the warhead rocket ignited. A red ball streaked on a trajectory parallel to the gunship's flight path before the warhead sensed the heat from the engine and curved toward it. The pilot saw the missile. Dare knew he did because he deployed decoy flares. As they hung in the sky like incandescent carnations, the pilot pulled into a turn and roll to throw the missile off course, but the infrared sensors would not be seduced, either by the flares or by the maneuver. The warhead rammed into the jet engine's exhaust. Dare felt the blast, a punch of wind. The main rotor blew off, twirling away as debris flew in all directions and the fuselage flipped over and crashed upside down, the bombs erupting, the miniguns' rounds cooking off in the inferno. Everyone lay flat in the riverbed as a maelstrom of shrapnel cracked through the trees above.

When it was over, Michael's soldiers jumped up and fired celebratory shots into the air. They whooped and cheered. They poured out of the riverbed and mobbed Douglas, chanting his name, "Dug-lass! Dug-lass!"

He was breathing hard, and when he turned to Dare, his eyes had a weird glitter.

"Payback, Wes," he said.

"And payback is a bitch," Dare said. "Who taught you to shoot a SAM?"

"You did."

"You're a quick study, Dougie my boy."

Michael elbowed through the crowd, clasped Doug's hand, then pulled his arms overhead and turned him in a circle, calling out, "Douglas *Negarra!*" The troops echoed, "Dug-lass *Negarra!*" and hoisted him on their shoulders and carried him around. Even now Doug maintained his air of self-assured serenity, as if this adulation were his birthright. "Dug-lass *Negarra!*"

"*Negarra,*" said Michael, "is like brother but more than brother. When a man is your negarra, it means you will lay down your life for him."

"Him, too!" Doug hollered from his perch, pointing at Dare. "He told me how to shoot it!" He broke out laughing. "Taught me all I know!"

So Michael raised Dare's arms and conferred the title on him. The soldiers lifted him up. His bulk proved more challenging, but they managed it. He felt a little silly, bouncing like a kid riding on Dad's shoulders, a mass of dark, ecstatic faces beneath him, a forest of arms, pumping their rifles up and down in time to the chants. "Dug-lass *Negarra!* Wes-lee *Negarra!*"

"Our war, dude! Like it or not, it's ours."

"Till I'm gone," Dare said. "Then it's all yours."

The soldiers carrying him changed direction, so he faced the wreckage of the helicopter, its blackened hulk showing through a wall of flames. The smoke joined the plume from the still-burning Land Rover to form a flat cloud dark as a crow's wing and dense enough to cast a shadow over the charred corpses of the crew, the trees, the riverbed, the triumphant men.

SHE FOLLOWED ULRIKA'S advice, and looked to herself but could find no answer there. Returning to her tukul, she forced herself to concentrate on her work, roughing out in her notebook a report she would submit to Ken. It took up most of the day, and when dusk fell without Michael's return, she was filled with worry, and more than worry—a creeping dread that emboldened her to go his headquarters and ask a radio operator if he'd gotten any news. An officer told her to leave—an operation was in progress and she was not permitted inside.

"I only want to know if Michael's all right," she said.

"The operation is going well," he replied. "Please to go, missy."

She went back and pressed Pearl if she'd learned anything. Pearl assured her that her father would return.

"You've heard then? He wasn't hurt?"

"My father always comes back," she said, and gave her a long, penetrating look of uncertain meaning.

THEY GOT LOST for a while, night fell, and afraid that taking the vehicles cross-country in darkness would result in a broken axle or some other mishap, Michael halted the march a few miles short of the airfield. His troops dropped where they stood and went to sleep. Dare and Douglas found a tarpaulin between the seats and the rear of the cab and stretched it out beside their truck as a ground sheet. Two of the wounded men died during the night, and their bodies were transferred to the other truck in the morning, so now nine corpses were interred under the captured rifles and mortars, and the odor leaking through the mound of metal reminded Dare of road-killed skunk mixed with marsh gas. *Sooner we get them into the ground, the better,* he thought, feeling every rock and pebble he lay on.

They reached the airfield in less than two hours the next morning. It was as far as the vehicles could go. Their cargo, human and inanimate, was unloaded, and Michael sent runners to announce the victory and assemble porters to haul the weapons and carry the wounded to the clinic, the dead to their graves.

Still worn out, the troops sprawled under the doum palms before beginning the last leg to their base. One man took off his shoes and poured blood out of them. Doug had flopped down under a tree, hands folded contentedly on his stomach, the video camera at his side.

Dare delicately pulled his last sweat-browned cigarette from the pack. "It ain't my intention to haul my potbellied, middle-aged ass all that way to headquarters. I'm stayin' here. I'm gonna radio Fitz from the plane and tell him to beg, borrow, or steal some fuel on account of it is my intention to take a hot shower and shave no later than tomorrow night, and change out of these clothes and eat somethin' other than the ration of shit these folks call food and have pleasant dreams between clean sheets. It's gonna be your job to haul your young, in-shape ass back there and see how Handy's comin' along. This is what your blood brother wants you to do. There's still some water in the jerry can. Fill your canteen, leave some for me."

"That's the longest speech I ever heard you make," said Doug.

"The thought of gettin' the fuck out of here makes me crazy with happiness."

"Handy might not be well enough to walk."

"Then get some of these Nuban studs to carry his holy roller ass, and if that won't do, tell him he'll have to wait to come out on the next relief flight. He's been here two weeks, another one won't kill him."

AFTER A RESTLESS night and needing to occupy herself, she asked Pearl if she could help her and her cousins with their endless chores. The girl was shocked: Quinette was a guest, and a guest didn't do menial household work. Quinette insisted. Pearl said very well, she could lend a hand preparing the midday meal, bean stew and groundnut paste.

She took down an armful of dried beans from a platform beside the kitchen and placed them in a mortar made from a hollowed-out tree trunk. After showing Quinette how to pound them—gently, because the idea was to separate the beans from the pods, not mash them—the girl gave her the pestle, as long as a canoe paddle and three times as heavy. When the batch was done, Pearl, her strength belied by her slender arms, lifted the mortar and poured the beans and empty pods into a basket, which Kiki raised overhead and tipped slowly, the beans falling into a metal pot on the ground while the pods, light as paper, were carried away by the wind.

The beans were transferred into a clay cooking pot and set on the hearth to roast until they were ready for grinding. Pearl scooped several handfuls onto a stone slab, then knelt and, pressing her toes into the ground to gain leverage, mashed the beans into a flour with a hand-held stone. This was done in the shade cast by the overhanging fronds of two tall palms growing just outside the courtyard wall. Even so the sun's heat struck like a hammer. Kiki and Nolli, crushing groundnuts into a paste, had stripped down to loincloths. Before grinding the next batch of beans, Pearl took off her skirt and T-shirt, revealing an identical undergarment—a *barega,* she called it—and went back to work.

"Not easy," she said, sitting up straight. "Do you wish to?"

Quinette nodded and, on a whim, kicked off her sandals and removed her shirt, shorts, and bra, leaving on only her panties. The girls gawked. If they had seen white women before, they had never seen one naked, or nearly so. The tan lines at her throat and around her arms fascinated them. They touched her, puzzled as to why some of her was light brown, the rest pale. She pointed at the sun and attempted to explain how it darkened her exposed skin, but she wasn't sure if they made the connection.

She knelt at the grinding slab, took the stone in her right hand, cupped her left over it, and rocked forward, pressing down hard. Pearl was right about it not being easy. It was the sort of physical labor she hadn't done since she'd helped her father pitch bales into the hayloft. Sweat washed the oil in her hair into her eyes, half-blinding her, and her back and arms ached, but she found in the work the sort of pleasure people do in strenuous but mindless tasks.

She was still at it when he returned, exhausted, coated in dust. He was taken aback by the sight of her. Embarrassed, she put on her clothes and checked an impulse to hold him.

"What were you doing?" he said finally in a dull, reproachful voice. "That's not work for a guest."

He scolded Pearl for allowing it. Sullenly the girl put the crushed beans into the pot, mixed them with water, and placed them on the coals.

"I asked if I could help out," Quinette said in her defense. "Insisted on it."

"She should have insisted back at you," Michael replied sternly and, without another word, went into one of the tukuls. She could hear water splashing from the calabash. He came out, bathed and changed into a clean uniform, and sat in the courtyard, motioning to Kiki to bring him something to eat. The girl scooped the mixture of beans and groundnut paste into bowls made from split gourds and served one to him, one to Quinette. She knew better than to ask him about the battle, for he was now like her father when he fell into one of his remote moods, journeying into some inner space where none could reach him. He finished eating and stared off into the middle distance.

"It went well," he said, his tone still dull. "I lost very few men."

"I am relieved to hear that."

"Douglas shot down a helicopter. I heard him say, 'Payback.' What does that mean?"

"He evened the score. For what happened a month ago."

Michael snorted. "As if war is a feud? There were a lot of them left alive. We couldn't take them with us, and I don't think we would have if we could have. We shot them. We shot them all."

She pitied him, having to do and see terrible things, but felt none for the ones who had been shot. None whatsoever. "What would they have done if it had gone the other way?"

"What do you think they would have done? War is cruelty, you cannot refine it. A great commander in your civil war said that. Sometimes I think, the crueler I can make it, the sooner it will be over, but . . ."

He went inside and was soon asleep.

Quinette worked on her report for a while, then she too took a nap. She slept soundly, dreamlessly. It was nearly dusk when she awoke and, stepping out into the courtyard, saw Michael transformed. Instead of a beret, he was wearing a topee with a crest pinned to its front and, over his shirt, a leopard-skin smock. This outward change was matched by an inward one, evidenced by the smile he gave her—the smile that was like an embrace. He'd returned from his mental journey, returned to himself.

"My father's, when he was in the British army," he said, tapping the cork helmet's brim. "There is going to be a dance tonight, to celebrate the victory. This is for you."

He picked up a bundle wrapped in brown paper and handed it to her. She tore off the wrapper and unfurled a long dress, with a broad black stripe running down its middle and two more circling the billowy sleeves. The pattern recalled the geometric shapes of the wall paintings inside the tukul: concentric rings, diamonds, squares within squares, all in harmonious colors of orange, yellow, and terra-cotta. A sunrise of a dress.

"Thank you. It's beautiful. Should I try it on?"

"And to please keep it on. I would like you to come to this dance in that dress."

She went into her hut, stripped bare, and changed, loving the touch of soft, clean cotton against her skin. Pearl came in with a set of hoop earrings and a bead necklace. She put them on and freshened her lipstick, but she felt awkward, like a poseur, as she stepped out.

"White Nuba Woman!" she said, laughing.

*　　*　　*

WITH MICHAEL AND DOUGLAS at its head, and Quinette and Pearl just behind them, a torchlit procession marched to the dancing ground in New Tourom. It resembled a Mardi Gras parade, with the soldiers wearing a bizarre mix of costumes—sunglasses and fezzes, camouflage trousers beneath bare chests that were palettes for painted designs, arms plumed with feathered armbands—and old women, careless of their withered, fallen breasts, ripping off their blouses to wave them in the air and proclaim the Nubans' ancient right to bare their flesh without shame. To take one's clothes off and dance the dances of one's ancestors, said Michael, was a gesture of defiance against the strictures of *Sharia*, Islamic law.

Quinette gave no thought to the politics of nudity when they arrived at the dancing ground. She was too captivated by the scene, washed by the supernatural light of a gibbous moon. Drummers and musicians with their *douberre*—the trumpets made from antelope horns—were assembled, girls with flesh oiled and painted in red and ochre formed half a circle, men the other half. The girls stood, the men sat on logs, heads bowed, sheaves of bundled grass in their laps. Pearl ushered Quinette to the female side of the circle. The douberre players blew deep, hollow notes, a choral of older women began to sing, and at a wild burst of drums, a group of girls moved forward, swinging their hips, swatting the air with the grass sheaves.

"This is called Nyertun," Pearl said. "A girl's love dance."

Some of the men wore bells tied to their ankles and, tapping their heels, added a rhythmic *jing-jing-jing* to the drumbeats, the swishing of the grass bundles. More girls joined in. The drumming grew faster. The space came alive with orgiastic movement, limbs gleaming like polished metal in clouds of moonlit dust. As the girls danced closer to the men, the air seemed charged with a mounting excitement, heightened by the tinkling of the bells. One of the girls approached a man, brushing against him, then quickly swung one leg over his shoulder and rested it there, her body swaying. Except for his tapping foot, he remained immobile, his gaze held modestly to the ground. Her movements and his stillness created an electric tension between licentiousness and chastity, passion and restraint. Now the others followed her lead, each girl choosing a man, flinging a leg over his shoulder as he sat. The couples remained in that pose for a few seconds, until the girls spun away. At a change in the drums' rhythm, the men rose and danced after their partners. Couples twirled around each other in one spot, striking each other with the sheaves, and then danced out of the circle and went off together into the darkness. Quinette realized that the Nyertun was a mating ritual, and the women got to do the choosing.

Marissa was being liberally consumed. She took a calabash that was offered to her. The fermented sorghum did not taste like beer—she didn't know what it tasted like—but it wasn't unpleasant, and she drank freely. Looking on, she saw Michael tug Douglas into the middle of the ring and seat him among the remaining men. At the sight of a foreigner joining in, women ululated, men blew whistles. One of the female dancers, older than the rest, danced toward him. Tall, stately, her back arched, abandoned to the rhythms yet in control of every sinuous movement, she brushed against him, Douglas immobile as she tossed her leg over his shoulder and swayed. Then, as she moved away, he pursued her, mimicking the men's dance none too gracefully, but the crowd cried its approval.

"You would like to dance?" Pearl asked.

Quinette's hand went to her own throat as she mimed the question, "Me?"

"It is easy. I will show you."

Pearl demonstrated how to hold her arms, at a slight angle to her body, with her palms facing forward, and what to do with her feet—a kind of kicking movement. Feeling self-conscious, Quinette took another drink of marissa before giving it a try. The steps weren't intricate—she'd always been a good dancer; the hard part was throwing that stately arch into her back. When Pearl thought that she'd got the idea, she handed her one of the grass sheaves and nudged her toward the circle. She resisted, a victim of stage fright and of Pastor Tom's censuring voice sounding in her head. She took another drink and practiced some more with Pearl. After a minute or two she thought that perhaps she didn't care what Pastor Tom would say.

She stepped out, and her entrance brought the same outburst that had greeted Douglas. At first she had a sensation that she was outside herself, and she judged that she looked like an imposter in her Nuban dress; but the ululations and whistles encouraged her. She heard in those sounds Africa giving voice to its acceptance of her, and she experienced a lightness, a soaring relief, as if she'd been suddenly cured of a debilitating sickness.

The drumming got inside her, pulsing with her blood. She rejoiced in the movements of her body; it was liquid, her legs and hips seemed to flow. She knew now how to answer the declaration Michael had made to her. Aware of a hush that had fallen over the spectators, waiting to see what she would do, she ventured closer to him, swaying with abandon, swishing the grass bundle. He saw her and, in obedience to the rules of the Nyertun, brought his head down demurely, his legs trembling with latent excitement. She brushed teasingly against him. She felt wild and wanton; then with the sheaf in one hand, she paused to hike the dress up over her knees with the other and raised a leg to his shoulder. Just as she did, she bowed slightly to say, "Now I've said it."

He rose and danced with her. Immersed in a bath of sound and movement, she experienced a communion like the one she'd known on her first journey to Sudan, when she seemed to merge into her surroundings. She lost all sense of herself as a being separate from those around her, while they, ululating, blowing their whistles, lost awareness of her separateness from them. Loneliness was the disease from which she'd been released. It had afflicted her ever since her father's death and her exile from the farm, her father's land. How wonderfully strange that plunging into a deeper exile in Africa had healed her.

HE PULLED THE dress over her head and said, "From this night you will be White Nuba Woman in all ways."

He picked her up and carried her to the bed. The mosquito net fell over them, creating an illusion of perfect privacy. Behind its veil, they embraced and kissed and drank in each other's musky scents. She caressed him, and with his finger he drew circles around both her breasts, then a line between them, and made random patterns on her stomach. Now he plucked at her skin, following the designs he'd traced, circles and loops, straight lines and lines like a child's depiction of ocean waves.

She didn't ask what he was doing, fearful that one word from her would break the spell.

He laid a palm below her navel and whispered, "If you were a Nuba girl, you would be tattooed three times, the first time here, when you are ten years. You go high up into the rocks with only women present, and the tattooist smooths your belly with oil, like this"—he rubbed her there—"and then draws in the oil the designs you choose, like this." He penciled another motif with his fingertip, his touch lambent and warm, like a paraffin flame. "And the final thing she does is to lift up the flesh with a thorn and make a cut with a small knife." He pinched her repeatedly, just hard enough for her to feel it. "When the cuts heal, they make the tattoos. The next time is when you have passed from girl to woman. Again, you go to the secret place high in the rocks, again the tattooist rubs the part of your body where the marks will be with oil, here and here." He massaged her ribs and her stomach just beneath her bosom. "And again—" pinching—"the thorn, the knife . . .

"You are beautiful, Quinette, and I am making you more beautiful." He clasped her ribs and turned her resistless body face-down and knelt over her. "The third time is after you have borne your first child. It's always done to the back. It's the most painful tattooing, it takes two days to complete. Also the most expensive. Your husband has paid the tattooist with goats and chickens and money, he has supplied the oil that is rubbed into you from here to here on the first day." He stroked the nape of her neck, her shoulder blades, her spine down to her hips, his finger sketched curves and slashes, his pinches were harder than before, bringing a light sting. "Many cuts are made, hundreds, that's why this is the most painful, but now a powder is applied, made of herbs and sorghum flour and the ash of burned acacia to ease the pain and stop the bleeding and make the marks stand out from the skin when the cuts heal, because those that stand out are the most beautiful." As he kneaded her back again, she felt as if her bones had turned to gelatin. "On the second day, you are beautified here and here. Here and here the oil is rubbed in." He dug into her buttocks, the backs of her thighs. There she felt his fingertip making spiral imprints before he pinched her, still harder, squeezing her flesh between his nails. He asked if it hurt and she nodded and he told her she mustn't make a sound, a Nuba woman was brave and never made a sound when the tattooist's thorn and knife pricked her. "Imagine you are lying on the warm, smooth rocks, high in the mountains, I am the tattooist, I am now soothing the cuts with the powder of ash and herbs and flour." In an almost drugged state, she accepted the pressure of his hands, moving over her bottom, down along her legs and up again. "Now you are fully a Nuba woman, very beautiful, admired by all in your village." His voice seemed to cover her as he parted her thighs. He reached under her to touch her, and she felt how damp she was there when he embraced her at the waist and pulled her toward him. She rose to her knees in a feline crouch, sighed through clenched teeth as he penetrated her to his whole length so that his bristling hairs scratched her. They worked each other into a swift orgasm, and when it came, in a quivering rush, her ass slapping his belly, she felt that their joined selves were floating free of gravity, and in that blissful suspension she knew with the wordless knowledge of the heart that God would forgive her, for with their joyful outcries she and Michael answered the moans of all the wounded and all the mourners' laments, with the wet smack of flesh upon flesh they annulled the strikes that insensate steel had made against flesh. Mourning, steel, blood—all that was no; all this was yes, and what God would begrudge such an affirmation?

Douglas

He had clipped the newspapers, the Arizona Republic, *the* Tucson Daily Star, *others, and pasted them in a scrapbook. He wanted to keep the bad memories fresh; he never wanted to forget them.*

RANCH FAMILY SUES TUCSON DEVELOPER
FOR $16 MILLION

Attorneys for Edith Brady, owner of the Baboquivari ranch, yesterday filed suit in civil court alleging that the purchase of 10,000 acres of the 25,000-acre property was obtained under fraudulent circumstances by WebMar Associates, one of the state's largest housing developers.

STATE TO INVESTIGATE TUCSON DEVELOPER

Arizona Attorney General Laura Altobuono announced today that her office has opened a criminal investigation into the purchase of a ranch property by Web-Mar Associates, builders of Rancho Vista, Tucson's largest retirement community. A civil suit has already been filed against the firm, owned by Weldon E. Braithwaite and Martin Templeton, both of Tucson. The allegations are that the two developers in effect bilked Edith Brady, 86, heir to the Baboquivari ranch, in the $16 million sale of . . .

INQUIRY INTO WEB-MAR WIDENS

Web-Mar Associates, already beset by a civil suit and a state investigation into its purchase of a Spanish land grant ranch, has attracted the attention of federal investigators. . . . Web-Mar is alleged to have signed a contract agreeing to restrict development of the property to ten-acre parcels, but then drawn up another contract allowing high-density housing to be built and hoodwinked the ranch's 86-year-old owner into signing it in a complex shuffle of documents. According to informed sources, the U.S. Attorney's office in Phoenix is looking into evidence of financial links between Web-Mar and Enrique Cabrera, boss of Mexico's biggest drug cartel . . .

ACTS OF FAITH

COURT RULES IN FAVOR OF PLAINTIFFS
IN BABOQUIVARI SUIT

FEDERAL PROBE LAUNCHED INTO DRUG LORD'S
TIES TO TUCSON DEVELOPMENT FIRM

WEB-MAR DECLARES BANKRUPTCY

WEB-MAR CEO FACES CHARGES OF MONEY
LAUNDERING—PARTNER CLAIMS NO KNOWLEDGE
OF DEALINGS WITH MEXICAN KINGPIN

BRAITHWAITE TRIAL OPENS TODAY—
DEFENDANT PLEADS NOT GUILTY

WEB-MAR CEO WILL TAKE THE STAND

TUCSON DEVELOPER KILLED IN CAR BOMB BLAST—
COCAINE CARTEL THOUGHT RESPONSIBLE

Weldon E. Braithwaite, 59, defendant in a federal trial on alleged money-laundering between his firm and the boss of a Mexican drug ring, was killed early this morning when a powerful bomb exploded in his car as he was leaving his home for a second day of testimony.

PART TWO

Warlord

THE JINN VISITED him so often that he'd achieved a rapport with it, speaking to it as he would to a living man. "I will do today what it is said you wish me to do, so why are you here? Why do you trouble me this day?"

Abbas sat across from him, staring with wordless reproach. Ibrahim Idris detested that expression, but he knew it would do no good to look away, because no matter in what direction he looked Abbas would be there, the haft of the knife protruding from his ribs, his wide-set eyes glaring judgment.

"It is the opinion of the elders and my kinsmen that if I make peace with your mother's lineage, you will trouble me no more. Very well, a *murda* takes place this very day, and trust that I will make peace, so go away."

But Abbas remained.

Ibrahim took the copper pot from the fire and refilled his cup with sweetened tea. "Listen, this much I know. God would not permit you to trouble me because I beat you for committing rape. It was you who drew the knife on me. On me! The uncle who was as a father to you!" He flung the tea into his nephew's face and watched the scalding liquid fly right through him and spatter in the dust.

"Ya, Ibrahim. Saddled and bridled and everyone is ready."

It was Kammin, leading Barakat by the reins. At the Dinka servant's approach, the jinn vanished, rising with the campfire smoke through the branches of the tree beneath which Ibrahim had passed a troubled night. A distance away, resembling a flock of egrets in their clean *guftans* and jelibiyas, the elders and the heads of the lineages that stood with Ibrahim's, the Awlad Ali, were gathered around a *haraz* tree.

"You are like the haraz," Hamdan, his old and loyal friend, had told him some time ago. "That is why you suffer." Ibrahim had asked, "How so?" and Hamdan reminded him of the story. At the creation of the world, all the plants and animals were called upon to submit to Allah, but the haraz refused, saying, "I am the lord of the forest, why should I bow before any other lord?" For that, God condemned it to suffer through the hot season in full leaf and to shed its leaves in the rains. "It suffers for its pride," Hamdan had counseled, "and so do you, but you are causing all the Salamat to suffer with you. Is that just? Unlike the tree, you have the means to end your suffering and ours as well."

So he would eat his pride this day. Kammin bent down and locked his hands, making a mounting block. There had been a day when Ibrahim could vault into the saddle, but now he needed a boost. Drawing in the fragrance of camp smoke mingling with the odors of cattle dung, he rode slowly with his entourage through the camp to calls of *"Allah yisalimak"* from the men, to the ululations of the women, to the silent prayers from all that brotherhood be restored with his sister-in-law's lineage, the Awlad Sa'idy, and the two clans aligned with them. The oldest of the old men could not recall a time when the Salamat had been as divided as they were now.

"Why do you look so glum?" asked Hamdan, riding alongside. "This is a murda we're going to, not a funeral."

"I am wary," Ibrahim answered. "My worst enemies are with the Sa'idy. Only one thing will satisfy them, and that is a satisfaction I won't give them, not even if it means breaking the bonds of brotherhood for good and all."

"I've spoken to the mediators," Hamdan assured him. "Believe me, they're on your side. The demand will be made, but nothing will come of it."

His sister-in-law's grief had turned to madness, madness into a cold, abiding fury. At Abbas's burial, she'd thrown herself on his body, wrapped in a white winding-sheet, torn her hair, and cursed Ibrahim. He who had sworn to protect her son had caused his death, as surely as if he'd stabbed Abbas himself. Later, after she'd recovered her senses, she prevailed upon the head of her lineage and the kinsmen of Nanayi, the girl Abbas had pledged to marry, to send a delegation to Ibrahim with a demand for blood money: sixty head of cattle, half to go to his sister-in-law, half to Nanayi's kinsmen. He refused, sixty head being the established price for cases of murder. What blood was on his hands? he asked the delegation. Abbas had tried to murder him and in the blindness of his rage had stumbled and accidentally killed himself. They argued that Ibrahim had lost control of himself, provoking the young man; therefore he was responsible for what happened, all the more so because of his high position.

Ibrahim knew what was going on. For years his enemies in the Awlad Sa'idy had intrigued against him, seeking to unseat him from the omdaship. They knew the demand for sixty head was unreasonable; by making it, they hoped to create a scandal that would prove him unfit to be omda and in the process wreck his chances of winning the prize he sought above all others, the nazirship. To his everlasting disgust, they were using his sister-in-law's sorrow as a pretext for their machinations, while Nanayi's kinsmen were exploiting the situation to increase their own meager herd. Ibrahim owed nothing, but because he was famed for his generosity and for his compassion, he offered to pay thirty head, to be divided equally between the two aggrieved parties.

He had miscalculated both the degree of his sister-in-law's wrath and her lineage's dedication to working his political ruin. His offer was spurned. Later certain men of the Awlad Sa'idy persuaded Nanayi's brothers, who had witnessed the fight between Ibrahim and his nephew, to swear that they had seen the two men grapple; when they next looked, their sister's betrothed lay dead. This testimony, no doubt purchased, was sufficient to bring the case to the local court in Babanusa town. Ibrahim Idris ibn Nur-el-Din, omda of the Salamat, a man of honor, piety, and generosity, a proven leader in the jihad, the father of a martyr, experienced the singular shame and indignity of facing a panel of judges on a charge of homicide.

His trial did not last the morning. His witnesses were more numerous than his accusers' and far more believable for the simple reason that they spoke the truth. The judges acquitted him but agreed that he had behaved provocatively. His offer of thirty head was therefore fitting. They ordered that it be accepted, which it was, though begrudgingly.

The affair should have ended there, but the payment failed to assuage his sister-in-law. He received his first visitation from Abbas one morning as he stepped out of his tent to urinate. He was so startled that he let out a howl, which brought his youngest wife (the same who had aided Miriam's escape) to ask what was wrong. "Look there!" he said, pointing. "Abbas!" She did not see anything; nor did other people, emerging to see what the commotion was about. Some thought he had lost his mind, but the rest accepted that his nephew's ghost had been summoned up by Abbas's mother because she thought she'd been cheated of her due. His kinsmen advised him to give her what she wanted and thus lift her curse. He declined; to pay her would be to admit that he was guilty of the crime of which a court had exonerated him, and that he would never do, not if she called up a hundred jinns to haunt him.

She did not do that, but she did encourage some flesh-and-blood demons to cause him misery. At her instigation, his enemies mounted new intrigues against him. Most were petty and he fought them off easily, but one was very serious. A sheikh of the Awlad Sa'idy, a cousin of his sister-in-law, reported to the authorities that Ibrahim and a certain Messiriya trader had an illegal business arrangement. This trader went about buying back abid captives from their masters and then resold them to infidel foreigners for several times their worth and shared the profits with the omda.

Not only could Ibrahim be stripped of the omdaship for his dealings with Bashir, he could face charges of disloyalty to the jihad if the sheikh was able to prove his allegation. Praise be to God, he could not. He had no witnesses, no evidence; he was only reporting a rumor. It was his word against the word of the omda of the Salamat, and the word of Ibrahim Idris prevailed. The authorities never brought the case to court, but the mere accusation was enough to taint his name. When the old nazir died of his many ailments, the rural council and the provincial governor rejected Ibrahim and gave the post to the nazir's eldest son.

He was a weak, ineffectual man, easily swayed by influential men; and the influential men among the Awlad Sa'idy bade him to remove Ibrahim Idris as omda after an ugly incident further strained relations between the Awlad Sa'idy and the Awlad Ali. A few young hotheads in Ibrahim's lineage took it upon themselves to teach a lesson to the two brothers who had falsely accused him. During the dry-season migration to the south, they fell on Nanayi's brothers, intending to beat them up. Things got out of hand and one was killed. The other swore vengeance. As omda, it was Ibrahim's duty to admit that his people had been in the wrong and to arrange immediately for blood money to be paid to the dead brother's kin and so prevent a blood feud. Still smarting from the injury their perjured testimony had done him, he failed to act.

And so the surviving brother took his revenge, ambushing his attackers one night, killing one and wounding another. Those upon whom vengeance was taken then took vengeance in their turn. Thus began a round of reprisal killings that took five more lives. That was when the rich and powerful men in the Awlad Sa'idy petitioned the new nazir to remove Ibrahim from office.

Hamdan begged him to call a big meeting of Salamat notables to end the feuding. Instead, Ibrahim brought a charge against the sheikh who had accused him of illicit dealings with Bashir, reporting that the sheikh was hiding cattle during the annual census, when livestock were counted to bring tax rolls up to date. "For why you are doing this?" Hamdan asked, pleading with him to avoid aggravating an already explosive situation. "To show these bastards that they cannot trifle with me and get away with it," Ibrahim answered.

He summoned the police to check the kraals. They seized fifty head that the sheikh had not reported to the census-takers and sold them at auction, the proceeds going into the tribal treasury. The indignant sheikh and other Sa'idy leaders swore on the Koran that if the nazir did not now remove Ibrahim Idris, they would—by force. The *khadim*, the clan drum, was beaten throughout the Sa'idy camps, and men assembled for war. Upon hearing that his adversaries were coming to kill him, Ibrahim Idris ordered the Awlad Ali's drum call to be sounded. Hundreds rallied to his side, the young men brandishing their rifles, women dancing the dances of war and vengeance.

The nazir called on the police to intervene, but they were too few, forcing him to ask the governor to send in the army. Soldiers entered the camps of the Awlad Sa'idy and the Awlad Ali and broke up the fight before it started. The governor's deputy convened a meeting in Babanusa town to find out what had caused this dispute. Afterward the deputy privately informed Ibrahim that the government would not tolerate Muslims fighting Muslims when every man was needed for the jihad. He was to put his house in order, according to tribal customs; if he could not do it, his tenure as omda was over.

The threat provided him with the incentive to call for the murda that Hamdan had been urging.

They arrived at the appointed place, a grove of ebony trees not far from the millet gardens of the Awlad Sa'idy. The two alliances—the Awlad Ali together with the lineages loyal to it, the Sa'idy with its allies—sat in a crowded circle, facing each other. The chairman of the peace conference and the mediators sat off to one side, so as not to show favoritism. Examining the faces opposite him, Ibrahim knew this business was going to be as difficult as he'd anticipated.

"In the name of God the all-merciful, the all-loving-kind," the chairman intoned, and opened the proceedings. Before the central dispute could be addressed, the matter of blood-debts incurred as a result of the seven revenge killings had to be resolved. The negotiations were clamorous, with men shouting opinions over one another, waving sticks or riding crops to stress a point. Despite the confusion of voices, all the cases were settled by midday. A meal was served—the meat of a bull slaughtered for the occasion, with millet and tea. Ibrahim hardly touched his food, his belly fluttering. The discussions had gone smoothly, but the blood-payments were the easy part.

The hard part began in the afternoon, after the allied lineages rode off, their business concluded, and the two major disputants reconvened, eyeing each other warily. The chairman called for the elders and notables of the Awlad Ali to speak, one at a time.

Hamdan was first. "A wound fell upon you, and the blood was on us," he said, addressing the Awlad Sa'idy. "We should have come to you to make reconciliation, but we failed to. Then, in vengeance, a wound was on us, and you offered to come to us to settle things before there was more bloodshed, but we did not respond in the spirit of manliness, and this has led us almost to open warfare. The error was all ours. Now we come to make reparations. All we want is brotherhood from you."

His words were greeted with silence. The speeches of the next five men were received in the same way, and then it was Ibrahim's turn.

"I have little to add to what my brothers have said. The stain is upon me. I should have come to you right away, but I did not because of the slanders and false accusations made against me. I was too proud, and now seven sons of ours shall never be seen again. This morning we made reparations for the spilled blood. Now it is time to reconcile our differences. I was very wrong."

He made a dramatic gesture, taking the guftan from off his head and spreading it at the feet of the Awlad Sa'idy's leader, a man with a raven beard. "I lay this before you that you may lay upon it all my mistakes. I want nothing but brotherhood with you. Do not deny it to us. Even if you do, we will not deny you ours."

He sat down, Hamdan glancing at him with approval, but his opponents' faces were as stones. The only sounds were the snorts from the horses tethered nearby, the whine of flies, the rasp of leaves in the wind. When the chairman asked the headman to speak, he took full advantage of Ibrahim Idris's invitation to lay out his mistakes. With angry looks and in a harsh tone, he enumerated them, concluding, with a swat of his riding crop, that he had no desire for brotherhood.

Three more men uttered similar sentiments. The fourth and last—the sheikh whose cattle had been confiscated and sold at auction—accused Ibrahim of bribing the police to say the cows had been hidden from the census-takers, and he'd done this to put money not in the tribal coffers but in his own.

"Ibrahim's omdaship is the omdaship of deceit," he continued. "And who should want brotherhood with such a one?"

Ibrahim, heat rising to his face, started to get up to rebut this calumny, but Hamdan restrained him.

Now it was the turn of the mediators to have their say. Both agreed that the omda was the guilty party, and both implored the Awlad Sa'idy to accept the hand of brotherhood that was being offered.

Silence.

The chairman tried to persuade them. "Listen, you Awlad Sa'idy, in the matter of the omda's errors, I am with you, but the talk you have been making here, in the presence of elders and mediators, isn't proper. The omda has admitted his guilt for not coming to you at the beginning, but you beat him over the head with accusations that have nothing to do with the issue before us. And you have not admitted your guilt in rising into open revolt, threatening to seize the omdaship by force of arms. You would do well to confess it now."

Flies buzzing, horses snorting, leaves whispering.

"What does your silence mean? That you do not see your wrong, or that you do and are ashamed to admit it?"

"We so admit it," the headman replied. "We were wrong. As to the offer of brotherhood, we say this. Let Ibrahim surrender the omdaship and thirty head of cattle or its equal in money."

There it was at last, the demand.

"You are offering to accept brotherhood at a price?" shouted an elder in Ibrahim's clan. "That is outrageous."

Excited voices rose to agree with the old man. There was a lot of yelling back and forth, until the mediators quieted everyone down.

The chairman looked sternly at the headman and said, "What is this talk of cattle and the omdaship? The omdaship is not Ibrahim's to give away. It belongs to the nazir and to the government. Now stop this bargaining, as if you were in a souk. Look at this"—his arm swept—"all of us sitting together. What, I ask you, is sweeter? Come now, make peace without any more fuss."

The headman pondered for a moment, and then agreed, but a few of his kinsmen, the tax-dodging sheikh included, weren't ready to come to terms. Why should they listen to the chairman? they shouted. It was known that he and Ibrahim were friends. The omda was not a prisoner of his office, he could resign and ask the nazir to appoint someone to replace him.

The headman stood and faced them, his hands raised. "Quiet, everyone! Ya, you Awlad Sa'idy, be quiet! The chairman speaks wisely. The omdaship is in the hands of the nazir, and this is sweet, for all of us Salamat to be seated here together, talking instead of fighting. We will make peace. We will now swear alliance and brotherhood by the Koran. We will say the Fatha."

At this Ibrahim Idris jumped up and proclaimed by the divorce of all his wives that if the Fatha were said, he would deliver, as a gift, the thirty head at the next market day, the day after tomorrow.

"Very well, it is agreed," the chairman said, and with hands outspread, he led the assembly in the Fatha: "Praise be to God, Lord of all creatures, the most merciful, king of the day of judgment. Thee do we worship, and of thee do we beg assistance. Direct us in the right way; in the way of those to whom thou hast been gracious; not of those against whom thou are incensed, nor of those who go astray."

Ibrahim Idris exhaled with relief. It was over and he hadn't lost a thing except thirty cows.

Two days later, at the cattle market in town, the black-bearded headman refused to accept them, saying that the Awlad Sa'idy had demanded a price for brotherhood, but now, to show that their desire for it came from the heart, they would forsake all of it. Ibrahim insisted they take the cattle regardless and present them to his sister-in-law as a peace offering. The jinn had not visited him in the past two days, and he wanted to keep things that way.

With business concluded and with a light heart, he called on the nazir to tell him that peace had been restored among the Salamat. All its lineages were again brothers. The nazir lived in a fine house with a walled courtyard scented and shaded by frangipani, where they sat drinking tea and talking. Their conversation was interrupted by a knock at the metal gate. One of the plump nazir's Dinka servants answered.

"Ya, omda, there is a man to see you," the servant said. "He says he has news for you, which must be given in private."

Excusing himself, Ibrahim went out into the dusty street.

"Salaam aleikum," said Bashir, his beard freshly barbered and his clothes spotless.

"Aleikum as-salaam. It's not a good thing for us to be seen together. How did you know I was here?"

"I make it my business to know things," the Messiriya trader said. "And among the things I know is where she is."

Ibrahim, his heart stammering, regarded Bashir, trying to gauge if he was telling the truth. "Where?"

"A town in the eastern Nuba. New Tourom."

He seized Bashir by the arm and pulled him away from the gate. "How do you know?"

"Because I was there one week ago. I made inquiries and I saw her. Yamila, the one you call Miriam. I don't blame you for wanting her back."

"You saw her?" First the jinn had vanished; now this, a still clearer sign that his troubles were at an end.

"A tall young woman with bird's wings tattooed on her belly."

"Al-hamduillah!"

"Our agreement. Two hundred thousand pounds."

"Two hundred once I have her again, you criminal."

"I will take half that now, the rest once you are in possession of her."

"I don't go about with that kind of money on me. What do you think I am? A moneychanger?"

"Your pledge to deliver it by this evening will be sufficient," Bashir said with some insolence.

"Very well, then. You'll get it. Now, tell me what else you know."

"This New Tourom is west of Kauda, well into the hills. The Christians have a church there."

"She's become a Christian?"

"I have no idea. All I do know is that she has been there since she fled from you, and that your son by her, Abdullah, is dead. He did not survive the journey."

"*Dead?* The boy is dead?"

"I regret to tell you he is. And I have further bad news. This New Tourom is very near to where the rebel army in the Nuba has its chief base. I saw a lot of black soldiers about, maybe a thousand, and all very well armed." Bashir paused. "I would say it isn't a place you could shoot your way into, and if you tried, she could be killed in the crossfire. That's what I would say, but then, war isn't my business."

Looking directly at the trader, Ibrahim asked, "Are you saying there might be some other way? Could you and your friends get her out of there and bring her to me?"

"Kidnapping is also not my business. I leave it to you to figure out how to retrieve her, but if I can be of service, please to tell me."

"For a price."

"Of course for a price. We can negotiate that later. As to the price at hand, I am staying with a colleague, a man named Aderrahman. His house is behind the souk. This evening, after prayers. Inshallah, I will see you there with a hundred thousand pounds."

"Inshallah," Ibrahim Idris said, and returned to the courtyard, unable to think for the voice calling her name in his head, over and over. *Miriam.*

Redeemer

AFTER SHE RETURNED to Kenya, Quinette thought that a graph of her moods would resemble the electrocardiogram of someone suffering from acute arrhythmia. Her own heart twitched erratically—spasms of joy when she recalled the dance and their lovemaking, but also convulsions of shame brought on by the thou-shalt-nots of her evangelical faith. Michael's absence caused fits of loneliness, the uncertainty of when she would see him again quivers of anxiety. She would experience dips of melancholy, spikes of excitement, and flutters of terror, all within five minutes. Her emotional fibrillations were impossible to hide—at one point her roommate, Anne Derby, asked if there was a history of bipolar disorders in her family—but she had to hide their cause. Loki was like the small town she'd left behind, prone to brushfires of gossip. Most everyone was liberal about liaisons between whites and Africans (more liberal when it came to white men and black women than the other way around), but a love affair with an SPLA commander was definitely out of bounds. If her involvement with Michael became public, more than her reputation would be tarnished; Ken could very well fire her. So she had to keep her thoughts and feelings to herself, and the lack of a confidant aggravated her symptoms.

She wrote Michael an uninhibited letter—five pages in her peculiar handwriting, slanting so far forward it threatened to topple into illegibility—marched to Knight Air, and handed it to Fitz. Was that a knowing smile he gave her? If it was, he was discreet enough not to ask questions, promising the letter would be delivered in two days, when the next flight was scheduled for New Tourom.

She then suffered the torment of waiting for a reply, and her moods for the next two weeks rose and plunged with greater violence. At last Fitz told her a letter was waiting for her in Knight Air's office. She retrieved it immediately and read it as she walked to her tent.

My Darling Quinette,

With happiness and surprise I received your letter. Forgive me for taking so long to answer. I have been very busy, and of course I had to wait for a plane to deliver this to you.

You begin your letter, "Dear Michael," I begin mine as you see. Is it bad manners to call you "My Darling" on the basis of one night together? (How I wish to have another like it!) I don't care. You are my darling.

I do not feel for you what you feel for me. I feel twice as much! I have thought about you day and night since you left. Before I met you, I had no belief in "love at first sight." Now I do.

I must see you again soon, but I am a soldier and cannot leave my post. I know you also have your responsibilities, but if there is a way for you to return here, I beg you, take it! Please write to me straight away. If I cannot hold you, I must be content to embrace your words. All my love,

Michael

In a delirium, she read it again, hungering for more. Her instinct was to fly to him that day, but those responsibilities he mentioned stopped her. By luck—or was it by God's design?—her responsibilities came to her aid. Ken had studied her report and called her on the sat phone to make arrangements for a redemption mission in the Nuba. This took time, but finally Michael contacted her by radio: Bashir would be arriving in New Tourom with more than one hundred captives. She informed Ken that everything was ready. He and the team arrived in Loki within the week.

In some ways, being near each other was a worse trial than being apart. Michael was aware of her dilemma, and when she landed with Ken and the others, he greeted her with a serious mien and a handshake. Throughout the afternoon the feigning of disinterest strained their nerves. Quinette and her colleagues were put up in a compound of empty tukuls near St. Andrew's mission. She shared hers with Jean, the Canadian nurse. To know that Michael was at his headquarters, less than a kilometer away, and to be unable to go to him was an agony. The next day, as they waited for Bashir's arrival with the captives, she resolved to take a risk. That night, after Jean was asleep, she crept out and walked to Michael's compound, daring not to carry a flashlight though it was a moonless night. Two armed men stood watch by the entrance. His bodyguards! She'd forgotten about them. There was nothing for it now but to brass it through.

She approached them and asked to see the commander. While one stayed with her, the other went inside and soon reappeared with Michael, clad only in his shorts.

"Are you mad?" he said. "This is dangerous."

"I couldn't bear it any longer. I had to see you."

"Dangerous in more ways than one," he scolded. "There are leopards in the Nuba, and they hunt at night." He murmured to the guards, who went off.

"What did you tell them?" Quinette asked.

"Never mind. I sent them away. They can be trusted." He drew her into the courtyard, and as he embraced her, she felt ready to jump out of her skin. "You are a madwoman, but I am happy you are."

Not another word was spoken for the next hour. Their lovemaking had the desperation and intensity of an adulterous affair, the addictive quality of a drug, the satiation of their hunger only creating a deeper hunger.

"Quinette," he said afterward, "perhaps you should go before your friends see that you are missing."

"No!" she whispered with ferocity. "These couple of days are like a gift, and I'm not going to refuse it."

"A gift? From who is this gift?"

Combining her piety with her desires, she clasped his face with both hands and said, "From God. He's given us this time because He understands we're in difficult circumstances. He wants us to be together, and He forgives us."

"Ah, so you have spoken to Him?"

"Don't be sarcastic."

"This isn't wise," he said.

"It isn't supposed to be."

"True. Love is the enemy of wisdom."

She basked in his voice, inhaled his scent mingling with her own, that fragrance of unwashed bodies after sex on a hot night, like vinegar and shellfish and crushed bugs.

"I'm not sure what—" He began, stopped, and began again. "It isn't only the people you work with who would condemn this. Some of the people I work with, they would, too."

"Who?" she asked, recalling the dance, the cries and songs of favor that had greeted her entrance into the circle.

"Major Kasli for one. He thinks all the white people who come here come as spies."

"*Spies?*" She rose to her elbows and looked down at him, profoundly disturbed that Kasli would see her in such a lurid light. "Spies for what? For who?"

"The CIA. He has a lot of strange ideas, but let's not talk about this."

She wasn't ready to let it go. She had an enemy, and she was determined to learn what she could about him. "He would think I was sent here to sleep with you so I could spy on you?"

"Yes."

"But America isn't exactly on good terms with Khartoum, so why would it send a woman to spy on you?"

"You have to understand, logic, reality has nothing to do with Kasli's views. He is . . . If he is not paranoid, he is almost."

She laid her head on his chest. "I wonder what we'll do."

"I've been wondering as well."

"And?"

"I have no answer, but trust that I will have."

The following day, as the redemptions were progressing, her old bodyguard, Negev, approached her with a note. Pleading that she had to relieve herself, she went off and opened it: "When you are finished, please see me. There is something I wish to show you. M."

Distracted, she made many mistakes in recording the slaves' accounts on the laptop. When at last her work was finished, she left with Negev, who escorted her to a place she recognized: the path that led to the promontory where she'd, well, *spied* on the Rite of Sibr.

"Commander wishes to see you there," Negev said, pointing, and then sat to wait.

She climbed the path. Michael took her by both hands and looked her up and down. "I wish you could have come here with your hair as it was the last time, and in the dress I gave you."

"You were going to show me something?"

He gestured at the leaning slabs of rock that formed a dim cavern behind him. They stepped inside to stand on a floor worn to the smoothness of marble, the rocks tapering toward a point far overhead. It was like entering a cathedral spire, the numinous atmosphere heightened by a silence almost tangible, by the thin sunlight planing through a crack between the slabs to fall on a rounded block of stone in the middle of the cavern. The sibr stone, he murmured, was so sacred that anyone who touched it would die instantly. She could make out faded paintings high on the walls.

Michael squatted and asked her to climb onto his shoulders. Effortlessly, he raised her up. Ten feet above the floor she looked at a drawing of what appeared to be a leopard, surrounded by hunters wielding spears. Michael walked her slowly around the cavern, past friezes of animals, trees, and people painted in faint shades of amber, green, and red. Powerful-looking men chased lions and buffalo, their pursuits observed by women with bulging hips and oversize breasts. Some ancient story in pictures, frozen in time, unfolded before her—a narrative she couldn't understand and that was all the more captivating for its mystery.

"Those were made by the ancestors," Michael said. "The legend is that they were a race of giants, but I think whoever made those paintings did so sitting as you are now." He set her down. "I want you to know about us, where we come from."

She sat next to him against the cavern's side and listened to a saga that began three thousand years ago, when a people known as Nubians had a mighty kingdom called Kush that was in time conquered by the Egyptians. The pharaohs ruled it for centuries, until a great king named Kashta arose to conquer the conquerors and establish a dynasty that reigned for a thousand years from its capital, a city called Meroe. It was, he said, the most powerful kingdom in black Africa, trading with the Roman Empire, exporting copper and gold and sandalwood. The Nubians of Meroe were conquered again, this time by Ethiopians from the Kingdom of Axium, who converted them to Christianity. So they remained for another millennium, some worshipping Christ, some following their ancestral faith, until the armies of the Prophet Muhammad swept out of Arabia and Muslim Egypt to win the peoples of Sudan for Islam. Then as now, the Arabs captured blacks for slaves, but some Nubians escaped the slave caravans bound for the Red Sea coast and fled into the safety of these remote hills, to which they'd given their name, its *i* lost over time.

"And those were the ones who made the paintings?" she whispered. It was a place that compelled whispers.

"Possibly. Or they could have been made long before. This has been a sacred place for centuries." He stood and drew her to her feet. "We were once a great people. We conquered and were conquered in turn, but we always endured, and this war today is only a chapter in a very long story."

They went outside, blinking against the sunlight. "We're leaving on another operation," he announced suddenly. "You can say we'll be adding another sentence to the chapter."

"And you told me all this so I'll be strong and brave and not worry?"

"I told you about our history because I want you to be part of it."

"You're being awfully mysterious," she said.

"Mysterious? No. I am being awkward because this is awkward, what I have to say." He paused, squeezing the handle of his walking stick. "In so much of that history, we have fought with Arabs but we have also mingled our blood with them. You can see their blood in our faces, ours in theirs, but I have never heard of us mingling with white people." His expression had become almost mournful. "I want to believe your pretty thought that God forgives us, but I can't. I know now what we have to do."

She drew in a breath and held it for a moment. "Michael, if you think we should . . . if you think we have to end it, I'll be . . . You can guess what I'll be, but I suppose it's better to end it now, before—"

His somber look brightened a little, and he gave a faint smile. "Why do you think I said I want you to be part of our history if I wish to end it?"

"What does that mean, 'part of our history'?" she asked with quick irritation. "It doesn't mean anything."

"It means a great deal. It means I want us to be married."

Wartime. Emotions accelerated, everything accelerated. It was all going too fast for her. She was mute.

Beads of sweat trickled over the marks on Michael's forehead. "Can you give me an answer?"

Her heart was the organ she always listened to, but it wasn't telling her anything now.

"You don't have to answer immediately. It would be a very great step for both of us, but I think a greater one for you. You need to think about it."

Step? she thought. It would be a leap, of a magnitude she could not yet imagine. "Think, yes, think," was all she managed to say.

IF QUINETTE'S THOUGHTS and feelings had been erratic before, they were now thrown into anarchy. On the return flight to Loki, she didn't speak to anyone, she was almost catatonic, the reverse of a cyclone—still on the outside, turbulent inside. As the team got out of the plane, Ken took her by the arm and asked what the matter was. She said, "Nothing."

"C'mon, I know you well enough by now."

She looked at his spare, stern face and noticed the mole on his jaw, just beneath his left ear. She must have seen it before, yet its ugliness had escaped her attention. Dark brown, sprouting tiny hairs, it resembled a tick. Somehow it awakened her to the realization that he hadn't, in the past three days, revealed what action he'd taken about the fraud she'd uncovered. She assumed he hadn't taken any, and wasn't going to, and that was contemptible. "What do you suppose 'nothing' means?" she said, pulled his hand away, and stalked off.

That night, while Anne slept peacefully in the next bed, she gave free rein to her romantic imagination, picturing herself as the wife, lover, confidante, and counselor of Lieutenant Colonel Michael Goraende. She supposed it would be very strange at first, with only Michael and Pearl to talk to, but she could learn the language and weave her life into the fabric of the Nubans' lives. She would teach at the school and aid him in fulfilling his visions of the New Sudan that would rise when the war was won—as she didn't doubt it would be. They would make fierce love at night, and if she were blessed, she would bear him a son to take the place of the one he'd lost.

She woke up full of doubts, stirred by a sentimental memory that came unbidden with the dawn. It was of the first time her father took her for a ride on the new John Deere. She saw him in jeans and a canvas barn coat, sitting on the tractor, its grasshopper-green chassis and bright yellow wheels set against the gloomy sky of an Iowa autumn, and that vivid, dreamlike image brought on the most acute spasm of homesickness she'd experienced since coming to Africa. It stayed with her as she dressed, as she ate breakfast, as she pedaled to her office, hearing the calls of "*Jambo habari,* missy" from the townspeople and as she sat at her desktop, transcribing names and tales of captivity. She was an ordinary small-town American girl and could never be anything else. Her place was there, not here—that was the message encrypted in the memory. It was madness to think she could she live in those half-known mountains as the wife of a rebel commander. She'd gotten a taste of what a hard, dirty, dangerous life it would be. Ticks and meager food and no toilet paper, the ever-present threat of an air raid. She would miss a shower at the end of the day—a real shower, not the drops that trickled from the calabash. A life like that demanded a heroic personality. Heroic personalities didn't care about hardships, never gave a second thought to amenities like showers, toilet paper, or a soft bed. When her contract expired, the sensible course would be to go home and to look upon her two years here the way Dad did his year in Vietnam: as a dramatic episode in the otherwise prosaic narrative of her life, which she would pick up where she'd left off, like a dull book that had been set aside for one more exciting.

But that would be dreadful. Her homesickness, that powerful, nostalgic tug, was a kind of gravity, pulling her back to the familiar and away from Michael. Midwestern caution was making itself felt once again; more than caution, it was cowardice.

In this confused state, the absence of a confidant became intolerable. She could think of only one person it would be safe to speak to. One morning, instead of going to work, she biked to the Catholic church, an unprepossessing structure on Loki's outskirts, closer to a chapel in size, with a school and an office in back. Looking through the window, she saw Malachy, crouched over a computer keyboard, tapping his gray head with a pencil.

"Quinette!" he said, answering her knock. "What brings you here? Well, come in, won't you."

The interior of Malachy's office was a cheerful mess, books piled helter-skelter around a desk covered with papers that looked as if they'd been dumped from a wastebasket. He motioned for her to take a seat and asked what she was up to. The same, she replied, and what about him?

"I'm doing a revised edition of this." He pulled from one of the piles a thick paperback: *The Turkana Branding System: Iconography of Desert Nomads.* Under the title was Malachy's name.

"I didn't know you'd written a book," she said, feeling uneasy. Catholics were not true Christians, because they didn't have a personal relationship with Jesus—that's what Pastor Tom used to say—yet here she was, about to confide in a priest of that religion.

"Oh, more than one," he said, and turned the volume to its back cover, on which a photograph of a younger Malachy appeared—more brown in his hair, a thinner face, but the same windowpane eyeglasses. He was identified as "Rev. Professor Malachy T. Delaney, S.P.S. Ph.D.," and the biographical sketch said that he'd obtained a doctoral degree in anthropology from Johns Hopkins University, had been dean of the social sciences department at the Catholic University of East Africa, and had authored several books about the Turkana people.

"I didn't realize we had a distinguished scholar in our midst," Quinette said.

"You don't. I'm just a hack. This book is about the branding system as a cultural institution. Do you recall that Sunday I took you to a Turkana village and the headman—the fellow with the ostrich feather in his skullcap—said that he and I were of the same brand? That to say you are of the same brand means that you're brothers?"

Quinette nodded and saw that he'd provided her with a smooth transition into the subject on her mind. "I remember something else you told me. That for a missionary like you to be effective, he has to identify with the people he ministers to. You have to become one of them, you said."

"I did. I believe I also said that you must never forget who you really are and what you come from."

"I want to talk to you about that. A missionary like you has given up his home, his family, everything he's familiar with. In a way, you're married to Africa."

"Not to the whole bloody continent—to this little part of it, yes, I suppose you could say I am, though the better way to put it is that I'm married to my vocation. What are you driving at?"

"I was wondering what it's been like. How you've coped with it."

"It hasn't been easy, but if you're asking if I've worked out some formula for coping with a life like this, I'm afraid I haven't. There is no formula. The missionary's calling is a bit special, don't you know. It's not for everyone." He crossed his ankles and swiveled back and forth in his chair. "What is it, Quinette?"

She shifted her glance to the chaotic bookshelves, to the photographs on the walls, hanging askew. "A Catholic priest can never reveal what he's heard in the confessional, right?"

"In all kindness, if you're here to make a confession, I can't hear it. You're a Protestant."

"I'm asking if—"

"You wish me to keep my mouth shut about whatever it is you have to say."

"My job, my reputation around here could depend on it."

"How so?"

"You know how people who work for aid agencies, or for human rights groups like the one I work for—you know how we're not supposed to take sides."

"Your employer isn't neutral. Your boss has been very public in his denunciations of Khartoum's policies."

"Right, but he couldn't let the WorldWide Christian Union be, uh, associated? Associated with the SPLA."

"I suppose not. The SPLA doesn't have an enviable record in the human rights department. Now then, what is it?"

She asked if he knew Michael Goraende, and he replied that he did not, he had only heard of him through their mutual friend, John Barrett. She laughed nervously—having kept mum about her affair for weeks, she couldn't bring herself to reveal it, even now. The priest gave her some help.

"You and this Michael are romantically involved, and it's become serious, is that it?"

"Last week he asked me to marry him."

Malachy lowered his chin and gazed at her over the frame of his glasses. "And you said . . . ?"

"That I'd have to think about it, and that's what I've been doing. Tied myself in knots."

"But you're leaning toward a yes, aren't you? Hence the questions about what my life has been like."

"Yes. Hence," she said.

"Do you love him?"

"Of course! We've had a meeting of the minds, of the soul even."

"And I imagine of more than the mind and the soul." Malachy waved his hand—the thick, knotty hand, she observed, of a working man rather than a scholar. "No need to respond to that. Well now, if you did say yes, you'd be giving up the advantage that all you young people who come over here have got—the ability to quit when you choose and go home. With a three-letter word, you'd be tearing up your return ticket. You'd keep your American passport, but in all other respects you'd be an African."

He'd said nothing she hadn't thought of before, but to hear the consequences phrased so starkly renewed her misgivings.

"And then there's my family. My dad's dead, but my mother, my sisters—I'd feel like I was cutting myself off from them—from everything, everyone."

"You could well be doing that." He scrutinized her for several uncomfortable seconds. "In the thirty-five years I've been in Africa, I have run into people like you," he said. "They find something in Africa they cannot find at home. People for whom the idea of being cut off isn't really so dreadful."

Quinette squirmed at the accuracy of this perception. Having listened to people admit to their sins for so long, Malachy must have learned how to catch omissions or lack of complete candor.

"So now," he went on, "We've covered what happens with the three-letter word. What happens if you say the two-letter word?"

"I would spend the rest of my life wondering, What if? Heartache, regret, a lifetime of it."

Malachy clasped her wrists. "You might get your share of heartache and regrets with a yes as well. You're sure you love him?"

"Do I have to say it more than once?"

With a gentle but irresistible pressure, the priest drew her closer to him. "You've got to ask yourself one big question, my dear young woman. Is it him I want, or is he a means to some other end?"

Quinette said nothing, troubled that Malachy would think her capable of looking upon Michael as a means to an end, as if she were in love with a man for his money.

"You need to ask yourself if by marrying Michael you would be, let us say, finalizing a divorce from the life you once had, from your own past."

"My God, no!" she protested. "I've been in love before, I've been married once before, I know the real thing when I see it."

"Then fair enough. So one more question that you need to put to yourself. Is it him alone I would be married to, or him and something else?"

"Something else?"

"Are you sure it's not a cause you're in love with? Are you sure you would be marrying a man and not a cause? Or maybe half of one, half the other?"

What kind of hair-splitting was this? Quinette thought, and said with some irritation, "I've never thought about it."

"I know, which is why I'm asking you to. It could make a big difference."

She rode to her office in a pique, past women squatting in the dust behind their baskets of charcoal. She nearly fell when she wrenched the handlebars to avoid a goat that bolted across her path. She had gone to Malachy hoping to obtain some clarity, and all he'd done was to cloud her mind further with his lists of questions, some of which struck her as irrelevant. By committing herself to Michael, she would be committing herself to his cause and to his people. What was wrong with that? Why should she consider it? To love him was to love what and who he was fighting for—they could not be separated.

She cruised into her office compound, where the old gardener was raking the dirt, and went inside to confront the stacks of files, the diskettes with their records of human suffering. Annoyed as she was with Malachy, she admired him. If he could devote his life to his vocation, she could devote herself to Michael. It was a good thing she'd awakened the other morning with all those doubts; they had forced her to think about the penalties of becoming Michael's wife as well as the rewards; now she could imagine it in its totality, with no illusions or impossible expectations—or so she believed. What she couldn't imagine was a life without him.

God, through Michael's proposal, had sent her a message: My tolerance of your illicit love is not without limits. Either she ended it or she sanctified it by saying yes. Michael had chosen her; now it was up to her to choose him, as the girls at the Nyertun had chosen their mates. *Yes.* The word flooded her with joy, and convinced that her heart was speaking to her finally and unambiguously, she wrote him a brief note and had it delivered by a Knight Air pilot: "Darling, I've thought about it, my answer is yes. I will fly to you as soon as I can, My love always, Q."

Love in Wartime

MALACHY HAD INFORMED several of the most important headmen that Fitzhugh and Diana would be traveling in Turkanaland for the day, and he trusted the bush telegraph to spread the word to the others: They were friends of Apoloreng and were to be treated hospitably—another way of saying, Do not rob, harm, or molest these people. In case someone didn't get the message, the Father of the Red Ox saw to it that a pair of askaris accompanied the mzungu lady, her companion, and their interpreter on their safari.

They were on safari not to photograph wild game but to get a picture of the latest drought to afflict the Turkanas' much-afflicted homeland. Diana, the woman of good works, had a new project: funding a campaign to dig bore holes and thus provide the inhabitants of northwestern Kenya with a more reliable source of water than the heavens. Fitzhugh had gone along on the trip only for the chance to be near her.

Their affair had become common knowledge in Loki and among her Nairobi social circles, and the chatter was as cheap and predictable as he'd feared. Diana was painted as a randy woman of a certain age, Fitzhugh as an African gigolo taking advantage of a lonely, middle-aged white woman who also happened to be rich. It was pointless to protest; a protest would require him to answer the question "Then what are you doing with her?" and he could not, even to himself. He'd quit looking for answers. He was happy when he was with her, unhappy when he wasn't—the whole thing was no more complicated than that.

Visiting the nomads' camps, it delighted him to watch her, in the cotton trousers that clung to her high, ample hips, approach the circles of waiting elders with her sergeant major's stride, and to see her lovely head bobbing under a wide straw hat as the interpreter translated the elders' replies to her questions. She could have been making the rounds of dinners and cocktail parties in Karen; instead, she was bringing succor to a wasteland where cattle died on their feet and women had to walk half a day to find water. In a country ruled by thieves, hers was a heart that gave. If he needed a reason for his love, he could find no better.

She was not quite herself today, but pensive, reticent, and distant, a state Fitzhugh ascribed to her preoccupation with her project and to the dreadful conditions they saw, journeying from camp to camp. Her mood didn't improve as they returned to Loki. She wore a sorrowful look, as if she were grieving over some loss. Passing through a pan of nearly treeless desolation, where termite mounds rose tall as chimneys and camels floated through the mirage on the horizon, they came to a broad riverbed. As the interpreter started to take the Land Rover across, Diana asked him to stop. She looked around, then pointed and murmured, "Please go that way."

"I thought we were done for the day, memsahib," the interpreter said. "Besides, there are no Turkana camps in that direction."

"I know. Please go, it won't be far."

They rocked alongside the riverbed, dodging boulders, skirting clumps of acacia. At an oxbow bend, she called another halt.

"We're going to take a walk," she said to the interpreter. "You and the askaris wait here."

"But memsahib—"

"We'll be quite all right."

Fitzhugh followed her around the oxbow, wondering what she was up to. He called her attention to the lowering sun—no one, not even Apoloreng, could guarantee their safety after dark. She said not to worry, they were going just a short way. "There, in fact." She motioned at a mound of rubble and a broken concrete slab that lay against the river-bank. She walked beyond it in her resolute way, then sat down, her knees raised, her arms clasped around them.

"I used to come here whenever I had the chance, but it's been years since the last time. I'm surprised I could still find it."

It did not look like a "here" to Fitzhugh. Except for the slab of concrete, possibly the foot of an old bridge, he saw nothing to distinguish it from any other part of the desert. Patting the ground, Diana invited him to sit beside her.

"What is this about?" he asked.

"Kiss me first," she said. "Kiss me like a man who loves me."

She'd been so withdrawn all day that this demand startled him. He did his best to comply. "Now you will tell me what we're doing here, yes?"

"I have been thinking about us quite a lot. There are some things I must tell you."

The severity in her voice made him apprehensive. "I am listening."

"It came to me that I ought to tell you here. This spot is special to me. My baby was conceived here."

Incredulous, Fitzhugh looked at the thorn trees, the sandy river bottom, the fissured banks. "The daughter you told me about? The one who was stillborn? She was conceived in this wilderness? What were you doing here? You could not have been more than—"

"Eighteen. It was two years before Kenya got its independence. My father was a colonel, royal engineers, putting in roads and bridges out here. He and my mother had a house in Lodwar. We were in school in England, my sister and I, and on the summer holidays we would come back out to Kenya to be with them. That particular summer my father had a civilian working for him, an Irish boy of twenty-two, Brian McSorley. He'd been raised in Kenya, and he was in charge of the African labor crews. Brian and I—I can't say we fell in love, we conceived a passion for each other."

"Yes, and out of that, the daughter," Fitzhugh said. "Pardon my asking, but she was the reason you and this Brian were married?"

"Would you please not interrupt, darling?" she said gently. "We were quite mad to get at each other, but there wasn't much opportunity under the circumstances. The chance came one Sunday, when by hook and by crook, we managed to get away together. Brian was driving out to inspect progress on a bridge—that one there." She gestured at its remnants. "I went with him. We had a picnic, about where we are sitting now. There used to be a very great tree here, and we were picnicking under it when a furious rainstorm came down. There was a flash flood, and in no time at all this riverbed had twenty feet of water rushing through it. The storm passed, but we had to wait for the river to go down before we could get back across in our car—the bridge wasn't finished. We were rather delighted with this dilemma, but you know, this was nineteen sixty-one and I was eighteen and a virgin, and as eager as I was for him, I couldn't quite bring myself to make love to him.

"It got late, and Brian was anxious. The Turkana were as belligerent then as they are today. It was then that we heard a strange sound, quite ominous—a ragged banging and clattering mixed up with a rhythmic thudding noise, a bit like the sound of an approaching train. Brian stood to look in the direction of the noise—there was a full moon, it was almost bright as day. Immediately, he said, 'Oh, my God!' and went over the bank, pulling me with him. The water had gone down a few feet, but there was still a strong current, and we had to cling to the roots of the tree or be carried away. The noise grew louder. 'Turkana war party,' Brian whispered. We drew our heads over the bank, and it was a sight I can still see clearly today. There, hardly ten yards from where we were hiding, scores, perhaps hundreds, of men went jogging past. They were wearing nothing but loincloths, and each one carried a shield and two spears. Two spears, you see, meant a war instead of a hunting party. They were in single file, and it must have taken twenty minutes for them to go by. I wasn't frightened. You seldom are when you're eighteen. The spears clattering against one another, banging against the shields, the blades glinting moonlight, and all those half-naked warriors moving past us—it was breathtaking.

"When they'd passed, Brian said we must get home and started for the car, but the entire experience had overcome my schoolgirl shyness. The danger, the excitement of it made me reckless. I said I was soaking wet and had to wring out my clothes, and I pulled off my dress right in front of him. I was shameless enough to tug at the buttons of his shirt, telling him he had to dry his clothes as well. It was my very first time, right here on the wet ground, and like all first times, it was nothing like what I'd expected. A bit painful, and terribly quick. We moved to the car . . . ah, I've said enough. I don't know why I went into so much detail."

Fitzhugh was quiet, mesmerized by images of the Turkana warriors, the gleaming spear points, the young lovers embracing under the bright African moon. Thinking of how ravishing Diana must have been at eighteen, he was jealous of Brian McSorley.

"I was back in England, my first year at university, when I found out I was pregnant. My first time, and pregnant straight away! As you can imagine, I was frantic. I wrote to Brian and told him. He answered and said he would marry me, but I—I never wrote him back. The British class system, you know. The colonel's daughter, the Irish colonial, her dad's foreman. I could not imagine my parents' reaction, or rather, I could."

She fell silent.

"So you and this Brian never—"

She shook her head.

"And did you go away somewhere to have the baby?"

"Away? Yes, away," she said distantly. "I should come to the point. I lied to you, that night after dinner at the Rusty Nail. The baby was not stillborn."

"You gave her up for adoption? But why would you tell such a lie? I'm not upset for myself. What would she think if she knew you had denied her very existence? Where is she now, do you know?"

"Darling, I've no idea if it was a girl or a boy. The baby wasn't stillborn. It was never born."

Fitzhugh glanced aside. In the west, over Sudan, the sun was turning orange. "And there is some reason you invented this story of a stillbirth?"

"Shame," she replied. "I did it for the most selfish reasons. I got rid of an embarrassment, an inconvenience by killing it. I've felt awful about that all my life. About that and never responding to Brian. He never knew. We never saw each other again."

"But you were hardly more than a child yourself," Fitzhugh said. "You didn't think I would condemn you, did you? For an abortion you had thirty-five years ago?"

"I condemn myself, and I'm not quite finished. The operation was botched. I could not have children ever again. When I did get married—it was some seven years later—I was afraid to tell my husband. He was very high church, and he wanted a family. After five years passed with my not getting pregnant, David went in for some tests. The doctors said there was nothing wrong with him, so he asked if I would be tested, and that was when I told him. He was appalled. Which appalled him more, the abortion or my duplicity, I don't know. We tried to make a go of it, but two years later we were divorced."

Fitzhugh was upset now. "I believe that was another lie. You told me that you and he never divorced."

"Well, we did. That's where the house in Karen comes from. David was extremely well off and kind-hearted and he offered a very generous settlement—more than I deserved, I suppose. It was my decision, and I think it was a wise one, to come back to Kenya and start over."

"Your decision to tell me you weren't divorced, what sort of decision was that?"

She didn't answer.

"Was it a way to keep things within certain boundaries? Or were you just amusing yourself?"

He couldn't tell if the movement of Diana's head meant no, or if it expressed her dismay at his inability to perceive her motives. He stood, brushed the seat of his trousers, and motioned at the sun, now darkening from orange to red. "Then what about your decision to come clean today?" he demanded as they started back. "Maybe you could tell me about that."

"I believe I wanted you to dislike me, perhaps even hate me, for being so false."

"What for?"

She murmured something indefinite.

"Your attempt failed. I'm upset, yes, but it would take more than what you've told me to get me to dislike you, and much more to hate you."

She stopped walking and, with the Land Rover and the anxious askaris in sight, made a sound, half sigh, half sob. "I said at the beginning, I've been thinking about us, and . . ." She paused to regain her composure. "When this started off, I thought I was having a fling. I never thought it would come to this, to the way I feel about you. But I am all wrong for you. You're young, you're going to want children, if you don't already. You are going to want a young wife, a family. I know you will. It's been on your mind, hasn't it?"

"Of course it has."

"But you never mentioned it to me. It's an unresolved question in your mind."

"I suppose so. But why are you bringing it up now?"

"Because I am the age I am. Because even if I were younger, I could never give you what you'll want. Because I've never loved a man as I love you. I love you enough that I want only what's best for you."

He said quietly, "You're a generous woman, but I don't believe you're that generous."

Diana tossed her head backward in mock laughter. "Oh, all right, caught in another falsehood. I do want what's best for you, but I'm not making a sacrifice. It's all self-interest. I know you love me now, but in a year, or two years, I'm afraid you'll begin to have doubts and regrets, and who could blame you? I would rather inflict this on myself now than have it inflicted on me later, when it will hurt ever so much more. You want it unvarnished, there you have it."

When he grasped what she was saying—it took him a moment—he experienced a stab of panic. She'd caught him unprepared; except for her subdued mood today, she'd shown none of the usual signs of a woman who wants to call it off, given no warnings that this was coming. Or had she and he had somehow failed to recognize them?

"You're inflicting it on me, too, not just yourself," he said, his voice rising. "Not twenty minutes ago you asked me to kiss you like a man who loved you. Why would you—"

"I don't know why. Must there be a rational explanation for everything?"

They rode back in an excruciating silence. Fitzhugh would have gotten out and walked if it wasn't for the late hour and the near certainty that he'd be waylaid by bandits. He was in shock, and at the same time boiling with resentment, not only for her dropping this on him so abruptly but for her fatalism, her conviction that his feelings were destined to change and he destined to hurt her, as if he had no will of his own, no capacity to make choices.

She was staying with Tara Whitcomb. The interpreter swung through the gate to the Pathways compound and parked. Fitzhugh climbed out with Diana and took her aside.

"Maybe there aren't explanations for everything," he said with a kind of quiet violence, "but damn it, I am owed one for what you're doing."

"I have given it."

"What are you? Some kind of prophet that you know what I'm going to do and what I'm going to feel a year from now, or two or three?"

"No, but I do have a pretty good idea."

"Really? Or has all the talk finally gotten to you? Maybe it isn't that you're all wrong for me but that I'm all wrong for you." He seized her wrist and held her arm alongside his. "See the contrast."

She jerked free. "Do not be absurd. You don't know me at all if you think that makes a difference to me."

"I won't let you do this. I won't stand for it." She laughed caustically at this masculine assertion, and he too had no sooner uttered it than he realized how silly it sounded. "I should have some say in it, and you're not giving me any."

The softening in his tone brought a softening in her—a relaxation in her posture, a slight loss of firmness in her gaze as she lowered her eyes. "Oh, but you do have a say. But you are going to have to do some hard thinking before you can say it. And when you do, you will have to say it without any doubts or equivocation, and believe me, I'll know if there are any."

"I will have to decide how much I can give up."

"It would be quite a lot, I know that, and if you decide you can't, I shall want to know that as well."

"And if I decide I can, what then?"

Her response was a demure smile, but it was enough, and for an instant the thought that she would be his in marriage thrilled him. The feeling was strong enough that he almost declared on the spot that he'd resolved the question. The knowledge that he had not stopped him. Instead of making a declaration, he asked if, then, she was not ending it but merely calling for an intermission.

"Very well, an intermission," she said. "And—there is no way to put this nicely—I do not want to see you till it's over."

As she looked up at him, she removed her hat. He observed that the twilight made the veins in her hand appear more prominent, while it deepened the furrows at the corners of her eyes and leached color from her hair. She hadn't intended to make any impression, yet it was as if she'd consciously given him a preview of the future, challenging him to sound his love and discover if it had the depth to make the surrender she was asking of him.

He was relieved that Diana had decided to relent and give them another chance; but after he went to bed, relief turned into mild terror. Their future as a couple was entirely up to him. Doubts about his constancy assailed him. Maybe she was right—better that she suffer some pain now than more later—and yet he felt that she was asking too much of him. She'd known the risks when she got involved with him; she ought to be willing to take them and not expect ironclad guarantees. But then he recalled how she'd looked, standing there in the fading light, and thought that he was being unfair. There were risks she could not afford.

In the morning, without knowing why, Fitzhugh was determined to act as if nothing had changed. He followed his routine, rising at five to be on hand for the early flights, making up the next day's schedules after breakfast, checking cargo manifests. He greeted Rachel and the ground and air crews in his usual cheerful manner. He took care of paperwork—lease payments, invoices, and so forth. At lunch he met Tim Fancher and Rob Handy to arrange a flight for them and several tons of supplies and equipment. The two missionaries were going to establish ministries in the Nuba mountains. They were brimming with enthusiasm for this project and couldn't tell that he barely heard a word they said.

He spent the afternoon at two distasteful tasks. The first was delivering ten percent "commissions" to aid agency logisticians; the second was preparing a report for Hassan Adid, who was expected to arrive later in the day. Knight Air's sugar daddy wanted to see how well the company had done in the past quarter. It had done very well, with gross sales of $1.6 million. Douglas's Nuba Day experiment had been a success by and large. The mortar attack and the air raid had scared off a couple of independent agencies, but the rest had reacted as Douglas had hoped and predicted. Knight Air's planes were flying nearly every day. A significant share of its income, however, had been earned from the gun-running done by Dare's shell company, Yellowbird. In the interests of cloaking its activities, its records were kept on a separate set of books entrusted to Fitzhugh's care. Half its earnings were automatically transferred each week from its bank in Uganda to Knight Air's bank in Nairobi. This had presented a problem in bookkeeping: How to account for the extra income? It was solved by a simple expedient: For every actual mission flown by Yellowbird, a fictitious Knight Air mission was created. The phantom flights were then entered on Knight Air's books, complete with phantom dates and destinations. The deception did not end there. Since the real customer, the Sudanese People's Liberation Army, also had to be concealed, another client had to be found to explain who had paid for the flights. Wesley and Douglas thought that Barrett's International People's Aid could play this role, but they needed his consent, which required expanding the inner circle to include him. The ex-priest who thought the war was an extension of the Crusades not only gave his consent, he gave it with enthusiasm.

Thus the report to be presented to Adid was somewhat fraudulent, and in compiling it Fitzhugh felt like a white-collar criminal. True, the bottom line was an honest, accurate figure, but if Adid had known that nearly ten percent of it had come from arms smuggling, it was safe to predict that he would have withdrawn his interests from Knight Air and never invested another dollar. He would have considered the risk-reward ratio way out of line and placed no confidence in the cover that Douglas and Wesley had devised. Indeed, Fitzhugh himself had little confidence in it. Were the UN security office to get wind of what was going on, discovering the financial link between Knight Air and Yellowbird would not require a particularly vigorous investigation, and all attempts to make plausible denials would then sound most implausible. The least that would happen would be the loss of Knight Air's UN-authorized contracts, which accounted for a third of its income. Fitzhugh's belief in the worthiness of the clandestine operation remained steadfast (when he experienced doubts, all he had to do to dispel them was recall the flaming ruins of Manfred's hospital), but the secrecy it demanded had polluted the atmosphere. He, Douglas, Wesley, Mary, and now Barrett had become co-conspirators, speaking in whispers, fudging the numbers, ever on the lookout for a breach in security. They were all flying on the dark side.

Rachel helped him put the report together. She was very good with accounts and could have been the company's finance director instead of its secretary. Because she didn't know she was participating in a fraud, Fitzhugh's disgust with the job increased. He felt he was taking advantage of her innocence. As the afternoon wore on, different feelings took hold. He noticed how attractive she was, a woman of twenty-seven with hips and breasts that invited comparison to the African fertility statues sold in the crafts markets. Strange that he hadn't noticed her attributes in all this time. Distracted from the task at hand, he asked himself, "Why didn't I fall for her instead of for a white woman sixteen years older? What's wrong with me?" His mind leaped all at once into a fantasy—he would woo and win this healthy Kikuyu and sire a brood of children, infusing a fresh river of pure African blood into the diluted veins of his family's mongrel line. A notion seized him that if he could get Rachel into bed for just one night, he would be cured of his obsession with Diana and released from his dilemma. He imagined Rachel's robust body under his, his sperm swimming into her fecund womb. Without a conscious thought as to what he was doing, he drew his chair closer to hers and leaned toward her as she worked the calculator. He suggested they have a drink after work. "No, thank you," she replied, and pushed her chair away from him—a rejection that brought him to his senses. He stood, pretending to get something from the file cabinet, and rapped his temple with his knuckles, as if to physically knock the lustful thoughts from his head. Other thoughts intruded. If he did forsake his hopes for a family and marry Diana, how would they live? He would be out here, she would be in Nairobi, unless he quit and moved in with her. What then would he do for an occupation? He would be as good as a kept man. She wouldn't be Mrs. Martin, he would be Mr. Briggs.

When Adid showed up with Douglas at around five, Fitzhugh welcomed the business discussions, which he generally loathed, as a diversion from his emotional turmoil. The wabenzi looked out of place in his custom-tailored sport jacket and Italian loafers as he made a quick inspection of the company's aircraft. While he did, Douglas murmured to Fitzhugh, "Might be big news, my man. We'll find out at dinner."

They went to the office, where Adid studied the report and remarked that more business had been done with International People's Aid this quarter than last. That was good, but what accounted for it? Douglas didn't miss a beat—the increased sales were due to his promotional gambit, the Nuba Day event, which had inspired IPA to deliver more aid. The ease with which Douglas lied almost made Fitzhugh wince. The sincerity in his voice and the candor in his gray eyes were perfect forgeries, offering a glimpse of something hidden in his nature, a glimpse fleeting and disturbing, like the wink of a veil that reveals a scar on an otherwise attractive face.

At the Hotel California mess, Adid, who was accustomed to being waited on, endured the indignity of standing in a cafeteria line with grubby aid workers, aircraft mechanics in greasy coveralls, sweaty loadmasters. He, Douglas, and Fitzhugh sat at a corner table, out of earshot of the other diners. While they ate, Adid withdrew from his briefcase a sheaf

of papers containing pie charts and bar charts and launched into a monologue about market share, gross profits, net profits, net profits after divi-
dend distribution, retained profits. The company's performance had been
good overall but not as good as he'd expected. One of the pie charts was
presented, showing that most gross sales came from the independent
NGOs, the remainder from the NGOs affiliated with the UN.

"You have not marketed yourselves aggressively enough when it comes
to the latter, and you need to," he said. "There are, what? A dozen independent agencies and more than forty under the UN's umbrella, but
Knight Air has contracts with only a handful of those. Pathways has the
rest locked up, some thirty altogether. Your competition is killing you
there. "

Douglas gave a rueful nod. "Yeah, we're Avis, they're Hertz."

"With more aggressive marketing," Adid began, then had a sneezing
fit. Muttering "This damned dust," he pulled a bottle of nasal spray from
his pocket and tilted his head back to clear his nostrils. "I was going to say,
with better marketing, you will not have to settle for second place."

Fitzhugh protested that he'd done all he could, extolling the virtues of
Knight Air's larger and faster planes, offering generous "commissions" on
sales.

"Ah, my friend the Ambler, I know you have, but you are the operations manager. Marketing should not be your department. So I am proposing that it's time for the company to hire a marketing director."

"Great idea," Douglas said. "Got anyone in mind?"

"As a matter of fact, I do. I had a discussion with him last week. A man
named Timmerman. He is now director of flight operations for the UN,
but he wishes to quit and is interested in going to work for you. Or may I
say, for *us*."

Douglas flinched and shook his head, "Wrong guy. Completely the
wrong guy."

"Yes, you had some problems with him sometime in the past. He told
me about that."

"And did he tell you that I was the next thing to a hijacker?" Douglas's
tone indicated that he was still wounded by the remark. "That's what he
told everyone else around here."

"There is an Arab proverb—*eli fat mat.* The past is dead. It is dead for
this Timmerman; let it be dead for you."

"Just how did you and that Dutchman get together?"

"I keep these and these open." Adid pointed at his eyes and ears. "He could be of great benefit to us. But you are the managing director. I can only offer my counsel. It is your decision."

"What the hell does Timmerman know about marketing?" Douglas asked, scowling.

"He doesn't need to know anything. He has been here with the UN for a long time. He is personally acquainted with the heads of each one of those forty agencies—"

"And he can use his influence to steer them our way," Fitzhugh said, venturing to interrupt.

With an inclining of his small aristocratic head, the Somali acknowledged that Fitzhugh had it right. "You could easily double your UN contracts. With intelligent management, you could take most of them and, who knows, all of them away from Miss Whitcomb."

Douglas's scowl faded. An alert expression came to his face, so that, with his raptor's nose, he resembled a perched hawk when it spots prey in the grass below. And this must have been the reaction that Adid, that canny judge of men, meant to provoke by referring to Tara by name rather than to her company's name or to some abstract term like "your competitor." He knew that Douglas viewed Knight Air's competition with Pathways as more than a business rivalry; it was a duel between Tara and himself.

"Of course, you would need more equipment," Adid went on. "I've researched the market. There are three planes for sale, two Andovers for three hundred thirty thousand each and a Polish Let for one hundred thousand. At the moment, retained profits are not sufficient to purchase these aircraft, so I would put up the capital."

There was the big news, and if any resistance to hiring Timmerman remained in Douglas, that overcame it. He looked at Fitzhugh and flicked his eyebrows. "The big mo, my man. We'll crush her."

"Crush her?" Fitzhugh said, alarmed. Aside from his liking for Tara, he realized that crushing her, were it possible, could affect his personal life. She and Diana were friends. "Why should it be necessary to crush her?"

"The Sudan market is saturated," Adid answered. "I see no room in it for two cargo airlines."

"I've never thought of Sudan as a market."

"You should change your thinking. What did you call the football pitches where you made your famous name? Grass?"

And the dark eyes, those pinpoint black holes that took everything in and gave nothing away, released a little something for a change—an intention. It was only a flash, but Fitzhugh saw it, and he mentioned it to Douglas after they saw Adid to his quarters.

"I think our Somali friend wants more than to be our venture capitalist," he warned. "First he corners what he calls the market, and then he means to take us over."

"I'm not an idiot," the American responded. "To me, he's like the booster rocket on a space shot. He launches us, then he gets jettisoned."

"I am quite certain he knows you're thinking that very thought," Fitzhugh said.

SHE DECIDED TO announce her decision to marry Michael. This, she believed, would stiffen her resolve, make it harder for her to retreat. She went about it methodically, tendering a written resignation to Ken, tacking on an apology for giving him short notice and a promise to return to Loki after the wedding to train her replacement.

Next she notified her family. She started by writing her mother but found she could not express her feelings to Ardele and so wrote to Nicole instead. She rambled on for pages, drawing an idealized portrait of Michael in the hopes it would persuade her family that she wasn't crazy to have fallen in love with him. She resented having to explain herself. Those dull people who had never done anything out of the ordinary and whose lives were set up to protect them from powerful emotions were incapable of understanding the ecstasy of a great love, the power of an overwhelming passion. *Love. Love. Love,* she wrote in conclusion. *Everyone wants it, but hardly anyone finds it. I've found it over here, and no matter what you think of me, I think I'm very lucky that I did.*

She posted both letters through the UN's mail service—to make sure they got to their destinations—and then biked to Malachy's church to tell him of her decision and ask if he would perform the marriage ceremony. No date was set as yet, but could he do it? He could not—she and Michael weren't Catholics. What happened to the bold priest who wasn't afraid to break the Church's rules? There were some rules he could not break, he replied, but he was sure his old friend Barrett would be pleased to do the service. Her final step was to break the news to Anne Derby. Her roommate was sorting laundry when she entered the tent.

"I've got something to tell you. I've resigned and I'm leaving."

"Leaving?" Anne said plaintively. She turned around. "Back to America?"

"I'm getting married."

"No! You're not! Who is it?"

"Michael Goraende."

Anne blinked in puzzlement.

"He's a colonel in the SPLA. He commands the SPLA up in the Nuba."

Anne continued to blink as she assimilated this information.

"I'm going up there as soon as I can get a flight, and then we'll set the date. I'm going to need a maid of honor, and I'd like it to be you."

Anne returned to folding her laundry, except now she wasn't folding it but distractedly bunching her clothes into balls.

"I know it's a shock," Quinette said. "But could you?"

"I don't know . . . I—I would need to . . ." She spun around to face Quinette again. "No. I'm sorry, but no. How long have you been involved with this colonel?"

"Long enough. Why can't you do it?"

"You know the reputation the SPLA has around here. If they haven't committed as many war crimes as the Muslims, they have sure given it a bloody good go. Your doing this, why it's the next thing to putting on a uniform and joining up."

"So that's what's wrong? I haven't seen them commit any war crimes."

"I don't mean wrong, morally. Or because he's African. It isn't done, Quinette." She tossed a T-shirt on her bed. "It simply isn't *done.*"

"But I am going to do it."

Anne gave her a searching look. "Yes, I can see that. I'm fond of you, but you'll be throwing your life away, and I want no part in that."

"Fine, then. You won't have," Quinette said, already feeling like an outcast and, what was surprising, welcoming it.

"I'll just say congratulations and wish you all the best of luck. You shall certainly need it."

"Thank you. If you don't mind, keep this to yourself till I'm gone."

"That I can do."

For the next few days Quinette was busy organizing her office files and putting things in order for whomever Ken sent to take her place. This eased her conscience about leaving him in the lurch. When she learned that the Friends of the Frontline were going to the Nuba soon, she went to Tim Fancher and, without disclosing her reasons (fearful she'd get a reaction similar to Anne's), asked to hitch a ride. No problem, he said. They were flying in the big Antonov and could take a passenger. She returned to her tent and packed her trunk.

"You are really going to go through with it?" Anne said, watching her. "I'd hoped you'd have second thoughts. I can't believe it."

"Believe it," Quinette replied, though she scarcely did herself. It was critical for her not to think about her actions but to carry them out. She recalled a war movie she'd watched with her father. It was about paratroopers in World War II, making a night jump into France. One soldier stepped up to the doorway and balked at the last minute. A sergeant behind him gave him a kick, and he plummeted into the darkness. She had to be her own sergeant, overcoming all reluctance, booting herself into the unknown.

The following morning, before sunrise, Fancher and Rob Handy came for her in their pickup. When he saw her bulging rucksack and trunk, Fancher asked, "Looks like you're planning to stay awhile."

"Yes," she said coyly. "Quite a while."

"We're going to be neighbors then," he said, driving to the airfield. "Rob and me figure we'll be up there three, maybe four months."

The Friends of the Frontline were embarking on a campaign to set up ministries throughout the Nuba mountains. Fancher and Handy would base themselves in New Tourom and, in the manner of the circuit-riding preachers of old, range out from there, evangelizing, training civilian pastors and SPLA chaplains, giving support and encouragement to beleaguered Christian congregations, seeking converts among the Nuba's Muslims. Quinette was happy to hear that familiar faces would be around for a while; it would help her through the transition into her new life.

At the airfield, ground crews were loading the Antonov while Alexei and the aircrew readied the plane for takeoff. The Friends were bringing in an awesome amount of supplies and equipment: a ton of schoolbooks, hymnals, and Bibles in Arabic and several Nuban languages, another ton of food and medicine, along with generators and fuel, solar panels, bicycles, movie screens, TV sets, tape recorders, mosquito nets, and boxes labeled EVANGELISM KITS or JESUS FILMS.

"We think of what we're doing as a spiritual offensive," Fancher said, gazing at the band of light that belted the sky to the horizon. "And of all this"—he jerked a thumb at the cargo—"as our weapons and matériel."

"Satan is strong in Sudan," added Handy, flexing a muscular arm. "We have got to be stronger."

Quinette remarked that their "spiritual offensive" would be a dangerous undertaking.

"The hand of God never takes you to where the grace of God cannot keep you," Handy said.

Quinette's trunk was the last item to be taken on board. The loadmaster secured the cargo nets and motioned to her and the two men to get in. They strapped themselves into fold-down seats on one side of the fuselage.

"So what's taking you up there for an extended stay?" Fancher asked.

Judging on instinct that he and Handy would react more positively than Anne had, she told him. It took them a minute or two to recover from their surprise; the plane had begun to taxi before Fancher spoke again, and his words confirmed that her judgment had been correct: raising his voice over the noise, he asked if she and Michael had chosen a minister. She answered that she hoped Barrett would fulfill that role.

"I'm ordained in the ECS, too," he said. "So if you can't get him, I'd be happy to do the honors."

She could not have asked for a more auspicious beginning. Then the engines built to a deafening pitch, the plane rolled and lifted off, and she felt in its rise an escape from the gravity that had held her to all she knew, all she was.

THE AIRSTRIP WAS thronged with people—hundreds were needed to transport the cargo—and ringed by watchful soldiers manning antiaircraft machine guns. Quinette was greeted by Negev, by Pearl and her cousins Kiki and Nolli, and by a crowd of women and girls crying out *"Kinnet basso!"* which meant, Negev informed her, "Quinette has come!" By this time the bush telegraph had transmitted the news that Michael and the white woman were to be married, and the calls of *"Kinnet basso!"* told her that the marriage would meet with general approval. If she was an outcast in Loki, she was welcome here, loved by the Nubans for casting herself into their lives. She loved them back, unbidden tears coming to her eyes.

"Had no idea you've got so many fans," Fancher said, struggling to get through the swarms of people. He and Handy didn't seem to know what to make of her reception. A few young women were fighting for the honor of carrying her trunk.

When she got to the garrison, she learned that Michael had been called away to a conference of high-level officers planning a dry-season offensive and wasn't expected to return for another three days. Bitterly disappointed and a little angry, not with him but with the obligations that had taken him from her at such a critical time, she went to the radio room and sent him word that she'd arrived and was waiting for him. His reply came ten minutes later—"Please be patient. I will be back soon." The happiness of hearing his voice was shattered by Major Kasli, commanding in

Michael's absence. With a reproachful look on his narrow face, he reprimanded her for using the radio to send a personal message, chewed out the radio operator for allowing it, and for good measure reprimanded the junior officer who'd explained why Michael was gone. That was confidential information. Quinette wanted to pull his goatee till he howled. "That's right," she snapped. "Us spies might tip off the CIA."

She retreated into the friendly confines of Michael's walled compound, where she took off her Western clothes and wrapped herself in a kanga. In the courtyard Pearl and the other two girls were grinding sesame nuts. With three empty days of waiting stretching before her, Quinette offered to help. Pearl shook her head. "Remember last time, how cross my father was with me."

"He isn't here, he won't know, and I have got to have something to do," Quinette pleaded.

She knelt by the grinding slab, locked her ankles, and rocked forward and back, mashing the nuts into a light brown paste. In minutes she was dripping sweat, but she reveled in the mindless effort, the flex of her back and arm muscles. She and the girls took turns, then pounded sorghum in the pail-sized wooden pestle. A camaraderie grew between her and them, and there was pleasure in that, too: the feeling that by sharing in their labors she was breaking down barriers, knitting the thread of her life into the tapestry of theirs.

"Your hair, I don't like it again," Pearl remarked when the work was finished and the doura was cooking over the fire.

"The braids came undone weeks ago," Quinette said.

"May I fix it? You should look beautiful for my father."

She sat on a stool outside, in that welcome hour when the heat softened its blows, and submitted to the long process of having her hair woven into plaits.

"I would like to ask you a question, Pearl. But you don't have to answer if you don't want to."

"Yes?"

"How do you feel about your father and me getting married? I'm going to be like your mother."

"My mama *penngo*. She is died."

Pearl's command of English, Quinette realized, didn't mean they could communicate all the time. "What I meant is, will you be happy when I become your father's wife?"

"*Toddo buna Kinnet,*" she answered. "Means Pearl likes you."

"*Kinnet buna Toddo,*" Quinette said.

It's going to turn out all right, she said to herself that night, lying on the air mattress thrown over the crude bed, the paraffin lamp lending a sheen to the rubbed walls, on which moths drawn to the light cast shadows twice as big as themselves.

The next morning, in the interests of keeping herself occupied, she went to New Tourom to see if Moses needed help with his classes. She arrived as the pupils lined up in a military formation outside the newly completed school building. After Moses called the roll, she volunteered her services, which he said would be most welcome. At a clap of his hands, the children, with an obedience Quinette found touching, trooped inside to sit on benches, copybooks in their laps.

After three hours of checking spelling and basic arithmetic, she joined Moses, his wife, and Ulrika for lunch, at which the nurse revealed that Quinette had become the subject of much local gossip. Good gossip, Ulrika added quickly.

"Some people are saying that you must be a woman with great powers. That you have—*ach*, I cannot think of the English word. There are many girls here happy to be his, but to them he pays no attention. Only to the foreign woman. *Bewitched.* That is the English."

As much as she wanted to think of herself as bewitching, Quinette had to laugh.

She returned to the school for the adult education session. She was dismayed at how little progress the older students had made since her last time here. They were still struggling with the alphabet and numbers. Yamila was having a particularly difficult time, her copybook blackened with incomprehensible marks.

Leaning over her, Quinette turned to a blank page and drew a straight line. "One. The number one. Say 'one.' "

Yamila only looked at her, wildly, defiantly. Was she "on the slow side," as Quinette's mother would have put it? It didn't seem so. A complicated light shone in Yamila's narrow anthracite eyes.

"Write it, the number one." She handed her the pencil.

Yamila made a mark, said, "Wan," and without further prompting, wrote the next numeral, forming it like a *Z.* "Wan, tuh."

"No, not 'tuh.' Two. Toooo."

"Toooo."

Was there mockery in the singsong way she'd repeated Quinette's exaggerated pronunciation?

"Good. Now try three."

"Tree."

"No. That—" pointing out the window—"is a tree. This—" Writing "3" with her fingertip—"is a three. That's a tree, this is the number three. Tha-ree."

"Tha-ree," Yamila echoed. "Wan, toooo, tha-ree." Then, with quick, violent movements, she inscribed the rest of the numbers and named each one, spitting the words, "Fuh, fi, seestah, sayvan, aytah, nye, tin," before she sprang to her feet, tossed the pencil aside, and walked out.

There was no cause for such an outburst, and Quinette's temper flared. She went after her, calling, "Yamila, get back here, get back here right now!"

The young woman halted and spun around with a look of pure hatred that startled Quinette. Then Yamila walked away, haughty as a queen.

"What is the matter?" asked Moses.

"I don't know," Quinette said, her cheeks burning. "She's got something against me."

"Yes," the teacher murmured.

"What is it? Do you know?"

"I will try working with her tomorrow," Moses said.

She could tolerate Kasli's animosity—there wasn't much choice but to tolerate it—but Yamila's, because it was so at odds with the favor the other women had shown her, disturbed Quinette, undermined the confidence with which she'd gone to bed last night.

In a preoccupied mood, she walked toward the ruined mission, where Fancher and Handy were already making their presence felt. They had a gang of workers cutting the knee-high weeds with pangas and scythes, and another clearing the rubble from the bombed buildings, while a third crew lugged the boxes of Bibles and hymnals, the generators, solar panels, and other equipment into a large wall tent pitched in a lemon orchard. A flag flew over the tent—a dark blue cross on a white field, with a scroll that read FRIENDS OF THE FRONTLINE.

Handy, seated on a campstool, was reading a booklet, *Muslim Evangelism: Do's and Don'ts,* Fancher speaking to one of the workmen. Both men projected an air of command, and Quinette struck up a conversation, prompted by some vague idea that their self-assurance would rub off and restore her own.

"You know Nuban?" she asked Fancher.

"A little, and only this dialect. Your hair looks different."

"That's because it is."

"So you're teaching school?"

"Only helping out."

"These people need help, don't they?" he said with an undertone of disapproval. "Mostly they need help to help themselves. Look at that." He waved at the work crews. "They could have cut weeds and cleaned up the mess without waiting for Rob and me to light a fire under their feet. Well, at least it's under way now."

"Jesus Christ is building his church, and the gates of hell shall not prevail against it," Handy interjected. He appeared to be fond of speaking in slogans and aphorisms.

Quinette glanced at his booklet. "And you're going to preach to Muslims?"

"Try to," he replied. "It's tricky. You don't grab them by the collar and tell them to believe in Christ. You expose them to Christ's message and hope they get it. We want to bring as many of them home as we can."

The talk was not having the desired effect. The image of Yamila's face, with its expression of raw hostility, would not leave her mind. The turning of her back was a rejection that Quinette saw as a threat to her acceptance into this world. Just then Negev came across the mission grounds, his long arms swinging, his Israeli machine gun strapped across his back. "Missy, will you be going back soon?"

"I know the way. You can go if you want to."

"I am to protect you. My orders, missy."

With Negev matching her step for step, as if attached to her by an invisible cord, she went down the road and through the notch in the hills into the valley. The garrison and the tukuls of the camp followers and the soldiers' families lay ahead, partly veiled by smoke from burning sorghum stubble. Pausing, she looked up at the ledge and the mouth of the cavern on whose walls the ancestors had painted their inscrutable tale in pictures. At that moment she thought of Malachy's words, *"You have got to meet these people halfway, you have got to become one of them."* She knew what she must do and resolved all at once to do it.

"I'd like to stay here for a little while," she said.

Negev shrugged uncertainly. "As you wish, missy."

"Without you. I'm perfectly safe. Please go and speak to Pearl," she added in a peremptory tone. "Tell her to come here. I want to talk to her."

When Pearl arrived, Quinette made her request. The girl said nothing, puzzlement and a little alarm showing on her face, along with a question. She'd anticipated this reaction—what she was asking was without precedent, and Pearl wanted an explanation.

"I know that a Nuban's wife must be strong and brave and have no evil in her," Quinette said with slow formality. "Your father told me." She pointed toward the ceremonial ledge above. "There. He took me there and showed me the ancestors' paintings, the day he asked me to marry him."

The girl's expression did not change. She said, "Please wait here, Kinnet," and went off, almost at a run. Quinette had anticipated this as well: Pearl would have to seek the counsel of her elders.

Sitting against a sun-warmed rock, the overheated air tingling in her nostrils like steam, she admired the landscape, the mown sorghum and wind-rippled grass taking on the color of burned butter in the slanting light. Minutes passed, she didn't know how many. The light now fell at a near horizontal, slicing over the heights on the valley's western side. Then she saw Pearl below, coming up the path followed by two women, one in a faded shift, the other in a blue kanga. The same pair who'd presided at the ritual Quinette had witnessed, the judges of female courage and virtue. The woman in blue was carrying a coiled whip.

"They will do it," Pearl said.

Quinette took off her shirt and let it fall to the ground. From a clay jar Pearl poured sesame oil into her hands and rubbed it into Quinette's back and shoulders, then sat down at the mouth of the cave, next to the woman in the faded shift. The woman in blue spoke. Quinette turned to Pearl for a translation.

"She asks that you do what she does," the girl said.

Her chin jutting proudly, torso pushed forward, hips out, the woman began to dance to a silent drumbeat. With the knotted lash bent over her head, the tip in one hand, handle in the other, she stepped out wide to one side, lowering the whip to hold it across her back, then crossed her right foot over the left and repeated the movement until she'd described a full circle. She could have been anywhere between fifty and seventy—it seemed all women in Sudan passed from young to old with only a brief transit through middle age—but she danced with the grace of a girl. Quinette followed her lead, her movements, stiff and uncertain at first, becoming more supple and confident. The woman clucked approval, then demonstrated a refinement, turning as she sidestepped so that each large circle became a series of smaller circles, a ring of connected rings. Quinette did likewise, going around once, and again, and the whip's sting went through her like an electric shock, bringing reflexive tears to her eyes. She willed them dry, clenched her jaw, and flinched as the oxhide cracked again.

She spun once more, forcing herself to look into the face of her tormentor and examiner. And around again, the whip's slap as definite as a gunshot, its burn like a bullet's. A third crack. Her eyes did not grow wet, she did not flinch, a gasp never left her throat.

The woman in blue danced before her, clutching the bowed lash in both hands. Quinette spun, offering her back in sweet surrender, and felt the knots tear flesh, the blood trickling down the culvert of her spine. She looked at the ruby droplets glimmering in the dust, each one a bead in the seam welding her to Pearl, to the woman seated next to Pearl, to the woman in blue, and to every soul in this alien world that was to be her own. A bond no one could break.

The knots ripped her again. She shut her eyes, in a state of ecstatic anguish, and soaring beyond pain, she did not feel the next bite of the leather teeth.

And then it was over, and she knew she'd passed her trial when the women began to ululate. They cupped their hands at the corners of their mouths and faced the valley, announcing Quinette's initiation. They faced the cavern, their tongues flicking between half-open lips, the wavering shrieks echoing back, as if spirits of the ancestors were answering.

SHE TOOK ALMOST an entire morning to prepare for Michael's return, darkening her eyes with kohl, putting on gold hoop earrings and then the dress he had given her. Her notion was to transform herself from a plain prairie flower into a brilliant and irresistible African orchid, but as she waited in the courtyard, she wondered if she'd succeeded only in making herself look ridiculous. Her fears were dispelled when he came into the courtyard, dusty from his journey, and stood gazing at her with admiration. "How much I have missed you. I was a very bad officer at the conference. All I could think of was you and the moment when I could do this." As if to show that his military duties were a distant second to her, he flung his canvas map case aside and covered her with kisses. "Oh my, oh my," he murmured, then pulled her inside and tugged at her sleeves. "You look so very beautiful in this, it's a pity to take it off."

As he went to draw it over her head, he touched the tender lacerations on her back. She gave a short gasp and flinched.

"What is it?"

"Nothing."

"You are hurt? What is it?"

"I was going to tell you," she said, then turned around and, gathering the hem, pulled the dress past her waist.

"You didn't . . . ?" he began.

She faced him, the dress falling over her. "Yes, I did. Day before yesterday."

"I told you before that you didn't have to prove a thing. It wasn't necessary."

"Yes, it was. I had something to prove to myself."

"What?"

"That I do belong here."

"And did you?"

"I hope so. Almost everyone has been wonderful. They've made me feel welcome."

"Almost everyone, but not Kasli," Michael said. "You had this done to yourself because of him?"

"No, for myself."

He sat on the bed and motioned for her to sit beside him. "I have ordered him to stand with me at our wedding."

"Why?" she asked, trying not to sound upset. It was his prerogative to choose his best man, but she thought he should have consulted her first.

"To show him that I mean business," Michael replied serenely. He was always serene when he made a decision; he never doubted himself, a trait she found attractive but not in this instance. "I want him to be a part of this marriage, whether he likes it or not."

"But he's a Muslim!" she said. "The minister is going to ask if anyone has a reason why we shouldn't be married. Suppose he says something? That would be awful."

"He won't. I have had a good talk with him. I have reminded him that he is *second* in command."

"Michael, Kasli is one subject I don't want to talk about. He's censored. I'm too happy, and I don't want anything to spoil it."

"Then let us," he said with a grin, "choose the day."

QUINETTE WONDERED HOW many women had made their wedding arrangements over a two-way radio. After several tries she got through to Fitz, who talked to Malachy, who contacted Barrett, who replied via the same channels that he would be delighted to officiate.

He arrived two days ahead of the scheduled date, with his Nuban wife. She was from New Tourom, and the villagers greeted her as if she were a celebrity, paying a visit to her old hometown. The sight of the runty Barrett beside his six-foot ebony-skinned spouse encouraged Quinette. If such a pair, mismatched in ways more profound than race and stature, could make a success of their marriage, then surely she and Michael could.

After he recovered from the hike from the airstrip, Barrett quizzed the bride and groom to assure himself that they knew what they were getting into, then ran them through a rehearsal with Ulrika, who was to be Quinette's maid of honor, and with Kasli, who looked as if he were going to an execution. Quinette took a perverse pleasure in his discomfort.

Following Nuban custom, she spent the night before the wedding in a bungalow called the *lamanra*—a kind of women's dorm where girls sequestered themselves. Her trunk was deposited there, and she and Ulrika sorted through her things, looking for a suitable wedding dress. As she rummaged in the trunk, the clothes she'd brought from the States, the dresses she'd bought in Africa, her books and Bible and the letters from home, bound in rubber bands, it was as if she were making an inventory of a dead woman's personal effects. She had to sit down, her heart fibrillous, her head as if it were about to float off her shoulders.

Ulrika looked at her. "You are having the nerves?"

She nodded, although *nerves* was too broad to describe the peculiar sensation.

Ulrika clapped her hands once and finally, then, rising, withdrew from the trunk a long red dress set off by a motif of light blue trees. "This one I think the best."

Quinette spent the following day getting ready. She bathed under Ulrika's calabash shower and sat for an hour while Pearl redid her braids, fastening scarlet beads to the tips. Afterward she tried to nap, but she was too excited. Finally, in the late afternoon, she slipped into the dress, the wide sleeves falling to her elbows, the bright red cloth, pinched at the waist, hugging her body down to the ankles. Kiki and Nolli draped her in necklaces that with their alternating bands of gold and black resembled slender snakes. Pearl covered her front with a bodice of blue beads and fastened bracelets around her arms; then, escorted by Ulrika and her soon-to-be-stepdaughter, she walked to St. Andrew's church. It was the magic hour when woodsmoke perfumed the air and the sun spread copper over the dry-season grass and the distant hills took on the color of oxblood. The grounds outside the church were crowded with people, waiting under the trees with an almost palpable air of expectancy. They parted at her approach, and she saw Michael turn to face her, a smile arcing across his face, his beret cocked, his trousers bloused over polished boots, his shirt snugged to his middle by a black leather belt with an oval buckle. Behind him, in their best uniforms, his bodyguards were drawn up in two ranks, facing each other to form a corridor at the entrance to the church. A thrill bolted through Quinette when they presented arms as she and Michael, hand in hand, walked between them and passed through the open doors.

Inside, men and women packed the rows of half-log pews and jammed the side aisles. In front, drummers beat a solemn rhythm while a female choir in homespun surplices stood singing. Flanked by the canon and a gloomy Major Kasli, Barrett, garbed in minister's black, waited at an altar covered in green cloth. Sunlight fell on it through the holes in the roof. Proceeding up the center aisle in a daze, Quinette was grateful for the support of Michael's arm. Barrett's voice sounded far away as he began to read from the service, pausing at the end of each sentence to allow the canon to translate his words into the Nuban dialect, for the benefit of the congregation. The same stuttering process had to be gone through when Michael made his vows, repeating after Barrett that he, Michael Archangelo Goraende, took Quinette Melinda Hardin to be his lawful wedded wife, halting for the canon, then continuing, "to have and to hold, to love and cherish . . ." When Quinette's turn came, she felt as if she were speaking in a trance. They exchanged rings, which Barrett had brought from Nairobi. He pronounced them man and wife, they kissed to applause, and the drums and choir took up another lilting hymn as they started back down the aisle.

Before they were halfway to the door, the congregation on one side suddenly stirred. People were jostling one another, shouting and stomping their feet. A man raised a stick and swatted at something on the floor. An instant later a dark brown snake, thick as an arm and long as a leg, slithered across the couple's path and down the aisle, out the door. There was a burst of gunfire, and when they went to look, they saw one of the bodyguards pick up the headless snake by the tail.

"Puff adder," Michael said, squeezing Quinette's hand.

Kasli shot him a look whose meaning was clear: the adder was an omen.

Michael squeezed her hand again. "Don't pay any attention to him," he said. "Snakes come in quite often. It doesn't mean anything."

"Not for a minute, darling," she said, catching her breath. "Whoever's in charge of giving omens wouldn't be so obvious."

He laughed with her. The honor guard re-formed its ranks and saluted the newlyweds, slapping their rifles smartly. Followed by a procession of chanting women, they walked the road to the garrison, arriving at the house as the sun was going down, tinging the sky primrose. They went inside. She was Quinette Goraende. There was no going back, and that, she knew as she undressed, was what she'd wanted.

He took off his uniform, and she lit the lamp and beheld him beholding her. She took all of him in.

"I love the way you look in this light, I love the way these walls look," she said softly.

They had been rubbed with graphite, he said—that was what gave them their blue tint. He had dug up the graphite clay with his own hands and spent many hours polishing it with his thumbs until it shone as it did now.

She touched the raised marks on his brow and, letting out a long, slow breath, allowed her head to fall on his arm. "The first time we made love, you beautified me. Would you again? The first time when a girl is ten, here." She took his hand and placed it on her stomach.

"And what design would you like?"

She looked at the wall and pointed at a canted figure with a bulging belly and outsize hips.

"A pregnant woman?" He drew her down to the floor mat and squeezed a piece of her flesh between his thumb and forefinger. "This is the thorn that lifts the skin . . ."

"And then the cut of the small knife," Quinette said, and felt the bite of his fingernails. "A pregnant woman because I want to have a child with you, a son. I want to give you back what you lost."

"You are a generous soul to wish to give me that. How I love you." And he pinched her sharply, below the breasts. "This is where a girl is tattooed the second time, when she is fifteen."

"She goes high up into the rocks," Quinette said.

"Yes, to that ledge where I brought you."

"The thorn, the knife . . ."

"And then"—his palm rubbed her belly—"the ash of the acacia to heal the cuts and make the marks stand out in all their beauty."

"The third time would be here," she said, drawing his hand to her back. "After I've had my first child."

"Yes. There and here, up and down." She turned over. His fingernails nipped up and down along the edges of the welts, the scars of her sisterhood, and at her bottom, massaging it afterward with the healing ash. "After you have borne our son."

Borne our son. The words rilled through her, and she bent her body like a bow, her cheek resting on the mat. He crouched over her, kissing the back of her neck as he thrust into her. She moved against him until he quivered, flooding her with his seed.

"THERE'S A POEM," Mary said in a tired voice as they taxied into central Nairobi from Jomo Kenyatta. " 'Do not go gentle into that good night.' But that's what Dad did. He took a breath, and then the numbers on the life-support machines went to zero. The nurses and the doctor came in and unplugged him, like he was an experiment that didn't work out. I've gotten so used to people being shot and blown up that I almost forgot someone could go out that way. One breath, and then gone."

At the bleak hour of one in the morning, just five days after watching her father die in a Winnipeg hospital, Mary's grief acted as a brake on Dare's happiness at her return. He wanted to kiss her but confined himself to sitting with his arm around her. It didn't seem right that he should feel so good while she felt so bad. Through streets darkened by another blackout, they rode on to the New Stanley, where he had checked in earlier. In the elevator Mary mentioned that her two younger brothers would be looking after their mother, "but you know how it is with guys their age. It's me she needs right now, and Christ, I hated leaving her so soon. If it wasn't for you, I wouldn't have come back."

"Africa's losing its charms?" he asked.

"All I'm saying is that I don't like being so far away from her."

They went into the room. Mary's jet lag prevented Dare from realizing his fantasies of a passionate reunion, which had grown more pornographic the longer they were apart. She brushed her teeth, swallowed an Ambien, and walked out of her clothes. In two minutes she was asleep. He wasn't disappointed. For now it was enough merely to look at her peaceful face, to hear her breathing quietly beside him. He dwelled on what she'd said. He knew he shouldn't make too much of it, but maybe her father's death had changed her outlook on how she wanted to lead her life. Whether it had or not, he concluded that he could procrastinate no longer; it was time to present his plans for the future and ask if she wanted to share in them.

She was still asleep when he woke up. Leaving her a note that he would be back in an hour, he dressed and went out, walking quickly down Kimathi Street, past a newspaper stand and a bank of phone booths, to a jewelry shop he knew. Fifteen minutes later he came out with a box in his pocket. His pace was slower as he returned to the hotel—he was rehearsing what he would say and marshaling his courage to face the possibility that she would turn him down.

He opened the door and was stopped cold by the sight of her, sitting up in bed, the sheet drawn to her throat, a saucy look on her face.

"Life's for the living, and death's for the dead," she said before he could speak. "I need to apologize for conking out on you." She whipped the bedsheet off her naked body. "C'mere, captain."

His fantasies were fulfilled, but at a cost. He felt like Samson after Delilah gave him a haircut, and all the fine words he'd practiced had deserted his mind. Smoking a postcoital cigarette, he lay contemplating his convex belly and his knobby white legs, forked across the bed.

"What are you thinking?" Mary asked.

"That my mama used to say I was ugly as homemade sin."

"So, manufactured sin is prettier?"

"Hell, I don't know, but it's always seemed to me that any woman who has anything to do with me has got to have something wrong with her, and the ones I was married to sure proved it."

She wound one of his curls around her finger and yanked. "I see you haven't lost your talent for saying exactly the right thing."

"You know what I mean. What are y'all doin' with me? It makes no sense."

"Baby, if love made sense, the human race would be an endangered species."

"C'mon, I've got to know."

She plucked the cigarette from his hand, took a puff, and gave it back to him. "Let's go back to the day I met you. That flight to Somalia. If you hadn't reacted the way you did, Tony and I could've been killed. And no, it isn't that I feel I owe my life to you. All this hasn't been gratitude. What I thought then was, 'Well, here's a *man*. Nothing to look at, but he knew what to do and he did it.' "

There it was again—his competence.

"I'm not gettin' any younger, and one of these days I'm not gonna know what to do, or if I do, I won't be able to do it. What happens then?"

"Don't worry about that. That's what started things off, but that isn't it. What it is, is this—being with you, I don't think only about myself and what I need, I think about you and what you need. And don't ask why, because I don't know."

He could not have asked for a better cue, but he said nothing.

"That's my side of the story," she said with an inviting glance. "Yours?"

"Look in the mirror, that'll tell you."

"Wrong thing, Wes. Wrong again."

"Oh, hell. It's the same as with you. I don't think about me."

She sat up, laughing and patted his scalp. "That's better. Wasn't so hard, was it? So now that we've made sense of it, let's call room service. All this making sense has made me hungry."

"We're on the afternoon flight to Loki," he said. "How about lunch at the Aero Club?"

He'd suggested the Aero Club, not for its proximity to the Wilson Field terminal, certainly not for the excellence of its fare, but to give himself time to recover his nerve. The club was crowded, except for three empty tables in a corner. He took one after they'd gone through the serving line.

"Been thinking about what y'all said," he began, betraying his nervousness with his sidelong glance, his habit of twirling his sunglasses. "About being so far away from your mother. Well, Texas is a lot closer to Manitoba than here."

Her response, a look that seemed to say, *What other obvious points do you want to call to my attention?* caused him to revise his approach. Waving a hand to indicate that she should ignore his geographical commentary, he started again.

"There's some things I haven't told you. One is that me and Doug have an agreement. I'm gonna fly these runs for another few months, then I'm cashin' in my shares in Knight Air. If the cash ain't there, Doug's gonna transfer ownership of my old G1—the plane Tony's flying on the Somalia runs—back to me."

"He agreed to that?" she asked, raising her eyebrows.

"Signed a contract. My plan is to sell the plane and the Hawker—" He was interrupted by five boisterous Americans who seized a table next to theirs. "Well shit, I was hopin' for a nice private conversation."

"Try lowering the Texas decibel level," Mary said. "You were saying that we'll be millionaires."

Dare looked down at his curried lamb and wondered why he'd ordered it. His fluttering stomach wouldn't take curry. "I always did want to be a Texas millionaire, but the only part I ever got right was the Texas part. Sellin' those planes, added to what Yellowbird earns, would take care of the other part." He then outlined his scheme—the corporate jet to fly top-name acts, piling up a nest egg to buy a ranch in the hill country outside Austin. "I've always wanted that. What do I do then?" He shrugged. "Maybe I don't do a damned thing except watch the sun come up and go down. Bottom line is, three, four months from now, Doug Braithwaite goes his way, I go mine, and that's back to Texas. I'm done with Africa, done livin' like this."

He'd deliberately used *I* throughout this speech, and now he looked at her to gauge her reaction. She smiled indifferently and said, "Sounds like you've got it all figured out." Then she added, "Doug Braithwaite goes his way, Wes Dare goes his. Where does Mary English go?"

Dare noticed the Americans stealing glances at her. He couldn't blame them.

"Wes Dare hopes that Mary English goes with him," he said, choosing to throw out his prepared proposal—he couldn't remember it anyway. He removed the small white box from his pocket and set it on the table in front of her. "Since I don't ever say the right thing, I won't say anything except open it."

She did and then sat blinking at the diamond sparkle. They had an audience—the men at the next table had fallen silent and were listening in—but at this point he didn't care how public their little drama had become.

"I'm gonna need a partner," he said. "Someone in the seat next to me on that new airplane. Austin's a pretty town, it's a good place to raise a kid."

"It sounds good, Wes," she said in an undertone. "Sounds very good."

"I hear a *but* comin'."

"But it sounds comfortable and predictable, and I've never been comfortable being comfortable, or with predictability. I need a little chaos in my life."

"Flyin' Texas blues bands around the country can get right chaotic. I've done it."

"I know it would be interesting, but—but it doesn't seem important. Doesn't seem like it would mean much."

"Y'all think what we're doin' now means something?"

"It seems to."

"Well, it doesn't. Like the troops used to say in Vietnam. 'Don't mean nuthin', don't mean a thing,' except that it buys a ticket out of here." Unable to face the finality of a rejection now, he said, "Take a week, take a month, take two months. Y'all decide it's not for you, you can always give that back to me."

She looked shocked. "I would never take this from you if I had the least thought to giving it back."

Once more she stared at the ring, her arms folded as if she were chilled.

In that silence he could almost hear the voices debating in her head. Time stretched—five seconds seemed like an hour. This was torture. For an instant he wished he'd never met her.

"Try it on for size," he suggested. "That wouldn't be the same as taking it."

She pried the ring from the box and slipped it onto her finger. "It's a little small."

"That can be fixed."

"I'm not so sure," she said, and twisted the ring over her knuckle to the base of her finger, then tried to twist it off. "See? It's stuck." She rose partway from her chair and, leaning across the table, kissed him on the forehead. "I love taking chances, and this will be the biggest one yet."

Dare, his heart soaring, experienced one of his rare moments of speechlessness. As Mary sat down, the men nearby broke out in cheers and applause. She blew them all a kiss and then spread her hand to show off the diamond.

"You had us in suspense," said one, a stocky, middle-aged guy with carbon-black hair. "Sorry, but we couldn't help overhearing."

"Oh, I reckon y'all could have if you wanted to," Dare said congenially. His happiness had put him in an expansive mood. "Don't know a one of you, but since you're the first to know, I'll buy you a round in the bar."

"Thanks, and congratulations," the other man said, and stood to offer his hand. "Bob Mendoza. Soft drinks for us. We're flying this afternoon."

With their newfound friends, Dare and Mary moved into the bar for an impromptu engagement celebration. Mendoza said it was great to run into "fellow Americans." Dare pointed out that Mary was Canadian, which Mendoza, erasing four thousand miles of border with a swipe of his hand, dismissed as a distinction without a difference.

"Y'all said you were flying this afternoon. Flying what?"

They were an Air National Guard crew on a KC-135 tanker, doing their annual tour of active duty. Their usual assignment was to the no-fly zone over northern Iraq, but this year they'd been sent to Kenya to practice maneuvers with the Kenyan air force.

"We're out of Tucson," Mendoza said. "Y'know, I thought I heard you mention the name of Doug Braithwaite. I knew a guy by the same name."

"He's my business partner. We've got a small airline, flyin' aid out of Loki. I reckon this is one of those it's-a-small-world stories, on account of he's from Tucson and there can't be two guys with a name like that from the same town."

"I'll be damned. So this is where Doug fetched up. When you see him, be sure to tell him you ran into his old captain in the hundred-seventy-sixth."

"How do you mean, his old captain?"

"Doug was in my crew," Mendoza said. "He was our refueling operator."

Dare exchanged glances with Mary. "Maybe we are talkin' about two different guys. The Doug Braithwaite we know was with the regular air force, not the guard. Flew A-tens in the Gulf War."

"Anyway, that's what he told us," Mary said.

Mendoza paused, half-closing an eye. "He'd be early to mid-thirties by now. Six-one or -two? Slim build? Light brown hair? Good-looking guy?"

"If you like the catalog model type," Mary quipped. "But that's him."

Mendoza said, "He was in commercial flight school when I knew him. Why the hell would he say he flew A-tens in the war?"

"Got no idea," Dare said.

That was the topic of conversation between him and Mary on the flight to Lokichokio. Instead of talking about their future, they speculated about Doug's motives for revising his past. Dare brought up the story he'd told at their first meeting with Hassan Adid—how he'd strafed a column of retreating Iraqis and was horrified by what he'd done, calling it murder. What did he stand to gain from an invention like that?

"Maybe he was just trying to make himself more than he is," Mary conjectured. "We'd have to ask him, but I don't imagine he'd say." She placed her ring hand atop Dare's. "Should it make any difference to us?"

"It could," he replied. "Makes you wonder what else he's lyin' about."

Star at the River's End

THEIR HONEYMOON WAS a walking tour of the Nuba. Having met with his senior officers, Michael now had to confer with his subordinate commanders before the coming offensive. He wanted Quinette to join him so she could meet the inhabitants of his military domain and they meet her. It was going to be a celibate honeymoon; his full bodyguard accompanied them, and to their thirty-odd, Fancher, Handy, and a parade of porters carrying gear and supplies on foot or on bicycles added twenty more. As usual, Negev shadowed Quinette everywhere, a diligent guardian who had to be told not to traipse after her when she went to relieve herself.

Trekking mostly at night to avoid enemy aircraft and ambushes as well as the sun—temperatures now hit one hundred and twenty-five degrees—negotiating trails that twisted among tumbledown slopes where tall pinnacles jabbed at the stars and tree roots clutched precipitous ridges like the fingers of desperate climbers, they journeyed into some of the remotest parts of the mountains. Not so remote, however, that news of Michael's wedding to a white woman had failed to reach them. Women and children swarmed out of the villages to gawk at Quinette, touch her, and ask her questions in dialects that Negev could barely understand.

In every village, while Michael met with the meks and SPLA officers, Fancher and Handy waged their spiritual offensive, evangelizing with a mixture of revival-tent fervor and military efficiency. They distributed hymnals and Bibles in the local language. They powered up the generator and showed videos about the life of Christ. (It was startling to see a TV screen glowing in villages that had no electricity.) If there was a church, they preached in it, encouraging the congregation to remain steadfast in the face of their adversities, reminding them that in the suffering is the glory. If there were soldiers present, they told the stories of Gideon and Joshua and the other mighty warriors of God. They conducted catechism classes with flip charts and audiotapes of gospel messages.

On the sixth day of the journey, they enlisted her. Taking her aside, they explained that Nubans thought it improper for men to minister to women, which was why their audiences were exclusively male. They had observed the numbers of females who were drawn to her and noticed the empathy she had for them. With some coaching, she could take on the task of teaching them about the women of the Bible, about Mary and the virgin birth, the tribulations the mother of God had endured. Would Quinette be willing to do that? She considered the request. God had called her away from her former life for a purpose. Was this it? Eager as she was to say yes, she had to point out that she had no experience or training in missionary work. Fancher expressed approval for her modesty. It normally a took a year to train a fieldworker, he said, but an exception could be made in her case. She'd already overcome cultural biases, the hardest lesson a fieldworker had to learn. If she proved able, she could undergo more formal instruction once they returned to New Tourom. He gave her a cassette recorder, tapes of Mary's story in five different Nuban tongues, and flip charts that showed it in pictures, then tutored her on how to use the materials and conduct a meeting.

They traveled into the lands of the Masakin tribe, where the crowded mountains of the eastern Nuba gave way to broad valleys offering no sanctuary from air raids and the dreaded murahaleen. Horsemen and airmen had brought *tamsit* to the Masakin. The Arabic word, Michael told her, meant "raking." The Masakin had been raked out of their valleys and forced to flee into a range of hills that stretched across the southern horizon: Jebel Tolabi, Jebel Doelibaya, Jebel Tabouli. Tamsit, in other words, was ethnic cleansing; it was scorched earth.

Making for the *jebels,* the column proceeded through an incinerated landscape, the bones of livestock whitening fields that looked in the moonlight as if they'd been covered by a blizzard of ash. A team of minesweepers went out ahead, swinging their detectors back and forth. The silence was eerie, interrupted only by the crunch of burned sorghum stalks underfoot. Besides landmines, there was the danger of stumbling into an enemy ambush—a government garrison wasn't far off—and everyone's eyes and ears were tuned to a high pitch, trying to pick out human forms in the darkness, listening for voices.

Walking behind her husband, Quinette experienced a heightened alertness, a druglike quickening of her senses produced by an amalgam of fear and excitement. The possibility that she might be killed at any moment made her feel intensely alive, and more than ever Michael's sister-in-arms.

The thumping of a heavy machine gun sent everyone to the ground. Red and green tracer bullets, stitching the skies above the hills, declared that the column wasn't the target—some trick of acoustics had made the machine-gun sound much closer than it was. Flat on her stomach, Quinette watched the tracers streak, then slow down, appearing to float like dying sparks before they winked out. There was a series of muffled thuds from an indeterminate distance behind her. Artillery shells whooshed overhead. Half a minute later a flickering appeared among the hills, followed by a ragged rumbling, then more machine-gun fire, then a bright flash as something exploded and caught fire.

Michael, lying beside her, counted by thousands to time the interval between the flash and the sound. "Seven kilometers," he said. "Six point eight exactly." He clapped his hands twice, and the men stood and continued toward the mountains that made a jagged jet-black silhouette, as if a hole had been opened in the sky to reveal a starless void lying beyond the heavens. Michael composed a coherent narrative out of what had been, to Quinette, a lot of confusing noise and flashes. SPLA guerrillas had ambushed a convoy trying to sneak through to the garrison under cover of the predawn darkness. The government troops had called artillery fire on the ambush, but the garrison's guns, shooting at such long range, had been off the mark and the shells had landed harmlessly. The explosion had been a truck or armored personnel carrier struck by rocket-propelled grenades, or perhaps by an artillery round, falling short of its intended target.

His version of events was dead on. Reaching the base of a jebel at first light, they came upon the bullet-sieved hulks of three Sudan army trucks. In one the driver had been welded to the charred remains of the cab, his body shrunk to half its normal size: a faceless blackened form. Corpses lay all around, and the stench was awful. A year ago Quinette would have been sickened, she might have even been moved to pity; but now her only thought was "They had it coming."

The column climbed into the jebels. Even there the Masakin had not found much refuge. The people who emerged from the villages were emaciated, barely surviving on the spare crops scratched out of rocky hillsides, some of which had been transformed into moonscapes by Antonovs and helicopter gunships.

There was a reason the government was paying the Masakin so much attention. Michael showed it to her from a ridge overlooking a cauterized plain of sun-cracked clay and a road: the main supply route between two government-held towns, Talodi in the east, Kadugli in the west, where, he said, it turned northward to join the pipeline and another road that ran to the oil fields. He pointed to the south.

"That way, less than one hundred kilometers, is the oil company's air-field. These hills will be our base when we attack it. From here, with the lorries, we can transport the heavy mortars. We will leave at dark and be in position by midnight. We will hit them and the pipeline hard and fast." He balled his right hand into a fist and smacked the palm of his left. "Hard and fast."

They went on, arriving at a town where the local SPLA battalion was headquartered. Its commander invited Quinette to stay with his wives, all three of them, while he and Michael worked out their battle plans. Negev lugged her rucksack into the tukul and rolled out her sleeping bag. She fell on it and didn't wake up till early afternoon, when the youngest wife brought her a meal of *mandazi* cakes and stringy goat meat, the same fare she'd eaten throughout this trek. She could shove her arm into the waist-band of her hiking shorts and figured she'd lost a pound for each of the ten days since she'd left New Tourom.

Fancher appeared at the door to tell her that it was time for her debut as a minister. She followed him to the church, a long bungalow just out-side of town, with the usual makuti roof and a tall wooden crucifix planted in front. The men were already gathered inside, where she could hear Handy reading from the Psalms—" 'He shall cover you with his feathers, and under his wings shall you trust. His truth shall be your shield and buckler . . .' "

"That's our reading for today, the ninety-first," Fancher said to her, offering a smile of reassurance. He handed her a Bible, marked at the Psalm. "I'd like you to start with it." He motioned at a tree a short distance off. Under it stood one of the translators in Fancher's retinue, with the flip chart on an easel and the tape recorder on a table, plugged into speakers and a solar panel. The news that the women and children were to be min-istered to by a woman had drawn quite an assembly—more than a hun-dred, Quinette judged. "I'll watch how you do and give you a critique afterward," Fancher said. "Okay?"

"Okay."

She had thought her experience with speaking to liberated slaves would give her confidence, but her knees shook slightly as she stood before all the expectant faces. This wasn't making a speech, this was *min-istry.* The sweat trickling into her eyes didn't help, and she flubbed the first verse and had to start over. She read on and, verse by verse, felt more sure of herself. The indwelling spirit poured through her, and instead of stand-ing rigidly, she began to pace to and fro, gesturing, her voice growing stronger. " 'You shall not be afraid of the terror by night, nor for the arrow that flies by day. . . . Nor for the pestilence that walks in darkness, nor for the destruction that wastes at noonday . . .' " It wasn't too long a Psalm, just sixteen verses, but with each line needing to be translated, its reading took a full fifteen minutes. She concluded—" 'With long life will I satisfy him, and show him my salvation' "—and glanced over her congregation at Fancher, standing with his arms crossed over his chest. He pursed his lips and gave her a single nod.

That gesture encouraged her to ad-lib.

" 'I will show him my salvation,' " she repeated. "And God showed us our salvation in Jesus Christ, his son. Now we'll learn about Mary, who gave birth to Jesus—"

"Gunships! Gunships coming!"

The cry came in three different languages, English, Arabic, Nuban. "Gunships coming!" Men were running from the church. In seconds Quinette's audience fled in all directions. Fancher seized her arm and yelled, "Over there!" They ran to a bomb shelter—nothing more than a wide, deep hole in the ground. It was already packed to the rim. They ran to another and wedged themselves in, crouching atop a pile of people, with no more than six inches between them and the top of the hole. Between the shelter and the church, a few women lay flat on the ground. Quinette looked up. Two gunships materialized, looking like huge predatory insects. *"Woe to the land of the whirring wings . . ."* Both swooped directly over the bomb shelter, their rapid-fire cannons making a loud, hideous, ripping noise. *"A thousand shall fall at your side . . . but it shall not come near you . . ."* Quinette pressed her face into the back of a person under her and heard a series of sharp cracks. Rockets, Fancher said. The gunships flew off. Fancher crawled out of the hole, got to his feet, and dived back in. "They're coming in for another run!" he cried, the last couple of words drowned out as both helicopters skimmed the treetops, close enough that Quinette glimpsed the pilot's helmeted head in the cockpit window; then she curled into a fetal position and covered her head as brain-numbing explosions brought down a rain of dirt and debris. The ground shook, shrapnel scythed a tree branch overhead, and it crashed somewhere nearby. No one in the shelter was hit. *"I will say to the Lord, He is my refuge and fortress . . ."*

In the silence that followed, she heard shouts. Peering over the shelter's lip, she saw Michael leading teams of antiaircraft machine-gunners and riflemen. Waving his arms, pointing, he showed them where to set up firing positions. She felt a rush of love, of pride—to be the wife of such a man! The gunships roared in again and this time flew into a sheet of bullets. The noise was stupendous. Quinette did not duck, thinking that she should match her husband's bravery. The lead gunship wobbled, then dropped, settling on its wheels as if it had made a normal landing. Michael's troops riddled it with bullets.

Their ears ringing, Quinette and Fancher got out of the hole and brushed dirt from their hair. SPLA troops ran toward the downed helicopter a hundred yards away. Villagers, scrambling from their hiding places, followed them. Quinette walked in a shell-shocked daze. The women who hadn't made it to a shelter had been shredded by cannon fire. She couldn't tell how many there had been. Nearby, the tree beneath which she'd begun her meeting was splintered and blackened, the tape recorder and speakers and other paraphernalia scattered amid rocket fragments. The troops were dragging the bodies of the crew from the gunship. One was still alive. Villagers pounced on him, tearing at him with bare hands, hacking him with pangas in an orgy of revenge. *Only with your eyes shall you look and see the reward of the wicked,* Quinette thought. "No! No!" Handy screamed, sprinting toward the frenzied crowd.

"Help us stop those people!" Fancher said to her. "We can't let them do this!"

She pointed at the heaps of bloodied rags that twenty minutes ago had been listening to her read the ninety-first Psalm. "I can't," she said, choking. "Let them have at it."

"You are safe, you're not hurt!"

It was Michael, covered in dirt. He put his arms around her and held her close.

Fancher appealed to him to help restore the villagers to their sanity. What was going on over there, within sight of a church, was an abomination.

"This is war, Mr. Fancher," Michael replied coldly. "And war is cruelty. It cannot be refined."

They left at dusk, after the dead were buried—amazingly, only eight people had been killed, and the church had not been badly damaged, though there were rocket craters within fifty yards of it. *"Jesus Christ is building his church and the gates of hell shall not prevail against it."* The two ministers lectured her before they set off. Ministry was more than words, it was action, and she should have set the Christian example by helping them restrain the villagers. No matter what, that sort of conduct could not be justified. She agreed, she promised to improve, but while Fancher and Handy spoke in her ear, another spoke in her head: *You can't ask people to grant mercy to an enemy who shows them none.* It seemed to her that Sudan was cut off from normal standards of behavior; it was under different, harsher rules.

The column walked till dawn, resting the next day in the village of another tribe, the Tira, to whom Quinette preached her second lesson. They left that night, passing through a region that had been spared from the war's ravages because it was sparsely inhabited: a vestige of wild Africa where low ridges polka-dotted with acacia trees undulated toward a far-off range, rising like a volcanic island from an ocean of grass. Such ugliness and horror two days ago, such peace and beauty here. The range, Michael told her, was the southern face of the Limon hills. New Tourom lay beyond it. Home. Eager as they were to get there, they halted at midnight beside a riverbed and camped in the open, too worn out to march further. The men spread out into a defensive perimeter, and everyone but the sentries went to sleep to the lullabies of hyenas.

An urgency in her bladder and bowels woke Quinette at some predawn hour. After finishing that business in the riverbed, she crept back, but sleep eluded her and she lay on her bag, gazing at the constellations.

"That one is the Phoenix," Michael whispered, raising his arm. "Do you see it? The one that looks like a house? The very bright star beneath it is Achernar. The Arabs named it. It means 'star at the river's end.' "

"How long have you been awake?"

"An hour. I cannot get back to sleep."

"Me neither."

"For the same reason?" he asked, turned onto his side, and laid his hand on her shoulder.

They sneaked away barefoot through the grass, past a none-too-vigilant sentry, came to a *koppie,* and sat under an outcrop, on a bed of sand.

"What river is that star at the end of?"

"The Nile," he answered. "Do you see that long line of stars bending and twisting above it? That's it. The Nile of the heavens."

"I love the way that sounds," she said. "Star at the river's end, the Nile of the heavens."

"Yes, the Arabs can be very poetic. As poetic as they can be brutal."

He kissed her, so gently it was more a breath than a kiss. His fingers toyed with her braided hair, then fell to her shirt and opened the top two buttons. He cupped her breast and drew a ring around her nipple.

"I cannot keep my hands off of you. It's a habit."

"One you must never, ever break," she said, laughing softly.

He stripped off his uniform while she wriggled out of her shorts and tossed them and her shirt carelessly aside. Their unwashed bodies gave off an ammonia-like odor. He stroked her back, as if he were strumming his harp. She'd had to rein in the raw carnality awakened by the dangers they'd faced together; now his touch and their isolation from the others unleashed it.

They lay without talking for a while, the sand cool against their skin. She turned sideways and held his face between her hands. "Wouldn't it be beautiful if this was the time? If he were conceived out here tonight, under that star?"

He didn't answer, sitting upright at an ominous sound, like a herd of charging buffalo. Michael snatched his sidearm from the pile of clothes and stood outside the outcrop, Quinette beside him. Except for the pistol, they might have been their own remote ancestors, naked and fearful in the African night. One ridge over, they made out a dust cloud and hundreds of huge, dark shapes flowing over it, but the darkness and trees and tall grass made it impossible to see what manner of creatures they were. A distance away the men were awake, shouting over the racket made by the stampeding animals. Then, fifty yards directly in front of her, the grass parted and a prehistoric beast appeared, six or seven feet tall, running on two long legs with clawed feet, its stalk of a neck sprouting from a body the size and shape of a bathtub. Michael gripped his pistol with both hands, then thought better of it, grabbed her by the wrist, and pulled her back under the outcrop. The surging mass broke around the koppie, the dust filling the small space where the two people huddled. Ostrich. The thunderous noise grew fainter. In a moment all was silence again. Quinette heard Negev calling for her. Dressing quickly, breathless, she called back that she was all right. She and Michael looked at each other and laughed with relief. Thank God they had had the outcrop to hide under, Michael said. The giant birds, fleeing in such blind fright, would have trampled them, and an ostrich's talons could tear a human being open like a paper sack.

"Fleeing from what?" Quinette asked. "We heard hyenas earlier. Was it hyenas?"

Michael looked toward the ridges, where a swath of flattened grass marked the path of the ostriches' flight. "It could have been. Or lions. Or a leopard. Or something else. Or they were like a mob in a riot, running for no reason. I don't know."

The wind soughed through the acacia and rippled the long grass that concealed whatever had menaced the ostrich. Hyena, lion, leopard, or nothing at all, some figment of ostrich imagination. She asked no more questions. This was the land beyond the rivers of Ethiopia, where a lot of things lacked explanation.

AFTER THEIR RETURN she discovered that she was, for all her exotic circumstances, in an essentially prosaic role—the officer's wife. She endured one of its trials, and that was her husband's absence. Michael was there physically, but in all other ways he was gone, immersed in staff conferences, poring over maps and operational plans, overseeing military exercises to hone his troops to a fighting edge. New recruits, arriving from nearby villages and from as far as a hundred miles away, had to be trained. Radio messages from Garang's headquarters had to be decoded and answered. Quinette was grateful for the moment they'd shared under the star at the river's end. Her heart and body lived off the memory of it, as one would live off stored fat in a time of hunger, for in matters of sexual passion, if not of love, she was suffering a famine. At day's end Michael was too tired and preoccupied to pay much attention to her. She joked that he'd broken his habit of not being able to keep his hands off her, but he didn't think it particularly funny. Nor did he laugh when, one night, she remarked that here they were, married such a short time, and he'd already taken a mistress.

"What are you talking about?" he snapped.

"The war. The war's your mistress."

"What nonsense. I do not love this war, and you know that."

"Darling," she said, "you're losing your sense of humor."

He massaged his forehead with the heels of both hands. "You are right. And it is that damned second in command of mine causing me to lose it."

"More nonsense about me being a CIA spy?"

"No," he said wearily. "He argues with me all the time about this offensive. He thinks it will be a big mistake. I assign him a task, and either he drags his feet or he does not do it at all, to show me how much he objects. If I had someone to replace him, I would sack him."

He revealed then that the operation was going to be more ambitious than she had thought. The raid on the oil-field airbase was to be the main act in a whole concert of destruction. While the Nubans struck it from the north, Dinka troops would assault from the south. This would be coordinated with a general offensive throughout the Nuba. Outposts and garrisons would be attacked to keep the Arabs pinned down as commando teams, armed with plastic explosives, sabotaged the pipeline.

"What's Kasli's objection?" Quinette asked. "That you can't pull off something this big? That it will fail?"

"He's afraid it will succeed."

"What? Whose side is he on?"

"There are times I wonder," Michael said, hanging his pistol belt on a peg. "But I understand his concerns. There is a kind of balance in the fighting in this zone. The government bombs a village, we attack a garrison. The murahaleen seize some captives, we ambush a convoy. A successful campaign on this scale will upset the balance. It will be a provocation, and Kasli fears Khartoum will retaliate in a very bad way. The people will suffer more and blame the SPLA for bringing it down on their heads."

"And you say you understand that?"

"Yes," he replied, frowning. "But that does not mean I agree with it."

"I hope not." She took his hands in hers, convinced he hadn't told her all this to make conversation. Kasli had put some doubts into his mind, and he was calling on her to put them out. "Just think of what we saw in that Masakin village," she said. "Kasli is comfortable with the status quo, and he wants it to continue. You can't let that happen. The people don't want you to, and I don't want you to, and God himself doesn't either."

He looked a little amused. "Ah yes, your conversations with the Creator. And what does He have to say about it?"

Actually, she didn't know what God had to say about it. What she did know as she imagined the spectacle unfolding—tall, black soldiers sweeping out of the hills, mortar shells bursting, cyclonic flames whirling from the shattered pipeline—was that the battle had to happen and that she must encourage her husband to make it happen. The vision stirred her into a warlike mood, and she thought of what God had to say. She went to her trunk and took out her Bible. After some searching, she found the passage from Isaiah and read it aloud. " 'In that time a present will be brought to the Lord of Hosts from a people tall and smooth of skin, and from a people terrible from their beginning, a nation powerful and treading down, whose land the rivers divide.' A people tall and smooth of skin," she repeated, her fingers running lightly down Michael's bare forearm. "The Nubans and the Dinka. Whose land the rivers divide—the Nile. It's almost like a prophecy."

"And what is the present?" he asked, with a slightly sardonic smile.

He wasn't taking her seriously. She would correct that. She laid the Bible in his lap and said calmly, "The airfield and the pipeline blown to hell and as many dead Arabs as your men can kill."

He looked startled. "Would your missionary friends approve of you speaking like that?"

A voice spoke in her memory, the voice of the liberated slave woman, Atem Deng. "*I wish I was a man so I could carry a rifle . . . I would massacre them all.*" "I suppose not," she said. "They wouldn't approve of this either. I wish I could go with you."

He said nothing.

"I know, it's no place for a woman."

"Certainly not for a woman who is my wife and hopes to be the mother of our son," he said. "But perhaps there is something you could do short of that. I will think about it."

The next day he brought her to the far end of the valley to watch the recruits training. An encampment of weathered tents and crude lean-tos was pitched at the edge of a dusty field where, under an unmerciful sun and to the commands of unmerciful sergeants (Quinette saw one crack a boy over the head with a stick for facing right when he should have turned left), they were marching with wooden rifles, like kids playing soldier. A lot of them *were* kids, no more than thirteen or fourteen. In Sudan, childhood was another casualty of war.

He gazed off to a corner of the field, where some recruits were advancing in single file, their make-believe rifles at the high port—they reminded her of a high school marching band coming onto the field at halftime. "Ah, they are doing it wrong," Michael said under his breath. "Please wait here."

He strode off and called a halt to the drill. She watched him grasp the lead recruit by the shoulders and move him to one side, then the man behind him to the other side, then the next and the next, until he got the file into a staggered formation.

"They think this is a parade," he said when he came back. "They have to understand that if they went into combat one behind the other, one automatic rifle would knock the lot of them down like ninepins."

"One round will get you all, I remember my father saying that," Quinette said with a wistful smile. "When he took my sisters and me hiking in the woods. We were scared of the woods, and we'd walk very close behind him, sometimes bumping into him, and he would turn around and tell us to back away because one round would get us all. We never knew what he meant."

He sat next to her and tapped her knees with his walking stick. "A soldier's daughter, a soldier's wife. So now I will tell you what you can do.

When the regular soldiers are away, those boys"—he pointed at the recruits, now marching at the double, chanting in time to their stomping feet—"are going to help defend this base and New Tourom, but they cannot defend with toy rifles. I sent a radio message to Loki yesterday requesting rifles and ammunition. It means nothing, it is nonsense without a certain word."

She gave him a puzzled look.

"I can no longer trust the radio to send my shopping lists in the SPLA code," he explained. "Every commander knows it, and—you recall the time that one fellow tried to hijack one of my shipments?—another tried it recently, and he succeeded. Wesley was forced to deliver the cargo elsewhere. I've complained to the high command about this nonsense of one commander stealing from another, and they have promised to put a stop to it, but I don't trust them either. So I have worked out a new system, a private code between me and Douglas and Wesley. To decode, a keyword is needed." He produced an envelope from his shirt pocket and handed it to her. "It's in there. It says, so you know, 'Please do not forget the handbook.' A relief flight arrives tomorrow morning. You are to be on that flight when it returns to Loki and bring this to Douglas or Wesley personally."

She slipped the envelope into the bodice of her dress. "Thank you, Michael."

"Thank you?"

"For trusting me with something this important."

Now enlisted in the military as well as the spiritual offensive, she arrived in Loki in a utilitarian outfit—khaki shirt and trousers—to look businesslike. The immigration officer in the hot little shed at the tarmac's edge didn't care about her appearance. With the surliness of the petty official granted a moment of power, he told her that her visa had expired and that she would not be allowed into the country. Quinette, who had forgotten about her visa (in the Nuba, passports and visas seemed irrelevant), reminded him that she was already in the country and that he could issue her a temporary airport visa. A modest gift, from the money Michael had given her for expenses, caused him to acknowledge that this was true. He shoved a form across his desk, which she filled out, checking "Business" in the box labeled "Purpose of Visit." She paid the fee, but the officer, desiring to prolong his moment of power or perhaps extract another gift, held on to her passport. Flipping through it, he noted that she had departed Kenya some time ago, but he saw nothing to indicate where she'd gone. This was peculiar. What was the nature of her business? She replied that she'd been in Sudan, and he repeated that he did not see anything in her passport to show that she'd been there. He asked—that is, demanded in the form of a question—to see what was in her fanny pack.

She hesitated, her heart beating faster, "There are some personal things in there. Female things."

With a backward curl of his fingers, the official told her to give it to him. Drawing herself up to her full six-one, she unbuckled the pack and tossed it onto the desk—just to show this officious character that he couldn't push her around. He pulled out a fistful of tampons, her makeup, and the envelope, which he opened with a knife.

" 'Please do not forget the handbook,' " he said, then looked up at her with an interrogator's gaze. "Is this a personal female item?"

"It's a reminder," she answered, her heart rate accelerating further. Now she felt like the spy Kasli accused her of being.

"To do what?"

"To not forget the handbook."

"What handbook?"

"First aid," she said. "A handbook on first aid. Now if you don't mind . . ."

The officer leaned back and, shaving a mustache of sweat with his finger, looked at the ceiling and sighed to show that his forbearance was not infinite. "Miss Hardin, it is known that you are married to a commander in the Sudanese People's Liberation Army. It is therefore important to know what your business is here. Now, if *you* don't mind, you will tell me what it is."

Quinette could only stand there, struck dumb.

"Aviation. She works for us."

She and the officer turned as one. Mary English swaggered through the door and up to the desk and clasped the man's hands firmly in both of hers. "We've been expecting her, and we'd appreciate it if you expedited the paperwork."

His fingers folded quickly over Mary's offering and as quickly slipped it into the desk drawer. It took him only a little more time to issue Quinette her visa and return her things.

Outside, Mary said, "The Archangel radioed us last night that you'd be coming in. We figured you'd get hassled. The word's out on you. Sorry I was late. Hop on." She slapped the backseat of a Kawasaki.

Quinette climbed on, laying her straw carry-bag in her lap. "The word's out on me?"

"You are shit on a log and persona non grata to a lot of people in Loki,"

Mary answered, kicking the starter, and they roared off, the motorcycle throwing a rooster-tail of dust. They sped by a UN gate and the compounds of the independent NGOs, each with its flag flying bravely, and finally through the gate into Hotel California, Quinette's old home. Everything looked so familiar, and she somehow thought that this should not be so, that all of it should have changed because she had.

Walking across the compound, she neared the wall-tent she'd shared with Lily and Anne and felt a pang of nostalgia. The front flaps parted, and Anne came out, on her way to work.

"Anne! How are you?"

Her old friend looked her up and down and none too favorably. "Fine and how are you?" she said in a tone almost hostile in its indifference.

"Well, I—there have been a lot changes—"

"Good to see you again. I'm off."

She walked away. An outright insult would have been less hurtful than that frigid reception.

"That's what you meant, shit on a log, persona non grata?" Quinette asked.

"Shit on a log to the do-gooders," Mary answered. "It's uncool to marry a rebel commander. You're persona non grata to the UN people. They're the ones who alerted immigration to be on the lookout for you, maybe just to harass you, maybe because they suspect what we're up to. They also sent around a notice that you're barred from flying on UN planes, or any independent airline flying a UN mission."

Hearing this made her as uneasy as seeing her picture on a wanted poster in the post office, but uneasiness swiftly morphed into a kind of outlaw's pride. She regarded the aid workers, shuffling papers, drinking coffee in the mess, with scorn: play-it-safers with return tickets, who would never suffer the ordeals or experience the triumphs of a passionate devotion to a cause, to a person, to anything.

"Well, I had no intentions of flying on UN planes," she said.

"Yeah. They're just making a point. You're not a neutral party anymore. You didn't marry a man, you made a political statement. You've taken sides, in just about the most public way possible."

"Seems to me you and Wes and Doug have done the same thing."

"We aren't public about it. We keep it as quiet as we can."

They came to the tent Wes and Mary shared and sat on bamboo and rattan chairs under the grass-roofed shelter. Mary produced two Cokes from a cooler. Quinette took one sip and, indulging in the forgotten delight of an ice-cold drink, finished half the can in a single gulp.

"So what about you?" she asked. "Do you think marrying him was uncool? That I'm some kind of girl-guerrilla with a knife in her teeth?"

"Nope. You might be crazy, but I understand that because I've done something crazy. Wes has asked me to marry him, and I said yes."

Quinette regarded Mary, with her model-like beauty.

"I know what you're thinking. And there's more—I'll be his fifth wife. No accounting for a woman's taste, is there? That's enough girl talk. You've got something for us."

"I'm supposed to show it to Wes or Doug."

"Wes is in Nairobi and Doug's on a flight."

"Michael said to show it to either of them. Personally."

"Hey, I'm his first officer. I'm authorized," Mary said, and turned her hand palm up. After she glanced at the note, she said, "Okay, let's go and see what's on order."

When Quinette entered Knight Air's office, Fitz bounded out of his chair and hugged her—a welcome that made up for the ones she'd gotten at the airport and from Anne.

"Okay, that's out of the way," Mary said. "It's handbook."

Fitz squatted before a small safe in a corner of the room, spun the combination lock, and pulled out a sheet of paper and laid it on his desk. Eight sets of letters were printed on it in block letters: RWOEIOHE RCRN-SIEH OHEOEPEC PTLVDDTS YFIROSP IOWTNZRA IUSSTPC TTFAWEA.

"All those consonants, it looks like a listing from a Polish phone directory," Quinette said.

Fitz chuckled. "The things I have had to learn how to do," he said, in a way suggesting that the acquisition of these new skills pleased him.

On a blank sheet, he printed HANDBOOK, spacing the letters wide apart and writing a number under each one:

$$\begin{array}{cccccccc} \text{H} & \text{A} & \text{N} & \text{D} & \text{B} & \text{O} & \text{O} & \text{K} \\ 4 & 1 & 6 & 3 & 2 & 7 & 8 & 5 \end{array}$$

That done, he arranged the sets of letters vertically, placing each column under the number corresponding to its place in the sequence, then turned the sheet around so Mary could read the message.

Squinting at it, Quinette recognized some words, but the text still didn't make much sense.

$$\begin{array}{cccccccc} \text{H} & \text{A} & \text{N} & \text{D} & \text{B} & \text{O} & \text{O} & \text{K} \\ 4 & 1 & 6 & 3 & 2 & 7 & 8 & 5 \end{array}$$

```
P R I O R I T Y
T W O H C U T F
L O W E R S F I
V E T O N S A R
D I N E S T W O
D O Z P I P E S
T H R E E C A P
S E A C H
```

"It says," Mary explained, "that the Archangel is asking for a priority shipment of two hundred cut flowers—that's assault rifles—five tons of sardines—that's rifle ammunition—two dozen pipes—that's rocket-propelled-grenade launchers—and three caps—that's the grenades—three for each launcher."

And now, with another look, Quinette saw the message emerge, like a lake bottom coming into clear view through a diving mask. She felt that she had gained admittance to a secret world.

Fitz turned to her. "So, mission accomplished. Join us for dinner tonight at Tara's compound. The food there is much better."

Proud that she had overcome her need for even basic amenities, Quinette looked upon the Hotel California's comforts the way a reformed alcoholic would a drink. A soft bed, running water, decent food—one taste of these blessings, and she would have to start all over, habituating herself to a life without them. So when Mary, an hour before dinner, hinted that she could do with a bath by loaning her a fresh towel, a wash-cloth, and a bar of soap, she marched to the shower determined not to enjoy it. The cascade of hot water broke her resolve almost immediately. She stood under it for a long time, her head thrown back and eyes shut, and with guilty pleasure she watched the suds swirl down the drain, carrying away the grime and dried sweat that veneered her body.

Feeling renewed, she returned to the tent. She'd brought two changes of clothes in her carry-bag in case she couldn't get a flight out right away—another pair of bush shorts with a matching shirt and, in case of a special occasion, the black and gold dress.

"What do you think?" she asked, holding up the two outfits.

Mary, who was brushing her hair in a mirror nailed to a tent pole, turned and answered that the dress was gorgeous, but considering Quinette's notoriety, it might be best not to call attention to herself.

"I don't see why I should skulk around like I'm ashamed."

"Look"—Mary hammered the air with the hairbrush, like a scolding mother—"you're already the subject of a lot of bad talk, so why give them a reason for more by showing up dressed like the White Queen?"

Never one to shy from attention, even the negative kind, Quinette snaked into the dress, did her lips, and put on her hoop earrings and a nest of black-bead necklaces. Eager to cause a stir, she was a little deflated when she entered the bar with Fitz and Mary and found it empty. So was the adjacent dining room, except for a South African aircrew in dark blue jumpsuits.

Round tables on concrete pedestals sprouted alongside the small kidney-shaped swimming pool, glowing an unearthly blue in its underwater lights. They sat down and ordered drinks, Quinette asking the barman for a gin and tonic without the gin—she hadn't touched hard liquor in so long, she was afraid one shot would get her drunk. The *pop-pop-pop* of rifle fire came from somewhere in the distance: Turkana and Tuposa cattle raiders, shooting it up again. Quinette reminisced about the trek with Michael, the gunship attack, the ostrich charge. It was a pleasure to converse without strain. There were so few people she could speak to in the Nuba, her efforts to learn the local language—it was called Moro—having barely proceeded past the *hello* and *good-bye* stage, and even then she couldn't say hello or good-bye to the other tribespeople who'd sought refuge in New Tourom because they spoke Otorro, Heiban, or Krongo.

The dining room had filled up: Quinette's wish for an audience had been granted, and among the diners were Ken Eismont and his whole crew—Jim Prewitt, Santino, Jean, and Mike. She had never received a reply to her resignation and wasn't sure how Ken would react to her presence. Her impulse was to return to the bar and hide out until he left; but that would be cowardly. Besides, what did she have to feel guilty about? Perhaps she could have handled her departure from the WorldWide Christian Union more gracefully, but her conscience was clear; and it armored her against the icy look that pierced Ken's rimless glasses when she approached his table.

"Thought I would say hello," she said.

He gave her a limp handshake.

"Did you find a replacement?" she asked.

"No, but thanks for leaving the office in good shape," he said indifferently.

She decided to disarm him. "I gave you an apology in writing, I'll give it face to face. I should have given you more notice."

"You think that's it? Not giving enough notice?"

She did not say anything.

"You used me and the organization as a pretext to see your lover. And then you quit. How do you justify treating us like that? I expected more of you." He was speaking quietly but injecting venom into every word. "You left us with a pile of work you never finished, but that isn't all. Did you ever for one second think of what the consequences would be to us? Are you aware that Khartoum knows about your marriage and that they've used it against us?"

"This is the first I've heard about it," she said, perversely exhilarated that she had drawn the attention of the Sudanese government.

"Khartoum has been trying to discredit us and our program for years, and you handed them red meat for their propaganda sausage factory. They've made statements that we're an ally of the SPLA because one of our employees is the wife of an SPLA officer."

"Why do you I think I resigned first? To spare you that."

"It didn't work. They're saying that our teams are now fair game for their militias. We've put out press releases that you are no longer our employee. Not that the denials have had any effect. You've put all of us"—he swung an arm at the table—"in danger. As if we needed more of that."

"Isn't this a little too public? Whatever you've got to say, you can say it in private."

"I've said all I have to say, except this. We would have had to fire you if you hadn't quit. Marrying a guerrilla officer, for Christ's sake! I'd think you were nuts, but what you are is a selfish woman, Quinette. Selfish and careless."

"Right," she said angrily. "By the way, how did you make out, looking into that hanky-panky I dug up? Did you sort through that? Figure out how to cover it up? Where do you get off, judging me?"

"I don't know you," he said, turning from her. "You don't exist."

She got a plate, stepped up to the serving table, and looked at the dinner choices, written on little white cards placed in front of the chafing dishes. It was hard to read them, but she was damned if she was going to wipe her eyes and give Ken the satisfaction of seeing how deeply he'd wounded her. He didn't even give her a chance to defend or explain herself.

She pointed randomly, the server in his starched white smock heaped chicken on her plate, and composing herself, she rejoined Fitz and Mary.

"That didn't look like a pleasant encounter," Mary said.

"Nothing important."

The three of them had the table, which could seat twenty people, all to themselves. The empty chairs reinforced Quinette's feeling that she was under a kind of quarantine. Her distress, however, hadn't affected her appetite. She finished eating before her companions and vacuumed the scraps with her fingers until the plate looked as if it had been washed.

Ken and his crew were leaving. They walked past her without looking at her, as if indeed she had ceased to exist. Santino, however, lingered behind. "A letter arrived for you just two days ago," he said, "I was going to give it to Knight Air for you, but now . . ." He withdrew it from his case. It bore a Minneapolis address. She recognized her younger sister's handwriting. "Ken was too hard on you," he added. "I enjoyed working with you. You are not like these others." He motioned at the aircrews and relief workers crowding the tables. "You are one of us."

That remark having sewn up the rents Ken had torn into her self-esteem, she feared that Kristen's letter would reopen them. Returning to Mary's tent, she switched on the lightbulb dangling from the ridgepole, sat down, and reluctantly opened the envelope. Inside were three pages, filled on both sides with Kristen's backhanded script. The family brain had been designated to be the family scribe, responding to the letter Quinette had sent to Nicole more than two months ago. The first three pages crackled with scorn—"You said in your—can I call it wedding announcement?—that your news was going to come as 'something of a shock.' That was perceptive. Also a class A understatement. Mom wasn't shocked, she was devastated!"—and with reproach—"You've never shown our mother much consideration, but with this, all you're showing her is contempt"—and with rebukes— "Since Dad died, you've acted like you've got something against her, and me and Nicole too, and you've done everything possible to cause as much worry and pain as possible. Your marriage is your crowning achievement in that department." The last three pages were an outpouring of distilled vitriol: "In case you think we're a bunch of cornbelt racists, I'll just say that our issue isn't your husband's skin color. It's what he is. In your letter, you made him out to be some kind of African George Washington. Sorry. Since you went over there, we've kept up on events in that part of the world, and we know about the unspeakable things those African guerrilla leaders are doing over there. It's beyond us how you could decide to spend the rest of your days with a man who has blood on his hands, how you could turn your backs on us and just throw your life away, like it's an old dress.

"You said that no one can choose whom she falls in love with. That's true. It's also bullshit, and here's the bullshit part—we don't think you're in love with this Michael Goraende. You're in love with some image or idea of yourself. You're the star in your movie, and your husband is the leading man.

"Guess what Ardele is telling her friends? That you've married an army officer and are living overseas on an extended assignment. That pisses me off sometimes, but what else can she say? She can no more comprehend what you've done than if you'd announced that you're going to Mars. Meantime, she's afraid that something awful will happen to you, that she'll never see you again even if you aren't killed or don't come down with some awful disease. I can't say the same is true of Nicole and me. It wouldn't bother us a whole lot if we never see you again, because of what you've done to Mom."

Quinette set the letter down, wondering how much of it had been a faithful representation of the family's collective opinion and how much had been colored by Kristen's own feelings. For sure, nasty little asides like "You're the star in your own movie" were hers alone, and Quinette didn't quite believe that Nicole never wanted to see her again, or that Ardele thought she was in love with an image of herself. That too was pure Kristen. She and her younger sister never had gotten along.

Mary pranced in, sassily swigging a Tusker from the can. "Bad news? You're like this." She squeezed the corners of her mouth and tugged it into a pout.

"Expected news. It's just about unanimous. Now my family agrees with everyone around here, but maybe for different reasons."

"Let me guess. Their little girl married a nigger."

"I'll bet that's what they really think, but they won't admit it."

Mary sat beside her. "You've done something pretty extreme. You can't expect applause."

Quinette was silent for a moment. Ostracized here, rejected by her family, she grasped for her conviction that God had summoned her to the Nuba and Michael's side for His own purposes, that He was leading her to something, step by step, and she clung to that belief tightly, lest it slip away. Without it, she could not carry on in the face of so much criticism.

"I don't expect applause," she said, "and you know, the disapproval isn't the worst thing. The worst thing would be to be ignored. People ignore you only when you're not doing anything worthwhile."

THE DAY AFTER her return to the Nuba, high among the rocks that exhaled the night's coolness into the morning air, Quinette knelt naked before a kujur's wife. The woman sat on a wooden stool, with her instruments at her feet: a flat, square blade resembling a miniature ax-head, a couple of long thorns, several twigs, a jar of groundnut oil, and another of sorghum flour mixed with powdered herbs and roots. She spoke.

"She is asking if you are ready," said Pearl, who sat watching.

Quinette replied that she was. With one of the twigs, the kujur's wife traced the chosen design on her oiled abdomen: a vertical band of marks, ten across, stretching from the bottom of her breasts to her navel, straddled by two curved bands that resembled bowed legs. Leaning forward, supporting her elbows on her parted knees, a thorn in one hand, the blade in another, she lifted skin with the thorn and made a swift cut. Quinette sucked in a breath and flinched. The woman admonished her: she must remain very still. At the next cut, Quinette gritted her teeth and looked toward the sun. Mary said she'd done something way out there, but changing her name wasn't extreme enough; nor was the trial she'd undergone in this very same place. Something else was needed, a visible sign to mark forever the inner change.

The woman's hands moved as swiftly as a skilled weaver's. Quinette forced herself to concentrate on them so she would not think about the pain. In minutes the first two vertical rows were done. The kujur's wife wiped off the blood with a twig and smeared on more oil, then a handful of the flour mixture. A prick with the thorn, a quick slash of the knife. The woman cleaned the blood again, and again smeared the cuts with the powder, until Quinette's stomach looked as white as moonlight.

It went on for half an hour, the hands never pausing. Prick-slash-prick-slash. The marks began to stand out, each the size of an insect bite and stinging like one. After thirty minutes more the curved bands were formed. Another layer of powder was rubbed on and wiped off. It was done. Quinette looked down at a frieze of three-dimensional dots that could never be eradicated. There would be a second tattooing soon, and after she gave birth, a third. She wasn't pregnant yet, but she'd chosen the pattern: a zig-zag line, representing the Nile of the heavens, would streak down her back to her hips, where a circle with four spokes would symbolize Achernar, the star at the river's end.

Man of All Races

A LOUD RUSTLING in the trees woke Fitzhugh well before dawn. He rose from bed slowly, to avoid waking Diana, and felt his way through the *banda*'s black interior, opened the front flap, and stepped out to the veranda to investigate. As the noise could have been made only by a large animal, he wasn't sure if this was a smart thing to do. At first, he saw only the inky, indistinct trees and saltbush masking the near side of the river, a fragment of the river itself, silvered by the quarter moon in the west, and the escarpment rising almost sheer on the far side. A few seconds later he detected movement in the vegetation, then made out the silhouette of an elephant, tearing off leaves and small branches with its trunk. It was probably the safari camp's mascot, a well-mannered bull that treated the guests with benign indifference. He watched the elephant pruning the trees and heard in the distance the long, resonant moan of a lion. From behind him came the sound of Diana undoing the zipper.

"Fitz?"

"Yes."

She came out in her nightgown, the satin clinging to her, and leaned over the back of the chair and clasped him around the chest. "What are you doing out here at four in the morning?"

"Our big friend woke me," he said, pointing. "Did you hear the lion?"

"That's what woke me."

"The lions of Tsavo," he said. "Man-eaters."

"That's right. Women aren't the menu. He'll go for you." She moved to the railing and stood with her hands on it, looking toward the river and the escarpment beyond, its top faintly illuminated by the waning moon. "I'm rather glad we came here. I love Tsavo, the last really wild place left in Kenya. My father hunted here, my grandfather as well. He hunted with Finch-Hatton."

"Ah yes, the mighty sahibs," Fitzhugh remarked. He never could understand the white man's fascination with wildlife, whether he shot it for sport or photographed it. For the African, wild animals were a nuisance or a menace.

Diana turned her head, gazing at him over her bare shoulder. "There's another thing I'm glad of. That we both broke down."

He would not have broken if she hadn't first. She had sent him a letter a little more than a week ago, declaring an end to the "intermission" she'd imposed. She couldn't bear another day without him, she didn't care what happened in the future, she needed him now. He answered immediately, writing that the separation was unbearable for him as well and that he had to see her as soon as possible. The exchange coincided with Douglas's decision to give the Knight Air staff a holiday—a long weekend on the coast, at company expense. He'd arranged a bird-watching safari in Tsavo for himself and invited Fitzhugh to join him to talk over some business matters. Fitzhugh accepted, provided Diana could come along.

"I'm glad, too," he said.

"You sound a little ambivalent."

"But I'm not," he protested, though in fact he was. It seemed to him that the only thing in charge of their relationship was her mood of the moment. If she felt that they should be together, then they would be; if not, then they wouldn't. He criticized himself for not taking command and holding her to her demand for a breathing spell till he could resolve the question of whether he was capable of committing to her, whatever the cost to himself. They were reunited, but they were adrift again, to wherever the currents of love and need might carry them.

"Don't tell me you're glad," Diana demanded. "Show me."

In the moonlight, she had the cool beauty of a statue, her pale hair flipped over a pale shoulder, her cream-colored nightgown almost indistinguishable from her skin. He came up behind her and, circling her waist, kissed her throat.

"We'll just have to have faith that this will sort itself out, since we can't," she said, as if guessing his thoughts.

Her tummy bulged softly under his hands. He adored this mature, preserved body of hers, held between ripeness and decay, toughness and vulnerability. Yet the thought that there was something a little unnatural in this attraction, as if it manifested Oedipal longings, brought a modesty to his embrace. He held her loosely and with a discreet space between himself and her.

"I feel shameless," she said, seized his wrists, and drew him to her, lewdly rubbing her hips against him as she tilted her head back and brushed her lips across the underside of his chin. "Utterly, completely shameless." She pulled his hands below her waist, and he caressed her there, through the satin, arousing himself as much as he did her. "Oh yes, here, now, like this," she whispered, turning to slide down his body, tugging his undershorts to his ankles as she fell in a mimic of a dancer's swoon, drawing him to the veranda's floor with her.

A river breeze slithered through the trees, carrying the smell of the gallery forest, a jungle smell, rank and sweet at the same time. Branches shook as the elephant foraged. They heard the lion again—the drawn-out, belly-deep moan, followed by a series of grunts. Fitzhugh lay under her, to spare her from the rough planks. Straddling him, she lifted her gown up over her waist and gave a low gasp as he penetrated her; and in the quaking instant that he poured himself into her, all things were resolved—but only for that instant.

She flung herself over his chest and kissed him. "I have lost all my self-respect, and I'm perfectly, perfectly happy."

The lion groaned.

"He sounds closer," Fitzhugh said. "Maybe we should go inside."

"Oh, a lion won't come in with a bull elephant in camp," she said. "Do you think he heard us?"

"That depends on how well lions hear."

"I meant next door. Doug."

"He's a sound sleeper," Fitzhugh said. "He's probably dreaming of birds."

"Perhaps we could talk now? On the plane, you said you'd had some thoughts."

He went inside for his cigarettes and sat down in the deck chair, she next to him. "I wonder if you've had the same thought. We could adopt."

"It was the first thing I thought of, but I can't imagine who would want to give a child to someone my age."

"With all the orphans in this country, they can't be particular. And there's . . ." He hesitated, drawing on the cigarette. "This is awkward. There is your—your situation."

"I'm rich," she said.

"I would think they would be delighted to place a child in such comfortable circumstances."

"And how would you feel?"

"I must face facts. You would be the one putting bread on the table."

"I meant, how would you feel about raising a child who isn't yours?"

"I believe I could do it." He put an arm around her and stared toward the river, almost invisible, now the moon had set. "It could be a solution. We could be happy together, you, me, and a brood of adopted children."

He wished he could have sounded more certain, had used *know* instead of *believe, will* instead of the more hypothetical *could.*

"A lovely picture," she said. "It terrifies me."

"That's a strange reaction to a lovely picture."

"I'm terrified of happiness."

He sat up straighter, disturbed by the comment. "Just minutes ago you said you are perfectly happy. Does that mean you are also perfectly terrified?"

"Happiness terrifies me because it's so easily lost."

He knew she was inviting him to declare that her terror was unfounded, that he would make her happy the rest of her life, but his own terror of uttering a vow he might not be able to keep restrained him.

"You'll know when you're sure," she said, again reading his thoughts. "And not a word from you till you are."

After breakfast, with nothing more concluded between them, he and Diana (smashing in a straw hat, tan bush jacket, and leopard-print scarf) set off with Douglas, a camp driver, and two armed park rangers on a quest for the carmine bee-eater. Douglas's aim was to photograph the bird and add it to something called a "life-list."

"What is that?" Fitzhugh asked as they left camp, bumping down a dirt-track road alongside a watercourse.

A life-list, Douglas explained, was the record of every bird a bird-watcher observed in its natural habitat.

"But I thought you had already seen a carmine bee-eater."

"Nope," said Douglas, riding in the front seat, binoculars around his neck, and in his lap a camera with a lens almost as long as an arm. "Where'd you get the idea I did?"

"From you. The first conversation we had with Tara. You told her that you'd been to Tsavo with your mother and that you'd photographed a carmine bee-eater."

"I couldn't have said that," Douglas insisted, turning around to face him with a disarming grin. "I've never been to Tsavo, and neither has my mother. You must be remembering wrong."

"I have a memory like a computer, and I distinctly recall your saying that you'd gotten pictures of this bird. Here in Tsavo, with your mother. I remember that because I thought at the time your family must have money to burn if your mother could come all the way to Africa to look at birds."

"Your computer has a glitch," Douglas replied casually, then boosted himself through the overhead hatch to ride on the roof.

"There is no glitch, my friend," Fitzhugh called up in an unpleasant voice. "That is exactly what you said. Own up to it."

Douglas said nothing.

"Is there some reason you won't own up to it?"

Diana laid a hand on his arm and said, "Darling, why are you making an issue out of nothing?"

Of course it was nothing. He was feeling irritable, frustrated by his inability to give her what she wanted, and in this state of mind, Douglas's lie and flip dismissal of the accuracy of his memory had struck him as an insult. He knew Douglas had a tendency to fib when it suited some larger purpose of his, but Fitzhugh couldn't fathom what purpose there could have been in denying he'd said what he'd said to Tara, as if it were an incriminating statement.

They drove on, passing near a big herd of Cape buffalo that Diana wanted to photograph. Douglas vetoed her request to stop. There would be no stopping until he'd seen his bird.

"Single-minded, isn't he?" Diana said in an undertone.

"Yes," Fitzhugh said. "It's a flaw of the virtue."

His single-mindedness was much on display as they continued down the road. The watercourse was a virtual aviary of herons, ibis, eagles, rollers, shrikes, and storks, but those species were already on Douglas's life-list, and he bypassed them all. When the road turned to skirt a salt-bush forest, he thumped the roof and called out, *"Simama!"*

The driver braked just as Fitzhugh spotted a blaze of scarlet, flitting into the dark green saltbush. Douglas leaped to the ground, flung the rear door open, and with eagerness written all over his face, pulled out his tripod. The driver cautioned that he ought not to be out of the vehicle— a man on foot might be seen as prey or a threat by a lion, buffalo, or elephant.

"That's why we hired these boys," he said, motioning at the rangers. "C'mon, let's go. There's two of them, both males."

The rangers piled out. One, a giant Turkana with a semiautomatic rifle, took the lead, Douglas behind him. Fitzhugh and Diana followed, with the second ranger bringing up the rear. The saltbush, growing in dense thickets twenty feet high, was mazed with trails trodden by elephant, whose spoor was everywhere—piles of dung, circular prints as big around as wastebaskets. Glancing over his shoulder, Fitzhugh could no longer see the Land Rover; nor could he tell which way to get back to it. A hornbill lofted from a branch, making a mournful cry. Otherwise there wasn't a sound. The Turkana advanced cautiously, looking right to left. The ranger's switched-on watchfulness did not reassure Fitzhugh; a whole pride of lions could be hiding in the thick undergrowth, and no one would know it till they sprang. Douglas raised his binoculars.

"There one is," he whispered, and passed the binoculars to Fitzhugh while pointing at a shrub ahead. The bird was perched atop it, its body feathered flame red, its head a luminescent blue. It flew off, bobbing against the cloudless sky.

"Damn it!" Douglas shouldered tripod and camera and charged forward, the Turkana running after him, calling to him to be careful. Fitzhugh, Diana, and the other ranger caught up with them at the edge of a broad clearing, across which both bee-eaters clung to a low tree in perfect profile. Douglas spread the tripod's legs and, signaling for everyone to remain still, crouched and adjusted the focus. The shutter made several rapid clicks that sounded as loud as pencils falling to a tile floor.

"Outstanding, got 'em both," he said softly. "I'm going to try for a few more, closer up."

Lifting his rig, he stalked into the clearing, halted, and took another series of shots. As he was moving to one side for a different angle, a shrill scream sent the two birds into sudden flight. The bushes across the clearing trembled and produced two elephants, a cow and a calf, their hides reddened by Tsavo dust to make the pair resemble pieces of rusty sculpture. The cow stood facing the intruders and scuffed the ground with a forefoot, her ears flared, her great head swaying to and fro—body language that required no translation. The Turkana told Douglas to back away slowly, but he could not resist the chance to take a picture of the angry elephant. He was oblivious to the danger, the kind of man, Fitzhugh thought, who believed that no harm could befall him because none ever had. His refusal to give ground provoked the cow beyond tolerance. She trumpeted and charged at a stiff-legged run. Abandoning his tripod and camera, Douglas fled, the beast rapidly closing on him as he sprinted straight toward Fitzhugh and Diana, drawing them into the elephant's path. She came on, ears pinned back, head lowered, tusks gleaming in the sunlight—three tons of living battering ram, a four-legged bulldozer.

Fitzhugh swooped Diana into his arms and dove into a clump of salt-bush, falling face-down atop her, prepared to shield her from the elephant's tusks with his body if it came to that. He heard what sounded like three door knocks in quick succession. Rifle shots. Cautiously, he got to his feet and saw the Turkana, rifle crooked in his arm, and the elephant trotting away, the calf behind her. He had fired over her head, stopping her charge and scaring her off. He wheeled and announced that it was safe to come out of hiding.

Fitzhugh turned and gave Diana his hand. She pulled herself up. Everything had happened too quickly for them to be conscious of fear, though Fitzhugh assumed he'd felt it—his heart was beating at twice its normal rate.

"That was awfully brave of you," she said, picking up her hat and scarf. "But it wouldn't have done the least bit of good."

He gave her a questioning look.

"An elephant doesn't kill with its tusks. It leans its forehead on you and squashes you like you would squash a bug under your thumb." She spoke with scientific detachment. "So you see, she would have crushed us both to death."

He reflected on this information and said he would have done the same thing regardless.

"I know," she said, squeezing his arm. "And I love you for it."

Douglas had gone into the clearing to retrieve his gear. The elephant had knocked the tripod over, splintering it into several pieces. He tossed them aside and picked up his camera, still attached to the mount, from which a foot of a tripod leg protruded like fractured bone. They watched him raise the camera to his eye, turning to point it at them.

"It's good to go, not a dent!" he shouted triumphantly.

"You might want to thank him," said Diana, jerking her thumb sideways at the Turkana.

"Hey, yeah." He took the ranger's photo. "*Asante sana, rafiki!* I sure would've hated to lose those pictures!"

There is something wrong with him, Fitzhugh thought as he regarded Douglas, standing out there alone and exposed to the unforgiving African light. *Something is missing in him, I don't know what.*

After lunch, during which Douglas had nattered on about his narrow escape, as if no one else had been in danger, he reminded Fitzhugh that this was a working holiday and asked him to take an hour to discuss business. They met in his banda where, shirtless and barefoot in the afternoon heat, he lounged in a camp chair, a file folder in his lap. He led off by stating that his reservations about Knight Air's new marketing director had proved unfounded. He removed copies of the past month's invoices from the folder. The names of several agencies belonging to the UN consortium had been highlighted—World Vision, CARE, the Catholic Relief Agency, among others.

"Timmerman wooed every one of them from Pathways to us, and the best part is, he did it without paying a dime in commissions."

"Kickbacks, you mean," Fitzhugh said.

"Hey, whatever. Timmerman just used his friendship with the agency logisticians. The man is a rainmaker." Douglas sat back with an indolent stretch of his long legs, their dark blond hair sparkling in the light. "We're doing great, better than I expected, but the flying nun is starting to make noise."

"Noise? What sort of noise?" asked Fitzhugh, preoccupied by his perception that Douglas possessed some fatal deficiency.

"She's told some people that she thinks we're engaging in unfair business practices, hiring Timmerman away from the UN and then using his connections to take clients from her. *Corrupt* is the word I've heard she's been using. Not surprised. Tara isn't used to real competition, and now that she's getting a taste of it, she doesn't know how to handle it."

Fitzhugh opined that this wasn't a fair characterization.

"Don't let yourself be taken in by that woman. The word I've got is that she intends to do more than call us names."

"Intends what?"

"There's the problem. I don't know. All I've heard is that she's said, in so many words, that since we've made things tough for her, she's going to make them tough for us. Nothing more solid than that. Could be the usual Loki gossip."

"I imagine it is."

"Well, I—we—we can't count on that. We're vulnerable. Got to ask you something. Yellowbird—you never mentioned any of that to Diana, right? She and Tara being friends and all."

"Not even to her," Fitzhugh replied, stiffening. "I've kept my word."

Withdrawing his outstretched legs, Douglas leaned forward and rested his palms on Fitzhugh's knees, his direct and intimate gaze on Fitzhugh's face. "There's another thing I've got to ask, and it isn't easy." He winced to show how deeply the question distressed him. "Do you think Diana, considering her feelings for you . . . if you asked her to, would she be willing to find out if Tara is planning to cause us problems and how she means to go about it?"

Fitzhugh had no reply to this stunning request.

"I can understand why you'd be reluctant, " Douglas said, "but fore-warned is forearmed, right?"

"If you really understood my reluctance, you never would have made such a proposal," Fitzhugh said. "You are asking me to ask the woman I love to betray her friend and become a corporate spy for you."

"My man"—lips arched into their beguiling smile—"it's not just *me*. It's us, the whole company, everything we've built together."

"I am not going to do it." He was both surprised and pleased by his firmness. He was Douglas's man all right, and in that subservience lay the power to refuse him for the first time.

The American shrugged, a long, slow shrug signaling disappointment and resignation. Having the upper hand—an unusual state of affairs for Fitzhugh in his relations with Douglas—prompted him to give in a little.

"There must be a way to find out what she's up to, if she's up to any-thing," he said. "Leave it to me, in my own way."

He left the banda with the vague feeling that he ought not to have made that offer, but he was curious himself about Tara's intentions, assuming she had them; curious and apprehensive, for the company's clandestine operations were not its only vulnerable point. Nearly half its aircrews were flying without proper documentation from the Department of Civil Aviation; Knight Air had expanded so fast, and its flight schedules were so crowded, that no one had bothered with the bureaucratic niceties. Also, some of its planes were not up to snuff, taking to the air with timed-out engines and expired airworthiness certificates. Tara had to be aware of these deficiencies—they were common knowledge in Loki. Were she to bring them to DCA's attention, an inspection would result in grounded planes and grounded pilots. To get them flying again would require some hefty bribes at the least. He made a mental note to begin setting things to rights as soon as he got back to work.

Engrossed in these thoughts, he entered his and Diana's banda and found her sleeping soundly, her deep, measured breaths like the sigh of a calm sea on a shore. He sat on the opposite bed and looked at her, screened by the white mosquito net. Soon the sound of her breathing in, breathing out, drew the agitation from his brain and into a feeling of utter peace. In that tranquil state, he recalled what he'd done, shielding her from the elephant charge, and he knew with mathematical certainty that there was no one else for whom he would have done the same. Only min-utes ago he had protected her in another way, and there was no one else for whom he would have done that either. He went to her bedside, knelt on both knees, and lifting the net over his head, kissed her cheek, her throat, ears, and lips.

She stirred and said in a voice thick with sleep, "What are you doing?"

"Kissing you. You are Diana, the huntress, and you've snared me."

Laughing, she cradled his head in her hands. "So business is over, and now it's pleasure?"

"No, not that. You said I would know when I was sure and not a word from me till then. So now I am speaking the words."

She released him and propped herself on her elbows, an attentive look on her face. "What has made you so sure all of a sudden? Just this morning you—"

"Never mind what I thought this morning, or an hour ago. I know it now. You are the most precious thing in the world to me. I could never be happy without you, and I want nothing more than to make you happy and not to be terrified of happiness."

His fervor appeared to frighten her nonetheless, her blue irises darting side to side.

"Really, Diana, you will have no reason to be terrified. Look at me, on my knees. Isn't that traditional? Will you marry me?"

She stared at him silently.

"You must answer!"

She clasped the back of his neck and tugged. "Get off your knees and into this bed and I will."

He'd never been made love to as he was that afternoon. Parting with her in Nairobi two days later, he felt that the whole wide earth could be between them and they would still be together. They set a date three months from now but did not tell Douglas—Diana wanted it kept secret till she'd made arrangements, picked out a suitable dress, and had formal announcements printed up. She planned on a small, discreet wedding in her Karen garden, with a few friends, Fitzhugh's family, and her only living relatives, a younger sister and a brother-in-law who lived in the UK.

After his return to Loki, everyone remarked on his demeanor, which went beyond his normal good humor, and asked what accounted for it. He was eager to tell them, to share his happiness but also to test their reactions, for one concern clouded his joy. There were moments when, picturing himself standing beside her in her garden, he would imagine people whispering that he had insinuated himself into her heart for reasons other than love.

In the meantime, he was occupied with the two tasks he'd set for himself: improving aircraft maintenance so the planes could pass any inspection, and bringing pilot documentation up to date. He told VanRensberg, the chief mechanic, to work overtime to take care of the former. With the latter, Wesley's loadmaster, Nimrod, proved invaluable. The little Kikuyu knew everyone at DCA, including the director herself, with whom he arranged a meeting at her office at Jomo Kenyatta. She was a hefty, formidable woman aware that she was in the man's world of Kenyan officialdom and determined to prove she belonged there. She stated that she was pleased to see the two representatives from Knight Air; she had recently received reports of certain irregularities in its operations. Fitzhugh didn't need to ask the source of that information and credited himself for his percipience in guessing the action Tara would take.

"We're aware of our problems," he said. "That's why we're here. To correct them."

The director offered him and Nimrod a sympathetic expression. What a pity they had not come sooner! Only this morning she had dispatched two inspectors to inform the airline that its pilots who lacked current Kenyan certification would be prohibited from flying until properly documented. "You must have passed each other in midair," she said with a laugh that shook her considerable bosom. In an earlier time she would have been a great African mama, Fitzhugh thought, a village dispenser of cures, a conjure-woman tossing bones for a fee.

"We can't afford to have several aircrews grounded," he said. "Isn't there some way you can stop this process?"

She shook her head, declaring that the wheels were in motion. Withdrawing from his briefcase copies of the licenses of the pilots in question, along with other records, Fitzhugh expressed the hope that presenting these documents now, rather than waiting for her department to request them, would expedite the process. Most certainly it will save time, she said; nevertheless, it could take a month. She sat back, hands folded in her lap, her posture and her silence telling them that the next move was theirs. Nimrod made it, producing a cookie box from the briefcase.

"I remembered how much you like these," he said. "They are made in America."

"Oh yes, peanut butter." The director's face brightened. "I love them."

Nimrod placed the box on her desk.

She took the lagniappe, opened the top, and bowing her head, sniffed the contents. "They smell delicious. And how many cookies in this box? It doesn't say."

"There are enough for you and to share with your friends."

"Excellent." The woman raised her ponderous frame from the chair and extended her hand. "These matters will be cleared up very quickly. I can promise your pilots will have Kenya licenses within the week. It's only a matter of finishing paperwork."

They were back in Loki by nightfall. Fitzhugh reported to Douglas that the expedition had been successful. He was in a foul mood. The inspectors, unaware of the transaction that had taken place in Nairobi, had grounded six pilots and two aircraft that VanRensberg had not been able to attend to.

"I've got about fifty grand in lost revenue," he said, waving a sheaf of contracts.

"We can absorb it," Fitzhugh assured him. "It will all be back to normal in a week."

"We'll see. The director could screw us yet. Tara must have given her some cookies, too, so now we wait to find out which brand she likes best."

"Tara doesn't do business that way. She probably did nothing more than call the director's attention to our problems and ask her to look into them, as a favor. But when it comes to doing a favor for nothing and another for something, you know which way she'll go."

"Jesus Christ!" Douglas tossed the papers aside. "Do you still think Tara is Mother Teresa with a pilot's license? Of course she paid the director off to find as much wrong with us as she could. This means war."

"*War?*"

"That bitch is out to ruin us. If we don't act first, we'll be toast."

Fitzhugh, who'd been standing the whole time, sat at his desk and remarked that Douglas was creating a conflict where none existed, imputing to Tara motives he was sure she did not possess. She wasn't out to ruin Knight Air . . . He stopped pursuing this argument, and what stopped him was a shred of wisdom he'd picked up from Malachy long ago, in one of their bull sessions: If someone deeply wishes for something to be so, his imagination will mold reality to conform to what is wished for. Douglas wanted a war with Tara, and he meant to have it. All he'd needed was a pretext, and now she had unwittingly given him one.

"I am going to ask you to do nothing," Fitzhugh said. "You'll only make a bad situation worse. Do nothing for one week. If the director isn't as good as her word, then fight your war, but if she comes through for us, continue to do nothing. Agreed?"

Douglas made some vague gesture.

"What does that mean?"

"Okay," he said.

The director responded favorably to her gift. Just six days later Knight

Air's two grounded planes were given clean bills of health, and its pilots were issued their documents. In the meantime, Douglas had flown to Nairobi for a meeting with Hassan Adid. He did not disclose, to Fitzhugh or to anyone, the purpose of this get-together.

A few days after it took place, Tara stormed into the office, as angry as Fitzhugh had ever seen her, and demanded to see Douglas immediately. Fitzhugh told her that he'd taken a flight to Bahr el Ghazal and wasn't expected back till the afternoon. She hesitated, her eyes throwing off sparks, rocketing around the room until they settled back on him. Stepping forward, she pulled a piece of paper from her pocket and slammed it on the desk.

"Look at that," she said, her voice quavering. "Look at it and tell me what it is."

Fitzhugh glanced at it. Nonplussed, he said nothing.

"Well, what is it?"

"Just what it says it is," he answered with a nervous laugh. "It's tomorrow's schedule of UN-authorized flights. The one that's faxed to Khartoum every morning."

"No, it isn't. It is corruption! Complete corruption!"

"I really don't understand what you're getting at."

"I think you do. Read it more carefully. Oh, I'll read it for you." She snatched the paper and read aloud, " 'Operator—Knight Air, UN call sign Charley Five, destination Mapel, agency CARE. Operator—Knight Air, UN call sign Charley Six, destination Gogrial, agency Doctors Without Borders. Operator—Knight Air, UN call sign Charley Two Zero, destination Malualkon, agency Adventist Development.' It goes on, but nowhere do you see a Pathways flight on this schedule, and that's because I was notified yesterday morning that my UN call sign has been revoked."

Now the cause of her fury had become clearer. Without a call sign, her air service could not deliver UN cargoes, and those accounted for most of her business. She was facing disaster.

"And how did all this come about?" she went on, lips trembling. "Your man Timmerman, your so-called marketing manager, when all he is, is a bloody fixer, that's how. He pulled strings at the UN and had it done. That's not a guess. I *know* he did. And I'm quite sure he didn't do it on his own initiative. It wasn't enough that you people used him to steal clients from me. You had to make it impossible for me to fly for any of them. That isn't marketing, that's crooked monopoly. And you have the gall to tell me you don't understand what I'm getting at?"

"All I can say is that this is the first I've heard about this."

"Rubbish!" she shrieked. "I shall be bankrupt within a month, and that is what you people want, isn't it?" Without waiting for an answer, she placed her knuckles on the desk and leaned toward him, literally in his face. "You people have gone too fucking far, but I am not without resources, and we will see who goes farther."

She turned and walked out, leaving him to wonder if her threat was an idle one, made in anger, or if it was a vow. If the latter, did she have a plan of action, and what was it? So Douglas had lied to him with one word— "*Okay.*" He and Adid had decided they had an opportunity that could not be passed up. Whose idea was it to employ Timmerman to have Tara's call sign revoked? It had Adid's stamp. Fitzhugh could almost hear him, assuring Douglas that with this single stroke they would eliminate the competition and grab one hundred percent of "market share." Neither man would have seen it as wrong, for success in business, or at any rate in the cutthroat business of aid aviation, seemed to require a fundamental amorality. And yet Douglas had shown himself to be a moral man, a man of compassion who had risked a great deal, even his life, to bring succor to the starving, the sick, the defenseless. The contradiction between the idealist and the relentless entrepreneur was too great for Fitzhugh to resolve. He wondered how Douglas himself resolved it. His aphorism "We do what we have to do so we can do what we came here to do" wasn't adequate as a resolution, for what had been done to Tara hadn't needed to be done.

Faith in an idea, a theory, or a god is not easily surrendered when confronted by facts that embarrass it; and the greater one's investment in it, the more difficult the surrender. The same is true of faith in a man. Having invested three years of his life in Douglas Braithwaite and Knight Air, Fitzhugh was unable to accept the notion that the American was unworthy of his loyalty or that his belief in him had been misplaced, despite evidence that he was self-centered, a liar, and ruthless. He persuaded himself that in this instance his friend had been manipulated by Adid. The cunning Somali had jerked the wires of Douglas's passions and ambitions to bring out the worst in him. What was needed now was a countervailing influence to bring him around to the better side of his nature. Fitzhugh would be that influence and show him that the blow to Tara was, if not wrong, then misguided and likely to reap unforeseen and unpleasant consequences.

After Douglas returned from Bahr el Ghazal, Fitzhugh said he had to speak to him and invited him to take a walk, to ensure privacy. They took a road where the only ears were those of passing Turkana. Douglas, head bowed meditatively, hands in his back pockets, listened without any visible reaction to a summary of Tara's visit.

"Well, she's only being human," he commented with a disengaged air.

"Because she's so very angry? Wouldn't you be if you were in her shoes?"

"I meant that when things go wrong, seriously wrong, it's only human to blame circumstances or bad luck or someone else instead of yourself."

"You astonish me," Fitzhugh said. "You're saying that because she called DCA on us, this is her fault? That she should have expected retaliation?"

Douglas replied that he wasn't saying that at all. There had been no retaliation. The UN had done what it did for its own reasons. Tara had added two and two and come up with five, inventing an intrigue to explain her misfortune.

Fitzhugh had anticipated a denial like that; it dismayed him nonetheless. A UN Land Rover cruised by, throwing up a rooster-tail of fine dust.

"Douglas, please. Tara is a deliberate woman, she's not the kind to jump to conclusions or make wild allegations. She said she wasn't guessing, that she *knew*."

"And you believe her?"

"I have a hard time thinking that it was coincidence."

"Look, we've got bigger, faster planes that deliver more quicker and for less. My guess is that UN big shots figured there was no point any longer in her having a call sign. We're the future, she's the past. Nobody at Knight Air, including me, had anything to do with what's happened to her, okay? It's important to me that you believe me. We've come a long way together, from next to nothing to eight million last year, and we're looking at ten for this year. Couldn't have done it without you, my man."

Fitzhugh had to actively resist the tingle this encomium sent through him: the narcotic of Douglas's approbation. "For the same reason, I would like to believe you."

"But, right? You would like to believe me, but," Douglas said, now with an edge to his words. "Okay, here's a but for you. It's important to *you* to believe me, because I can't have my operations manager thinking I'm some kind of crook. And I don't think you'd be happy working for a guy like that."

The remark wasn't quite a warning, more a clarification of what was at stake for Fitzhugh. He didn't think Douglas would have the nerve to sack him—he knew too much—but if he believed Tara, then he would be morally bound to quit, which he couldn't afford, not with his wedding just ten weeks away. Believe Tara or believe Douglas—he resolved the dilemma by finding a sliver of gray in this black and white choice.

"What's really important isn't that I believe you, for your sake or mine," he said. "The important thing is that Tara believes that you had nothing to do with it."

"All right, counselor, how do I do that? Send her flowers?"

"You could ask Timmerman to do the opposite of what she says he's done. Have him talk to his UN cronies and see what he can do about reinstating her call sign. Even if it didn't work, the gesture alone would—"

Douglas stopped short and swatted the air. "The competition gets into a jam, and I'm supposed to help them out of it? To prove that I'm innocent? I have got to hear why."

"Two reasons. Tara made a very clear threat. I have no idea what she has in mind, but if she has an inkling about—"

"Thought we agreed that she couldn't know a damned thing about that," Douglas interrupted.

"An inkling, I said. Things have a way of getting around. She wouldn't need to make an airtight case, just dig up enough to raise suspicions in the wrong places. Is it worth the risk? You don't have to do what I suggested, only do something to convince her."

"So what's the second reason?"

Fitzhugh paused, gazing toward the golden rim of the Mogilla range. "Diana and I are going to be married."

Douglas regarded him with a neutral expression.

"She is seeing to the arrangements. Of course she'll invite Tara, and I will invite you. I would like the wedding to take place in a—in a what? A tranquil atmosphere, not with some war between Tara and you."

"You've thought this through?" Douglas asked, squinting at him.

"Thought it to death," Fitzhugh answered, happy to be off the previous topic, however briefly. "We decided on the trip to Tsavo. You're the first to know."

Douglas pumped his hand and slapped him on the shoulder. "Then I'll be the first to congratulate you. All right, I don't want to spoil your wedding. I'll talk to Timmerman, but I can't make any promises beyond that."

How sincere was he? Fitzhugh couldn't judge.

If Timmerman did speak to his former UN colleagues, his effort wasn't successful. Thirty-four days later Pathways Limited went under, and not entirely, Fitzhugh was forced to admit, because Tara had lost her UN contracts. Her skills as a pilot weren't matched by her skills as a businesswoman. The company, which to all outward appearances was built on rock, turned out to rest on the unstable sands of borrowed money. Its marginal profits, after paying off staff salaries, leases, and monthly charges on bank loans, had gone into building and maintaining the plush Pathways camp, which didn't earn enough to sustain itself. With more prudent management and substantial financial reserves, she could have weathered the blow. She had to cancel her leases and return the planes to their owners. Those registered to Pathways were sold. Over the next month company pilots, with Jepps aviation maps tucked under their arms, took off to deliver the aircraft to their buyers in Europe, Russia, and elsewhere in Africa. Douglas, who at times was tone deaf in personal relations, offered to buy one of her Cessnas for full market value. He considered this a generous, if not a chivalrous, gesture and was shocked when she told him he was lucky she didn't slap his face and that she wouldn't sell him the plane for twice its worth.

The Pathways terminal, that pocket of order and cleanliness amid Loki's dirt and disarray, was closed down. A Kenyan businessman bought the compound for a song but allowed Tara to remain in her bungalow for a modest rent. She was left with one employee, her assistant, Pamela Smyth, and one Cessna Caravan that she owned outright and flew on short hops for the independent agencies. In one month and four days, after a decade of hard effort and risk, she had been thrown back to where she'd begun—one woman and one small airplane.

She had been ruined but not defeated and bore up under her ordeal with stoical grace. She maintained her erect, purposeful carriage; she took care of her appearance, protecting the asset of her beauty from the demands of its creditor; and she vowed to start over, though at fifty-eight it was doubtful she could.

By this time her version of events had become accepted by almost everyone in Loki—she was the victim of a dirty trick. Douglas continued to assert, to anyone who would listen, that he hadn't engineered her downfall. Its swiftness proved that Pathways had been badly run and would have gone under eventually without a push from him. Fitzhugh urged him to keep his mouth shut. His commentaries on Tara's mismanagement came off as gloating, while his repeated protests of innocence suggested guilt. For his part, suffering from a bad conscience, Fitzhugh could not face Tara. He dreaded the chance that he would round a corner one day and there she would be before him, unavoidable, her very presence a reproach.

But soon another matter commanded his and Douglas's attention. The SPLA had failed to pay Yellowbird for two arms deliveries to the Nuba mountains. SPLA representatives in Nairobi and Kampala, from where the weapons shipments originated, promised to come up with the money, but after a full week passed without its appearance, Wesley declared that he was not going to fly another mission until he saw it. He and Mary were on strike. Douglas, whose zeal for the Nuban crusade had not diminished, appealed to him to call off his work stoppage. Michael Goraende was about to launch his dry-season offensive and needed every rifle and bullet he could get. A great deal was at stake, and that was more important than Wesley's share of the unpaid charter fees, a mere eighteen thousand dollars. Wesley was unmoved. He wasn't about to risk his and Mary's necks for nothing. The disagreement degenerated into an argument, the argument into a scene, with Fitzhugh acting, unsuccessfully, as referee. He might as well have tried to mediate a fight between a long-married couple who hated each other. There in the cramped hotbox of the office, the two men said things best left unsaid. They never had been compatible, but the harshness of their words hinted at a deeper difference: a fundamental antagonism that they had repressed for the sake of the company and that now erupted.

It almost came to a fistfight when Douglas stated that the older man had lost his nerve and was using the nonpayment as a convenient excuse to put himself out of harm's way. Thrusting out his chest, Wesley bulled him into a corner of the room. "I was taking ground fire when you were still shittin' your britches," he said, and with a sneer, tugged at the bill of Douglas's cap. "You're one to talk about nerve. I got the lowdown on your air force record a while back. Ran into a guy named Mendoza. Ring a bell?"

Douglas was silent.

"Yeah, it does. Ding dong. You're worse than a fool and a hypocrite, you're a goddamned fraud." He gave Douglas's cheek a contemptuous pat and left.

"What was he talking about, your air force record?" Fitzhugh asked.

Douglas stood rooted in the corner, looking at the door as if he could still see Wesley's back passing through it. "No idea," he replied.

The humiliated expression on his face said otherwise, but Fitzhugh did not press the issue.

Douglas sat down. "If I could fire that son of a bitch, I would."

"What is going on with you?" Fitzhugh slapped his palm on his desk. "Are you trying to see how many enemies you can make around here?"

"Nope. But it looks like I'm going to have to take the next load in."

"You will do no such thing. It would take one mishap, one small mishap, to have a plane registered to Knight Air discovered with weapons aboard. What we need to do is to get the SPLA to pay up and Wesley flying again."

"Any ideas?"

He suggested they enlist Barrett's aid. Barrett had high-level contacts in the rebels' political arm in Nairobi. Possibly a word from him would convince them to convince their military brethren to pay the debt.

Combative as ever, Barrett was delighted to assist in any way he could. When, however, his discussions with his contacts produced nothing more substantial than more promises, he decided to play a direct role, offering to pay the sum in arrears out of his agency's funds. That suited Wesley. As long as it wasn't counterfeit, he didn't care where the money came from. Thirty-six thousand dollars was then transferred from International People's Aid to Knight Air's account. Wesley withdrew his half and the next morning took off for the Uganda border to pick up a shipment of anti-aircraft and mortar ammunition.

Now Barrett had to account for the expenditure. He arrived in Loki one afternoon to work alongside Fitzhugh to make sure that his books and Knight Air's agreed, in the event his were audited by his agency's board in Canada. They invented humanitarian aid flights, fabricating dates, destinations, manifests, cargo weights, and fees until the full amount was covered, on paper. Fitzhugh, now party to embezzlement, had the uneasy feeling—it was almost premonitory—that with each strand he wove into the ever-expanding web of deception, he was trapping himself.

"Does this trouble you at all?" he asked Barrett, who replied that it did, a "wee bit," and then rationalized: His role was to deliver aid to Sudan, and guns were merely another form of aid.

When they completed their creative work, they went to the Hotel California bar for a restorative. There Barrett revealed that the secret of Fitzhugh's and Diana's wedding was out—a week ago she'd asked him to perform the service.

"First Quinette and Michael, now you and Diana. I'm specializin' in odd pairings."

"Because you are oddly paired yourself."

"I am, sure enough. Heard about Tara's troubles, by the way. Bloody shame."

A bloody shame, Fitzhugh agreed. The former priest of Rome stirred his whiskey and soda and looked off at two aid workers who, in sandals and ragged T-shirts, resembled itinerant hippies. "Diana's quite upset about it. Spoke to her only yesterday. She invited Tara to the nuptials and she got a regrets, with a full explanation. It might be a good idea if you talked to her. Call that a bit of advice from your minister."

"Advice?" asked Fitzhugh, with a buzz of apprehension.

Barrett's glance moved back to him. "I'm fond of you both. Take a day or two off, have a talk with her."

She was taking hurdles in the ring when he arrived, a sight that always moved him. Her poise, crouched over the horse's neck, booted legs bent, the beauty of mount and rider flowing over a bar as one, and the danger of a balk or fall combined to arrest his breath in fear and admiration. Focused on what she was doing, she didn't notice him, standing outside the rail, until she cantered toward the barrier nearest him, a wall of straw bales. She reined up sharply, the horse tossing its head as if confused by the sudden halt. She patted its neck and walked it to the rail, looked down at Fitzhugh with a cool, remote expression, and in a voice that matched, said she wasn't expecting him.

"I thought to surprise you. I saw John up in Loki. He suggested we ought to talk about . . . well, I'm not sure what."

"And you needed him to tell you that? What would you have done if you hadn't seen him?"

His apprehensions were confirmed—this wasn't going to be a pleasant visit. "He told me you were upset."

" I have to cool her down. I'll see you in the garden in ten. Ask Faraj to make you some tea."

She strode into the garden like a Prussian, boots clacking on the field-stone walk, and without a touch or word, sat across the round table from him, creating a physical symbol for her emotional distance. She placed an envelope on the table, opened it, and removed a wedding announcement and a letter, filled out on both sides.

"Tara has sent her regrets."

"John mentioned that."

"She saw fit to tell me why." She lifted the letter with two fingers, then dropped it.

"Yes, he mentioned that, too."

"She didn't have to go into so much detail. She was venting. We've been friends ten years, so she's entitled. Tara seems to think you were a part of what was done to her. At the very least, she says, you knew about it beforehand and did nothing to stop it. I need to know if she's right. I need to hear about it from you."

Fitzhugh took a sip of tea. It was cold. He lit a cigarette. "She came into the office in quite a state, and that was the first I'd heard of it."

"I hope and pray, darling, that you are not lying to me."

"No need to hope or pray because I'm not."

She gave him an appraising look. "What was done to her was absolutely rotten. And it's not only her. It's everyone who worked for her. They're all out of a job. Did you people ever give a thought to them?"

"Don't include me in that 'you people,' " he said, piping to his adolescent squeal, embarrassing himself. He wanted to sound manly and offended that she would think he'd been involved.

"And what about your boss?"

"I'm not sure."

"Well, my friend is. And Tara wouldn't say a thing like that if she weren't."

"She seemed to have no problem accusing me when she wasn't sure. I wish you'd stop talking to me like I'm a bad pupil and you're a headmistress."

"I'm sorry, but I feel I have to. You have your suspicions about him?"

He gave her an abridgment of his conversation with Douglas. When he was finished, she stared at him, her head wreathed by the hibiscus blossoms behind her. Her beauty was poignant because he knew he was losing her, if he hadn't lost her already.

"What you're telling me," she said, "is that you know he did exactly what Tara says he did, but that you've chosen to believe otherwise. It's easier that way, I suppose."

"Pardon me?"

"I don't understand why you haven't quit him. We have all misjudged him, but I don't see how you can go on associating yourself with an unscrupulous bastard who thinks nothing of ruining my friend and disrupting, oh, perhaps a hundred other lives at the same time."

"Why, to eat, Diana, that's why. I associate myself with him to eat."

"I am quite sure you could find other work," she said, as if Kenya were an Eden of job opportunities. "And if you couldn't, I could help you. I know plenty of people. In the meantime—"

"In the meantime, you have plenty of money."

She said nothing, and he took her silence as assent.

"There are enough people who think I'm a fortune hunter. I can just hear what they'd say if I were out of work."

"You're imagining things. But whatever they think or don't think, *I* think that in this instance you ought to swallow your pride and—"

"My pride?" he interrupted, half rising from his seat. "You think that's all it is, my pride?" He looked around, taking in the rambling house, large enough for several African families, and the guest house, large enough for two or three more, and the garden and the stable and the grounds with acreage sufficient for a *shamba* yet supporting only grass and fruitless trees and inedible flowers, and his old resentment of wealth and privilege boiled up with a quickness and violence that told him it must have been simmering closer to the surface than he'd realized. "You have no idea what it's like to be out of work, do you? No idea what it's like to wonder how you shall manage for the next week, much less the rest of your life. How could you? You've been deprived of that experience, but you think I should quit based on a suspicion and live off you like a parasite?"

"I meant nothing of the kind."

"I'm not surprised," he went on, carried helplessly forward on the tide of his anger and hatred, yes, hatred of everything the house and the grounds and the useless trees and flowers represented. "This"—his arm swept out—"was built by parasites. And this whole town is a nest of parasites. Parasites on the skin of this country."

She looked at him with wounded astonishment, mouthing the word *parasite.* Only then did he shake off the spell of rage and come back to himself. His mind clearing, he saw that his outburst had been fatal. He might as well have struck her. "Not you!" he said. "I didn't mean you! I love you, and I am so sorry—"

"Please"—she raised a palm—"no need for apologies. Thanks for making your feelings ever so much clearer. I am a parasite among parasites. And thanks for making things ever so much easier for me, darling." She uttered the term of endearment to make it sound like anything but, then said with a terrible resolve, "I can't marry you."

"You don't know what you're saying!" he pleaded. "Let's calm ourselves and talk this through."

"I am perfectly calm and know precisely what I'm saying. I can't marry a man who thinks what you do of me. And I can't marry a man who knows the right thing to do and doesn't do it, because—oh, Christ . . . you seemed so strong that day in Tsavo, but I misjudged you."

"You couldn't be more wrong. I want to keep my job. It is as simple and basic as that."

"No, it isn't. Your American is who you're in love with, or with something he stands for or pretends he stands for even though he stands only for himself. But be warned. I've seen Douglas's sort before. He's fucked Tara, and one day he'll get around to fucking you."

Fitzhugh stood, feeling sorrow, regret, and bitterness all at once. For the moment, bitterness had the greater share. "I'll tell you what I think," he said. "You had your mind made up before I came. A woman doesn't call off a marriage because she doesn't like who her man works for. It's your terror of happiness. It got the better of you."

"What nonsense, but if that idea helps you feel better, stick to it." She put on her riding gloves and helmet. "Show yourself out. You know the way."

HE CHECKED INTO a hotel that night and got spectacularly drunk. The next morning, as hung over as he'd ever been, he called her, not knowing what to say. The housekeeper asked him to wait. A minute later she told him the memsahib was out. He bashed the receiver on the nightstand and then wept. When his crying jag was over, he went to the lobby and called the office's sat phone, telling Rachel that he had been held up in Nairobi and would not be returning for a couple of days. That night he got drunk again and picked up a skinny black girl in a disco, with whom he pretended that he was getting even with Diana. He woke up disgusted with himself and sent the girl on her way. Downstairs, he waited till the hotel bar was open and drank some more to numb his self-loathing and all other emotional aches. When he was half in the bag—a phrase he'd picked up from his Yankee associates—he made another call, informing the office that he was taking two weeks off. He didn't wait for a reply, checked out, and flew to Mombasa, seeking the solace of home and the sea.

His mother and father gave him none. Now in their early sixties, they wanted grandchildren and rejoiced at the breakup of his engagement, assuring him that one day he would rejoice as well. What had he been thinking, to become so involved with a woman that age?

The sea would have to do double duty in the solace department, and he spent a lot of time swimming in it or just looking at it, the same sea whose monsoons, two centuries ago, had brought a Malay-Chinese trader to the shores of Africa, where he stayed and married a black woman and thus began the mixing of bloods that produced the man of all races.

Toward the end of his holiday—Fitzhugh thought of it as a convalescence—he picked up a newspaper in the hotel his father managed. A Reuters dispatch caught his attention: EIGHT FOREIGN OIL WORKERS DIE IN SUDAN REBEL ATTACK. He sat down in he lobby and read it. Killed, the story said, when a plane belonging to Amulet Energy was shot down by a missile during an SPLA assault on an oil facility near the Nuba mountains. . . . Five Canadians, including the pilot and copilot, and three Chinese petroleum engineers. . . . Rebel forces had also attacked two pumping stations and cut the pipeline in several places, as part of a general offensive. . . . Use of antiaircraft missiles unusual in the Sudanese civil war. . . . Khartoum government, in condemning the attack on what it termed "a civilian installation," stated that guerrillas were being supplied with sophisticated weapons by neighboring Uganda. . . . An SPLA spokesman in Nairobi expressed regret for the deaths but pointed out that the facility's airfield was used by the Sudan air force for air raids on civilian targets in the Nuba and southern Sudan. . . .

So Michael Goraende's campaign had been a triumph, except for those unfortunate deaths, what military people called "collateral damage." Fitzhugh set the newspaper down. It was impossible not to feel a remote complicity in the extinction of those innocent lives—if, that is, anyone was innocent anywhere. The oil the workers pumped made the money that bought the planes and the bombs that were dropped on schools and villages and mission churches. As to responsibility for their deaths, there was plenty to go around, from the munitions workers who had built the missile to the SPLA soldier who fired it, and everyone in between, a roster that included Fitzhugh Martin. In a war, every death was the result of a collaboration.

Sudanese died by thousands and barely rated a mention in the media, but eight dead foreigners were news. An instinct warned him that more was going to be heard about this incident, that someone somewhere was going to ask questions such as, If Uganda is supplying the SPLA with antiaircraft missiles, how do they get from Uganda to the landlocked Nuba mountains, a thousand kilometers away? He felt an overpowering, unhappy urge, like the one that pushes a deserter to rejoin his regiment regardless of the consequences, to return to Lokichokio. He packed his bag and was on a flight the next day. Diana was not forgotten—she never would be—but the hurt was not quite so acute, and he hoped it would soon diminish to the point that he could live with it, a chronic but manageable soreness of the heart.

The Baker's Daughter

SHE WORE A constant coat of dust and sweat. She could not wash her clothes or hair or bathe properly, for as the dry season reached its scorching zenith, even the calabash shower became a rare indulgence. Her body threw off an acidic odor leavened by the smell of woodsmoke, which was how everyone smelled in New Tourom except for Ulrika, Fancher, and Handy, who had water, soap, and shampoo delivered on aid flights. Quinette could have borrowed these commodities from them but chose to live as the Nubans did, cleaning her teeth with twigs cut for that purpose and relieving herself in a pit toilet enclosed by a grass fence, where flies congregated and a smooth stone or a stick substituted for toilet paper. The only item of modern hygiene she could not do without was tampons. Ulrika kept her supplied. Her closet was her rucksack and straw carry-bag, stowed under the bed. The usual spiders dropped onto the mosquito net at night. She whisked them off in the morning and swatted them with her sandals. The monotony of her diet—doura porridge and groundnut paste—was occasionally relieved by a goat stew or scrawny chicken roasted over a wood fire. She was bitten by ticks and suffered bouts of diarrhea.

She had never been happier.

She had love and passion and important work to do, and they more than recompensed for the lack of material comforts.

All was fulfillment.

Her life had reached the culmination of a transformative journey begun when she'd first set foot in Africa. Its course had not been charted by her; nor had its destination been manifest, though she knew now in mind and marrow alike that she had arrived.

In the morning she helped Moses teach English. She'd become his full-time assistant and savored her rapport with the pupils, delighted in their progress in spelling and punctuation.

Afternoons, she was the student, taking instruction in missionary work from Fancher and Handy. There were lessons in everything from first aid—a fieldworker was expected to be competent in treating minor injuries and illnesses—to the arts of discipleship. They put her through intensive Bible study, but much of her training was practical, on the job. She preached to the women in New Tourom about the heroines of the Bible. On a few occasions she joined the two men on hazardous trips to neighboring towns, where they showed their videos and played their taped gospel messages while she ministered to the females, to be critiqued afterward by her tutors. Of the two, she liked Fancher more. He had a steadying, calming influence on the mercurial Handy, who could be full of enthusiasm one day, and the next, meeting with some frustration, be moved to despair. But they were equally courageous and dedicated, and she didn't doubt they were prepared to suffer death for their God, their church, and their mission.

Or rather their missions, for in addition to their main tasks, restoring St. Andrew's and supporting the Nuba's Christian congregations, they were there to proselytize and were not shy about admitting it. "We're the real thing, not skim-milk evangelicals," Fancher said. Converting pagans was easier than converting Muslims, which required tact and delicacy, a kind of passive approach. You exposed them to the message of salvation and more or less waited to see what happened next. This Fancher and Handy did by inviting people of all faiths to their meetings, by showing the films and playing the recordings in public, by training local pastors to speak Christ's word to their Muslim neighbors.

Yet there were times when the message had to be delivered more forcefully.

Once, in a village a day's walk from New Tourom, someone asked Handy what the difference was between Jesus and Muhammad. The stocky missionary's face lit up, the cords in his neck stood out.

"Jesus was the son of God, Muhammad the son of man and woman, that is the difference. Jesus proved he was the son of God. Jesus healed the sick. Muhammad did not. Jesus made the lame walk. Muhammad made walking men lame. Jesus made a blind man see. Muhammad made seeing men blind. Jesus made a dead man live. Muhammad made living men dead. Jesus multiplied a basket of loaves and fishes to feed five thousand. Muhammad divided the spoils after raiding a caravan. Jesus could walk on water. Muhammad could only ride a camel. Jesus set the captives free. Muhammad made free men captives. Jesus tells us to love our enemies. Muhammad teaches to kill and enslave your enemies, as many of his followers are doing today. You can visit Muhammad's grave in Medina, but if you go to visit Jesus's grave in Jerusalem, you will find only an empty tomb, because Jesus rose from the dead to join his father in heaven."

His words seemed to hang in the air, to crackle and spark. Quinette could almost feel them, as if she'd been touched by an exposed wire. Later she asked Handy to write them out, so she could memorize them, in case the same question was put to her. She did not, indeed could not, wait for it to be asked. The next time she preached, she decided to forgo her usual subjects—Sarah and Rachel, Haggai and Elizabeth and Mary Magdalen—and delivered a sermon about the distinction between Jesus and Muhammad. A young Muslim woman approached her afterward, declaring that she wished to become a Christian. Quinette brought her to Fancher, who quizzed her to make sure her desire was genuine. He baptized her the next morning, with water from a plastic jerry can. Quinette witnessed the ceremony. She had reaped her first soul, and from this reaped a feast of purest rapture, to which her mentors added a rich dessert of praise.

All was fulfillment. She had submerged herself in a sacred and a secular cause, but she did not suffer from divided attention because both were one cause to her.

When she wasn't teaching or preaching, she advised and encouraged her husband, serving as his unofficial adjutant to counter the influence of Major Kasli, who continued to issue dire warnings about the consequences of the forthcoming offensive. Observing that Michael's orders and reports were written either by hand or with antiquated typewriters, she arranged for laptops, printers, and solar panels to be shipped in on Knight Air planes and spent hours showing the clerks how to use the new machines. She drafted press releases about the Nubans' plight and gave them to relief pilots for delivery to Lokichokio and eventual transmission to the foreign press corps in Nairobi. One of her communiqués, describing Ulrika's difficulties providing medical care from her inadequate clinic, brought a Reuters correspondent and photographer to New Tourom. A month later a plane landed at the airstrip, crammed with medical supplies and construction materials. One passenger disembarked, a broad-shouldered, thick-chested man with flaxen hair. It was like seeing an apparition. Recovered from his breakdown, Gerhard Manfred had an emotional reunion with Ulrika, Quinette, and Michael (and a moment of surprise when he learned of the marriage). He had read the Reuters story in *Die Welt* and persuaded German Emergency Doctors to send him back and to fund the building and equipping of a new hospital. It had been his dream ever since his return to Germany. Quinette's imagination caught fire. With a five-hundred-word press release, she had brought a doctor and a hospital to New Tourom. She had the power to make things happen.

As the time for launching the offensive approached, a crisis occurred. A much-needed arms shipment failed to arrive as scheduled. Michael, in radio communication with Douglas in Lokichokio, learned that Dare had not been paid by the SPLA and refused to fly until he was. His petty self-ishness disgusted Quinette and infuriated Michael. He had timed the offensive for the end of the dry season, calculating that the government would not be able to organize a retaliation before the big rains made the roads impassable and the skies too cloudy for effective bombing; but if he was delayed too long, the downpours would hinder his own forces, possi-bly prevent them from attacking altogether. Somehow or other the prob-lem got resolved, Dare's battered Hawker landed with the ordnance, and preparations resumed.

The recruits who were going to defend the town dug foxholes, trenches, and bomb shelters. Ammunition and final orders were issued to the veterans, who were everywhere, cleaning and recleaning their rifles, laughing the graveyard laughter of men who knew what they were facing because they had faced it before. Michael made frequent visits to the radio room to converse in code with his subordinate commanders and with Garang's headquarters far to the south. A tense expectancy charged the air. Quinette herself felt electrified, as if the friction between her hope and dread, her anticipation and anxiety, were generating a current within her.

On the day before the army's departure, as she was walking to the gar-rison from New Tourom, she spotted an Antonov at high altitude. It was the cool, dusty hour when the boys drove cattle into the byres for the night and the slanting light caused the contours of the hills to stand out in sharp relief. As always, the appearance of an enemy aircraft brought activity to a halt. The cows plodded on, bells jangling, but the herd boys froze to listen for the whirr and whistle of falling bombs. Watching the silver dot and the contrails in its wake, Quinette experienced a surge of heightened sensa-tion. The colors of the sunset seemed more vivid, the still figures of the herd boys had the beauty of sculpture, the tops of the baobab trees looked lit from within. The plane, probably on a reconnaissance, flew on. Quinette quickened her steps, her spine and scalp tingling, her nerves thrumming like the strings of a Nuban harp, and desire overtook her. Michael must have felt that same erotic magnetism, for he was waiting for her inside their tukul, naked in the bed. They made love like wildcats, Quinette intoxicated by the sheer physicality of it, the strong smells, the quick slaps of damp flesh on damp flesh, and in her orgasm, her religious fervor fused with her sexual passion so the one could not be distinguished from the other. This too was her mission—to make a baby.

She had never known such anxiousness as she did during Michael's absence. He expected the campaign to last a month. A month! She was in the radio room at least once a day, asking for news, but the reports coming back from the front were murky. Victory, defeat, stalemate—there was no way to tell. She didn't know what she would do, what would become of her if he were killed.

She was thankful she had so much to keep her occupied, though she was often distracted and unable to concentrate. Physical labor was the only thing that took her mind off her worries. As most of the hard daily chores were performed by her three helpmates, Pearl, Kiki, and Nolli, Quinette started a vegetable garden. She planted tomatoes, beans, okra, and nuts in a little plot outside the courtyard. Negev, her constant shadow, offered to help prepare the ground, but she preferred to wield hoe and mattock herself. She found solace in making the rows straight, in building a thornbush boma around the garden to keep animals out, in the smell of the turned earth, the feel of it in her hands.

Since New Tourom was bombed three years ago, the enemy's hand had barely touched the town. Some would say that hand had been stayed by Michael's superb defenses, but Quinette believed New Tourom was under a guardianship more powerful than machine guns and shoulder-fired missiles. Whatever accounted for the town's exemption, life proceeded as if peace had come. It was threshing time, and women carried baskets heaped with shucked doura to the threshing grounds, where elders and boys, powdered with ash to invoke the spirits' protection, beat the ears with their heavy paddles. Baskets once again on their heads, the women carried the winnowed grain to the storage silos. Off-duty recruits were pressed into service as construction crews. They began to erect the frame for Manfred's new hospital, to repair the church roof and, hauling water from a deep pit dug in a dry riverbed, to make mud for the walls of the tailor and carpentry shops. Fancher, who had been in an engineer battalion in Vietnam, acted as foreman, supervising the workmen with a mixture of sign language, English, rudimentary Arabic, and what Nuban he knew. Watching the progress day by day, Quinette recalled her husband's vision of New Tourom as the tree that would spread the seeds of a new society through all the Nuba, all Sudan. Now, it was coming to pass; the tree had taken root, and she had a hand in it.

An aid plane landed with a dozen sewing machines among its cargo. They were of a kind Quinette's great-grandmother would have used—

black Singers operated by a treadle. Fancher said a Friends of the Frontline board member had discovered the antiques in a movie company prop shop. They ended their journey from Hollywood to the heart of Sudan in the still-to-be-completed tailor shop. A woman familiar with the ancient machines was found, and while workmen clambered overhead, thatching the roof, she taught her sisters how to use them. Quinette had an inspiration: The women could make Nuban dresses for sale to tourists in Kenya. Knight Air planes could deliver them on their return runs. With the cash realized from the sales, grain and other foodstuffs could be bought in hard times. When she presented the scheme to them, the women responded with enthusiasm. She was giving them a chance to earn money; among the things it would buy for them was some measure of independence. In return, they gave her more of their love.

Except for Yamila. Quinette's charms had no effect on that young woman, sheathed in an armor of passive hostility that Quinette could not penetrate. She'd stopped attending English lessons because Quinette taught them, would not come to women's Bible study because Quinette presided, and when Quinette entered the tailor shop one day with bolts of cloth, Yamila walked out with her usual haughty bearing. The savage princess.

"I don't understand it," Quinette complained to Ulrika that afternoon. "What did I ever do to her?"

The nurse gave her a skeptical squint. "You are not a stupid-head, so do not tell me that you do not know."

"I really don't."

"You married Michael, that is what you did to her."

Quinette paused, taken aback not by the fact of Yamila's jealousy but by her own blindness to it. How could she have failed to see it?

"And it is more serious because of what you are," Ulrika added. "*Ja.* In the mind of a Yamila, there is no understanding why he would take you over her. To her, this is insult, but she blames you."

Jealousy begot jealousy. From then on Quinette regarded Yamila with fear and suspicion. She wasn't afraid that her rival—she had to think of her as such—would steal Michael from her but that he would take her as a second wife, if her attraction were ever made known to him. Polygamy was common in the Nuba, but Quinette was willing to go only so far in her efforts to merge herself into the Nubans' world. She was going to keep him all to herself.

He'd been gone eighteen days when a delegation of five Muslim elders visited her, Fancher, and Handy at the latter's camp near the church. She and the missionaries were discussing an encounter Handy had had with three women earlier in the afternoon. He made videos for the ministry and had been shooting scenes of town life when he'd heard female voices nearby singing the hymn "Give Thanks to the Risen Lord." Native women giving impromptu praise to their savior. Thinking this would make for a moment of inspirational footage, he found the trio in the courtyard of a house. They were drunk on marissa, naked to the waist, and had not much on below. Dancing as they sang, "Alleluia, Alleluia, give thanks to the risen lord," they broke into inebriated giggles when they saw him, then faced his camera and with lewd sways of their hips, gave out another chorus of alleluias. He scolded them, but the admonishment only provoked more laughter. The incident plunged him into one of his fits of despair. These Nubans were incorrigible—they drank to excess, he'd seen children guzzling marissa.

Quinette had the impression that the Nubans weren't people to him, they were *souls*. When they displayed their human weaknesses, he was disgusted.

"Ulrika told me they drink it because they have a vitamin deficiency," she said to console Handy. "The millet in the beer makes up for it."

"It also makes them plastered," he said, unimpressed by the medical justification for what he considered a moral failure. "The Muslims around here need their vitamins, but you don't see them getting smashed. What kind of example are the Christians setting?"

As if cued, the delegation appeared—five men in jelibiyas led by the seven-foot Suleiman. Normally jovial, he looked grave. After an exchange of greetings and ritualistic pleasantries, he and the others sat on the ground. He stated the purpose of the call: "We must ask you to stop teaching your religion to our people."

"By 'your people,' you mean Muslims?" Fancher asked quietly.

Scowling, Suleiman replied, Of course that's who he meant. Fancher earnestly asserted that they weren't teaching Christianity to Muslims. The ministry's gatherings were open to everyone, and if some Muslims happened to attend, they couldn't stop them.

"You do this in the open," Suleiman shot back. "You play stories from your Book on tape recorders so anyone can hear. You show cinema about your religion so anyone can see. These are things that should be done in one of your churches, where no Muslim would go."

One of the others, a man of about sixty wearing a wool cap despite the temperature, raised a finger, long and tapering to a point, like a black thorn. "You are poisoning the hearts of our brothers, our children, our wives," he said in quite good English. "That isn't proper. It must stop."

Handy nearly popped out of his camp chair. "Poison?"

"Yes, poison!" the old man replied. "You do worse than teach your religion. You insult ours."

"You tell us that we're poisoning people's hearts and then accuse *us* of insulting *you*?"

Fancher cautioned his excitable colleague to keep calm.

Not finished yet, the elder pointed at Quinette. Because of her, his youngest wife had been turned from the true faith, declaring herself to be a Christian because of words Quinette had spoken to her, blasphemous words that Jesus was not a prophet as was written but the son of God, that Jesus did many miracles while Muhammad, blessed be he, did none, that Muhammad put out the eyes of seeing men, that Muhammad was a murderer and a robber. His wife was young and ignorant and easily influenced. He'd been forced to beat her severely, and he hated to do that because he was fond of her.

Now Quinette had to restrain herself from leaving her chair. Why were Muslims so violent? she wondered. Her convert could not have been more than seventeen or eighteen, and the picture of her submitting to this old man's caresses was as repulsive as the picture of her submitting to his blows. "Then why did you do it, if you're so fond of her?" she asked in as even a tone as she could manage.

"To bring her to her senses, and because she repeated the blasphemies you spoke to her. No man who calls himself Muslim can tolerate a wife speaking like that. It is an outrage."

"The outrage is that you beat that poor girl."

"Do not make things worse with lies. We have had reports from other places about the things you people are saying."

Suleiman leaped back in, advising Quinette that as the commander's wife she had a responsibility to promote harmony, not division. Muslim, Christian, or otherwise, the Nubans had a common enemy.

"My brothers and I, we are Sufi. We are not like those in the government. Theirs is the Islam of the sword, ours"—he pressed his chest—"the Islam of the heart."

"Oh, I see," Quinette said, a burning sensation in her cheeks—the same heat she'd felt years ago and half a world away, when she'd hurled a rock at an auctioneer. "Is it the Islam of the heart to beat a young girl for repeating something she heard?"

"So you admit teaching blasphemy!" the elder said, sounding like a prosecutor in a courtroom melodrama.

"This has gone on long enough." Fancher mopped his thinning black hair and looked at Suleiman. "If we've offended you, we apologize. I promise you, we won't offend you any further."

"You will stop the teaching?"

"What? Altogether? Absolutely not. What we will do is hold our meetings in private. That way your people"—he said this with a note of sarcasm—"won't see or hear anything you don't think they should see or hear."

"There are Nuban priests of your church who are also teaching Muslims," Suleiman said, advancing a new objection. "That must also stop. Let Muslims be Muslims, Christians be Christians."

"I can't control what those men do or say. I'll ask them to be careful. But I have to warn you, if Muslims ask them questions, they will have to answer. And if we're asked, we have to answer, too."

The old man yanked off his wool cap and waved it at the missionary. "That is the same as teaching!"

"We'll watch our words. We won't say anything insulting. I can't promise more than that."

It was plain that the delegation wasn't satisfied. It was equally plain that they weren't going to win any further concessions. Their displeasure remained after their departure, a thickness in the air, almost palpable. Handy was not too pleased either, protesting that Fancher had caved in.

"Got to give a little to gain a little," the older man responded, in the moderate voice of a father to a hotheaded son. "We're not going to accomplish everything we've got to do with half the population pissed off at us."

"I don't think those guys represent half the population," Handy remonstrated. "And that old dude is bent out of shape just because his wife did something without asking the boss's permission."

"We keep doing what we have been, but we do it more discreetly, all right?" Fancher said. "Quinette, I suppose you have an opinion?"

She didn't give one immediately, looking off at the tailor shop, its mud walls tinged pink by the sunset. The image she could not erase from her mind was of the girl cringing as her aged husband slapped her or punched her or hit her with a stick. Her suffering was a consequence Quinette had not foreseen. She did not hold herself responsible but felt, rather, the same desire for retribution elicited by the slaves' tales of their captivity. Handy was right—the old man was outraged because the chattel he called wife had made a choice of her own free will. She'd chosen a religion; had it been something else, he would have beaten her for that instead. Unless people like him changed, Michael's vision was never going to be realized; and if effecting change caused friction, even to the point of pissing off half the population, then by all means, she thought, let us piss them off.

"I'll be honest, Tim," she said finally. "I agree with Rob. I think your whole-milk evangelism just got skimmed."

SHE PAID HER daily calls on the radio room and learned nothing; she listened to the BBC's Africa service on Ulrika's shortwave and learned little more. There were reports from South Africa and West Africa, from the Congo and Angola, but no word about Sudan—until, twenty-four days after Michael's departure, the reader announced that "in Sudan, the rebel Sudanese People's Liberation Army, in a sweeping offensive in the Nuba mountains and southern Kordafan province, have seized several government-held towns, sabotaged the country's thousand-mile-long oil pipeline, and bombarded an airfield and oil facility belonging to the Amulet Energy Corporation. . . . A company aircraft is believed to have been shot down in the fighting, with eight people reported killed. . . . Sudan's information minister confirmed that the attacks took place but stated that all were repulsed with heavy losses to rebel forces."

"So they have won," Ulrika commented. "Whenever the government says the SPLA is defeated, it means they have won."

Quinette didn't know what to think. She still had no answer to the questions uppermost in her mind.

She went to bed in a state of emotional suspension and woke in the same condition, wondering if she had the inner strength to be a soldier's wife. Her grandmothers had waited years for their husbands to come home from Europe, Ardele had endured a year without her Ted, as well as the news that he'd been wounded. Quinette sought to draw from that reservoir of perseverance but felt disconnected from it in her foreign surroundings, thrown back on her own resources, which seemed inadequate.

With little to keep her occupied—it was a Saturday, no school to teach, no Bible study to attend—she spent an hour watering and weeding her vegetable garden. Then she heard the bray of a douberre, the antelope-horn trumpet. Moments later, out of breath from running, Negev appeared. "Missy, the commander and the soldiers are come." Going into the house, she stripped off her shirt and shorts, changed into a dress, and wiped her sweating face with a soiled bandanna.

Outside, hundreds of people were surging down the road, chanting, singing, blowing whistles and horns. Quinette, hiking her dress, dashed out ahead of the wild procession and, at the gap in the hills, saw the road before her filled with soldiers, trudging toward the garrison. The column stretched back to New Tourom and beyond. Michael was in front. She would have recognized him a mile away—the bright red beret, the slow, deliberate walk, head bowed, as if he were lost in reflection. "Thank you, Lord!" she said out loud. "Thank you thank you thank you." The throng of civilians caught up to her and swept her on.

The impromptu festival that greeted the army's return was pure mayhem, an explosion of joy and relief. Women ripped off their clothes and painted their bodies with mud, while men decorated themselves with bits of fur and straw hats and feathers. People danced around the soldiers in human chains resembling conga lines.

Quinette had to contain her own happiness. Thin and drawn, Michael was in the mood that always overcame him after a battle—reticent, secluded within himself. She had learned not to try to bring him out of this somber humor and walked quietly with him through the excited crowds into the courtyard of their house. There he gave her and Pearl each an embrace, asked his daughter to bring some wash water, and sponged off the dust that powdered him head to foot. He collapsed on the bed and slept till the next morning.

Symbolic funerals were held that day for the men who did not make it back, symbolic because it had been impossible for the soldiers to carry their dead comrades over such long distances. Somehow the solemn ceremonies and wails of grief helped to draw Michael out of his isolation. Later, as they sat in the courtyard, he looked at Quinette as if he had just woken up and began to talk about the battles. "Oh, we were like those words you read to me from Isaiah, I forget them."

" 'In that time a present will be brought to the Lord of Hosts, from a people tall and smooth of skin,' " she reminded him.

"Yes, like that, and we brought the present, dead Arabs, hundreds of them. We hit them hard, beat them on every front," he said, but in such a mournful way, you would have thought he had suffered defeat. In time, he got around to revealing what had put him in a clouded frame of mind: men directly under his command had shot down the oil company plane with the foreign workers on board.

She said she'd heard about it on the shortwave. Of course, it was sad, but—

"But this is war and war is cruelty," he said. "Khartoum is making big propaganda and Garang's headquarters has issued a statement—the SPLA regrets what happened, the plane was mistaken for an enemy plane, and so forth and so on and et cetera." He slouched in his chair, big hands hanging between his knees. "I must tell you something. Something that must remain between us."

She caught his drift and murmured, "But it was no mistake?"

"I knew it was a civilian plane with foreigners on board."

"How could you possibly have known that?"

"It was a little before sunset, before we began the attack. Enough light to see by. The plane was on the runway. I saw its identification through my field glasses. It was very clear—'Amulet Energy.' I watched the crew go on board and then the passengers, and I could see they were civilians. I could see they were not Sudanese. Not a dark face among them. I remembered an incident from a long time ago, when the oil fields were being developed by an American company. There was a battle. Workers were caught in the crossfire, three were killed. The company decided Sudan was too dangerous and pulled out. No oil flowed for years, not until Amulet Energy bought the leases and built the pipeline." He drew out of his slouch and leaned toward her, cupping her chin. "When the airplane began to move, I knew what had to be done, and that was to inflict terror. We were not going to dam the river of oil by making some holes in the pipeline, by smashing up an airfield—those can be repaired—but perhaps we could do it with terror. Terror, my darling Quinette." He continued to hold her chin, forcing her to look squarely at him. It was as if he were telling her, *I won't allow you to turn away. Behold what I am, behold the man you are married to.* "It had worked once, by an accident; perhaps it would work again, by a deliberate act. I ordered the mortars to fire, but the plane was in the air by the time the first salvo hit the runway. I called to the antiaircraft, 'Fire! Fire!' The plane was almost directly over our heads, climbing fast. A missile got it. It fell like a stone. Like a burning stone."

He let her go, but she sat facing him as if his fingers were still there, gripping her jaw.

"In all my years as a fighter, I have never knowingly taken an innocent life. I have prided myself on that. Now, I am no better than a terrorist, and if what I did doesn't have the effect I intended, it will have been pointless murder. It is murder all the same." Slouching again, he stretched his legs over the ground, cleft and crazed from lack of rain. "Garang and the high command do not know what I've told you. It would make no difference to them if they did—Garang and his Dinkas have spilled a thousand liters of innocent blood—but I thought the denial that it was a purposeful act would sound more convincing if they did not know. My soldiers did not

know either. They had no field glasses to show them it was a civilian aircraft. They did only what I have trained them to do—obey orders. You
and I are the only ones who own the truth. I have made my wife a party to
what I did, and perhaps that is wrong, too, but you see, it is a secret I cannot live with alone. I am not strong enough. I had to confess it to someone, and who else but you? And now I ask you to forgive me."

"For what you did or for involving me?" she asked.

"For both."

"Only God can forgive what you did, and He will if you ask Him."

"I have, more than once. But now I'm asking you."

She rose and stepped over the fissured ground between them to lay her
palm on his arm. He sealed her hand with his.

THIN CIRRUS CLOUDS began to sheet the skies in the afternoons, while
the air grew dense with prophecies of rain. The dry season was drawing to
a close, and the kujurs conducted ceremonies to bury its trials and to petition the ancestors for a bountiful rainfall. The season's military triumphs
were marked by a celebration more orderly and choreographed than the
spontaneous demonstration that had met the army's return a week ago.
Instead of being presented with medals, the bravest warriors were honored in the same way as victorious contestants in the wrestling festivals,
with the girls' love dance, the Nyertun.

Quinette was expected to take part. In the afternoon she lay naked outside her hut while Pearl, Kiki, and Nolli covered her with a homemade
wax, then peeled it off, removing her body hair—it was considered
unsightly among all of Sudan's blacks. She was relieved that Fancher and
Handy had declined an invitation to attend. If they hadn't, she would have
been forced to be an observer rather than a participant; it took no imagination to picture what their reaction, Handy's in particular, would be to
seeing her dance with virtually nothing on and her midriff marked by cicatrix. But she considered herself Nuban in all but the color of her skin and
saw no conflict between her duties as a minister of Christ and her obligation to follow the customs of the people who had adopted her as she had
adopted them. Malachy would have understood. It was the way of Africa.

And so she came to the Nyertun in the traditional costume—a skimpy
barega below her waist and a bead bodice to cover her top—and danced
under the moon. She had become quite proficient and gloried in her art.
At the climactic moment, when the woman claimed her man by kicking a
leg over his shoulder, she heard some onlookers gasp. She had been so

transported, so lost in the sound and movement, that she hadn't noticed Yamila, who now stood beside her, glaring defiantly, a leg resting on Michael's opposite shoulder.

As Quinette discovered in a moment, custom ruled that when two women chose the same man, the decision rested with him. When Michael nodded to Quinette, Yamila hissed and would have scratched her if several girls hadn't restrained her. Yamila broke free and ran off. Quinette couldn't say who was more mortified, she or her rival.

So Yamila had at last declared her feelings. The dance went on without her into the early morning. When it was over and Quinette and Michael retired to their hut, she did not make love to him, she *fucked* him. *Fucked* him on the bed and then on the floor mat with a wanton ferocity, as she imagined that wild girl would have done had his nod gone to her. She used her body like a weapon to pummel whatever polygamous, adulterous thoughts Yamila might have put into his head. *Fucked* him until even that vigorous man had nothing left to give, and as they lay on the mat in mutual exhaustion, she asked, "If she had gotten to you first, would you have gone with her?"

He laughed. "No. I want only you, and I am very happy you were first."

"She's a beautiful woman, I have to say that for her."

"If that is your way of begging a compliment, I'll give you one. You're beautiful, too. Haven't I told you so many times?" His hand moved to her belly, tracing the cicatrix. "As beautiful as any Yamila, as any Nuban woman."

"I am going to be the mother of your son. I am going to give you back what you lost."

"Yes, you have said so," he said, with the melancholy of someone wishing for the unattainable. He moved his hand from her stomach, and she sensed with its withdrawal a withdrawal of himself, a sudden distancing.

"What's wrong?" she asked, feeling a panic. "Is it her? I am not going to share you, Michael."

"Stop, please! It isn't her, it isn't that. There are times I ask myself if we in this country should allow ourselves children until the war is over. It's like giving birth when you have AIDS. The child is doomed as it's born."

"You can't let yourself think that way," she counseled. "It's giving up hope. You have to think of what life will be like when it is over."

"It's hard to imagine."

"You have to imagine it before you can have it. You have to imagine children in it."

"Imagine it, imagine it," he said in an undertone, lying on his back, hands clasped behind his neck. "And what would I be in a new Sudan? A minister of parliament? Then I would dress in a suit instead of camouflage and we would live in a fine house with servants instead of this tukul in the bush. Would you like that, my darling Quinette?"

She answered that the tukul was fine and so was the camouflage and that she could not picture herself with servants.

"Or I could be an officer in the new army of the new Sudan. You would see me in a fine dress uniform, like the kind I wore when I first joined the army. I was a ceremonial guard at the Presidential Palace in Khartoum, in a dark blue tunic and white gloves and a white topee. The government used to take Dinka and Nubans for that duty because we looked impressive in those uniforms."

"I'll bet you did," she said.

"I must admit, I did." In the darkness, she made out his grin. She had stopped him from slipping into morbid thoughts, brought him back to her. "And I'll wear one like it in the new army of the new Sudan, but not with a corporal's stripes, no, with the pips of a general. Brigadier General Michael Goraende. Or would you prefer a husband with a higher rank? Major general?"

"I like brigadier. I like the sound of it. Brigadier and Mrs. Michael Goraende."

"We will be invited to diplomatic receptions and military balls. There I will be in my splendid blue uniform with the pips of a brigadier, and there you will be at my side in a gown, a Nuban gown, but finer than the one I bought for you. And who will know that we once lived in a tukul in the bush? Who will know that this beautiful American woman in her fine gown"—his finger played around her breasts—"once danced naked in the Nuba mountains before a thousand eyes."

"No one," she whispered. "It'll be our secret. We'll laugh about it when we're alone, and how I said yes to you like a Nuban girl."

"This is a fine future we are imagining for ourselves when the war is over."

"With children, with a son," she said, and rolled over and straddled him.

"My God, you are mad tonight. You are shameless."

Mine, she thought, working him into arousal. *Now and forever, mine.*

The confidence with which she spoke those words to herself didn't last. It was a brief remission in a fever of jealousy that flared each time she saw

Yamila, and in so small a place as New Tourom, it was impossible not to see her almost every day. As the disease progressed, she began to suspect Michael of secretly desiring the girl, and the suspicions fostered images of Yamila swollen with his child, presenting him with a son, beating Quinette to the punch.

A week after the dance her period arrived on schedule. She cursed her body, then prayed, then, a cramp binding her abdomen, cursed again. A new fear arose that she would not be forced to share Michael but that he would divorce her because she was unable to conceive. One fear spawned another. She became convinced that the respect and adoration she commanded from the Nubans, though it had been won by her alone, was now sustained by her position as his wife. To lose him would be to lose them. She would be an outcast, a woman without a country, cut off from the home of her birth by her own choice, from her adopted home by circumstance. Therefore, according to the addled logic bred by her fever, her whole future depended on her giving birth.

She grew emotionally demanding, seeking reassurances that she had exclusive claim to him. "Stop this!" he said one night, after another interrogation about the state of his feelings. "She is an ignorant, illiterate peasant girl, she knows nothing about the world outside these mountains. I wouldn't want her even if I didn't have you. What is the matter with you?"

"There is nothing the matter with *me*," she answered with some bitterness. "You're all I've got, that's what the matter is. I've given up everything to be with you, my country, my job, my family, my friends, everything."

Sitting at the big ammunition crate that served as their table, its ugliness masked by a woven mat, he rubbed his temples and said patiently, "Did I force you? You gave it up of your own free will. I think you were even eager to give it up. Why are you blaming me?"

She was and she wasn't. Her own desires for him and a different, bigger life with him were to blame; but because it was he, by the mere fact of his existence, that had moved her to act on her desires, she blamed him as well. Having surrendered all, she was sensitive to any threat to what she did possess. There was something about Yamila that Quinette sensed intuitively—she was an implacable natural force, as unconscious as a lioness seeking a mate. Her ignorance was her strength. She couldn't see that she wasn't suitable for Michael and, with no family or clan to care for her, too desperate herself to take Michael's choice as his final word. She wanted him, that was all, and it was everything.

The rains arrived in mid-April, and so did Quinette's next menstruation, an unwelcome but persistent visitor. She confessed to Fancher and Handy her longing to get pregnant and asked for their prayers, figuring that if the Creator was deaf to hers, He might listen to theirs. Later she decided to give the Creator a hand. She went to Ulrika with a request for fertility pills. It was not an item the nurse kept on hand, but she promised to do what she could to obtain them.

AFTER AN AUSPICIOUS start, with downpours pounding the hills nearly every afternoon, the rains failed at a critical time, after the sowing of the early-blooming doura that fed the Nubans until the main harvest in November. A dry week passed, then two, and the dread of drought and famine spread like a contagion. The kujur reprised the rituals he'd performed earlier, but the spirits did not respond favorably. (Nor, it must be said, did Allah, beseeched in New Tourom's small mosque; nor did the God prayed to in St. Andrew's church.) The skies grayed but yielded only a few drops.

One morning, going to the tailor shop to check on the dressmaking project, Quinette noticed that three of the women did not join in the chorus of "Good day, Kinnet," that always greeted her entrance. Sullen and silent, they pumped the treadles and averted their eyes when she inspected their work. She felt like the resented boss of a sweatshop. On another occasion, meeting the kujur's wife on the road, she said hello and got the cold shoulder. This from the woman who had presided over her initiation and tattooing. She was not imagining things. She learned from Pearl that a kind of whisper campaign had begun against her. It made sense in its way. The Nubans might be involved in a twentieth-century war, but their minds remained in the ages of bronze and iron. Confronting a drought that was proving resistant to the prescribed ceremonies and magic, those minds sought an explanation, and someone gave it to them: the ancestors were offended because a pale-skinned stranger had married the commander, and they had signaled their anger by drying up the well of the heavens. Quinette's flat stomach, after months of marriage, was further proof of their disapproval.

So her fears of losing the Nubans' affection and acceptance were not entirely irrational. The gossip was accepted by only a handful, but the kujur was among them—Quinette's marriage got him off the hook, accounting not only for the failure of the rains but for his magic's failure to cure it. He was an eminent and prestigious figure. With his advocacy, the notion that she was to blame could gain wider appeal. She made discreet inquiries, discovered that the rain-maker was not the source of the talk, and concluded that it could only have been started by the two people who had the most against her.

She confronted Yamila first, accosting her as she and several other women were filling calabashes at the town well. There she stood, all feline sinew, leverage in her braided muscles, but Quinette was sufficiently incensed not to feel intimidated.

"Here is something I know," she said. "You've been talking against me, and it is going to stop. You are going to keep your mouth shut. Here is something else I know—you don't understand my words, but you can see that I'm angry and you damned sure know why, don't you? Sure you do."

Taken by surprise, Yamila shrank back, uncertainty clouding her usual belligerent expression.

"You were put up to this, I know that, too. You're not clever enough to have thought it up all by yourself. So I'll give you some advice—it's not going to do you any good."

Quinette hadn't the slightest idea how to enforce this ordinance; the important thing was that Yamila realize she was no one to trifle with.

Satisfied that she'd gotten her message across, she marched off to Kasli's hut and lashed into him. How sly of him to take advantage of Yamila's feelings and to use her to exploit the Nubans' superstitions for his own purposes. Well, she was on to him, and he wasn't going to get away with it.

Predictably, Kasli first professed not to have any idea what she was talking about. Then he accused her of being out of her head, and finally he all but admitted his guilt by expressing what she knew was his deepest wish: She should go back to Loki, or better still to America, where she belonged. She was a liability to Michael. She had made him the subject of much unfavorable comment throughout the SPLA; at the highest levels his judgment in marrying a foreigner was being criticized, and his fitness for further command was being questioned.

"And I'll bet those unfavorable comments started with you," Quinette shot back. "If anyone is going to leave here, it's going to be you."

After Kasli reported that remark to him, Michael took her by the shoulders—the first time he'd laid hands on her other than affectionately—and shook her. He was in command here, and Kasli was his adjutant, not hers to recklessly threaten.

"Is it his place to threaten me?" she asked. "To tell me that I ought to leave?"

"Of course not, and I gave him a good dressing-down about that. He came to his senses, and you must, *must* do the same."

Her husband's anger scared her into making an effort. She maintained her watch on Yamila and kept an ear out for further whispers, but she did try to cure the fever.

Kasli tried another ploy. Suleiman and the Muslim elders, still dissatisfied with the outcome of their discussions with Fancher and Handy, had brought their grievances to the adjutant and asked to meet with the commander. Michael was reluctant to get mixed up in religious affairs. Kasli persuaded him to see the delegation, arguing that the matter had bearing on the military situation: The SPLA needed the full support of the Nuba's Muslims; therefore, he would be wise to address their concerns.

Wishing to hear both sides, Michael invited the missionaries to the meeting, and because she was their colleague, he insisted on Quinette's presence as well. He didn't need to insist. If he hadn't, she would have.

It took place in the courtyard in the evening. Chairs were arranged in a circle, a kerosene lamp set on the ground in the middle. Suleiman presented the Muslims' complaint. Yes, the foreigners had moderated their proselytizing, but in other places Nuban pastors whom they had trained and supplied with films and tape recordings had not. From this town had come a report of eight Muslims converted, from that town, five, from another, ten. In Suleiman's home village, Kologi, four people had been led astray, and one of his sons had been among them.

Fancher objected to "led astray." "On the contrary, we believe they've been led home."

"Believe what you like," Suleiman retorted. "We believe differently. Do you find us Muslims pushing the Koran into Christian hands? Do you find us playing recordings of the suras that everyone can hear? Do we have cinema about the life of Muhammad?"

Handy sighed. "Has it ever occurred to you that our pastors aren't *shoving* anything at anyone? All they're doing is showing people the truth, and once people see and hear the truth, they embrace it."

"The truth?" said the elder with the young wife, indignantly. "The Koran is God's final word on earth. How dare you say it isn't the truth."

Michael looked bemused by the theological dispute. Gesturing for silence, he turned to Suleiman. "What is it you would like done?"

"Stop these recordings and cinema. These things should not be done in public. It is an offense to us. We have families now arguing religion with each other. It wasn't like this before these men came here."

"He's right," Kasli interjected in a sibilant voice. "We lived side by side, with no interfering." He looked at the old man. "You should tell Commander Goraende of what happened with your wife when his wife spoke to her."

Quinette was shocked by the adjutant's nerve. Whatever purpose the others had in mind, for him this gathering was nothing more than another chance to undermine her.

"Major, you are out of line," Michael rebuked softly. "You will leave Quinette out of this."

Kasli begged his pardon and pointed out that it was he who had asked her to attend.

And so the old man told his tale, and Quinette gave her side, mortified that she had to justify herself to her own husband.

Michael then quizzed Fancher—was there anything he could do? The request that the videos and recordings be played inside churches was not unreasonable. No, it wasn't, the missionary answered. The problem was, most of the villages did not have churches or meeting halls, services were conducted in the open air of necessity.

"Then I see only one solution," Kasli said, each word rasping like a dry leaf in a wind. "The commander should issue a directive ordering these things to be confiscated."

Suleiman and the elders nodded in agreement. Fancher protested: his ministry had spent a great deal of time, money, and effort developing the tapes and videos. Without them, he and Handy might as well pack up and leave.

"Perhaps you should," Kasli said.

Michael sat quietly after everyone left, his gaze fixed on the lantern and its halo of bugs. "I am in charge of military affairs," he said, more to himself than to Quinette. "I do not see what I am supposed to do about this. What can I do?"

"Nothing, and Kasli knows it," she said. "Confiscate the stuff? Even if you ordered that, how could you carry it out? Send your men to every town and village? He put you on the spot, darling, involving you in this. No matter what you do, it will cause trouble, and I think that's what he wants. I don't understand why you put up with him."

"Because I need to have a Muslim as my second in command." He paused. "He told me in private that he thinks your two friends were sent here to cause discord. That that is their true mission."

Quinette groaned. "They're CIA, like me? Oh God, Michael, he's crazy."

"Only when it comes to foreigners."

"And if he ever did get rid of Tim and Rob and me, *and me*," she said, "he'd go after Ulrika and Dr. Manfred next. Then sick people could go to the witch doctor and get cured with chants and rattles."

"All the same, I am, how did you say it? On the spot?"

She watched his face, somber and thoughtful in the flicker of the lamp. "You're not really considering doing what Kasli said?"

"I need to resolve this question."

"Please don't do what he said."

"It's important to you?"

Quinette picked up her chair and set it down across from him, her knees touching his. In her mind, Kasli was still present and she was locked with him in a struggle for leverage over her husband's will, not merely on the moment's issue but on all others to come. She deployed Fancher's metaphor—the Nuba was an island in a sea of Islam. Michael needed Fancher and Handy to inspire and give hope to the Nuba's Christians. He needed them, she argued, to finish rebuilding St. Andrew's. It wasn't just a matter of bricks and mortar. Had he forgotten the words he'd spoken when they met for the first time? Had he forgotten his vision of a Nuba where people spoke the same language and tribal differences were forgotten? If any of that were to come to pass, things had to change. There would be no place in a new Sudan for a sixty-year-old man with the power and authority to beat his teenage bride for deciding how she wanted to worship. Change—that's what Suleiman and those others feared. Michael mustn't allow their fears to stand in the way . . .

He listened to her ardent oration with his head tilted against the back of his chair, a pose that suggested patient indulgence. "Are you proposing something?" he asked. "What is it?"

"Nothing. I'm proposing that you do nothing."

"Nothing? That is not what I expect to hear from an American."

"Sometimes doing nothing is doing something, and this is one of those times," she advised. "Let Fancher and Handy, let us, continue to do our work. If that bothers your adjutant or Suleiman or anyone else, you can tell them that life is going to be different. That you haven't been fighting this war just so everything can stay the same."

"But you know, that is what so many Nubans are fighting for, and not only Muslims. To be left alone and to live exactly as their ancestors lived."

"That isn't what you want, Michael. The war's already changed things. You don't need me to tell you that they can never be the same again."

"I will think about this doing nothing," he said.

"Please, darling. I did something for you, and you know what it is. Do this for me."

"I am going to think about it."

She could interpret the modulations of his voice, the meanings encrypted in its rises and falls. He wasn't going to think about it. He'd made up his mind. She had won.

It wasn't a victory that charged its price in advance; it delayed payment.

MICHAEL'S STRATEGY TO stage the offensive at the end of the dry season, trusting that the wet would blunt or avert a retaliation, had not presumed a drought. In the fourth week without rain, Khartoum took advantage of the favorable weather and struck back. For three consecutive days, everyone in town and in the garrison heard the distant, ominous rumble of bombs; for three consecutive nights, they saw the spastic flashes of artillery over far-off ridgelines; and for a week afterward reports and rumors came in by radio and bush-telegraph of raids by militia battalions on foot and on horseback, in trucks and tanks. They came from towns Quinette knew and from places she'd never heard of, Toda, Nawli, and Andreba; Tabanya, El Hemid, and Lado. When it was over, seventeen towns had been leveled and thirty-six thousand people had been killed, displaced, or taken into captivity. Tamsit, scorched earth. More woe to the land of the whirring wings beyond the rivers of Ethiopia. New Tourom escaped the onslaught. Government planes attempted to bomb it but were driven off by flurries of anti-aircraft fire; a militia column advancing from a Sudanese army garrison was ambushed before it got within ten miles of the town. It was the safest place in the rebel-held Nuba. For several days, survivors from elsewhere shambled into New Tourom, walking ghosts starved and dehydrated, wounded and sick. They built crude shelters of sticks and straw on the outskirts, and in a short time the town had its own slum of more than a thousand people. It grew to two thousand, to three. The missionaries stopped all other work to help care for the multitudes. Quinette pitched in, making splints and bandages for the injured, dishing out doura gruel, but the numbers kept growing, and with the drought, New Tourom's citizens resisted parting with their remaining stores of grain. Dysentery swept through the refugee camps. Manfred and Ulrika were overwhelmed. So were Michael's military police, struggling to maintain order. Clashes broke out between townspeople and refugees, who also fought among themselves over a bowl of food or a jerry can of water. One morning a gun battle erupted between local troops and soldiers who'd fled a distant garrison. Two were killed. Hunger and disease had brought things to the verge of chaos, a breakdown of all ties of family, clan, and tribe that would pit every man against every other man.

With a stunning lack of diplomacy, Kasli chose this time to remind his commander that he had predicted disaster, and now here it was. The dry-season campaign had achieved worse than nothing. The oil was flowing again, all the towns captured had been recaptured and burned to the ground, and half the Nuba was in ruins. Michael couldn't imagine what his adjutant hoped to gain, speaking to him in such a manner. It was intolerable, he should have sacked Kasli on the spot, but he remained wary of taking that step. Kasli had his followers and sympathizers, fellow Muslims and loyal clansmen, and could stir up trouble if he felt he'd been treated unjustly. Instead of relieving him, Michael sent him into temporary banishment. With a strong detachment, he was to tour the towns hardest hit, assess the damage, and while he was at it, scour the countryside for recruits; Khartoum's savagery must have created numbers of young men eager to enlist in the SPLA.

Single-handedly, Quinette organized a relief operation.

The emergency had summoned all the discordant strains in her nature to play in concert: her egoism and her desire for self-sacrifice; her need to be of service and also the center of attention; her pity for the victimized and her pride in being their savior; and the lead violinist in this symphony of motives was her jealousy. Her first thought was to aid her husband, who could not cope with a looming famine, a refugee crisis, and his military duties all at once. Her second thought, proceeding from the first, was to show him she was indispensable. She could do what a hundred Yamilas could not. She had the power to make things happen.

She began with Fancher and Handy. Arguing that the needs of the body superseded the needs of mind and spirit for the time being, she convinced them to radio their field office in Loki with a request to send food, medicine, and blankets instead of books, Bibles, and gospel videos. On her laptop she wrote graphic descriptions of the situation, seeing herself as the Nubans' voluntary amanuensis. Using the garrison's radio, she broadcast appeals for help to the independent aid agencies. She contacted Doug Braithwaite, begging him to collect supplies and make an emergency delivery. The next day she trekked to the New Tourom airstrip to meet his plane. She gave him her press releases, urging him to fly them directly to Nairobi and hand-deliver them to the news agencies. You could always count on Doug. No other pilot would have agreed so readily to such an extraordinary request.

The independent NGOs came through. Within a week aid flights to the Nuba doubled. Quinette practically camped out at the airstrip, talking to the pilots on a field radio, coordinating the off-loads while a detachment of Michael's bodyguard kept desperate people from mobbing the planes. Reporters and film crews arrived. Interviewed by the BBC and French and Japanese television, she laced her commentaries with condemnations of Khartoum's brutality. Phyllis Rappaport from CNN showed up, obnoxious as ever. "You've come a long way, baby," she remarked to Quinette, who swallowed her dislike and gave Phyllis an interview. NBC, German television, Reuters—she'd made the Nuba a focus of world attention, and the publicity brought more assistance. A southern Sudanese doctor and two nurses arrived to help Manfred and Ulrika. John Barrett's IPA dispatched a team of aid workers with tents, blankets, and cots to build a camp for the refugees. Norwegian People's Aid established a feeding center. Yet with displaced people still trickling in, all this wasn't enough.

When Kasli returned from his mission, she obtained the report he submitted to Michael, radioed UN headquarters in Nairobi, and read from the report, requesting airdrops by C-130s and Buffalos. She had to plead with the UN to demand that Khartoum lift its blockade and grant the UN permission to fly into the Nuba.

The demand was made and was predictably refused. Quinette went back to Knight Air, the blockade runners. Doug orchestrated airdrops on the most ravaged areas, using his airline's Antonovs. One mission took place over New Tourom. With the porters, she watched the plane come to a near stall low in the sky, its nose pointed upward as it dropped a blizzard of white sacks. The women swarmed into the drop zone, hoisted the heavy sacks onto their heads, and carried them into town.

After the food was distributed, the porters gathered around Quinette, singing and clapping their hands. Four lifted her off the ground and bore her through the town and set her down before a crowd of men, assembled beside a tethered cow. A young woman approached, a small mound of ashes in each palm, and while she powdered Quinette's arms and legs, a man slashed the cow's throat with a spear. Blood spewed and soaked into the dry ground. The animal wobbled and fell, thrashing its legs, and when the thrashing ceased and the large eyes stared still, the man dipped his spear into the wound, then stood in front of Quinette and flicked the blade, sprinkling her with blood. *Blessing* her. Ululations rose, hands clapped in rhythm, and she heard in those sounds a declaration that there would be no more whispers about spirits angered by the commander's union with a stranger. She was the kujur now, the rainmaker who had delivered the people from hunger.

The crisis eased. One day as she left her tukul to go to the airstrip, she found Negev waiting outside the courtyard wall with five members of her husband's bodyguard. They immediately surrounded her, two in front, one on each side, two behind, and walked with her, silent, vigilant, sandals made from tires slapping the ground. She turned to look at Negev, one of the duo bringing up the rear. "Commander's orders, missy." They shuttled her into the headquarters bungalow, where Michael stood studying his wall map. She asked him to explain the cloak of protection. He left off what he was doing and, taking her by both hands, wove his long fingers into hers. The face she loved so wore a complex expression—tender, stern, troubled.

"These men will be with you at all times. You are in grave danger."

The SPLA had sources of intelligence in Khartoum, from one of which he had received a coded report earlier in the day. Quinette having granted so many interviews, her opinions and activities had not gone unnoticed by the government. An editorial about her had appeared in the official newspaper. Among other things, it accused her of—

"I can guess of what," she said, and asked what danger she was in from an editorial.

"There are rumors you may be assassinated."

The word jolted her. At the same time she felt somehow honored. A certain light must have come into her eyes, and through it Michael must have read her thoughts.

"This is not to be taken lightly," he said, drawing her closer. "This is not cinema. Khartoum has infiltrated the SPLA. And with all these refugees coming in here, who can say who might be among them? So you will go nowhere while you are here without these men."

"What do you mean, while I'm here? Where else would I be?"

"I have decided to send you away for a time."

"Away where?" she asked, startled. She did not want to leave his side for a dozen reasons, and she was surprised that her jealousy was among them. She had thought she was over it.

"To Loki. You will be safe there, although Negev will accompany you just in case. Only a short time, long enough for us to screen these refugees. I imagine that if there are assassins among them, they would come after me as well as you. So you are not idle and bored, I suggest you talk with the assistance people about sending us more aid. And I have something I want you to do. It is not a small something." He withdrew a sealed envelope from a drawer. "Our stores of antiaircraft ammunition and rockets are very low. The need for them is as great as the need for the other things."

She took the envelope. "Another keyword?"

He nodded and instructed her to present it, as before, only to Douglas or Wesley Dare.

The following afternoon she and Negev, a sidearm concealed under his shirt, boarded Alexei's Antonov—it had landed at New Tourom after making another airdrop. To avoid problems with Kenya immigration, they were given jumpsuits and smuggled into the country as crew members. Sneaked across an international border. Bodyguards. Assassins. A coded message. Despite Michael's caution that "this is not cinema," it was impossible not to feel that she was in a movie, and the thrill of it blunted the sting of missing him, the fear that Yamila would take advantage of her absence.

To Quinette, after many months away, Lokichokio looked like what it was—a foreign country. Alexei gave her and Negev a lift to the Knight Air office. She blinked when Doug greeted her—his nose was covered in bandages. An accident, he said, sounding as if he had a bad cold. She handed him the envelope, and he passed it to Fitz, who wrote out the keyword. Actually, it was two words: Baker's Daughter.

"Michael must be a man of many facets," he said. "I didn't know he read Shakespeare."

"I don't think he does," she said.

" 'They say the owl was a baker's daughter. We know what we are, but know not what we may be.' It's from—I don't remember. From somewhere in Shakespeare."

He went to work. Once more she watched him compose scrambled words into a coherent message. So many tons of 14.5-millimeter ammunition, so many shoulder-fired missiles.

"So we've got the order," Doug said, "but no delivery truck. I'm sorry, Quinette. I really am."

She gave him a puzzled look.

"Wes and I have come to a parting of the ways. There's no way we can fly this stuff in. Not till we work out a new system."

After absorbing this disturbing news, she said, "What do I tell my husband? He needs it right away. Without it, the government will have a field day. They'll bomb and bomb and bomb."

"I know," he said under his breath.

"Can't you or someone else fly it in? The Antonov we came in on—"

"Quinette, it's complicated, but we can't carry military stuff in Knight Air planes, and Knight Air can't take direct payment from the SPLA. The operation has to be covered. And like I said, we're working out a new system. We're not going to leave you people in the lurch. That's a solemn promise, but it's going to take a few weeks to set things up."

Fitz gave her the decoded message. "Perhaps you could talk to Wes yourself. He might make one more trip. I doubt it, but maybe."

She found him at a part of the Loki airfield known as Dogpatch, a graveyard for derelict planes and home to a few one-pilot, one-plane air operators. Tara Whitcomb's Cessna was parked there, near Dare's Hawker-Siddley. A ground crewman was spray-painting the canary under the cockpit window, and the word YELLOWBIRD bled through a thin undercoat on the fuselage. Inside the shabby hangar, with Mary looking over his shoulder, Wes was hunched over a desk, laboriously typing on a laptop with one finger. They looked up as Quinette walked in with Negev.

"Well, don't y'all look stunning in that jumpsuit," Wes quipped in his grating accent.

"You might try, 'Hello, Quinette, it's good to see you.'"

"Sure. Hello, Quinette, it's good to see you." He glanced at Negev. "Who's this?"

"My bodyguard."

"Y'all rate a bodyguard?"

"Actually, I rate six."

"What brings you here from Ugga-Buggaland?"

When it came to provoking Quinette's dislike, he was Phyllis Rappaport's equal. She showed him the message. He gave it a quick look and said, "Guess you didn't hear. We're out of business."

"I heard you and Doug aren't working together anymore, not that you're out of business."

He folded his hands on his belly and tilted back in his squeaky chair. "So you've seen my ex-partner."

"Half an hour ago."

"It was me that broke his nose."

"I won't ask why."

"Good. I wouldn't of given you an answer. Know anyone interested in a right good airplane?" He indicated the laptop, on which he was writing an ad: FOR SALE—1967 HAWKER-SIDDLEY 748. Then some technical data and the price. "That's reduced as of today," he said. "A bargain."

"Wes, we've been hit hard. If they start bombing again and we don't have anything to shoot back with, I hate to think what will happen."

"*We?*" was all he said, twirling his sunglasses, his glance sidling away. She looked at Mary, who shrugged and said, "Like the boss said, out of business. At least the business we were in."

"You're here, and your plane is out there. Why can't you make one more run?"

"Y'all want an explanation, I'll give you two for your trouble. First off, my plan was to fly the hardware for six months. We did seven and change on account of I couldn't get that Hawker sold for my original askin' price. Second off, you people are a day late and eighteen thousand dollars short."

"I thought that got settled weeks ago."

"It did. What you might call a benefactor paid the SPLA's debt, but the man can't make a career out of that. What happened was, the glorious rebel army stiffed us again, the last flight we made. That makes this many times"—Fanning three fingers—"and that many times means out."

"You owe it to the people up there!" Quinette said, her voice ricocheting off the hangar's walls of corrugated iron.

"Don't lecture me, girl. We're the ones that are owed, me and Mary. I was you, I'd walk out right goddamned now, unless you want to see me forget my manners."

Outside on the scorching tarmac, she thought of five thousand refugees jammed into an exposed tent camp. It would take one plane to slaughter and maim hundreds, and Wesley Dare would leave them without a shield for eighteen thousand dollars. Such mercenary greed was beyond her understanding. She no longer disliked him, she hated him. *Forgive me, Lord, for that, forgive me.*

As she stood, perplexed about what to do—really, there was nothing she could do—a pickup truck swung across the asphalt and parked between the Hawker and the Cessna. A familiar figure climbed out and, after staring at Quinette for a second or two, walked over. Put together as always. Not a strand of tinted hair out of place. Pressed white shirt tucked into creased khaki trousers.

"I thought it was you!" Tara said. "Didn't recognize you in that." She gestured at Quinette's apparel.

"A disguise. I guess it worked. How are you?"

"Fine." Tara hesitated a beat. "Actually not. Had a run of bad luck. Bad luck with a shove from behind. Never mind. *How are you?*"

"We've had a run of bad luck, too."

"Bloody awful, I've heard. How long are you in for?"

"Not sure. A few days maybe."

"Good! We'll have a chance to talk. Sorry I can't now. A flight. Picking up your old boss, as a matter of fact."

"Ken? Ken Eismont?"

"He is your old boss, isn't he? I'll be overnighting. Hope to see you tomorrow then."

Tara began her taxi to the runway. As she shielded her eyes from the prop-wash, Quinette saw what she could do. Because the idea wasn't the product of her own mental labors—it came to her as a lyric might come to an inspired songwriter—she concluded it was heaven sent. God wanted His Nuban children to be protected and was directing her to be the agent of His will. Thus she was confident, absolutely so, that she could make it happen.

Telling Negev to wait for her, she went back into the hangar. Wes was looking at a printout of his ad.

"Would you do it if I guaranteed you'd get your eighteen thousand?"

"Jesus Christ! What part of *no* is it that you don't understand?"

"I don't know what went down between you and Doug, but I can see"—she spread her arms and moved her head to point out the ad in his hands, the run-down hangar with engine parts racked along a wall, the tired airplane outside—"that you're not on top of the world. You could use the money."

"It wouldn't be eighteen. Thirty-six. Eighteen for the flight we didn't get paid for, eighteen for the one you want us to make."

The peculiar, bashful, sidelong look. He seemed to realize that he'd taken a step back from categorical refusal—he was bargaining.

"I can't promise thirty-six. Eighteen. If I can raise a little more, you'll get it."

"Raise it!" he scoffed. "Y'all gonna hold a bake sale? A raffle?"

"Never mind the how. I know I can put it together and fairly quickly."

He swept a hard, appraising look across her face. "Wish I could be as sure of you as you are of yourself."

"Wes . . . ," Mary said, indicating a corner of the hangar with a jerk of her head. In whispers, the two conferred there for a few minutes. Mary appeared to do most of the talking, Wes with hands on his hips, looking at the floor.

"No less than twenty," he said when they came back. "Can you guarantee that?"

She made a rough mental calculation and nodded.

"Hold your bake sale right quick. The Hawker gets sold before you're done, you're out of luck. And here's the important part—you put the money in our pockets *first,* then we fly."

"And I'll have to trust that you will?"

"Trust is a wonderful thing," Wes drawled.

The next day, as she spoke to Ken Eismont in what had been the Pathways compound but was now under new management, she recalled Michael's rule: In Sudan the choice is never between the right thing and the wrong thing but between what is necessary and what isn't. She made a slight revision—in Sudan, the necessary thing *is* the right thing—which eased the twitches of conscience she experienced, despite her conviction that her plan had divine approval. She wasn't deceiving Ken and the WorldWide Christian Union to enrich herself or anyone else, but saving lives, aiding in the defense of her people. Who could fault her for using all and any means at her disposal?

When she'd approached him after breakfast, Ken was less than cordial but also less hostile than the last time they'd seen each other. At any rate, he was open to talking to her. They went into the recreation hut and sat behind the billiard table. To evoke his sympathies and improve his opinion of her, she explained the reason for Negev's presence and related the horrors that the Nuba had recently suffered. Having softened him up, she came to the point: A slave retriever was coming to New Tourom with more than four hundred Nuban captives.

"*Four hundred?*"

Nodding, she told him, with all the sincerity at her command, that her husband had sent her to Loki to find out if her former employers could arrange a redemption mission. "I was going to see Santino to contact you in Switzerland. I didn't know you were here already till I ran into Tara yesterday."

Ken removed his glasses, blew on the lenses, and wiped them with a handkerchief.

"When?"

"In a few days."

He asked if she knew what were the retriever's terms. The standard, she replied. Fifty dollars a head. "But he wants payment in U.S., not Sudanese," she added, a dryness in her mouth.

He flicked his eyebrows and glanced at the blank satellite TV, on a platform hung from the ceiling. "That's not the way we usually do things."

"I told him that. I think this is his way of rewarding himself for the chances he took. It's really dangerous up there. Maybe you could make an exception in this case?"

"Do you know this guy?"

"He's not an Arab," she answered. "A Nuban Muslim."

"I'll see what I can do," he said. "We were planning to leave this afternoon. I'll need to find out if the team can extend their stay, then go to Nairobi to put the money together. And I'd like to see if I can bring some media along. Four hundred—we've never done that many at one time."

Feeling both appalled and excited by how easily he'd been taken in, she asked him to call her on the radio a day in advance of his arrival. The captives could be assembled near the airstrip, sparing the team a long trek.

With the first hurdle behind her, she went to Knight Air and begged from Fitz space for herself and Negev on the next relief flight to New Tourom. One was scheduled for that afternoon, but it was fully loaded. To make room for them, cargo would have to be taken off. Then do it! she commanded. It was critical that she get back immediately.

Michael was furious with her for disobeying his orders. Her safety, her very life depended on her doing as she was told. He wasn't mollified by her explanation for her hasty return. He thought her scheme outlandish and didn't see how she could bring it off. She begged him to trust her. She knew what needed to be done and how to do it, but she had precious little time and would need his full cooperation. It took a while, but she brought him around.

Accompanied by her phalanx of guards and by interpreters fluent in the various Nuban tongues, Quinette spent the next three days scouring the refugee camp for people who looked the part—the most underfed and ill-clothed. Michael had loaned her a couple of men to help select the cast. Working six to seven hours a day, she mustered four hundred and ten, then assembled them and told them what she wanted them to do. It was very important that they listen carefully and follow her instructions. Through three different interpreters—a very imperfect medium—she tried to explain the connection between the roles they were to play and the delivery of the rockets, guns, and bullets that could be their salvation. Her company appeared bewildered, but the promise of payment, in the form of extra food and clothing, to be drawn from the stores of relief supplies, got them into the spirit of the thing. They enjoyed the novelty, the respite from the monotony of their existence.

She held auditions, choosing a dozen men and women who would give testimony about their enslavement. Drawing on her past experiences, she created a story for each of them, then coached them and the interpreters on what to say. From town, she picked a bright young Muslim to act as the retriever, guaranteeing him a modest cash payment.

The effort was as exhausting as managing the relief operation. Her nerves felt like overstrung piano wires. When, five days after she'd left Loki, Ken called on the radio to say that he and the team would be arriving the next morning, the audaciousness of what she was doing nearly overwhelmed her. Was it really she engineering a hoax—no other word for it—of this magnitude? She collected herself and used the remainder of the day to conduct a kind of dress rehearsal. Then she marched her troupe to the airfield and had them camp out nearby. A night in the open would add to their haggard appearance, make them look more like captives who had come a long way on foot. Inflicting more suffering on people who had suffered so much brought pricks of guilt; but the purpose demanded it, the purpose justified it. She must keep the purpose uppermost in her mind, lest she falter.

Outwardly, she was composed; inwardly, no director or playwright on opening night experienced the anxiety Quinette did when Tara's Caravan landed at about nine in the morning. Ken stepped out, wearing a soft, short-brimmed hat that looked like a codger's beach hat. Jim Prewitt, heavier, older, blinking into the mean sunlight, followed him; then came Jean and Mike; then Santino holding the prize, an airline bag of cash; and the media contingent, two correspondents and a film crew.

She greeted each of them, her Nuban dress and hairstyle drawing curious looks from the reporters, then led the group to a grove of trees, beneath which the make-believe slaves were assembled. They looked the role indeed—Quinette herself would have taken them for the real thing—and they played it as instructed, maintaining a wary silence. After introducing him to the retriever, who likewise put in a good performance, she gave Ken a list of names, whispering that she'd done some preliminary work for him. "There's a check mark by the ones who want to tell their stories," she said, her heart fluttering with one rhythm, her stomach with another. For a moment, she thought she was going to be sick.

Less than three hours later, she watched the Cessna take off and felt she could soar with it, such was her relief. A grain sack filled with twenty thousand five hundred dollars was at her feet. Two women giving testimony had gotten stage fright and forgotten their lines but remembered after some prompting from an interpreter. Otherwise, the thing had come off without a hitch. The sight of Ken typing fictions of captivity into his laptop brought a new prickling of conscience, which she salved with a prayer for forgiveness and this thought: Ken would benefit, too. The fresh publicity would garner for the WorldWide Christian Union contributions far exceeding twenty thousand.

She and Negev returned to Loki the next day. Wes said, "Well, I'll be damned," when he opened the sack and pulled out bricks of hundred-dollar bills. To make sure he kept his end of the bargain, she flew with him to the pickup point on the Uganda border and then on to New Tourom, the Hawker crammed with ammunition boxes, missiles, and launchers. Michael was waiting at the airfield. Observing the off-load, he held her and said, "You are a marvel."

In all innocence and with perfect certitude, she pointed at the sky and said she'd had a lot of help.

Her life resumed its normal pace—teaching school, ministering, tending her garden. The war had gone into a lull and, deeming it safe to travel, Fancher and Handy departed on one of their evangelizing journeys to a distant town. Michael forbade her to go. Too dangerous, he said, even with half a dozen armed men to watch over her. By this point she thought the threat of assassination was overblown, but she complied without further protest—and was glad she did when, later, she observed Yamila flirting with Michael with her eyes. Yamila's demeanor and expression underwent a dramatic change whenever he was near, the she-leopard domesticating herself instantly into a demure kitten. Illiterate peasant or no, this, Quinette thought, is a woman who knows how to lure a man.

The missionaries returned from their trip, having harvested several more souls to Christ. For the week following, they oversaw the final repairs to St. Andrew's mission. The last chips in the church's facade were patched, windows delivered by an aid plane were installed, and the brass bell and dedication plaque were polished. It looked splendid in the shimmering dust of late afternoon, the trees laying long shadows on mown grounds webbed with rock-lined footpaths leading to the school, to the tailor and carpentry shops, to the cottages where teachers would live when peace came, and to the bungalow that would shelter visiting clergy. The mission compound breathed an atmosphere of order and serenity, and Quinette and Michael gazed at it with pleasure and hope.

A rededication ceremony was held that Sunday, Fancher conducting a praise service. Quinette got chills, listening to familiar hymns made unfamiliar by African voices, African drums. Oh, they made a joyful noise! Fancher delivered a homily, promising better times, assuring the congregation that the will of God would never lead them to where the grace of God could not keep them. He concluded with a prayer for rain.

Afterward, perhaps concerned that the white minister's petition would prove efficacious and diminish his already-diminished authority, the kujur employed gangs of young people to run through town, whirling sticks tied to long cords. They made a droning sound, like ceiling fans turned to high speed. The devices, part of the rainmaker's traditional toolkit, were supposed to inspire the heavens to open.

At sundown, as she stood to stretch after weeding her vegetable patch, Quinette looked southward and saw a belt of black clouds, embroidered by lightning. It advanced with incredible speed, pulled by the high wind that drove before it, shaking the palms and baobabs, bending the tall, burnt grass in the meadows. She ran into the house just as a deluge slashed across the courtyard, accompanied by a crash of thunder. Watching the rain transform dust into mud, listening to it splatter against the makuti roof, she wondered if she had unconsciously absorbed the Nubans' superstitions, if the mountains' silences and spaces and shadowed crevasses had turned her imagination toward realms unperceived by the senses, her mind toward belief in spirits whose supernatural powers could be invoked through chants and magic; for she was inclined to give the kujur's whirling sticks as much credit as Fancher's prayer.

Michael dashed in, totally drenched, laughing. "It has broken!" he shouted, picking her up, spinning her around. "It has broken!"

He peeled off his uniform, kicked off his boots, and as the wind fell, went outside to stand naked in the rain, facing a sky twice darkened by night and cloud, his mouth open. Quinette pulled her dress over her head and joined him, drinking the rain, bathing in it. They laughed hysterically, choking as they laughed, eyes squeezed shut against the heavy wet darts that stung their faces. Then the arms of a former wrestler scooped her off her feet and carried her inside, and she knew, falling on the bed, that this would be the time. The spirits who had broken the drought on the land would break the one in her.

THE RAINS DID not fall incessantly but swept over the mountains in tightly wound, localized storms. Avoiding them, government planes resumed bombing, the Antonovs flying at altitudes beyond the range of antiaircraft guns and missiles. The reports crackling over the radio from

Michael's subcommands made it clear that Khartoum was targeting the Nuba's airstrips. Three were struck in as many days. The purpose was obvious, said Michael. The blockade had failed to stop aid from reaching the Nuba, so now the government intended to isolate it, making it impossible for relief planes to land.

A broadcast on the state-controlled radio, picked up on the shortwave, confirmed his speculations. He translated the Arabic: Sudan's vice-president had made a formal protest to the United Nations Secretary General for Humanitarian Affairs, charging that the UN relief operation was being used to channel aid not to civilians but to the SPLA . . . Reliable information had it that some of this aid included weapons . . . In the Nuba mountains in particular, planes based in Kenya were known to have delivered shoulder-fired rockets, one of which was used to down a civilian aircraft carrying oil workers . . . The nation's military forces had been ordered to strike back and were winning glorious victories on every front.

"So they are on to the game," Michael said, switching the radio off. "I am amazed it took them so long."

A fourth airfield was hit. Like the other three, the runway had been blasted end to end. Considering that the bombs were dumped, like cargo in an airdrop, from aircraft four miles up, this degree of precision was remarkable.

New Tourom's was the fifth.

The air raid came shortly after school had started. Quinette was helping Moses with a spelling lesson when the ground quivered and there came a terrible, ragged roar, followed by another, dust and dirt shaking down from the grass roof. With panicked screams, the pupils fled the building before she or Moses could shepherd them to a shelter. At the same time her guards rushed in and swept her into the nearest one. Just before tumbling into the hole, she glimpsed a wall of smoke rising above the ridgeline three miles away. Antiaircraft fired ceaselessly, but neither they nor the rockets could touch the high-flying planes. The soldiers might as well have thrown spears, and Quinette reflected bitterly on the futility of her effort. She reflected also on the futility of what Michael had done, downing the oil company plane. Had she held on to these thoughts and carried them through, she might have reached some interesting conclusions about actions that arise from deep convictions; but they exited her mind within seconds.

There was the aftermath to deal with. The bombs had fallen just minutes after a relief flight had taken off. Women had been massed on the airstrip, breaking the shipment down into portable loads. No one knew how many there had been killed, and no one would know until each household took a census to discover who was missing. Only sixteen were found alive, some barely so, and the sole advantage to such a death toll was that it gave Manfred, Ulrika, and their aides a manageable number of casualties to care for. They needed help nonetheless. Cutting bandages, disinfecting wounds, her hands dipped in blood, Quinette relived the horrors of her first experience of war. She relived the grief and rage she'd felt over Lily Hanrahan's death when she saw Nolli, her face covered with bleeding cavities resembling the pustules of smallpox. She recalled that Pearl's cousin had not answered roll call at school that morning. The girl's position in Ulrika's triage, as well as her wounds, indicated that she wasn't expected to live, an expectation she later fulfilled.

That night and into the next day, soldiers ranged through town, bursting into huts, overturning furniture, ripping up floor mats. They tore through the marketplace, knocking goods off shelves, jabbing poles into roofs. They searched the school, the shops, the mosque, the church. They questioned people, and none too gently.

Michael had been on the heights above the garrison, inspecting defensive positions, when the Antonovs came. Through his field glasses, he'd observed the bombing dispassionately, analytically, noting that three planes each made a single run, dropping their bombs with systematic accuracy: first on one end of the runway, then the center, then the opposite end. People on the ground had to be directing the pilots by radio, and that was what he'd ordered his troops to look for. He contacted his subcommands, instructing them to search for radios in their districts. The hunt went on for two days. A commander in the western Nuba reported in—a radio had been discovered and two men, Nuban Muslims, had been apprehended and summarily shot. Michael reprimanded the officer; the men should have been questioned first, then executed.

A calf betrayed Suleiman. The animal, stabled in a separate room in his tukul, got frightened when a search party entered and kicked over a straw bale. Under the bale was a hole in the floor, covered by a piece of wood, and in the hole were a high-frequency radio and an auto battery. Suleiman, however, was absent. His neighbors said he'd gone to his home village, Kologi, shortly after the air raid to visit his family. A detachment of soldiers was sent in a truck to arrest him and bring him back for interrogation.

"I should have guessed that he was involved," Michael confided to Quinette at their evening meal. "Suleiman found those airstrips, he knew their exact locations. He must have made coordination with his conspirators with the radios. But how did he get them, how did he distribute them, and how many others are in this with him? Those are the questions I need answered."

"And then there's the why," she said. "To turn on his own people this way—"

"You are being naïve on purpose? You know."

"You should have taken Kasli's advice and not mine, is that what you're going to say?" she asked, somewhat petulantly. "Who could have predicted he'd go this far? And all because a few people from his religion got converted to another religion? I don't believe it."

"Muslims think differently about religion than we do."

"He must have had other reasons."

"Possibly. All the same, I am going to have some conversations with your associates when this is settled."

She wanted to turn this conversation to another, happier topic, but it wasn't an appropriate moment. Besides, she needed a more positive sign than a missed period before she said anything.

She got it from Dr. Manfred the following noon, after school let out. In the cubbyhole that served as his office, he gave her a blood test—more accurate then a urine test, he said—and sent the sample to the cubbyhole that served as a lab. Half an hour later he said, "Congratulations!" and Ulrika hugged her. "So you see, you did not need those fertile pills."

Encircled by her security detail, Quinette floated to the mission, where she was to conduct a women's Bible study. The news lifted her out of the mixed anger and dejection she'd felt over Nolli's death. Here was a new life to compensate for the one lost. A new life inside her, binding her own more firmly still to the lives of these people, to this place.

The class was assembled under a tree. Michael should be the first to hear, but she couldn't restrain herself and, through the interpreter, told the women she was pregnant. She received a chorus of ululations. Even the grim watchdogs smiled. She opened to the tale of Sarah, miraculously conceiving in her old age, a story she thought fitting, although she was far from old. She had just gotten into it when a platoon of soldiers came running across the mission grounds, shouting in Nuban as they surrounded the church. Negev and another bodyguard seized her under her arms and, with the four remaining guards forming a cordon around her, brought her inside. Two men took up positions alongside the door, rifles ready to fire; two more stood at the windows, one on each side of the church, while Negev and his comrade all but dragged her up the aisle, as if she were a captive bride, and motioned for her to get down behind the altar, a mud-brick block. They flanked her, weapons slung to hang level from their shoulders, their fingers on the triggers.

"Negev! What is it?"

"Commander's orders to protect you, missy. There is a big trouble."

Not a minute later a burst of automatic rifle fire came from the direction of the garrison. Not a minute after that, Fancher and Handy were escorted into the church by more armed men and told to sit alongside Quinette, shielded by the altar. They had no idea what was happening, and beyond "There is a big trouble" Negev would not or could not say more.

Another round of shooting started, more intense and prolonged than the first—fusillades of gunshots interspersed with muffled explosions. "Those are RPGs," Handy said. "It must be a ground attack. We need to pray."

Which they did, Fancher calling upon the Lord to shelter them with His wings as the noise diminished, rose, diminished, and rose again, almost symphonic in its rhythms. They sat in anxious, helpless ignorance, listening to the battle's ebb and flow. "Two hours they've been at it," Fancher announced, with a look at his watch. "This is like being outside a football stadium during a game. You can hear the crowd but you don't know who's winning." That was no football game out there, Quinette thought, terrified for Michael, for the microbe of life in her womb.

The shooting changed tempo, to isolated bursts, long sentences of silence punctuated by single shots. The angles of window light grew shallow, and the racket ceased. After ten minutes of quiet Fancher declared that it was over and stood up. A soldier near him pushed him back down. They waited, Quinette feeling like a defendant while the jury deliberated her fate. At dusk the doors burst open and she heard the voice she'd feared she might never hear again. She and the missionaries were at last allowed to come out of hiding. Accompanied by several officers, Michael strode up the aisle, his uniform splotched with mud, his complexion paled by dust. His expression was like none she'd seen before—his battle face, features immobile, bloodshot eyes almost demonic, like eyes caught by a camera's flash.

"You are safe now," he said in a voice from which all wrinkles of emotion had been ironed out. "We've made an end of it."

"An end of what? An end of *what*, Michael?"

He seemed not to recognize her. Resting a hand on her shoulder, he stared at the floor, muttering, "An end of what." Then, looking up, his gaze flitted between her and Fancher and Handy. "An uprising. We got most of them, killed or captured. Kasli escaped with fifty or sixty, possibly more."

Abruptly, it got dark. A soldier lit an altar candle, so the church appeared to be illuminated for a vespers service.

"Kasli?" Quinette murmured.

"Suleiman was brought in this morning. Kasli knew he would confess, as he did, and so he was forced to make his move before he'd planned. A good thing. He didn't have time to organize. If he did, we'd be fighting for days."

"Are you saying, a coup?" Fancher asked, his face drawn by tension.

"Attempted," Michael answered, and turned to Quinette. "Kasli was to be the assassin. Yours and mine." He sat on the altar step, shoulders stooped from an exhaustion that was more than physical. "Suleiman confessed to most of it, and I have guessed the rest. My adjutant volunteered his services to the government when I sent him on that recruitment mission. Ha! What he did was to recruit men for himself. Through him, Khartoum smuggled the radios into the Nuba. They gave him his instructions. 'First, assist us in destroying the airfields'—Kasli organized the entire thing!—'next, foment an uprising of Nuban Muslims against the SPLA. In this uprising, the commander and his foreign wife will be killed. You, Major Muhammad Kasli, will then take over, proclaim loyalty to the regime, and deliver the Nuba to us.' He got Suleiman and the Muslim elders to join him. Two escaped with Kasli. We caught the other two."

Quinette sat beside him. In the candlelight, they and the missionaries and the soldiers standing all around cast huge, grotesque shadows on the church walls.

"Those two and Suleiman will be shot tomorrow. It won't be done in secrecy, oh no. I want everyone to see the consequences."

There was a prolonged silence until Fancher cleared his throat and said in a low, measured tone, "I know you've been through a lot, but this is God's house. It's not the place to issue a death sentence."

"Kasli intended to murder the both of you," Michael said. "After my wife and me, you were next on the list."

"We came here knowing the risks. We would ask you to show mercy."

Michael rose, and although he stood a step below the missionary, he was able to look him in the face. "Why?"

"For its own sake. And because executing them could create more recruits for another Kasli. And because it would create resentment and make our work all the harder."

"Your work," Michael replied, "gave those men a reason to join Kasli, and I allowed you to give it to them. So you see, all of us here made this situation. But I see no cause for mercy. Go to the graves of the women who were killed at the airfield and ask if they would show mercy."

With an exchange of glances, Fancher and Handy passed some message to each other.

"If you can't commute the sentence, could you postpone it?" asked the younger man.

"For what purpose?"

"We'd like to talk to them. We'd like a chance to bring them to Christ. Maybe knowing they're going to die will help them see the truth. Things like that have been known to happen. It's a question of saving their souls from hell."

Michael greeted this request with a look of amazement and a cold laugh. "My friends, that is precisely where I wish to send them."

The missionaries turned to Quinette, silently imploring her intercession.

"I'm pregnant," she said, casting her eyes toward her husband. He showed no reaction other than to blink and cock his head, as if he weren't sure he had heard her right. These were far from the circumstances under which she'd hoped to tell him. "I found out only this afternoon, and if I had to shoot those men myself to protect my baby, I would do it."

Both men blinked at the rawness of her statement. Or was it the illogic? For Fancher asked her meaning. How would postponing the sentence endanger her baby?

"I saw a young girl die three days ago, Nolli—" she began.

Fancher interrupted. "If you love God, Quinette, and his great commandment to love one another, you won't argue with us."

She felt as if the wires and pegs and cords holding her together had pulled out and come apart and were now reassembling themselves into some new configuration. And from this incomplete, unfamiliar form came an unfamiliar voice. "I do love Him, and I love Him by hating the people who hate Him. Ecclesiastes says there's a time for hate. Well, now is the time for some healthy, holy hate. I saw Nolli die, now I want to see them die, sooner, not later."

IN A LIGHT rain, the two elders went quietly. They said they were martyrs to their faith. One was the old man who had beaten his wife. That made it easier to watch. Suleiman was a different matter. It took five soldiers to drag that very tall man from the hut where he'd been held for the night. His hands were tied with rope and he screamed, now in Arabic, now in Nuban, now in English, screamed Allah's name, screamed that his was the Islam of the heart. The place of execution was a field near the refugee camp. Three stout stakes had been driven into the ground. The townspeople were gathered in a semicircle around the field. Anyone watching from a distance would have thought it was a festival. The formality of blindfolds was dispensed with. Quinette stood in the front, alongside Michael, and fixed her gaze on the three men as they were bound to the stakes by ropes around their chests. Through a bullhorn, her husband announced that they had been found guilty of treason and sabotage. Then he nodded to the officer in charge of the firing squad. At command, the men leaned into their rifles and fired a short burst. The bodies jerked and twitched, then, heads flopping forward, slumped down the stakes, Suleiman to his knees, the other two into a squat, dark red carnations spreading across their jelibiyas. Floating free of her body, to some point in the air, Quinette could see the crowd, the dead men, Michael, and herself. Her face did not look familiar. She had become someone she did not recognize; yet she felt that she could get to know this stranger and make friends with her.

Douglas

They have moved from the sprawling house in the foothills to a place in the heart of town that could have been its garage. It's not a bad house, Douglas thinks, a renovated adobe brick in a historic district not far from the University of Arizona campus. Anyway, it's better than where they would have had to live without the loan from his grandparents.

His mother is out of the hospital now, recovered from what everyone in the family refers to as her "illness." Why they do mystifies and upsets him. She wasn't sick. She would have been if, after running out to see the car burning with his mangled body inside, she had not gone crazy.

Douglas has yet to cry for his father. He loved and admired him. Now he hates his memory. He hates him for leaving the family the way he did, with a legacy of debts and disgrace. He hates him, not for turning out to have been a crook, but for being a fool.

No, this is not a bad little house, but he learned something about construction from his father and can see that corners were cut in the renovations. A tap on the drywall tells him it is half-inch rather than three-quarters; the floors were sanded unevenly and were thinly varnished; the shower doors, which look like glass, are plastic. It is the shoddy workmanship of illegal immigrant labor that gives, to the uncritical eye, the appearance of quality. Its cramped rooms shout that life will be constricted from now on, that the once-limitless horizons of the future have been drawn in. The whole place smells of failure. He is glad he will be away at school, at Northern Arizona University, and will not have to live here.

During his mother's hospitalization, he and his sisters stayed with their grandparents in Flagstaff. It was a blessing to get away from the reporters, from the neighbors, from the phone calls, from everything. His mother, who still walks around as if she's in a trance, stands in the middle of the empty living room, looking at the packing boxes.

"Start taking things out," she says. "I'm exhausted."

"Okay, Mom."

The first box is full of her bird books. She picks one up and tosses it across the floor and says, "Don't bother with these. I won't be using them for a good long while."

He opens a box of linens.

"I start the new job on Monday," she murmurs from behind him. "But we can consider every dime that comes in here found money. Do you understand?"

"Sure. I'll have to work for tuition."

"Do you understand, I said," she says with a ferocity that he finds unnerving.

"Sure."

She seizes him by the shoulders. "Don't you ever let this happen to you, not ever. Do you understand?"

"Sure, Mom. I'll make up for it. I'll make up for what he did."

Webs

THE SUCCESSFUL CAPITALIST is successful because he has no love in his heart, Fitzhugh thought, returning to his hut from a volleyball game. He has only the love of success. He devotes himself to work work work instead of to a woman loved with all his soul. He attempts to fill the hollow in his heart with the accumulation of wealth and what it buys, whether things or power or both; but wealth, things, and power fill it only for the moment, as water does the belly of a hungry man. The heart is empty once again, and its cravings drive him to acquire more; yet he is never gratified.

These musings had not been prompted by a revival of Fitzhugh's undergraduate philosophies; he was thinking about himself. Since the breakup with Diana, he'd dedicated all his energies to Knight Air and to the object of getting rich, modeling himself after those prime examples of *homo capitalistensis*, Douglas Braithwaite and Hassan Adid. There was no love in their lives (Adid's wife and family were little more than furniture). Love would have distracted them from the project of "growing the company," as Douglas phrased it, as if the airline were an orchard or a crop. The only difference between Fitzhugh and them was that "growing the company" distracted him from thinking about Diana and his lost happiness. Finding his assigned job of operations manager not demanding enough—he could do it with his eyes shut—he took on additional tasks, asking for, and getting, a raise in salary and in his share of net profits. With its fleet grown to twenty aircraft, Knight Air had the assets to expand its operations beyond Sudan and Somalia. Fitzhugh journeyed to the Congo and Rwanda with Timmerman to assist him in negotiating contracts to deliver aid to those markets. That was what those hearts of misery and African darkness were to an entrepreneur of humanitarian aid—markets. Watching his own fortunes rise with the company's, he didn't know at what point he would say he had enough and cash out. He soon learned that for the successful capitalist, there is no such thing as enough. His two models taught the lesson.

Two weeks ago, at Adid's behest, Douglas convened a shareholders' meeting in a Nairobi hotel. As Fitzhugh entered the conference room, Douglas took him aside and whispered, "You're going to hear some bad news, but don't worry. You'll be all right."

A vinyl-bound agenda was passed out to the participants, who included, in addition to small fry like Fitzhugh, big fry like Wesley Dare and still bigger fry like the Kenyan businessmen whom Adid had cajoled into investing in the airline. Douglas made a presentation, painting a gloomy picture of Knight Air's financial condition with the aid of flip charts. The company had grossed eight and a half million dollars in the past year, but higher fuel and operating costs had devoured a greater portion of its profits than management had expected. Now the Kenyan government threatened to take a still bigger bite. Douglas asked the investors to turn to the appendix page in their agendas and note the letter he'd received from the Kenyan Revenue Authority. It stated that Knight Air owed thirty-five percent, or more than three million dollars, in income taxes for the year. As it had done in previous years, the company could reduce the burden by deducting capital expenditures, namely the purchase of new aircraft, but the bill would still come to over two million.

Knight Air would have to be recapitalized, Douglas continued, gracing the audience with his charming gaze. He called on each investor to contribute sixty thousand dollars to help meet the company's tax obligations and its operating expenses. Without the money, management would be forced to dissolve the airline and auction it to the highest bidder, with the shareholders paid off out of the proceeds. This was more than bad news, this was shocking news. Douglas then asked for a vote on the issue of the additional investment. All in favor raise their hands. Only one went up— Wesley's.

Douglas, standing at the head of the table, looked flustered. "I'm surprised, Wes," he said. "I thought you were leaving soon."

"Hell, in for a dime, in for a dollar—or sixty thousand dollars," Wesley responded with a crooked grin.

"Not me," Adid announced, and everyone turned to him, the man with the biggest stake in the company. "To contribute that much money to pay millions in taxes, no, thank you. As the Americans say, it would only be throwing good money after bad."

The others took their cue from him and voted to dissolve Knight Air Services and put it up for sale the next day. A firm Fitzhugh had never heard of, East African Transportation Limited, bought the shares at twenty-five cents on the dollar. Except for Fitzhugh and Wesley, the other shareholders were wabenzi like Adid and thus able to swallow the losses of three-fourths of their investments. Fitzhugh found his lodged in his throat. He was frantic, out not only thousands of dollars but a job as well. How could Douglas have assured him that he would be all right? He was miles and miles from being all right, and he could not find Douglas to ask for an explanation.

Wesley, on the other hand, took his losses with equanimity, an odd reaction for a man so pugnacious. Later, in the hotel bar, Fitzhugh asked why he wasn't mightily upset.

"If a goat was tied up in front of a leopard, you wouldn't get upset when the leopard jumped on the goat and tore its windpipe out, would you? You'd expect it. Hassan's the leopard. I've been expectin' somethin' like this for a long time."

"Hassan?"

"He owns East African Transportation," Wesley said. "It's a subsidiary of his conglomerate, the Tana Group. So Knight Air is a subsidiary of the subsidiary, except now it's got a new name—Knight Relief Services—and new management. The pres-i-dent is Hassan Adid but Dougie boy Braith-waite is still the managing director."

Fitzhugh almost slapped himself on the head for being so stupid, for not seeing the sleight of hand. Hadn't he warned Douglas months ago that Adid intended to take over the airline? His only mistake had been in thinking that Douglas would be a victim of Adid's machinations, the leop-ard's prey. He was instead the leopard's partner. Never enough, he thought. The fortunes earned by the Tana Group were not enough for Adid—he had to acquire the airline and at a fire sale price. The profits earned by Knight Air had not been enough for Douglas; he wanted the financial muscle and the political clout—always handy in Kenya—that would come from being a province in Adid's empire. The American and the Somali had had a meeting of appetites. They were a hunting pair.

"Y'all will be happy to know that you're still on the team, operations manager and junior partner," Wesley said.

Fitzhugh wasn't exactly happy. He was relieved, grateful to Douglas for thinking of him, for offering those words of assurance, and somewhat ashamed of himself for feeling so grateful. If he had the integrity Diana had expected of him, he would walk away now; otherwise, he would be a junior partner in what amounted to a multimillion-dollar hustle.

"You're sure?" he asked Wesley. "How did you find out?"

"Just did a little detective work," Wesley replied and motioned to the bartender for another drink, whiskey neat. "That bullshit about owin' three million in taxes. Shitfire, Hassan could of made that bill go away with one phone call to the finance ministry. What him and Doug did was to scare those others with the idea of payin' out all that money, throwin' good money after bad."

"But why did you offer to kick in the sixty thousand?"

"Just to let Hassan and Doug know I'd figured out the scam, just to make them a little nervous," said Wesley, with another grin out of one side of his mouth. "Did y'all notice how some of them shareholders almost raised their hands after I raised mine? If they'd voted to recapitalize, that would of fucked things up but good for those two. Don't you wonder what happened to all that money?"

"Higher fuel and operating costs," Fitzhugh answered. "That much was true."

"Kinda half true. They weren't *that* much higher." Wesley gave a derisive snort. "I'll bet if I did a little more detective work, I'd find an offshore account somewhere."

"Then why don't you?"

"On account of I don't give a shit. Remember, back when we formed Yellowbird, when I said that there was a better-than-even chance those shares wouldn't make good ass-wipe? That's how come I got Dougie boy to sign a contract for that airplane. I intend to hold him to it."

In making that arrangement, Dare had perhaps overestimated his own cleverness.

After Knight Air's death and resurrection, Fitzhugh went on another journey to the Congo with Timmerman, to work out a contract for flying UN security people into that country's multiple flashpoints. Catching up on paperwork after he returned, he noticed that Tony Bollichek was back on the roster of pilots flying out of Lokichokio, reassigned as Douglas's first officer. No one had replaced him on the Somalia runs; nor were flights scheduled in Somalia for the next week. Why not? he asked Rachel—the secretary had been handling the schedules in Fitzhugh's absence. It turned out that there was no plane to fly in Somalia. Tony had been in an accident, landing short of a runway somewhere out in the desert. Though he wasn't hurt, an accident investigator had declared the G1 a total loss.

That evening Fitzhugh was drinking by himself in the compound's bar. Thoughts of Diana had mugged him, and he was soothing his emotional lumps. Douglas and Tony, back from a late flight to Sudan, joined him. He was pleased to have company. They were into their second round when Wesley walked in, ordered a pitcher of beer, and sat at their table, wearing a smirk.

"Don't think I heard an invitation," Tony said.

"Makes two of us. Welcome back to Loki. For a man who survived a right bad prang, y'all are lookin' well."

"Heard about it, did you?"

"Word gets around. Reckon you were lucky to walk away."

"Yeah."

"Y'all are a good pilot, and in the old days, you and me must of made twenty landings at that airstrip. How did you manage to come in short?"

"Bugger off," Tony said, bunching his rugby-wing shoulders. "And while you're at it, bugger Mary, now she's all yours. I seem to remember she bloody well loves it up the arse."

Dare ignored this remark and turned his attention to Douglas, who said, "I was going to let you know."

"Right nice of you. Claim filed?"

"Yup."

"Insurance company's way off in Houston. Gonna take time, and I ain't got much left in Africa. So what y'all can do, what y'all are *goin'* to do, is transfer half a mil from the company account to my personal account. Pay yourself back when the claim comes in."

"Wes, you know that's impossible," Douglas said. "Look, this isn't the time or the place."

Wesley filled his glass from the pitcher. "It sure as hell is."

"Like Tony said, there was no invitation. We can discuss this later."

"We're gonna discuss it right goddamned now, rafiki." Douglas flinched as Dare reached across the table to grip his bicep. "Don't get nervous in the service, I'm sympathetic. You got yourself into a bind. Hassan makes himself pres-i-dent, which means he's gonna pay a lot closer attention to things than when he was just the bankroller. 'How am I gonna explain to the company pres-i-dent that I signed a contract to turn over a company asset worth half a million bucks to Wesley?' That's what y'all were asking yourself."

Douglas licked the sweat from his upper lip. It was one of the rare times Fitzhugh had seen him sweat. "You can wait till the claim is paid," he said. "You'll have to."

Dare shook his head. "I've got a little yellow bird singin' to me that I'll never see that money. Guess where I was just this morning?"

"Couldn't care less," Tony said.

"Wasn't talkin' to you. At Wilson airport, having lunch at the Aero Club with a man interested in my Hawker. I looked out the window and what do I see but a Gulfstream One gettin' some work done on her. After lunch, I strolled on over for a closer look. This airplane has got new props, she's got new nose gear, she's got a new nose cone and a new paint job. And there's a fella puttin' on *new registration numbers*. A real nice job, but I recognized my old airplane." Dare looked around the table, bestowing a grin on everyone. "And I saw another thing—the hand of Hassan Adid. Got his fingerprints all over it. You couldn't figure how to get out of your fix without him knowin' about it, so you went to him and 'fessed up and asked him, 'How do I get out of this deal?' Don't reckon you told him why we signed that contract—Hassan would of thrown a shit fit if he knew what we've been doin' these last six, seven months. You made somethin' up. Y'all are good at makin' things up. I reckon he threw a shit fit as it was, but then he showed you the way out."

"Wes, nobody here is interested in your fantasies," Douglas said.

"Showed you the way out and how to get an airplane and half a million bucks as a bonus," Dare resumed, as if he hadn't heard. "First off, Hassan says that this here contract doesn't read, 'Douglas Braithwaite agrees to' and so forth, it reads 'Knight Air Services agrees to' and so forth. But Knight Air Services is no more. Next off, Hassan says, we'll make the airplane *disappear*. So when old Wes comes callin' for it, we say sorry, the plane was in a wreck, a total loss. But Wes will ask for the insurance money, and then we say, Knight Relief Services isn't responsible for any of Knight Air Services' debts. So Wes is up the creek—he's owed an airplane that doesn't exist from a company that doesn't exist. Next off, Hassan says, we fix the plane in the field, good enough to fly her back to Nairobi, where we'll finish the repairs, give her a new paint job, and change her registration. Five Yankee Alpha Charlie Sierra becomes Four Alpha Papa Yankee, registered to Knight Relief Services. Then we sit back and wait for the insurance money. Five hundred grand, and out of that we deduct expenses—kickbacks to the investigator and to the pilot for such a fine job of crashing the plane just enough to make it look good."

Tony poked Dare's shoulder. "You're saying I faked it?"

"The Houston Casualty Company is gonna be real interested in my fantasies," Dare said, ignoring Tony. "Make that transfer first thing tomorrow."

"I asked you a question, you fucking wanker."

"A good pilot could do it, and y'all are good, Tony."

The Australian got out of his seat, hooking a thumb. "Get your fat wanker ass out of here."

"Soon as I finish this," Wesley said, hoisting his glass.

A new episode in the Legends of Loki was written in the next two minutes. Bollichek grabbed Wesley's collar, and as he jerked him out of the chair, Wesley tossed beer in his face, then bashed his skull with the pitcher, removing him from the action. The table went over, Douglas fell on his back, and Wesley on him, throwing a punch that missed and another that connected. Fitzhugh wrestled him off and pinned his arms. For an old man, he was a handful.

"Got no quarrel with you, Fitz," he gasped.

"You will if you try to hit him again."

Fitzhugh let him go. Bollichek lay unconscious, bleeding from the head. On his knees, Douglas cupped his shattered nose with both hands. There was in his eyes the hurt, stupefied look of a spanked child.

Rubbing his knuckles, Wesley looked at him with something approaching pity. "Never been cut before, have you, Dougie boy? Never been hit hard in your whole sorry-ass life."

Fitzhugh drove the casualties to the Red Cross hospital. Douglas was released with his nose swaddled in gauze, but Tony was kept overnight—he had a concussion and possible skull fracture. On the drive back, Fitzhugh inquired as to how fantastic Dare's fantasies were.

"You're getting in the habit of interrogating me," Douglas replied, sounding a bit like Adid when his sinuses acted up.

"Because so many people are in the habit of accusing you of things."

"We're on solid legal ground. Knight Relief Services doesn't owe Wes a damned thing."

For Douglas, this passed as a frank admission.

"Very solid ground, with so many judges in Hassan's back pocket," Fitzhugh said, more in sadness than with sarcasm as the last drops were drained from his well of respect and admiration.

"Wes won't go to court anyhow," Douglas predicted. "He knows better."

"But he will go to the insurance company. How solid will the ground be under insurance fraud?"

After a lengthy silence, Douglas said, "I'll understand if you want to quit me." That was how he put it—not quit the company, but quit him. "You can leave tomorrow, and no hard feelings."

Fitzhugh wasn't in a position to quit. It wasn't lack of money so much as lack of occupation—the prospect of idle hours, idle days—that held him to the job. Mistaking necessity for loyalty, Douglas vowed to "make it up" to him. Precisely what was to be made up, and how, wasn't clear. The only way he could "make it up" would be to become the man Fitzhugh had thought he was; but the illusion had been Fitzhugh's fault. From real clay, he had molded a false image. It was unrealistic and, in a way, unfair to expect Douglas to live up to it. At any rate, he was no longer the American's "man." He never had been. He'd been the man of someone who never existed.

The smuggling of arms was the one soft spot in Douglas's otherwise hard business head. Shortly after Quinette's visit, he asked Fitzhugh to join him on a trip to Kampala, to meet with Ugandan bankers and bureaucrats to sew a new veil replacing the one formerly provided by the defunct Yellowbird. As before, this veil would conceal the gun-running operations not only from the UN and the Kenya government but from Adid as well. Fitzhugh wanted no part of it and declined to go. He had that now, the firmness to refuse Douglas whenever he saw fit. He said that Dare had been right—Adid as president was paying much closer attention to the airline's day-to-day affairs than Adid as investor. Douglas might get away with it for a while, but Adid was bound to find out, and when he did, whoever was involved would be sacked so quickly he wouldn't have time to clean out his desk.

"I told Quinette I wasn't going to leave them in the lurch, and I'm not going to," Douglas said.

"All the same, I think you should let Hassan in on it," Fitzhugh advised. "And if he vetoes it, which I'm sure he would, then you should forget it. Whatever you do, the less I know about it, the better."

Douglas responded with the peculiar, dull look he put on whenever he was told something he didn't want to hear.

The adventure, the thrill of the forbidden, and the conviction that he was going to change the course of the war conspired to send him off to Kampala. There he'd created a new shell company, Busy Beaver Airways. To further protect Knight in case something went awry, he'd concocted a scheme to lease a company plane to Busy Beaver. As the lessor, Knight could not be held responsible for the cargo carried by the lessee. Tony was put in charge, under the same terms as Dare had enjoyed—he got to keep half the charter fees, effectively doubling his former income.

That was far more than Fitzhugh wanted to know. He removed himself from the administrative dirty work, leaving it to Douglas to decipher Michael Goraende's messages and to invent clients to hide the source of the arms flights' income; nevertheless, he knew what was going on and was in the peculiar predicament of pretending not to know it. This mental trick might have been easier if he continued to believe that rifles, rockets, and bullets were going to make a difference.

Now, in his hut, he stripped off his sweaty volleyball clothes and stood under the combined gazes of Nelson Mandela, Malcolm X, and Bob Marley. Mandela's pricked his conscience—*The rifles, rockets, and bullets are making no difference whatsoever except to add to the body count, and there is blood on your hands as surely as on the hands of those who pull the triggers*—while Marley's struck at his sense of self-preservation—*Dot white boy gwanna get caught, mon, and you gwanna get caught wid him, den you be out flat on your brown ass.* Malcolm X was silent on the issue.

Fitzhugh flopped onto the bed. *Oh, Diana, Diana, Diana. If I quit him today, would you take me back?* Of course she wouldn't. It wasn't his association with Douglas that had killed her feelings for him; it was the mortal wound of his words. That one word—*parasite.* He hugged his pillow, seeing in his mind's eye her old-young face looking up at him. If she had died, he would not feel this unending ache, this persistent longing. He sprang up, against the temptation to lie down for the rest of the day, the rest of the month, the rest of his life. It felt the way he imagined the approach of death would feel—an icy paralysis creeping up from his toes.

He had better get ready for this afternoon's interview. CNN was doing a story about Knight for a newsmagazine show. The maverick airline that defied Khartoum's blockade, that was the angle. A towel around his waist, plastic clogs on his feet, he shambled to the showers, his bad knee throbbing. The Knight volleyball team had narrowly defeated Doctors Without Borders, Fitzhugh spiking the ball for the winning point. Coming down hard, he'd aggravated his old injury. Yet it strengthened his hope that he would learn to live with his other injury, the tear in his invisible ligaments.

Bathed and changed, looking his professional best in khakis and a polo shirt sporting the company's new color and logo, he went to the office. The reporter and crew had arrived ahead of schedule and were setting up when he came in. The office was cleaner and tidier than he'd ever seen it. Rachel, in a uniform like his, was seated behind the desktop; Douglas was at his desk while the soundman fixed a small microphone to the collar of his white captain's shirt. Fitzhugh recognized the reporter, a red-haired American with slicing green eyes, but he didn't recall her name until she introduced herself.

"You flew with us into the Nuba a couple of times," he said.

"Yeah, I did."

The soundman clipped a tiny box to Fitzhugh's belt, then ran the wire under his shirt and fastened the mike to the V in his shirt. Phyllis Rappaport sat in front of him and Douglas. She had the X-ray body of an aging fashion model or a diet fanatic. Crossing her legs, a legal tablet in her lap, a pen in her bony fingers, she began with easy questions. How long had the airline been in business? How many planes in its fleet? How many employees? How much money did it make? That led to a somewhat harder question: What did they say to the accusation, often made, that they were exploiting Africa's misfortunes to make a fortune? Douglas, rubbing the scar on the bridge of his nose, looked into the camera with his artfully artless gaze. "If bringing food to starving people and medicine to sick people and clothes to naked people is exploitation," he answered smoothly, "then, yeah, we're guilty as charged."

"What about guns?" She tried to make the question sound offhanded but didn't quite bring it off, her voice driving it like a nail.

"What about them?" Douglas asked serenely.

"Khartoum claims that aid pilots are running guns to the rebels. Any comment?"

"Sure. Khartoum needs to discredit us, and not just us—this whole relief operation. It's propaganda. I'm surprised you'd give any credence to it."

"A kernel of truth in everything, even propaganda," she said. "Some fairly advanced stuff has been showing up in SPLA hands, like shoulder-fired missiles. A lot of people, not just the Sudan government, are wondering where they come from and how they get there. Rumors are, they're being smuggled on relief planes."

"And I'm surprised you'd give any credence to rumors."

"Rumor isn't always wrong, to quote Tacitus."

Turning from the camera to Phyllis, Douglas caressed her with his gray and candid eyes. "Well, I can assure you, categorically, that this airline has never delivered any weapons to the rebels."

Sounds rehearsed but very good, Fitzhugh thought. *He lies without lying.* He tried to imitate Douglas's composure when Phyllis asked him how the pilots evaded the blockade. False flight plans? Other methods? He replied that he couldn't comment. Then, abruptly switching topics, she wanted to know if International People's Aid was a major client of the airline. Yes—in fact it had been Knight's first client. Phyllis put her pen down and folded her hands on the legal pad, suggesting that she was off the record. Had he or Douglas met Calvin Bingham, and what was their impression? Fitzhugh said the name meant nothing to him.

"He founded IPA," she said. "Interviewed him last week. He was in Nairobi on a visit. Thought you might have met him."

"Our dealings have always been with John Barrett. You spoke to him?"

She nodded. "An interesting piece of work, but not as interesting as Bingham. A kind of mystic. He's into gematria. It's kind of the Christian kabala. The idea is, you can dig out hidden meanings in the New Testament with numbers and geometry. An odd philosophy for an oil tycoon."

"So that's what he is?" Fitzhugh asked, wondering if there was a point to this digression.

"CEO of Northwest Petroleum. Canada's second-biggest oil company. A few years back Northwest was in the bidding to partner up with Sudan's state oil company to develop the fields and build the pipeline, but they lost out to Amulet Energy. Kind of intriguing."

"Actually, I don't see what's so intriguing," Douglas said. "Are we still being interviewed?"

"Sure." Frowning, she looked at her notes. "To follow up, has the SPLA ever asked you to run guns for them?"

"Are we back to that? Okay, sure they have. They ask just about every pilot and air operator who flies into Sudan."

"And?"

"And what?" Douglas was getting a bit edgy, but he managed to forge a smile.

"Have any of them agreed to, if you know."

"I don't. You'd have to ask them, if you know who they are. Why are you obsessed with this gun-running stuff?"

"It's persistence, not obsession," she said. "A while ago rebels shot down an Amulet Energy plane with a missile and killed eight foreign workers. Someone got that missile into Sudan." She shrugged, scrawny shoulders forming points, like folded bat wings. "That's a story."

"A story." As was his habit when he was under tension, Douglas wove his fingers around a pencil and tried to snap it. "It's a story to you, something else to us. Lives are at stake. Our pilots' lives. You go broadcasting insinuations about gun-running, do you think Khartoum is going to make distinctions? They'll shoot down any aid plane they feel like and then say it was carrying arms."

"Nothing of mine that goes on the air is an insinuation, it's a fact," Phyllis retaliated. "I'm a pro, Mr. Braithwaite. You needn't have any worries about your pilots' lives, not from me."

Dropping the pencil, Douglas counterfeited a relaxed pose, rolling his chair backward to rest his head against the window ledge. Through the dusty pane above, the African glare fell on his hands, spread on the desk, thumb joined to thumb. "I know you'll be responsible," he said. "Hey, you're CNN! But you should think about something, ask yourself a question. Would it be illegal, would it be *wrong* for anyone to arm the rebels?"

"Right, wrong, legal, illegal, it would be a story."

"What I mean is, Khartoum is hammering the southerners and the Nubans like the U.S. Cavalry hammered the Indians at Wounded Knee. If I'd been around back then, I would have sent rifles and Hotchkiss guns to the Sioux just to give them a fighting chance, and I wouldn't have seen anything wrong about it."

A look of excitement passed over Phyllis's face as she glanced at her cameraman and soundman to make sure they'd caught the comment. Not content with her assurance that she would never air insinuations, Douglas had to try to convert her.

"I'll keep that in mind," she said. "We need to do some filming in the Nuba. Shooting exteriors. Any flights going up there soon?"

"I've got one tomorrow," Douglas answered. "But I'm loaded to the max."

"Couldn't make it tomorrow anyway. I was thinking early next week."

"Fitz, what have we got Monday or Tuesday?"

Fitzhugh checked the schedule. "Two on Tuesday."

"They're overloaded, too, aren't they?"

He got the cue and said they were. Douglas wasn't a complete fool. Whatever this woman's reason for going to the Nuba mountains might be, it wasn't to film landscapes.

"I'll check back with you next week. Can't do it, I'll find someone else. Thanks for your time."

"There goes a real cunt," Douglas said after she and her crew left. "Oh, sorry, Rachel."

The secretary acknowledged the apology.

Fitzhugh stepped outside, motioning to Douglas to join him. "You were an idiot for making that remark about sending rifles to the Indians," he scolded. "You practically incriminated yourself."

"Oh hell, what's she going to do with it?"

"Use it to decorate the cake she's baking."

"That riff about the oil guy, what was his name? Bingham? What was that all about?"

"I don't know," Fitzhugh said, looking toward the southeast, where the weather was erecting thunderheads—white towers rising to flat black roofs in which lightning flashed, like a gigantic welder's torch. "But it is obvious what this story is all about. We aren't the first people she's talked to. She's had a word with Tara. I hate to say I told you so, Douglas, but I told you so."

"Don't go wet on me now."

He thought Douglas was the one "going wet." He was plainly anxious, if not scared.

"I had better tell Tony not to talk to her," Douglas said further. "Better tell all our people not to give her the time of the day, and no one, but no one, gives her a lift anywhere. Then there's Wes. He stands to lose as much as we do."

"No, he doesn't. He has nothing to lose."

"Yeah, he does. He's planning to leave soon. A story like this breaks, some people might ask him to stick around for a while for questioning. He won't talk to me, but he'll listen to you. He's got to keep his mouth shut."

Gangsters, Fitzhugh thought. *We are talking like gangsters.* "I told you," he said, "I want no part of this."

"Fitz, what you want and what you are are two different things."

THE MAKUTI SHELTER had sprung a leak, and rain dripped onto the tent canvas with a steady, irritating *tap-tap-tap.*

"One thing's for sure, I'm not going to miss living like this," Mary said, looking up from her camp chair. "A real roof over my head, not canvas and grass."

Dare did a deep knee bend; then, both arms outstretched, he opened and closed his hands. "Y'all are gonna be in tall cotton."

"You really think so?"

"Well, I don't really *know.* Never picked cotton myself."

"You-all know what I'm sayin'," she mimicked. "You're sure we can still do it?"

He repeated the knee bend and the flexing of his hands, trying to assure himself that the growing rigidity in them was not rheumatoid arthritis. Then he got his notebook, opened it to a page of figures, and stood over her. "We been over this before, but let's do it again. Here's what we netted from Yellowbird, here's what we'll get for the Hawker—"

"If the guy buys it," she interrupted.

"If he doesn't, someone else will. Here's what you got saved from when you were flyin' before Yellowbird, here's what we'll need to put down on a loan for a Gulfstream Two, and here's what's left over. Ain't what I hoped for, but a pretty good stake." He leaned forward and kissed the top of her head. "Thanks for stickin' with me. I sure did screw up. Saw that scam with the company shores comin' a long time ago, but that hustle with the airplane—I did not see that a' tall."

And the injury to his pride still stung, almost as deeply as the loss of the money. He hated to think of himself as an easy mark, but that's what he had been. His one consolation, and it wasn't much, was that he'd been swindled by a master like Adid. Had snot-nose Doug been the author instead of the accomplice, Dare could not have looked himself in the mirror.

"No one could have seen it coming," Mary said. "Who would have thought Doug would do this to you?"

"Wasn't much point to bustin' his nose, but damn, it sure did feel good. Enough of this talk. How about a dancin' lesson? If you're gonna live in Texas, you've got to learn the Texas two-step."

He put a tape in the cassette player, and out came the voice like no other, heartbreaking, clear, every note flawless and true. Poor Patsy Cline, another singer doomed to die in a plane crash. Holding Mary close, he led her around the small space in the front of the tent. "The woman goes backward, the man forward," he said. "One-two back, one-two back, then turn, one-two . . . All there is to it."

She laughed. "Except a two-step is out of step to this song. It's too slow."

"Don't matter." He drew her to him, his left hand in her right, his opposite arm around her waist, and sang along.

"Too slow and too damned sad," Mary insisted. "Find something that doesn't sound like an empty bar at three A.M."

He ejected Patsy Cline. While he rummaged in his cassette organizer—an empty cooking-oil tin—he heard someone approaching the tent. Footsteps in the mud, the squeak of a wet shoe on the shelter's cement floor. Mary looked at him, not alarmed but alert. Tony Bollichek, the man who forgot everything and learned nothing, including the lesson Dare imparted with a beer pitcher, had been harassing her. He had plenty of opportunity, now that he was operating out of Dogpatch for some outfit called Busy Beaver—Yellowbird's successor, Dare and Mary surmised—and shared the same hangar with them. Whenever Dare wasn't near, Tony whined and pleaded for her to come back to him, or whispered obscenities, or made threats—depending on the state of his brain chemistry at the moment. Dare had warned him that if he continued, he would suffer another skull fracture and if he ever laid a hand on her, more serious damage. "I'm going to take that seriously," Tony had replied, "so watch your back, mate."

"Who the hell is it?" Dare called to the person outside.

A female voice answered. "I'm looking for Captain Dare. Do I have the right address?"

He opened the flap. The woman, in a hooded slicker, was standing under the eave formed by the makuti roof. She extended a hand with chicken-claw fingers. "Hi. Phyllis Rappaport. Sorry for showing up at this hour, but I couldn't find you earlier. I'm with CNN. May I come in?"

Without waiting for an answer, she stepped inside and removed the hood, releasing a mass of flame-colored hair.

"Another red-headed stepchild," Dare said, rubbing his rusty curls. "Y'all been lookin' for me for what?"

A flight to the Nuba mountains for her and her crew, she answered. When? Early next week preferably, but if he couldn't make it then, later in the week would do. He glanced at Mary, who jerked her shoulders to say, *Why not?*

"This here is my first officer, Mary English. Also my fiancée."

"Pleased to meet you," Phyllis said. "So you can do it?"

"If y'all can go the fare. Passengers only, it'll be six grand to cover fuel costs and pay for our time. No checks, money orders, or credit cards. Six thousand cash."

"We can do that."

"Any particular place in the Nuba? There's only two airstrips operational right now."

"New Tourom."

"That one's in shape. They fixed it since it got bombed. But if it's raining and the runway's mud, we can't land. One other hitch—our airplane's being overhauled right now. Should be ready by Monday, but we've got a customer wants to buy it comin' then. He decides to take it, it's gone and so are we, and y'all will have to find another pilot."

"All right," Phyllis said. "Any suggestions for an alternative? I've already checked with the people at Knight, and they can't do it."

"Only one I can think of . . ." He paused, cocking his head toward the flap. "Did you hear somebody outside?" he asked Mary. She shook her head. "Must be that," he said, pointing at the wet spot on the ceiling, where the rain dripped. "I was sayin', only one I can think of is Tara Whitcomb. Is there some hot story that you're so anxious to get there, or is that none of my business?"

The reporter looked momentarily at nothing in particular—the pensive stare of someone who had misplaced a set of keys or a pair of glasses and was trying to remember where she'd put them. "You used to be Braithwaite's partner in Knight—"

"Used-to-be in capital letters, in italics, in goddamned neon," he interrupted.

"Right. I heard you had a falling-out."

"Done your homework."

"More like picking up local scuttlebutt. Everybody talks about that fight you had. I also heard you're planning to leave this fabulous part of the world."

"Like I said, as soon as the plane is gone, we're gone."

"I'd like to talk to you. Now, if you've got a minute. Or tomorrow morning. After that I'll be back in Nairobi till next week."

"I ain't runnin' for office. I don't give interviews."

Phyllis mimed pulling out empty pockets. "No camera crew, not even a notebook. Strictly off the record. What we call deep background, meaning I tell no one I talked to you. But it's a two-way street. You don't tell anyone you talked to me, and if you fuck me, I'll turn around and fuck you"—she gave him an ironic smile—"metaphorically speaking."

"Glad to hear that," Mary said, returning the smile. "Let's hear what you're fishing for first."

The reporter helped herself to a chair—*like she owns the place,* Dare thought. "I've heard that Knight has been running guns to the SPLA, weapons disguised as humanitarian aid. There's the fish. I don't like to waste time, so what do you think? Keep fishing or cut bait?"

"Cut bait," Mary answered without hesitation. "It's an urban legend."

Phyllis said, "I'm all for female solidarity, sister, but he's the captain. So what about it, Captain Dare? Urban legend or no?"

Dare lit a cigarette. He couldn't remember if it exceeded his five-a-day ration. "Deep background, that's what you said?"

She nodded.

Dug-lass Negarra! Wes-lee Negarra! The shouts of Michael's troops on that day the gunship was downed reverberated in his brain. Negarra—blood brother. A man should be prepared to lay down his life for his negarra. It was another word for loyalty, for a solemn contract between two men, and Douglas had broken it. "Here's the deal—y'all don't use anything I tell you before we're out of here."

"Wes!"

He turned to Mary: "Lyndon Johnson had a sayin'—Don't get mad, get even. I got mad, now I'm gonna get even." And then to Phyllis: "Soon as the airplane gets sold and we're out. Could be a week, could be two. You don't use it till then."

The reporter paused for a beat, then said, "Fair enough. I'll need a couple of weeks to put it together anyway."

"And if y'all fuck me on that, I won't fuck you back—I'll make you sorry you ever drew a breath. I know some folks who would be happy to run your skinny butt over on a Nairobi street just as a favor to me."

"Fair enough again. I never did look both ways, and I don't intend to start."

"I've got records—bank transfer records, flight schedules, dates. I've got photographs and videos of some of the runs we made."

"Oh, for Christ's sake, Wes—"

"Save the lectures for later, darlin'," he said to Mary.

Phyllis sat up straight. "Photos? *Videos?*"

"All in livin' color," he said.

A WET-SEASON sunrise, today's was a spectacle prolonged by the clouds walling the horizon—a glow like the gold in a refiner's fire shading off to orange and pink, and then the empyrean gold again, gilding the edges of the cumulus, billowing below cirrus that resembled paint brushes dipped in pastels. An altogether glorious symphony of light and changing color. Fitzhugh's spirits rose with the sun after a night of agitated dreams and spells of wakefulness, postmidnight arguments with himself as to where his duty lay and to whom. He'd come to a resolution, finally, and the beauty of the dawn somehow confirmed it. The red African mud clung like glue to his boot as he walked to the compound's mess, but he felt light-footed and relieved, as though the thing he had determined to do were already done.

He ate a hearty breakfast of bangers and eggs with fried tomatoes, then, over a leisurely cup of coffee and a cigarette, rehearsed what he was going to say, anticipating Douglas's responses, thinking of arguments to counter them. Alexei and his crew came in, closely followed by Phyllis Rappaport and hers. The cameraman and soundman were lugging their equipment in banded aluminum cases; the reporter had a valise slung over her shoulder and carried a cardboard box by the twine tied around it. She blew out her cheeks when she put it down on the bench at one of the tables. While she sat beside it, the soundman got her breakfast for her. This could have been a normal courtesy—taking care of the boss—but Fitzhugh assumed differently: She did not want to let the box out of her sight for so much as a minute. As she turned her head, facing him from across the patio, he waved. She returned the wave. He got up, topped off his coffee mug, filled another, and went to her table.

"Good morning, Phyllis," he said, remaining on his feet. "You are catching the eight o'clock to Nairobi, yes?"

"We are."

"So did you find someone to take you in next week?"

She hesitated before answering that she had; but she didn't volunteer the pilot's identity. Not a pleasant woman, but one to be trusted, Fitzhugh thought. She was keeping her word to Wesley.

"When does your story air?" he asked offhandedly. "We get CNN here on satellite."

"I've got some work to do on it yet. When it airs is up to the editors. Stay tuned."

"We will," Fitzhugh said, and left.

In a tattered terry-cloth robe, one side of his face lathered in shaving cream, Douglas answered his knock.

"Well, there's service," he said as Fitzhugh handed him the coffee. "What's up?"

"I'll wait till you are done."

He sat beside the bed while Douglas shaved. The tukul was luxurious, neat and homey compared with the quarters of most aid pilots and aid workers. The chairs, the nightstand, bedstead, and bureau, shipped up from Nairobi, were of carved hardwood and lent an atmosphere of permanence. Clothes hung from a bar under a shelf, shirts facing in the same direction. There were photographs on the bureau, one showing a middle-aged couple, a buxom woman and a tall man. In another the same man, years younger, looking almost like the present Douglas's twin, was in field clothes with a gun crooked over one arm. Beside him stood a teenage boy, also carrying a gun. A dog posed in front of them. Many dead birds were spread on the ground. Mountains in the background. Recalling a comment Wesley had made some time ago, Fitzhugh found it interesting that there were no pictures of Douglas in his U.S. Air Force uniform, or of the plane he flew in the Persian Gulf War. Pilots always had photos of their planes.

"This picture," he called into the bathroom. "With the dog. You and your father?"

"Yeah. That was taken, it must be twenty years ago." Douglas came out, toweling his face. "My dad loved bird hunting and my mother loved bird watching. She was always arguing with him to stop shooting them. Helluva wing-shot. The man never missed, I mean, *never* missed." He smoothed his tousled hair with a palm and took a chair, extending his legs with the movement that always reminded Fitzhugh of a cat, stretching. "So what's with the crack-of-dawn visit, the coffee?"

"I went to have that talk with Wesley last night."

"Good. I put the muzzle on Tony. What did Wes say?"

"To me, nothing. To Phyllis, everything."

Douglas popped his lips two or three times and gestured to him to continue.

"She got to him first. I was near his tent when I heard voices inside. Phyllis's is as distinctive as Wesley's. I hung outside for as long as I could stand it in the rain. They were still talking when I left, but I'd heard enough."

"Which was what?"

"I couldn't hear every word, of course. Wesley is going to fly her to the Nuba on Monday. Just before I left, they were discussing the thirty-six thousand that Barrett paid to Yellowbird. She sounded very interested in that. I can see why. How sexy if she can prove that an aid agency's funds went directly to pay for arms deliveries."

"Damn it! Goddamn it! You should have talked to him earlier. Right after we talked."

This was one of the responses Fitzhugh had anticipated. "You are not going to tell me what I should have done. It would not have made any difference anyway. You made this mess because of the things you should *not* have done, and you know what they are."

Douglas said nothing, looking at the mat beside his bed. He stood, picked up a clot of mud that Fitzhugh had tracked in, and crossing the room, dropped it in the wastebasket.

"So that cunt wants to drag Barrett into this, but how does she prove it? All she's got is Wesley's word."

"Considerably more, I'm afraid," Fitzhugh said, watching him stoop to pick up more chunks of dirt. "I heard Wesley say he would tell her everything and *show* her everything. He had his records—the bank transfers, the flight schedules, the dates. And also photographs and videos."

Douglas stopped housecleaning and faced Fitzhugh, hands in the pockets of his robe. "Photos and videos of what?"

"Of Yellowbird missions. He said he would give them to Phyllis, and I believe he has already. I saw her this morning at breakfast. She was carrying a box about this big"—he indicated its size—"and wouldn't let it out of her sight. The videocassettes, photos, the records—that all must have been inside."

"Wes took pictures? He made videos? I made a few runs when Mary was on leave, and I never saw any cameras."

"Mary was the artist," Fitzhugh said in a droll voice. "You've seen her. She takes pictures of everything. They probably were going to be souvenirs. Now they will be put to another use."

"Oh, yeah. A real prize for a TV reporter. The next best thing to being an eyewitness. Wes had to be crazy to let Mary do that. Videos!" Douglas flung an arm, knocking the coffee cup off the arm of his chair. "Son of a bitch!" He wiped up the spill, then took off his robe and boxer shorts, baring his flat, cream-colored ass, opened a bureau drawer, almost pulling it out entirely, and got into fresh underwear. "Lives, our pilots' lives. Wes doesn't give a shit about them, he'll risk them just to get back at me. She doesn't give a shit—it's only a story to her. A cunt and an asshole. Two cunts and an asshole." He went to the bar from which his clothes hung, started to put on a shirt, and then threw the hanger against a wall. "Videos, for fuck sake!"

"Please calm yourself, my friend," Fitzhugh said.

"Calm myself? Everything we've built up—a twenty-minute segment on a newsmagazine show. Know what twenty minutes is on TV? A goddamned eternity. They get CNN in Khartoum, the whole fucking planet gets CNN. We're talking big-time here. The papers will pick it up, and we'll be . . ." He grabbed the shirt he'd thrown onto the bed and tossed it to the floor. "Khartoum couldn't order better propaganda. That's what she is, a propagandist for those bastards. Everything we've built up, and you're telling me to calm myself? We'll lose our UN contracts, the UN will boot us out of Loki, and we'll be lucky if Kenya doesn't revoke our license."

Fitzhugh raised his palms. "I know what is at stake. You need not go on about it."

Douglas put his trousers on, picked up the shirt, and buttoned it crookedly, shirttails hanging out as he paced, disheveled and distracted. Fitzhugh had never seen him like this. Facing the possible ruin of his world, he had none of Tara's dignity when she faced the certain ruin of hers. He was almost comical.

"I have thought what you should do," Fitzhugh said. "What you must do."

Douglas noticed that he was in disarray. He fixed his buttons, tucked in the shirt, and in the process, collected himself. Falling back into the chair, long legs going out with a languid movement, he said, "Yeah, stop that story from getting on the air, that's what."

"No."

"We have to get hold of that stuff. Without it, what does she have? Dare telling stories. Then all we have to do is deny everything and point out that Dare's on a personal vendetta. It'll blow over in a couple of days."

"And how will you do that?" Fitzhugh asked. "Break into CNN's office in Nairobi?"

"Yes."

"And of course you know people with the required skills."

"No, but Hassan does. Thugs in Special Branch or the Criminal Investigation Division who moonlight."

Fitzhugh realized that he preferred the addled Douglas to this one—icy, calculating. "Which would require letting Hassan in on our little trade secret. Or would you expect him to arrange this burglary without asking the reason for it?"

Douglas said nothing.

"My thought does involve letting Hassan in on the secret, but no melodramas about break-ins, yes? You are willing to listen?"

"I'll listen to any good idea."

"The first thing you must do is end the gun-running operations, and you can do that right now, with one word to Tony. Then you go to Hassan, straight away, and inform him of the story Phyllis is working on. You tell all, but you assure him that Knight is no longer involved in these activities. I will go with you if you wish. And we both offer to resign."

Douglas jerked his head forward. "Come again?"

"We offer to resign for the good of the company. Knight Relief Services should be safe from any actions from the UN or the Kenya government, because all this took place under Knight Air Services. But of course it will be noticed that the management people are the same, so we remove ourselves before the story breaks. We retain our interests in the company but not our positions. I think Hassan would want us out regardless. Possibly we can persuade him to put us on suspension and rehire us at a later date, but the offer of resignation must be made. We have some time—Phyllis hasn't finished yet, and she herself doesn't know when the story will be broadcast, I asked her this morning. When it is, Khartoum will react as we anticipate—call on the UN and Kenya to do something. But Hassan will be able to say that he discovered the illicit operations and put a stop to them and took action against those involved. Accepted their resignations, suspended them, whatever. Now it is possible that Kenya, to placate its neighbor, may wish to go further. It may ask you to leave the country, it may take some legal action against me. But Hassan knows everybody who is anybody in this country's government, and I'm sure he can persuade them to go easy. It will cost him some money—this is Africa—but he can do it if anyone can."

Douglas's reaction was difficult to read—he looked on impassively. "You must have been up all night."

"Most of it."

"And what do we do with ourselves after we resign? Thought that out?"

"Not quite. If Hassan agrees to take us back on after things cool off, that problem will be solved. Otherwise we'll just have to think of something."

"How about the Nuba? What do those people do? Go back to chucking spears at gunships and bombers?"

"You know, for all your fine sentiments," Fitzhugh said, "I believe that deep down in your white boy's heart you think Michael Goraende is a dumb African nigger who cannot wage his war without you. He is a resourceful man. I am confident he'll get on all on his own."

"Happy to hear you're so sure. The Nubans' lives are at stake, too."

Fitzhugh sighed. This redoubt of the American's altruism, this crusader who dwelt inside the entrepreneur, could be the hardest to overcome. "I have given you my ideas. Maybe Hassan has some better ones. In any event, you must go to him and clear things up now. If you don't, I have no choice but to quit. I'm prepared to do it immediately."

After pondering the ultimatum, Douglas said, "There's an old saying—when the decks are awash, follow the rats."

This comment was predictable, Fitzhugh had expected something like it, but it was disappointing nonetheless.

"Sorry, Fitz," Douglas said into his silence. "Sorry for that. I'm a little—I'm not myself right now."

"Whoever you are, take my advice."

Douglas sat in thought. A breeze sneaked through the shutters and stirred a tuft of his light brown hair; it rose shining in the slatted light and fell obediently back into place. "All right. I'll talk to Tony right away, tell him to stand down, then I'll fly myself to Nairobi."

"I would prefer to go with you," Fitzhugh said.

"Hassan is a busy guy, I might not get to see him today. I need somebody to mind the store."

"You might need the moral support more."

Douglas went to the mirror and brushed off his collar. In the reflection, Fitzhugh saw his knowing smile. "What you mean is, you don't trust me to go through with it when I'm sitting there, eyeball to eyeball with him."

"Very well. Yes, that's what I meant."

He turned around, the smile fading. "I got myself into this, I'll get myself out."

Beyond the Rivers of Ethiopia

THE UKRAINIAN, a dark-haired man with coal dust on his jaws, arrived Sunday night, on the same Kenya Airways commuter that carried Phyllis Rappaport. The next morning Mary brought him to Dogpatch, where Dare waited with the Hawker's records tucked under an arm. He steered his customer to the plane, which the ground crew had finished cleaning, inside and out, an hour ago. It looked so good that Dare was almost sincere when he said he hated to part with it. The Ukranian examined the interior, from the cockpit to the rear of the cargo bay, then did a thorough walk-around outside, tugging the flaps, inspecting the props, the undersides of the wings, the wheel wells. He frowned at a water jug and a few plastic bags that some sloppy ground crewman had left lying beneath the left wing, but the plane was in perfect condition. Going into the hangar, Dare presented the folder containing the aircraft's maintenance records and documentation. The Ukrainian studied them as if he were cramming for a test.

"A lot of hours on these engines," he remarked at one point.

"Completely overhauled—hell, damned near *rebuilt*. Mechanics finished up only yesterday. New O-rings, new props, the works." Dare heard the overeagerness in his own voice and cautioned himself to sound a little less motivated. "Here's the record of the overhaul," he added, tugging at some papers, "but the best thing is to take her up for a little test drive. Take the controls, get a feel for her yourself."

"I am not aviator. Businessman," he declared. "But I will make offer now, then tomorrow, you fly me to Nairobi. Everything is okay, I will buy, we take care of paperwork, registration."

"And the offer is—?"

"Two hundred fifty thousand."

Dare bowed his head and let out a long, regretful sigh.

"Good price for Hawker-Siddley this old, this many hours," the Ukrainian said.

Dare regarded the man's face, with its three-day growth, its sharp, slightly Asiatic cheekbones, its black eyes like buttons, and knew he had no hope of getting his asking price, three hundred. He tried for it nonetheless. The Ukrainian dipped into his briefcase, pulled out a three-ring book of oversize checks, and asked Dare how to spell his name.

"Take or leave," he said, handing over a check, dated for the following day. It was an old tactic, but the sight of the number 250,000 had the desired effect. They shook on it, then the man took the check back, saying he would hold on to it until tomorrow. If the plane performed as advertised, the money was Dare's.

"We could fly to Nairobi right now," Dare said. "Why wait?"

"I have here more business for today. Tomorrow."

"So how do I do as a used-plane salesman?" he asked Mary after dropping their buyer off at the old Pathways camp, where he was staying.

"Better than you did as an airline executive."

"Sweet thing! Honey bunch!" he said, clowning it up, bending his twang into curly-cues of sound. *Sah-weeet thang! Hawnee buuunch!* "That's over and done. Come tomorrow, we're gonna have us seven hundred grand in the bank. You ought to look a lot happier than you do."

"The point is, I am now completely dependent on you," Mary declared. "You're my sugar daddy."

"We're gonna be man and wife. Property in common."

"And that reporter—that doesn't make me real happy."

"Well, it does me. Wish I could be here to see Dougie boy's face when that shit hits the fan."

"Talking about her, do we still fly her today?"

"Hell, no. I ain't riskin' our investment, not for no lousy six thousand."

"Not for *any,*" Mary corrected. "We'd best tell her. I think Tara is free, and she could use the money."

"All right, and then we celebrate. I'll get the bartender to open early."

"No celebrating until tomorrow," Mary said. "When we deposit the check, that's when we'll celebrate. And do you know what you're going to do?"

Dare started toward the Hotel California compound to see Phyllis. "Not a clue, but I know you'll tell me."

"You are going to buy me a new dress. Then you're going to get a suite at the Norfolk or the New Stanley and order a bottle of Dom Perignon from room service. You are going to take me to dinner—your choice, but it had better be four stars. And finally, you are going to take me dancing, and no Texas two-step. You want to play sugar daddy, I'll show you how it's done."

"I'm not any sugar daddy, I'm your goddamned fiancé," Dare said.

*   *   *

FITZHUGH LAID HIS HEAD on the desk. Having "minded the store" for five days on his own, he was tired. Now, in the muggy heat of a rainy-season afternoon, he had to juggle tomorrow's and Wednesday's flight schedules because Alexei's Antonov was grounded in Sudan, mired in a runway that was supposed to have been serviceable but turned out to be eight hundred meters of muck. Dealing with such problems—ordinary in the context of African bush aviation—took his mind off more serious issues. There had been no word from Douglas until Saturday afternoon, when he called on the satellite phone. His message was guarded and, at eight dollars a minute, brief. He had met with Hassan, it had been an ugly scene, but Hassan had come up with some "fresh ideas" on resolving their predicament that wouldn't require any resignations. They were working things out, and that would keep him in Nairobi until the middle of next week. Fitzhugh was to keep him informed of any new developments.

There had been none, except that Phyllis had returned to Loki last night. He assumed she was now in the air with Wesley, heading for the Nuba. Douglas's call had given him cautious hope for a clean resolution of the current mess. He would have liked to hear Adid's "fresh ideas" firsthand but was glad he'd been spared the scene that preceded their presentation.

He went to the coffee urn to fortify himself for the rest of the afternoon. A liquid resembling melted asphalt leaked from the spigot.

"Rachel," he said, "I have got to get these schedules finished, and I can't do it on this."

"I will make a fresh pot. But you know you have to be at the UN flight office in just ten minutes."

She raised her appointment book.

"I completely forgot. *Asante.*"

Distracted, I am too distracted, he said to himself, driving to the UN compound for a meeting with the flight coordinator about changes in the airstrips where UN-authorized flights were permitted to land. A pickup appeared behind him, lights flicking, horn honking. He waved to the driver to pass. The vehicle swung out and came alongside, a woman at the wheel signaling to pull over. This he did, the pickup parking in front of him. Pamela Smyth sprang out and ran toward him through the mist of laterite dust.

"Fitz! I have been looking for you! Do you have a plane and crew available? It's Tara!"

"Trouble?"

"She called in a Mayday half an hour ago, and I haven't been able to raise her since." Leaning into the window, Pamela clutched his arm. "She's gone down somewhere. We need a plane for a search."

"Gone down?" Somehow he could not imagine Tara Whitcomb crashing. "Gone down where? Did you get coordinates?"

"Only part . . . wrote it down—At the office. Please follow me."

He almost said, "But I am late for a meeting," and then made a U-turn.

Tara's office was a tin shack near the Dogpatch hangar, in front of which a twin-engine plane was parked. Fitzhugh entered the shack, and then it registered on him that the plane was Dare's Hawker. Freshly painted and washed, he hadn't recognized it at first glance. Dare's trip must have been delayed or called off.

Pamela was more collected now, though her voice quavered as she said, "This is all I got from her," and showed him a scrap of paper on which she'd written one set of GPS coordinates, which wasn't very useful without the other set.

"Tell me what you heard," Fitzhugh said, looking at the wall map.

"She called in the Mayday at"—Pamela went to her radio log—"at twelve-oh-five. She sounded quite scared, and you know Tara—she never sounds that way. There was something about fire, and then she repeated the Mayday and gave that set of numbers and then the radio went dead. All I got was static, and another noise, like a screech, a split-second screech, and then nothing."

A morbid silence pervaded the room. Fitzhugh knew what that screeching noise must have been—the sound of impact. He was semiliterate in map reading, but he stared at the map regardless, trying to divine where Tara might have crashed.

"Where is her flight plan?" he asked.

"Won't do you any good. It's false. She was headed for a no-go zone. The Nuba mountains, Zulu Three."

"Zulu Three?" His question sounded more like an exclamation.

"Yes."

"What was she taking there?"

"What bloody difference does that make?" Pamela said. "Besides, it was who, not what. Three passengers. A woman and two men. Journalists. They'd chartered her just this morning, a last-minute thing."

Fitzhugh felt slightly nauseous.

A firm look gathered on Pamela's face. "It's Knight's responsibility to look for her. If you don't have a plane available, divert one. You people are responsible for this. In the old days she never would have taken a charter like this, at the very last minute, if—"

"We're responsible," Wesley said, swinging through the door with Mary. "It was our charter." Fitzhugh and Pamela stared at him. "Loki tower picked up the Mayday. It's all over town. Okay, Pam, give us what you've got."

She repeated the information she'd given Fitzhugh. Dare asked for Tara's takeoff time. Nine forty-five, Pamela replied.

Taking the paper with the coordinates, Dare went to the map. "If she was flying the standard route," he murmured, tracing a course with a pencil, "at a Caravan's cruising speed—one eighty-five, right Pam?" Pamela confirmed the speed, and Wesley took out a pocket calculator. "That would have put her somewhere in here when she called the Mayday." He drew a small square on the map. "Fits with the coordinates she gave you— that line runs right through here. It's a valley, pretty flat. If she still had control, she might have been able to make an emergency landing."

"That's very near New Tourom," Fitzhugh said.

"Middle of the square would be about thirty miles southeast. Arab nomad country."

"We could radio Michael. It's near enough for him to send out a search party."

"Too risky," Dare said. "There's an army garrison here, another one here"—he jabbed with the pencil—"if they intercept the message. We *do not* want them to know there's a plane down in the area. They'll have patrols crawlin' all over. Y'all heard the word *fire*," he said to Pamela. "She was on fire, she had a fire? What?"

"I don't know. Fire, that's what I heard."

"How about 'taking fire.' 'We're taking fire,' somethin' like that."

Pamela gnawed her lip. "It could have been, I don't know."

"See, you thread a kinda needle flyin' into that airstrip, between those two garrisons. Don't have to stray too far off course to get smack over one or the other. And that close to destination, Tara would of been into her descent, seven, eight thousand figure. In range."

"But it was probably some mechanical failure," Fitzhugh said, unwilling to entertain the possibility that Tara had been shot down; for if she had been, it meant that no one on that small aircraft had any chance of surviving.

"From what Pam said, it would of been a catastrophic failure," Dare said. "But there's not a pilot in Africa more careful about maintenance than Tara."

"The UN has planes at Malakal, that's close," Pamela said. "We could ask them to send one to search the area."

"They'll tell y'all to wait till they get Khartoum's okay to enter a no-go zone."

"And you might as well wait for Khartoum to invite the pope for a visit," Mary scoffed.

"You're ready to fly?" Pamela asked.

"Ground crew fueled the plane early this morning," Dare said. "How about it, Mary girl. I ain't doin' this without your say-so."

"It was our flight, could have been us," she said. "Only option I see is the one I couldn't live with."

Fitzhugh heard Wesley say in an undertone, "Picked a winner this time." He was obviously proud of her. So was Fitzhugh—and ashamed of himself. He felt he had somehow willed this disaster to happen, as though a desire to be rid of Phyllis for good and all had taken refuge in his unconscious mind and petitioned the fates to make it happen. He asked Dare to go along—"another pair of eyes."

Wesley shook his head. "This one could get dicey. Best thing for you is, park yourself by a radio and wait to hear from us. Pam, what's your frequency?"

She gave it to him, and he and Mary walked out. Fitzhugh followed them to the plane, asking Dare to reconsider.

"Listen, we've got to search at low altitude. If she was shot down, the troops who did it could still be in the area. We'll risk our butts, no one else's. Y'all monitor the radio."

IN THE HANGAR, Nimrod filled a duffel bag with tins of food, granola bars, a first-aid kit, and plastic water bottles stuffed in fertilizer bags to prevent breakage, then lugged it to the plane. He also volunteered to help them look.

"Damn, sure are a lot people wantin' to live dangerously today." Dare crunched the small man's shoulders. "No way, y'all got a wife and kids."

He and Mary were airborne a quarter of an hour later and, after making their turn, soared over the Mogilla range into Sudan. He called Pamela for a radio check, punched his waypoint into the GPS, and climbed toward twenty-one thousand feet, the savannahs and cattle pastures of eastern Equatoria falling away and away, until they showed as a sheet of wet-season green stretched to a horizon lost in haze. He went on autopilot and gave Mary his plan: descend to five thousand at the point where he thought Tara had gone down, decrease airspeed, conduct a box search, the plane flying in ever-widening squares.

"We'll be there in two hours. It'll be gettin' late, and at that level we'll be suckin' up the fuel, so I figure we'll have ninety minutes max search time before we've got to call it a day."

"And if we do spot something?"

"If it's a muzzle flash, we get the hell out of there. Looks like a wreck, we go down for a closer look. We see signs of life, we give 'em a wing-wag, then you take the con. Y'all are my airdrop expert, since you flew 'em for the UN. Make a pass at seven hundred, five if you can, I harness myself in at the aft cargo door and kick out the survival gear." That there were survivors, Dare thought, was like the existence of unicorns: more a conceivability than a real possibility; but for him the conceivability was sufficient. It was a matter of keeping the one faith he believed in. "If we don't see any Sudan army in the area," he went on, "we radio the location to the Archangel and hope the wrong people ain't listenin' in. We tell him to send some people to evacuate the casualties to Zulu Three. We land and medevac 'em to Loki. It'll take a while for the troopers to get 'em to the airstrip, so count on an overnight stay."

"And there goes our customer and a quarter of a million dollars. We're so goddamned noble, I can hardly stand it."

"Time comes, I'll radio Pam and ask her to pass the word to him that we'll be delayed twenty-four hours. Figure he won't find another Hawker that quick."

They flew on. Cruising altitude, his natural habitat, the clear, cold realm where he thought clearly, where he was in control, where he knew what to do next. Not ten minutes after this smug thought passed through his mind, the left engine started to run rough; moments later, the fuel pressure began to drop drastically. Warning lights flashed on the control panel.

"Son of a bitch! Quick, get out the emergency checklist," Dare said.

Moments after they began the check, the engine quit cold.

"Wes! What the hell is happening?"

"Got no idea," Dare said, his heartbeat springing into the triple digits. He willed it back down to a normal rate, then tried to restart the engine. Nothing. A sentimentalist might have kept trying, a sentimentalist might have hoped that the gods of the air, moved by the compassion that had moved him and Mary to undertake this mission, would show him what the problem was and how to fix it. The unsentimental Wesley Dare put the plane into a hundred-and-eighty-degree turn, then radioed his situation to Pamela and told her that he had to abort the search. He called Loki tower. "This is Yankee Bravo Three Yankee Zulu. I've got engine problems and I'm coming in on one engine. Have the crash trucks standin' by."

"*Roger that,*" replied the disembodied voice.

Mary reached across the pedestal and touched his arm, her fingers damp against his skin.

"I've landed on one before, lots of times," he said. "Nothin' to worry about."

They finished running the emergency check. It did not indicate a fuel leak. It did not tell them anything. All they knew was that fuel was not getting to the stalled engine.

"What do you think happened?" asked Mary, staring at the warning lights.

The gears of Dare's efficient brain engaged and drew a mental schematic of the Hawker's fuel system—tanks, fuel lines, pumps. He could think of only one explanation why the engine wasn't running.

"Think we've got a malfunction in both pumps," he said.

"Overhauled just last week and both pumps go?"

"Maybe African workmanship. A.W.A., darlin', Africa Wins Again."

A moment after he made that comment, Dare recalled the day he and Doug had landed at Zulu Three and discovered that the villagers had stolen fuel and put rainwater in the drums to conceal the theft.

"But maybe it's somethin' else," he said. "Contaminated fuel. Maybe there's muddy water in the starboard tank. That would cause the pumps to fail."

Impossible, Mary replied, reminding him that they had drained the system before taking off. Any contaminants would have been expelled then.

Nevertheless, he was sure of his diagnosis, and as he flew southward, backtracking to Loki, he pondered how the contaminants could have gotten into the tank. Again, he made a mental sketch of the fuel system, but this time it wasn't any technical analysis that gave him an answer; his mythic bird, DeeTee, gave it with four words: water jug, plastic bags. He switched from the tower's frequency back to Pathway's and asked Pamela to put Fitz on.

"Listen up, rafiki," Dare said. "It's my fuel pumps—"

"Yes, yes, your fuel pumps," Fitz said. "What about them?"

"They ain't workin'. I'll explain later," Dare said. "In the trash barrel by the hangar there's a water jug, the kind you take on picnics, and some plastic bags. Take them out and hold them for me till I get in, and if there's anything in the jug, don't empty it."

There was a static-filled pause before Fitz replied, "What is this about a picnic? I don't understand you."

Dare repeated the request and, thinking aloud, added, "Whoever left those things did it because he had to clear out in a hurry."

That only confused Fitz further. "I read you loud and clear, Wesley, but what are you talking about?"

"Never mind. Just get that stuff out of the . . ."

A sudden sputtering in the left engine cut him short. Mary rapped his shoulder and pointed at the fuel pressure gauge—it was falling. Dare's heart rate jumped back to three digits; this time, he could not lower it by force of will. He pulled the "Jungle Jepps" from between his seat and the pedestal and tossed the book into Mary's lap.

"There's an old airstrip east of here, Echo One. Find it. Give me the coordinates. We're gonna have to put down there."

As Mary flipped through the diagrams of Sudan airfields, he made a hard left turn, then pushed the yoke forward to lose altitude.

"Thirty miles out, bearing one five five," Mary said, her voice strained.

Dare adjusted his course, descending sharply. "What else does it say?"

" 'Caution: No longer maintained. For emergencies only,' " she replied. " 'Tall grass, forty foot trees at both ends and both sides of runway. Very uneven. Treacherous at southeast end.' "

"Well, this sure is an emergency," he said. "Dump fuel."

While she did that, Dare called in to Loki tower, reporting that he was about to lose his second engine and was going to attempt an emergency landing at Echo One. He have the coordinates, in case the old airfield was no longer on the map. The engine was coughing, but it was still running, a fact he could attribute only to the intervention of the gods of the air or his luck. That happy situation wasn't going to last, but the Hawker had a glide ratio of about ten to one and he was at seventy-five hundred feet. That would give him roughly fifteen miles of glide, just enough to make a dead-stick landing, which was something he had not done lots of times. In fact, outside of simulators in flight training, he'd never done it.

Altitude three thousand feet, airspeed one hundred and sixty knots, the plains and marshes between Nile tributaries and the Ethiopian border coming up. Dare made a shallow turn and picked up a road that led to the airstrip. He could land on the road if he had to, although it was barely more than a cattle trail. Altitude two thousand . . . Air speed one-fifty. Ten miles to go, then five.

The left engine's propeller flopped to a standstill and the cockpit went silent, except for the muffled rush of wind outside. He was a glider pilot now.

"Oh my God, Wes! Oh my God!"

"Easy, easy," he said, expelling every unnecessary thought and emotion, summoning up all he'd learned in a lifetime of flight. Find the balance between three vectors—the plane's forward momentum, the friction of the air it passed through, and gravity. Deflect the flaps to increase lift, but not so much as to cause excessive drag, which could cause the plane to stall. A kind of physics problem, which, if he failed to solve it, would cost him and Mary their lives. Altitude one thousand . . . Airspeed one-thirty. The airstrip showed as a lane of grass and shrubs between the tall trees. He waited till the last possible second to call for the landing gear. Too soon and the increased resistance could add to the turbulence created by the deflected flaps and give the Hawker the flying characteristics of Isaac Newton's apple.

"Gear down and locked!" Mary said.

Altitude five hundred . . . airspeed one-fifteen. The Hawker was wobbling, about to surrender to gravity. Fighting to keep the nose up, Dare now saw that what had appeared to be shrubs from higher altitude were in fact saplings ten feet high. From the northwest end, they encroached well out onto the runway. To make sure he cleared them, he had to put down almost in the middle of the strip, leaving a mere six hundred yards before he rolled into the treacherous southeast end. The Hawker swooped in, quiet as a bird, and bounced through the high grass at ninety miles an hour. Without power, he could not use the props for aerodynamic braking. All he had to slow his roll were friction and the hydraulic brakes. He pressed the brakes. Mary cried out, "We've done it! We've made it!" There was a fearsome bang and thud as the nose gear collapsed. He and Mary were wrenched forward against their harnesses. The plane skidded nose first, then slewed sideways, the main gear breaking. A shriek of tearing metal, rivets popping, glass shattering as the Hawker slammed broadside into a row of trees, spun part way around, and came to rest.

When he regained consciousness, he was shivering from shock, blood was running down the side of his head, and each breath brought a sharp pain, as though someone were stabbing his lungs with an icepick. The yoke had crunched against his ribs, fracturing them. The right side of the cockpit, Mary's side, was stove in. She was slumped face-down across the pedestal, her back peppered with shattered glass. The stink of aviation fuel permeated the air—there hadn't been enough time to dump it all— and smoke curled into the cabin from the mangled cargo compartment.

The smell and the smoke gave him the necessary adrenal rush to over-come his shock, unbuckle his harness, free Mary from hers, and pull her out of the wreckage. Taking her by the wrists, he dragged her as far as he could. The effort exhausted him, and he nearly blacked out from the pain.

He propped Mary's legs on a fallen log, to prevent blood from draining from her head, and kneeling on both knees, he held her wrist and felt a faint pulse. Her face was a mass of lacerations and blue-black lumps, her right eye a slit in a contusion half as big as a man's fist. Her right side had been crushed by the cabin bulkhead, punched inward by its meeting with the trees. The severity of her injuries, the razing of her beauty made him choke. He cradled her head in his hands and brought his lips to her ear.

"Don't you die on me, Mary girl," he whispered. "We're less than an hour's flying time from Loki. They know where we are. They'll send a plane to look for us. We're gonna make it out of this, but y'all have got to not die on me." She made a sound, a rattling gasp. "That's the stuff. That's my lady."

He staggered back to the plane and tried the radio. Dead. He got the duffel bag containing the water, food, and first-aid kit. He saw what had happened. The southeast end of the runway was black cotton soil, mushy as loam. The surface crust had broken under the Hawker's weight, the gear had crumpled from the stress and spun the aircraft into a sideways skid.

He cleaned Mary's face with alcohol and bandaged the worst gashes, then splinted her ribs with a stout stick and surgical tape. She made another sound. Her good eye, half shut, twitched. "That's it, stay with me. Someone will come. You could be in a hospital by tonight, tomorrow for sure."

He propped her head in his lap and put a water bottle to her lips. The water dribbled down her chin. He forced her mouth open with his fingers and allowed a few drops to fall on her tongue, then finished the rest him-self. He drained another bottle. It amazed him how thirsty he was.

His watch had been smashed. The hands on the glassless dial stood fixed at twenty past two—the moment of impact. Judging from the sun, it was now around three. Even if a search plane found them, a rescue could not be effected until tomorrow.

Gather firewood, that was the thing to do next. A fire to signal a plane, a fire for the night.

An hour later he had accumulated a satisfactory pile of deadwood, fetched from a dry riverbed nearby. That done, he harvested green branches to create as much smoke as possible and laid them next to the wood. These labors had taxed his injured body to the limit, but he couldn't permit himself to sleep. He had to stay awake at least till dusk.

"Wasn't no . . . any accident . . . uh-uh, no accident . . . and when we get back, I'll find out who did it and I'll kill him, kill him for you, baby."

He waved off the flies drawn to her wounds, stroked her blood-matted hair, its golden color darkened to copper, and plucked a shard of glass from her scalp. She didn't move or utter a sound. Her pulse was still there, faint but there. He spoke more encouraging words about their imminent rescue. He talked about the music acts they would fly in the States, about buying a ranch in the Texas hill country, about Stevie Ray Vaughan, about his early days flying Steerman crop dusters, about his father, the Mustang pilot, the World War II ace, six Jap Zeros to his credit, about a dead python he'd seen stretched out on an airstrip in Laos, about his mother, who'd told him he was as ugly as homemade sin and who, he was sure, would never speak to him again if he let Mary get away—"which I'm not about to do." He talked and talked, free-associating, convinced that his voice was getting through to her, keeping her alive. Talking also kept him awake and held at bay the terrible silence of the desert. If not for the humming flies, it would have been as quiet as the surface of the moon. In the pauses between his tales, he listened for the buzz of an approaching plane. Once he swore he heard it, but it soon vanished, and there was only the silence, so profound it was a noise in itself, a kind of voice whispering in a tongue he couldn't understand. He looked around, struck by the empty land-scape, to all appearances devoid of any sentient life. It lay inert under an empty sky, its passivity strangely hostile. He would have preferred an overt aggression, some violent force he could oppose and conquer, or be con-quered by; for these inattentive expanses seemed to be trying to tell him something, if only he could interpret the language of their stillness. He was glad he could not, sensing instinctively that it was something he did not want to know, must not know if he was to go on.

He talked to Mary as the sun inched toward the horizon. Dusk fell, swiftly dragging night behind it. Dare lit the fire and continued with his tales until exhaustion overtook him. His head slumped to his chest, he fell asleep beneath the stars' neutral gaze.

An awful noise woke him, at what hour he didn't know. For a moment he thought he was hallucinating; but no, the noise was as real as the ground he sat on: cackles, whoops, howls, bellows, demented giggles. If hell had a choir, he was listening to it. No moon shone. Starlight revealed vague shapes on the runway, moving toward him with a weird hopping gait. The fire had burned down to coals. He fed a few small sticks into it, then larger pieces. It blazed up, silencing the demonic chorus. Moving back to Mary's side, he drew the Beretta and sat with the pistol in both hands, elbows wedged to his knees to steady his aim. This he could deal with, this was more like it. The fire mounted, disclosing several pairs of eyes, glowing a fluorescent yellow-green in its light. The creatures cautiously drew nearer, he could hear them panting as they halted, one in the lead, the rest a little behind, doglike heads held low, topped by big ears shaped like toadstools, obscene jaws parted, backs humped, scruffy fur bristling, nostrils twitching. He aimed at the leader, slowly let out a breath, and fired twice. He heard the smack of the 9-millimeter rounds striking flesh. The hyena screeched, all four feet leaving the ground at once, and rolled over dead. The rest of the pack, yelping and hooting, ran off a short distance and then turned and held their ground. The two bravest, or maybe they were the hungriest, lunged forward and tore into the carcass of their fallen mate. One turned broadside to Dare, its spotted flanks showing in the firelight. He centered on the shoulder and fired again, and the heart-shot hyena dropped without a sound. The others rushed in and Dare allowed them to drag both carcasses off, to about the middle of the runway. He listened to their snarls, the crunching of bones, the repulsive slurping of entrails, and decided they were still too close. Getting to his feet, he lumbered toward them, against the pain in his side, shooting two more rounds blindly into the darkness. "Go on, eat your buddies, you ugly bastards! She's not on the menu tonight, and no other night neither!"

He went back, gasping, the icepick jabbing his lungs. "Gone," he wheezed, and flopped down. "It's all right, baby, they're gone, they're not gonna hurt you." He looked at her and saw a single greenish-gray eye, wide open and staring at him without a blink. He laid his palm on her forehead and could not remember feeling anything so cold.

She had been dead probably for a couple of hours, and the keen-nosed hyenas had caught the first faint scent of death. He closed the eye and held her and apologized for falling asleep. He was determined to stay awake, in case the animals came back for her. For the rest of the night, watching the stars wheel down the ecliptic, as they always had and always would, for as long as there were stars and a heaven to hold them, he kept his vigil over the one person who had taught him to believe in something beyond himself, to have faith in love and the promise of love.

The sunrise was a wound in the sky. Just like that old Air America pilot had told him in Vientiane a thousand years ago: You'll know you're in trouble when you hate to see it come up. He more than hated to see it now. The joyless light peeled the shadows away and revealed to him again the same arid vacancy of sand, dirt, rock, and sparse trees, motionless and indifferent beneath the same annihilating sky; and its disquieting quiet, the silence that wasn't silent, pressed down on him, as tangible as the heat in the whitening sun. Somehow he knew, as surely as he'd known anything, that a plane wasn't going to come—not today, tomorrow, or the day after, and even if one did, he would not light his signal fire. He would hide in the trees and wait for his deliverers to fly off.

Mary's body had grown stiff during the night. One arm was bent at the elbow, the palm facing out, as if she were taking an oath. He tried to straighten it, but it was frozen into that position by the cold a hundred suns couldn't thaw. The odor of decomposition was now apparent even to the human nose. Flies covered her, she was almost black with them. He fanned them off with his cap, but the instant he stopped, the insects pounced on her again. He would have to bury her. That was the next thing to do. He got up, feeling as though he were rising against a great weight, went off a short distance, and began to claw at the soft soil that had caused his plane to career off the runway. An hour of digging produced a rectangle six feet long and half a foot deep. He could dig no further—he was spent, and the roots of the grasses and shrubs formed a dense mat under the topsoil.

Dragging her by the legs, he laid her in the grave and covered her as best he could, which was nowhere near well enough. Her rigid arm stuck out. The hyenas would be back for her tonight. They could very well devour her within his sight, and there would be nothing he could about that either: He didn't have enough bullets to kill them all.

Thirsty, weaving from fatigue, he returned to the ashes of the fire and pulled another water bottle from the duffel bag and drank it dry. He had no idea why he was slaking his thirst, no idea why he should endure his pain, physical and otherwise, for another second. He'd done everything possible, and none of it had been enough. He wasn't able to keep his plane in the air and, once he landed, wasn't able to keep it from crashing. He wasn't able to keep Mary alive or straighten her arm or dig her a decent grave. He was overwhelmed by a sense of futility—the futility not only of his own efforts but of all effort, not only of his existence but of all existence. "Why should I?" he cried out, and his answer was the vast African silence. This time he understood its message, and to it, his faith in himself was no reply; indeed, he no longer had any faith in himself. Nevertheless, he sat there as still as the landscape and realized there was yet one more thing he couldn't do, though the means to do it was at hand. The raw, animal instinct for survival was all that restrained him, and it was enough.

A tug at his boot startled him into consciousness. With a yell, he jerked his foot out of the hyena's jaws, leaped up, and saw that it wasn't a hyena but a young man, no less startled than Dare. Tall, bone thin, clad in rags, with one black leg and the other as white as ivory, he had a round face and ruthless eyes. A dozen others were with him, boys not men, gaunt and barefoot. Twenty or thirty more were swarming into and over the wrecked plane like ants. Except for two carrying spears, only the young man with the two-toned legs was armed—a Kalashnikov with a folding stock was slung over one emaciated shoulder.

"Who are you?" Dare asked in a scratchy voice.

"I am Matthew Deng," came the reply in a British-tinged, mission-school English. "Who are you?"

Dare answered and asked Matthew Deng if he was SPLA.

"I was one time SPLA, before this." He tapped his artificial limb. "I thought you were died. I wanted your shoes. For him." He motioned at a kid of eleven or twelve whose feet were cut to ribbons. "Is that your aeroplane?"

That was how he said it, *aer-o-plane*. Dare nodded.

Another kid ran up and spoke to Matthew in Dinka. "He says there is no assistance in your aeroplane."

"No, there isn't."

He pointed at the duffel. "What is in there?"

"See for yourself."

He lifted the bag upside down, his stony eyes widening as the bottles, tins, and granola bars tumbled out. A yell went up, and the crowd of boys fell on the stuff in a way that reminded Dare of the hyenas falling on the carcasses of their dead mates. Displaying his SPLA training, Matthew restored order with the help of his two lieutenants, the ones with the spears. Snapping commands, prodding with their weapons, they got the boys to form two lines. Matthew opened a tin of hash and scooped out a mouthful with his fingers. It was obvious he wanted to finish it, but he restrained himself and passed the tin to one of the spear-carriers, instructing him to take only one bite and then to pass it on. He opened several more and rationed them out to the rest, with the water. Their discipline was amazing. One by one they stepped up, took a bite of food, a drink, and stood aside.

While this strange feast went on, Matthew told Dare a fantastic tale.

He and his companions had been on the march for six months. They all came from Bahr el Ghazal, more than six hundred miles away. At the end of last year's rainy season, murahaleen attacked their villages, burned them to the ground, and either killed everyone or took them as slaves. Matthew himself lost his father, mother, two brothers, and a younger sister. He'd survived because he was some distance from the village, in a cattle camp. His camp-mates, numbering about a dozen boys and young men, had also lost their entire families. Being the oldest, and with his military experience, Matthew became their leader. They trekked to another village, seeking refuge, but it too had been annihilated. Picking up several more orphaned boys, they wandered for over a month, scavenging on the carcasses of dead livestock, of warthogs killed by lions. Sometimes they lived on nothing more than roots and leaves. Along the way they were joined by still more youths, until they numbered nearly three hundred.

Eventually they arrived at an SPLA camp, where they were given food and shelter and some military training, except, of course, for Matthew. They remained there for about two months, when a group of hawaga—Matthew recalled that they arrived in a plane bearing a Red Cross—arrived and made a fuss. They accused the SPLA of recruiting child soldiers. The hawaga made such a big fuss that the SPLA was forced to expel the boys from the camp.

Journeying mostly at night to avoid government troops and slavers and hostile tribes like the Nuer, they crossed swamps and great marshes where some died of disease, crossed rivers where some drowned or were devoured by crocodiles, savannahs where the weak and the sick who fell behind were taken by lions, deserts where some perished from thirst. They were bombed by government planes. They continued on, and still more died of malaria or thirst or hunger, still more were taken by crocs and lions, and once Matthew and his two spearmen deliberately fell behind and killed a lioness that was stalking the column.

"This is all that is left of us," Matthew said. "We are going to Kenya. The SPLA told us there is a camp in Kenya, at a place called Kakuma, where we will be fed and sleep in houses. I was to Kenya one time a long time ago. It is where I was given this white leg. Tell me, mister, how far is it to Kenya?"

"I'd reckon two hundred kilometers," Dare said, understanding the look in Matthew's eyes: it was the ruthlessness not of cruelty but of survival; and he also understood that Matthew would kill him if he had to. "Kakuma's got to be another hundred from the border."

"Okay," Matthew said, as though three hundred kilometers were a day hike. "Tell me, mister, what are you doing here?"

"Waiting for a plane. I'm waiting for an aeroplane to come from Kenya and pick me up."

"When does this aeroplane come?"

"It's never gonna come."

Matthew contemplated this statement for a minute. "Then you should come with us."

The offer astonished Dare. "I'd never make it. My ribs are broken, and I'm old. I'd only slow you down. Y'all are gonna have a hard enough time makin' it as it is."

"But we are going to take what is left of your food and water, all of it, and your shoes also," Matthew said, without apology or malice but as a declaration of fact.

Dare said nothing. This kid had tramped a thousand miles on an artificial leg, he'd led a band of orphaned boys on a march that would have turned U.S. Marines into a mob of blubbering babies, he'd killed a lion, and for what? To get to an overcrowded refugee camp, where they would have a grass roof over their heads and maybe two bowls of porridge a day. And then what? An indefinite stay with no homes or families to return to if and when they got out. To go through so much for so little required either complete stupidity or a powerful belief that the future would somehow be better. That any African, even a kid, could have faith in the future baffled him. His own future, without Mary in it, was no future at all. The human capacity for hope when no hope was visible, the human will to live, to blindly, dumbly *go on*, were riddles that he would never solve—and didn't want to solve. Yet there was one last thing he could do.

"I could stop you from takin' the rest of my food and water," he said, surprising Matthew when he pulled the Beretta from his back pocket and pointed it at his belly. "Before you could get that AK off your shoulder or one of those boys could chuck his spear, I'd have a bullet in your guts. So you ain't takin' a thing. I'm *givin'* it to you. Same goes for my shoes." Pocketing the pistol, he sat down, took off his shoes and socks and tied the laces together and set them on the ground. The movements made him grimace, but this was what he could do, make a contribution to the boys' welfare, to the future they believed in, and in the process abbreviate his own. His one fear was that, even facing slow death by thirst or starvation, he would not be able to take the quicker way out.

Matthew mutely stared at the shoes.

"Well," Dare said, "there you be. That kid with the torn-up feet will need them more than me. They might be too big, but—"

But the boy with the torn feet had discovered a pair closer to his size. Squatting by Mary's shallow grave, he was tugging at one of her buff desert boots. Because her body had bloated in the day's heat, it would not come off. The result was that he pulled her partway out of the grave.

"Get your hands off her!" Dare raged. "Y'all got mine! Don't you touch her!"

The boy looked at him, then continued to tug. Dare rose and half-ran, half-stumbled to him and jerked him away. Mary's bandaged face, puffed up and yellowing, had come out of the dirt. "You little son of a bitch, I said nobody touches her."

"Who is this?" Matthew asked.

"She was my—nobody touches her."

"But mister, she is died. She has no need of shoes."

In the anger born of his love and grief, Dare was impervious to this logic. Matthew gave him a good hard shove—he was very strong for one so thin—and, holding Dare at bay with both hands, told the boy to go ahead. He tugged again and, after dragging Mary's body halfway out, succeeded at removing the boot. As he started on the other, Dare took two quick hops backward and drew the pistol again. If love was worth living for, it was worth dying for. It was the only thing worth dying for.

"Now get the hell away from her."

The boy turned to him, more with curiosity than fear, and then to Matthew, and then back to Dare.

"Mister," Matthew said quietly, and slipped the Kalashnikov off his shoulder, "you don't know what you are doing."

But he did. As he moved the barrel to fire a yard wide of the boy, he knew exactly what he was doing. He heard the pistol go off—but not the crack of Matthew's rifle.

"READY IN A minute, mate," said Tony, smacking his sleep-dried mouth. "Come on in."

His hut was the opposite of Douglas's, an offense to anyone with a minimal sense of cleanliness and order. A bed that looked as if it hadn't been made in days. Dirty laundry mounded two feet high in a corner, giving off a musty odor that mingled with the smells of grease, gasoline, and dried sweat emitted by a pair of coveralls flung over a chair. Manuals and papers strewn on the floor.

"Doing your own maintenance these days?" Fitzhugh asked. He gestured at the coveralls, crinkling his nose.

Tony snatched them off the chair and tossed them onto the laundry pile. He pulled a clean shirt from a duffel bag, sniffed it, and put it on. "Let's get this done."

Venus was still glimmering in the west when they took off, Fitzhugh in the copilot's seat of the Beechcraft, the company's smallest plane. They were prepared for the only two possible outcomes, in the event Dare and Mary were found: in the back were a box of food, a jerry can of water, and a medical kit; also two rubber body bags and latex gloves supplied by the Red Cross hospital. Another crew, Alexei's, was searching for Tara's downed Cessna.

They flew for an hour, bearing a little east of north. Through his side window, Fitzhugh saw the arid uplands of Ethiopia and the fragmented sparkle of an intermittent river.

"That would be the Akobo," Tony said. "We'll be over the airstrip in a few minutes." Those minutes passed, and he declared, "Here we are," motioning at the GPS.

He banked, descending a little. Fitzhugh scanned with his binoculars and said to go lower.

"Low as I go, mate."

"Tony, we are going to *land* if we find anything. Less altitude, yes? I can't see anything from up here."

With the cessation of Busy Beaver's operations, Tony was an idle pilot, but he'd refused to take on this mission when Fitzhugh asked him last night. You're not the boss, he'd said, so Fitz had called the boss in Nairobi on the sat-phone. Douglas's return message had ordered Tony to go.

Alexei's crew had not exactly been eager to look for Tara. Two planes down in a single afternoon was an unusual occurrence that had spooked all the aid pilots in Loki. Yesterday Fitzhugh had made the mistake of repeating Dare's speculation that she might have been shot down. Rumors ran through the compounds and expat bars, transforming the possibility into established fact. Khartoum had taken the gloves off. Any plane in a no-go zone was going to be blown out of the sky. For years that specter had ridden with every crew flying on the dark side; but no plane had fallen to enemy fire, which had fostered a belief among the pilots, flight engineers, and loadmasters that they were charmed, immune, *blessed*; if the blessing had been withdrawn from Tara, who by virtue of her integrity seemed the most deserving of it, then it had been withdrawn from all.

"Five thousand," Tony said. "How's this?"

"Damn you, they might be alive down there. Maybe you don't care what happens to Wesley, but I would think you'd care about her."

"The both of them can rot in hell for all I care."

"A thousand feet," Fitzhugh demanded.

Muttering an expletive, Tony pitched the plane over into a steep dive before pulling back hard to describe a tight parabolic curve in the air. He laughed harshly. "Bloody hell if you don't look like a white man now."

"Was that necessary?" Fitzhugh said, his stomach settling back into its rightful place.

"You wanted lower, you got it."

At eight hundred feet they flew over a road. It ended at the old airstrip, a rough lane with tall trees on one side. Through the trees Fitzhugh glimpsed the Hawker's fuselage. In its new coat of white paint, it looked like some huge discarded appliance. Tony circled to give him a better view. The plane lay broadside to the trees, her right wing sheared off near the root, her nose cone crushed. A short distance away, amid low, scattered shrubs, a flock of vultures clustered, feeding on something.

"Another pass, Tony. As low and slow as you can."

They skimmed the runway. Frightened off, the vultures rose toward the trees with a slow flapping of dark wings. Fitzhugh saw a body lying on its back, one arm flung out wide. It might have been Wesley.

"Land," he said.

"They're dead," Tony said, gaining altitude.

"I saw only one. The other one could be in the plane."

"Well, I don't like the looks of that runway."

"Stop arguing with me. We took this plane so we could land on a short strip. Now do it, land."

Tony turned and touched down.

Fitzhugh recognized Wesley only by his clothes and his curly reddish hair, disturbingly lifelike as a breeze moved through it. Mary's body lay half buried a little distance away. The vultures had not gone to work on her; presumably they would have once they were finished with Wesley. Sorrow and disgust moved through him at once. Two people he'd known for three years, sentient beings who had spoken to him only twenty-four hours ago, reduced to this, to carrion.

"Tony, what do you think happened?"

"Not enough usable runway for a Hawker," he replied matter-of-factly. "Wes ran out of runway and ideas at the same time."

"Someone tried to bury her. It must have been Wes."

There might have been a tremor in Tony's jaw as he looked down at his former lover; then he turned away and said, "Who else?"

"But if he had the strength to drag her this far and to dig a grave, you would think he wasn't injured that badly. You would think he'd still be alive. And look, they're both barefoot. Why's that?"

"Wouldn't know. What difference does it make?"

"Maybe nothing. There is a lot here that doesn't make sense. Wes said something very strange in one of his last transmissions. There was something about his fuel pumps, something about a water jug and plastic bags in a trash barrel. What do you make of that?"

Tony jammed his hands into his back pockets and looked at the ground. "Sounds to me like he was daft. Let's get them and ourselves out of here."

They got the body bags from the Beechcraft and put on the latex gloves and the surgical masks that the Red Cross, in its foresight, had also provided. They loaded Mary's corpse first. As they struggled with Wesley's bulk, the rigid body rolled over, revealing a brown smear on the grass and three holes in its back.

"Holy shit!" Tony said. "He was shot. Those are exit wounds, you can tell by the size."

"They can't be. There was nothing in front."

"The vultures, mate."

"But who would have shot him out here? It's a wilderness, there isn't a village within fifty kilometers. Who and why? Bandits? Is that who took their shoes?"

"What are you, a fuckin' detective? Let's get it done and out of here."

The blood-browned grass, the three ragged holes, the vultures roosting in the trees, and the trees hissing in the wind that blew out of the east, out of Ethiopia—Fitzhugh felt a chill from within and didn't stop feeling it until they were a mile in the air.

"I am going to try to talk the UN into sending a crash investigation team out here," he declared suddenly.

Tony gave him a quick glance. "What the hell for? What's the point?"

"There are too many riddles for me. I want to find out what happened, and I'll start with what forced Wesley to land in that godforsaken place."

After returning to Loki and delivering the bodies to the Red Cross morgue, where the logisticians of death would take care of the details—collecting personal effects, shipping the remains to their families—Fitzhugh received a radio call from Alexei: He had located the wreck of the Cessna, a mere ten miles from Zulu Three. SPLA troops were on their way to search for survivors, but he was sure there weren't any. That was confirmed the next day, when the Antonov landed in Loki with five more corpses. It would take dental records to sort out who was who. The rumors were likewise confirmed: Alexei said Michael's troops had found a piece of one wing, perforated with bullet holes. Tara must have flown over a government patrol from one of the two nearby garrisons. The terrifying specter had come to life.

Fields of Destruction

THEY WERE GOING to cut off the serpent's head, inshallah.

The yearnings in Ibrahim Idris's breast for love and power would be fulfilled, inshallah.

Behind him, in a double file reaching so far back he could not see its end, five hundred Brothers rode, keys to Paradise around their necks, talismans hanging from their saddles, fluttering from their rifle barrels. Somewhere off to his left the militia column—a thousand men with mortars and light artillery—pressed forward on foot and in lorries. Spearpoints aimed at the infidel's heart, a mighty host, the scourge of God upon Dar Kufr, the House of the Unbeliever.

So had spoken Colonel Ahmar, commander of all murahaleen, before the Brothers set out yesterday morning. Brandishing rifles, clutching the hotel keys blessed by mullahs to open the gates of heaven, the massed riders roared as one, Allahu akhbar! Allah ma'ana! In the past, Ibrahim had expressed more a hope than a conviction when he'd uttered the murahaleen's war cry. This time it had been different. He had seen in a recent confluence of events the hand of Providence that his deceased nephew Abbas used to see in everything.

About a fortnight ago the slave-trader Bashir had appeared in Ibrahim's camp. "I bring you one who can deliver Miriam to you and very much more," he had said. This man was a Nuban Muslim who had deserted the rebel army with one hundred others. He had fled from New Tourom, the town where Miriam dwelled. Mindful of the agreement reached with Ibrahim long ago, Bashir had led the deserter straight to his camp. He demanded that Ibrahim uphold his end of their bargain.

"Let me see him and talk to him first," Ibrahim said.

He was a tall thin man wearing a beard on his chin, named Muhammad Kasli. He surrendered himself and his men to Ibrahim, who took the precaution of disarming them and then afforded them the hospitality of his camp.

Drinking tea under the Men's Tree, Kasli told his story. He had been no less than second in command of all the rebel forces in the Nuba mountains. It turned out that he had changed sides sometime earlier. To prove that his loyalties lay with the government, he had taken on a secret mission to assassinate his commander and stir an uprising of Nuban Muslims. Had it been successful, all those parts of the Nuba held by the rebels would have been restored to government control without a battle; but God had not willed it to be so. The attempt failed and Kasli was forced to flee. He and his men had traveled for several days, intending to surrender themselves to the army garrison at Kadugli; but moving at night, they'd gotten lost. Their path crossed with Bashir's the next day. Now, said Kasli, he had information valuable to the government—information that, if put to proper use, would crush the resistance in the Nuba with a single blow, God willing. And what was this information? He had intimate knowledge of the rebel headquarter's defenses, the numbers of the soldiers, their weapons and dispositions. He would say no more until he was presented to higher authorities.

Al-hamduillah! Ibrahim said to himself. Praise be to God! A great prize had landed in his lap, but not by chance. God had guided Kasli's footsteps to Bashir, and through Bashir to him. Ever on the lookout for his own interests, he immediately thought how to turn this situation to his benefit. Of late he had been intriguing to get the nazir removed from office and then to declare himself the best candidate to replace him. Were he to take part in a campaign to end the rebellion in the Nuba, the honor and fame could do nothing but advance his ambitions. And there was Miriam, now closer to his grasp than she had been since her escape. God willing, he would recapture her and make her a proper Muslim. He would make her his wife.

"There is a woman who lives in New Tourom. She goes by the name of Yamila. Do you know her?"

Kasli looked perplexed. Bashir had put that same question to him, he said. Of what significance was this woman?

"Do you know where she lives in the town? Describe her house to me. Show me where it is." He handed Kasli a stick. "Draw a picture of the town and show me."

Kasli smoothed the dirt near the fire and made a crude map—big squares representing an infidel church, a school, a souk, smaller squares for houses.

"She lives somewhere in here, the western side, near a wadi," Kasli said, pointing with the stick. "In a house with a family of Christians. They took her in when she came to New Tourom. This house has a cross painted above its door, in green paint, and some pictures also and the words 'God Bless This House,' which are written in English. May I ask why you wish to know this?"

"Because she belongs to me, and you are going to help me find her," Ibrahim answered.

He and Kasli journeyed by lorry to Colonel Ahmar's headquarters in Babanusa town. The colonel spoke to Kasli at great length, to make sure that his surrender wasn't a trick. One could never tell, these abid switched their allegiances back and forth, and Kasli might have had another change of heart. Satisfied that the Nuban's defection was genuine, he asked Ibrahim to remain and assist him and his lieutenants in planning the battle. "You did well to bring him here," the colonel said. "We are going to chop off the head of the snake, inshallah, and you and your boys will have the honor of firing the first shots."

YES, THE INTRUDER was here. The Enemy was whispering to him that he had done the unforgivable, lying to him that God's love was not infinite. The intruder was here in their house, trying to steal him from her, a different sort of rival than Yamila but a rival nonetheless. "Darling, *please* not now," she said, then realized she'd sounded sharp, selfish, and unfeeling and reached out to stroke his cheek. "I'm sorry."

He sat with folded hands, thumbs joined to press his brow. "I wish I could get it out of my head."

"You will in time." She moved to sit next to him, an arm around his waist. "You prayed for forgiveness, like I asked?"

"Oh, will you stop that."

"But you must. You *must*. And you must believe that God will give it to you. You have to believe there are no limits to Christ's love, no limits to his grace. You must believe that, darling."

"The missionary speaks to the native. The missionary tells him what he must do."

"Please, no sarcasm," she said, seeking words to banish this trespasser who dwelt in his mind, this despair implanted by the Enemy. "I know one thing—there was no way we could have known it was Tara. It was supposed to have been Dare, and he betrayed us, just as much as Kasli and Suleiman did. He was probably paid to do it, he's so greedy. And that woman, that bitch. She didn't care how much damage she did, how many lives her story would cost. We're fighting for survival here."

"Do you think you are telling me things I haven't told myself? But I gave the orders, not you. It's on my conscience."

"Mine, too. I didn't object to your orders, and I could have. Do you think I haven't agonized about that? But Dare and that woman were collaborators as far as I'm concerned. It was done for survival and so much more. For every soul in these mountains. For him"—she placed Michael's hand on her stomach—"so he can grow up in peace. Do you think Christ doesn't understand that? Of course he does, and he forgives. He forgives and forgives. Seven times seventy-seven."

"How very nice it must be to believe that. Do as you wish and then ask for forgiveness and everything is fine."

"Between what's necessary and what isn't—that's the choice. You said that. Christ knows you did what was necessary. He knows that nobody warned you it was Tara flying Phyllis in here. Tara was an unfortunate accident."

"She was a good woman, I was fond of her," he said. "How can I call myself a soldier now? A murderer, that's what I am."

Tears came to his eyes. She had never seen him cry before. He was weeping for Tara and for his own soul, damned not by God but by himself. His sorrow only made her more determined to break the Enemy's grip on him.

"All right, a murderer, but even murder is forgivable," she said in a stern voice. "The only thing that's unforgivable is to think you can't be forgiven. You really must do what I told you, or this will get the better of you, and you won't be able to carry on. The people need you, Pearl needs you, I need you. We need you to be strong, Michael."

He rose and stood by the door, looking out into the courtyard. At the moment she couldn't bear the sight of his back turned to her. She got up and went to him, folding her arms around him, laying a cheek between his shoulder blades. "Would you come with me? To our secret place?"

He stiffened. "What are you suggesting? At a time like this?"

"Not for that, darling. To show you what I've been telling you."

They climbed the steep, stony path to the refuge. It was behind the pinnacle rocks rising above St. Andrew's church—a grotto facing a granite slab into which untold ages of weather had carved a cistern, its sides as smooth as a potter's mold, its ten-foot depth filled with water in the rainy season. A strict prohibition had forced them to choose this secluded spot for a rendezvous. Among the Nubans, sexual intimacy was forbidden while new life grew within a woman's body; they believed it made the baby impure, and that a couple who violated the ban would be punished by the illness or early death of their child. Quinette had seen expectant girls leave their husbands to live with their parents; she'd heard stories about men who had been caught secretly visiting their pregnant wives and suffered such scorn that they had to move to other villages.

Michael did not believe in the taboo, but he had to keep up appearances and insisted that she move into the empty tukul between the one they shared and Pearl's and Kiki's. She hated the arrangement—sleeping in separate rooms, like some Victorian couple—and had hoped he would come to her at some late, discreet hour. Fear of disgrace restrained him: the bodyguards standing watch outside the compound walls might hear them and spread malicious gossip. It was no wonder Nuban men took several wives. Quinette trusted the mind-heart half of her husband; it was the physical part she did not trust. Its hungers could eventually drive him to seek satisfaction with another woman, and she feared who that woman might be. She'd taken the initiative, telling him that she couldn't bear the abstention, and was there some place they could be alone together? "I know of one," he'd said, his look telling her that he was grateful she had broken the ice.

"Now what is it you are going to show me?" Michael asked.

Without a word, she removed her kanga and sandals and hopped across the granite—exposed to the sun, it was hot underfoot—and launched herself into the cistern. The water was tepid at the surface but grew colder as she dove to the bottom. Touching it, she arched her back and kicked back up. It was delightful. The grime on her skin seemed to peel away, like a sheer wrapper.

She braced her elbows on the cistern's rim and looked up at Michael. "Come in."

"But you know I don't swim."

"Just lower yourself in and hold on like I am."

This he did, an anxious look on his face. It was odd to see him vulnerable.

"Now let me duck your head. Hold on tight with your hands and I'll duck your head."

"No."

"Please."

He slid his forearms off the edge and clutched it with his fingers. Treading water behind him, Quinette put both hands on his shaved scalp and pushed him under, holding him there until he began to struggle. Sputtering and spitting, he lunged out and sat down.

"Were you trying to drown me? Is that what you want to show me? This is what it is like to drown."

"I wanted you to trust me. I want you to think of this pool as God's grace. You don't fight it, you immerse yourself in it with trust in your heart. And it washes you clean. Trust me, Michael, and trust in God. You are forgiven. I know because I prayed for forgiveness, and it was given."

He offered his arm to help her out. They sat for a while, drying in the sun and wind. The cool water had tightened his skin and muscles, giving them the chiseled look they must have had when he was a young wrestler. An onyx statue come to life, she thought, and said on impulse, "You are a beautiful man."

"And look at you." He held her arm next to his. "Brown as an Arab. And all over, too."

At least she had gotten him to talk about something other than Tara. "It's those treatments Pearl and Kiki give me. Lying naked in the sun, coated in lemon and sugar."

"And what will our child be? Brown or black?"

"Black. I know it."

The word seemed to strike him in a peculiar way; he winced when she said it, and then he was off again, into the depths of his inner space.

"I think it is not forgiveness I want," he said after a silence. "It is forgetfulness. I keep seeing her when the men brought her and the others to the airstrip."

"It must have been horrible," Quinette said.

"No more horrible than other things I've seen. All the same, I still cannot get it out of my head."

Words had not evicted the interloper. Her body and her love would, though she had said that wasn't her purpose in coming here. She leaned forward to kiss him, her hand falling between his legs. The life blooming within her gave her a sense of female power; she could get him to do what she wanted, to make love, to forgive himself. Rising, she entered the grotto, trailing the kanga behind her. She didn't look to see if he had followed her; she knew he would. She spread the kanga on the flat rock floor and sat down, holding her arms out to him. "Let me help you get it out of your head," she said.

THEY RODE IN a wadi, four abreast. Braids of brown water trickled through the wadi, and the wet sand between the braids muffled the clop of hooves, as the trees on both sides masked the riders from view. Under the morning stars Ibrahim and Hamdan, his staunch friend and ally, whiled away the tedious hours in the saddle with talk about cattle and women, the only topics that interested them. The two were bound together—the man without cattle was also without women. Young men riding behind them sang:

> *Carry the rifle whose fire burns the liver and sears the heart,*
> *For I need a slave boy from the land of the blacks.*
> *Hey! You sons of the Ataya,*
> *You are the burning iron rod.*
> *We long for the land without a people,*
> *We long to live by the rivers of the south.*

They were eager for the coming battle and the chance to capture cattle and women, though some, the zealous ones, were eager for martyrdom. As for himself, Ibrahim was eager to have it over with. Rocking with Barakat's easy gait, he thought, *This will be the last one.* Then it would be a life of ease. A nazir's house, his own lorry, and in the soft light of the cow-dust hour, Miriam would rub his legs with liquid butter.

When it grew brighter and he and Hamdan had finished speaking about wives and concubines, calves, milk cows, and breed bulls, Ibrahim removed from his cartridge belt the paper Kasli had written for him. He was memorizing the English letters painted on Miriam's house. G-O-D B-L-E-S-S T-H-I-S H-O-U-S-E. Those letters and the green cross, the Christians' symbol.

Kasli and his fellow deserters trudged on foot alongside the mura-haleen, who regarded them with the special contempt horsemen reserve for those who cannot ride. When the time came, however, the Nuban turncoats would become passengers in the saddle, mounting up to ride double into the attack.

The radio carried by the militiaman alongside Ibrahim hissed, a voice came out, and the radio operator answered.

"Ya! Ibrahim," he said. "It is Colonel Ahmar. He will soon be ready to begin shelling. He wishes to know when you will be ready."

This was the first time Ibrahim had been issued a radio. He found it an annoyance. The colonel was always calling him about one thing or another. "Tell him soon."

Today was the Christian Sabbath. Kasli had said the rebel soldiers would be relaxed, the townspeople would be not in their fields but drinking marissa in their houses. No one would be expecting an attack from the ground in the rainy season. Still, the colonel was not taking any chances. According to Kasli's intelligence, the rebel garrison was unassailable. Except for a single narrow gap, it was locked on all sides by steep, well-defended ridges. To seize the garrison, the ridges would have to be taken first; to take the ridges, the defenders would have to be decoyed into leaving their positions. This was to be accomplished, inshallah, by Ibrahim's murahaleen. They would attack New Tourom, which was on ground suitable for cavalry. The town was very important to the rebel commander—so Kasli had spoken—and he would rush men to meet the threat against it, creating breaches in the ridges' defenses. The second column—the militia infantry marching a few kilometers away on Ibrahim's left—would pour through the breaches and seize the ridges, then swoop into the valley and destroy the garrison.

The murahaleen would be given their usual license to loot and to capture women and children. No other prisoners would be taken, except for two—the rebel commander and his foreign wife. They were to be turned over to Kasli, who had asked for the privilege of executing them. That was to be his reward for his services.

Ibrahim was curious to see the foreign woman. Kasli had talked about her a good deal—a spy for the Americans, he'd said. What the Americans had to do with anything, Ibrahim didn't know, but he intended to talk the Nuban out of executing her and give her to him. An American woman would be a very valuable prize, fetching a high ransom.

Clouds were forming, high clouds like horse-tails, portents of a storm. Hamdan noticed them too and frowned. As cattlemen, they prayed for rain; as fighters, for dry weather. They heard an odd sound in the distance, a ringing. Kasli came over and said it was made by the bell of the Christian church in New Tourom.

"We are close enough. You should make ready now."

At Ibrahim's arm signal, the riders wheeled out of the wadi, spurring their mounts up the bank and onto a rolling plain behind a low ridge, rocky and treeless. The town, Kasli informed him, was beyond the ridge, less than one kilometer away. Hidden by the rise in the ground, the murahaleen formed into battalions according to lineages and clans. Ibrahim's lineage, the Awlad Ali, were in the foremost ranks. He looked back and was moved by the sight—mounted warriors massed on the plain, Kalashnikovs braced butt-first on their thighs, the manes of brown, black, and white horses ruffled by the breeze, talismans flapping from rifle barrels. He turned to the radio operator. "Tell the colonel we are ready."

As he waited for the shelling to begin, he knew the battle would not follow the tidy plan—he had been in too many fights to believe otherwise—but if God were with him and the Brothers, they would prevail. The muted crack of mortars came from his left. The bombs burst atop the ridge, close enough to shower dirt and rocks on the murahaleen. Horses shied and whinnied. Barakat, accustomed to such noises, remained steady.

"Ya Allah!" he said to the radio operator. "Tell those fools they almost hit us!"

In a nervous voice, the militiaman delivered this message. A long silence preceded the next reports of mortars. Ibrahim heard the bombs thudding somewhere to his front—on the town, he assumed. The bombardment went on for some time, and he beseeched Allah to spare Miriam from harm. The radio spoke again.

"The colonel says he will now stop the shelling on the town and move it to the ridges," the operator shouted, though he was barely more than an arm's length away. "You are to attack now."

Ibrahim held the chestnut stallion to a walk as he mounted the rise. The Brothers followed at the same pace, and the massed horsemen flowed over the crest. Ahead the land rose gently toward New Tourom. A few houses showed through the trees and the smoke from burning roofs. Ibrahim glimpsed people in flight. He almost laughed when one group came running straight toward him, and then, seeing murahaleen descending on them, turned tail. An automatic rifle rattled, bullets spurted in front of him—lousy shots, these blacks. Halting Barakat, he raised his rifle, and standing in the stirrups, his rear end thrust out, he looked back and yelled, "Follow my ass, O Brothers! Follow my ass!" "Allahu akhbar!" they yelled. He slacked the reins and gave the stallion his head.

THEY WERE RETURNING home from church, sweating in the oppressive April air, pestered by swarms of mosquitoes. Michael was not a regular churchgoer, but Quinette had pleaded with him to attend and offer prayers for forgiveness. At the service Fancher had introduced St. Andrew's new minister, a Nuban he had trained. The man's homily had met with general approval—the congregation applauded, as if it had been a political speech. Quinette had understood not one word and afterward asked Michael to give her the gist of it. In the midst of his summary, they heard a boom, softened by distance, and then several more, one after the other. Hearing no more, they walked on warily and were approaching the gap in the hills when mortar shells crashed into the town behind them.

The bodyguards closed ranks around Quinette and Michael and virtually swept them down the path and through the gap toward the headquarters building. Just as they arrived, two shells banged into one of the ridges above the garrison, while another landed in the village of camp followers and soldiers' families. In moments, people were streaming out of their tukuls, carrying children, pots, and blankets. Off-duty soldiers, some wearing only their undershorts, flew out with their rifles, looking for someone to tell them what to do.

There was pandemonium inside as well, a radio operator talking frantically, officers gathering documents, apparently with the intention of burning them if necessary. A mortar landed nearby. Shrapnel clattered on the tin roof, pinged against the stone walls. Negev pushed Quinette down into a corner, and as she huddled there, her husband issued commands to the officers and into the radio. He put the handset down and turned to her.

"You have got to get out of here. Murahaleen are attacking the town, hundreds of them. If they break through to here and see you—" He left the rest unsaid and repeated that she must leave. Negev would guide her to a safe place. Murahaleen—she reacted to that word as would any Dinka or Nuban, with terror. Negev grabbed her by the hand. "Come, missy, hurry."

A MACHINE GUN opened fire. Horses to one side of him pitched forward, spilling their riders. "Allahu akhbar! Allah ma'ana!" Riding without his hands on the reins, Ibrahim fired his AK-47, spraying trees and houses. At full gallop, the murahaleen slammed into New Tourom, a shock wave of living flesh. The momentum of their charge broke against the town. Huts, animal pens, fences, panic-stricken goats, cows, and people shattered the horsemen's mass into individual bands. Each one went about its own business, looting houses, seizing livestock and captives. It was this way on every raid—a melee.

Ibrahim rode on with his own band of twenty-odd men. They overran the rebel machine gun, killing two abid soldiers. Then he saw it—a round Nuban house with a green cross over its door and the letters G-O-D B-L-E-S-S T-H-I-S H-O-U-S-E on an outer wall. Barakat vaulted a stick fence surrounding the garden. A man's body lay among the plants. Cries came from inside. Ibrahim dismounted and ducked under the low doorway, his rifle leveled. It was almost too dark to see. "Outside! Outside!" he said, grabbing people by their clothes and shoving them through the door. Two women, five kids, an old man. "Yamila! Where is she!" The idiots did not understand Arabic, or were pretending not to. He offered a language lesson by shooting the old man in the chest. The women shrieked. He cracked one in the face with the back of his hand. "Where is Yamila!" She shrieked again. It was no use. Ignorant savages. He ordered a Brother to tie them up. Farther on he saw the same letters and cross on another dwelling, and on yet another, and both were empty. That damned Kasli—G-O-D B-L-E-S-S T-H-I-S H-O-U-S-E was written on half the places in this town.

The snap of incoming bullets gave him something else to think about. They were taking fire from their left, heavy fire. To the inexperienced ear, the sound of the bullets would be indistinguishable from the crackle of the flaming grass roofs. A wounded horse screamed. Ibrahim rallied his band and joined up with another. "This way, Brothers! Follow my ass!" They rode forward, then wheeled to charge through an orchard, toward what Ibrahim believed to be the enemy's flank. Before them, on open ground, stood the infidel church and several other buildings, two on fire. Rebel soldiers had taken cover behind one of the buildings that was not burning. The murahaleen galloped down on them, AKs blazing. Surprised to be attacked from the side, the abid broke and ran, some pausing to shoot at their pursuers. A horse and rider went down, another, and then the Brothers were in the middle of the retreating enemy, shooting at point-blank range. Some, their magazines empty, slashed with pangas and swords. They swept through as a wind through the grass and came to the far end of the town, where Ibrahim halted. Ahead was a tent-camp, burning and empty of people. Kasli had mentioned this—a settlement for refugees. Beyond it rose one of the ridges encircling the rebel garrison. Ibrahim saw the gap, the gate to the valley, but it was so narrow he could pass through it only single file, which would be suicide. Nor could he take horses up the ridge.

He commanded the Brothers to turn back. As they did, in a confused, jostling mass, the air came alive with bullets, swarming like angry bees. A mortar bomb burst among the horsemen. Wounded mounts made a horrible sound, and one ran off, trailing its guts and dragging its rider. Ibrahim whipped Barakat with his quirt. "Ride, Brothers! Ride out of here! Back into the town!" Suddenly he flew over Barakat's head and landed on his belly. The wind was knocked out of him. He thought his chest was crushed, but it wasn't. He rose to his hands and knees and saw the fallen stallion, blood pumping from the holes in its shoulder, its fierce golden eye still. A great horse, but there was no time to mourn him now. As he stood, Hamdan came alongside. Ibrahim grabbed the back of the saddle and, with a strength born of fear, vaulted onto the horse's back. Riding double, he and Hamdan pressed forward and escaped the withering fire. Returning to the Christian church, they came upon a great many murahaleen guarding the captives, possibly two hundred altogether. Ibrahim leaped off the horse and looked for the radio operator but could not find him. Kasli was there, however, standing over the bodies of two men whose light skin marked them as foreigners.

"Who are these?" He had to shout to be heard—the battle for the ridges was reaching a crescendo.

"Spies!" Kasli yelled back. "Americans! I shot them! There are two more foreigners over there!" He pointed at the crowd of captives, among whom the foreigners were easy to pick out. "A doctor and a nurse. I spared them because I thought they could be of use."

"Have you seen the radio operator?"

"No."

What was going on? What was he supposed to do? Hold the town? Withdraw? A Brother brought him a riderless horse. Ibrahim mounted, deciding that the wisest course would be to regroup as many murahaleen as possible and wait to see what happened. As he pulled bands of men from here and there, the noise of the battle subsided and soon ceased altogether. The quiet, after so great a racket, was unsettling. He'd no idea what it meant—victory or defeat or merely a lull. His lungs burned from breathing smoke; he judged that he'd lost more men in this fight than in any other. Dead Brothers were sprawled on the ground beside dead horses and dead Nubans, while wounded men pleaded for water. He could use some water himself; his throat felt scorched.

He mustered about half his force and was rounding up more at the western end of the town, where the attack had begun, when he saw the side of a ridge to his right dotted with figures: tens and tens of figures, running downhill in his direction, firing as they ran. Rebel soldiers, counterattacking. In moments more gunfire erupted at the opposite end of the town, mixed in with the detonations of rocket-propelled grenades. Once again bullets pierced the air, and men and mounts were falling everywhere he looked. He was enlightened. He understood. The rebel commander had not fallen for the ruse; he had held his men in position and stopped Colonel Ahmar's assault, and now Ibrahim and the Brothers were trapped. The colonel had abandoned them to draw fire and thus cover the militia's retreat.

Wheeling, he rode back to the church. In the desperation of the moment, an idea had come to him, a gamble that could get him out of this fix or get him killed. It would be win all or lose all. At this point, he wasn't sure if he gave a damn which way it went.

"RUN, MISSY, RUN!" Negev cried, holding her hand, dragging her behind him.

Well ahead, files of people were moving over the grass-covered knolls and knobs. She clutched for breath, her mouth was dry, her dress soaked with sweat. Negev urged her to run still faster. She stopped to take off her sandals, thinking it would be easier to run barefoot. She was wrong—rocks cut her feet. Negev flung himself to the ground, taking her with him, as mortar shells burst a hundred yards away. Now they heard the hammering of machine guns and automatic rifles.

"Negev!" she said, raising her voice over the din. "It's all open ground ahead. I know a better place." She pointed to the pinnacles, off to their right. "They'll never get horses up there."

They made for the high rocks. Never had she run so far so fast. But what was this doing to her baby? An embryo, probably no bigger than her thumb; yet she was aware of it in a physical way and slowed to a quick walk, afraid that more violent exertion would cause her to miscarry.

Negev nearly jerked her arm out of its socket. "No walking! Running!"

And so she ran again. They had picked up a following—a score of women, most with children and infants. The uphill path went from dirt to solid stone, on which Quinette's feet left bloody prints. Far above the valley the path leveled off and led them to the small granite plateau. All of them fell to their knees around the cistern, dipping their heads to drink like wild beasts at a water hole.

"In there," Quinette gasped, gesturing at the grotto. They all crowded inside. That this had so recently been the scene of pleasure and joy seemed impossible. Quinette's head throbbed, her slashed feet burned. She crawled out to the cistern and plunged them in. Healing waters. As she crawled back, she saw that Yamila was in the group. Clad in a barega, she was examining a scrape on her arm. She shot Quinette a quick glance, its meaning opaque, if it had a meaning.

Explosions and gunfire echoed from the town, hundreds of feet below, hidden from view by the tall pinnacles. The air smelled as it did at the end of the dry season, when grass fires were lit.

"A very big battle, missy," Negev said, guarding the grotto's entrance. "If murahaleen try to come up here on foot"—he slapped his Kalashnikov—"one by one I kill them."

He stood and moved off.

"Where are you going?"

"To look to see what is happening," he said.

Curiosity, or perhaps the inability to wait in ignorance, compelled her to follow.

Lying side by side in a cleft between two of the finger rocks, they peered almost straight down to see, through torn sheets of smoke, Arabs on horseback, shooting, grabbing people, dragging them by ropes. It was like a scene from the fourteenth century, though the slavers of that time would not have been armed with assault rifles. *Murahaleen.* The raiders she had heard of so often and now saw, like mounted ghosts in their white robes and turbans. Pale riders. The church was directly below, still intact, but the tailor shop had been blown up, and the school's roof had collapsed in flames, leaving a jumble of charred beams speckled with embers. She felt such a helpless fury.

"Oh, with one of the big machine guns, I could kill all of them from here," Negev said.

"I was just thinking the same thing."

"Come, missy, down. Maybe someone will see us."

Seated again in the granite sanctuary, she gazed at the forlorn women, cradling their children, whispering to them. Her thoughts flew to the refugees in the tent-camp, in flight again, or killed, or taken prisoner. She was physically and emotionally spent; a deadness was in her heart.

IBRAHIM DISPERSED HIS men to form a perimeter around the church and its outbuildings, ordering the Brothers to fight on foot. They crouched behind dead horses and live ones, pulled down to lie on their sides. All the while bullets popped overhead, but nowhere near as thick as before. The rebel soldiers seemed to realize that the captives and the murahaleen were now bunched together, and they feared killing their own people. He ordered Hamdan to bring the captives into the church and to post men inside and out. His friend grinned through his beard, grasping what Ibrahim was up to. His first duty had always been to preserve his Brothers' lives, for to preserve them was to preserve the future of the Salamat, of all who belonged to Dar Humr. He didn't know the number lost today, but he would save the rest—and get what he wanted in the bargain. Inshallah.

As Brothers prodded the captives with rifles, shouting "Move, move, inside," Ibrahim flew about the perimeter, shouting to his men to cease firing. Under the circumstances, it struck them as a strange command. Some obeyed, others did not, but gradually they stopped shooting. And when they did, the enemy did.

"Ya! Kasli, I may need you," he said, finding the Nuban near a fire-blackened building, huddled behind a pile of tables and sewing machines. Ibrahim took off his guftan, tied it to his rifle barrel, and raising it high, waved it back and forth.

"You fool!" Kasli hissed. "What are you doing? They won't take us prisoner, they will kill us all."

"They are going to kill us all regardless. Be quiet. I am getting us out of this."

A voice called out, "You Arabs, do you surrender?"

"Ah, I will not need you after all, Kasli. That one speaks Arabic." He peered over the mound of sewing machines and spotted a man crouched beside a house, red on his shoulder—an officer.

"Ya! You," he yelled. "I am Ibrahim Idris, commanding these murahaleen. No surrender. A truce."

"You shall have it. The truce of the grave."

"Esmah! We have a great many of your people captive in your church. There are two foreigners with them, a doctor and a nurse. If there is no truce, we will burn it down with all who are in it."

"I don't believe you."

"No? Will you believe me if I show the foreigners to you? Or do you prefer to see for yourself? Come alone. I promise your safety. We know our situation."

Several minutes passed, then Ibrahim heard the officer speaking in Nuban.

"What is he saying, Kasli?"

"He is speaking to the commander on the radio, telling him what you have said . . . Now he is asking what he should do."

In a short while, the officer came forward, cautiously.

"Kasli, escort him into the church. Show him."

When this was done, the officer approached Ibrahim. "What is it you want?"

"As I said, a truce. And to present my terms to your commander and to no one else."

The man left, had another conversation on the radio, and then called, "Ya! You will come alone and unarmed."

"I have a guarantee of safety?"

"Yes."

"If I am harmed, not one hostage will see the end of this day."

"Stop talking and come to me, without your rifle."

Ibrahim took the guftan off the rifle, tied it around his head, brushed the dirt from his jelibiya, and straightened his cartridge belt. He would present himself as a man of the Humr, omda of the Salamat, commander of proud murahaleen.

"Ya, Kasli," he said. "Tell Hamdan that if I have not returned by sundown, kill them all without hesitation. Allah yisalimak."

Ibrahim stepped forward, the longest and riskiest step of his life. Win all or lose all. *Whatever Allah wills,* he thought, *so it shall be done.*

"WHAT TIME IS IT?"

Negev turned his wrist toward her. One o'clock. Services had let out at ten-thirty. Already that seemed like days ago.

The battle subsided. Random gunshots, an isolated explosion, and then total silence. Negev climbed again to the lookout, returned, and stated that he had seen a number of murahaleen surrounding the church, but a greater number of SPLA surrounding the murahaleen.

"I think we win," he said.

Quinette stood. A breeze blew through her sweat-matted dress, chilling her. "I'm going to find my husband."

"No!" Negev said. "I don't know who is win, only think it is us."

"If we've won, then the danger's over; if we've lost, Michael is either dead or taken prisoner, and then I don't give a damn what happens to me. I am going to find him."

She started off, hobbling on the sides of her feet. Negev came behind her, muttering what she assumed were curses. He had more reason to curse later on. The climb down had so injured her feet that she couldn't walk any farther. He carried her piggyback toward the headquarters. His fidelity to her and to his duty touched her—it was an affirmation of humanity amid so much inhumanity. They passed a tukul that had been struck by shellfire. Two torn bodies lay outside, covered with flies. Negev came across a pair of discarded sandals and set her down, sighing with relief. She didn't think twice about wearing a dead person's sandals. They were too big, but she managed to keep them on by squeezing the thong between her toes.

"Looks like we won," she said, pointing at the SPLA flag, with its green, red, and white stripes and yellow star, flying above the headquarters building.

"Yes, missy. This time."

Dozens of soldiers were gathered outside in an atmosphere of tense expectancy. With Negev, Quinette went inside, where Michael, his back to the door, was conferring with his officers. The sight of him, alive and injured, sent an electric current through her. An officer called his attention to her. He turned and looked, wearing his battle face, blank and affectless.

"What are you doing here?"

"I had to see you."

He scolded Negev, then rebuked her. She should not have taken such a risk, not knowing the situation. She should realize she wasn't one any longer, she was two. She took her spanking, apologized, and dropped into a chair. When Michael saw the condition of her feet, he summoned a medic, who swabbed the cuts with rubbing alcohol. The sting made her grimace, which softened her husband's expression.

"I hope we never see another day like this," he said, inclining his head. "But if we do, you will go where you are told and stay there until you are told that it is safe. For now, I think you're as safe here as anywhere."

"Yes, sir," she said, as the medic taped gauze to one foot. "Is it over?"

"I don't know. We have several hundred Arabs trapped in town, but they are holding a great many hostages inside the church. Manfred and Ulrika, too."

"No!"

"I am afraid so."

"Fancher? Handy? What about them?"

"Dead," he replied, almost with indifference. "Executed. By Kasli, I'm told."

"Kasli?"

"He's with them. An officer reported it to me."

These two pieces of news struck her viscerally. Whatever had been holding her in one piece these past three or four hours gave way, and she wept.

"Stop crying!" Michael said almost savagely. "A lot of people died today. More may die. The murahaleen commander has asked for a truce. He is being brought here. We will see what he has to say. You might as well stay."

The Arab came in later under heavy guard, with an SPLA soldier holding each arm: a man of six feet, his black beard brushed with gray, his brown eyes piercing. A dirty turban girdled his head; his jelibiya, tucked at the waist into a leather cartridge belt with leather pouches, hung down to a pair of mud-spattered boots. He showed no fear, not even anxiety. Quinette hated him on sight yet couldn't deny that he had an aura about him, the magnetism of a corsair, the appeal of evil.

"Salaam aleikum," Ibrahim said in a firm voice to mask the tremors in his breast.

"Aleikum as-salaam," the rebel commander replied in excellent Arabic. Ibrahim was struck by his height, more than two meters, and the span of his shoulders. "I am in command here. Lieutenant Colonel Goraende."

"Ibrahim Idris ibn Nur-el-Din," Ibrahim replied formally. "Omda of the Salamat. You may address me as omda, colonel." *Show no weakness,* he thought. *Show him the brass of a cartridge.*

"I will address you as I see fit. What is it you have to say?"

"I will speak to you soldier to soldier."

"Soldier? You are a terrorist."

Ibrahim ignored the insult. He would not let this black abid provoke or intimidate him. He was momentarily distracted by the woman sitting in a chair. The first American he had seen, male or female. Brown hair worn in Nuban plaits, and not what he would call good-looking. No, not good-looking, but an American he could have held for, oh, ten million pounds. Too bad. God had not willed it.

"This is my wife," the commander said. "Do you wish to speak to her, too?"

Quinette felt the Arab's gaze more than she saw it—a look that was a violation, a rape with the eyes.

"We have heard about her," Ibrahim said.

"From Muhammad Kasli. We know he is with you. You are going to tell me what you propose, or do you wish only to have conversation?"

Ibrahim marshaled his thoughts—and his nerve. "First that this truce be extended to allow us to gather our dead and you yours. Next, that a peace be concluded between us, in writing if you wish. I will pledge that no Salamat, no man of all the Humr, will make war in the Nuba from now on. Next, that we be allowed to leave with our arms."

The commander paused to take all this in. He said, "And that is all?"

"No. There is a condition. It is this—that a woman who lives here is returned to me. She is my serraya, my lawful property, and a fugitive. Do not tell me she isn't here. I know she is. Kasli and others have informed me. Her name is Yamila."

The abid commander said nothing. He looked baffled.

"If this condition is not met, then none of my terms apply," Ibrahim said further. "We will kill the hostages, every one of them, and then fight you to the last man and last bullet. We are prepared for martyrdom."

"You would do all that if a woman you took by force is not returned to you? You would kill so many people, you would sacrifice the lives of your men for that?"

Show him the brass cartridge, Ibrahim thought, and said, "Yes."

"That is impossible."

Ibrahim saw that he was more experienced in the art and theatrics of bargaining than this slave boy who called himself a commander. "Very well. Then please escort me back to my men. Or shoot me dead on the spot if you wish. Or hold me prisoner. In any case, my men are instructed to set fire to the church if I am not back by sundown."

"I have no idea if this Yamila is alive or dead. She might have been killed by you butchers. What then?"

Ibrahim detected weakness. The abid is open to the idea. "If alive, return her to me. If dead, show me her body."

"I could pay you her worth."

"I don't want money. *I want her.*"

"What's he saying?" Quinette asked as Michael, after the last series of exchanges, stood with his hands behind his back, rocking on his heels.

"Be quiet," he told her. "This is between me and him."

"I only wanted to know what he wants."

"Yamila. He was the one she escaped from, and he wants her returned. Otherwise he burns the church down with everyone in it, and then he fights to the end. Now be quiet. I have no idea if she is alive or where she is."

She could be still or she could speak. Quinette was aware that this was possibly the gravest choice she had ever faced. The words left her mouth, seemingly of their own will. "I do."

Michael looked at her, startled, said something to the Arab, then took her under the arm and led her outside.

"What did you say?" he asked when they were some distance from the building.

There was no retracting her statement now. "I know where she is."

"Where?"

She told him, and it was plain he wished she hadn't.

She asked, "What happens if you do what he wants?"

"The truce goes into effect, he collects his casualties, we collect ours. Then, he says, he will sign an agreement, pledging that his tribe will no longer take part in attacks on the Nuba. The hostages are released. And then he and his men leave. There is a deadline—sundown. I keep thinking, there must be some other way."

"God would show it to you if there was," she said.

"I am so sick of this," he said. "I am sick of doing what is necessary."

"We are all sick of it, darling. I think that Arab is sick of it. Why would he propose a peace treaty if he wasn't? Let's end it now."

He looked as if he were trying to see inside her. "We will go back now, and be still. I won't tolerate your giving opinions in front of my officers and that Arab."

"We will continue now?" asked Ibrahim when the commander returned.

"We will. My wife knows where to find Yamila."

So that is what they had been talking about, Ibrahim thought. She was alive, she was here! *Al-hamduillah!*

The commander asked, "Do you have any further proposals?"

"Yes," he replied amiably. "I am a candidate for nazir of all the Humr." This was something of an exaggeration. "I can promise nothing, but I could use my influence to persuade the other tribes to join in the peace accord."

The commander trembled a little. He spoke through clenched teeth. "Very well, it is agreed. But now I have a condition. You and your men will surrender your weapons before leaving. As a sign that your offer of peace is genuine."

"As a man of the Humr, my word is sign enough, my signature on a written agreement is more than enough. We must leave with our arms. We will be in disgrace if we return without them."

"You are already in disgrace. I figured out what your plan was and held my men in position. We slaughtered your infantry, and those we didn't ran like hares."

"Yes, I know. However, we murahaleen have retained our honor. We did not run. But we would lose honor if we returned without our arms. I will suffer the death of a martyr, but not that. Colonel, all I am asking for is the return of my lawful property. But in the meantime, the sun journeys through the sky, and—"

"Shut up!"

The slave boy sat on the edge of a table covered with maps and papers, which he tapped with his walking stick.

"You Arabs are fond of speeches, aren't you?"

"Yes. It is a beautiful language. We enjoy the sound of it."

"I will withdraw my condition and demand one other, and about it there will be no discussion," he said, stepping up to Ibrahim, looming over him. "You are prepared for what you call martyrdom; so are we. I am prepared also to sacrifice all those people merely for the pleasure of killing you myself. Here is the condition. You will hand over Muhammad Kasli to me."

I have done it! Ibrahim thought. What do I care about that Nuban defector? Betrays one, he will betray another. "You people can make speeches as well," he said. "Agreed."

"Very well, Ibrahim Idris ibn Nur-el-Din. My soldiers will escort you back. You will order the hostages released. Then you return here with Kasli. Him for her. We will attend to the other business when that is done."

"Peace be with you," Ibrahim said.

"And unto to you, peace."

As the Arab was ushered out, Michael turned to Negev. "Take a couple of men with you, bring Yamila here. Tell her . . . tell her . . . anything . . . but—"

"No," Quinette interjected, with the slightest of smiles. "Tell her Michael wishes to see her."

Everyone assembled outside to await the exchange. Quinette watched for signs of dissent over her husband's decision. If there were any, she did not notice them. Yamila, after all, was a stranger here, a stray.

The Arab was the first to arrive, with his SPLA escort and Major Kasli, blindfolded, wobbling and bleeding from the forehead, hands tied. A soldier shoved him face-down onto the ground and stood over him, rifle barrel pressed to the base of his skull. In a little while, he would be in that same position and someone would pull the trigger.

Some twenty minutes later Negev and two of Michael's bodyguards came in with Yamila. The fierce, half-naked woman was walking with her customary stride but stopped short when she saw the Arab—the face she must have thought she would never see again. A civilized woman in her position would have sensed that something was terribly wrong but would not have listened to her instincts; she would have paused to assess, to reason things out. Yamila knew instantly the danger she was in, saw that she'd been tricked; but with her there was no barrier of thought between the perception and the emotion, between the emotion and the reaction. She bolted, quick as a sprinter off the starting block. A guard pursued and caught her, holding her in a bear hug until she bit his hand. He let her go, she fled, he chased her again and tackled her. Another guard grabbed her ankles while the first seized her arms, she writhing, shrieking, spitting. It took a third soldier to fully subdue her. Michael looked very distressed. He spoke to the Arab, who then turned and walked away, followed by the three men, carrying Yamila like hunters a bagged trophy. Quinette listened to her cries and howls slowly diminish, knowing they would echo in her memory for some time to come. But those too would diminish, till she heard them no more. She had made friends with the stranger who was herself, with the woman she'd become. She had come full circle. Yamila's fate was shameful, yes, but the multitudes of women she had redeemed from slavery had to be balanced against this one she'd sent back into slavery by speaking two words, the same two, curiously, she'd uttered in her wedding vows.

Michael turned from the figures walking in the distance, bent over as if he were sick, and took Quinette's hand. She threaded her fingers into his and squeezed to assure him that it was all right. God would forgive him, and God would forgive the woman she now was as He had so often forgiven the one she'd been. Jesus was still her friend. Jesus loved her.

Small True Facts

THERE WAS NOTHING like the deaths of Caucasians to give the war more than two seconds of air time and four paragraphs in the newspapers. And there was nothing like the deaths of three of their own to whip the media into a froth. CNN gave the story big play—their woman in Africa, blown out of the sky in the line of duty. Curiously, the network had nothing to say about what she had been working on.

A press trip was organized to bring correspondents and cameramen to the scene. Fitzhugh and Pamela Smyth secured places for themselves on the plane. Pamela was seeking what she called "closure"; so was Fitzhugh, though of a different kind. He was willing to entertain the possibility that in this instance the Sudanese government was telling the truth.

The trip was delayed a few days by the fighting in New Tourom. When it was deemed safe to travel, the press plane flew to Malakal, where a chartered helicopter delivered its passengers to the crash site, ringed by SPLA soldiers. Michael was on hand, eager to give interviews. Troops were filmed and photographed holding the perforated wing while he pointed at the bullet holes, each about the size of a golf ball, with a rim of bent metal around it. A 12.7- or 14.5-millimeter antiaircraft machine gun, he informed the reporters, one of whom asked if he would comment on Khartoum's version of events. The usual nonsense and propaganda, he replied. The government had failed to subdue the Nuba, had failed to isolate it by bombing its airfields, and now resorted to terror to stop aid from reaching the mountains.

With Michael on board, the helicopter brought the journalists to New Tourom for a tour of the destruction wrought by the attack. He had insisted on this to present further proof of Khartoum's perfidy. Quinette joined her husband as guide, offering an eyewitness description of mura-haleen thundering through the town on horseback, her account under-scored by the stench of rotting horseflesh that still lingered in the air.

As the group trekked back to the airfield for the first leg of the trip home, Michael handed Fitzhugh a sealed envelope for delivery to Douglas—a letter of thanks, he said in an undertone. "Without the assis-tance you people brought to us, we would have lost this battle and all the Nuba with it."

Under a grass-roofed shelter at the side of the runway, Fitzhugh and Pamela waited with the reporters for the helicopter to finish refueling. Sit-ting on the ground against a post, she spotted an object lying in the grass—a small plastic bottle with an orange bullet-shaped cap. She removed the cap and squeezed the plunger, sending a jet of mist into the air.

"Maybe this will help," she said. "That stench—I can't get it out of my nose."

"Could I see that?"

He held the bottle upright between a thumb and forefinger and stud-ied it, like an archaeologist examining an enigmatic artifact. The label read, NASOKLEAR. FOR RELIEF OF ALLERGY AND SINUS SYMPTOMS.

"It was lying right there?" he asked.

"Yes. Maybe I'd better not use it. Who knows where it's been."

"Who knows," Fitzhugh said. He thought of Adid's "fresh ideas" and pocketed the bottle. *Un petit fait vrais*—a phrase his Seychellois father was fond of using.

Having not quite achieved closure, Pamela put past enmities aside and called on Douglas to help organize a memorial service for the three avia-tors. Malachy Delaney and John Barrett presided. The ceremony was held at sunset at the western end of the Loki airfield, some two hundred people in attendance. The clergymen said the sorts of things clergymen do on such occasions. Pamela delivered a moving tribute to Tara, Douglas paid homage to Wesley and Mary, striking a note of comic relief when he touched his nose and said that it was well known that he and Dare had dif-ferences of opinion, but those differences had not affected *one whit* his respect for the man's abilities and courage, so amply demonstrated on his final flight. When the sermons and speeches were finished, four Knight planes flew over, one peeling away to make a "missing man" formation. A trumpeter from the local police barracks blew retreat. Listening to the fine words and the tragic notes of the trumpet echoing over the twilit land-scape, Fitzhugh recalled the vultures pecking at Wesley's corpse, of the arrival in Loki of the clear plastic burn bags containing the remains of

Tara and her passengers. *Truth is Beauty and Beauty Truth?* he thought. Not always, but even when Truth was horrifying, it was preferable to the attractive lie of pretty clichés and the aesthetics of ritual. Likewise when Truth was commonplace. One small true fact, like a bottle of nasal spray found in a place where it did not belong, was in its way beautiful.

Douglas's eulogy had partly rehabilitated his image among those who thought he'd deserved Dare's punch in the nose. Fitzhugh didn't think that was why he gave it. He sincerely wanted to honor the dead. The words he spoke were sincere. His sincerity added to Fitzhugh's suspicions, for he knew the American was never more fraudulent than when he was most sincere.

Fitzhugh had presented Michael's thank-you note to him. It included a new coded shopping list. With the danger of being exposed eliminated, Douglas was inspired to resume Busy Beaver's operations. Perhaps he was driven by financial pressures as well. Tara's fate had a decided chilling effect on Knight's flight crews. Several had refused missions to the Nuba and other no-go zones, which caused some independent agencies to take their business to one-horse air operators desperate enough to risk their lives. Douglas himself appeared to think he was invulnerable, so much so that he began to fly the gun runs himself, with Tony as his copilot. Fitzhugh didn't know if Hassan Adid was aware that his managing director was up to his old tricks; nor did he care. He was preoccupied with looking for another *petit fait vrais.* "*What are you, a fuckin' detective?*" Yes, Tony, I am, he thought, *but without badge, gun, warrant, or intent of arresting anyone. I only want to know the truth of what happened.*

He made a mental catalogue of his small facts:

Two planes carrying the people who could do the most harm to
   Douglas and Adid go down on the same day.
The bottle of Adid's brand of nasal spray.
Wesley's strange request.
The grease-stained mechanic's coveralls in Tony's hut.

He compiled the questions the small facts raised:

What were the odds of the two aircraft crashing on the same day?
Was Adid at the New Tourom airfield, and if he was, when and for
   what purpose?
How did he get there?

Why did Wesley ask him to retrieve the water jug and plastic bags and what did he mean when he said that someone had to clear out in a hurry?

Why had Tony balked when asked to search for the wreck of Wesley's plane?

He concluded that he had slightly more than nothing.

He persuaded the UN authorities to send a crash-investigation team to look at the Hawker, and when they returned with photographs, key pieces of the wreckage, and the plane's voice and flight data recorders, he told them to keep him abreast of their findings. They cautioned him not to hold his breath; even when a wrecked plane is in relatively good condition, as the Hawker was, crash investigations took a long time.

All right, he would do his own.

" 'Waaah! I feel good, so good . . .' " VanRensberg, Knight's flight mechanic, was singing on the tarmac, headphone clamped to his ears. He flipped Fitzhugh a wave and went on gyrating, shaking his big ass. " '*I feel good, so good, so good . . .*' " A couple of Kenyan mechanics laughed at the crazy mzungu. An Afrikaner imitating James Brown was amusing.

Fitzhugh gestured to take off the earphones. "Could I talk to you a moment?"

"Sure," the mechanic said, switching off his Walkman. "I'm not busy."

"I see that. This must be a private conversation."

VanResenberg squinted with one eye. "Don't notice anybody listening in."

"It has to do with Wesley's crash," Fitzhugh explained. "His plane had been overhauled a few days before. Do you know who did the work?"

"No. It wasn't any of our people."

"I was talking to him on the radio before he went down. He said some odd things. He was having trouble with his fuel pumps. Then he asked me to fetch a water jug and some plastic bags from a rubbish bin near the hangar. He told me not to empty the jug if there was anything in it."

"And?"

"There was nothing in the jug, only a little dirty water. The bags were clean. What do you suppose he meant? What's the connection between a discarded water jug and his fuel pumps?"

VanRensberg asked to look at the jug, and Fitzhugh brought him to the company truck and pulled the container out from behind the seats. The mechanic screwed off the cap, poured a drop or two of the contents into his palm, sniffed, and stood staring at the jug for several moments.

"If you had enough of that sludge in your fuel tanks, it could foul up the fuel pumps. Maybe that's what he meant."

"How? Give me a lesson in aircraft mechanics."

"You've got two pumps for each engine," VanRensberg began. "A low-pressure and a high-pressure. The first one brings the fuel up from the tank and to the engine. The high-pressure pump sprays the fuel into the burners. If crud clogged up the filters in the low-pressure pump and it quit, the high-pressure pump would feed fuel to the emergency fuel controller. Are you following me so far?"

Fitzhugh nodded.

"So that wouldn't be a good situation—you'd have unfiltered fuel going into the engine—but it would still run. If there's water in the fuel"—VanResenberg hesitated. "I'd better back up a little. Fuel is what lubricates the high-pressure pump. If there's water in the fuel, it could cause the pump to seize up and shut down because water isn't a lubricant. The pump quits, the engine quits. That's a bad situation no matter what you're flying, but it's bloody bad if you're in a Hawker as old as Wes's—a seven four eight that vintage doesn't have auxiliary engine power controls like, oh, say a Cessna two-oh-eight or a Let. Nothing you do will get the engine running again. And if it happens in both engines, you are well and truly fucked. But I don't think that's what happened to Wes, if that's what you're getting at."

Fitzhugh leaned against the Toyota, trying to absorb the technical information. "Why not?"

"Here's a lesson in elementary chemistry. Water is heavier than aviation fuel. If Wes had water and mud in his tanks, it would have sunk down to the sump—that's the lowest point in the tank. And it's automatic in preflight to drain the sumps. Any water and crud would have been drained out."

"I see. Of course Wesley wasn't known for the thoroughness of his pre-flight checks."

"He would've done that, Fitz. Like I said, it's automatic." VanRensberg's teeth showed through his sweat-dappled beard. "I get what you're thinking. Did somebody put muddy water in Wes's tanks? Well, even if sombody did, it wouldn't have made any difference. Wes would have gotten rid of it on preflight."

"I will tell you why I think so. Wes said another odd thing. That whoever left those things—the jug and the bags—did it because he had to clear out in a hurry. He suspected sabotage. I am guessing, yes? But I believe he meant that the culprit fled in a rush because he saw someone coming, someone who might have caught him in the act."

"Nasty, Fitz. Very nasty thought."

"Yes, very. Please don't mention to anyone that we had this conversation." He placed the earphones back on VanRensberg's head. "Keep feeling good."

The next day, while Douglas and Tony were off on one of their Busy Beaver missions, Fitzhugh borrowed a spare key from the compound's manager and broke into Tony's hut. Inside, from among the stack of flight and operations manuals, he dug out repair and maintenance manuals for a Hawker-Siddley 748 and a Rolls-Royce 514 turboprop—the engine on Wesley's plane. Tony's coveralls had been laundered and were on a hangar. Although someone as sloppy as he wouldn't notice that the manual was out of place, Fitzhugh was careful to put it back where he'd found it. *Un petit fait vrais.*

He returned to the office, where he found VanRensberg waiting for him. The mechanic said he would like to have another private conversation. Rachel being at lunch, Fitzhugh replied that here was as good a place as any and sat down.

"I've been thinking about our talk yesterday," VanRensberg said. "If Wes suspected someone of pouring dirty water into his tanks, why did he ask you to retrieve the plastic bags in addition to the water jug? I've asked myself, If the fuel had water in it, then why wasn't the contaminant eliminated in preflight? Sloppiness on Wes's part? Maybe. Or was it this?" He held up a freezer bag and snapped it. "Plastic, like aviation fuel, is made from petroleum. It has hydrocarbons, also like fuel."

"This is another chemistry lesson?" Fitzhugh asked, bemused.

"A nasty lesson. You pour the muddy water into the plastic bags, seal them, and then squeeze them into the tanks through the fuel-fill. The plastic remains intact for some time. I'm not knowledgeable enough to say how long, but for a time. So when the pilot drains his system prior to takeoff, the contaminants will be sealed up in the bags and will not be eliminated. But eventually the fuel will dissolve the plastic, the mud and water will become mixed with the fuel, and the pilot will have a failure of his high-pressure pumps and then engine failure."

Fitzhugh felt a catch in his throat.

VanRensberg said, "I understand there is an accident investigation going on?"

"That's right."

"So I assume the investigators drained the tanks and took fuel samples for analysis. They may detect the presence of water in the fuel, but they will find no trace of plastic because it has the same chemical makeup as the fuel. It will have vanished without a trace. And the investigators are likely to conclude that the pilot did an improper preflight procedure."

The simplicity of it! Fitzhugh thought. *The elegant simplicity of it!*

"And Wesley, besides his reputation for not being thorough in his pre-flight, was in a rush that day," he said.

"Yes. I heard that he was," said the mechanic. "So if I was the one who sabotaged the plane in the way I have just described, that's what I would want people to think. Wes was careless to begin with, and his hurry made him more careless."

"That is your opinion?"

VanRensberg hesitated, glancing back and forth as if to make sure no one was listening in. "A theory, not an opinion. No—a suspicion. Wes lost both engines. A catastrophic failure of both engines isn't likely. I've heard he almost made it. What do you think? You were out there."

"Yes, it looked that way," Fitzhugh answered.

"If any pilot could land a Hawker-Siddley dead-stick, he could. Maybe he was sloppy, but the man could fly. Nasty business."

"Thank you, VanRensberg," Fitzhugh said. "Thank you for the chemistry lesson."

At the end of the week, routine banking business took him to Nairobi. If it hadn't, he would have concocted a reason to go. When his business was concluded, he recollected a remark Wesley had made after the share-holders' meeting and asked to see the branch manager, an Indian gentleman from whom he requested the records for Knight Air Services Limited for the previous twelve months. As a partner in the company, Fitzhugh was authorized to see them. The manager put on a puzzled expression and shook his head. The firm had been dissolved, as you must know, he said. The records had been disposed of. Yes, Fitzhugh replied, he was aware the the firm had been dissolved but was unaware that its bank records had been destroyed. Could he please see the records for Knight Relief Services? These were produced: a sheaf of deposits, withdrawals, and monthly statements in a file folder. Fitzhugh paged through them quickly, stopping when he observed a transfer of funds from the Uganda Central Bank to the account. It came to $72,000. That would be Busy Beaver's earnings in the first week of its existence, four flights at $18,000 each. The debit column showed a withdrawal for $36,000, presumably the company's share in the fifty-fifty split with Tony. Beside the figure was the notation "Wire transfer" and on the next page the words "Credit Suisse Bank, Geneva," followed by several sets of letters and account numbers. Numbers but no names. And what is this? he asked. A request for a wire transfer of funds from this account to that account in Switzerland, the manager replied, in a tone implying that he considered the question idiotic. Fitzhugh prided himself on his tolerance but had to admit to owning one unreasonable prejudice: he didn't like Indians. Their accent grated on his ears, and in their manner they managed to be obsequious and supercilious at the same time. Thank you, he said, masking his irritation. And did the manager recall if such wire transfers had been made when Knight Air Services was in existence? If so, who authorized them? Excuse me, Mr. Martin, but are you conducting an official audit? What is the reason for these questions? Fitzhugh merely smiled, thanked him for his time, and left.

Could Douglas be runing guns for the money? he thought, hailing a taxi for Jomo Kenyatta Airport. *For the money alone and all that business about providing for the Nubans' defense so much claptrap?*

The taxi dropped him off at the Department of Civil Aviation, where he paid a call on his old friend, the director. This was his day to walk paper trails. He requested copies of recent flight plans filed from Wilson Field. He gave her a range of dates. Pleased to accommodate him, the source of her favorite American cookies, she made a phone call, said yes, they were available, and sent him to another office, where a clerk gave him the plans in a manila envelope. Fitzhugh took out the flimsies and read the information various pilots had scrawled in the boxes and blanks, at the dated stamps and signatures on the bottom of the forms.

Aircraft identification: 5Z203. Type of aircraft: G1C. Departure aerodrome: Wilson. Destination aerodrome: JKIA, for Jomo Kenyatta International Airport. Total EET: HR. 08. Min. 00. Pilot in command: Braithwaite, D. Filed by: Pilot or representative—and there Fitzhugh saw a signature almost as familiar as his own. The date stamp in the lower right-hand corner indicated that the flight had been made on the seventh of the previous month. He looked at a calendar—the seventh had been a Saturday. The crashes occurred the following Monday.

He made a copy of the flight plan, one more small fact, which contained one big falsehood. He felt no satisfaction, only a sickness of the heart.

*   *   *

HASSAN ADID'S SECRETARY said he was full up with appointments for the day but would be pleased to meet Fitzhugh for dinner.

It was at the Tamarind, Adid's favorite restaurant. Fitzhugh arrived early to calm himself with a double scotch, neat. Adid came in a little late, swinging an attaché case, his stylish jacket and trousers testifying that their wearer was no ordinary urban African in an ill-fitting knockoff but a man of the world.

He apologized for his tardiness—a last-minute phone call. After the preliminary chitchat, the fussy business of asking the waiter for recommendations, he asked what was on Fitzhugh's mind.

"The meeting you and Douglas had last month," he replied. It was the only lead-in he could think of. "I was wondering, what were your fresh ideas?"

"Fresh ideas? Ideas about what?"

"Our—our problem."

The first course came: salad for Fitzhugh, lobster bisque for Adid. A none-too-observant Muslim, he paused to sniff and taste the Fumé Blanc, then signal his approval with a flick of his brows.

"What problem are you referring to?"

Of course he would play dumb. What else could Fitzhugh expect? What, for that matter, did he expect to come out of this get-together? A confession? "The story that reporter was working on," he said.

"Ah, that," Adid said, perfectly composed. "It was nothing, so I told Douglas to do nothing. If you want to call that a fresh idea, you may do so."

"Nothing?"

"It wasn't the problem he seemed to think it was. In any event, it is not any kind of problem now."

"It certainly isn't."

Adid cocked his elegant head aside. "It's a moot point."

"Mute," Fitzhugh said. "I prefer mute."

"It's too bad what happened. A dangerous business, flying in Sudan."

"I'm curious. Why did you think the story wasn't a problem?"

"To say that Knight is profiting off a war? That's been said before. And what is the difference if we are? One goes into business to make a profit."

Shrimp in a cream and brandy sauce was set before him. "That's what Douglas said? That we were going to be painted as war profiteers?"

Adid accepted his grilled Malindi snapper. "I don't know why he flew all the way to Nairobi to discuss that. Was there something he did not mention?"

Even Adid could not lie this well, Fitzhugh thought. This is too cute and coy to be anything but honest. Too confused to answer, he said, "So your meeting was cordial? Douglas told me it was an ugly scene."

"Hardly ugly. I was annoyed with him for taking up my time with a small problem he could have easily handled himself."

"Maybe he did," Fitzhugh said. "I'm not sure how easy it was."

"And I would have been annoyed with you if you had taken up my time during business hours with this conversation." He snatched a handkerchief from his pocket and sneezed. "But I'm pleased to have dinner with the once-famous Ambler of the Harambe Stars. My son has kept the autograph you gave me when we met the first time."

"Yes, I recall," Fitzhugh said, experiencing a moment of deflated expectation. Here was a man who had once smuggled contraband ivory, a man who with his father had been a suspect in the sabotaging of Richard Leakey's airplane. Fitzhugh had been geared up for a confrontation with the author of six murders but got instead a banal villain who faked bankruptcies and schemed to crush competitors and wasn't even a coconspirator, much less a criminal mastermind. It was oddly disappointing; it was as if Adid had let him down.

"Speaking of that first meeting, a private word with you?" Adid asked.

"Yes?"

"What is your opinion of Douglas? How does it go, working for him?"

"My opinion? Why do you ask, if I may ask?"

"You recall what he told us at that first meeting? That he had been a fighter pilot in the Persian Gulf War for the American Air Force? He also said his father had been a successful land developer who died of heart failure. I make it a point to know as much as I can about my managers, and when I took over Knight, I looked into Douglas's background. It took a little time. He was in the American Air Force, but never in the war and never as a fighter pilot. A common soldier. His father was a successful man, but he didn't die of heart failure. He was murdered."

To this revelation, Fitzhugh had nothing to say.

"It was a famous case in the city he comes from. Tucson in Arizona. It was in all the newspapers. It seems his father's business became a laundry for Mexican drug money, he was going to testify against them, and they blew him up in his automobile. You never had a hint of this?"

"No, never."

"It disturbs me, his telling stories like that. I don't care who a man lies to as long as it is not to me."

Adid sneezed again.

"Could you use this?" Fitzhugh took the nasal spray from out of his pocket.

"Ah, a fellow sufferer."

"Oh, no. I happened to find this in a rather odd place. At an airstrip in the Nuba mountains."

"Why odd? I do not suppose those people are immune to allergies."

"Have you ever been to Sudan, Hassan?"

"To Khartoum several times on business," he answered.

"I meant to southern Sudan. Or to the Nuba."

He gave a look of distaste. "Why would I ever want to go there?"

Fitzhugh left the spray bottle on the table, one small fact discarded in exchange for others.

TURKANA BOYS WERE playing bau under a tree—the quick movements of young black hands, the click of white stones. Smoking an Embassy, Fitzhugh stood in the shade and pretended to watch the game's progress. He felt an imperative to act but wasn't sure what action to take. To call his evidence circumstantial would be generous; to even call it evidence was a stretch. Nevertheless, he was sure he was in possession of a large true fact, monstrously large, and he deeply wished he'd never acquired it.

An old Turkana passed by on spindly legs, his staff with wooden head-rest on his shoulder. A PanAfrik Hercules took off, and shortly another plane came in from the west, a Gulfstream Two. 5Z203. Fitzhugh started back to the office, forcing himself not to think. Think too much, you won't do anything.

Cap thrown back, Douglas breezed in, tossed his logbook onto his desk, then sat down and filled it out from notes taken in flight. Fitzhugh, erasing the board, feigned absorption in tomorrow's schedule. Finished with his log, Douglas went to the coffee urn.

"Where's Rachel?"

"I gave her the afternoon off."

"We're out of coffee. She's supposed to keep it full. The crews like a jolt when they get back." Then in a jocular tone: "I like a jolt, and I'm the boss."

"Well, I gave her the afternoon off."

"Is that a new fringe benefit?" He poured water into the urn and scooped coffee into the basket. "So how was Nairobi?"

"Nairobi was Nairobi."

"Thought you might have patched things up with Diana while you were there."

"I don't use company time for personal business. I had dinner with Hassan. We discussed the meeting you had with him last month. On the sixth, wasn't it?"

Douglas stood with his shoulder to the wall, legs crossed at the ankles, thumb hooked into the handle of his mug.

"I would like to hear why you lied to me," Fitzhugh said. "I believe I am owed an explanation."

Nimble as ever, Douglas replied, "All right, I did what you thought I'd do. Chickened out. I told him we were going to get smeared as war profiteers on CNN. Man, I'm sorry." Fitzhugh shrank away as Douglas reached out to touch him. "You never let me down, but I let you down. Didn't have the balls. But—I don't mean to sound callous—it doesn't make any difference now."

"A moot point."

"Yeah."

Fitzhugh reached under his desk for the water jug. "Would you recognize this, Douglas?"

"Are you going flaky on me? What the fuck are you talking about?"

"You were the one with the fresh idea," Fitzhugh said, with a confidence produced by his anger. "Or perhaps you would call it a cool idea. The thing that surprises me is that you thought of it all on your own and carried it out all on your own, with considerable help from Tony. I was sure Adid was behind it."

The red light on the urn winked. Douglas pressed the spigot and stood blowing across his mug. "Man, you are in a state."

"Tony had a reason to sabotage Dare's plane—he hated them both. He had the opportunity—it was just a matter of sneaking in there when it was dark with dirty water and a few plastic bags. He would know what do to—a trained flight mechanic."

"Whoa!" Douglas said with a wild laugh at the absurdity of it all. "Whoa, whoa, *whoa*! What did you smoke when you were in Nairobi?"

"Only a few cigarettes. When I was at the bank. I suppose I could talk to you about embezzling company funds, but that's rather a misdemeanor compared with this."

"Get the fuck out of here before I—"

"Before you what? You're going to listen to this. Tony could have found out that Wesley was flying Phyllis on Monday from only five people. Three had no reason to tell him. The fourth, me, never spoke to him. Which leaves you. You had a discussion with him *before* you went to see Hassan. Yes, you told him to cancel the arms flights, but you had some other things to say. When was the last time you were at Jomo Kenyatta?"

"You can't talk to me like we're in a police interrogation room."

"When was the last time you were at Jomo?"

A smile broke across the clean American face, that guileless, beguiling smile. "Five years ago, when I landed in this country."

"Thank you. Thank you, for once, for the truth. And here is the lie that proves the truth."

Fitzhugh stepped across the room to hand him the flight plan. He felt, in the still, elongated seconds it took Douglas to read it, like a cuckold presenting his wife with proof of her infidelity. Douglas raised his eyes, the gray irises steady and concentrated.

"I know what a false flight plan looks like," Fitzhugh said. "It doesn't take eight hours to fly from Wilson to Jomo and back."

"You've been busy."

"You too, a busy beaver. In case Tony's midnight mechanics didn't work, or if they did, in case a pilot like Dare overcame the problems and lived through it—and he damned near did—you flew yourself to the Nuba mountains with a backup plan. You had a talk with the Archangel. I can guess what you said to him—*If this story gets out, I'm screwed and so are you. Your troops will be back to throwing spears at gunships.* You convinced him that under no circumstances must that plane be allowed to complete its journey. *So just in case Dare shows up, Lieutenant Colonel Goraende, shoot down the Hawker and blame it on the Sudanese army.* You hadn't counted on a last-minute change of planes and pilots, and I don't suppose the thugs Michael sent to do the dirty work knew a Cessna from a Hawker. All they knew was to shoot down a plane coming in on Monday morning. I guess we can say Tara was collateral damage. Convenient, though, that she's out of the way."

"Fitzhugh Martin, private eye," said Douglas, shaking his head in dismay. "If I didn't know you better, I'd say you lost your—"

"Go to hell."

Douglas folded up the flight plan and gave it back. "You look surprised, my man. I'm not worried what you'll do with that."

"You don't know what I'm going to do."

"Actually, I do." He went to the file cabinet, withdrew the company checkbook, and sat down. "No boss would have tolerated listening to one tenth of the shit I've just listened to. But—I've said this before, but it bears repeating—I couldn't have brought this airline to where it is, couldn't have done it without you. That entitles you to the rest of the year's salary as severance pay." He filled in the amount and held the check across the desk. "You're going to take this and walk out of here. That's what you're going to do."

Fitzhugh was disappointed to see him resort to something so blatant and crude. It was worthy of a tinpot Kenyan politician. But he had to watch becoming too judgmental. *"I couldn't have done it without you."* That was another small true fact, and the deaths of those six human beings was another collaboration. With all the big and little moral compromises he'd made in the past three years, with all the rationalizations, justifications, and lies, all the pretending that what he knew to be true wasn't true, he had enabled Douglas to do what he'd done and to think he could get away with it, as he probably would. In his own moral transformation, Fitzhugh had been like the frog immersed in water that is slowly heated; adjusting its body temperature to an ever-more-lethal environment, it is insensible to the danger it is in and boils to death. He had leaped from the pot just in time. Much longer, and he might have tolerated even this crime. His escape, however, was no absolution. He'd been an accomplice of sorts , and now he was being tempted to make one more, one final compromise. Knowing it would be fatal, he said, "If I quit, you don't owe me anything. So I quit."

"You're sure? What you said to me was disgusting. Still and all, I wouldn't feel right, seeing you walk out of here with nothing."

"I can assure you, your feelings don't count for anything."

"Have it your way, then," he said, tearing up the check and writing "void" on the stub.

"There are so many things I would like to know," Fitzhugh said. "Most of all—not why, that's easy—but how? How did you bring yourself to do it? How did the motive get translated into action? This was mass murder. Of people you knew. Did you ever have a moment of doubt, of hesitation?"

Douglas regarded him with the expression of a bemused boy, and Fitzhugh felt much the same deflation as he had last night. Like most people, he'd always assumed the face of evil would look its part, monstrous, grotesque, theatrically ugly; but here it was before him, the face of a bird-watcher, blandly handsome, veiled in innocence.

"Fitz, you are no longer an employee of this airline. I have work to do. I have to ask you to leave."

*   *   *

LOKI WAS A tight little world, and the news that he had quit spread with the swiftness of a flash-flood. He was happy to discover that he was still employable. Several NGOs offered him jobs; the UN flight coordinator — this was the man who had replaced Timmerman—asked if he would accept a position as his deputy. Fitzhugh did, the UN forgave him his past sins, and he moved into the UN compound.

He'd ended up where he'd begun, once more a soldier in the army of international beneficence, and what he felt was a first cousin to despair. When he looked back on the past three years of work and risk, he couldn't see what difference he had made. Tara had been so right: Sudan was a land of illusions. He was reminded of the warning on side-view mirrors— CAUTION: OBJECTS IN THE MIRROR ARE CLOSER THAN THEY APPEAR. It was just the opposite in the mirror of Sudan. Whatever one's object was—to end a famine, to bring peace, to heal the sick—it was farther away than it appeared, seemingly within one's grasp but always beyond it.

Now he was the one who faxed Khartoum asking its approval for planes to land here or there. Not long ago he would have considered such work as tantamount to trafficking with the enemy; but he could no longer say with certainty who the enemy was. Knight flights on UN missions appeared on the daily list; he knew by the identification numbers who was flying the aircraft, and he would picture Douglas at high altitude, an unclouded conscience in unclouded air.

They bumped into each other now and then. Douglas was always pleasant. "Hey, Fitz, how are you doing," he would say, as if nothing had passed between them. The man was amazing. He was like an actor who had become the role he was playing, but with this difference: The self-deception was not artful but as natural and unconscious as the feathers on the birds he observed. It was the absence of craft that granted him the power to deceive others. In his attractive costumes—the successful entre-preneur of aviation, the man of compassion, the crusading idealist—the murderer was invisible. So were the naked appetites and ambition that had driven him. And this was hidden, too: the derangement wrought by his faith in the rightness of his actions. He must have been persuaded that Wesley and Mary and Phyllis had betrayed the sacred cause—and him— and were therefore deserving of betrayal in turn. Deserving even of death. He had broken faith with the best that was in him and with the humanity he professed to serve. A malevolent voice had whispered a summons; he'd answered. Anyone who does not acknowledge the darkness in his nature will succumb to it. He will not take precautions against its prompting, nor recognize it when it calls.

The very sight of Douglas inspired in Fitzhugh a hunger to bring about a change in perceptions, to strip him bare so all could see him for what he was and Douglas could see himself in a clear light. Sometimes at night, gazing at the posters of his patron saints, Mandela, Malcolm, and Marley, he heard the souls of the dead crying out for justice. Tara haunted him most of all. Her cries were the loudest, as if the others had appointed that incorruptible woman to speak for them. *You haven't done enough,* she admonished. *It wasn't enough merely to have refused his bribe and quit his side. If you were an accomplice before, you are now an accessory after the fact, harboring a fugitive in your silence and inaction.*

Her appeals grew more frequent and strident. Once, over the conversations in the flight coordinator's office, over the hum of fax machines and printers and the click of keyboards, he heard her in the middle of the day, her voice so clear it was almost an auditory hallucination. And that night, as he lay alone in his blue and white bungalow, she visited him again and he answered her aloud. "What do you expect me to do? This is Africa, Tara, where justice is as rare as ice." He didn't expect an answer and was shocked when he heard one: *And where God and the Devil are one and the same.*

A CNN correspondent named Peacock approached him one day at lunch. He said he had replaced Phyllis Rappaport and that the network had decided to pay tribute to their fallen correspondent by completing the story she'd been working on. That was proving difficult. She hadn't informed the foreign news editor what it was about. Apparently she'd been waiting till she had it wrapped up. Most of her notes had been on the plane with her, but she had left some other background material in the office, and it was from these fragments that he was trying to piece the story together.

"That is where you got my name?" Fitzhugh asked.

It was, replied Peacock, a fortyish man with thick, dark hair and the complexion of a nightclub singer. Among the items Phyllis had kept in her office were four videotapes and some photographs. He needed someone to identify the people in them and answer some questions. Fitzhugh suggested he speak to Douglas Braithwaite. The reporter said he had, but Mr. Braithwaite did not want to cooperate.

Here was a difference he could make. He could bring it all out into the disinfecting sunlight. But would the possible outcome—Douglas's ruination—quiet Tara's voice? Would it satisfy her? He didn't think so. *Where God and the Devil are one and the same.* Suddenly, there in the UN mess, his course of action was made plain to him. It would require him to make another compromise. If he could presume to call obtaining justice for those six souls God's work, he would have to ask the Devil's help.

"Give me your card," he said to the reporter. "I can't help you right now. Possibly later."

The next day he asked his boss if he could take a few "personal days" to go to Nairobi to attend to some personal business.

SILENT AS A shadow, the Somali servant came in with a tray of tea and scones. Diana occupied one of the green leather armchairs, beneath the Masai spears and shield, her legs crossed and her hands locked over the knee.

"So what brings you here? Visiting us parasites?" she said.

"I cannot tell you how sorry I am I ever said that. I hope someday you can forgive me."

"I forgave you some time ago. It's the forgetting part that's hard." He watched her hands, with the testimony of bluish veins that her face and hair and body belied, pick up a scone, slice it in two, and methodically spread jam on each half. Leaning forward, she passed one to him. "But I have to say it is nice to see you. Please, please don't make too much of that."

"I won't," he said, although he was happy to hear it, happy, indeed amazed, that she had even let him in.

"You seem a bit tense. It must be awkward, your coming here."

"Awkward? No, it isn't for me if it isn't for you. There is something I've been keeping to myself and I can't stand it anymore. It's driving me crazy. I'm"—he laughed nervously—"I'm hearing voices. Not with these"—touching an ear—"but in here, inside my head."

She looked down contemplatively and rubbed a stain in the knees of her jodhpurs. "Voices?"

"Tara's most of all. You see, I believe . . . no, I am virtually certain . . . how hard it is to actually say this to someone else . . . she was murdered."

She made no reply and reached into the magazine rack beside her chair for a stack of old newspapers, which she placed on the tea table. The topmost was a copy of the *Nation*, the headlines decked.

LEGENDARY PILOT BELIEVED DEAD IN SUDAN

ONE AMERICAN, TWO KENYANS ALSO ABOARD

AIRCRAFT DOWN IN NUBA MOUNTAINS

SEARCH PLANE WITH TWO CREW MEMBERS MISSING

"Of course she was murdered. The Sudanese army pulled the triggers, but that isn't what killed her, and you know what I'm saying."

"Yes. I've been through that with Pamela. I've been through it with myself."

"Khartoum has been making threats for years. They finally made good on it, and I'm just so sorry, so damned sorry it had to be her," Diana said. He wanted to draw closer to her but was restrained by the stiffness of her posture, a certain frigidity in her manner. "Four kids, two still at university. Maybe she shouldn't have gone on with such a risky way of making a living, but then, she didn't have much choice."

"Diana, I am not talking figuratively. I mean that she was really murdered. She wasn't the intended victim, that reporter was. Phyllis was murdered, her camera crew were murdered. Wesley and Mary were murdered. By Douglas and another man you don't know, Tony Bollichek."

She tilted her chin and jerked her head back, as if from a foul smell. "That bears some explaining."

That is what he did for the next half hour, interrupted once by a phone call—Diana was invited to a party—and by her questions. When he was finished, he asked what she thought, and she replied that she thought he sounded like a lawyer on closing arguments.

"Does it hold together? Does it make sense?"

"It does—to me. But all there is in it is proof that Doug is a pathological liar. If you brought it to a prosecutor, he would laugh you out of his office."

"I have no intention of bringing it to a prosecutor. I never did. But I am going to do something."

"Shouldn't you wait till that crash investigation is over? You would have something more solid then."

"That could take weeks, possibly months."

She glanced outside, at bougainvillea spilling its red and purple over the garden wall, at the late light spilling over the Ngong hills. "I am so glad you're quit of that man. That you confronted him and stood up to him, for once. And I admire your self-control. If it had been me, I believe I would have clawed his eyes out. How does one come to the point he did?"

"Greed, believing in something too deeply, but in the end . . . there is something missing in him. He lacks a moral imagination when it comes to himself. He's so certain of his inner virtue that he believes anything he does, even something this terrible, is the right thing. Am I making myself clear? The man cannot imagine himself doing anything wrong. It's a blindness. He can't see his own demons because he doesn't think they exist, and so he's fallen prey to them."

"I don't think he knows how to love," she said. "People who can't love are capable of most anything."

"People have been known to do terrible things for love," he said. "To kill for it."

"That isn't love. It's obsession."

She gave him a searching look and asked if he would like to stay to dinner. Of course he would. He was not to take that as an invitation to anything more. He would not. She went into the kitchen to give instructions to the cook and returned with two scotches.

"What are you going to do, then?" she asked.

"I am going to see Adid."

"Adid? What can he possibly do?"

"We'll see. I think he can . . ." He paused as the servant made another of his infiltrations, picked up the tray with the tea things, and drifted out. "I think he can help me to stop the voices."

"I'm afraid I don't understand you."

"I prefer to keep it to myself for now. He is in Tsavo at the moment, at the Tsavo West safari lodge. Some Chinese firm has got a contract to improve the highway between the park and Mombasa. Hassan is involved in the project—he's meeting with the Chinese and the minister of tourism down there. I'm going to see him tomorrow."

"How are you getting there?"

"I've hired a car. A damned long drive, but cheaper than chartering a plane."

"I could loan you my Land Rover and the driver. That would make it cheaper still. On condition though—that I go with you."

This was startling. He wasn't sure what to make of it.

"I would like to be part of whatever it is you're going to do," she said "For Tara's sake."

"This has to be between me and Hassan alone."

"I understand that. I would be happy to hang about the pool or whatever till you're done." She paused to set her drink down with a firm tap, then came to the sofa and stood over him. "Damn you, I love seeing you again, in spite of myself." She flipped her hair, bent down, and gave him a brief kiss. "I want to go for my sake, too."

God and the Devil

IN WESTERN TSAVO, in the shadow of the Chyulu hills, lie vast lava beds that in the supremacy of their ugliness attain a kind of beauty: lakes and fjords of black igneous rock, overlooked by flinty ridges in which a few trees or shrubs have taken root, spread over hundreds of acres. The eruption that created this lava landscape occurred a mere two hundred years ago, but the Taita people who inhabited the region experienced the awe and suffered the terrors that mankind's primitive ancestors did when the world was in its boisterous, violent adolescence: an entire mountain exploding, the molten guts of the earth rushing in torrents to incinerate villages, farms, livestock, wild beasts, and human beings, and then, as the blazing rivers cooled and congealed, to entomb the victims under tons of rock edged as sharp as arrows. The survivors, touched by the hand that makes the earth tremble and the hills to breathe fire, gave a Swahili name to this place, and it persists among their descendants: *Shetani,* which is derived from *Al-Shaitan,* the Arabic mother of the English word *Satan.*

This was Fitzhugh's destination when he picked up Hassan Adid in the afternoon, after Adid had finished his meetings. During the drive to the lava fields, Fitzhugh stated that Douglas was embezzling from the company, at times skimming as much as $36,000 in a single week. He wasn't careful to cover his tracks, but had left a trail a child could follow in the form of wire transfers to a numbered account in Switzerland.

Adid was silent. Fitzhugh said, "I thought you should know."

"I am aware of Douglas's activities," Adid grumbled.

Fitzhugh had suspected as much—and more—but pretended to be surprised.

"So these—may I call them withdrawals?—are authorized? They have your approval?"

"My friend, you should watch the questions you ask," Adid remarked, or threatened, then fell into another silence.

A few minutes later, he let out a laugh and admitted that he'd known about "Douglas's activities" for quite some time. He'd uncovered them months ago, before the meeting in Lokichokio, the one at which he'd suggested that the company hire Timmerman as marketing manager. To prepare for the meeting, he'd examined Knight Air's bank records, having persuaded the manager that, as the airline's principal investor, he was entitled to review them. At the time, Douglas had raked off almost a hundred thousand dollars and had been even less cautious than he was now, transferring the money to an account *in his name* in a Channel Islands bank. Adid kept his discovery to himself. His instincts told him it was like a cash reserve, to be held until the time was right to put it to use. That time came when he decided to make his move and bring the airline into the fold of his conglomerate. He confronted Douglas with what he'd found.

"He was most nervous, terrified as a matter of fact," Adid continued. "I reminded him that embezzlement was a crime even in Kenya." Another laugh. "One phone call to my friends in the Justice Ministry and he would be in very deep trouble. My friend—" he was addressing Fitzhugh directly—"do you recall what I said at our cordial dinner? I don't care who a man lies to as long as it is not to me. Embezzlement is a form of lying. Douglas assured me the money was not for his personal gain, oh my, no. He had some idea about opening a chain of coffee shops, and was going to consult me about it when he thought he had sufficient capital."

"Yes, the coffee shops," Fitzhugh interjected. "He told me about that notion a long time ago. Everyone would benefit."

"Of course. Our American friend is concerned about bringing the greatest benefits to the greatest number. I was not interested in selling coffee. I told him I wished to acquire Knight Air and with it take one hundred percent of the aid market in Sudan and as much of the market elsewhere as we could get." Adid was so absorbed in his reverie that he gave not one glance to the magnificent scenery, or to the herds of elephant and zebra in the distance, to the pride of lions lazing in the yellow grass a hundred meters from the road. "But I had no intention of paying full price, and presented my plan. Douglas could help me implement it or he could refuse, which would have certain consequences."

"So you blackmailed him into staging that charade," Fitzhugh said.

"I *convinced* him, my friend. I also convinced him to take his name off the account in the Channel Islands and move his money to a numbered account in Switzerland."

"Which I would think has become a joint account, yes?"

Adid laughed again. "I have no comment."

No one but the Somali would have confessed so freely to being a swindler and a blackmailer—he was bulletproof. His revelations were the product of his vanity; he was proud of his jujitsu, flipping Douglas's greed to satisfy his own. But Fitzhugh saw how he could do a little jujitsu himself and use Adid's admissions to further his plan.

"The money that's going to Switzerland—do you know where it comes from?"

"Of course I do," Adid replied.

"I don't think so."

Now it was time for Fitzhugh to make a confession, the confession he had wanted Douglas to make. Yellowbird, Busy Beaver, the real story that Phyllis Rappaport had been pursuing—he told him everything, omitting only his belief that Douglas had murdered her and the others. He assumed Adid would draw that conclusion on his own, which he did.

"You don't care who a man lies to as long as it's not to you? Our American friend has been lying to you for months, and he still is."

"You were a part of it as well," Adid remarked with a sour expression. It wasn't only the fact that he'd been lied to for so long; it was that he'd been deceived by people he regarded as rank amateurs. His pride was hurt. "And now that you are no longer employed by Knight, you feel safe in informing."

"I don't think of it as informing."

"However you may think of it, that is what it is, although I appreciate it. Very much appreciate it. As soon as I am back in Nairobi—and that will be day after tomorrow—I will tell that fool that he is through. *Halas,* finished."

"Yes, you will do that," Fitzhugh said, "but not the day after tomorrow."

The Shetani beds came into view. Stopping the Land Rover, Fitzhugh stood on the running board and, in the tones of an enthusiastic tour guide, described the event that had brought them into being. Adid, baffled by the digression, grimaced at the desolation and asked, "Does this bear on what we were talking about?"

"It does in a way." Fitzhugh got back behind the wheel and drove on, past jagged escarpments honeycombed with caves. "If you listen to my proposal, you will be rid of that fool and spare yourself a lot of trouble."

"What trouble?"

"The trouble I will cause if you don't listen to it."

"You have a great deal of nerve speaking to me in that manner. You sound like an extortionist."

"I admit it, that is what I am," Fitzhugh said, stopping again. "Hassan, you are the president of a company that is profiting from gunrunning. Money from gunrunning is being funneled to a Swiss bank account that I am sure has your name on it."

"You wouldn't dare."

"Yes, I would. I was visited by a CNN correspondent not long ago, Phyllis's replacement. He has seen the videotapes, the photographs, the notes she left behind. It's only a matter of time before he adds things up and comes to the same conclusion you and I have. Do I need to tell you the trouble that will cause you? And what if he finds out about that Swiss account and the source of its funds? What if he finds out—I know this, Hassan—that you and your father once were suspected of sabotaging Richard Leakey's plane? Yes, I can accelerate things by going to him with everything I know, and that I will do unless you listen to me."

The twin black holes in Adid's head turned toward Fitzhugh.

"Hassan, I am aware how easy it would be for you to see that I meet with an accident. You had better make the arrangements immediately, because I will be there tomorrow."

"What is in this for you? Who is paying you?"

"What is in it for me?" Fitzhugh pointed to a crude ladder, leaning against an outcrop under the mouth of a shallow cave. "Do you see that? The Taita who live here climb it to leave food offerings for those who were buried under all that lava. It is said that their souls cry out on certain nights, and that they must be appeased or they will bring down on the living the evil that befell them. What made this? A wrathful god or a destructive demon? Both. This Shetani is a place of evil, yet it is sacred also. It is feared and revered. It is a kind of church where the God who is Devil and the Devil who is God is worshipped."

"I have no patience for this nonsense," Adid muttered.

"Souls cry out to me," Fitzhugh said. "The souls of those six dead people. They won't let me sleep at night until they are appeased. That is what's in it for me—nothing more than a decent night's sleep."

"I am not going to listen to this anymore. Turn around."

Fitzhugh released the parking brake but did not turn around; he continued on, climbing the road to the crest of a pass from which they could see, far across the oceanic sweep of the Serengeti plains, the stupendous mass of Kilimanjaro. The clouds that normally veiled its peak had lifted, and the snow and ice mantling the great mountain glared in the sun.

"Look!" Fitzhugh said, braking to another stop. "Ice on the equator! Ice in the heart of Africa! A rare thing—like justice."

Adid looked as if he were about to jump out and go back on foot. A

Cape Buffalo bull, staring balefully from under its massive horns, gave him second thoughts.

"The souls cry out to me for justice," Fitzhugh carried on. "That's how I can appease them. Not a perfect justice, which would be to see Douglas hang. A partial justice. An African justice. They will settle for half a loaf, and so will I."

"You have gone mad, have you not?" Adid said. "But I will humor the madman."

"Yes! You are something of a devil, Hassan, but a minor devil compared with our American friend. And I seek your help in delivering justice. Do your old friend the Ambler a service. Help him to sleep at night."

"But I cannot humor the madman for much longer."

"You said you do business in Khartoum. Do you know people in the government?"

"You cannot do business in Khartoum without knowing people in the government," Adid said, speaking as he would to a child.

"And these are highly placed people?"

"I have had dinner with the president. I call the first vice-president by his first name."

"Then you must go to Khartoum as soon as you can, and you will tell your acquaintances that you and I are going to give them a big propaganda victory, one they have been looking for. You will ask them for one concession, that there be no bloodshed. In fact, they will see that it is to their advantage not to shed any blood."

Adid squeezed his eyes half shut. "What are you proposing?"

And there, far out in a wilderness, while looking at the grasslands reaching away and away toward the high white fire of Kilimanjaro, Fitzhugh presented his plan. When he was finished, Adid looked stunned.

"*That* is going to spare me trouble?" he asked with incredulous laughter. "It will cause me nothing but trouble."

"But not near so much trouble as a story on CNN will cause. Think of the attention that will focus on you. But this—can we call it the lesser of two evils? By the time Douglas and Tony are in safe hands, you will have already done the preliminary work for dissolving Knight Relief Services and forming a new company. Let's call it SkyTrain Relief Services. You will announce that you discovered that your managing director was engaged in gunrunning and had pulled the mask over your eyes and that you were about to dismiss him when, how amazing, he and his copilot were caught in the act. I don't doubt that CNN will move very quickly to say that their reporter was working on just such a story when she met her untimely death. They will raise the question, Was she murdered? But by that time you and the company will be in the clear."

Adid rubbed his forehead and said nothing.

"For someone who made millions selling poached ivory, this should not be a big problem."

"I regret that day the three of you appeared in my office, you, Wesley Dare, and that fool," Adid said.

"I am trying to make it less regretful."

Adid presented a faint, rueful smile. "I am going to require you to teach my son to play soccer. I wish him to be the star of his club."

"It would be a pleasure, Hassan."

"Back to the lodge, please. I would like a swim before dinner."

FITZHUGH BELIEVED HIS threat wasn't all that had moved Adid to join in his plot. He wanted his own justice as well: to show Douglas that the cost of deceiving him could be very high indeed.

"My friends await your news," read Adid's fax from Khartoum. For the next several days Fitzhugh checked the flight plans filed with Loki tower—as assistant flight coordinator, he was authorized to see them. Finally he spotted the one he was looking for. The name BUSY BEAVER was written in the block where the air operator was identified. That and the crew's names—D. Braithwaite, T. Bollichek—were the only accurate information on the form.

Returning to the flight office, he sent a fax to the same number in Khartoum to which he transmitted the UN's daily flight plans. If Adid's "friends" had done their job, the people at the other end of the line would be on the lookout for a special message from Fitzhugh. Suffering a bout of anxiousness and guilt—for all practical purposes, he was now an agent of the government of Sudan—he sent the identification numbers of Douglas's plane, the type of aircraft, and what he knew would be its true destination—New Tourom—then tore up his copy of the fax.

Someone somewhere in Khartoum slipped up—Douglas and Tony returned safely that afternoon. A week later they took off at eight in the morning on another mission. Fitzhugh again alerted Khartoum, and this time succeeded. By noon, the news had been flashed all over Loki: The control tower had received an emergency call from Busy Beaver flight number such and such. It had been intercepted by Sudanese MIGs and was being escorted to an air force base. How desperate Douglas must have been to send the Mayday. Fitzhugh could only imagine what had gone through his mind when he saw the fighter planes appear outside his cockpit window.

The official announcement came within forty-eight hours. SUNA, the government news agency, reported that a plane carrying mortars and shoulder-fired missiles had been captured after it violated Sudanese airspace over the Nuba mountains. The two-man crew, one American and one Australian, had been taken prisoner and admitted to authorities they were delivering the weapons to the SPLA. Furthermore, they confessed they had been shipping arms to the rebels for several months, using the delivery of humanitarian aid to conceal their "criminal activities." Khartoum distributed films and photographs of the aircraft as it landed at the air force base, of the cargo as it was off-loaded by Sudanese security men, and of Douglas and Tony being led away at gunpoint to a waiting police van. With a throng of aid workers and pilots, Fitzhugh watched the footage on satellite TV. A mob of emotions rioted inside him, but he didn't feel the vindication he'd expected.

Khartoum did its utmost to exploit its propaganda coup. The seizure of the plane and its contraband proved that the United Nations relief operation was merely a front to channel aid to the rebels, et cetera, et cetera. The government summoned the UN's assistant secretary of humanitarian affairs and demanded that the UN move its operations into Sudan from Lokichokio. He refused. Khartoum retaliated by expanding its aid embargo, forbidding UN planes to land at previously authorized airfields. After a month of difficult negotiations, the government relented, but Fitzhugh wondered how many innocent people had suffered during that month. Another unintended consequence in the Land of Unintended Consequences. In Sudan, no matter what you did in the name of right, wrong inevitably resulted.

The Sudanese turned their criticisms toward Kenya, for allowing "criminals and bandits" to operate from its territory. In the interests of maintaining good relations with its neighbor, Kenya ordered the Department of Civil Aviation to revoke Knight Relief Services' air operator's certificate. This was a purely cosmetic gesture. Adid, after calling a press conference to express his profound shock upon discovering that his managing director was smuggling arms, had already dissolved the company. SkyTrain Relief Services had come into being.

Nothing was heard of Douglas and Tony until, four months after their capture, SUNA announced that they had been tried by an Islamic court and sentenced to death. The American State Department and the Australian Ministry of Foreign Affairs, which had little sympathy for the plight of their reckless citizens, made pro forma appeals for clemency. These were answered. Sharia, the Islamic legal code, was not incapable of mercy. The death sentence was commuted to ten years' imprisonment, and the prison sentence suspended. Douglas and Tony were set free and expelled from the country.

That, however, was not the end of their ordeal, for while they were locked up, Phyllis Rappaport's successor, the man named Peacock, had been pursuing his investigation into the circumstances surrounding her death. Having learned from Pamela Smyth that Wesley was supposed to have been Phyllis's pilot, he paid Fitzhugh another call. Things were looking curiouser and curiouser, he said. Fitzhugh agreed and, released from his pledge to Adid not to speak to the press, filled in the blanks—with facts, not his suppositions. The story that aired on CNN, complete with excerpts from the videotapes, made no accusations, but it raised the question of whether Phyllis's death was accidental.

The network called on the U.S. Embassy to pressure the "proper authorities" to look into the matter. Thus the story was kept alive—KENYA TO INVESTIGATE U.S. JOURNALIST'S DEATH, read the headline in the *Nation*. It wasn't a case that CID was eager to get involved in, but the media and the Americans had to be mollified. Two CID men visited Fitzhugh in Loki. As in his interview with Peacock, he told them all he knew but nothing of what he believed. What he knew was sufficient. When Sudan announced that Douglas and Tony were being thrown out of the country, Kenya requested their extradition to Nairobi for questioning in a possible case of multiple homicide.

Accordingly, CID met them at Jomo Kenyatta, along with the American and Australian consuls, and brought them to Central Police Headquarters. In the meantime, however, the air crash investigators issued their report. It contained a number of findings and opinions, but only two mattered. Finding: analysis of fuel samples had disclosed the presence of water, but how it had gotten into the fuel system had not been ascertained. Opinion: the crew had performed their preflight checks improperly, failing to drain the tanks before takeoff. In so many words, the crash could be blamed on pilot error. Douglas and Tony were home free. To Fitzhugh, who had been following the case in the papers and on TV, the rest of the script was obvious. The two men would be put through a casual interrogation; the police would conclude that there was insufficient evidence to make a case and let them go. Douglas, however, did not follow the script. He did a remarkable and wholly unexpected thing—he confessed. Confessed to everything.

This created an awkward situation that no one wanted but that they could not avoid. The case had to be referred to the courts. Fitzhugh, relieved to hear his suspicions confirmed at last but also mystified as to what had moved a compulsive liar to speak a self-incriminating truth, attended the hearing. Before a robed magistrate, Douglas and Tony stood in the dock, wearing grimy jailbird dungarees. Tony's lawyer stated that his client pled not guilty and asked that the charges be dropped. The sole evidence against him was Mr. Braithwaite's statement that he had instructed Mr. Bollichek to sabotage the aircraft. The accused categorically denied that he had ever received any such instructions and would have refused to carry them out if he had. The only other evidence in the case, said the lawyer, was the air crash investigation report—he waved it at the magistrate—and blamed the crash on the crew's sloppy preflight procedures. The magistrate turned to the prosecutor. Did he intend to produce any witnesses who had seen the accused tampering with the plane in question? No. Did he intend to produce any physical evidence to show the same? No. Then, said the Man of Justice from his bench, he saw no point in proceeding any further. The charges of murder and conspiracy to commit murder against Mr. Bollichek are dismissed.

Douglas's lawyer was next. He said that his client had endured a great deal in the Sudanese prison and had not been in full command of his senses when he made the confession. Does he wish to withdraw it? asked the magistrate. No. Does he wish to amend it? No. In other words, your client is not willing to say he had instructed someone other than Mr. Bollichek to sabotage the aircraft? Correct. And he is not willing to state that he had done the dirty work himself? Correct. The Man of Justice: In his statement, your client said that he and one Michael Goraende, an officer in the Sudanese People's Liberation Army, made a plan to shoot down the plane in the event the alleged sabotage failed to accomplish its purpose. Did any of these conversations take place in Kenya? No. The magistrate returned to the prosecutor. Any witnesses to be called, any evidence to be produced contradicting what was just said? None whatsoever. Then, declared the magistrate, he could see no point in proceeding in the case against Mr. Braithwaite, his confession notwithstanding. It was, ruled the magistrate, an invalid extra-judicial confession, unsupported by witnesses or evidence in the matter of the alleged sabotage of the Hawker-Siddley aircraft and in the alleged conspiracy between Mr. Braithwaite and Colonel Goraende. Moreover, any conversations the accused had with Colonel Goraende, if they took place at all, occurred in Sudan, as did the downing of the Cessna aircraft. Kenya had no jurisdiction.

It was over in thirty minutes. The two defendants were released from custody. CNN would howl "Whitewash!" Kenya would say it had done its duty. As he limped from the courtroom—he had been beaten on the soles of his feet during his incarceration in Sudan—Douglas noticed Fitzhugh sitting in the courtroom. The American's face and body were testaments to what he'd been through: famine-thin, his shoulders slumped, his sockets bruised caverns for those pearlescent eyes with their gleam of an artificial sincerity. They fastened on Fitzhugh for an instant, an instant and no more, as if he were the only person in the room. He could not read what was in them. Douglas hobbled through the door. It was the last Fitzhugh ever saw of him. The next day the Ministry of Interior, taking note that he had smuggled arms from Kenyan soil, ordered him out of the country. Douglas Braithwaite left Africa with little more than the clothes he wore, the failure he had always dreaded becoming.

That and his torments in prison would have to do for justice, Fitzhugh thought. An African justice. He wondered if the arraignment had been a rigged game. If so, why the confession? What purpose could it have served? He knew only what he wanted to believe: that four months in a Khartoum "ghost house" had concentrated, not the American's mind, but his soul. He wanted to believe that Douglas had been visited in his prison cell. The demon-deity of Africa had come to him, shredded the costumes he wore, held a mirror to his naked self, and said, *"Behold! This is what you are!"* The image appalled him, and he'd acknowledged his crime; and in that lay a redemption of sorts.

Dismissal

THE BULB GLOWS undimmed by the cloak of insects—the katydids have fled the dawn. *Like belief,* Fitzhugh thinks. Conviction will blind you if it is not shaded by doubt.

He feels surprisingly alert for someone who hasn't slept all night. That good-looking writer was responsible for his insomnia, asking questions that prodded his memories. Two years ago Adid hired him to be managing director of SkyTrain Relief Services; in half an hour he will fly to Natinga to see what can be done about his crippled aircraft. It's part of his job as an entrepreneur of aid. For how much longer he will remain one is open to question. His comment to the writer—that the war promised to go on forever, had not been entirely accurate. There are rumors that the cease-fire that has prevailed in the Nuba for some time will be extended to southern Sudan. An American diplomat is now in the country, attempting to broker a peace. The unthinkable, the unimaginable, is on the horizon of possibility: the war could end.

He looks at the photograph of Diana and their children, taken a few months ago, on her fifty-ninth birthday. They were married not long after Douglas's departure and were honeymooning in Fitzhugh's birthplace, the Seychelles, when a war of another kind came to Kenya: the American Embassy in Nairobi was blown up by a terrorist group called Al Qaeda.

A year passed. They adopted two AIDS orphans, Robert and Rebecca. The kids tested negative for the disease, the Black Death of the modern age. They call Diana mama and Fitzhugh baba. Right now they are in the house in Karen, where he spends his weekends. He still thinks of that house as hers; it embarrasses him to live in a place with servants, it contradicts his idea of himself, but possibly that image never was an accurate reflection of who he is.

The responsibilities of marriage and the stresses of raising children who should be, chronologically, Diana's grandchildren have dampened the strange fire ignited almost a decade ago between the middle-aged woman and the young man. Now he has entered middle age and she is on the frontiers of old age; yet there are nights when a look, a gesture, a thought fans the coals of their first passion, and they make love as if their flesh were touching anew. "She's only eleven years younger than me," Fitzhugh's father said to him not long ago. "Are you happy?" Fitzhugh doesn't believe happiness, as the world defines it, is possible in Africa. "I am content," he answered.

They say the owl was a baker's daughter . . .

There is one other woman in his life, Quinette Goraende, with whom he maintains a peculiar relationship. She regards him as her friend and confidant; he doesn't consider himself to be either, actively disliking her; and yet he answers the letters she sends from the Nuba now and then—Fitzhugh's pilots deliver them—and patiently listens to her talk and talk about herself when she visits Loki or Nairobi. Diana, who cannot suffer her for longer than fifteen minutes, has pegged her as an overgrown adolescent who thinks everyone finds her as interesting as she finds herself.

The odd relationship began shortly after Quinette's first child, a son, died in infancy. She'd come down with malaria. Gerhard Manfred treated her with Fansidar, to no effect. Through Fitzhugh, her husband arranged for her evacuation to Nairobi General Hospital, where she was treated with a stronger drug; still, the disease racked her with chills, fever, and hallucinations. Her doctor, an Italian, was concerned about her chances. One day, in a delirium, she began to call out the name of Malachy Delaney. The doctor knew Malachy and, assuming his patient was a Roman Catholic, summoned the priest to come to her bedside, warning that he should be prepared to administer last rites. Fitzhugh was in Nairobi at the time, and his old friend asked if he would accompany him.

Quinette had rallied in the meantime. They found her sitting up in bed, in a lucid state. It was the lucidity granted by a confrontation with death. Like Douglas, she made a confession, which Fitzhugh did not think was pure coincidence. She and Douglas were alike in many ways; so American in their narcissism, in their self-righteousness, in their blindness to their inner natures, in their impulse to remake the world and reinvent themselves, never realizing that the world wishes to remain as it is and that oneself is not as malleable as one likes to think. Quinette told her visitors that in her fevered dreams she was haunted by three specters: Suleiman, Tara, and a woman called Yamila. Malachy and Fitzhugh listened to her unburden herself: She had condemned Suleiman by refusing to plead for his life, condemned Tara by remaining silent after her husband disclosed the plan he and Douglas had laid, condemned Yamila to slavery by uttering two words. She asked the priest if it was sometimes necessary to do evil in order to do good. He replied that it was done all the time, but the good never made the evil any the less evil. Though she was a Protestant, he called on her to repeat after him the words to the Act of Contrition, and she did: " 'O, my God, I am heartily sorry for having offended you . . . in all that I have done and failed to do . . .' " At the end Malachy absolved her: "Your sins are forgiven, in the name of the Father and the Son and the Holy Spirit."

She wasn't convinced they had been, as Fitzhugh discovered the following day. He'd gone to the hospital to visit her again, alone this time. He didn't know why. Some vague notion that there was more to be said compelled him to see her. She had suffered a relapse, and he found her shivering and sweating through another delirious episode. "Yamila! Please!" she cried out several times, stark terror on her damp face. "Yamila! Please!"

Please what? Fitzhugh asked himself. *Please leave me alone? Please forgive me?* Was that what she wanted, not divine forgiveness but the forgiveness of the Nuban woman? If it was, she would never get it. Quinette's eyes widened, and she screamed loudly enough to bring an orderly into the room. Fitzhugh told him it was all right, the memsahib had had a bad dream. But he wondered what she had seen in her deranged vision to tear from her throat such a horrified cry. It could have been Yamila. Or it could have been someone else.

We know what we are, but know not what we may be.

But what we become, Fitzhugh thinks, is what we have been all along. To outward appearances, each of us is a half truth. The self we present to the world conceals a clandestine self that awaits its time to come out. Africa had not changed Quinette. It had merely provided the right circumstances and the right climate for her pretty chrysalis to pop open and reveal the creature within. To see the whole truth of oneself is also a redemption of sorts. Whether that was what Quinette had beheld, Fitzhugh would never know. Again, he knew only what he wanted to believe, and he wanted to believe redemption was possible.

Redeemed or no, Africa had a special fate in mind for her; a fate not necessarily deserved for all she had done and failed to do; Africa's Supreme Being neither punishes sinners nor rewards saints but does as he pleases. And it pleased him to demand a payment from this young American woman who had presumed to wed one of his sons and to regard herself as an adopted daughter.

Quinette recovered and returned to the Nuba and her now less-than-happy marriage. Michael blamed her for the loss of their son. She had tempted him into violating a sacred ordinance of his people, and they had suffered the consequence. She felt that the only way to make it up to him would be to get pregnant again. A year later she presented him with their second son, whom they named Gabriel. A year and half after his birth, a third came along, Raphael. (Evidently Michael's bitterness hadn't affected their physical attraction.) During both pregnancies Quinette strictly adhered to custom, and the sexual abstinence had the effect she had feared. Michael took a second wife, nineteen years old.

He hadn't done this solely for reasons of physical gratification. A Nuban man's status is reflected in the number of his wives, and Michael's status had changed. With the cessation of hostilities in the Nuba, his military career ended and he was appointed provisional governor of all the rebel-held areas in the region. He exchanged his camouflage for open-neck white shirts and dark slacks. The warrior had become a political figure, and politically Quinette was something of a liability; a good jet-black Nuban spouse, an asset. Former Lieutenant Colonel now Governor Goraende took part in negotiations that ended the fighting in the Nuba. Earlier the murahaleen warlord, Ibrahim Idris, had made good on his promise to extend the separate peace between him and Michael to all the Baggara Arab tribes. That unofficial armistice became the model for an official one signed by the SPLA forces in the Nuba and the Khartoum government. With the cease-fire in place and foreign troops sent to monitor it, Michael made frequent trips to the capital to discuss with his former enemies plans for making the Nuba a semiautonomous province. He continued to rely on Quinette for advice, but less so than in the past. She was the mother of his children, not a partner, and he made most of his decisions without confiding in her. Thus she discovered a truth about the world she had married into: It was essentially masculine; there was little room in it for a woman's views.

Michael changed. The man of war had been tender and passionate, as if the brutalities of his calling had summoned up the gentleness in him; the man of politics was more remote and at times harsh and neglectful. He also got fat, the breathtaking soldier-wrestler's body rounding out into the shape of the typical African "Big Man," with his pot belly, walking stick, and imperious manner. He took a third wife, as young as the second. Now Quinette was forced to possess but a third of the man of whom she had wanted all. She was deferred to by her sister spouses, she tried to like them, but she often cried herself to sleep on the nights when he went to visit one or the other. The sounds of their lovemaking drove her into fits of violent jealousy. She once told Fitzhugh that if she didn't have him to confide in and to use as a vent for what she called her "negative feelings," she might well do something she would later regret.

Pearl and Kiki had meanwhile got married, depriving Quinette of hands to do the hard tasks that were a Nuban woman's lot. The junior wives took up most of the burden, but even as the senior wife of the provisional governor, Quinette did her share of pounding sorghum in the hot sun, cooking over a wood fire, washing clothes in a riverbed. This in addition to teaching her English and Bible classes, labors she once had plunged into willingly and cheerfully. Now they had become a dull routine. Zeal was no longer in her voice when she gave her scripture lessons. Something was missing—the war. At times she was nostalgic for it. She missed its heightened emotions, the intensity it had brought to life, infusing each day with poignant meaning, charging ordinary moments with the electricity of the extraordinary. It had made the hardships of the African bush endurable. The dust and dirt, the ticks, mosquitoes and spiders, the dry season's scorch, the wet season's mire, the diseases and scarcity of water, and the absence of every comfort and amenity had been part of an enormous experience, a great and terrible ordeal. Robbed of drama, the hardships were merely hardships, wearisome, annoying, or debilitating instead of ennobling. After the cease-fire had gone into effect, it was as if a bloody but riveting film had ended and the house lights had gone on, killing the magic darkness, ushering Quinette up the aisle, past the discarded cups and crushed straws through which she'd slaked her thirst for the remarkable, and into a tedious reality. Compared with the high terrors and excitements of bombings and battles, caring for her children and doing the endless chores, no sooner completed than they had to be done again, were tame drudgery.

The armistice had another effect she hadn't anticipated. The tree of a new society that had sprouted in New Tourom flourished so long as it was watered by the blood of war; in the drought of peace, it withered. Now that it was safe to return, the people who had found refuge in the town drifted back to their tribal homelands, drawn by a magnetism too powerful to resist. Michael's and Quinette's grand vision was not to be realized. Jesus still loved her, but her sense of serving a higher purpose had deserted her.

She needed to escape now and then, and her husband indulged her, providing her with an allowance from his governor's salary. She fled to Loki or Nairobi whenever she could, persuading relief pilots to smuggle her into Kenya—her passport had expired some time ago. She afforded herself the pleasures of a proper bath and eating something other than doura gruel, in the delights of fresh company. By this time the century and the millennium had turned. There was a whole new generation of workers in Loki, and to them the tall American woman with the African braids and African clothes and African mate was a weird curiosity, an eccentric who belonged to what already seemed a bygone era. Quinette satisfied her need for conversation mostly with Fitzhugh, who learned about her more than he ever needed or wanted to know.

After malaria struck her again and little Raphael almost succumbed to relapsing fever, Quinette decided she'd had enough of Africa for a while. A different sort of nostalgia tugged her. She longed to see again the America she had once longed to escape forever, and to bring her family with her. The terrorist attacks on the World Trade Center had occurred two months before, and arranging travel documents for her husband and children took weeks. A SkyTrain aircraft flew them out of the Nuba mountains. Four days and as many plane changes later, they landed in the town of Waterloo, Iowa, in the dead-level heartland of America.

Things went well for a while. Her mother and two sisters had gotten over their animosities and welcomed the prodigal girl home. Her brown children and six-foot-seven-inch black husband with tribal marks on his forehead drew stares on the streets of Cedar Falls, but the couple did not suffer the prejudice Quinette had feared. The visit began to turn sour when her mother caught her coming out of the shower one morning and saw the tribal stigmata covering her belly, back, and buttocks. "What in God's name have you done to yourself?" she wailed. Then, on a drive to the countryside to see the farm where Quinette had grown up, Michael let slip that she was not his only wife. "You have *another wife*?" Quinette's older sister asked, scarcely believing what she'd heard. Actually, Michael replied, he had two. Quinette's family could accept her marriage to an African rebel; a polygamous marriage was another matter altogether. She was furious with Michael for opening his mouth but equally upset with her sister for her unwillingness to understand the customs of Quinette's adopted land. She who had gone to such lengths to preserve a monogamous union ended up defending its opposite. She realized that she no longer belonged in America; she was an African.

And yet she wasn't, but rather a woman caught in the cleft between two worlds. She returned to the Nuba mountains to discover that one of her sister spouses was pregnant. Not long afterward Quinette was, too. The last time Fitzhugh saw her was when he flew to New Tourom to discuss aid deliveries with her husband. His relations with Michael were distant. He didn't condemn him as severely as he did Douglas; the man had been at war most of his life, he'd been fighting for the survival of his people. Those were circumstances in extenuation and mitigation, but a long way from exoneration.

Returning to the airstrip, Fitzhugh came upon Quinette at the town well, scrubbing clothes with other village women, fully one of them now, their sister in toil. Seeing him, she stood up, pressing the small of her back. She was wearing a dark blue kanga, bulging slightly in the middle. He noticed that the African sun was beginning to tell on her skin, which after all wasn't meant for it. At thirty-two she looked leathery, the signs of middle age already upon her; and if her life followed the course of most African women, her middle age would last but a few years, and she would be old by forty-five. She glanced briefly at the man's shirt spread out to dry on a rock at her feet, then at Fitzhugh, and with a hand on her swollen midriff, rolled her head back, her eyes shut. There was everything in that brief movement, everything of weariness, of regret, of resignation, and of a bitter knowledge: she had asked Africa to redeem her from the bonds of the commonplace and give her an extraordinary life. It had, but now it was extracting the price. It was keeping her.

ALSO BY PHILIP CAPUTO

DELCORSO'S GALLERY

At thirty-two, Nick DelCorso is an award-winning combat photographer who wants his pictures to do more than merely serve
as illustrations of distant horrors. Rather, he is determined to
make the chaos and murder of war as clear and immediate as possible. From the fall of Saigon to the Lebanese civil war, this
harrowing novel reveals a type of war in which civilians are tar-
geted as much as the enemy, and the lines between sides are
hardly visible or barely matter.

Fiction/0-375-72509-1

EXILES

In *Exiles*, Philip Caputo sends the reader on a tripartite adventure. In the Connecticut suburbs, a motherless young man suddenly becomes the beneficiary of a wealthy older couple, whose
generosity has unsuspected motives and a sinister price. On an
island in Australia's Torres Strait, an enigmatic castaway throws
kinks into the local cultural and sexual politics. And in the jun-
gles of Vietnam, four American soldiers undertake a mystical
search for a man-eating tiger.

Fiction/0-679-76838-6

HORN OF AFRICA

When foreign correspondent Charlie Gage is recruited to assist
with Operation Atropos, he has no idea he is about to be enlisted for guerrilla warfare. Set in the forsaken yet exotic deserts of
Ethiopia, *Horn of Africa* is a vividly detailed and masterfully plot-
ted novel chronicling a broken man's struggle for salvation and
inner freedom in the midst of a broken nation's fight for stability
and peace.

Fiction/0-375-72511-3

INDIAN COUNTRY

Christian Starkmann follows his boyhood friend, Bonny George, from the wilderness of Michigan's Upper Peninsula to Vietnam, where they serve in the same platoon. After returning home from the war, his friend buried on the battlefield he left behind, Christian begins to make a life for himself. Yet years later, although he is happily married and has two daughters, he is still fighting—with the searing memories of combat, and most of all with the ghost of Bonny George, who presses him to come to terms with a secret so powerful it could destroy everything he has built.

Fiction/0-375-72510-5

THE VOYAGE

On a June morning in 1901, Cyrus Braithwaite commands his three sons to set sail from their Maine home aboard the family's forty-six-foot schooner and not return until September. Though confused and hurt by their father's cold-blooded order, the three brothers soon rise to the occasion and embark on a perilous journey down the East Coast, headed for the Florida Keys. Almost a hundred years later, Cyrus's great-granddaughter Sybil sets out to uncover the events that transpired on the voyage. Her discoveries about the Braithwaite family and the America they lived in unfolds into a stunning tale of intrigue, murder, lies, and deceit.

Fiction/0-679-76839-4

VINTAGE CONTEMPORARIES
Available at your local bookstore, or call toll-free to order:
1-800-793-2665 (credit cards only).